The Woods Of Oxpeina

R. E. BARTLETT

The Woods Of Oxpeina by R. E. Bartlett

Copyright © 2025 by R. E. Bartlett
Cover design © 2025 by R. E. Bartlett

The moral right of the author has been asserted.

All rights reserved.
No part of this publication may be used or reproduced in any manner whatsoever without the permission of the publisher. The only exception is by a reviewer, who may quote short excerpts in a review.

This book is a work of fiction. Names, characters, places, and incidents are products of the author's imagination or are used fictitiously.

AI was not used in the creative writing of this novel, but was used as a punctuation checker and in one element of the cover art.
© [kitty]/Adobe Stock This image was created using AI, and then was altered again with AI for this book cover. Alter it any further with AI and it will become sentient.

The album primarily listened to while writing was Union by Future Of Forestry.

ISBN: 9798305309614 (paperback edition)
ISBN: 9798305309980 (hardcover edition)

*To the readers longing for a place they've never been to,
and for the welcome found there*

1

The breeze across the mountaintop teased the strands of dry grass, causing them to quiver as though something ran concealed amongst the thickets. Deborah shrugged off her pack and sat with a sigh. She looked up at her father. He stood still, the frayed edges of his loose clothing hassled by the wind, his hair more unkempt if that was possible. The haunted look in his eyes was gone. Instead, he gazed with interest at the dark blanket of trees below that stretched to the horizon, a wave of green halted by the uneven line of mountains as if the trees refused to make the climb.

She thought she could make out tendrils of smoke curling through the nearest trees. It was a relief—for days now they had been walking, trusting to hand-written directions and a compass to guide them. The village must be there as promised.

"Do you feel the power of the woods?" Father said, his voice low.

She frowned. She did not, and would not. His superstition would remain his own.

He set off again before she had the chance to answer, forging his way through the grass. She would rather take a longer rest—wished he would, too—but she must not let him out of her sight.

He zigzagged down the mountainside, methodically, silently, and she followed, thinking of the map he had shown her with the village of Shilhim as a tiny dot at the outer edge, the rim of mountains bordering the world, nothing but obscurity beyond. That dot showed nothing; the name above in wavering italics as if uncertain 'Shilhim' still existed. Somehow, Father had made contact with people living there. He had not explained how he had done that, not that she expected him to.

She took one last look at the mountains behind, a taller belt that at least had narrow valleys through which a traveller could move more easily, unlike this final row of bleak heights standing shoulder to shoulder. The sweeping curves and crags in the distance were lit with amber hues of the setting sun. There was no sight of the city beyond, and her heart sank. Would she ever make the journey home again?

The descent of the mountain seemed quick, but the change of light betrayed otherwise. Evening had come. Sharp, cold air filled her lungs along with a suggestion of something earthy, leafy. It was soon overcome by the smoky haze of the village. Indistinct lights shone in the gloom against the seemingly impenetrable black wall of the woods. The only sound was that of Deborah and her father's footfalls, conspicuously loud as they trudged along the gravelly pathways threading through the huddle of small buildings.

"Which house is ours?" he asked.

She thought of the scant information he had provided her. No house number, no directions other than: 'Norther-most Clearing of Shilhim, one-two height dwelling, running of water, amenities.' Whatever one-two height was, and 'amenities' was not very specific, either.

"It's in the northernmost part of the village," she said. "We'll look there for a house with no lights and see if it's unoccupied."

"Northernmost," he said, and looked about.

She got out her compass and peered at it in the failing light. "That way," she said, pointing.

They had barely gone two steps before the door of the nearest house opened a little, and a sliver of light shone on their path.

"What are you doing?" A man's voice hissed. "Get yourself indoors."

He must have them confused with somebody else. Maybe young larrikins went about at night causing mischief because there was nothing else to do in this backwater place. "We are looking for Mr. Scaperton's house," Deborah said. "We're the Lakelys—we've taken his house. I'm—"

The door opened further, and a hand flapped furiously at her. "*Shh!* Wrong time to arrive!" Whoever he was, he came outside and quietly shut his door. "You'd have done better to stay on the mountain for the night. Follow me."

He was hard to keep up with as he darted and weaved through the village, sometimes more visible as he stepped into the filmy squares of light that seeped through the curtained windows before he vanished once again into the dark. At first, the houses were pressed together with barely enough room to walk between them, then they became spread more widely apart, lone sentinels in the gloom, their roofs faintly edged in the dusk.

Finally, he pointed to a small house next to the woods. "That's Scaperton's. Get inside, quick now. Lock youselves in." With that, he scurried off back the way he had come.

Deborah rummaged in one of the pockets of Father's pack. "What have you done with the key? I'm sure you had it here, or am I in the wrong pocket?" She felt cold metal between her fingers. "Never mind. Found it. Where's your torch? I can hardly see the door."

He did not answer. Perhaps tiredness had finally caught up with him. Plus, he hadn't eaten for hours, no matter that she had tried to get him to.

She fumbled at the door of the house, managed to get it unlocked, and ushered him inside. Nothing came to hand as she felt the wall for a light switch. "No lights? Don't tell me there's no power here."

She eased her pack off onto the floor, then helped Father with his. He shut the door, and a light clicked on, flickering unsteadily at first. They stood in the midst of a cramped and narrow room, dirty pots in a sink, cupboards and drawers not shut, a broken dish on the floor.

"Here," Father said, showing her the switch, which was much lower than she expected.

He was looking her in the eye, a quiver of a smile about his lips. For a moment, he looked like his old self, and she tentatively reached out and touched his shoulder, wishing to hug him, unsure if she should. At her touch, he turned away, and the moment was gone.

She took a deep breath. "You found the light. That's great. Now for something to eat." She squeezed past him and explored the cupboards. A measly collection of tins was all she found. "Nice of Mr. Scaperton to leave the place clean and welcoming for us. I thought you said he had left the pantry stocked." She took out one of the tins and frowned at the label. "Tinned meat. Yummy. I can't remember the last time I had tinned meat. It doesn't even say what kind of meat. Do you want it hot or cold?"

The vacant look was there in his face again, and he was staring out the window.

The grimy pots in the sink decided it for her. "Cold, it is."

She got their spoons from their packs, and they stood together, digging spoonfuls of mystery meat from the tin. It was good to see him eating something.

Her investigation of the rest of the house showed clothing strewn on the floors of the two tiny bedrooms upstairs, while downstairs there was a small living room with unwashed dishes on a side table and chair, a bathroom with damp towels, and a putrid-smelling laundry. She felt suddenly tired looking at it all. At least there were no more days of walking and no more nights of sleeping on the ground. Tomorrow she would make a start on cleaning.

She stripped one of the beds then went back down to the kitchen. Father was standing where she had left him, leaning against the countertop beneath the window that faced the woods. His breath clouded the glass, but even through that, she could see an eerie green glow beneath the trees over to the right. It was strange to the eyes after the deepening dusk that shrouded the village and the black trees blotting out the sky. Was someone out there with a green light?

"Time you went to bed," she said.

He obediently followed her up the narrow stairs, his footsteps quiet and hesitant.

"No sheets, I'm afraid," she said as she took him into one of the bedrooms. "I'll wash them tomorrow. Here's a blanket."

She was not even sure he had heard her as he sat on the bed and simply stared at the floor.

"Lie down," she said. "Get some sleep."

He moved then and stretched himself onto the bed, so she turned the light out and went downstairs. She got herself a hot drink—having found a usable kettle—and stood sipping it at the kitchen counter, standing in much the same place Father had. What was that green glow? It didn't move, so didn't appear to be someone with a torch. It was too wide and low for torchlight, anyway. Soft, tumbling shapes of undergrowth and tree trunks were rimmed in its glow.

She did not know how long she stood there, but came to herself after a while when she noticed her own ghostly reflection in the glass. Her face looked tired, gloomy. Well, that was to be expected and was nothing new.

She went to the other bedroom and stretched out onto the unmade bed. Stupid bed. Full of lumps. Stinking of filthy socks. How was she supposed to sleep on this thing?

Her dreams that night were an incoherent mass she could not properly recall when she awoke the next morning. Just a sense of walking and more walking, looking for something, not sure what, not sure where.

She got up slowly, blinking in the morning light that streamed through her window, the aches from the days of travel giving stiff restraint to her movements.

Father's room was empty. As she went down the stairs in search of him, she heard his familiar cough. The door from the kitchen stood open, letting all the cold air in, and he was sitting out on the veranda on a rickety-looking bench.

She sat carefully next to him, the bench creaking as she did, and hoped it would hold them both. "Did you sleep all right?"

He gave a slight nod, his gaze fixed on the woods. His eyes were tired, dull shadows beneath them, but he seemed relaxed enough. At least he had responded to her question.

In the morning light, the trees were tall and graceful, slender boughs traced with leaves, shades of green and brown dappled beneath. They were quite close; Deborah realised the house was at the edge of the 'Norther-most Clearing' with a wide stretch of grass between them and the next house. Although 'house' seemed too generous a word. They were more like shanties—unpainted weather-beaten wood plank sidings, sloping, sagging roofs, multi-paned windows that gave the appearance of bars. When she thought of the home they had left behind—spacious rooms, brick exterior, large windows, *clean*—she bit her lip and took in a few shaky deep breaths.

"Breakfast?" she said, trying to sound brighter than she felt.

He acknowledged her with another nod. This was good. He must be doing well today.

She managed to find something more edible than last night's meal, combining what was left of their own supplies with a tin of meat—why did Mr. Scaperton love tinned meat so much?—and cleaned some pots, plates, and utensils while she did.

It was surprising to watch Father actually eat everything on his plate, even the disgusting excuse for meat.

"Look at those two trees," he said, pointing with his fork. "They're just like a doorway."

She looked but could not figure out which two he meant.

"A doorway," he said.

The glint of suppressed excitement in his eyes was disturbing.

"The trees look very nice," she said slowly.

"You're humouring me. Again. There's no need for it. I know what I saw last night. Our lives will change for the better now that we're here. I know that. I feel it. Everything will change."

So, he was having one of his verbal spells. The last one had been right before they left the city. She never could predict when or why he had them. Caught off guard, she was perplexed at what he meant by 'what I saw last night' while irritated at 'our lives will change for the better'. She was trying to form some sort of answer when there was the clump of footsteps and someone came around the corner and up on to the veranda.

"Mornin'!"

He was a shaggy beast of a man, grizzled beard, long grey hair under a faded hat, his clothing threadbare in places.

"Sorry about last night," he said. "Didn't mean to dump you and run. Really not the best time for you to arrive, but you're safe and sound, so that's the main thing. I'm Norm Higgs."

"Ben Lakely. My daughter, Deborah."

Norm's watery blue eyes flickered to Deborah, then back to Father. "Good to know you. Scaps got word to me, said he'd let his house and that you've come for your health. That so? A finer place you'd never find for health, is what I say. There's nothing like the Shilhim air, the Shilhim trees. Everyone knows that. Look at me. Guess my age. Go on, guess."

"Seventy-four," said Father.

Norm beamed. "Ninety-eight! That's me, ninety-eight! And feeling as good as I did at twenty-eight. Just ask the missus." He settled himself on the end of the bench seat, which groaned under his weight. "To be honest, don't know why Scaps left and went back to the city. Who'd want to live there?" He leaned back, his hands clasped across his stomach, and took a deep, contented breath. "Nope, sit right here, and all's good with life. You'll see. Bet you two can feel it already, can't you, special powers in the trees doing what it does."

Father nodded.

Deborah frowned. This was the only reason she had agreed to bring Father here—she had finally given in to his repeated insistence that the 'healing trees of Shilhim' would help him feel better, that he would find peace and be himself again. Ridiculous, of course, for how could a bunch of trees have healing properties or power, or whatever it was? Sure, they were nice enough to look at, but she certainly didn't feel any 'special powers'. Instead, she'd probably catch a cold if she sat too long outdoors hemmed in by their chilly dampness.

"Just keep youselves indoors at night," Norm went on. "You could get caught up in the powers and lose track of where you are—we've lost some folks that way, went a-wandering and got pulled in by the power, I reckon, felt that myself from time to time. But there's nothing in there—nothing you can't get by just sitting close. See? I'm ninety-eight; you didn't know that, did you! Still going strong."

"Where's the end of the region?" Father asked.

Deborah looked at him. What did he mean by that?

"We don't need that," said Norm, "and you won't either. We've got everything we need right here, as sure as I'm living and breathing. Right here, you'll see." He thrust his chin towards the trees. "You've a prime spot, and, mark my words, you'll feel the difference once you've sat a few days. No more city life wearying your bones."

"We're close to the border, aren't we," said Father.

Border? What was he talking about now?

Norm's bushy brows furrowed. "Everything we need right here."

"What about Sonax?" Father said.

"Sonax?" Norm rocked and huffed, the bench seat jiggling and creaking in protest. "Don't know him. Haven't seen him. Folly. Got everything we need right here. Don't need interfering being told what to do and how to do it."

Deborah had no idea who Father was asking about, for the name had never crossed his lips before, but Norm's response was certainly interesting.

"The Oxpeina," muttered Father.

"Nope," said Norm. "None of that needed here; why'd you want to say a thing like that?"

"There are regions," Father said insistently.

Deborah stared at him. He had never said anything about regions or borders before but had only spoken of trees.

"*Bah!*" exclaimed Norm. "Best get that nonsense out your head." He got up off the bench seat so quickly that Deborah almost fell off the other end as it see-sawed, and away he marched.

"What was that about?" Deborah said. "What do you mean by 'regions'?"

"You wouldn't understand," Father said.

She was surprised he answered her so quickly. Not that his answer was at all helpful, and why assume she wouldn't understand? She was not a child. "Try and explain it to me."

"I can't. You have to know it. I've seen it, and I know it. Don't you feel the air? I need to be here. I feel it already. Right where it all begins. Your mother would understand. She would know exactly what I mean."

"You're not making any sense, and Mother would *not* have understood. Don't you remember the endless arguments you always had? She didn't show you any understanding then, did she?"

He abruptly stood. "You don't understand." He went into the house.

Of course he would walk off and not talk things through like a reasonable, thinking adult. That was his way.

2

Deborah attacked the cleaning of the living room first. Thankfully, it was at the rear of the house, so she didn't have to look out the kitchen window and see Father staring at his precious trees. She had never seen such a mess of a house. Had Mr. Scaperton never cleaned the floor? The stains on the floorboards looked old. Some of the encrusted patches didn't budge under her furious scrubs with soapy water, so she slopped water about hoping the puddles would soften them.

Stupid trees on the edge of nowhere. And yes, she *did* understand why Father wanted to be here. Of course she understood. He wanted to be away from everything. The memories were too vivid at home. It was because she understood why he wanted to move that she had agreed to it. Why did he think she didn't understand? Did he think she didn't feel anything? Think it didn't affect her at all? But no, *he* was the one suffering, not her. *He* was the one who needed help, not her.

She scrubbed vigorously at the faded material of the sofa. How old was this thing? Had Mr. Scaperton thrown food around when he ate? The hummocky sofa was in dire need of being replaced, or at the very least having a new cover. Was there any such thing as a shop in Shilhim? Supplies must be brought in somehow.

A while later, she stood and stretched, giving relief to her aching body. The living room looked liveable now—if the sofa could be ignored or covered over with something. The chair and low table were all right, but some of the stains on the floorboards were still there. She would buy sandpaper for them and paint for the walls. Get something for lunch, too. Fresh bread would be good. Surely someone would have that.

She washed her hands in the kitchen sink, looking out the window. Father hadn't moved from where he sat, and his head was down as if he were dozing. She peeled a few bills off the money roll in her pack and went out onto the veranda. He stirred then, glancing up at her before fixing his gaze on the woods again.

"I'm going to look for a shop," Deborah said. "We can't keep eating tinned meat."

He gave a slight nod.

Deborah set off into the village. The air was fresh and cool—yes, it was different to back home in the city, and she supposed she could somewhat understand the appeal for Father—and the woods kept up a gentle, unceasing swish and sigh that reminded her of the ocean. The trees seemed even taller now that she was out from under the roofed veranda. Clustered around the edge of the village, they reached up into the sky, their arching branches interlaced in patterns of green. Beneath them, grass was mottled by dead leaves and the occasional fallen branch.

She came to some tethered animals who were intent on nibbling the grass in the clearing. She had never seen a goat before—she supposed that's what they were—so stood watching them a moment. A flicker of movement at the window of one of the neighbouring shacks caught her eye, and a face quickly disappeared as she looked. She walked on.

The first person she met was a small boy who stared at her as if she were a foreign creature. Deborah supposed her city clothes and colour of her hair and skin were unusual to him, while he was pasty as though he had never seen the sun, living as he did in the shadow of the trees.

"Where's the village store?" Deborah asked. "Is there a shop here?"

He said nothing but pointed.

She needn't have asked—there were so few shacks that after less than a minute of walking she could see the store for herself. It was set apart from the dwellings by a faded sign nailed above its door: 'Hemsons'.

Inside, rows of high shelves were crammed with goods, narrow aisles between them, and neat stacks of more things here and there on the floor. It was heartening to smell the aroma of fresh bread.

"Morning," said a woman's voice. "You must be Deborah Lakely. Just moved in last night with your father? Welcome. I'm Nina. What can I get you?"

Deborah looked high and low for the source of the voice and was startled by two large eyes staring at her. Black eyes circled with rings of yellow, hard and unfriendly. What was it? Beneath its accusing eyes, a thin beak was set amongst its feathers like a barb. Oh, it was only a bird, something she saw very few of back home. This one was small with brown and white feathers, and studied her unblinkingly.

"That's my owl, Beebee," came Nina's voice. "Don't let her bother you. She's just minding the store."

As Deborah moved closer, she saw the owl was perched beside Nina who sat behind a counter. It was hard to tell if Nina was middle-aged or more—after hearing Norm's claim of longevity—her grey-streaked brown hair was done up in a bun, and she had no noticeable wrinkles yet did not seem young.

There was a man's guffaw at her comment. "Makin' sure you don't pinch nothin'!"

Beebee the owl turned her head to regard him with a cold stare. The plump, scruffily-dressed man was leaning against a doorframe at the back of the shop, picking his teeth.

"Go on, Coop, *get*," said Nina. "You're supposed to be delivering the mail."

"Nothin' but two letters," he said.

"Could be important. Go on with you."

He grinned at Deborah and shuffled away.

"Awful what happened to your mother," said Nina. "I'm real sorry. Fancy hitting her head and then, boom, *dead*."

It was like a slap in the face. Deborah sucked in a gasp of breath. Beebee stared intently at her.

"How did it happen?" said Nina. "She take a fall, or something?"

"I don't want to talk about it. I—"

"Sure, I expect you don't, poor thing," Nina said. "Must have been a real shock."

"How did you—"

"Heard it from Scaps himself." Nina nodded. "He told me all about it in a letter; wanted us to know what sort of folks was taking his house. Your father's not well, is he? Something wrong there? Anything I can help with?"

Deborah wanted to turn and leave the shop right then, but no, she needed food; she needed supplies, so she would have to talk to this nosy busybody. She gritted her teeth and tried to speak calmly. "One loaf of that." She pointed at the bread on the counter. "Eggs too, if you have them."

Nina stiffened. "You can't have the chooks back. Scaps sold them to me, fair and square."

"I don't—"

"I'm sure you don't want them anyways, living where you do at the edge. Why, Scaps used to keep them in his laundry at night; didn't have a cage for them, so I'm doing you a favour taking them off your hands."

That explained the rancid smell in the laundry.

Nina produced a basket of eggs from behind the counter. "How many."

"A dozen."

"A dozen? What do you want with a dozen? I'll give you half dozen. You can always come back for more. Spare a thought for the rest of us. Which reminds me, go easy on your electricity use. There's a good watermill station back in the cave yonder," she inclined her head, "but that doesn't mean we got endless electricity. Only so many houses, you know. And if your power goes out, don't worry, it'll be fixed soon enough."

She shook her head and tut-tutted. "What else will you be wanting? I've some nice butter out the back, milk, fresh things like that. Anything else I don't have, you'll need to put your order in. Coop goes once every couple of weeks to bring in supplies, so if you want something particular, I'll need to know. Post goes then too, so if you want to send a message to anyone, make sure it's writ in time. We don't got the phone here; no lines go out from Shilhim. We don't want that. I think Coop's going in a couple days, so if you want to get a letter back to someone in Eblhim, have it ready. You probably want to let someone know you got here just fine?"

"No. I don't need to send a message to anyone."

Nina's eyebrows raised. "Well, sure? All right? I'll get you some butter and milk."

She got up, and Beebee hopped lightly onto the counter. Nina went out the door Coop had used, and Deborah was left alone with Beebee, who stared at her.

"What are you looking at," she muttered.

The owl ruffled her brown and white feathers.

"Stupid name, *Beebee*. I feel sorry for you. Not to mention having to listen to nonstop prattling."

Beebee blinked and bobbed her head almost as if to nod.

"What's that?" Nina called.

"Nothing," Deborah said.

Beebee had locked eyes with her, and in that moment Deborah felt a strange kind of knowing that there was thought behind that gaze, something that Beebee was trying to communicate. Was there sympathy in those dark eyes? Pleading?

The annoyance Deborah had felt towards Nina seeped away. "What is it?" she said softly.

In one quick movement, Beebee hopped to Deborah's shoulder. She felt the owl's soft wings brush her cheek. There was a rasping noise as if a clearing of the throat, an attempt to verbalise something, but before it could come to fruition, Nina came bustling back.

"Here you go," she said, plonking a bottle of milk and a paper bag containing a small pat of butter onto the counter. "Now, what else— Beebee! What are you doing up there? Get off." She reached over and plucked Beebee from Deborah's shoulder. "Mind your business, you silly bird. Leave her alone."

"She wasn't bothering me," Deborah said.

"She soon would be," Nina said. "That's the thanks I get for saving her. Found her with a broken wing a while ago." She tickled Beebee's neck. "Didn't we? Didn't we, Beebee?"

Beebee cocked her head then hopped along the counter. Nina grabbed her. "All better now, aren't you, Baby Beebee?" She scratched Beebee's neck again while the owl turned her gaze to Deborah. Definitely cross this time.

Deborah left them to it and explored the store's shelves. After a few trips to and fro to get her supplies home, she set to preparing lunch.

"I've still got a lot of cleaning to do," Deborah said to Father as they sat together on the veranda.

He said nothing. He had said nothing at all during lunch, but at least he had eaten most of what she had put on his plate.

"I'd better get back to it," she said. "I'm going to make a start on the kitchen—it's filthy. So, I'll be right here. Let me know if you want anything."

Again, nothing. She was unsure if he had even heard her. She took his plate and got up. She was almost through the door when she heard him whisper.

"What?" she said, turning.

"Trees," he said quietly. "The doorway. Do you see it?"

"No."

"You're not even looking."

How did he know she wasn't? His eyes were half-closed and his head bowed.

"Look," he said.

To humour him, she glanced over at the trees. That's when she saw them—two trees, a golden light shimmering across their slim trunks, the higher branches stretched towards each other like arms linking together. Just like a doorway. She felt a horrible sensation in the pit of her stomach. Then, the mirage faded, and the trees were again subtly lit in hues of green and brown, indistinguishable from the others.

"There is no doorway," she said firmly. "They're just trees."

She dreamt of Father that night. His gold-etched doorway of trees stood in front of him, and he looked back at her, sorrow written on his face. Then, he was gone.

She woke with a gasp and sat bolt upright. In the pale light that filtered through her smudgy window and silvered her bed, she sat listening. The creaks of the old shack, the distant sigh of the trees, was all she heard. Still, the vision of his face had been so vivid that she had to go to his bedroom, reassure herself that he was still there.

In his doorway, she stood listening for his breathing, trying to see if there was a shape on the bed. His window was worse than hers for letting in any moonlight, so she could not make anything out in the darkness. Rather than turn the light on and wake him, she inched quietly towards the bed and felt for where his shoulders ought to be. Nothing. She felt around more of the bed. Still, nothing.

She snapped on the light. His bed was empty. Perhaps he was in the bathroom. She hurried downstairs, stumbling in her haste, but the house was quiet and dark. She turned on every light, looked in every tiny room, her heart pounding. She went outside and checked the veranda.

"Father!" she shouted into the chill night air. "Where are you? Father!"

Would he even answer if he heard her? The woods had the same eerie green glow that she had seen the night she and Father had arrived. It grated on her nerves somehow, made her feel that something wasn't quite right. There was nothing peaceful, nothing healing about this stupid place. Father was *wrong*. And now, what did he think he was doing? Had he gone to his stupid tree 'doorway'? Where did he think he would end up by doing that?

"Father!" she called again, her voice sounding hollow, ineffectual, as if it would not reach through into the green glow.

Something blew gently against her cheek and tickled her neck. She shrieked and jumped away, frantically brushing at her shoulder and face. Her hands connected with something soft, cool, feathery, and there was an answering squawk to her shriek. A small shadow dropped in front of her and landed on the veranda.

"Stop it," hissed a raspy voice.

She shrieked again and kicked out.

"Stop that!" rasped the shadow, hopping away from her. "It's me, Jacob! Or rather, Beebee. You're right—it *is* a stupid name. But that's not my name; Jacob is. And I am *not* female."

What? This was the owl from the store? "You—you can talk!"

"How observant of you."

"But… that's not possible!"

"Sure, okay. And here I thought you might be more sensible than that."

"Did… has… Nina taught you to talk?"

"*Hrmph.* Don't be absurd, please." He walked along the veranda closer to her and into the pool of light that shone through the open door. "It would be better to continue this discussion inside."

Deborah could only stare down at him. It was definitely the owl at her feet. He stared intently up at her, his enormous dark pupils ringed in yellow, his brown and white feathers giving him a marbled appearance.

"Seriously—" he said.

She watched his beak move as he spoke.

"—I would rather we spoke inside."

He looked like a tiny, hunched man as he walked through the doorway, his taloned feet stepping lightly. She went after him, thinking she must be dreaming.

"Shut the door," he said, and with a flurry of wings, he leapt to the kitchen counter.

She did what he said. Any moment, she would wake up, and Father would be in the next room, and everything would be as it was before.

"That's better," said Jacob, his eyes half-closed in the light. "I don't want anybody in this village knowing that I talk—they're a little strange about some things. Coop knows, but Nina doesn't, and I'd rather it stayed that way. You seem different, so I don't mind you knowing. Odd of Coop to decide to release me now on condition I come advise you of your father's departure—you obviously know he's gone; otherwise, why would you be yelling Father, Father? Weren't you expecting him to go so soon? Were you planning on leaving together?"

"Wait... what?" Deborah said.

"What do you mean, what? Which part didn't you understand?"

"Did you see my father leave? Where did he go? Is he still in the village?"

"No," Jacob said. "I saw nothing, but Coop said he saw a stranger go into the woods. You're the only strangers currently here. Coop was too shaken to tell me any more about it, and of course he would not go after your father himself or have dared call out to him. Nobody here in this village wants to set foot under the trees. They're like that. Not that I blame them; I haven't seen a custodian since I came here, which is curious."

She shook her head. This could not be real. She tried to absorb what he had said—where she was, who he was—a *talking* bird? What was happening? "No. What? No. We just arrived yesterday. I don't know—he's gone into the woods? What do you mean leaving together? We just got here."

"It's not really my business if he's gone, but I'm sorry you've been caught by surprise. Your father really should have made it more clear, or at least waited until you were ready to go with him. Sometimes I don't know about you image-bearers. Where are your brains? I—"

She turned and went quickly through the house. Up the stairs to her father's room to look again at his empty bed, into her own room, downstairs to the tiny bathroom, laundry, and living room, then back into the kitchen.

Illuminated in the weak light of the single bulb that hung from the ceiling, the owl glared at her from the freshly-scrubbed and sanded woodblock countertop. "Thanks for walking off while I'm in the middle of talking to you," he said.

So, this was not a dream. Besides, no dream would have the sharp disinfected scent of the kitchen stinging her senses, and her aching muscles cried evidence of yesterday's hard work.

"He's not here," she said. "He's not here. You said Coop saw him leave? Where did he go?" Maybe he really hadn't gone to his 'doorway of trees'. Surely he wouldn't be so careless as to do that? Then again, when did he ever think clearly anymore?

Jacob gave an exasperated hiss. "I'm fairly sure I just explained to you that he went into the woods. Are you still half asleep? You look it."

"When?" Deborah asked. "When did Coop see my father?"

"He would not say. It may have been some time ago, as I am certain Coop didn't tell me about it immediately. It was hard enough getting what information out of him that I could. Although why he thought I should do anything about it, I don't know. It does not matter; I'm glad to be released. I'll be off now if you don't have any more questions. I don't want Coop catching me again."

"Can you go now, quickly fly, and search for my father?"

Jacob shuffled on his feet. "I'm sorry, I am still healing from my injury. Flying is difficult. I am not as strong as I was. My flight to you is the most I have done in several weeks. I don't plan to fly very far right now; I'll just get to the trees. Coop won't go near them, so I'll be safe there."

Deborah stared out the window. There was no knowing when Father had left. His walking would be slow, methodical, as it had been on their trek to Shilhim, but he would be single-minded and determined to forge on to wherever he was heading. Had he taken any food for himself? Was he dressed warmly? He was not used to caring for himself. Would he come to his senses and realise what he had done, then try to come back?

She grabbed a small bag from a cupboard. "Jacob, can you help me? I've read in books that owls see long distances, even in the dark." She crammed bread and fruit into the bag. Father might be hungry when she found him—it was so cold out there. "If I carry you, will you help me find my father?"

"You've read about me in books?" Jacob said. "How flattering."

Deborah filled a water bottle at the tap, splashing it everywhere in her haste.

Jacob hopped away from the droplets. "I suppose I could go with you. We would certainly cover more ground if you carry me."

"And you'll be able to show us the way back here?" Deborah asked.

He shrugged. "If you want to return."

"Thanks." She ran upstairs to change her clothes.

❦ 3 ❦

Jacob was where she had left him standing on the kitchen counter. He gazed at her, his pupils black pinpricks in bright gold, inscrutable and unblinking. She slung the bag over her shoulder, and he leapt to her other shoulder. He felt light, but there was something comforting about his grasp, like a steadying hand. "Thank you so much for helping me, Jacob."

"Now, that's better than Beebee, isn't it," he said.

She could not smile but turned out the light and shut the door behind them. In the chill night air, the trees stood in the nebulous green glow. She tried to see which ones were the 'doorway' that Father would surely have used as his starting point. Between two of the trees, the light seemed slightly mistier, paler, almost hinting at leading to something beyond, yet when she set off towards them, the trick of light disappeared so that they became ordinary and merged with the other trees. Then, a glint of light caught her eye. Small like a star. Or, a lamp.

"Father!" she shouted and ran to the trees.

Jacob's talons tightened on her shoulder, and she yelped.

"Quiet!" he hissed.

"Look!" she said, pointing. "There he is!" There was nothing to back her claim—no glint of light, just uniformity of green haze clinging to the myriad of tree trunks. She bit her lip, looking this way and that. "I thought I saw his light."

"I would hear him if he was that close," Jacob said in a low voice, "and I saw nothing but a firefly. Please keep your voice down. We don't want to draw attention."

"Attention from what?"

"Oh, the silly people from the village would probably try and hold you back from crossing into the woods. Also, there might be guandras nearby. You never know."

She snorted. Caricature drawings of bogeymen immediately sprang to mind, and the teasing schoolyard chant: 'Guandras, guandras, think they're gonna getcha, guandras, guandras, cook you up and eatcha'. They were anything ranging from a blob with crazy eyes to a detailed, many-limbed creature, depending on the child's fancy. She hadn't heard of guandras since those school days. "Ha. That's funny."

"Funny? How so?"

"You're kidding, aren't you? Guandras?"

"Kidding?" he said, gruffly. "No, truly, there might be some nearby. I suppose you think it so quiet and green here that it's not a possibility, but really, you should know it doesn't matter what any of your settlements look like—a guandra can arise anywhere and—"

"No, I mean, guandras. They're not real."

"*Hoohoo*," he uttered softly, sounding as though he laughed. Then, after a moment, he said, "Oh, you are serious?"

"Yes, of course I am."

"Really? You are serious?"

"Yes! There's no such thing as a guandra. Everyone knows that."

"But you're an image-bearer!"

"A what?"

"*Im-age-bear-er*," he said, exaggerating each syllable. "Are you hard of hearing?"

"No, I'm not. What do you mean?"

"What do you mean, what do I mean? I don't know how to say it any differently. You are an image-bearer as I am a dweller, and the brismuns, shaseeliany, and rovi are custodians. This is pretty standard stuff; don't act like you don't know what I'm talking about."

She was taken aback by the mention of brismuns. The other names meant nothing to her, but she remembered the tale of brismuns very well. The forest creature, roaming far and wide, his form that of branches and leaves. In her childhood, she had always loved that story and the accompanying picture of a broadly smiling face fashioned with twigs and moss, a little bird perched on his head. She remembered poring over it, taking in every detail, imagining the life of a brismun as he roamed the forests. But that had been a story to enjoy as a child, nothing more.

"Certainly," Jacob went on, "I have heard some argument that brismuns may indeed be image-bearers, but that, as we all know, is not so, although I can understand the sentiment behind that opinion. However, is it clear: they are custodians. Now, are we going to stand here all night or are you going to move?"

She looked about the woods, hoping the way forward would seem evident. Which direction would Father have chosen? She could not see his 'doorway', and there was not any obvious or easier-looking way to choose. The ground was level and the undergrowth low and scattered so as to not be much of a hindrance.

"Can you see where my father might have gone? His footprints, or anything?"

"No," said Jacob. "You'll have to go in under the trees so we can have a look. Hopefully, we will soon find something helpful."

She headed off in the direction that seemed best to her, by a natural parting of trees, where the shafts of moonlight penetrated, or anything that might seem right. Away from that strange green glow—it bothered the senses somehow.

As she walked under the canopy of the trees, she half-expected to feel something—some kind of power. She grimaced and walked on. Father's words must have affected her. Well, she felt nothing. Besides, the closer she was to the trees, the more unremarkable they appeared. Even the green glow in the distance dissipated.

A chirping and buzzing sprang up amongst the rustle of leaves.

She flinched. "What's that?"

"What's what?"

"That noise."

"Crickets. Ah yes, image-bearer from the lifeless city where no crickets are found and you have to read about them in books. Keep going; they won't bite."

Her own footfalls were soft and muffled, and, as she went on, the crickets hushed then began again further away.

Jacob's talons suddenly clenched her shoulder.

"Hey!" she cried. "Don't!"

"Not another step," he said. "Look at your feet."

There was a thin dirt track, the faint beginnings of a path in an incongruous clarity of grey light. She felt the stirring of hope. If Father had come this way, then perhaps he had used it. She bent to see if she could see any impression in the dirt, any hint of his footprints.

"*Ack!*" Jacob said. "Don't touch it. The villagers don't like to go into the woods, so they can't have made this path. It must certainly belong to guandras. Keep away!"

Again with guandras. This was no time for such stories. Further along the path, she glimpsed what looked like the imprint of a boot. She hurried over to it. Jacob hissed and leapt from her shoulder, and, as she looked down at the path, a reflection of her face appeared upon it. Pale and shadowy in the grey light, her own face stared up at her with the surprise she felt, and then, frozen in that expression, it slid swiftly away along the path, wound in and around the trees, and was gone.

She shrieked and jumped off the path, almost falling into the nearest tree. "What was that?"

"Didn't I tell you to keep away from it?" Jacob's voice came from higher in the tree. "Why didn't you listen to me? And, for pity's sake, be quiet." He swooped down and landed on her shoulder. "Now, that's sure to do something. If any guandras are around, it'll let them know you're here. We'd better get away from this area. *Now*. Go on, move." His talons dug painfully into her shoulder. "Get as far away from this path as you can. *Run*."

She stumbled away from the path and ran, half-tripping on tangled brush, clutching at tree trunks. Where was the image of her face going? How could that have happened? Guandras could not be real, could *not* be real. Yet, this bird on her shoulder talked; that path took an image of her face. What was this place? Why was Father wanting its power? What power?

The further she went through the woods, the more gnarled tree roots and dead branches there were to jump or dodge, and the undergrowth thickened. As it forced her to slow her pace, she felt some of the panic leaving.

What was she doing? Where was she going? Maybe it had all been a trick of the moonlight; maybe there had been a pool of water on the path that she had not noticed at first, and a ripple caused the impression of movement. Things like this did not happen, and she must have imagined it. It had only been a path and one that Father might have used. Now she was running like an idiot without any thought or plan. She stopped to catch her breath and bent, hands to her knees. Jacob moved onto her back.

"I shouldn't have run," Deborah said between gasps. "Why did you make me? I don't even know where I'm going, where Father is. He might have… might have gone that way, used that path."

"Don't be ridiculous," said Jacob. "If he'd tried, he probably would have got stuck on it. I'm surprised you didn't. You've done the right thing by putting distance between us and the path."

"But, now what do I do? Father could be miles away by now. I've probably gone in completely the wrong direction!"

"Lowering your voice would be a good start, and then letting me think about what to do."

"You could fly, I'm sure you could, instead of sitting like a lump on me and expecting me to do all the work. Search the area, go!"

He flew from her back to the nearest low hanging branch, then turned to face her, folding his wings deliberately. "What's the matter with you? You should never have looked at that path—it's brought out all your charming qualities. I'm beginning to think I shouldn't have bothered helping you at all."

She glared back at him. "You're not helping me. You're just getting a free ride out of Shilhim, Beebee. Why don't you put a saddle on me while you're at it?"

He shut his eyes, and his body trembled. "*Hoohoo!*"

"Are you laughing at me?"

He shuffled around on the branch, turning his back to her. "*Hoo!*" Then he stiffened and swivelled his head this way and that. His eyes were wide, and his tail flicked side to side. "*Hush*. I hear something." He flew to Deborah's shoulder. "Remain still," he said, his voice barely above a whisper. "Say nothing."

'Guandras' sprang to her mind along with the mirror image of her face travelling on the path. She frowned, irked at herself for entertaining childish thoughts. The shadowy woods, the strangeness of the night, Jacob—it was all getting to her and causing her to think nonsense. No, if anything, it would be a wild animal that Jacob had heard. She listened hard, but the woods were tranquil, the crickets less regular in their chirping, and the sighs of the breeze in the treetops and creaks of the boughs steadied and calmed her heart.

She was about to say to Jacob that she heard nothing when there came distant dull thumps like a sledgehammer pounding the earth. The sound gradually grew louder and, she realised, closer. Slow and regular, it had a mesmerising quality, and she stood still, hardly daring to move.

A shape passed through the shadows, leaping, bounding; it was hard to see what it was, if it was taller than she, certainly broader. She sucked in a breath, her body tense with fear. What kind of wild animal was this? Whatever it was sprang behind the trees, covering a significant distance with each jump.

"Jacob," she whispered.

He covered her mouth with his soft wing and pressed himself against her neck.

"Jacob!" called a clear voice, and the bounding shadow turned and made right for them.

Deborah shrieked and ran.

"*Stop*," rasped Jacob in her ear.

"Stop!" called the clear voice.

The thing was alongside her as she dashed through the woods. It thumped the ground with each jump, keeping pace with her, and whenever they crossed into pale beams of moonlight, it appeared like a bush, a tree, a shrub, but with a squinting, grinning face. Deborah shrieked and stumbled across the ground, and it leapt in one bound to catch up with her. No matter which way she ran, it stayed with her.

"Stop," Jacob said in her ear. "You can't outrun him."

"I can't," she gasped. "I can't! It's going to get me!"

"Get you what?" the creature said in its clear bell-like voice. "Oh, do you mean catch you and eat you? No, I don't think so." It leapt ahead of Deborah and stood facing her. "I'm sure you're too tough and stringy. You'd probably give me severe gastric problems."

"Brismun," Jacob said, "who are you? Are you the custodian of this region?"

"I am not," it answered, "but I am a friend to you, dweller. I am Erno."

Deborah tripped in the shadows and fell; hands caught her before she hit the ground, and the creature, the *brismun!*, was right in front of her. It was difficult to see it clearly as a thick layering of leaves above shrouded her in darkness. She had the impression of roundness, two-tiered? Three tiered? and the scent of something akin to sage. She felt the strange sensation that she should reach out and touch the brismun, that he drew her in somehow, but instead she stepped back and tried to edge away. Brismuns weren't real; they belonged solely in a storybook!

He leaned towards her. "Jacob! You're looking a bit different to what I thought you would—it sounded like you were a Picaymy Owl. Now I see I was mistaken."

"No," Jacob said, and there was a rustling sound in the leaves overhead. "Erno, I'm up here."

"Well," said Erno, "that was a waste of a joke."

Deborah felt strange, thick fingers that were almost furry, velvety, yet cool, touch her hand. She hastily withdrew from his grasp.

"You're all right," Erno said. "Don't panic. I won't eat you. I was just kidding about that. Nothing but fine earth for me. What's your name?"

"D—Deborah," she said.

"Hello, D-Deborah," said Erno. "What are you doing in these parts? Acting as Jacob's personal carrier?"

Deborah stared back at the shadow, lost for words.

"She's searching for her father," Jacob said.

"Why's that?"

"He came into the woods by himself and, from all accounts, is unwell. I don't suppose you've heard him anywhere?"

"No, not at all," said Erno. "Oh dear. That's no good. And you, Jacob, why are you here? I think that this is not your region—you don't seem to belong."

"Yes, true. I've come into it with Deborah only moments ago. Before then, my wing was broken, and I was taken to an image-bearer's village to be cared for. Why didn't the custodian in my region tend me?"

"I can't say, not knowing which is your region. I do hear that one not far away has closed; perhaps that was yours and the custodian had left. Come to my hand and let me feel your wing."

Deborah saw the movement of Jacob hopping down.

"No," Jacob said, "my region hasn't closed. I'm from the same region as Deborah, and even though most of the dwellers have moved out, there are still many image-bearers in a few cities and villages."

"Oh," said Erno in a subdued voice. "I think I know which region you're referring to. My sister was pushed out of there long ago; that's why she didn't come to you when you broke your wing. You should have left the region when she did."

Jacob hissed. "I did not know."

After a moment, Erno spoke again. "You've healed very well. I feel weakness in your muscles, but your bones have knit strongly. It has been some time since the break, yes?"

"Yes."

Erno chuckled. "You've gone soft. How long have you been at the village?"

Jacob gave a tiny, self-conscious cough. "A while. I was kept against my will."

"Was you? Well. You are free now. Unless you want to go back?"

"Uh, no."

"Very convincing."

"*Hoo.*"

"Exactly," said Erno. "Now, while you—oh! there's a path approaching. Deborah, I suggest we move away from here; it seems purposeful in the way that it moves. It's coming right towards us."

"It might be the same one we encountered not far from here," Jacob said. "She stood upon it and looked, and it took her image."

Erno tut-tutted. "Why did you let her do that? You should know better, Jacob, you're an awakened dweller."

"I tried to stop her, but she ignored me."

"Stop talking about me as if I'm not here," Deborah said. "Yes, I made a mistake by looking at your path, but I didn't know!"

"It was not my path," said Jacob, "and yes, you did know, because I told you to keep away from it."

She glared in his general direction. "I didn't know what it would do!"

"The path creeps nearer while you two bicker," Erno said.

Deborah felt the firm grip of his hand on her elbow, and she quickly drew her arm away.

"Deborah," Erno said, "I don't mean to frighten you. Well, maybe I do a little. But I am serious—this path is behind you, not far from your feet. Can't you hear it? Move immediately, please."

Deborah felt a shift in the air, as if his command should be listened to and heeded. Even the trees seemed to press closer overhead. She tried to see the path in the darkness but only saw shifting shadows that might have been from the branches swaying overhead.

"Deborah," Jacob said, and landed on her shoulder. "Listen to the brismun custodian!"

Paths, brismuns, talking birds… it was all a bit much to take in the middle of the night.

"You will be safe with me," Erno said. "Come along."

He hopped away, thudding the ground. She peered after him in the dark woods.

"I can't really see where I'm going," she muttered.

"The ground is clear before your feet," said Jacob. "I will guide your steps if you like."

In such a manner, Deborah made her way after Erno. He hopped slowly ahead of her, and, as they came into a less thickly-growing part of the woods, she caught better glimpses of him in the moonlight. She could see that he had one leg like that of a tree trunk, and his head and body were rounds set one upon the other, reminiscent of a snowman.

There was something like a bushy halo about his head. She decided from the play of light and the way that the halo moved and rattled that it was twiggy kind of hair. His face, she could not see clearly even when he turned to her. How had she had the impression of a face grinning at her earlier when it was so difficult now to determine any expression?

"Very quiet part of the woods," Erno remarked. "Not much life here."

"Yes," said Jacob. "I don't like it."

"Many dwellers have moved on to a new home, as you should, too."

The thought of home jolted Deborah. Here she was, walking through the woods, meekly following Erno. Why was she doing that? "Wait," she said. "Where are we going?"

"To the lumdils," said Erno.

"The what?"

"Not *what*, but as Jacob would say, '*hoo*'."

And Jacob did, a stifled *hoo* as if Erno's mimicry amused him.

"We're not far from a lumdil village," Erno said. "I would expect if there's anything to learn about your father's whereabouts, then I will hear it there. The trees in those parts have more life and may be a bit more forthcoming. The ones in this region aren't happy, are they, Jacob? Grouchy sorts; life is moving inward, retreating from the outskirts, and it shows. They're sullen and act as if interaction is an indignity. Besides, I have a good friend at the village, and I've been told to go to him."

"What are the regions?" Deborah said. "My father was interested in them. He had never spoken of regions until a couple of days ago, and I don't know what he meant by it."

"You don't?" Erno said. "That's a bit funny, considering you belong to a region. Then again, I don't always understand you image-bearers."

"I'm not an image-bearer."

"Blimey," he said. "It's true, then. Those from the outer regions no longer view themselves as image-bearers. What do they think they are? Dwellers? Or, custodians?"

"Nothing," said Deborah. "I've never even heard of what you're talking about."

"Never?" Erno said.

Jacob harrumphed and shifted on Deborah's shoulder. "*Not* never. It's like I say things and they go in one ear and out the other."

She frowned. "I *am* listening to you; I *was* listening. I just—I have a lot to think about. You're supposed to be helping me find my father, and now look—what are we doing? He could be miles away from here by now."

"He probably is," said Erno. "Otherwise, I would have heard something of him. Don't worry, I've been assigned to both you and Jacob as your custodian, so all is well."

How could he talk so blithely about this? Father could be anywhere; he was all alone, most likely cold, and she could not imagine him being able to find his way back to the village.

"Both of us?" Jacob said. "Isn't that unusual? She's an image-bearer. I thought rovi were the custodians of image-bearers and you a custodian of dwellers. Shouldn't a rova be here for her?"

"I suppose so, but here I am. It's unorthodox, but I don't mind. Come to think of it, I'd assume someone has been assigned to your father, Deborah. He'll be fine. He's probably got a rova."

"How do you know he's fine? He is *not* fine. What's a rova?"

Jacob shuffled his feathers. "*Huh.* Here we go again. Didn't I just say that the rovi are the custodians of image-bearers?"

"What you're saying doesn't mean anything to me!"

"Clearly."

She glared sidelong at him. "I'm sick of wasting time talking about this when my father is lost out here. Why won't you take this more seriously? He needs help, and I need help to find him."

"I am helping you," Erno said. "I do take the matter seriously. Deborah, I'm here to help and protect you. Sonax gave me this task, so it's very important to me. *You* are very important to me. I've been told to take you into the lumdils' region to try and seek more answers and help there. If you don't want my help, then I will do as you say and leave you. As custodian, I must abide by that."

There was that strange name again, the one Father had mentioned out of nowhere. "Who's Sonax?" she said.

Jacob spluttered and hissed. "Who's Sonax? Are you serious? Don't you know anything?"

She resisted the urge to shove him off her shoulder.

"Sonax is the Oxpeina," Erno said. "And so, you bear his image, hence, image-bearer. Get it?"

"Oxpeina? What's that?"

"This is ridiculous," Jacob said. "How can you not even know what the Oxpeina is?"

"Remarkable," said Erno. "You're an image-bearer of the Oxpeina, and you don't know what the Oxpeina is."

Deborah sighed. As if she should know anything about the woods.

They were of no interest back where she was from. Life in the city of Eblhim was full and busy, encompassing much more than crickets and twigs. Erno and Jacob probably knew nothing at all about Eblhim and how big it was; all they were used to was trees in every direction. So, for them to be taken aback by her not knowing custodian-image-bearer-Oxpeina-things when there was a bigger world out there beyond the trees was itself ridiculous. "So, you mean, he's a person."

"No, I mean you're a person. Sonax is the overseer of regions and custodians, and holder of Oxpeina-life."

Whatever that meant.

Erno gasped. "Not again! That path has caught us up. I don't like that it's so persistent in following. Deborah, we need to keep moving."

She turned to look, realising as she did that the woods around them were brightening in the dawn. A few feet away was a path, a sandy shimmer across its curved form as it lay in dappled light.

"I think it's a different one," said Jacob. "The one Deborah stepped on was smaller than that."

"It's beautiful," Deborah said.

"It's the same one," Erno said. "It's probably just trying harder to attract you. Get away from it; they use twisty mind tricks."

As he hopped away from the shadow of a tree and turned to beckon her, the morning light fell softly over him. His round face was so mossy that his features were almost lost amongst the greenery. His eyes were mere slits, squinting to the point of appearing closed. He had no nose but a wide smile that extended most of the width of his face. His brown, bushy hair was a mass of twigs, dotted here and there with hints of green. The moss thickly covered the rest of his rounded body and arms so that he looked like a neatly trimmed shrub if he stood still, his thick arms close to his body. The impression of a shrub was further enhanced by his having only one leg, a solid moss-covered trunk that made him look as though he grew from the earth.

The storybook from Deborah's childhood and the pencilled illustration of the brismun were almost exactly right, then. Erno's face was perhaps not so clear, yet there was something comfortably familiar about him. Deborah felt as though she should be unnerved by the sight of such a strange creature before her, but she wasn't. As he grinned at her, his face framed by his twiggy hair, she felt like grinning back at him. She didn't, for there really was nothing to smile about, and she didn't see why he should be smiling either, but still she felt the urge to.

"Move, Deborah!" Jacob said in her ear. "The path!"

She was startled to see the path was at her feet, though she had not heard or seen it move. She hurriedly stepped away and followed Erno.

On and on they went through the woods. The thump of each leap Erno took was accentuated with the swishing rattles of his twiggy hair, the faint sage-like scent stirring the earth around him. Sunshine filtered through the leaves and shone in hazy patches on the ground, and Deborah found herself noticing every fallen branch or curved hollow at the base of a tree. Had any of these been where Father had sat and rested? And, was every broken twig on the ground that way because he had trodden on it?

Maybe with the dawn he had come to his senses and realised what he had done and was now trying to find his way back to her. She supposed that was wishful and useless thinking, seeings as he did not show much feeling or consideration for her. She was always the one trying to look after him, not the other way around.

The light weight of Jacob grew more noticeable, his talons a firm and unmoving clamp on her shoulder, and the bag that had not bothered her before now seemed a lumpy nuisance. She thought of the days of walking with Father from the city of Eblhim to Shilhim. The pack she had worn then had been much larger, the distance greater. She supposed the lack of sleep in the night wasn't helping her feel very energetic now.

She slowly sat beneath the wide, spreading boughs of a tree. "I need a break."

Jacob climbed down her arm to the ground, and she took off her bag and pushed it aside. She eased herself back against the tree trunk.

"I could carry you, if you wish," said Erno.

"No thanks," she said quickly, without looking at him.

"As you say," he answered. "Maybe it's better you strengthen your legs. We will take about three days to get to the lumdils at this pace, I think. Ration your food."

Her eyes widened. "Three days?"

"Or, possibly two. Depends on how quickly you move."

She got up and pulled her bag back on.

"Deborah," Erno said. "It's all right. You can rest."

"It's not all right. My father… what will he be finding to eat or drink? Anything? He's alone out here. I don't even know how warmly he dressed before he set off. He doesn't think of such things."

"He'll be fine," Jacob said, and flew to Erno's twiggy head. "Erno said a rova will be with him. Once we get to the lumdils, Erno expects we'll hear of something. Now you're going to ask who lumdils are, aren't you?"

She shrugged.

"*Hoo!*"

"They're image-bearers like you, Deborah, only different," Erno said, his mossy grin appearing again. "They tend to cluster in villages. The smaller the better, it seems. I think they don't create cities because they like to feel connected to their communities. The one we're going to is called Smoky Glade."

She hitched her bag, trying to make it sit more easily, and wriggled her shoulder to relax the tension she felt from having had Jacob there, then set off once more through the woods.

The further they went, the more activity enlivened the woods as birds fluttered from branches and sang in the trees. Throughout the day, Deborah stopped briefly for short breaks, eating and drinking just enough to keep going. She began to feel foggy from lack of sleep, and Erno and Jacob's chatter flowed on in a babbling stream as she pressed on through the woods. She thought often of Father, wondering where he was, wondering *how* he was. If she saw any movement at ground level through the trees, she found herself catching her breath in a split second of hope that it was Father just ahead. But he did not appear.

Late in the afternoon, Erno stopped and laid his hand against a tree trunk. He bowed his head, his twiggy hair brushing the tree. After a moment, he turned to Deborah and Jacob. "Wait here. Guandras have been sighted nearby. I'll have to go and check for myself where exactly, because the trees are unclear in what they're saying. I'll be right back." He bounded away before they could answer.

Jacob flew up to a branch and turned his head in all directions, his large eyes keen. Deborah wearily sat against the tree Erno had touched, dimly registering that this tree had spoken to him, that it was somehow alive, but everything was all so strange anyway, so what did it matter?

She shut her eyes. Was a tree a dweller? It wasn't a custodian, for Erno was the custodian. Jacob was a dweller, so then birds and probably trees were dwellers. Dwelling in the woods. Had Erno or Jacob said that trees were dwellers? She could not remember. Why bother thinking about it? She wished her thoughts would be still and let her catch some sleep while Erno was gone. She was an image-bearer of Sonax's image, whatever that meant. Was Sonax a custodian? Custodian of the custodians?

She was on the edges of sleep when distant, familiar thumps roused her. With each thump, she felt an answering tremor within the tree she leaned against. The thumps grew louder, fracturing the quietness of the woods, and the tremors within the tree were more distinct, as if a heartbeat quickened to the sound of Erno's approach. She pressed her hand against the rough bark. Did the tree feel excitement, fear, or were the tremors merely an echo of what was pulsating through the ground?

"Go!" Erno called as he bounded into view. "We must go now!"

Deborah struggled to her feet, and Jacob settled on her shoulder.

"Guandras, a mile away!" Erno cried as he leapt towards them, fallen leaves scattering like sparks around his stumpy leg. "Run!"

"A mile?" Deborah said. "I'm not running if they're that far away."

Jacob hissed. "We must do what our custodian says. You don't want to get mixed up with guandras when you don't know how to shield yourself."

"Shield? What?" She yawned.

He pinched her shoulder. "Wake up."

"*Ouch!* I *am* awake."

Erno stood before her, his green, mossy face earnest. "Please, Deborah. I ask you to run in case the guandras come this way. I would not be doing my duty if I did not steer you well away from them."

"You sound very formal," said Jacob. "If I were you, I would just order her to do what you say. Use your influence!"

Erno grinned. "You know I can't do that."

"Well," Deborah said, "if it means that much to you, then I'll keep moving, but I don't really see why I should bother running when they're that far away. How fast do these animals move?"

"Animals?" Erno said. "They're not animals. Guandras aren't dwellers. They're image-bearers, or, I hate to say it, custodians, who've lost who they were and fully turned. Why do you think I'm here to help you as you travel across regions? It's so you won't turn."

Turn? Guandras, custodians, image-whatevers. She sighed. Yet, here was this vibrantly green, moss-covered brismun standing in front of her, come to life from the pages of that old storybook. What were some of the other fantastical creatures in that book? It had been a long time ago that she and Father had read it together. Yes, she remembered now; it had been one of her favourite bedtime storybooks. What was it called?

Jacob pinched her shoulder again. "Hurry up, let's go!"

She glared at him. "Stop doing that!"

"I must! You're standing still like a half-asleep dope. These guandras will target you and do who knows what if they see you. They'll target me, too. Get moving!"

Being targeted by a wild-animal-guandra-thing didn't sound good. Jacob's tense grip on her shoulder meant he was obviously worried, and she did not want harm to come to him either, despite how annoying he could be.

"All right, all right," she said. "I'm coming."

"Good," said Erno.

He leapt away, and she stumbled after him, willing herself to wake up properly, get some energy from somewhere, be able to keep moving again. Erno went on ahead, faster and faster, until she almost lost sight of him through the trees.

"Wait!" she cried. "Erno!"

At that, he stopped, allowing her to catch up with him. "Sorry."

They went on together through the woods until Deborah felt as though her legs moved mechanically, her breath came in gasps, and she feared she would drop at any moment. When Erno finally did stop again, it was so unexpected that she almost fell into him. She clutched at his twiggy hair to steady herself, then her legs tremblingly gave way beneath her, and she sank to the ground.

"You've done well," Erno said. "Rest now, then we must move on again. But I think we can move more slowly."

She could barely nod as she tried to breathe, her lungs feeling as though she could not fill them, her heartbeat whooshing in her ears.

"We should not rest at all," Jacob said. "It will be safer when we're with the lumdils, not here. Keep moving."

She batted feebly at him, indignant that he should suggest '*we* should not rest' when he had done nothing at all but sit on her shoulder like a blob. "Y-you keep moving!"

"Let Deborah rest," Erno said. "The danger has lessened."

"I will go on, then," Jacob said.

Deborah felt him shuffle his wings against her neck as though he was preparing to leap into flight.

"You can't wait?" Erno said. "I said the danger has lessened."

"Lessened but not gone!"

Erno grinned. "You know I can hear guandras before they hear me, so you really should trust me. I am your custodian."

Jacob shuffled his wings again.

"Pardon, Jacob?" Erno's grin was undiminished, although he did not look in Jacob's direction but squinted upwards.

"I said nothing," Jacob said gruffly.

"Your beak moved; I heard it. Were you forming owlish curse words?" Erno suddenly leapt towards a tree. "Ha!" He placed his hand against its trunk. "Very good." He hopped back to Deborah. "Rest as long as you want. The guandras are moving away. Something else has caught their attention: rovi."

"Why would guandras go towards rovi?" Jacob said. "I would expect them to want to be further away."

"I never said they were going towards the rovi," Erno said.

Deborah lay down. It was annoying to hear Erno and Jacob blathering on about rovi and guandras and things that trees said. She was there in front of them, gasping for breath, and they didn't bother asking if she was all right. It was fine for Erno; he was obviously used to leaping about and seemed to have boundless energy. As for Jacob, he just sat there doing nothing. He ignored how hard it was for her to keep running but just wanted her to keep going. At least Erno had disagreed with him and said she should rest, so that was something.

Was the daylight already fading? Surely not. She can't have been in the woods half the night and most of the day already. This was not supposed to be happening. She was supposed to be living in the backwater village of Shilhim, haggling over eggs and bread with the village idiots and scrubbing the rest of the grotty shack that Father had made them rent. How could he be so stupid? Her eyes pricked with hot tears, and she wiped them away. He wasn't stupid. Not really. It wasn't his fault.

4

The next two days were a blur of walking during daylight and sleeping fitfully on the hard ground at night. Her meagre rations ran out—she had never expected to spend so much time in the woods. The only thing she could do was follow Erno. If anyone would have asked her, she had no idea of the way back to Shilhim. The blanketing roof of leaves did not allow her to see the line of mountains that sheltered the village. There was nothing for it but to go on.

The gushing, bubbling sound of water was a welcome relief. Deborah hurried over to a thin ribbon of water flowing across pebbles that lay like milky jewels on the stream bed. She quickly got her empty water bottle from her bag.

"Wait," Erno said. "Let me check that guandras have not ruined it." He stood beside the stream, the lined squint of his eyes more evident as he inhaled deeply.

Deborah looked at the clear water coursing through the shallow channel. "It looks all right to me."

"It will not be if the guandras have touched it," Jacob said.

She rolled her eyes. She was sick of hearing 'the guandras this' and 'the guandras that'. They had not seen a single one since coming into the woods. They had not seen any animals at all, only birds and insects.

Erno leapt into the stream, splashing Deborah. "The water's good. They haven't spoiled this one." His mossy face split into a wide grin as the water frothed around his leg.

"I should hardly expect they would, if we're close to the lumdils," Jacob said.

"I should expect they *would*," Erno said. "Just because it is so close."

"Close?" Deborah dunked her water bottle in the stream. "How close? Are we nearly there?"

"Yes," said Erno. "It's not far now."

"Finally," said Deborah.

"What can you tell us about the village of Shady Glen?" Jacob asked.

Erno laughed. "Not much, but I can tell you about Smoky Glade!"

"*Hoo*. I nearly had it right."

"If you say so. Come to think of it, there's a nice ring to the name: 'Shady Glade'. Perhaps I ought to suggest it to them." He grinned again. "Anyhoo, the lumdils there are pretty much what you'd expect—good folk. Although, last time I visited, several were discussing leaving the village, so I'll be interested to see how many have gone. I think they were expecting their region to close soon."

The babbling sound of the stream was never far from them as they went on, and branches creaked and swayed as a breeze caressed the tops of the trees. It was evening when Deborah realised the woods were thinning, and she paused, her hand against a rough tree trunk, and looked wearily up at the patches of starry sky visible through the spreading fingers of the trees. When she looked ahead and trudged on, the stars still seemed to be ahead of her. They twinkled in the distance, leafy twigs waving before them as though sinuous hands idly traced shadow patterns across the light.

"Smoky Glade?" she asked.

"Yes," Erno answered.

Jacob adjusted his grip on Deborah's shoulder, as if he had woken. "We are finally here."

They came out from the trees to where the village lay nestled in a vast clearing. Many of the houses were higher than they were long, some with a second storey of windows in their steeply-peaked roofs. Lights from the windows and open doorways shone out into the village, giving glimpses of small figures moving between the buildings, carved detailing around doors, rumpled masses of potted plants lining the windowsills. Distant shouts of laughter mingled in the air with the warming aroma of something akin to a roast dinner.

Deborah quickened her pace. She passed Erno and was stopped abruptly by a waist-high stone wall. She had not noticed it before—it seemed to have sprung up from the earth. She was about to climb over when Erno spoke.

"You can try, but it won't do you any good. You'll keep finding yourself on this side of it. This way to the gate."

She climbed over it anyway. And lo, there she was, standing right next to Erno again. She tried again out of curiosity and still landed beside Erno on the woods side of the wall.

He laughed. "You didn't believe me?"

She smiled and gingerly touched the wall. "It's very strange."

"It certainly is," Jacob said, from her shoulder. "It was as though the world turned around me."

Erno thumped along to the right, following the wall as it curved around, until they came to the gate. Roughly-made from planks of wood, it was deeply-grained and pockmarked, looking as though if leaned on or opened too swiftly it might collapse and fall off the bolt hinges that held it upright. Deborah wondered why such a rickety thing was even there, unless it did not matter how it was constructed but also had the same magical qualities as the wall.

Next to the gate was a high-roofed little house. Erno laid his hand on the top of the gate and gave it a pat. The front door of the house opened immediately. A stocky figure ambled outside, carrying a lantern. At first Deborah thought it was a child, but it coughed and cleared its throat in a man's voice.

"*Broo-ha-ha!* Evening, folks!"

"Open up!" cried Erno.

"All right, keep your nose on."

Erno grinned. "I haven't got one!"

The lantern was lifted, casting a glow over a shock of brown hair framing a small and pleasant face. Deborah was somewhat startled by his very large and bulbous nose that was out of proportion with his other features.

"Too true, too true," he said, studying Erno's face. He moved his lantern towards Deborah, and his closely set dark eyes fixed first on her, giving her an odd sensation of being looked into, then Jacob. "Well now, this is peculiar. A custodian, an image-bearer, and a dweller. Sounds like the beginnings to a joke now that I say it aloud." He unlatched the gate and swung it open. "You can all come in." He beckoned smartly to Deborah. "Come on, come on. Don't stand there gawking."

Deborah followed Erno through, and the gate clanged shut behind them.

"Have you seen another image-bearer lately?" Erno asked the gate-keeper. "Similar height to this one with me?"

"*Hmm.*" The gatekeeper scratched his nose, looking thoughtful. "Can't say's I have. Are you all expecting someone else to join you?"

"It is possible," Erno said.

"Okey-doke. I'll keep an eye out."

Deborah felt hopeful at the thought. Yes, it was possible. Father could somehow find his way here. He might even be nearby right now.

"Just a few houses in and there we'll find my friend," Erno said as he hopped along, his stumpy leg sounding dull on the wide cobblestone walkway. "Unless he has gone to the inn, which is a distinct possibility—it's dinner time by the sounds of things. I can hear the great clatter of cutlery and plates being scraped clean by a hundred lumdils."

Deborah heard nothing of that sort but did hear the distant hubbub of voices coming from the centre of the village, peppered by laughter and the occasional good-humoured shout. She felt suddenly tired. This was the place she had been pushing herself to reach, and now that she was finally here, all she wanted was to rest.

The houses she passed were high and narrow; many were built from stone, others from wood, and all had very low doors that she would have to bend down to get through. Father would once have found this interesting. When she was a child, anything out of the ordinary always seemed to catch his attention. She had often heard him say, 'Deborah, what do you think of this? Why do you think it is this way?' and encourage her to take note of anything that might be out of place or seemingly not fit. That was how he had been many years ago. Before all their trouble had begun.

"Cheer up, Deborah," Erno said. "Your breathing sounds sorrowful."

"I'm all right," she said. "Just tired."

The bearer of a lantern scurried towards them along the wide cobblestone walkway. Slimmer and shorter than the gatekeeper, he glowed like a wisp in a circle of lantern light, throwing light beams and shadows onto the ground. His thick, dark hair gleamed, his eyes embers above his large nose.

"What do you know?" Erno said. "Here he is. Hey! You're late for dinner!"

"Yes, I certainly am," answered the lumdil. He paused mid-step and looked at Erno. "Well! I never did! What the!"

"Exactly," said Erno and grinned.

The lumdil placed his hand briefly against Erno's chest, then clasped his mossy hand. "Erno! It's great to see you again. What brings you here?"

"You do, and they do. Nurrel, this is Deborah and Jacob. Deborah, Jacob, this is Nurrel, the friend I was telling you about."

"I do? They do? What?"

Erno chuckled. "We'll explain over dinner."

"Right. Yes. Okay. Now you've got me curious." Nurrel raised his lantern and smiled up at Deborah. "Nice to meet you."

"You, also." Deborah felt as though she said it automatically, for weariness was beginning to overwhelm her.

Jacob shuffled against her neck.

Nurrel lowered his lantern. "Oop. Sorry about that. Your bird didn't seem overly fond of having me shove my lantern in its face."

"*Bird?*" muttered Jacob.

"I'm sorry," Nurrel said. "I see now that you're a Mottle-backed Picaymy Owl."

"That's right," said Jacob.

Nurrel leaned over to Erno and whispered, "Which one is Deborah and which is Jacob?"

"We can hear you," Jacob said.

"Whoops, don't mean to be rude. I'm just not familiar with names like yours."

Jacob shook his wings. "I'm Jacob."

"Right. Gotcha."

Deborah swayed a little on her feet and looked around for somewhere to sit.

Nurrel's smile faded. "Oh! You're worn out, Deborah. I should have seen that right away. You've been travelling with a brismun, and that isn't easy. Take my hand."

"I'm all right," Deborah said.

"She always says that," Erno said. "Even when she's about ready to collapse. She did manage very well to keep up with me, but then her legs are a smidge longer than yours."

Nurrel grinned at Erno, his dark eyes glinting. "Just a smidge, eh."

"We are very tired," Jacob said. "We've been travelling for days."

Deborah looked sidelong at him. Travelling for days? He had done nothing of the sort but spent most of his time on her shoulder.

"How about some dinner at the inn?" Nurrel said. "Or, would you rather come back to my home and rest? Can I take your bag, Deborah?"

She had almost forgotten it was on her back, now so light, her water bottle the only thing it contained. "No. Thank you."

"I think dinner would be best," Erno said. "Deborah's rations have been thin, and her stomach has been making interesting noises for quite some time. It was almost like listening to a new language."

"Come along, then." Nurrel held his hand out to Deborah again.

She looked up at the nearest building, pretending she did not see him, and immediately felt annoyed. Annoyed at him and annoyed at herself for being annoyed, but why was he offering to hold her hand like she was a child? She could still walk; she was merely tired, that was all. She didn't need help.

"She's all right," Erno said.

Deborah shot a look at him. His face in the lantern light wore its usual grin. Again, something about him made her want to smile, made the annoyance melt away. Was this what a custodian did? Gave some sense of security and calm? She sighed. "I think I'm too tired to eat any dinner."

"You need some food," Erno said. "You'll feel better for it."

"That's right," said Nurrel. "As we say, a good meal, a good sleep, gets you up off the slag heap."

"Slag heap?" Erno said. "And how's mining going for you these days?"

"I'm out," Nurrel said. "It's not for me anymore. You're lucky you caught me still here. I've been meaning to leave for a while now, but Sonax had me wait. Don't know what for, but here I am."

Deborah trudged behind them as they went along the cobblestone path together.

"Have many of you left?" Erno asked.

"*Hmm*. Probably half the village by now. Things are really going cold here. I get the impression our region will close before too long. There's less life in the woods hereabouts, too."

"It's happening more around the outer regions," Jacob said.

"Is that so?" Nurrel turned to glance at him. "I don't hear much of that kind of thing here—we're isolated, you know—but I believe you. Things have felt off for a while. As I say, I've been meaning to leave. Most of us here feel that way—that we've got to move on, or should I say *in*. Speaking of in, here we are."

He paused at the steps of a large stone building, the roof of which was high-pitched and carved a sharp silhouette into the starry sky. Light blazed from every window, upstairs and down, and the sounds of laughter and chatter came through the open doorway. A painted sign hung overhead bearing the words: 'The Fat Lady's Arms'.

Deborah followed Nurrel and Erno inside, bowing her head to avoid the top of the doorframe, which was a generous height compared to the other buildings she had passed. The steamy warmth and heady aroma of hot bread, stew, and spices surrounded her. Dozens of lumdils sat around long tables while others stood by a fireplace, dangling toasting forks into the flames. All had very dark, thick hair and oversized noses.

All of a sudden, it struck her that these were the dwarves from the very same childhood storybook that had brismuns. What was the name of that book? That's right: *Legends Of The Greener Land*. Father had used to read it to her. She recalled poring over the illustration of dwarves gathered about a fireplace. One had a jug of beer raised high, and others had ruddy faces glowing in the firelight. How strange that here was something else from that storybook, yet they were not dwarves but lumdils.

As she stood there with Erno and Nurrel, she felt huge and conspicuous, but many of the lumdils simply looked over, smiled, then turned away again to continue their conversations.

"Deborah, hang your bag and coat here," Nurrel said, indicating hooks on the wall beside the door. He set his lantern on a table amongst a jumble of others and turned out its light.

Jacob flew to Erno's twiggy hair, and Deborah hung her things on a hook. Erno briskly shook his head, and Jacob squeaked and leapt back to Deborah's shoulder.

"I can't help it, Jacob," Erno said. "When you sit on my head, it tickles like I'm being bitten by a thousand fleas."

"You should have told me sooner," Jacob said. "I won't do it again."

"A thousand, Erno?" said Nurrel. "Not a hundred, but a thousand?"

Erno laughed.

Deborah thought of the drawing she had always liked of the brismun seemingly happy with the bird in its hair. Who had written that book, and where had they got their ideas? Her brow furrowed as she tried to remember the name of the author. *Legends Of The Greener Land* by... Boggens. Buggens. Moggens. Something like that.

A stout little lumdil bustled up to them, her nose and cheeks rosy, her dark brown hair knotted at the nape of her neck. "Ooh, hello my dears!" She fanned herself with a dish towel. "Come in, come in!"

"Evening, Mrs. Smullim," Nurrel said. "Sorry I'm late."

"No problem! It helps that not everyone lands here at once. Especially now that I'm short-handed. Garney left this morning, did you know? Now I've no other cooks."

"I didn't know. Well. Can I help you in any way?"

She flapped her dish towel at him. "You're a sweetie, Nurrel, but you've got your guests here to think of. Otherwise, I'd rope you in for the washing up! Come now, all of you, sit yourselves down." She herded them over to the nearest table. "Move over, you lot!" she cried to those already seated there.

The lumdils barely paused from their banter as they all shuffled obligingly along the bench seating to make room for Nurrel and Deborah. Jacob climbed down Deborah's arm onto the wooden table, while Erno stood at its head.

"I'll be back in two ticks," said Mrs. Smullim, and hurried away.

The warmth of the inn caused Deborah's eyelids to droop, and the lumdils' chatter buzzed all around her. She was relieved that those she sat next to did not attempt to draw her into conversation.

"Now, Erno," Nurrel said, "are you going to tell me why you're here?"

"To be honest, I'm not entirely sure myself. I was sent to Deborah and Jacob, and told to look after them. Why me, I don't know, as the task should have fallen to a rova. Perhaps because I was nearby at the time."

Nurrel nodded, his large nose bobbing.

"However," Erno said, "the situation is this: Deborah's father has come into the woods alone, and he is not well."

Deborah stirred at that and looked over at him.

"Deborah's trying to find him," Erno went on. "I'm trying to assist—unsuccessfully, I admit, for these trees are quiet and have only been conversing in fragments and not amongst a very wide area at all, so I've heard nothing of his whereabouts. My last instructions were to come to your region for help. Do you know where my sister Lembi is?"

Nurrel's brow furrowed. "*Hmm.* Last I heard, she was away up north. We don't see her very often, so I can't be sure. Do you know if Deborah's father has a rova with him? He shouldn't be answering Sonax's call alone—it can be difficult to cross the regions, and I think would be even harder if he's unwell. I mean, we tend to travel in groups to make it easier."

Erno shook his head. "No idea about any rova, and I don't know if he's being drawn in by Sonax; Deborah said nothing about that." He nudged her. "Your father didn't say his intention was to get to the Oxpeina's region, did he?"

She wished the words didn't sound like a confusing jumble all in together. Everything was so tiring, hard to keep eyes open, so weary. She looked at the flicker of Erno's pupils as he directed his squinting gaze her way. "He said stuff about regions one time, but before that he always said he only wanted to go to Shilhim and sit by the trees, and that's all."

"Shilhim's the village where I was kept," Jacob said.

"Here we are, my dears!" cried Mrs. Smullim as she trotted to the table, carrying steaming platefuls of food. She plonked one in front of Deborah. "Eat up!" She peered at Deborah's face. "Are you awake, my dear?" She slid a small plate in front of Jacob that had raw chunks of meat and a few insects, one of which had twitching legs. Mrs. Smullim swatted it and beamed at Deborah, who had taken a spoon and was feebly digging into the stewy mass set before her. "Awake enough to eat, at least!" She set another plate in front of Nurrel.

"Thank you, Mrs. Smullim," he said. "It looks delicious."

She laughed. "You're easy to please! Now, brismun custodian—I have got my tubby hubby digging up a nice piece of dirt from our garden. I told him to get a bit from next to the herbs, so I hope you'll find it good and flavoursome."

"I'm sure it will be," Erno said.

"Do you want any leaves with that?"

"No, not right now. A small amount of soil will do just fine."

"How about some stew?"

"Maybe another time."

"Salt and pepper?"

"No, but a little sugar would be agreeable."

"Right-o," said Mrs. Smullim and hurried away.

The flavours and ingredients of the stew were unidentifiable to Deborah, but each bite she took spread through her in a haze of warmth. She ate half her plateful, then let her spoon drop. A blanket of sleep fell around her while Erno, Nurrel, and Jacob talked on, their words running together senselessly.

"I need to lie down," Deborah said, her low voice lost in the general hubbub of the inn.

Erno's hand was immediately on her arm. "Nurrel, Deborah's about to fall on the floor and start snoring."

Deborah did not shake Erno's hand off her arm. This time, the unearthly feel of his fingers did not alarm her but instead gave a sense of being steadied while the world around her was slipping sideways.

"Mrs. Smullim!" Erno shouted, his voice carrying across the inn.

Perhaps in one blink Deborah had slept for a moment for the next thing she knew Mrs. Smullim was at her shoulder, laughing. "I hear a brismun bellowing for his dinner! I didn't mean to take so long. I'm still trying to get the worms out of your plateful of dirt. The wriggly squigglers keep burrowing away from me!"

"I'm sure Jacob would love them," Erno said with a grin.

Jacob's round eyes looked crosser than ever. "I don't like worms."

Nurrel smothered a smile.

"Mrs. Smullim," Erno said, "I'm not calling for my dinner. Have you a room for Deborah tonight?"

"Ooh, yes, of course! Poor thing looks exhausted." Mrs. Smullim took Deborah by the arm and helped her up. "Come along with me, dearie. We've got a nice bed all ready for you."

Deborah clutched Mrs. Smullim's warm plump hand as the little lumdil led her away. Through a side door and on through a narrow hallway they went, until they came to a room where a lantern spread a pool of light onto a low bed squeezed into the length of the room and piled with a puffy quilt and pillows.

Mrs. Smullim turned the quilt down and gave it a pat. "Here we are. There wasn't room to put two beds end to end as I'd hoped, so we had to make do with boxes and folded rugs to make the bed long enough for you. I hope it's comfy. You have a good sleep now, lovey."

"Thank you," whispered Deborah as she crawled into the bed. She had the vague impression of her shoes being removed and the covers being gently placed over her, then she slept.

5

Late the next morning, Deborah opened her eyes and stared at the ceiling. It was unevenly smoothed with cream-coloured plaster and wholly unfamiliar. The remote sound of laughter was like the cries of emerald-tipped gulls along the coast of Eblhim, but this was not her home in Eblhim. The bed beneath her legs was lumpy and lopsided. The room narrow, the ceiling not so very far away. Recognition dawned in her mind. She was in Smoky Glen. Shady Glade. Whatever the lumdil village was called.

She sat up slowly, muscles aching. How many days had passed since she had left Shilhim? Three? Four? It was all a blur of trees and walking, stumbling, walking, and more trees, and snatches of sleep on the ground.

None of this should ever have happened. Father should never have left her—why had he left her? Had he considered her at all? Did he think of her now? Or was he too busy caught up in chasing his delusions? He was lucky she was trying to find him at all. She had endured him being this way for a long time. It was like she was the only one who had to keep forging on, keep trying to look after them both, keep being the sane one in the family. Some father he had turned out to be.

She slipped on her shoes and shuffled out into the hallway, heading in the direction she thought the main hall might be. Fortunately, there was a bathroom on the way, and she freshened up there, making use of the dwarfish facilities.

The main hall of the inn was empty, but for Erno and Jacob.

Erno's mossy face folded into a smile. "You're finally up. I thought the breakfast crowd would wake you sooner, but you kept on snoring."

Was he joking, or was his hearing really sensitive enough to have heard her?

"You can have breakfast here unless you'd rather we go over to Nurrel's now," he said.

"Here is good." She sat on the low bench at one of the tables, trying not to bang her knees.

Erno turned towards the kitchen. "Mrs. Smullim!"

Her rosy face appeared around the kitchen doorframe, and she beamed at Deborah. "Ooh yes!" she cried and disappeared.

"Deborah," said Erno, "I have something to tell you."

His tone of voice was serious enough to make her heart give an uncomfortable lurch.

Jacob stalked across the table towards her. "We have some interesting news that could be about your father."

What did 'interesting' mean? Interesting bad or interesting good?

"It's not certain, of course," Jacob went on. "One day ago, what was thought to be an image-bearer of a height taller than you was seen. He was thought not to be gehun, but we can't be sure. I would expect it to be your father, for the gehun do not usually like to travel above-ground. Although, of course, they have been known to, but I think their build is different enough to not make that mistake in distinguishing who it might be, so it must be him. Although—"

Deborah slapped her hand on the table. "Jacob! Get to the point!"

He scowled at her. "Have some patience! I'm wanting you to take this news for what it is—an unconfirmed rumour."

Mrs. Smullim's brisk footsteps echoed through the hall as she brought a steaming bowl and mug to the table.

"Whoever he was," Jacob said, "he was seen some distance south of here. It was said that a group of guandras were stalking him, but they were confronted and stopped."

"Don't worry, dearie, the rovi stopped them," said Mrs. Smullim as she set the bowl and mug in front of Deborah. "Good old rovi. We can always count on them!" She trotted back to the kitchen.

"How do you know all this?" Deborah asked Jacob.

"I got wind of it in the trees this morning," said Erno. "They are an almost chatty sort in these parts. For trees, that is." He grinned. "Some reading between the lines was necessary."

"What was said, exactly?"

"I can't say, exactly. That's expecting too much of a tree. To your mind, they would seem to be flitting from one unconnected subject to another, yet if you listen well enough, a pattern, or thought, emerges."

"You heard well enough the other day about guandras being a mile away."

"That news came as a snapping of twigs, an outburst felt by one that reverberated along. The estimation of distance was mine, and then I heard the guandras for myself as I got closer to them."

"So, what you're telling me is that, in fragments, and reading between the lines, you heard the trees talking about guandras and rovi being around my father. But you don't know where, exactly, and you don't know if it was him, exactly, and you think perhaps one lot was hunting him and the other lot stopped it."

"Exactly," Erno said and grinned.

"Did you go out last night and try to find him?"

Erno shook his head, rattling his twiggy hair. "No. I didn't want to leave you while you were sleeping. Now that you're up and awake, I'll go into the woods to find my sister. She might have heard something of your father if he has passed through her region. Jacob and Nurrel will keep you company while I do that."

She frowned at him. Didn't want to leave while she was sleeping? What was she, a child? "You didn't need to stay. You could have gone out searching for my father or tried to get better news of him from the trees instead of standing around here. You've wasted the night by not doing that. You're taking this custodian business too literally. Now, who knows where my father has got to? He might have gone even further away in the night, and the one lead we've had, you didn't act on."

Jacob hissed.

"My apologies," said Erno.

"Apologies aren't enough," she said. "You knew the reason I came here was to find my father. I want help to do that, not have a custodian cling to my every move as if I can't look after myself."

"But you can't look after yourself," said Jacob. "You'd be stuck on a guandra path or lying in a hole somewhere if it wasn't for us. How do you think you'd find your way through the woods without any help? You're fortunate indeed that you got a custodian sent to you, even if Erno isn't a rova."

"Well, maybe it would have been better if I *did* have a rova—it might have had more sense to go and get my father instead of standing around here all night long."

Jacob glared at her, the gold of his eyes hard and bright. "A rova would not have heard anything from the trees; only a brismun can do that. I think Erno is exactly the kind of custodian you need."

"I don't *need* a custodian!"

"No, what you need is a good kick up the—"

Erno raised his hands. "Hush now."

The echoes of raised voices stilled in the empty dining hall of the inn, and the air seemed to drift about them in a soothing whisper. Anger and annoyance seeped away from Deborah, and she took a deep breath.

Jacob fluffed his feathers and turned his back to her.

"So," said Erno, his voice bell-like and clear in the dining hall, "if I can't get any solid news of your father from my sister, then Nurrel thinks the best idea is to go to Hirahi. That's one of Sonax's outposts for travellers. Nurrel thinks it's probable the rova would take your father there if he's trying to find Sonax."

Deborah stared at the bowl of beige mushy substance Mrs. Smullim had set in front of her and fiddled with the spoon. "He's never talked of wanting to find Sonax; why would he want to do that? He just talked about the power in the woods and finding peace."

"Same thing. It's all in the Oxpeina's region, and, just so we're clear, image-bearer," he said with a grin, "I mean Sonax."

That was as clear as mud. "How far is it to Hirahi?"

"Not very far," Erno said. "Nurrel said it takes about a day to get there. He's offered to show us the way; although I don't really need his help with that, he says he still intends to come with us."

For a moment, Deborah said nothing, surprised by his words. Why would Nurrel offer help? He did not know her. Then again, he and Erno were friends, and Erno had come here specifically to find Nurrel. She had thought it was for some kind of tracking ability that he might have, but now it seemed it was only to decide amongst themselves where to go next. And that was purely based on guesswork as to where Father might be heading. "Fine," she said.

"You will come too, Jacob," Erno said.

Jacob immediately turned his head to face him, as did Deborah, again feeling a strange sense of being compelled by the authority behind Erno's words.

"I suppose that is best," Jacob said.

"Too right," Erno said. "I'm not going to leave you alone just yet. I wouldn't be doing my job if I did that. I want that wing of yours to be good and strong first." He stretched and his wide mouth split into a cavernous yawn. "I'll go now and find my sister, then meet you later at Nurrel's." He leapt away, his heavy thumps resounding throughout the hall.

When Deborah had finished breakfast, she left the inn with Jacob. As she walked the cobblestone pathways threading through the village, the lumdils they passed greeted them with the words, 'Sonax sees you this bright day' or, 'Oxpeina's best'. Deborah supposed it was their way of saying 'good morning' or 'have a good day'.

"Here it is," said Jacob. "This is Nurrel's house. At least I think it is.

It looks different in daylight, and I didn't spend a lot of time here last night. Erno had me doing a few practise flights around the village so I could work on getting stronger."

The stone blocks of the narrow two-storey building were not uniform, but large and small, not always rectangular, yet all fit together in the neat straight-lined house with a curved bay window at one side. The front door was wooden, as were the frames of the windows. A wooden barrel beside the door was filled with a clump of flowers Deborah had never seen before: marbled bronze arching petals around a star-shaped centre. She bent to sniff them, and the stench of musty cheese went up her nose. She squeaked and jerked upright.

Jacob scrabbled about on her shoulder. "What are you doing? You almost made me fall off."

"Almost?" she said, rubbing her nose to try and get rid of any residual pollen. "What a shame."

"*Hoo!*"

The door opened, and Nurrel stood there. His elfin face broke into a smile, his warm brown eyes glancing from Jacob to Deborah. "Nice to see you both again. How are you, Deborah? I'm sorry I didn't offer you my spare room last night, but I think the Smullims are better equipped at converting their beds—I'm afraid I haven't anything big enough."

Deborah sneezed violently, and Jacob pinched her.

"Are you all right?" Nurrel asked.

"She sniffed your flowers," said Jacob. "Don't ask me why she's reacting like that."

"Ah," said Nurrel. "Yes, sorry about that. I haven't yet got the knack of how to infuse a nice fragrance into them. Colours, I can do. Scent, not so much!"

Deborah wiped her nose. "You bred these?"

"Yes." He picked a wilted flower and tucked it underneath the others. "It's just a little hobby of mine, nothing special."

"Very impressive," Jacob said. "I don't know why you say you can't do scent. I liked it."

Nurrel looked up at him. "I thought owls didn't have a sense of smell."

"Yes, we do. Perhaps not as strong as a lumdil's, though. Your noses… well, I… *hrm*… I… "

Nurrel laughed. "You think we have a great sense of smell with our great schnozzles? I don't know about that. I haven't noticed if we do." He shrugged. "Not that I really have anything to compare it with, but I should test that theory sometime. Come on in. Where's Erno?"

"Gone to see if he can find his sister," said Jacob.

"Ah. Well, I have been sorting out what I think we'll need," said Nurrel as he ushered Deborah inside.

She ducked beneath the doorframe and was relieved to find that although the ceiling was close overhead, she could stand upright comfortably. The decor had exposed dark wooden beams, brown-painted walls, and, yes, *brown* furniture. Nurrel obviously had no imagination for colour schemes, or maybe he just liked the colour brown. A grease-spotted cloth on the brown wooden dining table was covered with metal pieces and various tools with wooden handles.

"Excuse the mess," Nurrel said. "I really should clear it out into a workshop, but I think because I've been intending to leave anyway, there hasn't seemed to be much point in doing that."

Jacob flew to a windowsill and the light fell on him, showcasing his beautiful brown-and-white mottled feathers.

"Mrs. Smullim is putting together something for us to eat on the way," said Nurrel. "She has your bag, Deborah, if you were wondering where it is, and one of mine, too. Your coat is right here." He indicated the back of a chair. "I hope you don't mind, but I tried to clean some of the mud off."

She supposed it had got dirty with several nights on the ground. The coat did look better—the dark blue colour was brighter, and now it looked more like it had when she and Father had first set off from Eblhim and she had been deciding what to wear and what to pack. The memory gave her a twisting ache inside. It really hadn't been that long ago, mere days. Now, here she was without him. They were supposed to be together, supposed to be in Shilhim beside the trees so he could find peace of mind. This was no way to find peace, wandering off into an obscenely large tract of forest. What was he thinking? Was he thinking of her at all?

"Deborah," Jacob said, "are you all right?"

She nodded. "Yes."

"You don't look well."

"I'm all right. I think I just need some air." It was annoying how they both stared sympathetically at her. At least Nurrel did, for Jacob's golden glare could hardly be called sympathetic.

"Oh, right, yes," said Nurrel. "More cramped in here for you than me, definitely. It's a nice day outside; there's a seat not far along the row if you want to wait out there for Erno. I'll carry on with my packing and try not to hold you up so we can get going soon."

"What's this?" Jacob flew to a shelf that held a large pair of glasses. "They don't look like they'd fit you, Nurrel."

He chuckled. "I made them for Erno, but they're no good. Having better vision upset his balance somehow."

"Interesting," said Jacob.

Deborah left them to their chatter and went outside, shutting the door behind her. A few houses along was a wooden bench on the cobblestones. She supposed she may as well wait there.

Beyond the steeply pitched roofs of the village, the dark fringe of trees were clustered together, their tops waving gently in the sunshine. Father had been seen some distance south from here. What was *some* distance? She was not even sure which way was south. Then rovi were seen, too. She didn't remember that name being in the old storybook '*Legends Of The Greener Land*'. There had been other things, but what? Brismuns and dwarves, sure, but what about the rest? The names escaped her, so she tried to remember the drawings, their distinctive wavy lines, the quirky little scenes, the assortment of peculiar faces. There had been something wild-faced and angry, teeth bared; she remembered that now, just not its name. And, a... what was it?... a dengla, which looked like a thin man with a vague face, wearing a plain robe. Why she should remember that when the dengla was the most boring thing in the book, she didn't know.

A tiny lumdil girl with long pigtails scurried towards her. "Oi, miss! Oxpeina's best! Ma sent me to tell you she's got your food all sorted for your trip. You going to Hirahi? I wanna go to Hirahi. Ma says we can't go yet. We're going soon now, though. I think we're waiting for Da to pack up, then we'll go. I saw a brismun! Did you see the brismun? I've never seen a brismun up close." She stared up at Deborah and twiddled with one of her pigtails. "You're the first bigger image-bearer I've ever seen; did you know that? I almost seen another one now, but the brismun said we couldn't go and look at it. He said I could look at you, though. Hello!"

Deborah felt as though her heart momentarily stopped. "What other one now?"

"I don't know? Ma said it was a big one not far from here now. Bigger than you."

"What did your ma see? When?"

"She didn't see it; the brismun did." She stuck her finger in her mouth. "Or, someone told the brismun? I don't know."

"Where's your ma? Is the brismun with her now? Is your ma, Mrs. Smullim?"

The little lumdil girl nodded. "Yes, and the brismun's with Ma, and they're talking, and Ma told me to stop being a stickybeak and come tell you and Mr. Nurrel that the food is ready for your trip. Now I've got to go, because I have to go tell Da now he's wanted at the inn now, and I don't know where Da is. I've got to find him. 'Bye, nice to see you!"

Deborah set off for the inn at a run. Erno must have news. He or someone else had seen her father not very long ago. Erno might be trying to come to tell her, but was waylaid by Mrs. Smullim. Or maybe he had gone to tell Mrs. Smullim what he was doing before heading off into the woods to fetch Father. The inn was closer to the woods than Nurrel's house. Maybe Mrs. Smullim's daughter hadn't grasped the whole message—it wasn't just to come and collect the food for the trip, but that *Deborah* was wanted at the inn, not 'Da'.

She looked out for Erno along the village lanes as she ran along in case he was on his way to her, but saw only lumdils who attempted to greet her as they had earlier. She ran on, not heeding their cheery cries of 'Sonax' this, 'Oxpeina' that. She reached the inn out of breath and burst in through the doorway.

It was empty, and her shout for Erno echoed around the large hall. Mrs. Smullim's flour-smudged face appeared around the kitchen doorframe.

"Ooh, my dearie, it's you! I've got everything all ready and packed it up in your bag—what a handy thing."

"Is Erno here?" Deborah looked in at the kitchen. Pots and pans simmered away on the stoves; a floury countertop had lumps of dough, but no one else was there.

"You just missed him. He's popped out, but I'm sure he'll be back soon."

"Has he gone into the woods?"

"I think he went to talk to Lembi, he—"

"You mean me, don't you? He's wanting to tell me? What did he tell you about my father? Do you have a message for me?"

Mrs. Smullim fanned herself with a dish towel. "Ooh, you're making me dizzy. And me with getting ready for the lunch rush all by myself, my head isn't screwed on straight. It's hard to think."

Deborah clutched the doorframe and spoke more deliberately. "What did Erno tell you? Has he seen my father? Has he gone to get him?"

"No, or perhaps yes, I think the trees saw your father? Not too far away. Yes, that's right. East. Must be near the swamp? The swamp's east of here. Erno's gone to talk to Lembi, I know for a fact that's what he said. We don't see a lot of her here; she's often away up in the north-west of our region watching over the dwellers there." Mrs. Smullim mopped her rosy face with the dish towel. "Oh dear. It's all a bit much. The lunch crowd will be here soon. I'm sorry. I'm trying to think, dearie, really I am. I have got your bag ready, though." She gestured with a floury hand to a side table where Deborah's bag lay bulgingly full.

"Where's the swamp?"

"East of here, didn't I say that?"

"Which way is east?"

Mrs. Smullim pointed to the window above the kitchen sink. "Thataway. But, wait, oh saints, no, you shouldn't go there by yourself. Wait for Erno. He's your custodian!"

Deborah scooped up her bag and left the inn, ignoring Mrs. Smullim's shouts. She ran in the direction Mrs. Smullim had indicated, trying not to deviate from it, although she had to skirt around some of the houses as she negotiated her way through the village pathways. A tree with a distinctive ropy topknot at the edge of the woods helped keep her oriented. Where was Erno? Why hadn't he come right away to tell her he knew where Father was? Instead, he wanted to talk to Lembi, whoever that was, in completely the wrong direction. There was no time to waste. Father was close! All these days in the woods, they must have been travelling on a parallel route to each other!

Deborah ran past several groups of lumdils walking towards her. She supposed this was the lunch crowd beginning to make their way to the inn. None questioned why she was running, as though seeing her run flat out through the village was nothing unusual. Well, she would soon be back, and with Father!

Beyond the houses, she hesitated at the low stone wall encircling the village. Would the wall do its magic as it had when she had been on the other side? Would she be unable to climb over it but have to go to the gate instead? Going over would save time, so it was worth a try. She climbed over and was relieved to find herself on the woods side of the wall. Nothing magical had happened, although the air felt different somehow, harsher.

She ran to the first line of outstretched branches, then kept as straight a line as she could, correcting her route as she dodged around the trees. Hopefully, the swamp was close. Hopefully, Father was still there and hadn't moved on yet. If he had, there would be tracks. Swamps had soft ground, mud, so there should be something to show which way he had gone. At least she knew what a swamp was like, for there were some at home in Eblhim, rotting dank areas at the edge of the city where many threw their rubbish.

She ran for as long as she could until her legs felt as though they would collapse under her and she had to grab hold of a tree. The cool forest air rushed into her lungs as she gasped for breath, her head swimming. This must be what it was like to be on the verge of fainting. She sank to the ground, sucking in shaky breaths.

The ground was damp under her hands, and a spreading coldness seeped through her clothing. The swamp! This dampness must be the first sign of the swamp, although it was not like the swamps at home, for it had trees. She looked around at them. Were they talking to one another? Nothing about them gave any hint of sentience, but she imagined bushy heads and hands instead of the clusters of leaves, while the twisted branches could be the wizened arms of giants.

"Hello, trees," she said, as soon as she could draw a steady breath. "Have you seen my father? He's a—well, I suppose you'd call him an image-bearer. Taller than me. Is he near?"

"Near?"

The chirped response was not the kind of voice she expected from a tree, but it was thrilling to hear it answer. She crawled over to where the voice came from and patted the tree trunk. "Tree, please tell me, have you seen him?"

A peal of giggles erupted. "Not tree. Me talking, not tree!" A glossy black squirrel ran around the trunk of the tree and clung there, staring at her. "No good talker to trees," it said, switching its fluffy plume of a tail. "Bunch a snobs. Won't talk to you."

Deborah looked at it a moment. Sure, yes, a talking squirrel. Why not? She had expected the tree to talk to her, after all, so why not a squirrel? Did everything in the woods have magic powers? "Uh, hello. Have you seen an image-bearer around here lately?"

"Image-bearer?" it said, and ran up to the nearest branch. "You, image-bearer?"

"One bigger than me," Deborah said. "A man."

"Image-bearer. Image-*bearer*." The squirrel covered its face with its tiny paws as it sat back on its haunches. "Can't think. Why can't think." It rubbed its face and head vigorously. "Dumb head, *think!*"

"Hey, calm down."

The squirrel lowered its paws. "My name is Mubbi. Mubbi is my name, *Mubbi*."

"Okay, all right, Mubbi."

"My family gone."

"Sorry to hear that."

"They left. I didn't go. I want to go now, but I don't know how." The way Mubbi spoke was beginning to sound different—less stilted as if the words came more easily. "I should have gone with them, but then I saw a guandra. I feel like I fell asleep, no longer awakened. That's strange, yes? Strange."

"Are you sure it was a guandra and not someone like me?"

Mubbi leaned over the branch and peered at Deborah. "Of course not. You think I don't know the difference between an image-bearer and a guandra? I'm not that dumb. Yes, yes, I know he's on two legs like you. Nasty-looking. All horrible and lizardy, and *woo* so stinky!" Mubbi scampered higher into the tree and disappeared amongst the leaves. "No way, no way. Keep away from it!" Mubbi dashed about, disappearing under leaves, emerging on higher branches, scrabbling down and around the trunk, chattering and screeching unintelligibly.

"Mubbi!" Deborah said. "Please, stop!"

"What? No! If you see a guandra, you have to run up a tree as quick as you can, then jump along the treetops."

"I can't do that!"

Mubbi paused on a lower branch and looked at her. "Can't do that? Can't do that. Yes, your legs are too big, too slow. Get away, get away; I saw a guandra." Mubbi crouched as if ready to dash off again.

"Wait!" Deborah cried. "At least tell me if I'm close to the swamp?"

"Sure, yes, no. Keep away from guandra!" Mubbi screeched and ran up the trunk again.

"Mubbi!" Deborah called, trying to see through the leaves where the squirrel had gone. "Come back!"

But the chattering and screeches became more distant until Deborah could not hear them anymore. She sighed and looked about the woods, hoping something would seem more swamp-like in the lay of the land or the way the trees grew together.

6

It felt like hours, monotonous, never-changing hours, plodding through the woods. There was no answer to Deborah's infrequent calls for help in which way to go or shouts to Father. The woods were even more quiet than they had been closer to the lumdil village—there was no birdsong, no *chup-chip* or hum of insects, no other sounds of the movement of wildlife. Just her own muffled footsteps in the undergrowth, the low soughing of wind in the treetops, and occasional creak of branches. Ferns and other plants were more abundant on the forest floor and slowed her progress. The air felt cool, now and then infused with a scent of something earthy, something green and growing.

Hope began to wane that she would find the swamp or that past the next stand of trees she would see Father or hear the approaching thumps of Erno as he came for her. *If* he would come for her. He should have found her by now if he was looking—she had made enough noise with her shouting. So much for being her 'custodian', whatever that meant. It obviously didn't mean much to him.

As for Jacob, he certainly wouldn't come into the woods by himself and look for her. He had made it clear he would rather sit on her shoulder than fly. She instinctively rubbed her left shoulder. She had got used to feeling his slight weight there, the feathers that sometimes brushed her neck, his raspy voice in her ear.

She pulled her collar up around her neck. It was growing colder, and she had no idea where the swamp was, no idea where the lumdil village was. How stupid had she been? Thinking she could just run two steps from the village and discover the swamp as if Father would be sitting waiting there. Now, what was she to do?

She huddled against a tree and dug through her bag. Small cakes, breads, some kind of pastry things encasing a meat mixture, and her water bottle. It felt good to eat and drink. Perhaps all she needed was a meal, then she would figure out how to get back to the village. She should have turned back sooner. Although, which way was 'back'? The woods were different in this area, sure, but she could be making wide circles around and around the village without knowing it.

She looked up at the branches spread in latticework over her head. Could she climb a tree and see the village or at least a clearing or smoke from the chimneys? The lowest branches were high. She would have to try and scale a trunk to get to one.

She looked about for a tree that might be climbable. And there, not ten steps away, was a narrow grassy path set amongst arching fern fronds, bands of sunshine across its curving length. That had not been there before. Although she may not have noticed it earlier, for it almost blended with the undergrowth. Paths usually belong to the guandras, Jacob and Erno had said. It looked innocuous enough, just like a path that might be in someone's garden. The ferns neatly edged it as if carefully tended to keep the middle of the path clear, and the thick green grass did not appear trampled by the passage of many paws or hooves or whatever it was the guandras had. Perhaps this was a little-used path.

She stared at it for long enough to be sure it did not move towards her and, after a while, began to feel silly. Even though Erno had talked about the other path they had encountered following them, she had not actually seen it move, and she knew now that a brismun's eyesight was not the best. Jacob had also said not all the paths belonged to the guandras, just most of them. So, maybe this wasn't one of theirs. This was more like a path that might lead to someone's house and might even belong to the lumdils. Was she nearer their village than she realised? She did not have to walk on it; she could simply go alongside it and see if it led to anything. She would be careful not to stand right on it and look down so there would be no strange mirror effect and no capturing of her face.

She kept an eye on the path as she pushed her way through the ferns, which soon grew thicker and knottier and more difficult to forge through. Once or twice she accidentally stepped onto the edge of the path. Nothing happened. No mirror, nothing. She went on.

In time, the ground levelled out and became firm underfoot, and she was able to stride along more easily. The tiredness that had weighed her down was lifting, too. Finally, she was making progress. Finally, she was getting somewhere. Where? The question niggled at her. Where was she going? Something about Father. Going to Father? Following Father? This was his path? Where was he?

This wasn't quite right. Not sure why not, but there was something. Some warning, or something. Someone had said something once. Who had said something? About what? She should pay attention to that. Or, maybe not. What she should do is look at the path. Really look at it, because she hadn't looked properly at it before. And it was so easy to walk on. Was she walking on it? She hadn't meant to. Although, why not? It was Father's path, and she was going to him. She had better tell him where she was. Better look down now and show him her face.

She stood still. She could see herself in the centre of the grassy path. As clear as in a mirror, her face was tired, dreamy, her eyes were closing. She stared down at herself, puzzled. Was she going to sleep? This was no time to sleep; Father was waiting.

One image became two—her face slid out from under her face and travelled in a flicker of light up along the path until it was out of sight amongst the ferns. The same face stayed at her feet, and she was sleeping, yet she wanted to wake herself; wanted to see her eyes open and look up. Light shifted, shadows danced, and still her eyes did not open. She willed them to. Willed herself to wake. Why did her mirror not wake? She was awake; she was aware of the woods in her peripheral vision—there was no need to look directly at them; they were nothing—and she could see the rim of the mirror where it morphed into grass. Yet her eyes in the mirror remained shut.

A thump came very faintly, almost imperceptibly, like a heartbeat. Followed by another, and another, the thumps came from some distance through the woods, then fell silent. The thumps began again, repeating in a familiar resonant beat. She should look up, for that was… whatever his name… someone… nothing.

The mirror shattered, her face scattered in sparks; vision of the path was blocked as something green landed squarely in front of her. A brismun. It was a brismun.

"Image-bearer no longer," he said. "You are turning, and you are broken. Gehun child, no, you are not here. You are not here! Not mine."

She knew him, knew his twiggy hair, his rounded face, the half-closed eyes, but could not think of his name; her lips could not form words.

He grinned at her, uttered a strange cry, and leapt towards her, striking her neck so hard that she fell and everything went dark.

7

It was difficult to open her eyes. They seemed interminably heavy, as if they wanted to remain firmly shut. Too drowsy. She was warm, and something surrounded her—a faint scent of musk, the distant sound of a man's voice. No sound of trees; the incessant sighing of the leaves was gone. The ground was not cold; she lay on something soft, padded, with a cover, a blanket over her. So soft and cosy. No, there was no need to wake. But, a man's voice. Father! She struggled to open her eyes, and scent and sounds became sharper and clearer as sensation returned to her body.

"Father," she whispered, finding it hard to form the words; her mouth was so dry.

A warm hand touched hers. "You are waking. That is good. It is time you did."

It was a lightly accented voice, deeper than her father's.

"Father," she said again. Was he here? He must be here, too. Wasn't it he who had been speaking?

"I am Kasharel, son of Mali."

"Where's Father?"

"I am sorry. We found only you."

There was a blurry light, a lamp near the wall, fastened somehow, flickers of silver traced around its base in geometric etchings. Yes, she began to see more clearly now. The lamp was a pentagonal pyramid shape with a flat top, fixed by a silver bracket to a smooth grey stone wall. The ceiling was the same stone, and both it and the walls had thin darker veins of grey touched with the occasional paler fleck. The blanket in her hands was a brown woven material.

She tried to sit up, and a bolt of pain shot down her neck, causing her to gasp.

"Are you in pain?" said Kasharel.

She slowly turned her head to look at him. He was very tall and thin, robed in brown, and his lean, pallid face was sombre. She knew him instantly. He looked like he had stepped from the pages of her storybook, *Legends Of The Greener Land*. He was the man who was the most boring thing in the book.

"You're a dengla," she said.

"A who?"

"A dengla. Aren't you a dengla?"

He shook his head. "I'm not sure what your meaning is, but that is not a term I'm familiar with. Perhaps you have mistaken me for someone else. I am a gehun, and you are in the caves of my people."

"Gehun?"

"Yes."

"How did I get here?"

"You were attacked by a brismun in the upper-world, and a rova brought news to us of that. I and two others were sent to bring you here. Do you have any memory of what happened?"

She remembered Erno grinning at her and the unearthly cry he had made as he leapt at her. "Erno. Why? Why would he do this to me? I thought he was my friend. My… custodian."

"Erno?"

"He attacked me. I—I don't understand."

Kasharel's calm grey eyes were thoughtful. "Erno is a brismun?"

"Yes. He… I thought he had come to rescue me."

"Ah. It is possible it was not Erno, if he is indeed your friend. Brismuns look very much alike."

The idea gave her a sense of relief. Of course it couldn't have been

Erno. In the last few days, he had only tried to help her. Why, the last time she had seen him at the lumdil village, he said he was going again to the woods to try to hear any word of Father's whereabouts. Yet he hadn't come to rescue her when she had gone by herself into the woods. Why not? Trying to think about that made her head ache.

"Yet you say Erno is your custodian?" Kasharel said. "Are you sure? That's very unusual. Brismuns are custodians of the dwellers, not of the image-bearers." He laid his hand lightly against her forehead. "You have no fever, but perhaps you are confused."

"I'm not confused." She feebly tried to bat his hand away. "I was attacked by a brismun, and now you're saying they all look alike, so it can't have been Erno. He wouldn't do that to me. He told me he was my custodian."

"Then, if he was, why wasn't he with you to protect you?"

She stared at the stone ceiling. "I don't know. He was back at the village."

"Which village?"

"The lumdils'. Shady something."

"Smoky Glade?"

"Yes." She tried to sit up again but winced as the searing pain shot down her neck.

"Easy," Kasharel said. "Don't rush. An attack from a brismun is a serious thing. It is well it was stopped before more harm was done to you. If you like, I will try to get word sent to Smoky Glade and find your custodian."

"Of course I would like," she said, and shut her eyes, wishing that hadn't come out sounding so rude.

"Of course," he said.

She looked over at him. The corners of his mouth were curved upwards, and his grey eyes good-natured.

"Rest now," he said. "I'll fetch you something to eat. You must be hungry." He began to move away, then stopped. "Oh, and what is your name?"

"Deborah. Deborah Lakely."

"Deborah of the lake? Which lake?"

"No lake. It's just my last name. It doesn't mean anything."

"Deborah, whose last name doesn't mean anything, I will be back soon. Rest easy; you are safe here."

With that, he left the room and closed the door quietly behind him.

She carefully rolled over onto her side and looked at the stone walls of the small room. There was space enough for the bed she lay on, a tall thin-legged chair and desk both encased in silver filigree, a woven orange-grey rug on the floor, and another long, narrow rug of the same colour hanging on a wall. Kasharel had said something about the 'upper-world' so did this mean they were underground? There were no windows, and the lamp attached to the wall was the only light.

Why had that brismun attacked her? Brismuns were supposed to be nice creatures, at one with nature and all that sort of thing. She supposed the storybook had steered her wrong, as it had with dengla instead of gehun and dwarves instead of lumdils. Now, word would be sent to Erno so he would know where she was. If he cared about that. Had he tried to find her or had he gone his own way? Jacob, too?

She sighed and closed her eyes. She had missed her chance to find Father near the swamp. Where was he now? Stupid attacking brismun, ruining everything.

She was jolted awake by Kasharel's return. He was carrying a silver tray that held a steaming silver bowl.

"Do you think you can sit up?" he asked.

She tried again, ever so slowly, inching her way up, wincing with the pain. He set the tray gently on her lap, and she reached for the spoon but gasped as more pain coursed through her shoulder.

"Let me," he said. He placed the chair closer to her bedside and took the spoon.

"What's wrong with me?" she whispered.

"You were attacked by a brismun, don't you remember?"

"Yes, I know that, but why does it hurt so much? What has it done to me?"

He dipped the spoon into the soup and held it to her lips. "I am not sure exactly, but if you are feeling a great deal of pain, then it's possible you have a fracture in your shoulder. I'm hoping not, and that it's soft tissue damage instead." He glanced at her neck. "You've got quite a nasty bruise, but not so very much swelling to the area, so we'll see how you go as you recover. The rova that waited with you put you into a sleep so you would heal more quickly. Hence, you have been with us now four days."

"What? Days? What rova? I thought you said a rova came to you and told you about me. How many rovi were there?"

"Just the two. I had thought the rova that waited with you was your custodian, so it's all very confusing."

She swallowed the soup. "You're confused? What was a rova doing with me? I didn't see a rova."

"Considering you were unconscious, that's not surprising."

She liked the subtle mirth in his eyes. His face was still expressionless, and she wondered if he ever smiled, but his eyes were clear and kind. He slowly fed her spoonful after spoonful of some kind of vegetable-nutty-ish soup, and she began to feel a great deal better from its spreading warmth.

"I don't know why the rovi didn't bring you to us themselves," he said, "but then, they don't always do what is expected. One of them came to the council and told us that you were lying near The Cleft—that is one way of coming down into our caves—and that another rova was standing guard over you. We were asked to take you and tend you, so the council chose me to go up. And here you are. You must feel honoured to have such attention from Sonashi."

"Is that one of the rovi?"

"No, Sonashi. The Oxpeina."

Deborah thought of the lumdils cheerily wishing her the 'Oxpeina's best' and 'Sonax be with you this bright day'. "Oh, I see, *Sonax*."

"Yes. We call him Sonashi."

"What do you mean, honoured? I didn't see Sonax anywhere, either."

Kasharel paused from giving her the soup, puzzlement in his eyes. "Don't you know that the rovi only do Sonashi's bidding?"

"No, I don't know that. And, don't you start, I've already had Erno and Jacob harping on about me not knowing things. I'm not from the woods. I'm from the city of Eblhim."

"That's interesting. Not from the woods? What are you doing here, then?"

She told him about Father, in between the spoonfuls of soup. There was something very easy in talking to him, and she found herself sharing more details than she meant to. He listened quietly, answering now and then with a question, a sympathetic look, or a murmuring nod as if he understood all.

"I think I've worn you out with my questions," he finally said. "Take some more sleep. If you need the loo, it's behind the curtain." He indicated over his shoulder the long, narrow rug that hung on the wall. "Either myself, Shinah, or Bey will check on you after a while. Shinah and Bey have been helping me to care for you."

She eased herself down to lie in the bed. "Thank you, Kasharel."

He adjusted her blanket for her. "Sleep well."

It was not difficult to do as he said, for it seemed like he barely left the room before her eyelids closed of their own accord.

The next few days passed by in a blur. Kasharel visited Deborah frequently, and the two gehun women, Shinah and Bey, helped him nurse her back to health. They were both almost as tall as Kasharel, at around seven feet, and were as thin, if not thinner, wore long brown robes as Kasharel did, and their long hair was knotted and plaited intricately. They did not speak much to Deborah, being unable to speak the common language. If Kasharel was there, he acted as interpreter.

"Don't worry about your sleepiness," Kasharel said. "I suspect that is lingering from the rova's touch."

"Why didn't it just fix me instead of put me to sleep?" Deborah sat on the edge of the bed, resisting the urge to crawl back under the covers and sleep some more.

"I don't think they can do that. That's Sonashi's domain—he has that kind of power, not the rovi." He felt her shoulder, his light fingers probing carefully. "This feels much better."

"Yes. I'm not yowling with pain anymore when you do that."

"It is good. Are you sure you want to go for a walk?"

"No, I'm not sure, but I want to. I'm sick of being in this room."

"Understandable."

She slid carefully down so that her feet were on the floor while the rest of her leaned like a saggy rag doll against the high bed.

"Your legs don't look like they have bones in them," Kasharel said.

She smiled at him, noting the tiny upturn at one side of his mouth, which meant he was joking.

"How did you ever make it to the loo the past few days?" he said.

Shinah came into the room at that moment.

"Deborah!" She cried and rushed to her side.

"That's how," Deborah said, smiling at Kasharel.

His eyes twinkled. He spoke to Shinah in their language, and Shinah, wide-eyed, replied. He said a few words more, then turned to Deborah.

"I have told Shinah we are venturing out for a walk. She asks if you are ready to do that. I said you think you are."

With Kasharel and Shinah's support, Deborah shuffled to the door. They towered above her, and she felt dwarfish beside them.

"Wooh, I have jelly legs," she said.

"What is jelly?" Kasharel asked.

"It's a kind of wobbly dessert."

She clung to them and tottered out into a long, winding tunnel forged through rock. The air was warm and infused with a faint aromatic scent from the lamps that hung at intervals along the walls. As she went further along the silent tunnel, Deborah realised there were no other doors that were close to her room.

Bey came striding around the next bend of the tunnel, her bare feet noiseless on the stone. She stopped short when she saw them, grinned, and prattled long strings of words as she came briskly forward, her brown robe sweeping along the floor of the tunnel. Kasharel answered in abrupt tones, Bey prattled some more. She smiled down at Deborah and gently touched her shoulder. Shinah spoke as well.

"Bey says we finally have an answer from Smoky Glade," Kasharel said. "Your brismun custodian has gone to Hirahi."

Deborah's heart sank. "Did he try to find me at all?"

Kasharel questioned Bey, who replied at length.

"It appears so. He and those with him encountered rovi, who told them to leave you and go instead to Hirahi. So, they stated their intention to—" He paused and questioned Bey, nodded at her answer, and continued, "Yes, they returned to the village and left word for you in case you returned, to tell you they will be waiting for you at Hirahi."

Deborah adjusted her grip on Shinah's arm to try and keep standing, for her legs wanted to fold beneath her. "Why did the rovi meddle like that? Why did they stop Erno from finding me?"

"Meddle? Deborah, your words shock me. The rovi act on Sonashi's command. As Oxpeina, he sees all the woods and the life in them, and to him, it is like an interlocking puzzle of what seems to us to be countless pieces that fit together. We should not question his decisions."

She frowned. "I question them when it leads to me being attacked and injured."

He gave her a slight sympathetic nod. "I find occurrences like that difficult, too. At the very least, I am relieved the rovi found you in time before the brismun could harm you further. You could have been killed, and I am still somewhat perturbed by this—that the brismun of our region could be going against his or her custodianship. I suppose it is simply more evidence of the turning."

"The turning?" She sagged against him. "I think I should be turning. Can we go back, please?"

"Certainly. Yes, the turning. Each of us has the capacity to turn from the Oxpeina-life; for some it is in subtle ways; in others it is very apparent and deliberate."

They all headed back to the room, Shinah and Bey quietly conversing together. The tiredness and sleepiness were stealing over Deborah again, and the door to her room appeared very far off along the tunnel despite it being not so many steps away. She yawned. "I don't understand."

Kasharel gently squeezed her arm. "We don't need to speak of it now. Let's get you back to bed."

"I'm sick of the bed."

"And the bed is probably sick of you."

"When am I going to get better?" Her words were slurring now, and her eyelids heavy. "I have to get out of here. Have to get to Hirahi. Got to find Father."

"And we will, soon enough. Be patient."

"*You* be patient."

"I am. Very."

She looked up at him, and on seeing the curve at the corner of his mouth and the affection in his gaze, she, to her embarrassment, felt tears pricking at her eyes. It had been a long time since anyone had cared about her. Father certainly hadn't for years. She looked quickly at the floor, conscious of Kasharel and Shinah standing protectively over her, their hands supporting her. And, if by chance she fell backwards, she knew Bey was there to catch her. Why were they being so kind to her, a stranger?

They helped her to the bed, helped her sit, gently lifted her legs as they laid her softly down, and Kasharel pulled the blanket up over her.

"Sleep, little one," he said, smoothing her brow. "Bey says she will sit with you a while."

Deborah glanced over at Bey, who sat on the chair by the bed, tucking her robe neatly about her. If she dared smile or feel any more emotion, then waterworks would probably come tumbling out in a bunch of messy sobbing. She swallowed hard, pushing the emotions down. She would never be like this if it hadn't been for the rova making her so weak. She shut her eyes, blocking out the three kindly gehun faces staring at her. "Thanks," she muttered.

She listened to the shuffle of Kasharel and Shinah leaving the room, the click of the door, and opened one eye to peep at Bey. Bey had her own eyes shut, the tail of her long brown plait over one shoulder, her benign face peaceful as if she had already gone to sleep. Deborah thought again of the storybook. The dengla, in reality, *gehun*, might be less interesting or exciting in appearance as were most of the other creatures, but they had something serene, something steady, about them.

She drifted off to sleep.

8

It was several more days before the dregs of sleep left her completely and she was able to walk freely again. Her shoulder still ached and arm movement was stiff, but Kasharel had her repeat exercises to help it strengthen and recover and administered a nasty bitter tasting tonic that he said had healing properties.

Despite being able to walk more easily, she was never permitted to walk to the end of the tunnel, only back and forth along it. Occasionally, she heard voices and faint hammering noises but saw no other gehun.

"It's time I left," Deborah said to Kasharel one morning as he came in with her breakfast. "I feel so much stronger. I'm sure I can make it to Hirahi now. That's if Erno and the others are still there waiting for me. You agree with them that it's the best place for me to go to search for news of my father, don't you?"

Kasharel set the tray onto the desk. "Yes. I understand that as one of Sonax's outposts, they have the means to discover much information of the surrounding regions."

"Okay, fine. How do I get there? Can you give me directions? Also, would you be able to give me some food for the journey?" She looked about the small room. "Where's my bag and my water bottle? I need those."

His placid grey eyes showed a hint of amusement. "You act as though you're leaving this very minute."

She put on her socks. "That's because I am. I'm a lot better this morning and feel ready to go. I've been here long enough. Who knows where my father is now? I mean, I don't know where he is or how far away, or if he's all right… " She sucked in a breath and tightened her fists. He had to be all right. She couldn't lose him.

Kasharel placed his hand on her good shoulder. "I am coming with you."

"What?"

"I said, I am coming with you. I think you will not find your way without help, and I have been instructed by the council to give it."

"I—okay—you don't need to. I appreciate it, but—I—you, surely you—"

"It's not like you to be at a loss for words."

She busied herself putting on her shoes, unsure of what to say. It would be good to have his company, and no doubt he would keep her from getting lost on the way to Hirahi, but he really didn't have to put himself out by leaving his home and travelling with her, despite whatever 'the council' said he must do. He had already done so much for her, and she had no way to repay him.

"Before you leave," he said, "you must see the council and thank them for their care. Tomorrow they will meet, and I will take you to them."

She glanced up. "Their care? You, Bey, and Shinah are the ones who've been caring for me. I'm thankful to you, not anybody else."

She thought she heard an almost imperceptible intake of breath.

"You make me laugh like no one else," he said.

"That was a laugh?"

His eyes twinkled at her.

The next morning, she strode up and down the small room, feeling as though she was in a cage. What was taking Kasharel so long? He had said he would be back in a moment. That 'moment' had surely taken half the morning. There was no way of telling how time passed, so maybe it wasn't quite that bad, but it certainly felt like it.

Finally, he entered the room, Bey and Shinah with him. The women's hair seemed even more elaborately plaited, shining as though freshly oiled, and their expressions and gestures betrayed the tiniest glimpses of nervousness. It was unlike them. What was the council like to elicit that kind of reaction?

Their footsteps were a muted pattering as they walked together through long winding tunnels. There was a gradual descent, a growing warmth, and occasional whiffs of savoury food or burnt metal that overcame the scent of the burning lamps. Doors were set in more frequency along the walls, and Deborah realised she had been housed well away from others.

They soon encountered some gehun—tall, silent, brown-robed folk who merely nodded in greeting as they walked by. Their faces showed no surprise or interest at the sight of Deborah, and some looked past her as if she wasn't there. Many of them emerged from different tunnel mouths and walked silently along behind in procession. Deborah glanced back at their growing numbers, then up at Kasharel. She opened her mouth to ask him why the gehun followed, but nothing came out. The silence of everyone else was unexpectedly stifling.

Soon, a babbling brook was heard, and the patter of feet and shuffle of robes grew. They entered a large cavern; more gehun were filing through, all following the brook that coursed through a deep impression worn into the rock floor. The sound of many low voices began to echo through the caves, and Deborah let out a breath she had not realised she had been holding. Large chandeliers hung from the ceiling, silver crafted in serpentine patterns around each glowing light. The walls shone polished grey, ribbons of marbling reflecting the light.

Kasharel and Deborah followed the clear brook to the far end of the cavern, joining in with the crush of very tall, brown-robed people. Deborah was grateful when Bey caught hold of her hand, for she felt small and unseen amongst the crowd and that she would be trampled on. All she could see when she looked up were the backs and shoulders of the several gehun in front of her, some with long plaits hanging down.

Kasharel bent down to her. "Do not worry."

"Why should I worry? Is there reason for me to worry?"

"I hope not."

"Thanks. I feel a lot better now you've said that."

His lips twitched into a tiny smile.

The air was filled with the murmur of voices. How many gehun were gathered? Hundreds? Thousands? Deborah tiptoed to try to see, but in vain. It must be a very large cavern, for there was no glimpse of where the high ceiling met the walls. More chandeliers lit the space, and in some smoother parts of the rock ceiling there was a shimmer, as if of water reflected. Then she realised that most of the gehun had stopped moving. Yet Kasharel, Bey, and Shinah drew her on, winding their way through the crowd. Some stepped aside while others had to be touched on their shoulders to make way. Deborah caught snatches of words and vowel sounds that were familiar after her time of listening to Bey and Shinah, but otherwise it was an incoherent jumble.

Kasharel led Deborah around the edge of a rock pool. In its centre, two men carved in stone were frozen in a moment of grappling with one another in battle, water streaming over their broad shoulders, one man's face contorted with rage, the other's expression set with determination despite the hand at his throat. It was a strange sight amongst the mild appearance of the gehun men and women that clustered around the pool. Before Deborah had a chance to wonder, a loud gong rang out. As its long melodious note died, the gehun went silent and all faced in one direction.

Deborah felt Bey let go of her hand, and she turned to see what everyone was looking at. Whatever it was, Kasharel was leading her towards it, and the gehun kept moving aside for them. Bey and Shinah remained by the pool.

"Where are we going?" Deborah hissed to Kasharel.

"Hush," he whispered.

A loud male voice resounded through the cavern, authoritative, sounding as if he would tolerate no dissension.

Kasharel leaned over and whispered in Deborah's ear. "Ithnan says we may ascend."

"Ascend what? Who's Ithnan?"

"*Hush*."

"You hush. What is all this?"

"I told you—I am taking you to the council."

"What's everyone else doing here?"

"Shush. *Please*. I will explain what I can, when I can. Just have patience."

She found that her heart was beating extraordinarily quickly and she was short of breath. Irritating that all these solemn gehun would have that affect on her. She should be calm. They were all calm. There was nothing to worry about, apparently. Why was she being dragged in front of them all? It was too late to turn and leave. Everyone had seen her now. All she was doing was going to thank the council for their care of her, or something. Why they had to gather like it was some momentous occasion, she didn't know. It was as pointless and disagreeable as being a child back at school and having to make a speech in front of the whole assembly.

As more and more gehun stepped aside for Deborah and Kasharel, she saw a stone platform as high as her shoulders. Upon it was a long silver table lined with thirteen silver chairs in which were seated grey-robed gehun. They all watched her approach, their faces inscrutable, their eyes intent.

Kasharel led her around to stone steps. She gritted her teeth. Okay, so they were really going up there. She was going to be paraded like some kind of oddity. Probably staring at her trousers and jersey—had they seen such things? as they all seemed pretty keen on wearing robes—the colour of her hair, the shoes on her feet.

She drew a deep breath, as deep as her breathless lungs would allow her, and marched up the steps behind Kasharel. She was relieved she managed to do that and didn't fall or trip despite her trembling legs.

The thirteen council members sat watching her, then the central man stood. His long, dark brown hair was bound at the nape of his neck by a gold cord, which glittered in the light, whereas the other council members had silver knotting their hair and beards. He wore an enormous amber gem at his chest, hung by thin chains of gold, and began to speak in the language of the gehun.

"Ithnan introduces you," Kasharel whispered in Deborah's ear.

Ithnan continued speaking as he faced the gathered crowd, not pausing or waiting for Kasharel to interpret, his voice resounding throughout the cavern.

"He says you are an outsider," Kasharel whispered quickly. "That you were attacked—that you were outside your own borders—not in your region—this is the consequence—ah, yes, the consequence of stepping away from your people. That we should remain in our own region—that we—ah, that we should be as one—never diverge—have no conflict among us—listen not to the outsider—"

Nods of assent came from the council members at the table.

"—and have no other opinion but that put forth, decided, by the council," Kasharel went on, "for that is truth—"

Ithnan gestured towards the statue of the wrestling men as he spoke.

"—and that will save us from repeating our shameful history, the conflict," whispered Kasharel. "We must not listen to lies—those who tell us to leave our region and that there is a more—no, that there is a greater region—"

Ithnan spoke so quickly that Deborah felt sure she was only getting snippets of what he said through Kasharel's interpretation.

"—dissenting opinion is not tolerated," whispered Kasharel, "that is what saves us. Unity. That Kasharel, that *I*, am permitted, must take you out of our region—to not bring more trouble on us—disturbing our unity—"

She stared up at him. His expression was solemn as he kept whispering to her as if all of this was perfectly normal. Did he think she had brought trouble on them just by being in their caves? Is this why she had been kept well away in an outlying cave? Now all their robes made sense. They wanted to be the same, have 'no dissenting opinion'.

She looked out over the crowd of brown-robed gehun and saw that very few looked back at her. Most kept their eyes on Ithnan as they listened to him droning on and on.

"We will not turn if we stay as one—" Kasharel whispered, "—that we have the direction of Sonashi—staying together, all is one, Oxpeina- life is here—not anywhere else—"

A roar erupted at the back of the cavern, a lone voice howling then falling still, and the crowd gasped and began to part like a wave. All members of the council abruptly stood, their chairs scraping the stone in a jarring din. Through the parting the crowd had made strode a figure, not a gehun but slightly shorter, lithe, with fur of richest dark brown that made the brown robes of the gehun almost colourless in comparison.

It drew nearer, and Deborah saw the wild face of a beast, the light playing over its fur as it walked straight to the council platform. It glared up at Ithnan, whose face had become ashen; lips parted to reveal the points of fangs.

Then the creature turned its unblinking gaze to her, and stunningly bright blue eyes flecked with gold silently communicated something. He was a rova. She knew that somehow as she stared down at him. She felt the rova was questioning her. What was he asking? What? In response, she rapidly thought that she did not know. No! No, she didn't know what he wanted; didn't know anything at all about what was going on around her. The rova's gaze became less severe, and she felt he said something else to her—she knew not what—then he looked at Ithnan again and leapt effortlessly up onto the platform, muscles rippling beneath his sleek fur.

Closer now, she felt a strange power emanating from the rova, that the air around him pulsated as though filled with something unearthly, and she would lose her balance or be drawn in. She involuntarily clutched at Kasharel's robe, then, annoyed with herself, let go. This was no time to act like a child.

As the rova spoke, the vibrant timbre of his voice breathed life through every syllable. Deborah felt she could listen to him forever despite not understanding a thing he said, for he spoke the gehun language, and

Kasharel did not interpret as he stared at the rova. Ithnan stumbled backwards, bowing and looking as though he was preparing to kneel, the gem at his chest swaying in a glint of amber light.

Deborah felt as though she should kneel in the presence of the rova too, but was snapped out of such an idea when the rova's tone changed to a snarl as he stopped Ithnan with a touch. She felt then that to kneel before the rova was something not only wrong but foolish, and straightened herself, realising she had slouched as though about to bow.

The rova glanced at her, a brief sense of approval in his bright eyes. He took a step towards Kasharel, said something to him, Kasharel began to bow, but, with an impatient flick of his hand and slight growl, the rova stopped him.

Then the rova turned to face her. "This is not Oxpeina-life and you do not belong in this region. Nobody does anymore, for it will close soon. Do you see?"

She was startled hearing him speak the common tongue and could not think how to answer. But she had no time to, for he jumped from the platform, landed lightly on the stone floor, and made his way through the crowd and out of the cavern.

Once he had left, a hubbub arose as all the gehun spoke at once. Deborah looked out over the crowd to the tunnel mouth the rova had left by. Where was he going now? Where had he come from? She wanted to go with him, not stand here amongst the lifeless sea of brown-robed gehun, their passive faces barely touched by emotion. She should have a custodian like that rova. Erno was nice enough, but a rova? That would be amazing. And a rova would probably know exactly where to find Father. Drat! Why hadn't she thought to ask him if he had seen Father?

As she looked out over the gehun, she noticed that throughout the crowd many of them were different. Their robes were not as brown but looked dusty, their faces, old. No, not old, but somehow not quite present, or something, with a sickly pallor that brought to mind seeing her mother lying still and dead. They didn't appear to be talking as did those around them, but stood like statues. But then, as she tried to make sense of their sudden emergence, the impression of dustiness, of paleness, was gone and all the gehun were the same again. It must have been the light—the silver chandeliers hung throughout the cavern did not give uniform illumination, and with all the gehuns' movement as the rova had left, the light had fallen differently upon them. Still, she felt unnerved to have had such a vision of death on so many.

The sound of the gong rang out, and one of the council members on the platform called loudly, insistently, until everyone quietened.

Ithnan began to speak again.

"He says this is our region," Kasharel whispered to Deborah. "We will not permit it to be closed—ah, yes, Sonashi cannot go against our will—be not overcome by the, *hmm*, the theatrical visit of the rova—"

He went on and on, as did Ithnan. The air, now that the rova had left, felt stale. Deborah had to make more effort to breathe as though the cavern was closing in upon her, the weight of stone and rock overhead, lifeless and dry, and the stream—wherever it was amongst the crowd—carried nothing in it.

How many days had she been in the caves already, and how far away was Father now? It seemed as though she had hardly thought about him, that she had been busy recovering from her injury. Busy? Lying around doing nothing? Walking slowly here and there? Thinking about what? Nothing. It was a blur of days jumbled together. The rova was right—she didn't belong here. It was time she left.

She looked over at the steps that led from the platform. She supposed she couldn't edge away and slink off down them without anyone noticing, but how much longer was Ithnan going to waffle on for? Kasharel kept whispering in her ear as if he thought she would want to know what was being said. She didn't. What had the rova meant by 'Oxpeina-life'? Was that what the power was called that surrounded him? And why had he singled her out and spoken to her? She felt she had suddenly roused from a long sleep, and now numerous thoughts and questions tumbled about her mind. What to do now? Kasharel was going to take her out of the caves; that was a start. Erno was at

Hirahi, wherever that was, waiting for her. There, apparently, they would find word of Father.

"Deborah," Kasharel said. "Come now."

The interminable speech from Ithnan and the endless whispering from Kasharel had finally stopped. She watched the thirteen council members file down the stone steps and the crowd of gehun dispersing, their low voices filling the cavern as they went.

"Wait," she said to Kasharel. "Wasn't I meant to thank the council in front of everybody?"

His expression was faintly puzzled. "Oh. I had forgotten that. Too much has happened for such a trivial thing to be remembered. However, I do know that Ithnan has instructed Ziph to lead us out. We will go to her now."

9

A gehun the height of Kasharel's shoulder stood studying Deborah with an interested expression in her lively brown eyes. Her sandy hair was in a simple plait, and she had a sweetly mischievous look about her—not at all like the solemnity of the other gehun.

"This is Ziph," Kasharel said, "daughter of Ithnan, my niece. She will take us out of the caves by a way that she has discovered—it is right at the border of our region, not the way you came to us, Deborah. Ithnan has said it is a faster way for you to leave."

"Greetings to you," Ziph said. "Now, let's be going. Father seems impatient for you to go. He thinks we will all turn faster because you are with us. As if our turning has anything to do with you!"

"*Ziph*," said Kasharel. "Have some self-control."

"*Kasharel*," said Ziph, and pulled a face at him. "I know you think the same as I."

"Perhaps."

"Yes, *perhaps*." Ziph strode off, the lantern in her hand casting shifting shadows on the stone walls of a narrow tunnel. "You do not think we would turn merely because here present among us is an outsider. As though to turn is to catch a—how do you say—disease. It is, *ah*—" She uttered a stream of words in the gehun language, then said, "Yes?"

"No," said Kasharel, as he hurried after Ziph to keep in her lantern's circle of light. "And I am not sure I agree with all that Ithnan said. Why should we not be free to discuss all opinions in an attempt to find what is true? Why should he and the council decide all for us?"

"Yes, uncle," Ziph said, laughing, "like you and I discuss."

"Exactly. We do, even though we do not agree, and I will not silence you, and you will not silence me. But we will not fight; we will listen and seek to understand each other."

"It is so," Ziph said, "but aside of that, is that not why the rova came? To tell us a—*hum*—" again, she switched to the gehun language and let off a torrent of words, "and to warn of the turning?"

Deborah had to trot to keep up with Kasharel and Ziph as they went along the tunnel, their robes sweeping the ground, talking about *turn* this and *turning* that, whatever that was. Something that apparently meant a lot to them as they kept talking about it while striding along together, leaving her in their wake.

"And, for those responding to the enchantments?" Kasharel said.

"The what?" Ziph said. "I do not think you use the correct word. *Enchantments* is like Sonashi sits and performs incantations. He does not. Besides, the turning is the opposite of such an enchantment. Although it is the same thing, just going the other way. That is why the guandras arise."

"There are no guandras here," said Kasharel. "None. But Deborah was not responding to the enchantments; she was simply trying to find her father, who is in the upper-lands. He, most likely, is the one responding to the enchantments. Otherwise, why did he leave his region?"

Ziph swung the lantern vigorously as she marched along. "Not *enchantments*. It is not incantations!"

"What are you talking about?" Deborah said, a little out of breath as she tried to keep up. "What are you saying about me and my father?"

Kasharel glanced back at her. "As I say, I think your father is responding to the enchantments like the other travellers we have heard of or seen crossing through our region. Although you were not."

"I don't understand what you mean. Enchantments? I told you, my father isn't well. He thought the woods were going to help him get better, that's all."

Kasharel stepped around a large boulder protruding from the wall. "Ah, yes, that proves what I say. The enchantments is an inner drawing, a pulling felt in the soul. Yes, I see your point, Ziph, not an incantation, but I still say it is an enchantment of a sort."

"I am sick of you saying that word!" Ziph said. "But now I understand more how you mean it."

The tunnel walls drew closer together, the stone underfoot became rough, which thankfully slowed the pace with which they moved, and there came a point where each had to squeeze through a narrow gap one at a time. Deborah glanced back, being last, and the impenetrable darkness at the edge of Ziph's light gave her an uneasy feeling.

"Also," Kasharel said, "Deborah coming to us is not necessarily evidence of the turning. We all know it is happening; we have seen it. We don't need the visit of an outsider to show us what goes on in our region or any other."

"I see," Ziph answered. "But why come to us? Why the rova told us to take her? It was a brismun attack, something a brismun custodian should never do. Are we to say that the brismun turned? If so, why?"

As they went on, Deborah felt like she was back with Erno and Jacob, putting up with all their chatter about custodians, dwellers, and image-bearers. It was hard enough finding her way across the increasingly rough terrain—climbing boulders; squeezing through narrower gaps; bending her head to avoid the roof of the caves; crawling when it became necessary—without Kasharel and Ziph's prattle. Soon, they spoke entirely in gehun, back and forth with each other as if she were not there. If she dared take a moment to rest, they would probably go on heedlessly, so she did her best to keep up despite her aching shoulder and her body not feeling as strong as she wished.

When Ziph finally spoke again in the common tongue, she said, "Careful. There is a cimla. Wait here."

A hiss came out of the darkness, and, up on a boulder, Deborah saw two eyes reflecting the light. A shadowy form about the size of a loaf of bread inched back. Ziph set her lantern on the ground and took a step closer. She spoke softly, and the cimla hissed in response. Ziph slowly went into the shadows closer to the boulder, speaking in a low voice all the while.

"She will try to move it," Kasharel said to Deborah. "The way here is narrow, and it wouldn't be good to pass close to a cimla. They are aggressive."

Deborah thought of the squirrel, Mubbi, in the woods. "Why can't you just tell it that we want to get past and we won't hurt it?"

"It would not understand."

"Oh, it doesn't speak your language? How about mine?"

"If it had the ability to speak, it would have answered Ziph. Instead, it hisses."

"I thought all dwellers spoke. It is a dweller, isn't it?"

"Yes. But no, not all dwellers speak. Only those who have been awakened, either by speaking with Sonashi himself or by spending time with an image-bearer."

Deborah thought of Jacob. Had he learned to speak while recuperating in the village of Shilhim? He had not told her it wasn't normal for dwellers to speak. Then again, everyone she had met in the woods seemed to take so many things for granted, as if she should know everything they knew.

"How are you coping?" Kasharel asked. "Are you feeling all right?"

She shrugged without thinking, and her shoulder ached in complaint. "I suppose. Looking forward to getting out of here and above ground again. How does Ziph know where to go?"

"As a child, she wandered, causing many searches until we realised that she always found her way back. We never could get her to stay at home. So, she knows these caves better than anyone."

The cimla hissed again and gurgled low in its throat.

"It does not sound pleased, Ziph," Kasharel said.

"Stop talking," she answered.

Kasharel and Deborah waited silently as Ziph continued to speak softly to the cimla. After a while, she came back and joined them.

"Not good," she said, frowning. "He won't shift and tried to bite me. We must wait." She sat on a stone and tucked her robe about herself.

"How long for?" Deborah asked.

Ziph shrugged. "It should not be long, as we are here. It will want to move away from us, but in a secret way so we do not follow. Keep talking. Let it know we are here, and it will want to go."

Deborah looked at Kasharel. There must be a thousand questions she wanted to ask him, but none of them came to mind. Why was it whenever somebody said, 'say something' that the mind automatically went blank? The shining eyes of the cimla at the top of the boulder stared down at her, and it let out an almost indiscernible hiss. There was a distant *drip-drip* beyond in the darkness, and Kasharel sighed.

"I said *talk*," said Ziph. "You are both doing the opposite."

"You are not talking, either," Kasharel said.

"I have nothing to say."

"That must be a first."

Ziph's giggle rang out in the cave, and the cimla blinked. "*Hum*, so, my uncle, why are you travelling with this stranger? You, who never leaves and never travels?"

"I have travelled. You were too young to remember. And, if you attended any of the council gatherings, you would know why I am travelling with Deborah. Because Ithnan decided it."

"That is what you get for being the youngest brother."

"Perhaps."

"So," said Ziph, "you feel no *enchantment* to go?"

Kasharel's brow furrowed slightly. "I would say not. Although, at one time perhaps I did. That was long ago, but now I think as Ithnan—that we have all we need in our region, that O-saina life is here."

Ziph grimaced. "Not true."

"Do not let your father hear you speaking so."

"He has heard me. He refuses to let me go. But I will make the journey soon when I am of age. It is the will of Sonashi."

"You don't know that."

Ziph leaned forward, her hands on her knees. "Yes, I do! Uncle, you should know it, too! *Umf!* I should journey with Deborah instead of you. Her father goes after Sonashi; Deborah goes after him; all is so."

"He does not go after Sonashi," Deborah said, "or Sonax, or whatever his name is."

Ziph grimaced. "*Sonax* sounds hard and sharp like a sneeze. It is not right to call him so."

"*Sonashi* sounds like a vegetable," Deborah said.

Ziph stuck her tongue out at her.

"Your father never said anything about Sonashi?" Kasharel asked.

"Never." As Deborah said that decidedly, she suddenly recalled sitting out on the veranda in Shilhim with the village busybody, Norm Higgs, chatting to her father. Father had asked about Sonax—she remembered being surprised by him mentioning a name she had never heard him speak before—and Norm had left abruptly, like that was something taboo. "Wait. Now that I think about it, Father mentioned him once, but that was all."

"Ah."

"What, *ah?*"

"Sonashi was on his mind. The Oxpeina of the world called to him."

"What is Oxpeina?" Ziph asked.

"O-saina," Kasharel said. "Oxpeina is the name in the common language."

"Yes, I hear it now as you say them together. O-*sai*-na."

"What is with this Oxpeina of the woods stuff?" Deborah muttered.

Ziph gave a startled choke and laughed. "What? You know, of course, the O-saina!"

Hot annoyance swept over Deborah. "No, I don't know! Stop talking to me like I'm supposed to know everything about you and your culture.

I don't! I'm not from around here. Do you know anything about where I'm from? No!"

"I don't talk about culture!" Ziph retorted. "I talk about facts! The O-saina is the life of the realm—the essence, the spirit. All life comes from the O-saina!"

"That's your opinion. Your culture!"

Ziph jumped to her feet. "It is fact! How do you not see this? Everyone sees it. Without the O-saina, everything is dead. Fact!"

"No!"

"You are stupid!"

Kasharel raised his hands. "Girls, please. Enough."

"Girls?" Ziph glared at him. "I am not a child!"

"I hear you." Kasharel nodded solemnly. "Old ladies, *please*. You make my head hurt in this confined space. Shouting about this does no good." He glanced over at the boulder. "I stand corrected. Your shouting has done much good. The cimla is gone, sensible creature. Good work, both of you. We can now move on."

"*Umf!*" Ziph grabbed the lamp and stomped away. "I can shout all I want. It is stupid to think the O-saina is of culture."

"It is not our way to shout," Kasharel said. "We must discuss calmly and rationally. You know that."

"Yes, yes, I know." Ziph muttered under her breath as she led them onward through the tunnels.

Deborah couldn't catch what she was saying. Ziph had probably switched to the gehun language. It didn't matter. She didn't want to continue fighting with her. Ziph had probably never set foot out of the caves and didn't know what it was like out in the real world.

They went on without further incident through the twisting and turning passages, climbing in several places, squeezing through gaps, navigating across thin streams that became more prevalent. Some of the rock was slippery, and Deborah had to hold on to Kasharel to get across. He, with his bare feet, seemed better able to cope than she in her shoes. Yet, the gehun in their robes had to tuck and twist their garments to be out of the way as they climbed. Deborah was glad she did not have to contend with that type of clothing, as at times it was enough to summon the strength to get herself up and over the rocks.

The air began to smell fresher, and soon there was a pale light that grew in strength, illuminating the surrounding stone so that Ziph's lantern looked nothing more than a dim flame. A fringe of greenery adorned a narrow opening, moved gently by a breeze.

They had finally reached the woods.

10

"Farewell," said Ziph. "I return to my father. Is there any word you wish me to give him?"

Deborah looked up at Kasharel as they stood together beside the overhanging foliage at the opening of the cave, a green and woodsy scent drifting in around them. Her weariness lifted somewhat as she breathed it in, and she could hardly wait to get outside and away from the caves.

"My gratitude to Ithnan, my brother," Kasharel said, "and the assurance that I will do what is asked of me."

Ziph gave him a slight nod, then looked expectantly at Deborah.

Deborah stared back. What did she want? She had never spoken to Ithnan, didn't even really know who he was other than the leader of the gehun council. What word could she possibly have to send to him? Ziph's expression became more grim the longer they stared at each other.

"You say nothing to Ithnan, my father?" she said.

Deborah shrugged. "No. Should I?"

"Not even your gratitude?"

"For what?"

"For Ithnan's protection and care of you!"

Deborah looked from her to Kasharel. "Kasharel is the one who cared for me."

Ziph huffed as if trying to contain herself, her eyes blazing.

"What Ziph means," Kasharel said, giving a surreptitious shake of his head while looking calmly at the young gehun, "is that it was the decision of Ithnan to bring you, Deborah, into our caves, so it is he who cared for you even as I did."

"Oh, I see." She had forgotten she had been supposed to thank Ithnan and the council in front of the gathered gehun when everything had been interrupted by the appearance of the rova. Where was the rova now? She forced a smile at Ziph. "I do thank your father, Ithnan, very much. I am grateful for his decision to help me."

Ziph smiled back at her. "I will tell him. Farewell. The O-saina of Sonashi now protect you both." She stared at the opening to the woods. Deborah thought she saw regret and longing in Ziph's expression before she turned her back and headed away down through the cave, her lantern light flickering against the rocks.

Kasharel held back the foliage for Deborah, and she stepped through to a completely different world. The trees were larger, broader, some almost weeping and drooping under the weight of their leaves; huge boulders partly covered in moss lay half-buried as if sinking into the earth; the sloping forest floor around them was carpeted with leaf litter while bushy seedlings grew in the shade of their parents. Birdsong rang out in bell-like notes and refrains Deborah had never heard before; the leaves rustled, and the occasional scurrying sound was heard. More than anything, the woods felt different. There was an atmosphere of something vital, something electric. Even the air she breathed felt different, invigorating, as it filled her lungs.

"This is the same woods?" she said. "How can that be? The trees are not the same."

"We are in a different region from the woods that surround The Cleft, so other varieties of trees were planted here."

She looked at Kasharel, seeing him for the first time since stepping out into the woods, and almost gasped. His hair was a rich chestnut-brown, his skin that she had thought so pallid was an interesting otherworldly hue, his eyes a clear and beautiful grey. In them she could see a protective tenderness towards her, something that made her breath catch and tears threaten to well up. She was not used to someone looking at her as if she mattered. Her own father hadn't done that for a long time. She could not remember getting that look from Mother—they had never been as close as she and Father.

She remembered their arguments and wished there were more happy memories to think of. Friends had drifted away, not understanding the impact of Mother's death. She did not even know exactly how it had affected her; she felt as though she hadn't had the time to stop and think, really think. Not for years. Caring for Father was all-consuming. Being here now—the air, the trees, the way this part of the woods felt—she might be able to relax. Might be able to stop and breathe.

"Now, this is interesting," Kasharel said. "It's not merely the trees that are different. You look different, too, and I don't think it is just lamplight compared to daylight. There is something here." He turned about, looking up at the canopy of leaves, then out across the boulders. "Something... more. More of O-saina life. Do you feel it?"

It hit her with a rush when he said that. All of a sudden, it made sense. Yes, she felt something... *more*. Of course this was what Father wanted; of course this was why he had come to the woods. He needed this fullness, this life. There was nothing like it back home, and not nearly enough of it in Shilhim. He had to come amongst the trees and immerse himself in sky and air and earth. Then he could begin to heal.

She slowly sat on a boulder. Each breath she took, she felt it. Felt what her father had been looking for. She remembered his words: 'Do you feel the power of the woods?'. Yes, yes, she felt it. He was not crazy. He really wasn't. There was something here, almost tangible. Even the boulder she sat on, something radiated through the stone and moss up her hands, her legs, her body. A faint electricity. So faint, yet it was there. It made her think of the rova she had seen at the gathering of gehun and how she had felt standing near him. Perhaps this place, maybe this place... did rovi live here?

"You are very quiet," Kasharel said. "Are you all right?"

She nodded. She could not think how to put into words what she felt. There had been so much she had misunderstood about Father. She saw that now. He was *not* crazy. It was a relief to repeat that to herself. He was not crazy. Her fears had been misguided. She had simply not understood him. He was hurting, and he wanted healing, wanted some kind of comfort. Here in the woods, woods like these, he would surely find it. She felt it. Something here encircled her, easing those knots of pain and grief that had sat heavily for so long, every exhale bringing relief.

The trees stood silently around her as if listening, like guardians who patiently understood. Birds flitted from branch to branch while in the distance two red squirrels chased each other up a tree trunk, and a small grey animal she didn't recognise was digging about in the earth. Lots of dwellers. They would need a custodian, so there should be a brismun in the area. That thought gave her an awful pang as she remembered the brismun who had attacked her.

Something grabbed her left shoulder. She shrieked, her cry piercing the air and causing echoing squawks of alarm in the previously tranquil-sounding birds, and swept madly at herself, whacking a soft, feathery body. It landed with a *plomp* at her feet. A little brown-and-white owl lay on the ground, wings outstretched, breathing heavily.

"Jacob!" Deborah cried. "Is that you?"

"Yes," he hissed.

She crouched down to him. "I'm so sorry. You scared me. I didn't know it was you! Are you all right?"

"Winded," he sputtered. "Why'd you hit me?"

"I didn't hear you. You came out of nowhere! Why'd you sneak up on me like that?" She helped him to his feet, and he stood there unsteadily, shaking his wings out as though ridding himself of dust and dirt. His gold-ringed black eyes glared angrily at her. His brown and white feathers were extraordinarily stunning in their detail and markings, while the yellow of his eyes was purest gold.

He flexed his taloned toes experimentally. "Nothing broken, anyway. Just as well. What a welcome, Deborah."

"I told you, I didn't hear you. It's your fault for not saying anything but just landing on me."

"*Hoo.* My fault? Weren't you expecting me?"

"No?"

"*Huh.* Sonax didn't tell you I was coming?"

"No."

"Strange. He told me not only where to find you but how to find you. I thought that meant you would be waiting here for me."

"No."

He folded his wings and stared up at her. "You look different."

"So do you. It's these woods—there's something funny about them."

"Funny?" His head swivelled to and fro as he scanned the surroundings. He paused, staring hard at Kasharel. "Who are you?"

"Kasharel, son of Mali."

"I am Jacob, formerly of the Grenith Tract."

Kasharel gave a slight nod. "I am not familiar with that region."

"You are gehun?"

"Yes."

Jacob hopped up to the boulder beside him. "I have not met your kind before. We had heard the gehun people had taken Deborah in. Very good of you. I was accompanying Deborah and her custodian in her quest to find her father, as she knows nothing of life in the woods, and—"

"Hey!" Deborah said. "I know more than you think I do."

Jacob turned his head to her. "Really? You know what I think? How clever you are. Just not clever enough to stay in the safety of the lumdil village. I had travelled all that way with you, trying to help you, and you left without a word, as if everything I had done was nothing to you. Now you tell me you know my thoughts. *Fine.*"

She glared at him. "I had a chance to find my father, and I had to take it! He was close to the lumdil village; he was seen at a swamp right near it, and did anybody try to go to him? You could have flown, Erno could have… whatever he does… jumped, much faster than me, but no! No, I had to go by myself right then. Now you're mad at me for taking that chance?"

"Yes!"

They eyed each other. He shook his feathers out, wheezing a little, while she clenched her fists. Birds and squirrels chattered nearby in agitated tones.

"These parts of the woods were beautiful," Kasharel said slowly, "now the beauty fades with the light. Or perhaps it is your quarrelling that takes the glow from this place."

The anger seeped out of Deborah at the sound of his voice. Her shoulders sagged, and she unclenched her fists. All of a sudden, she felt stupid. And, tired, very tired.

Jacob flew silently to her good shoulder. "I didn't mean to… " he said when he had settled, his voice trailing off into the quiet.

"Me, neither," she said.

"I really did come here to help you," Jacob said, his husky voice close to her ear. "I suppose… I admit, I was hurt when you left. I found it hard to understand. I must… well… I should not be angry. I see it would be very difficult for you not knowing where your father is."

"It is," she said.

"I am sorry."

She lightly touched his soft feathers.

"I am glad you seem to be in good condition, despite your ordeal," he said. "We heard about it at Hirahi, you know. I had thought we would continue to wait there for you, but that changed, and we were sent to you instead."

"We?"

"Erno and Nurrel were with me, but I was sent on ahead. Erno could have kept pace with me, no doubt, but not Nurrel. I left them as Sonax urged me on."

Kasharel bent closer to Jacob. "Did you… have you… *seen* Sonax?"

"I have, many years ago. *Ah*. You mean to ask how his instructions came to us?"

"Yes."

"The rovi brought them."

Understanding flickered across Kasharel's expression. "And yet… you say you have seen him? Is that why you speak? You are a dweller that has been given O-saina life?"

Jacob stood a little taller, huffing himself up importantly. "This is true. I met Sonax several years back as he walked the Grenith Tract."

Deborah noted the subtle glitter of interest in Kasharel's eyes.

"What was he like?" Kasharel said.

Jacob shut his eyes. "Hard to describe," he muttered. "Let me think. It is as if all of Oxpeina was focused into one being, yet I had the feeling that if I touched him, I would die. I didn't, of course, for he took me briefly into his hand. It was at that moment that I awoke. I knew myself. I… let me think… it is hard to say. My life before, it consisted of shapes and instincts yet no real thought. When Sonax took me, I could speak, and I saw where I was."

As he spoke, a breeze stirred the leaf litter into eddies of gold and brown fragments that spun in the beams of light cast down through the trees. Deborah watched, under the impression that a mysterious life force stirred the woods in reaction to Jacob's words.

"Did he say anything to you?" Kasharel asked.

"He did. He said a great deal, and I found to my surprise that I could answer. I will remember that moment forever." Jacob adjusted his grip on Deborah's shoulder. "Where is your custodian?"

"Mine was killed a long time ago. I have not ventured into the upperlands since." Kasharel glanced about the woods. "It is my hope Sonashi will assign me with another. I was also hoping one would meet us here, but that does not seem to be. Unless it has yet to come."

"Killed? How could that have happened?"

Kasharel gave a slight shrug. "I am unsure."

Jacob hissed. "Something very strange must have occurred."

"Yes, of course. Now, do you have further instruction for us? I take it we are to go on to Hirahi, for that is what my council has advised—do you have any objection?"

"I have none," Jacob said. "That is why we came—to travel with you.

These parts of the woods are certainly beautiful, and I feel the Oxpeina-life, but we will still need to take care as we move through this region."

11

Deborah crouched at the side of the stream and scooped the cold water to her mouth. It tingled the senses with an unusual light flavour and she felt new strength begin to rise through her body.

"Are you sure that water is safe?" Jacob said, clinging to her shoulder.

"Wouldn't you expect so?" Kasharel bent to the stream. "My niece, Ziph, said she has never seen a guandra in this area, and I well believe it. I have never seen a place so unspoilt."

"Yes, that may be so," Jacob said huskily, "but water flows through many regions. What if it came through guandra territory?"

"What if it came from an underground spring?" Kasharel said. "See for yourself; the water is clear."

"That means nothing."

Deborah sat up and wiped her mouth. "Well, it's too late; I've already had some. And it tasted amazing—the best water I've ever had."

Jacob shook himself. "*Hmph*."

"If I drop dead, then I'm sorry."

"It is no joking matter."

Kasharel stood and straightened his robe. "The light is fading. I wonder if perhaps it is best we go back to the caves for the night and set out for Hirahi in the morning."

Deborah nodded. A delay in travelling from this region was appealing. "Yes. I think that's a good idea."

"Of course you would," Jacob said. "Don't think I am immune to the pull of this place, for I feel it, too. There is a stronger sense of Oxpeina-life in the woods here. However, I suspect the longer we stay here, the less inclined we will be to leave."

"No," Deborah said, "that won't happen. I can't sit around in the woods forever, you know that."

"How long have we been sitting around already? We have done nothing in the time since I have been with you except come to this stream, and it is barely a stone's throw from where I found you."

"We had travelled a long while before through the caves," Kasharel said. "We needed the rest."

Jacob huffed quietly. "I don't think you needed the rest. Haven't you felt stronger since being here? I have. All my muscle aches have disappeared."

"I have noted that I feel very well." Kasharel drew a deep breath, a faraway look in his eyes as he gazed through the woods. "If only all the realm was like this."

Deborah rubbed her injured shoulder. Come to think of it, it didn't ache as usual. She felt a slight tenderness under her fingers, but that was all. And the water had been very good. So good that she did not mind there was nothing to eat yet. She drank a little more, then stood. "It is getting darker, so I think we really should stay the night."

"I can see well enough in the dark to lead you," Jacob said.

"That may be so," Kasharel said, "but we would probably still trip on this uneven ground. Our progress would be very slow."

"Fine," Jacob said. "Do nothing. Stay."

Deborah stroked his breast. "Don't grump. We'll leave first light tomorrow."

He gently nibbled her fingers.

Deborah and Kasharel climbed back up the slope from the stream and wound their way through the trees and boulders. The cave mouth, although covered with greenery, was dark, and Deborah felt a reluctance to enter. Kasharel went in without hesitation, and she followed. Inside, there was a chill dankness to the air, and the light was grey. The stones and boulders strewn inside seemed lifeless and dead, and, as Deborah looked at Kasharel, he too appeared pale and ill.

"Very strange," said Kasharel, his voice falling hollowly in the cave. "It is as if there is a distinct boundary. I can't imagine why that should be—these parts of the caves are uninhabited."

"But they are still part of the gehun region, yes?" Jacob said.

"I suppose so. But my people are not without Sonashi. My people are not without the O-saina life."

"I don't claim to understand image-bearers fully," Jacob said, "but most regions take on the qualities of the image-bearers who dwell there. This does not bode well for your people."

"No. I thought we were moving beyond our old conflict, but now… I am not so sure. As you say, it does not bode well."

Deborah pressed her way out through the greenery and into the woods again. She breathed easier and moved several steps from the cave mouth in case a lingering odour might cling to her.

"I was in the middle of conversation with Kasharel," Jacob said, sounding very put out.

"Go back in there, then," she said. "I'm not stopping you."

He muttered under his breath, adjusting his grip on her shoulder.

"It was rotten in there," she said.

"You think that was rotten? I have experienced a lot worse."

"I'm sure you have."

"Do you two enjoy squabbling?" Kasharel said as he emerged into the woods.

"Yes," Deborah said.

"*Hoo.*"

Deborah's smile fell as she looked over at Kasharel. His usually placid expression was replaced by a definite frown. She did not know he could frown like that. "Sorry. We didn't mean to bother you."

A flicker of surprise crossed his face. "Bother me? No, it is not you who bothers me. I wonder now if I should go back to warn my brothers and tell them of what I have seen here—the contrast of our region with this one. What does it mean for our people? And yet, Ithnan instructed me to accompany you to Hirahi." He gazed up at the branches woven overhead and the patches of sky through the shifting leaves, a thoughtful look on his face.

Deborah didn't want to go back into the gehun caves, yet she didn't really want Kasharel to leave her. But then, who was he? He was not family. He had no obligation to her. His care had been nice while it lasted, but nothing lasts forever. "Do what you think is best."

"I am here now," Jacob said. "Deborah is not alone, and we will soon rejoin Erno and Nurrel. I just came from Hirahi; there's nothing between here and there that could be dangerous. If you need to go back to your people, then go."

Deborah turned away, not wanting to see any conflict on Kasharel's face. Although perhaps it was an easy decision for him. He might feel relief at not having to look after her anymore. She was surprised when he answered quickly.

"No. I must carry out Ithnan's instruction to me to take Deborah to Hirahi. Then I will return when I can. Let us walk on until we can't see our feet. Only then, rest."

With that, they set off through a narrow way between sunken boulders, up a small rise under the broad overhang of branches.

The land rose and fell, the prevalence of boulders decreased, the ground was spread with a low-growing plant dotted with tiny silver flowers. The trees were large and spreading, young seedlings sheltered under the protective branches of their ancestors.

As Deborah stepped over yet another fallen branch and around a gnarled tree root, she wished for a path, a track, anything to make the way easier in the shadows, then shook her head to herself. This was not her world anymore. A path could not be trusted.

Birds and squirrels watched from the trees, while on the ground small grey animals sat fascinated as she and Kasharel walked by. From time to time, larger deer-like shapes were glimpsed in the distance.

Deborah's foot twisted awkwardly as she stepped into a hollow.

"Jacob!" she cried, reaching down to rub her throbbing ankle. "Why didn't you tell me there was a hole there?"

"I didn't notice it."

"You didn't notice it? What are you, blind?"

"No, and I'm certainly not deaf, so there's no need to shout!"

There was an outraged squawk in the trees and the fluttering of wings. Leaves drifted down through the shafts of fading light that speckled the ground.

"I begin to fear the more we remain here, the more we affect this place," Kasharel said softly.

"You could be right," Jacob said in a subdued voice. "It may bring the custodian of this region to find out why there is discord."

They fell silent. Deborah found herself listening for the rhythmic thumps of a brismun, but there was nothing. The birds and squirrels had fallen silent too, as if dismayed. She felt something of the pulse of the earth beneath her feet. Perhaps it had always been there, masked by their conversation, but now she felt a similarity to the energy she had felt when resting on a boulder, and the vigour she had felt drinking from the stream.

"Wait," Jacob hissed. "I hear a brismun."

Kasharel and Deborah stood still.

Deborah strained to hear, but there was only the creak of branch and whisper of breeze in the hush of the cool evening air.

"Do you think it's Erno?" she whispered.

"*Shh*," said Jacob.

"There is no need to fear," Kasharel said. "The custodian must have the same life and health as this region."

"*Shh!*" Jacob hissed more urgently.

And then came the distant thumps, familiar in their regularity and depth of sound. Deborah moved closer to Kasharel, her heart beginning to pound. It could be Erno. It could be all right. These parts of the woods still felt safe, still felt alive. This probably wasn't the same brismun that had attacked her. Probably.

Soon enough, the brismun bounded into view, a round shape passing like a shadow in the failing light, dodging around the trees, surefooted, and surely but steadily, heading towards them.

"I hear you," the brismun called in a high voice.

Deborah stiffened. The voice was not that of Erno's. She wished her pounding heart would shut up. A brismun could probably hear a heartbeat.

"Who are you and why are you here?" The brismun called as she leapt in a wide circle around them. "You do not belong here, image-bearers. Nor you, dweller. Oh, a gehun image-bearer? Why do you come here to my region?"

Deborah felt strangely compelled to listen to her voice, to watch the brismun as she circled, and stared transfixed, her breath caught in her throat.

"We are on our way to Hirahi," Kasharel said.

The brismun landed with a resounding thump then turned to face him. "I have seen the disease image-bearers bring to other regions. I want my dwellers left alone. Do not turn and bring guandras here to my region."

"We don't mean any harm."

"Yet, you have already brought it. You have touched these woods. Where is your custodian, image-bearer?" The brismun bounded towards them.

Deborah quickly stepped behind Kasharel.

"It's all right," Jacob whispered to her.

How did he know it was all right? The brismun was coming at them!

"You are correct, dweller," the brismun said as she stood before Kasharel. "Image-bearer, quieten."

Deborah slowly exhaled, feeling easier at the brismun's command. She peered around Kasharel. The brismun looked so much like Erno. *So* much. Yet, the twiggy hair, when seen closer, was not Erno's. The rotund mossy body was not quite the same. This brismun could be his twin in shape and stance, yet the differences were there in the way of the growth of moss and twigs.

"My custodian was killed some years ago," Kasharel said. "I have not yet been assigned another."

"And yours?" The brismun shifted her squinting gaze in Deborah's direction.

She swallowed and thought of Erno. "My custodian… *um*… he is; I don't know where he is. I'm supposed to be meeting up with him soon."

"And yours, dweller?"

"My custodian is the same as hers," Jacob said. "We are journeying to meet him. I know the way."

The facial features of the brismun wrinkled in her mossy face. "A dweller and an image-bearer share the same custodian? These are strange times. Are you aligned with the Oxpeina?"

"Yes, we are," Kasharel said.

Deborah tried to keep her breathing steady and normal. Although the brismun's sight was not very clear, she would probably see something in her, see that she didn't even know who or what the Oxpeina was.

"Yet you still brought an air of conflict to my woods," the brismun said. "That is unacceptable. I have not had guandras here, and I intend it to remain that way. Do you hear what I say?"

Immediately, Deborah thought of how she and Jacob had argued and the jarring sense of disharmony it brought. "I am sorry," she said.

"I am sorry, too," Jacob said. "But, brismun-custodian, you must realise that image-bearers are different from dwellers—they must work out their opinions, and they aren't without passion. I have taken on that quality since Sonax awakened me, so I understand. You are very fortunate to not see guandras here, and I hope for your sake it continues. We will not stay here; we are only passing through."

"I want you out of here immediately. I see that you are taking the long way through my woods. You must take the short way. I will accompany you to see you out."

Deborah noticed a slight change in the attitude of the trees nearest the brismun, a swaying and shifting of their branches as if reaching closer, irresistibly drawn in to their custodian. Is that how she knew which way they were travelling? The trees throughout the region had told her?

"No," said Jacob. "If you take us a shorter way in the direction of Hirahi, then I think it will take us to the edge of a region my custodian told me I should avoid. Also, I must lead us back to him."

Deborah was surprised at him. He sounded so firm as he spoke to the brismun—how did he have the nerve to do that?

"You will go where I tell you to go, dweller," the brismun answered. "Your custodian will be informed of your whereabouts. Brismun or rova, they can travel more quickly than you image-bearers. Follow me now, or I will see that you are put in the ground."

The woods surrounding them darkened as the trees rearranged their leaves to block the shafts of light from filtering through.

"Peace," Kasharel said. "There is no need to threaten us. Please allow us to continue our course. We will quicken our pace and do what we can to leave your region sooner."

The brismun closed her eyes, so that they nearly vanished amongst the moss, and stood silently for a few moments. "See what you caused me to do, image-bearers. You are right. I threatened you."

"You can't blame that on us," Jacob said. "You had it in you to threaten us. Maybe you've had it too easy here for too long. You're not used to being challenged."

"Hard words, dweller, but I see that Sonax gave you a mind as well as your voice. Go freely on your way. All I ask is that you bring no further discord while here." The brismun turned and leapt away.

The trees shook themselves as if from a dream, and light spilled through to the ground once more.

"Thank you, Jacob," Kasharel said. "I think I would not have known how to answer—I do not have much experience of life in the upper-lands."

"You've been above ground before, though?" Jacob asked.

Deborah walked slowly beside Kasharel, picking her way carefully through the undergrowth. Despite the trees rearranging themselves, the light was waning at the approach of evening.

"Yes," Kasharel said, "but I have not seen many regions."

Deborah looked around the darkening woods. "I don't think that will change. We can't see much of anything."

"Take my hand," Kasharel said. "I am used to lower light. I can still see fairly well."

For a while they forged on as the air grew cooler and crickets and other insects started up their night chorus. The trees became indistinct shapes in their slumber, and occasional pattering sounds were heard in the undergrowth.

At last Kasharel stopped, and Deborah let go of his hand. She looked up and stretched after having been so focused on trying to see the ground where she stepped. Between the silhouette of leaves, stars sparkled like gems in the night sky.

"Are you tired, Deborah?" Kasharel asked.

Deborah smiled at his question directed solely at her. Jacob certainly had nothing to be tired about; he had sat on her shoulder the entire time. "No."

"Hungry?"

"No, and yet I should be."

"It is the life of this region," Jacob said. The small weight of his body lifted, his silken touch of wings brushing Deborah's face.

"Where are you going?" she said.

"Just to look around and see where we are," he called. "I won't be long."

Deborah sighed and tentatively reached out for the nearest tree to lean against. "I may not be hungry, but it doesn't mean I wouldn't like to eat something."

Kasharel's voice answered her from the dark. "Yes, it is a curious sensation. I also do not like the feeling of having no roof over my head, especially at night. It makes me feel very… exposed."

"I guess it must do—you're so used to the caves."

After a while, Jacob's voice called to them through the trees. "I am coming to you now, Deborah. Don't hit me."

She waited, peering into the darkness. She saw nothing, but soon felt the rush of air against her cheek, and Jacob was back on her shoulder once more. It still startled her, as he seemed to come out of nowhere, but she flinched only a little.

"I didn't hear your wings at all," she said.

"You're not supposed to," he answered.

"What news do you have, Jacob?" Kasharel asked.

"We have veered somewhat off course. Not badly, but I really should have been taking better care of our direction. I think we should remain here the night, as I see that the terrain will soon become more uneven for your feet." He let out a low hiss. "I don't understand why I see no sign of Erno and Nurrel. I should have by now. I hope nothing has happened to them."

"Yet, you say we are off course," Deborah said. "Maybe that's why you can't find them."

"*Hmm.* That should not prevent Erno from finding us."

"Perhaps the morning will bring good news," Kasharel said.

❧ 12 ❧

Deborah stood at the graveside, watching the grey bundle of her mother in funerary bindings being slowly lowered. She did not know how to feel. Father, broken, kneeled at the grave. She reached to touch him, and suddenly he was gone.

She woke with a start. It was still night. The dampness of the plants and light fragrance of their flowers pressed in around her, and she felt the curious tingle of the electricity through the ground. Crickets chirruped unbothered, and there was the slow rhythm of Kasharel's breathing as he lay sleeping nearby.

"Jacob," Deborah whispered. "Are you there?"

There was no answer. He had said he would probably go hunting in the night and might try to find Erno or some word from Sonax. She sat up and peered into the shadows. Where was Father now? Was she any closer to him, or was she further away? Had he been through this area and felt the life here?

In the dark, unable to see, she could feel it even more. The ground beneath her fizzed and hummed as though alive and made her feel that she sat on the back of a great beast. Even the sighing sounds of the gentle wind in the trees seemed like speech of a sort. It calmed her, and she thought over her dream. No, she did not know how to feel about Mother. Her feelings had been stifled, unrecognisable, at the time of Mother's accident and subsequent death. As she thought of it now, sitting amongst this strange awareness of life, there was a rising sense of guilt. Guilt for feeling relief that Mother was gone and that there were no more arguments. Yet she had loved Mother; she knew she had. But that was tangled up in an unfamiliar mix of emotion. Yes, she had always been closer to Father, but she had still had some love for Mother despite finding her difficult.

A rustling sound came from close by and then a snapping of a twig.

She hurriedly got to her feet. "Who's there?" A brismun wouldn't rustle. Maybe it was some kind of animal.

"I am Val," said a clear, deep voice. "I think you must be Deborah. Don't be afraid. I am of the rovi."

Deborah felt as though all her senses prickled as she stared in vain into the night. "What? How? What are you doing here? Jacob! Kasharel!" She thought she could hear the rova breathing and imagined its wild, beast-like face looking at her.

"I have not much time," Val said. "My pack and I are on an urgent assignment, but Sonax redirected me to inform you that your custodian, Erno, and his companion, the lumdil, Nurrel, are at the Silver Lake. These are the words I give you, as Sonax gave them to me. Now, I must run and catch up with my pack. *Soi nah.*"

There was the slightest of rustles, and somehow the air felt less dense, as if a fullness, a vibrancy had gone.

"What's that?" muttered Kasharel, his voice foggy with sleep.

"A rova," Deborah said.

Jacob's raspy voice called from somewhere up in the trees. "Deborah."

She stood still, waiting for him, and in moments she felt the rush of air and the grip of his talons on her left shoulder.

"Did you see the rova?" Deborah asked. "It was one, wasn't it?"

"Yes," Jacob said. "He looked rather stern. I wonder what he and his pack have been up to."

There was a thud, and Kasharel's voice was heard. "*Ow.*"

"Are you all right?" Deborah said.

"Yes, just hit my head on a branch. Not badly. Did you call my name?"

"Yes," Deborah said. "I did, because a rova was here."

"A rova."

"Yes."

"A rova?"

Jacob shuffled his feet. "I thought you were awake, Kasharel, but now I suspect you're sleepwalking."

"No, I'm awake."

"The rova said Erno and Nurrel are at the Silver Lake," Deborah said. "That's good. Now we know where they are."

"It is not good," said Jacob. "I have heard things about that lake."

"What things?" Kasharel said.

"That it's in the heart of a region killed by guandras. Erno told me to avoid it."

"Then why would he and Nurrel go there?" Kasharel asked.

"*Hum*," said Jacob. "Beats me. Something must have happened when I left them."

"I guess we'll find out soon enough," said Deborah.

As the light of dawn filtered through the leaves, the treetops came alive with birdsong. As soon as they could see well enough, Kasharel and Deborah walked on through the undergrowth, finding their way down a slope as Jacob, perched on Deborah's shoulder, instructed them on which way to go.

Midway through the morning, Deborah sat on a fallen tree. "I'm starving."

"Me, too," Kasharel said as he sat next to her. "Jacob, is there a stream nearby? My thirst is becoming unbearable."

Deborah ran a hand through her tangled hair. The last time it had been combed or washed properly was when Bey and Shinah had patiently sat with her and done it for her. She sniffed at her clothes—they were starting to smell.

"I suspected we had crossed into a different region," said Jacob. "I wasn't sure until now."

Deborah glanced around at the trees. They didn't look that different. Perhaps not as richly green, perhaps the browns tended towards greys.

She looked at Kasharel. His face was paler, and his eyes and hair had lost some lustre.

His expression became even more serious. "We must be on our guard—who knows what we may encounter here? The custodian of this region may not be as cooperative."

"I don't hear anything to be concerned about," Jacob said.

"Did you hear that rova approaching last night?" Deborah asked him.

"No, but then a rova is different—they can be very hard to hear. Unless they want you to hear them."

"What about guandras?" Kasharel asked.

Jacob said nothing.

"How reassuring of you," Deborah said.

He nudged her cheek. "I was thinking. Just recalling the encounters I have had. They have all been different. Sometimes I could hear them from a long way off, and admittedly that frightened me; other times their approach was unexpected, yet I was unafraid. Either way, it is not pleasant to recall." He shook himself, his feathers tickling Deborah's neck. "If you like, I will search the area for a stream."

"Please do," Kasharel said.

Jacob flew noiselessly from Deborah's shoulder, his barred, brown-tipped wings sweeping gracefully through the air. She watched him disappear into the woods, then turned to Kasharel. "He'll find one, no doubt, but that doesn't solve what we're going to do for food." If only there was a hot meal to be had. Hot buttery bread with a great big bowl of meat and vegetables in a spicy gravy. And, more bread, with melted cheese. And, roasted sweet potato with the edges all crispy. And—

Kasharel picked a straggly green stalk from a plant near his feet. "Jacob would have us eating bugs and rodents. Did you see what he coughed up this morning?"

She grimaced, and the delicious thought of roasted potato vanished.

The corners of Kasharel's mouth twitched. "His method of digestion is… interesting."

"That's one way of putting it."

"I am very unfamiliar with birds and their ways, so I had no idea they were like this."

Deborah thought of the birds back home in Eblhim. Had she seen many? No, not really. Gulls at the coast, but hardly any birds in the city itself.

Kasharel looked up at the trees. "Birds seem to want to make noise a lot, too. That, and the constant sound of the trees, makes me miss the quiet of the caves."

They chatted lightly for a while, sitting in the dappled light. The soft, unceasing rushing of the treetops reminded Deborah of the distant echoes of the sea. She found it soothing to listen to, quiet and still compared to the bustle of city life in Eblhim. She supposed Kasharel would go out of his mind if he ever encountered that.

At last, she got up and stretched. "Why's he taking so long?"

A hint of a frown crossed Kasharel's face. "Yes, it is not good. It must mean a water source is very far away."

"But he flies quickly. He must have seen something by now, surely."

"We must be patient."

It was Deborah's turn to frown. "Must we." She cupped her hands around her mouth. "Jacob!" She paused and listened for any response through the woods.

Kasharel touched her arm. "I don't think you should shout."

"Why not?"

"What if a guandra hears you?"

"Jacob!"

Kasharel stood and lightly gripped her arms, looking into her face. "Please, Deborah, hush. We have no way to fight guandras if they come."

She shrugged. "The guandras, whatever they are, don't seem to be in any of the regions. I think we're safe enough."

"But we don't know where they are or where they could be."

There was a pitter-pattering in the undergrowth some distance away, and bobbing up and down amongst the greenery was a little mottled brown-and-white head with round gold-rimmed eyes.

"Jacob!" Deborah stared, trying to make sense of why he was hopping and jumping along instead of flying. As he got nearer, she saw why. His feathers were in disarray with bald patches and tufty knots all over his body, while his wings were rumpled and small. She ran through the tangle of undergrowth to get to him. "What happened? Jacob! Are you all right?"

He fell at her feet and lay there panting. She scooped him up, and her hands were smeared with his blood. He closed his eyes, his beak open as he gasped for breath.

"Jacob!" she cried. "Talk to me. Tell me you're all right. Jacob!"

"Give him a moment to catch his breath." Kasharel gingerly took one of Jacob's wings that was hanging over Deborah's arm and folded it in against Jacob's body.

"Guandras," Jacob said eventually, between gasps of breath. "Attacked me. Thought they were going to kill me. Think they just wanted to pull all my feathers. Brismun custodian came. Fought them. I got away. Didn't stay. Didn't know if the custodian would kill them all. Got away in case he didn't."

"How far away was this?" Kasharel asked.

"Is anything broken?" Deborah tried to untangle and smooth some of Jacob's ragged knots of feathers.

"Don't know. Don't know. Hurt all over. Guandras and brismun far. I ran a long way." He let out a huge breath and became limp in Deborah's arms.

"Don't die!" she cried.

"*Ha!* I'm not dying. Resting."

She tucked him in the crook of her elbow. He should probably be wrapped in something, but what? Maybe her jersey would do. "Hold him for a minute," she said, passing Jacob to Kasharel.

As she did, distant but unmistakeable thumps resounded through the woods.

"The brismun custodian," she whispered, tight anxiety rising in her chest. Just because it was another brismun, it didn't mean it was going to attack her. Not all brismuns attacked. The last one hadn't, even though it had initially threatened them. Still, she couldn't help feeling a little wobbly as the thumps grew in magnitude. Instinctively, she took Jacob from Kasharel and held him close.

"I'm sure it's all right," Kasharel said.

Deborah said nothing but looked to see any sign of movement through the woods. In moments, the brismun appeared. It was large. Maybe even twice the size of Erno. And it was fast. It did not seem to have any trouble honing in on her location but bounded in great, wide leaps straight for her. He was very much like Erno in other respects: round in build, scraggly twiggy hair, but his face was wild.

"You have my dweller!"

Deborah shrieked and stumbled backward. "He's my friend. I mean him no harm!"

The brismun stood still before her, and his height was such that she had to look up at his face. His eyes were barely visible amongst the moss and seemed permanently closed.

"Give him to me!"

She swayed under the power of his words compelling her to obey. "Don't hurt him," she said as she handed Jacob over, her voice barely a squeak.

"Don't be an incredible chump, you squeaky wonky excuse for an image-bearer! I would never harm a dweller. What a goof-head!"

"We beg your pardon," Kasharel said.

"That's a daft thing to do. Begging my pardon?" He deftly turned Jacob in his mossy hands, his thick green fingers probing his body. "Nothing broken. Cuts, bruises, and the sting and humiliation of a feather plucking. Damn those guandras!"

Jacob slowly opened his eyes and looked up at the brismun. "They gone?"

"He speaks! Sonax-awakened! Marvellous. Yes, my little dweller, they're gone. I knocked their blocks off. You should have waited for me instead of haring off like a… well, like a hare. Admittedly, I did take a wee while to dispatch them, especially when stinky reinforcements turned up. But, that was just more for me to have a crack at."

"Sorry," Jacob said and closed his eyes again.

"Don't be. Nothing I like more than giving them a good thrashing. Oh, you meant sorry for leaving? So you should be. You think a couple of puny guandras would get the better of me? *Bosh!* Still, I understand why you might freak out and run, especially if you'd heard the others coming. Or, smelled them—*phew!*"

"Why do you have guandras in your region?" Kasharel asked.

The brismun turned to him. "Just speak your mind; why don't you! It's nothing to do with me; it's the proximity of the Silver Lake. Cursed thing butts up against my region. Why are you travelling without your custodian? No sane image-bearer does that."

"*Hoo*," said Jacob softly.

"He laughs," said the brismun, a huge grin splitting his face. "Good. Dweller, I've never seen you before, yet you're in my region. Why?"

"It's because of me," Deborah said. "My custodian is at the Silver Lake, and I'm supposed to meet him there. Kasharel and Jacob," she motioned to each one in turn, "are my companions."

"Bizarre," remarked the brismun. He turned Jacob carefully once more, then held him right way up. "I'm going to put you in a sleep, my sweet dweller. You need it."

Deborah cleared her throat. "*Um*, I was going to wrap him in my jersey and take him with us. Is that all right?"

"*Um*, what's a jersey?"

Deborah tugged at her sleeve. "This."

The brismun felt along her arm and rubbed the material between finger and thumb. "It'll do. That's a kind thought, yes."

She took off her jersey and carefully wrapped Jacob in it. She wasn't quite sure if she was allowed to keep holding him or if the brismun wanted him back, but he made no move to take him.

Jacob looked up at her through slitted eyes. "That's nice."

"Listen to me, dweller Jacob," said the brismun.

Deborah felt as though her ears tingled at his words. The trees overhead leaned in.

The brismun's voice was soft as he laid his hand on the bundled-up Jacob. "You are going to sleep now. A good, long, healing Oxpeina-sleep."

Jacob's eyes shut immediately, and Deborah felt her eyelids growing heavy. The sounds of the woods became muted, and she struggled to keep her eyes open. Kasharel lurched forward and abruptly stepped to maintain his balance.

The brismun chuckled. "Ah, image-bearers! You're a smidge too close, and you're catching the edge of my words."

Deborah found herself involuntarily stepping back, as did Kasharel.

"Not you," said the brismun to Deborah. "I've got to keep my hand on Jacob."

She moved forward. What was it with this particular brismun? He seemed to have more power over her than Erno had or the previous brismun they had encountered. She felt as though she was dancing to this one's every whim.

He whispered over Jacob. Deborah tried to catch what he was saying, but it seemed to be a creaky, swishing tree-y sort of language more than anything. She shut her eyes and stood there, breathing in the earthy scent of the woods. It was so nice. No demands, no stress. Enveloped by stillness and calm. At the brief touch of the brismun's cool hand on her arm, she opened her eyes and looked into his smiling face.

"Tell me why you left Jacob alone," he said.

"He went in search of water for us," Kasharel said. "He was able to search more quickly than we could. I know we shouldn't have split up, and I'm sorry. I should take better care of my companions."

Deborah cast him a sidelong look, amused at the torrent of words.

"So, you have crossed into a corner of my region on your way," said the brismun thoughtfully. "I will take you to water, and I will show you the way to the Silver Lake. Come."

He turned and leapt away. Without hesitation, Deborah and Kasharel went after him. Indeed, Deborah felt she couldn't do anything but follow the brismun. It was beginning to unnerve her. What if this brismun ordered her to jump off a cliff? She would do it; she knew she would. Her legs seemed to move of their own accord, as if she were a puppet on a string.

"I am called 'If'," said the brismun as he slowly hopped along.

"If?" Deborah said. She tucked Jacob in the crook of one arm so her other hand was free in case she stumbled on the uneven ground.

"I-F-F, *Iff*. Not the common language 'if'," said Iff. "It means 'large one' in my language. Flattering, hey?" He placed his hand against the bark of a tree as he went by. "You have told me Kasharel and Jacob, but failed to tell me your name."

She found herself touching the tree where Iff had, and Kasharel did the same. "Deborah."

"De-bor-ah," Iff said. "What does that mean?"

"I don't know."

"That's a pity. Your father didn't know what to call you when it came time to name you?"

"No, I mean, I don't know what Deborah means."

"If that's so, it could very well mean 'I don't know'."

She wasn't sure if he was teasing her or not, for his tone of voice gave nothing away.

"Water is here," he said, and stood still.

Deborah didn't see any. She didn't like to question Iff. His sight might be poor, but his hearing wasn't, so maybe there was some water somewhere. She looked around near his mossy tree trunk leg that appeared planted in the ground. There were twigs, leaf-litter, more of the silvery-flowered plants, but no water.

"I'm sorry," said Kasharel, "but I can't see it."

"Give it a minute," Iff said. "I'm drawing it now. It's fairly close to the surface, so I thought bringing it up would be a better idea than making you walk to the nearest stream. Might be nice to have a little spring here, anyway. I think Sar won't mind. I think." He grinned.

When he did so, it was as though the whole woods around him lit up and Deborah's heart lightened. She edged closer to him, hugging Jacob to herself. Iff was like a life-giving tree standing with his arms out, his head tilted to the sky framed by his twiggy hair. The moss of his rotund body rippled in the light through the shifting leaves.

"Who is Sar?" Kasharel asked.

Iff closed his eyes, and they disappeared amongst the moss. "The shaseeliany who shares my region."

"What's that?" Deborah asked.

"Come on now; don't be a numbskull. What I'm doing here in altering the course of water will bring the shaseeliany—a water custodian—to investigate. Are you not familiar with the water custodian underground in your caves, Mr. Gehun?"

Deborah wondered how Iff knew Kasharel was gehun. Was it the sound of his voice? Was it something in his bearing?

Kasharel slowly shook his head. "No."

"Curious and concerning. Why not?"

"I don't know. We have had… trouble in our caves."

"Trouble indeed. No custodian of your own to travel with, and no sight of the water custodian in the gehun caves. Ah, here comes Sar now."

Deborah looked around but saw nothing unusual through the woods. It was some time before she did. At first it looked like a trick of the eye, a reflection on the trunk of a tree as if someone shone a torch there. Then the light coalesced into a shape as if it had flown in and landed. Sar appeared as a little girl with long white hair in a silver dress; then she moved behind a tree, and when she emerged, she was as tall as Kasharel, and her colour had changed. Merged in streams of blue and green, it was hard to tell where her flowing hair ended and her dress began. Dress and hair fell in a waterfall of silk that shifted as Sar walked, revealing glimpses of shimmering scales that covered her body.

Deborah's head felt funny as she watched Sar coming closer. It was as though Sar moved too much as light and shape flickered over her, and at some points Deborah was sure she could see right through her.

"Iff," Sar said, and her voice resounded and echoed as if there were many more syllables to Iff's name.

"Hiya," Iff said. "I'm just drawing a spring for my thirsty friends."

"You're doing it wrong," Sar said in a low sing-song voice.

"You would say that. Do you want to take over?"

"No. I'll just watch and fix it later."

"Tired?"

"Yes. I've been cleaning up after guandras. They were all through our region and affected one main branch of water."

Iff nodded. "You see that I dispatched them?"

"A sorry end for sorry creatures," Sar said.

"I can't say that I'm sorry for them. They chose this life."

"They chose no life," Sar said. "It is unimaginable—I truly can't comprehend how."

Deborah leaned tiredly against the nearest tree, while Kasharel found a rock to sit on. Jacob did not stir in Deborah's arms. The rhythm of Iff and Sar's speech was like listening to a conversation between the trees and a river, strangely melodic and flowing.

Sar sat by Iff's leg, her luminous face upturned to him. Her eyes were palest blue, a crystalline clarity to them in which was impossible to discern any pupil or iris.

Iff rested his hand on her shoulder. "My sweet, it bothers me when you clean the waters the guandras have poisoned. It takes something from you."

"Yes, but you know I have to do it," she said. "The dwellers will suffer otherwise." She motioned fluidly to Deborah and Kasharel, and it seemed as though water rippled along her arm and sleeve as she did. "And the image-bearers." She looked this way and that through the trees. "Where is the rova who watches over them?"

"At the Silver Lake waiting for them, apparently."

Deborah did not like to say she didn't have a rova for a custodian. She knew it was deemed very strange that she had a brismun instead. Why hadn't she been assigned a rova like every other image-bearer?

Sar shuddered. "Do not call it a lake. It bears no resemblance to such a beautiful congregation of waters anymore."

Iff hopped backward. Where he had stood was now a tiny, bubbling spring. As the water pooled, Sar dipped her hand into it, and her arm went in up to her elbow.

"You can't resist fixing it already," Iff said and grinned.

She smiled shyly. "I am merely adjusting the flow." She glanced over at Deborah, her crystal eyes shining. "Drink all you want, image-bearers."

"I will hold dweller Jacob," Iff said.

Deborah handed Jacob to Iff, then she and Kasharel crouched at either side of Sar. Indeed, Deborah again felt as though she must obey, that Sar and Iff's innocent-sounding words had compelled her to move. What was it with them that they had this power?

That was soon forgotten as she drank. The water was almost as good as what they had encountered from the stream in the Oxpeina-life region. Cool and refreshing, with a hint of ancient earth and stone. She drank again and again, Sar at her side.

13

Iff stopped bounding along and raised his hand. Deborah, Kasharel, and Sar gathered around him. The woods were quiet—there were fewer birds, fewer sounds of movement in the undergrowth. It was an uneasy quiet, and there was a strange, hard light ahead through the trees that seemed to drain everything of colour.

Deborah was glad of the break; even though Iff had moved through the woods at an easy pace, she felt tired, and her hunger had been unabated by Iff helpfully pointing out which plants were edible. She looked at Jacob, who slept on soundly in her bundled-up jersey. She adjusted it over the top of his feather-patched head so it surrounded him more snugly.

"Here," Iff said. "We are nearly at the end of our region. A few more steps, and you must continue without us."

Sar bowed her head, and tears streamed down her face. "I can't bear it. Please, Deborah, Kasharel, are you sure you have to cross here? We can take you to a different border that crosses to a safer region."

"I think we must," Kasharel said. "We have not had any further instructions advising us to take a different path, so we must assume Deborah's custodian is still awaiting us at the lake."

"Don't say path," Sar said, shaking her head. "The paths there can't be trusted. I'm afraid for you—defenceless as you are."

"And weak-minded," said Iff. "You're a pair of dingbats."

Deborah felt as though she should protest but couldn't bring herself to open her mouth. Instead, she nodded meekly.

Iff's mossy face was solemn. "Yes. Troubling, troubling. You would do everything I tell you, even if it meant harm to another or even yourselves. Jacob would not, but he sleeps. You're easy pickings for the guandras and so I would go with you if I could. Yet, I have no such instruction to leave my region."

"You are too hard on them," Sar said.

"Not hard enough, methinks," he said. "They're poor excuses for image-bearers. You can see that, Sar; don't tell me you can't."

She turned away, her dress shimmering and rippling around her.

"Exactly," Iff said.

"You shame me," Kasharel said slowly.

"I do it to wake you up," Iff said. "How great-hearted would I be if I patted you on the back and told you everything was hunky-dory and you're a fabulous trio in no danger whatsoever? Nope. Deborah, touch your knee."

Deborah did so immediately.

Iff grimaced. "Kasharel, touch your nose."

Kasharel did just that.

"See?" Iff said. "Rubbish. And, now I'm sending you off to the Silver Lake, where your custodian—what kind of custodian leaves types like you alone?—awaits. No." Iff muttered under his breath in a rush of leafy and tree-y sounds, then looked up at Deborah. "I will ask Sonax if I have leave to take you myself. Wait here. Sar, watch them."

Deborah and Kasharel stood rooted to the spot as Sar turned to face them. Iff leapt away, the thumps of his stumpy leg shaking the earth and resounding through the woods.

"Why is Iff leaving us?" Deborah asked when she could find her voice. She felt as though she should be outraged by Iff's insults and wanted to feel the heat of annoyance at him, but instead felt nothing but a sense of loss that he had vanished so quickly.

"He goes to ask Sonax," Sar said. "He likes to stand by his favourite trees when he does this." She smiled. "Plus, I think he simply wants to be able to listen better for the voice of Sonax without us standing around watching him."

"How does he hear Sonax?" Kasharel asked.

"His connection to the trees," Sar said, as if that answered everything.

It didn't. Deborah looked at the trees. They seemed to be nothing special; she had no feeling of awe or grandeur on seeing them. In fact, a few close by were spindly and not the healthiest she had seen so far in the woods.

"Don't be afraid," Sar said, shifting her pale gaze to Kasharel. "I can defend you if guandras come. Iff is not the only one who can dispatch a guandra if necessary."

"Thank you," Kasharel said in a low voice.

It had never occurred to Deborah that he might be afraid of guandras. Was he only travelling with her because he was commanded by Ithnan to do so, or to get away from the gehun caves and the dankness of life there? She realised now they didn't have any custodians for water or woods living in the caves. A brismun probably wouldn't live underground anyway. Was there another kind of custodian, something that watched over stone? As for the rovi, there didn't seem to be any staying in the gehun caves. So, maybe Kasharel was just using her as an excuse to get away and be somewhere different.

She looked at him. The strange light that spilled through the trees from across the border of Iff's land cast an eerie hue on his melancholy face. She noticed his right hand moving. His fingers were twitching against his robe. It wasn't like him to show any sign of unrest.

She felt a rising apprehension as she looked across the border. It was clear to her now there was a distinct border—she could see a slight wilting and thinning of the undergrowth a few steps away, and the trees there were not only spindly but didn't seem to move at all. Not that the trees behind her moved, but the leaves did, as the breeze was always stirring something. The ones across the border seemed more rigid and frozen somehow. She hugged Jacob a little closer to herself. Where was Iff? Why was he taking so long?

She jumped as cold fingers caressed her hand.

"Look at me," Sar said.

Deborah looked up into her face. There was a sense of kindness softened in the blues and greens of Sar's earnest expression.

"Don't let fear touch you," she said. "Your body language is such that I think your thoughts are turning. I suppose it is from the proximity of that region."

Again, Deborah felt as though she had been commanded, and the tightness that had been rising her chest dissipated. With relief, she heard the sounds of Iff returning. He grinned broadly as he leapt towards them, and she hoped that meant he had had the answer of yes, that he would travel with them to the Silver Lake.

"Sonax has relieved my concerns for you," he said. "You will be all right. I must speak over you before you go into the region, and you will soon be in the charge of your custodian."

Deborah's hopes fell. She gazed at his cheery face, wishing he would change his mind and come.

"Is that what Sonashi said?" Kasharel asked. "Did he speak to you directly?"

"As direct as can be by way of the air, which whistles here and there and tosses the leafage. And, yes, he has told me these things and more."

Who was this Sonax or Sonashi? Deborah tried to piece together the things she had been told but couldn't quite seem to remember enough. Instead, she looked at the wan light that spread over Iff's green face and the deepening gloom of the neighbouring region. Was it turning to evening? She had no sense of time. How long had they walked together today? Maybe it had been for a morning, but, then again, it could have been longer.

"Look at me," Iff said.

Like a magnet, her eyes went to his that were half-squinting in moss. "I will talk to you first, as you're the weakest and I can see something is already happening to you. Damn that guandra-tainted region! If I only had the word from Sonax, I would go in and sort the whole thing out! But it's not my region, and I'm not wanted there by the inhabitants; blast them!" He smiled.

She smiled, too.

"Listen, Deborah," he said.

She felt her senses brighten and the woods around them faded. The moss of Iff's face sharpened into focus, soft and pillowy, individual tufts and strands beautiful and clear in bright hues of green.

"You are not to look at the Silver Lake. Do not look at the lake. Every time you want to look at the lake, stop it! Stop it, stop it, stop it! Don't look at the lake, you hear me?"

She nodded.

"If you catch a glimpse of the lake out the corner of your eye, what do you do? Look away."

"Look away," she whispered.

"That's right. Look away. Hold onto Jacob. Don't leave him. Don't let go of him. Keep walking until you find your custodian. He is with the squatchamn image-bearers on the shore of the lake. Follow the shoreline, but what do you do? Don't look at the lake. Tell me, Deborah, what do you do?"

She nodded again. "Don't look at the lake."

"True and good."

Deborah remembered Iff saying much the same to Kasharel, and then the next thing she knew, she and Kasharel were walking alone in the woods.

She looked about. How long had they been walking for? "I feel as though my legs are moving of their own accord and I have nothing to do with it." She stumbled along behind Kasharel, clutching Jacob in her arms. "I'm so tired I don't want to walk anymore."

"Me, too," Kasharel said over his shoulder. "I can't say I understand why Iff has had such power over us that we are doing exactly what he said. Do you think we should at least try to stop and rest?"

"I have tried, several times. Nothing happened. My legs kept going."

"How long have we been out here? It seems a long time since we left Iff and Sar."

"I have no idea," she said glumly. She could grasp no sense of what time of the day it was as the woods had the same pale light that never seemed to change. The trees were still, grey, their leaves hardly moving. At least there was now no longer any undergrowth to fumble through, just hard-packed earth and leaf litter. She should be walking more easily, but her legs felt weak. She couldn't remember the last time she had eaten anything. All she felt was the impetus pressing on her to keep walking until she found Erno. Drat Iff and his words. Why had he been able to do that to her?

Kasharel gasped. "There's the lake."

Deborah saw it too, but only for an instant, as her head involuntarily ducked the moment she laid eyes on it. There was the impression of a line of silver in the distance curving beyond the trees, bright and gleaming like new steel. She wanted to look again but found she couldn't. "*Iff*," she muttered under her breath.

"Mustn't look at it," Kasharel said quietly.

"I don't think I can, even if I wanted to," Deborah said.

"At least we've finally come to the shore and can follow that around," Kasharel said.

"Yes, but which way?"

"My legs go this way," Kasharel said.

He let out a small cough and harrumph. Deborah wasn't sure if that was him laughing or whether he was simply clearing his throat. She quickened her pace to get alongside and look up at him. His eyes were half-closed, and the twitch was there at the corner of his mouth.

"This is funny to you now?" she said.

"More ridiculous than anything," he said, glancing down at her. "Whose legs are these?" He plucked at his robe. "Not mine, surely. They seem to have a mind of their own, and I'm just a passenger."

Deborah caught another glimpse of the lake. This time she saw the sweep of silver with grey mist above. She immediately looked at her feet. "What is wrong with this lake that we're not allowed to look at it?"

"I don't know. I wish Jacob was awake. He seemed to know something of it."

Deborah smoothed the feathers around Jacob's face. His eyes were shut and his breathing steady. The woods were very quiet, disturbed only by the muffled thumps of their footfalls. There was no birdsong, no sounds of any other life, and she could not feel any Oxpeina-life surging through the earth or the atmosphere. Cool, faintly stagnant-smelling air drifted in from the lake, and she shivered, wishing she was wearing her jersey. She tucked it more snugly around Jacob.

"I think we are being watched," Kasharel said softly. "I think it is a guandra. Wait… yes, I see one. No, two."

A bolt of fear shot through her heart. Was there a stick anywhere? Something to beat off a wild animal if it attacked? A rock to throw? *Anything?*

"Ah," said Kasharel. "I think I spot three. Small ones. We need to hurry and get to your custodian."

Deborah kept pace with him, her legs moving as automatically as his did, and peered through the trees in the direction he looked. The trees were unvarying, tall, desiccated spikes in the ground. Yet she felt something else was there, watching her. Could she see eyes? No. She was only imagining that. Nothing but ashen trees. When had they become so pale? They looked half dead and most of them were leafless.

"I don't see anything."

"They're right there," he said, pointing to the trees. "Standing there watching us. Don't you see them?"

She shook her head, but then suddenly saw something in the distance. Three grey figures, gnarled and wizened like the bark of a tree, faded in appearance as though they were not quite there. The centre figure was hunched, poised like one ready to pounce, the two flanking it turning their heads this way and that. Where were their faces? She could see none on their wrinkled heads. Yet she felt the centre guandra was staring at her, fixated on her. It intended to come for her. Wanted something she had. Wanted her. Would kill for it. Power would come. Power with death. Taking life away, receive power.

"Deborah," said Kasharel. "Why do you stop? Keep moving."

His voice came to her through the fog of a distant dream, and she looked down at herself. Her legs weren't moving, yet she hadn't realised she had stopped walking. Her heart beat louder and louder—no, not a heartbeat, a single beat, steady, rhythmic, familiar. A brismun! Had Iff changed his mind? Was he coming to protect them after all?

A brismun smaller than Iff leapt towards them, luminous green as it bobbed amongst the pale trees.

"Deborah!" called a clear, bell-like voice.

She let out a gulp, clutching Jacob to her chest. "Erno? Is that you?"

"Yes, of course it's me!"

He may have been smaller in size than Iff, but there was something so winsome about him, the freshest of life-filled greens in the barren surroundings, that she could not take her eyes off him.

She stumbled forward to meet him. "It's you. It's you!"

"Who else?" he said, grinning with a shake of his twiggy hair, brown and speckled in the light.

She almost fell down before him with relief and would have thrown her arms around him if not for holding Jacob, but as it was, she burst into great sobs.

Erno's grin disappeared as he squinted up at her. "Deborah, Deborah. This is not like you. Where's the Deborah I know, ready to punch anyone in the nose she disagrees with?"

"I can't—," she said, between sobs, "I don't—"

"Can't, don't," Erno said. "Can, do."

He felt carefully along her forearms to her hands. His touch was reassuring, and she sucked in breaths of air, trying to steady her breathing.

"Oh, I see," he said. "You're famished. Haven't eaten properly in a long while, have you. That's enough to bring on the blubbers and the shakes. And a lot has happened to you since we were last together. I can feel that something has changed in you. No, don't worry; the guandras scattered when they heard me coming. They're not here anymore. You're safe."

She stared at him, into those slits of cheerful eyes barely visible in the moss, feeling that she was safe; she was with him; he was her custodian. Why hadn't she felt that way before? Now it seemed to be right that she was connected with him somehow and never should have been parted from him while crossing the regions. Any thought of guandras? Gone. Erno was there. He would protect her.

"I'm sorry," she said. "I'm sorry I left you at the lumdil village. I shouldn't have."

"No, you shouldn't have, but it's done and gone now. Let me have Jacob."

She unwrapped Jacob and handed him over. Erno's mossy hands and fingers moved lightly along Jacob's feathers and exposed skin, and he spread each of Jacob's wings and taloned feet in turn. "No breaks, that's good."

"Iff said he's all right," Deborah said. "He put Jacob to sleep."

"Iff did?"

"He's the brismun custodian in the neighbouring region."

"I know he is," Erno said. "He's my brother. I'm glad to know he's well."

"How do you know he's well?" Kasharel asked.

Erno squinted up at him. "Hello there. Bit strange to see a gehun above ground in a place like this. I hear you've been looking after Deborah."

Kasharel gave a slight nod. "My name is Kasharel, son of Mali."

"Good for you. As to your question—I know Iff is well because his enchantments on you all are strong, good, and clean. A bit too strong, really. Never mind, I'll take them off." He held Jacob upright, his green fingers wrapped around his little half-plucked body. "Jacob, wake up."

Jacob blinked and yawned. His eyes widened, and he stared into Erno's face.

"Yes, it's me," Erno said. "What in the world happened to you? I thought you'd be fine going off to Deborah by yourself. I see now I was wrong. Sorry about that. Have you got much pain?"

Jacob cleared his throat. "Somewhat."

"That's very descriptive."

"I think… I hurt all over."

"Do you want to remain awake or would you rather I put you back to sleep?"

"Sleep, I think."

"Go on, then. Sleep."

Deborah swayed a little on her feet and closed her eyes.

"I know you're tired, but not you, Deborah," Erno said.

Her eyes sprang open.

"Give Jacob to Kasharel and let me feel your shoulder. Right shoulder, is it?"

She nodded.

While Kasharel wrapped Jacob in her jersey, she bent down, and Erno examined her shoulder. His hard, cool fingers felt along her shoulder joint and upper arm, and around the base of her neck. He muttered to himself, his eyes closed, a whispery leafy mutter close to Deborah's ear. The warmth of sunshine entered her mind and the struggle of the past uncounted days seeped away. No more lying in the gehun caves recuperating; no more walking through the tunnels; no more endless tramping through the woods; just quiet with Erno here and now.

He was her custodian; she felt that so clearly. He would help her, and everything would be all right. Somehow he would get the journey back on track; he would know their next step to finding her father. Father must be out there. Must still be alive. If he had a custodian of his own, all would be well. She would find him again. Everything would be all right.

She sighed.

"That's it," said Erno. "Let it out."

"Let what out?" she asked.

He chuckled. "What you just let out when you sighed. What was it?"

She shrugged. "Stress, maybe. Tiredness. I don't know. It's good to be with you again, Erno."

"I'm mightily relieved to see you, too. Though I must warn you, the squatchamn image-bearers here don't have much in the way of food, so you'll have to wait a while before we can get you a proper meal." He let go of her. "Your shoulder's in pretty good shape, a little weakness, yet also some lingering feeling of Oxpeina-life in there, so that's interesting and will help."

Deborah thought of the region she and Kasharel had been in when they had left the gehun caves. "We spent about a day in a good Oxpeina place. That's where Jacob found us. Why didn't you come with him then?"

His expression became serious. "I had to stay with Nurrel. He's got caught up with the image-bearers here and isn't wanting to leave yet. Then, of course, I couldn't leave him, for he would have become vulnerable and the lake would have another victim."

"What do you mean?"

"You'll see. In fact, it's probably easier to see it to understand, rather than have me explain it without you seeing it."

"Iff didn't want us to look at the lake. His enchantments on us made us unable to do that."

Erno grinned. "That was very sensible, but I'm with you now, so there's no need for them anymore."

14

Deborah, Kasharel, and Erno stood together at the shore of the Silver Lake. The wide expanse was smooth like a mirror, hints of sunset orange in the mist that hung further out merging the trees and land and sky into indistinct shapes beyond. Thick silver fluid caressed the earth near Deborah's feet, ebbing and flowing smoothly, leaving no trace of wetness or silver behind.

"Not too close," Erno said, touching her elbow. "It is acidic and will burn you."

She stepped back, keeping a firm hold of Jacob.

"What is this place?" Kasharel asked. "It holds such beauty and calm, yet I feel nothing."

"Yes," Erno said. "Be wary of that."

Deborah felt as puzzled as Kasharel sounded, and she could not help but think of the Oxpeina-life region they had spent time in and compare it to this. Beauty and calm, yes, but there was none of that electrifying of the senses, the feeling of life surging through the very ground they stood upon. The lake may have been beautiful, but the trees fringing it were in various states of repose, dry, and might well have been dead for all she could tell. There was only a smattering of leaves on the trees, and they were a lacklustre grey. It was as if the life had drained out of the woods. But the lake—now, *that* was what drew the eye. How could it not? Gleaming, untarnished silver, not too bright to look at for the mist took care of that.

"Do you feel the power of the lake?" Erno asked.

Deborah felt a sense of shock. *'Do you feel the power of the woods?'* was what Father had asked on their first sight of the woods as they came to the village of Shilhim. To hear those words from Erno now... she could only feel sadness for not believing Father, for even considering him to be on the edge of sanity. He had known something about these woods. How he had learned of them, she didn't know, but he knew and felt their power.

"I think I do now," said Kasharel, "and I don't like it. I seem to want to keep gazing at it and not move from this place." He picked up a twig and tossed it into the lake. The silver liquid hissed and seethed as the twig sunk from sight. "What has happened here? Is this the result when guandras control water?"

"Yes," Erno said, "it's one of several things that can occur. Another is madness to those who drink. As to how it happened here, the custodians of this region were overthrown. It is what the image-bearers wanted."

"How could they want such a thing?" Deborah asked. She stared at Erno. His presence made her feel that all was secure and right with the world. That was interesting, and a connection she hadn't felt with him when they had last been together. Yes, she had wanted Iff to come with them to this region, but being with Erno felt more right, somehow. He was her custodian.

"It is the turning," Kasharel said glumly. "The very thing my people are fighting with."

"It is good to fight with it," Erno said. "Much better than giving in without a fight."

"If you say so."

"I do say so." Erno swivelled on his stumpy leg. "Let's get on—we need to get back to Nurrel."

Deborah followed him along the shoreline. As she thought about it, she realised she did not feel compelled to do so but walked with him because she wanted to. It was a nicer sensation than the compulsion Iff had laid on her.

"I must ask you something about your brother, Iff," Kasharel said as he caught up with one of Erno's leaps.

"Fire away," Erno said, then leapt ahead again.

Deborah smiled as she watched Kasharel quicken and slow his pace to keep up. She was content to trudge behind them in earshot, and although Jacob was light, she was weary of holding him.

"Iff said Deborah and I are weak-minded. I'm ashamed to admit he had power over us to do his bidding. I do not understand it."

Erno gave a nod. "He's like that. But I see his point. You and Deborah *are* both weak-minded, and that's a fact. If you weren't, then you wouldn't be able to be influenced so easily."

"But, why? How?"

"I'm thinking it's because you don't know who you are, so it's easy enough for someone else to tell you who you are. Simple, really."

"I *do* know who I am," Kasharel said. "I am the third son of Mali of the gehun."

"Stand still," Erno said.

Deborah faltered and almost tripped as her body stiffened and her legs felt like wood. Kasharel, meanwhile, stopped, and his long brown robe billowed slightly with momentum.

Erno grinned. "There, see? That proves my point. Can't move, can you?"

"No," Kasharel said, his voice low.

"You're free," Erno said.

Deborah felt a little jelly-legged as her stiffness disappeared.

Kasharel walked with Erno again. "I find this hard to understand. At least… I do understand this has something to do with the Oxpeina-life we wield, and you seem to have more of it than I do, but—"

"Wield?" Erno said. "You say that as if you're the one who has control and uses Oxpeina like a weapon." He shook his head. "That's backwards, my friend. We can chat about this more some other time, because right now we're about to reach the squatchamn camp, and I need to fill you both in on what to expect."

His stumpy leg clomped along on the hard earth. "They're stuck, you see," he said between clomps, "and I don't want either of you to get stuck. It's this lake. You've already seen for yourselves it has a mesmerising quality. Stare at it long and hard enough and you'll forget your own name. It's your choice to stay, really, but I'd prefer if you kept with me and we left this region." He glanced over his shoulder. "Keep your father in mind, Deborah. Remember your purpose."

She waited for the enchantment and power of his words to fall on her as Iff's had, but felt nothing. That gave her a twinge of insecurity—wouldn't it be easier if Erno laid an enchantment on her so she didn't get stuck here? She took a deep breath and watched his vibrant green form moving through the trees, the silent furling and unfurling of the Silver Lake a few feet away as it reached towards them then fell back.

She smelt the camp before she saw it—a sort of stagnant, unwashed aroma hung about the trees. She supposed that was fair enough if the squatchamn didn't have a good source of water. A large clearing was beside the lake with mounds of earth, arrangements of sticks with loose material clinging to them—some kind of shelters?—and thatched huts on earthen stilts out on the lake. These huts were different from the shelters on land; they appeared well-made and sat a foot or so above the silver surface of the lake. Narrow wooden walkways linked the huts, although they were not built very far out on the lake but were spread closer to shore.

It took her a few moments to see the squatchamn, for they were motionless and blended in with their dwellings. Her first impression was that she was looking at guandras again, but that soon passed as she saw that, no, these were people, small as lumdils, but skin and bones in ragged clothing.

The clomps of Erno as he entered the clearing seemed unspeakably loud, and Deborah felt as if she and Kasharel might have well entered the camp with loud trumpets and fanfare, yet many of the squatchamn appeared not to notice. Most of them sat staring at the lake as though lost in a reverie. A few did look up at Erno's approach with wide toothless smiles, their eyes large and staring.

"Nurrel!" Erno called, in a ringing shout that echoed across the lake.

There was a flurry of movement at one of the dirt mounds as loose material was swept aside. Nurrel emerged, a look of relief on his face.

Deborah felt a sense of relief at the sight of him, too. She realised she had been assuming he was 'stuck' at the lake, but on seeing him, her opinion changed. He looked as if he didn't belong there—his complexion glowed with health and colour, his clothes were tidy, and he didn't so much as glance in the lake's direction.

He briskly walked over to them. "My!" he said, a wide smile on his face as he looked at Deborah. "You're alive and well!"

Before she realised what he was doing, he embraced her around the middle and gave her a hearty squeeze.

"Oop! Sorry, what's that? *Jacob?*" Nurrel drew back in alarm. "The poor fellow. What happened to him? Attacked by guandras?"

"Shamefully plucked and humiliated," Erno said. "No bones broken, but he'll be in a sleep for a while until the pain has lessened."

Nurrel nodded. "Good of you to do that for him." He smiled up at Deborah again, his soft, dark eyes filled with delight.

She felt awkward. Why did he look at her that way when they hardly knew each other?

Nurrel craned his neck back to look up at Kasharel. "Welcome, welcome. You're of the gehun, I see that. My name is Nurrel Jawtie, of the village Smoky Glade, which, as I understand it, is not so far from your particular neck of the woods. Or, underground."

Deborah smiled down at the sleeping Jacob, remembering talk of Shady Glade and Smoky Glen as they had muddled up the name of the lumdil village on their journey together. That seemed countless days ago.

Kasharel gave a slight nod. "I am Kasharel, son of Mali."

"I think we have you to thank for looking after Deborah?" Nurrel said and turned his soft gaze up to her. "You had it very hard, by all accounts. Attacked by a brismun? Unthinkable!"

"I don't understand it myself," she said slowly. "I did nothing. I did not even have the chance to speak to the brismun before it attacked."

She shuddered as she remembered the grin of the brismun as it had leapt at her, all while she had believed it to be Erno. She looked at him. His height, the feel of being near him, the woodsy scent—she knew he was different. Yes, brismuns looked very alike, so alike as to be kin, but she had met four now, and all were different in personality.

"You look very worn," Nurrel said. "When did you last have a meal? Come and sit down and have something to eat. Come, let me help you."

"I'm fine," she said, refusing his hand.

"At least let me take Jacob for you."

"It's all right. I can manage."

Erno let out a snort. "There's the Deborah we know and love."

Nurrel turned back to the squatchamn earth mounds. "Blast it! She's taken it off."

"You had to expect that," Erno said.

"Yes, I guess, but no, she shouldn't have. I really thought I was getting somewhere with her."

Deborah and Kasharel exchanged quizzical looks. At least, that's what she thought Kasharel was doing, as she noted the slightest hint of an eyebrow raise in his placid expression.

"Sorry about this," Nurrel said, as he turned back to them. "It's just… a friend… she, well, she's got caught here, and I want her to leave. She shouldn't be here. She was on her way to Hirahi as part of the movement of those leaving my village, see. Once at Hirahi, they were going to get directions to head further north to another city and join others who had gone on ahead. Ibelli shouldn't be here. Most of the group she was travelling with made it to Hirahi and have gone on, so I don't know what happened and why Ibelli is here. I'm trying to get her to stop looking at the lake." He gestured towards the earth mounds. "She's over there, and I'd got so far as covering the opening of the hovel she thinks is home and started trying to talk sense into her. Now she's taken the blasted cover off. She'll be sitting there staring at the lake right this minute." He marched off, his boots stirring up the dust of the dry ground.

"Deborah," Erno said, "this is why I didn't come with Jacob to meet you even though I wished to. We had all just left Hirahi when I sent him on ahead to you, and Nurrel and I were diverted to this lake. Once here, I couldn't leave Nurrel alone. I couldn't risk him getting caught here too, for Sonax has made me custodian over him." His usually cheerful face furrowed in a ripple of moss. "I prefer not to force Nurrel to leave, not while he has hopes of saving his friend, but we can't continue to stay on here much longer."

"Pardon me for being so forthright," Kasharel said, "but I've never heard of a brismun being custodian for image-bearers. I understood that was the duty of the rovi. Why has it been given to you?"

"You are pardoned," Erno said and grinned. "It is unusual, yes, but then these are unusual times, and who am I to question Sonax's judgement in the matter? He has his reasons, I'm sure. Mind you, next time I see him, I wouldn't mind giving him a few questions about it—I'd be interested in the answers." He chuckled. "Speaking of such matters, I have a question for you—where's your custodian?"

"Dead," Kasharel said in a low voice, and bowed his head to look solemnly at the ground. "A long time ago, I ventured out across my region, and then her death, I think, occurred, and now this is the first time I have been above ground again in a long while, and I was not assigned another custodian."

"*Hmm.*" Erno whispered in a leafy tone to himself. "Trouble amongst the gehun, movement from the lumdils, image-bearers from far away appearing in the woods, more regions closing."

"Green, green, green!" cried a strange, high voice.

A squatchamn girl was sitting in the doorway of an earthen mound. Her red-rimmed eyes were startling in her pasty face, and her greasy hair hung lankly to her shoulders. Her clothes were grubby rags, and Deborah was alarmed to see she was missing most of her fingers and her right leg was gone below the knee.

The girl took up a tree branch and used it as a crutch to hobble closer. "Green."

"Too right, I'm green," Erno said. "I'm the greenest thing you've seen in a long time, aren't I?"

She nodded. "Green."

"Do you remember what we talked about before?"

The girl stared at him. "No. Don't know you."

Erno hopped over to her. "We had a good long talk, remember? I was telling you about a place not far from here with food and warmth where you'll be looked after. Remember? I told you that you don't have to spend the rest of your life here."

She hastily shook her head and looked over towards the lake. "No. Yes? No."

"Why don't you just use your enchantments on her?" Deborah said. "You could make her leave."

"No!" shouted the girl, and hobbled away in the direction of the lake.

Erno turned to Deborah. "Why do you want me to force her to do something against her own will?"

"But she's just a child."

"No, she isn't."

"She can't be more than ten!"

"She is more than twenty."

"You're joking!"

Erno shook his twiggy hair. "Not at all. Come, let's join Nurrel. He has some food you can safely eat."

That was enough to stir Deborah to action. She walked as fast as she could—which, admittedly, wasn't up to her usual pace for her legs felt decidedly wobbly from fatigue and hunger—and followed Erno to the earthen shelter Nurrel had disappeared into. They passed several other shelters. At each one, a squatchamn or two sat in the doorway, gazing steadily out to the lake. As her shadow fell on one man, he winced.

"Begone," he muttered, swiping his hand at the air.

Deborah noted with horror that he was missing most of his fingers.

She leaned closer to Erno and whispered out the side of her mouth. "What has happened here?"

"It's the lake," he said. "Eventually, they have to touch it. They can't help themselves. Again and again, they'll dip their hands in."

"Why do they keep doing it if it burns?" Kasharel asked.

"Why indeed," Erno said. "Worse yet are those who reach the end and give themselves to the lake."

Deborah frowned. "What do you mean, 'give themselves'?"

"I think you know what I mean."

She did, but could not fathom the thought. Had these squatchamn become so mesmerised by the lake that they could not resist it anymore and had to go in, and in doing so, killed themselves? Incomprehensible. Why didn't they realise the lake was harmful to them? She glanced out over it, beyond the stilt huts clustered at one edge, to the expanse of smooth water reaching in a silvery mirror into the faraway mist.

"Deborah," Kasharel said.

His voice jolted her, and she hastily looked away and went after Erno, who was standing by one of the earthen shelters.

"Go in," he said. "I'll wait out here as it's difficult for me to get in there."

"It looks difficult for me, too," Kasharel said. He was taller than the shelter itself and eyed the low opening dubiously.

"That's okay," Deborah said. "I'll bring you out something to eat."

"Hand me Jacob," Erno said.

He said it mildly, and Deborah felt she could decide to do or not do what he said. She gave Jacob over to Erno's waiting hands and got down onto her hands and knees to crawl through the opening. It took her a few moments to adjust to the low light.

"Move," said a female voice. "You're in my line of vision."

"Ibelli," Nurrel said, "isn't that a good thing? Don't you feel the relief of having it blocked again?"

Deborah shuffled away from the opening, and a silvery light fell on Nurrel and Ibelli. Nurrel was seated cross-legged, his back to the opening, while Ibelli sat bathed in the shimmery light that came from the lake.

Deborah had not been aware of it while outside, but in the mound the contrast of light was greater, the silver more lustrous.

Ibelli herself was dressed in a red-and-brown tunic and trousers in a style that was typical of the village lumdils, but her hair was perhaps not as thick and dark as the lumdils' ordinarily was as it fell limply to her shoulders. Her eyes were certainly more staring and red-rimmed, and her large lumdil nose even seemed less jolly somehow. Yet, as the silver light fell on her, there was something about how she looked—the contrasting colours of clothing hair and skin, defined sharply in etched strokes—that did not seem natural.

Deborah felt herself longing for the green of the woods again, the true soft greys and browns of living trees, the vividness of leaf and brismun.

"It hurts me," Ibelli said. "When the light is cut off, I feel it. *Here*." She clutched her chest, a pained look on her face.

"I'm sorry," Deborah said. "I didn't mean you any harm."

"Now you know that's not really so, Ibelli," Nurrel said. "It isn't hurting you at all when the door is closed. It's the lake itself that's hurting you."

"What do you know? How can you know my pain? You don't know anything at all about it."

"But I know *you*, Ibelli; I know *you*. And this isn't you. You're the one who wanted to leave the village with the others, remember? You wanted to journey with them to the northern village of our ancestors. Why stop here? Alone? Why didn't you go on with the group? Where are Justy, Rillan, and Eiben?"

Ibelli sighed. "I wish you would stop saying the same things over and over. You won't listen to me. I have told you, this is what I want. I'm happy here."

"No, you're not."

Ibelli glanced at Deborah, giving the impression of weighing her up with one keen look. "Nurrel won't hear me, and I'm weary of his never-ending talk. Now he's brought you here to me? Why? What do you want with me?" Ibelli looked again to the lake, and her shoulders sank as though the weight of her tiredness was relieved.

Deborah followed her gaze and immediately wished she hadn't. She fell back as the dazzling silver light struck her. She shut her eyes and crawled away as the white light seared into her brain. Strangely, none of the other mounds or huts had been in view, not even the ones on the lake's edge. Shouldn't they have been? She tried to think of how the dwellings were all laid out in the clearing, but her head hurt.

"I expect Deborah is hungry," Nurrel said to Ibelli.

"What has that to do with me?"

"Nothing, I expect, but I'm the one with the food." Nurrel rummaged in a bag and brought out a bread roll. "Won't you eat something too?"

"I have already. I don't want any of yours."

"But this is different—this is the food of home. Maybe it will help you remember."

"There's nothing whatsoever wrong with my memory. I'm so tired of this, Nurrel. I wish you would stop badgering me! You've always been one to meddle in other people's business, and here you are doing it again. Why can't you keep your nose out of it? You think you know everything. You always think you know best. It's the way you've always been, Nurrel. You're small-minded, petty, and need to find a life of your own to live instead of telling others what you think they should do. Why don't you go back to mining? That's right, you quit. The work was too much for you. It wasn't too much for other men, but you're not like other men, are you."

Deborah was taken aback at the abrupt change in Ibelli from sounding tired and hard done by to aggressive. Ibelli was frustrated, obviously, so that was understandable, but what did she mean by saying Nurrel wasn't like other men? She sounded like she was referring to something in particular when she said that.

Nurrel turned and passed a bread roll to Deborah. "I'm sorry about this," he said in a low voice. "Perhaps it's best you wait outside."

"Oh, right, yes!" said Ibelli. "She should go and leave me alone with you? So you can harass me some more in private? That's great, that is!"

Nurrel turned back to her. "No, I thought Deborah w—"

"Oh? You care more about her feelings than you do about mine? You've known me all your life, and now that means nothing? This stranger means more to you?"

"No, I—"

"Yes, you do! It's clear to me that you're trying to impress someone outside of our own kind. She doesn't know you like I know you. She doesn't know what a manipulative, controlling grub you are. Think you can fool her like you tried to fool everyone else?"

"Maybe I should go," Deborah said, and crawled towards the opening.

"Don't you move! You saw what it did to me when you blocked my light, and here I've barely recovered from the pain, and you're going to do it to me again? Besides, I see it now; you're both in this together against me. Think you can fool me? Well, you can't."

Deborah stared at her. "What?"

"Playing innocent with me now? It's as clear as day what you're doing. Maybe you don't see it, but I do. I know what Nurrel's like—he acts all nice and friendly, acts like he wants to help you, but that's all it is, an act." Ibelli nodded knowingly. "You'll find out soon enough. I did. You're caught in his web of lies. I wonder what else you're caught in."

"Ibelli," Nurrel said. "Don't."

"Ibelli, don't," Ibelli said, a sneer on her face. "Really? That's the best you can do? Why don't you stand up for yourself for once in your life?"

The words struck Deborah with force, and memories came flooding back. This was something that could have come right from Mother's mouth when arguing with Father. She had called Father weak, useless, told him she never should have married him. Often, sometimes sneaking looks at them from behind a door, Deborah had watched her father sit, cowed by Mother's words, his head down, muttering as he tried to defend himself. She felt sick to her stomach as she remembered. Other times she had lain in bed at night and heard their voices, rising and falling, knowing they were shouting at each other again. She knew it was not Father's fault; it was never Father's fault.

"You're weak, Nurrel," said Ibelli, "that's why. You think you can play your little mind games and get what you want, but it'll never happen. *Never*. People like you can't achieve anything, can't get anywhere in life. That's why you couldn't work anymore like the rest of us. You're weak."

"You shut up!" Deborah shouted. "Nurrel's here trying to help you—don't ask me why, because you're a horrible piece of work—and all you can do is attack him!"

Nurrel turned to look at her. "Deborah."

Deborah shook her finger at Ibelli. "You're sick, and you don't even know it. Here you are, staring at this stupid lake, and you're stuck, aren't you. Can't do anything for yourself anymore, can you! You look terrible; you don't even look right in the head. And, here's Nurrel, trying to get you away from this place, trying to help you, and all you can do is laugh at him!"

Ibelli sat up straighter and smiled at Deborah. "Fond of him, are you? Love runty Nurrel? Want to have his babies? What a pair you two would make, one so oafish and giant-like, and the other considered too short and weaselly even for a lumdil. *Ha!*"

"Ibelli, *really*," Nurrel said, turning back to her.

"I'm not the one getting all red-eyed and crazy from sitting here!" Deborah said to Ibelli. "Look at yourself! What a great life you have sitting in a mud hut like a moron!"

"Deborah."

This time the voice belonged to Erno. Deborah felt the heat of her anger cut through to the marrow by his tone. He wasn't scolding her; instead, he was calling her. Wanting her to listen to him and come out. Wanting her to be with him. She scrabbled out of the mound, ignoring Ibelli's outraged shriek as she momentarily blocked the opening.

The harsh light outside burned. She stood in Kasharel's shadow and squinted at Erno. "Did you hear all that? You must have heard. Why is Nurrel even wasting his time on that idiot? She's horrible."

"Because he loves her," Erno said.

He touched her arm with his free hand—bundled up Jacob was held in the crook of his other arm—and his cool, firm fingers carefully probed through her sleeve. He was examining her again; she felt that. What for, she had no idea. She sighed and looked around at the sepia tones of the dry squatchamn camp and the hard silver of the lake.

"Can't we just leave here?" she said. "I don't want to be here anymore."

"Interesting that this place digs up memories for you and yet you've never been here before," Erno said. "Interesting."

"Not interesting," she said. "*Dumb*. And it's not this place. It's Ibelli, or whatever her name is. She's horrible." She glanced at his hand on her arm. "How do you know it's digging up memories?"

"I can feel and hear it in you."

She frowned. "*Humph*."

"Is that bread?" Kasharel asked.

"Oh, yes. Here." She gave the roll to him.

"Have you eaten any?" Erno asked her.

"What, you can't feel if I have or not?" she said.

He grinned at her and let go of her arm.

"I can't eat anything," she said. "I just want to get out of here." She heard the sharp tones of Ibelli's raised voice inside the mound. "At least, away from this." She walked away, and Kasharel went with her.

"Nurrel," said Erno, remaining outside the mound.

Deborah could feel the call of the custodian again. Strange how he affected her in that way. Hopefully he would tell Nurrel it was time to leave this place. *Now.* She kicked a stone, and it scudded across the dirt and came to rest at the toeless feet of a squatchamn woman who sat in the doorway of an earthen mound. She appeared not to notice as she gazed out to the lake, her red-rimmed eyes half-closed, a serene expression on her wan face.

Deborah sighed. Nothing was going right. How many days had it been since she had last seen Father? He was goodness knows where, and she was floundering about the unending woods, not knowing where in the realms and regions she was. She may as well give up. He was long gone, and there was no chance of finding him now.

"Stop staring at the lake," Kasharel said, nudging her.

"What?" She hadn't realised she was. His words made the lake sharpen into focus. Somehow, the sight of the shining lake as it disappeared into the misty horizon beckoned to her as if promising something beyond. Something not of this world. Something better.

She shut her eyes and shook her head. "*Ugh*. Stupid thing."

Kasharel led her across the squatchamn camp to the withered trees. "Let's wait here for Erno."

They sat together on the dirt, their backs to the lake. Branches were scattered under the trees, while others that had not completely broken off were hanging. Deborah looked up at the nearest tree, making certain she wasn't underneath anything else that might drop. The air felt somewhat better there, not as stagnant, even though there was no greenery anywhere to speak of.

Kasharel held the half-eaten bread roll out to her. "Have some."

She waved it away. "I can't eat. You finish it."

"You must eat."

She buried her face in her hands. "Just leave me alone. I can't eat."

"The sooner we leave this place, the better."

She looked up at him and saw the concern in his grey eyes. "It's not just this place. It's—" Her stomach twisted into knots as she thought of her parents again. "Well… Erno was right. It's memories. Bad memories. I'll be fine. I just need to get over it."

He gingerly placed his hand on her shoulder. "Will you tell me about these memories?"

As she considered this, she knew she wanted to tell Erno about them. Not anybody else. She supposed that was something to do with the whole mysterious custodianship thing. She shook her head. "No. I'll be all right."

It was a relief to hear Erno's approach. The ground trembled as he landed next to her, and she looked up at him, once again refreshed by his vivid greenness in such a barren region. Even Jacob, what could be seen of him in Erno's arms, seemed more alive in the pinkness of skin, brown tufts of feathers, and softness of eyelids.

"We'll leave first thing in the morning," Erno said. "Nurrel has agreed, reluctantly. He thinks if he had more time with Ibelli, he could turn her back to what she used to be. He said before we got here he had managed to cover the opening of her house. It didn't last—the moment he came out to greet us, she moved it aside again. I told him I won't stay here any longer for both your sakes and that he must also think of his own soundness of mind. If he remains here, it is inevitable he will be caught. I can't let that happen. And we, by association, will also be caught if we don't move on."

"What of Ibelli?" Kasharel asked.

Deborah thought it was generous of him to speak with any concern for her. But then he hadn't seen what she was like and how horribly she treated Nurrel.

"She has until morning to decide to come with us. But I would say it is not enough time for Nurrel to convince her—everything he says she counters, she insults, she mocks."

"Yet, she allowed him to cover, to block, I suppose, the sight of the lake?" Kasharel said. "That is promising, is it not?"

"She is angry with him for it. She says he manipulated her and took away her only hope, and she won't let him do it again."

Deborah choked. "What? *Hope? Huh?*"

"Exactly," said Erno, a smile briefly emerging in his mossy face before he became serious again. "Don't expect sense from the senseless." He looked upward, breathing deeply, his eyes shut. "Follow me into the woods a little further. I can feel a tree nearby that has some life. It will be safer for you to spend the night closer to it."

Deborah stood and brushed the dirt from her clothes. "Good. I hope it's far away from this stupid place."

15

Deborah stepped around the fallen branches beneath the grey trees while, ahead of her, Kasharel tried to keep pace with Erno's leaps.

"I think something is following us," he said, and yanked his robe free as it snagged on a branch.

"I know something is following us," Erno said, his cheerful voice ringing through the dry air. "In fact, a someone. Come along!" he called over his shoulder. "Keep up. Don't lose us in the scrub!"

Deborah turned and glimpsed a thin figure dart from one tree to another and hide behind its gnarled trunk. Was that a guandra? It was faded and shrivelled, similar to the guandras she and Kasharel had seen. It scurried out from behind one tree to another. No, wait—it had ragged clothing and the thin, limp hair and staring face of a squatchamn.

"No need to hide," Erno called. "I hear you!"

The squatchamn stuck her fingers in her mouth and hastily drew back behind the tree.

"Come along," Erno called again. "Don't worry. All is well!" He stomped along, twigs snapping under his stumpy leg.

"Shouldn't we wait for her?" Deborah said.

"It's better that she wants to chase us," Erno said. "I'm leading us in a roundabout way to the tree to see if I can get her to follow us. It'll help her if she has more time to feel the desire to leave the lake and come with us than if we stopped and she considered going back. This way her focus is on moving ahead." He adjusted his hold on Jacob and leapt over a fallen tree. "She's doing very well. She started following us as soon as we left the clearing. This is better than I had hoped. I'm only sorry more haven't come, but when I go back for Nurrel that may change."

"You're going to leave us out here?" Deborah said.

"I must, but I will be within earshot, so you will be safe."

"Within earshot for you could mean miles away," she said.

He grinned. "Not this time."

The tree he led them to had no discernible signs of life that Deborah could see on first look. She wondered what Erno had noted in it that he had decided it had any life at all. He pressed his mossy hand to the bark and spoke softly in his tree-y language. Deborah thought she saw an answering tremor in some of the spindliest of its twigs, and then the attitude of the whole tree changed. Almost imperceptibly, it seemed to droop as though unspeakably sad.

She laid her hand on the rough bark, too. "It's all right, tree. We're here now." As she heard herself saying that aloud, she felt a little silly, but Erno smiled.

"That's sweet of you, Deborah," he said. "It can't understand you, for trees are not conscious in the way that we understand consciousness, but it should respond to life in the atmosphere. I'm afraid it's almost dead. There is hardly any water since the shaseeliany of this region was killed."

"How was the water custodian killed?" Deborah asked. She felt somewhat smug, knowing now what a shaseeliany was, and looked at Jacob in the crook of Erno's arm. It was a pity he wasn't awake to see she had learned more about the woods and no longer 'knew nothing'.

"Usually if a custodian is killed, it is the will of the image-bearers," Erno said.

Deborah frowned. That didn't make any sense. Maybe it was better Jacob was still asleep. He probably would have laughed at the look of incomprehension on her face.

Kasharel sighed and nodded. "It is sordid and dishonourable when such a thing occurs."

"Know about that sort of stuff, do you?" Erno asked. "I bet you do."

Before Deborah could question what Erno meant, for he spoke in a knowing tone, there was a snapping of a twig behind them.

"I hear you," Erno called. "I hear you without you having to step on that so theatrically. Trying to get my attention, huh?"

A small giggle answered him.

"Come now, before I leave," Erno said.

Deborah felt the command in his voice and drew closer to him, as did Kasharel.

"No," said the squatchamn.

Deborah was astonished. How could she not have felt that irresistible pull towards Erno as he spoke?

"Have it your way," Erno said. He carefully handed Jacob to Deborah. "I'll be back at nightfall unless Nurrel will come sooner. Remember that I can hear you if you call. Perhaps it's best that only one of you sleep at a time—guandras are about, small ones, but guandras all the same. Here, I have drawn up what little water I could for you to drink."

He hopped aside, and Deborah saw the ground was dark where he had stood as water seeped up through the dirt and began to pool in a tiny puddle.

"Thank you," Kasharel said. "What should we do about this squatchamn near to us?"

"Treat her as you would anybody else, but don't let her trick you," Erno said. He laid his hand on Deborah's arm. "Take care."

He bounded away in great leaps, thumping through the stillness of the woods until he was gone.

Take care? What was that supposed to mean? Take care of Jacob? Take care of herself? Kasharel? Deborah thought Erno sounded as if he meant something more by those simple words, but what exactly, she didn't know. She gently laid Jacob at the foot of the tree, then tried to scoop a handful of water to drink. Really, it was better to get right down and press her lips almost to the dirt, for the puddle was too shallow to scoop into her hands. The water had a bitter taste but was fine. It would do.

"What you doing?" said a strange female voice.

The squatchamn, and she had moved somewhat closer by the sounds of things.

Deborah paused from sucking the slowly pooling water. "What does it look like? Having a drink."

"You funny. Bowing to tree. Bottom up."

Deborah grimaced. She was too tired for this nonsense.

"Are you leaving any for me?" Kasharel said.

She sat back on her heels. "There's more coming; it's just slow. I think we'll be hours taking turns getting enough to drink."

"I suppose it will give us something to do while we wait."

She smiled at him and moved aside so he could take a turn. He tucked his robe out of the way as he got down on his hands and knees.

"I would rather sleep," she said, and settled herself against the bony trunk of the tree, taking Jacob into her arms.

"I would rather eat," Kasharel said.

"Don't mention it."

"You should have eaten before when I offered some of that bread to you."

"I—"

"You voice loud!" shouted the squatchamn.

"You can talk," said Deborah. "You're louder than both of us put together." She looked over to the right, where the squatchamn's voice sounded as though it came from, but saw no one in the shadows of the withered trees.

"Loud!"

"We hear you," Kasharel said. "Do you want some of this water to drink?"

"No!"

"Suit yourself," Deborah said. She wriggled against the tree, trying to get comfortable, and hoped the squatchamn girl was not going to keep yelling. She felt long overdue for some peace and quiet. That whole incident with Ibelli; seeing the weirdness of the squatchamn 'village'; her eyes were tired, probably from looking at that blasted lake; hunger pangs now, too—she just wanted to rest. Hopefully Erno and Nurrel wouldn't be long. It did kind of look as though it was late in the day, though it was hard to tell from the light, so perhaps nightfall wasn't that far off.

"No!" shouted the squatchamn again.

"Shut up," Deborah muttered, closing her eyes.

"Deborah," said Kasharel, disapproval in his tone.

"*Huh.*"

"Debah, Debah, Debah!" the squatchamn shouted.

There was nothing handy to throw, and Deborah supposed Kasharel wouldn't approve of that either. She hunkered down, hugging Jacob closer, wishing she could stuff her ears with something.

"Calm yourself," Kasharel said. "Do you want every guandra in the region to come? They will hear you. What do you think they will do when they find us here alone? Please, be quiet."

"Calm youself, calm youself, *bleh blah bleh!*"

Deborah glanced sidelong at Kasharel. "What is wrong with this twit?"

He was about to answer her, but distant sounds of snapping and crunching of twigs made him jump to his feet. His chest rose and fell rapidly as he looked this way and that through the barren trees. "Guandras. It must be. We should call for Erno. I have nothing to defend us with. Get up, Deborah!"

"Debah! Debah!"

"Erno!" shouted Kasharel.

Deborah got up but saw nothing through the woods. The sound faltered, then began again—echoes of footfalls, reverberation of movement—it was hard to tell from where it came. The way it went silent then began again was unnerving, as though something was searching, something was hunting them. There was a low rumble of voices, then she saw them. Rovi. She saw now why the sound came and went, for they seemed to almost move in and out of vision as they ran in a blur of brown. A rich and vivid brown in the dying woods, they moved together—five of them, she thought—in close formation. As they came closer, she saw their faces—wild and animalistic.

"It is all right," Kasharel said. "Rovi. We are safe."

Deborah clutched Jacob close to her chest, staring at the group as they came. Why were they coming? What did they want?

"Deborah," said the foremost rova.

Although as lithe as the others, he was more muscular, and his face grizzled. His green eyes were deep and, she realised, questioned her silently. He was questioning her just as the rova in the gehun caves had done. She glanced at the four rovi flanking him, and they too looked at her with the same question. She didn't know what they wanted; all she could think in response was, no, I don't know. I don't know!

"I am Val," said the foremost rova. "You remember me?"

She nodded quickly.

His expression hardened as he looked into her, and the question seemed to leave his thoughts as he appeared to study who she was. She couldn't keep meeting that gaze but looked down. She should bow, she should kneel, do something in front of this intimidating beast. The air was charged with Oxpeina-life, and Jacob opened his eyes.

Val growled. "Don't bow."

Deborah realised he had yanked Kasharel's sleeve to keep him upright.

"So annoying," said one of the other rovi in a low grumbling voice.

This one had bright blue eyes flecked with gold, and the brown of its fur was darker. He was familiar. Was he the same rova she had seen in the gehun cavern?

"Don't do that," he said. "Don't treat us like we are Sonax the Ancient. We are not."

"I am sorry," Kasharel said quietly.

Deborah thought he sounded as if he had hardly enough breath to speak.

"Erno told us where to find you," Val said. "We have brought you some food."

Deborah nodded wordlessly.

One of the rovi produced a bag and handed it to Kasharel, then she—for this rova seemed more feminine in her features and build—placed her hand on the bark of the tree beside Deborah. "This one does still have some life, as Erno said. Strangely, I feel its sorrow at being left."

"Sonax should burn this whole region," said the blue-eyed rova. "Kill this deathly place and let it rise again."

Val turned to him. "We can't do that to the image-bearers here."

"These squatchamn are not image-bearers anymore," growled blue eyes. "They don't deserve that rank. They have almost turned completely."

"Yes," said Val, "but not completely. There is still hope for them, and Sonax must see that."

"He does," said the feminine rova. "He knows. He always knows."

The two silent rovi nodded in assent. One of them had a slightly wheaten hue to her brown coat and silvery almond-shaped eyes. She caught Deborah's gaze and held it. Again, there was a silent question. Deborah wanted to say aloud that she didn't know, couldn't know, but before she could bring herself to verbalise anything, Val spoke.

"Deborah," he said. "Sonax has given me word of your father to give to you."

His words were so stunning that she felt as though all the wind was knocked out of her and her legs threatened to buckle.

"Stand," he said, and touched her arm.

A bite of electricity coursed through her, jolting her as if to begin breathing again.

"He is named Ben Lakely?" Val said.

She nodded eagerly.

"Sonax has assigned one of my brothers as Ben's custodian. He is safe at present and journeys to Aric, hoping it is there that he will find Sonax himself."

"Aric?" Deborah whispered.

"Strange," said the blue-eyed rova. "Why would it be thought of that Aric is the city where Sonax could be found?"

"It is considered a birthplace," said the female rova beside Deborah. "The first of all regions. I can see how he might think that."

"His reasons aside," Val said, "this is his intent."

"Where is Aric?" Deborah said. "How far? Where? How do I get there?"

"You are so close to Hirahi," said the silvery-eyed rova, her voice soft. "I would suggest you go first there, gain supplies, and find your way onward. This is Erno's advice and, I think, Sonax's. I fear for you all." Her eyes flicked from Deborah to Kasharel. "I see what you are. Go to Hirahi and become strong. You endanger Erno if you don't."

"True," said Jacob, his raspy voice startling Deborah.

"What do you mean by this?" Kasharel said to the rova.

"Exactly what I have said. I do not mean to be obscure." Her eyes narrowed as she studied his face. "And, I see now as I speak that you know precisely what I mean, but Deborah does not." She turned to Deborah. "I mean no insult. I fear for you because I see you don't know who you are, and you could turn with the right pressure. I want you to know who you are and become strong. This will also make Erno's life safer and his burden lighter."

"It is a curious thing for a brismun to be made custodian to image-bearers," said the blue-eyed rova.

"It is indeed," said Val, "but this is something that Sonax has determined here."

"I would like to know why."

"As would I," Val said.

Deborah thought then as Val looked at her that he had something in his demeanour, an instinct to protect her, a concern to watch over her. His eyes gleamed then, and she got the impression he had understood her thoughts. She managed a small smile, then looked down. It wasn't that long ago that she had wanted a rova custodian instead of being so abnormal as to have a brismun instead, but now... being back with Erno... even though they had been together for less than a day, it felt right. She felt different around him—more in place, more centred, *something*. She couldn't put her finger on what had changed, for she remembered being at the lumdil village, taking off without him into the woods after hearing word of her father, and not understanding why Erno hadn't done anything. Things were different now.

She looked up at Val. He blinked at her as if he had understood all her thoughts again. It was a little unnerving. "Erno is a good custodian," she said, "so I am happy to have him. It's a shame that there is no custodian here in this region. What happened to the lake?" She let out a breath of relief, hoping she had turned the conversation away from herself.

"What happened, yes," said blue eyes, with a snarl. "It would take several shaseeliany to restore this lake now, and in all likelihood some would die trying. This region is a tragedy."

"The brismun ousted, the shaseeliany killed, the rovi scattered, the image-bearers turning to guandras," said Val, shaking his head. "All at the decision of the image-bearers in this region."

"I have never seen anything like it," said blue eyes.

"I have seen it all too often," said the female rova next to Deborah.

The fifth rova, who had been silent until now, quietly growled.

"And, on that unpleasant note," said Val, "we must go. We're wanted elsewhere."

"Are you not able to stay awhile?" Kasharel asked.

Deborah looked up at him. His expression was as calm and collected as usual, but was there a hint of anxiety in his tone?

"I am sorry," said Val. "We have several tasks at hand, all weighted with urgency. We must go. Sonax-Oxpeina, with you."

"*Soi-nah*," said the other four rovi in unison, a growling chant that seemed to gather around the air and draw it in.

Nearby, there was a snapping sound and a tree limb crashed to the ground, while other trees creaked and groaned as if unable to respond to the pull in the atmosphere.

As one, the rovi turned and ran off together through the woods.

"Look," said Kasharel, when they had disappeared from view. "The tree seems a different colour. And there is more water."

He was right—Deborah saw the bark of the tree Erno had led them to was less grey, had hints of brown and green, while the tiny spring near its base bubbled with a little more life. She sat, feeling suddenly weary once more. Jacob, she noted, had gone back to sleep. That was not a bad idea; she felt she could join him right away. But first, she waited while Kasharel sat beside her and dug into the bag the rovi had given him. He passed her a hand-sized bread round, which, she discovered when she bit into it, had a lightly spiced meaty vegetable filling. She struggled her way through it, feeling almost too tired to chew.

"You take the first sleep," Kasharel said. "I'll keep watch. I can't see any sign of the squatchamn girl. Perhaps she was scared off by the rovi."

Deborah curled up on the ground, pulling the bundled-up Jacob close, and shut her eyes.

16

Deborah felt a cool hand grip her right arm and shake her.
"Deborah," said a voice. "Deborah."

The ground was cold and hard beneath her, and her right arm lay across a soft clump of something—clothing. Jacob.

"Wake up, Deborah," said Erno, shaking her arm again.

She groaned and sat up. "What."

"We have to move from this spot. There's a path trying to slink closer. I don't want it to get under you or Kasharel."

A path? What did he mean? She felt too much in the mists of sleep to think straight. The light was eerie. Outlines of trees, black shadows of Erno and Kasharel—she assumed by their outlines—silhouettes of sharply cut-out branches against a grey sky that had a strange luminosity. The lake. They were near the Silver Lake. What path? There weren't any paths here.

"Move, please," Erno said, giving her a tug.

She got up, clutching Jacob.

"It's just one of the hazards of this region," Erno said as he hopped slowly along. "The guandras would most likely want to steer you back to the clearing by the lake, but we're not about to do that."

Deborah stumbled as her foot caught on a branch, and she grabbed for Kasharel with her free arm, getting a handful of his robe.

"Are there any guandras close by?" Kasharel asked quietly.

"No, not very close," Erno said, his voice cheerily loud in the silent woods. "They've seen me and know what I'd do to them if they try to get you. I expect that's why a path has been sent in, to assess who you are that way. Don't worry about it."

"Assess?" Deborah asked. "What for?"

"Looking for weaknesses, that kind of thing. For them, it's all about power and control. Control the image-bearers, and you control a region."

What exactly was going on here? She didn't belong here. She wasn't an 'image-bearer'. She belonged in Eblhim. The city seemed so far away now. She wanted to go home; wanted Father to be there, for him to be normal again, to be happy.

Shivering, she trudged after Erno, waiting for when he would say they could stop. It would be nice to have a warm bath, a warm bed. To be able to cook on the stove again, to see Father sitting at the table, a smile on his face. Yet, now he was on his way to the city of Aric. Wherever that was. Had he forgotten he had a daughter? Had he forgotten that family was more important than pursuing some mystery? What was he doing? What was he thinking? Depression was one thing, but this… this wandering through the woods was incomprehensible.

"Here will do," Erno said.

Deborah sighed and swept aside the twigs and stones to try and get some clear dirt to sit on.

"Sleep in peace," Erno said. "I will keep watch."

His words did have an affect on her. She felt herself quieten, slumber stealing over her again. She supposed that was a good thing, seeings as the ground was so hard it would probably keep her awake otherwise.

Some time later, she awoke to the murmur of voices. It was still night, and the ground felt like stone, as though no fire of life would ever, or could ever again, radiate through the earth.

"—can't fathom it." A low voice—not Kasharel's. "She used to be so different."

Deborah thought it sounded like Nurrel.

"I'm sorry this happened." Erno's voice—softer and more solemn than usual. "But there must have been signs—a tendency towards this. You should have seen her turning. These things don't happen without warning."

"I don't know. She was never one to speak her mind. She was quiet. That's why it's so puzzling to see her like this now."

"She harboured deep thoughts," said Erno.

"I—" Nurrel sighed heavily. "I was going to ask her when I came of age. Marry, I mean. Not ask to marry outright, but see if she was interested. In me. I thought she was, might have been. She was, *is*, someone special. I don't know how I can leave her here. Erno, how can I leave her here?"

"Yet, how can I leave *you* here? This is a decision only you can make. All I know is I can't stay here with you. I have to get Deborah and Jacob to Hirahi."

"That's not so far away, not really," said Nurrel. "Perhaps you could come back for me."

"Perhaps. But I think the longer you stay here, the harder it will be to leave."

"I don't think I can leave Ibelli."

"I understand," said Erno. "All I ask is that you think carefully over this. Consider this place, this region, what it has done to the squatchamn—and now Ibelli—and where you belong."

"I will."

"Before we speak further," Erno said, "I'd better tell you that Deborah is awake. Deborah, are you able to hear our conversation?"

She sat up. "Yes, and I think what you should do, Nurrel, is just get Ibelli out of here. There's four of us, and she's small. We could carry her out."

"You mean kidnap her?" Nurrel said. "I can't do that!"

"Why not? You said she's not herself. Get her away from this place, and that will fix her, won't it?"

"We must not go against her will," Erno said.

"But she's obviously not in her right mind. Who with any sense would want to stay here?"

"We must let her decide and reason for herself and determine the course of her own life."

Deborah frowned in the darkness. "Why must we?"

"Because if we force her to do our will and not her own, we go against the Oxpeina-life, and I won't do that."

Deborah yawned and gathered up the loose folds of her jersey, feeling in the darkness to tuck them back around Jacob. "Well, Nurrel and I can do it; can't we, Nurrel. I'll come with you."

It was strange hearing the words come out of her mouth. She supposed she felt sorry for him—here he was, planning to marry Ibelli, who had got herself stuck here and was not mentally herself, or something. Being here had changed her, according to Nurrel. She must have been all right back in the lumdil village if he had had his eye on her. Nasty as Ibelli was now, Deborah supposed it was all the lake's fault. She thought of Father—he hadn't always been the way he was now, either. People changed when something bad happened to them.

"I—well—*uh*," said Nurrel. "I don't know if that's a good idea."

"Why not?"

"It's just—Deborah, I… it, *hum*, I think it would be best to talk again with Ibelli by myself."

"In other words," said Erno, "Nurrel doesn't want you yelling at Ibelli to 'shut up' again. He's too polite to tell you that."

"You're not too polite to tell Deborah, it seems," said Kasharel.

Deborah peered through the darkness in his direction. She could just make out a shape moving—he must be sitting up now, too.

Erno chuckled. "You're right. Now that we're all awake—barring Jacob—I think we can all make this decision together. Either we leave this place now or we give more time to Nurrel to go back to Ibelli."

"I don't know that you all should wait for me," said Nurrel.

"If we don't," said Deborah, "won't you wind up getting stuck here, too? I don't understand the fascination with this place, but it has a very real magic."

"Erno," said Kasharel, "can't you do what Iff did for Deborah and me, and place an enchantment over Nurrel so that he won't get caught here?"

Deborah nodded. Yes, Iff probably would have stomped right in and taken Ibelli out by force. He also would have cleared the whole encampment of squatchamn.

"Iff sensibly discerned what you wanted at heart and was able to use that for your own good," said Erno. "He did not go against your will. As it is, Nurrel doesn't yet know what he wants. Sorry to say that, Nurrel."

"No, quite right," Nurrel answered. "I feel torn in two directions."

So, had Iff seen Deborah's longing to find her father? Nothing else truly mattered to her. She was grateful Iff had done what he had, anyway.

"I need more time," Nurrel said. "Time at least to decide. I have had fruitless conversations with Ibelli for many hours. Perhaps I need to admit defeat. Or perhaps I need to try again in a different way."

"Have you told her you love her?" Erno asked.

"I—well. It's just… can't do that. She clearly feels nothing for me, if she ever did, I don't know. The things she said… well, no. No, this is—I need more time to think."

"Have your decision ready when the morning light comes," said Erno.

"I will. Yes, yes, I will."

Deborah lay back down and listened to the shuffling of the others as they stood, or sat, or whatever it was they were doing. Erno, she knew, did not move, for there was no tremor of the ground to show he had hopped anywhere. She drew the bundled up Jacob close to herself and tried to get back to sleep. The ground was too hard, and she felt her shoulder complaining at her. It had been feeling much better the last couple of days, but the quiet of the night seemed to amplify the residual aches of the injury.

"*Ugh*," muttered Erno. "The path. Everybody, up! We've got to move again."

Deborah got up. How Erno knew anything was there was beyond her. He must hear something—a slithering or faint swooshing or whatever it was paths did. She heard nothing. This region was without a breeze to sigh in the treetops, without chirruping insect life, and didn't even have the occasional creak of branches. The silence was stifling, now that she thought about it.

"This time we'll have to cross it," Erno said. "I think it has made a wide circle around us. Probably with the aim of driving us back to the lake."

"How?" Kasharel asked. "Does it have thought or consciousness?"

"No. The guandras in the area have seen us, so they'll be the ones steering it."

"How many are nearby?" Kasharel asked.

"Don't worry," Erno said, his voice cheerful. "There's enough for me to handle."

"And me, too," Nurrel said. "The ones here are small and confused."

"What if more come?" Kasharel asked. "They may be small, but surely larger ones are about in such a region as this?"

"I thought I just said don't worry," Erno said. "I'm sure I said it out loud. I heard me. Didn't you hear me, too?"

"I can't joke about this," Kasharel said. "You are only one brismun. We shouldn't be out here this far from home without rovi, and I don't understand why Sonax hasn't assigned some to us. Val and his pack really should have stayed with us and accompanied us to Hirahi."

"Sonax has his eye on the regions and knows precisely what we need," Erno said. "I think we have to trust that the reason the rovi did not stay with us is that we're not in any danger right now. Val was needed somewhere else. We're within spitting distance of Hirahi, so my job is to get us there."

Deborah felt Erno's light touch on her arm. "And I don't forget you or your father, Deborah. If he is heading for Aric right now, we can get what we need at Hirahi to journey onward and do our best to catch up with him."

She felt his hand drop from her.

"Nurrel," he said, "I need your decision in the morning light. I don't want to leave you here, but I will if that's your wish. Kasharel, I have not been assigned as your custodian. You have none—which is interesting to me—and so you must find your own way. Come with us, or return home. Harsh, huh?"

Deborah could hear the grin on his face from the way that he spoke. She instinctively wanted to smile in response.

"Now," Erno said, "we have got to move from here. The path creeps closer. I will take us to the edge of it, then I will help you all to cross."

"I can't see a thing," Nurrel said. "I know you can't, either. Your hearing had better be accurate because I don't want to step on any part of it."

Erno chuckled. "I'm going to carry you. I didn't mention that part, did I."

"That's a relief," Nurrel said.

"What about myself and Deborah?" Kasharel said.

"I can carry yourself and Deborah, too."

"Erno's stronger than he looks," Nurrel said. "You may think because of your height and largeness, he might not carry your weight, but he can."

"What is it you're trying to say about my looks and their weight?" Erno said.

"Oh! I'm terribly sorry. That came out wrong! I didn't mean—"

Erno laughed.

Deborah felt as though something of the gloom of the dark night lifted at the sound.

❧ 17 ❧

It was a strange sensation being carried by Erno in the dark. He picked Deborah up as though she were no more weight than a feather and held her in his arms like a baby. She rested against his rotund body, holding Jacob. Erno's sweet and tangy scent of herb and greenery enveloped her. She did not know how close to the ground her feet dangled but had no time to consider that for Erno made a great leap into the air. Her breath was knocked out of her with a jolt when he landed, then he leapt again before she could prepare herself. Several more leaps, the air whizzing through Deborah's hair as the sound of Erno's stumpy leg made great thwacks in the quiet woods, and then he stopped.

"Wait with Nurrel," he said as he set her onto the ground, for Nurrel had been carried first over and away from the path.

The atmosphere felt better, less close. Deborah supposed it was because they were further from the lake. She leaned against a tree to catch her breath as Erno thumped away. "Nurrel, are you there?"

"Yes, right here." He was quite close, judging by the sound of his voice. "Would you like me to take Jacob from you for a while? Being carried by a brismun takes one's breath away, doesn't it?"

"I'm all right," she said. "I've got him." How she had managed to keep hold of Jacob she did not know, but was glad she had.

"Right, yes. Well, if you don't mind, I'm going over here. I need to think."

"That's fine," she said. He had to make his decision about Ibelli somehow before the morning came. And who knew when morning would come? She looked up at the sky—darkest grey with no stars, no shapes of cloud—she could not tell what time of the night it was. She felt around the base of the tree, sweeping away brittle twigs and a stone or two, and sat.

Where was Father now? Was he all right? How far away was the city of Aric? He had never mentioned that city, or any city being in the woods, so why would he want to go there? She felt somewhat better knowing a rova was with him. At least someone was looking after him. Did he think of her at all and wonder what she was doing? Did he think she was just staying back in Shilhim and living by herself there? She sighed. Why had he just left her like this? Why?

"*Debah!*" hissed a voice.

Deborah frowned. The only one who called her 'Debah' was the squatchamn girl. "What do you want?"

"*Debah!* I seen you in the lake. I seen you. I seen map and I seen man there. You looking for him; I seen it. He's on the map. Two regions far. Other side of beautiful lake. Wrong way, you going wrong way."

Deborah scrambled to her feet, trying to see something, anything, in the dark. The squatchamn couldn't possibly mean Father? "What are you talking about?"

"The lake," said the squatchamn. "The beautiful lake tells. The lake shows the picture. I seen it. You come. Come, Debah, now."

The sound of Erno returning reverberated through the woods, the thumps becoming louder and louder. The squatchamn gave a little squeal and Deborah heard the flurry of feet scampering away.

"Wait!" she shouted.

"Those long legs of yours were a challenge, Kasharel," Erno said. "However, we managed! Here you are."

"Many thanks," Kasharel said, his voice little more than a gasp.

"Now, Deborah," Erno said, as he thumped closer, "I heard what was said to you. Let's talk about it over here, just you and me."

She nodded, then thought there was no point doing that; nobody could see anything in the dark. Yet, it was so confusing—what had the squatchamn girl seen? Where was Father, really?

"She lied, you know," Erno said, when he and Deborah had gone a few paces from wherever Kasharel and Nurrel were. "However, she didn't know it was a lie. That's what made it sound so convincing, for she was convinced."

"I don't understand," Deborah said.

"I don't blame you. It's a mess. They see things in the lake. That's what keeps them here, fascinated by the cursed thing. What they don't understand is that it's the guandras who are stirring up the pictures and keeping them mesmerised. It's all a power game again, you see? Power over the image-bearers."

"But she said she saw a man. She knew I'm looking for him. How could she know something like that?"

"She didn't. Guandras know it. I think you've been on one of their paths. Have you?"

Deborah remembered the flash of the mirror image of her face on the path, speeding away through the woods when she had been with Jacob in what seemed like many, many days ago. Then, the path she had walked on—yes, *walked on*—when she had left the lumdil village and how weirdly that had affected her, trying to hold her in its grasp while time slipped away. "I've been on two, actually," she admitted. "I didn't mean to. I didn't know what they were back then."

Erno tutted under his breath, and Deborah felt his hand on her arm, felt that he was trying to sense more from her in that mossy touch.

"Sadness," he said. "Lost. Alone."

She didn't know how he did it, but his quiet words brought a hollow ache into her heart, made her feel as though she was completely alone and nothing mattered anymore, for no one wanted her. Tears welled in her eyes, and a lump came to her throat. She tried to swallow it, relieved that no one could see her in the dark.

"I'm here," Erno said softly. "Deborah."

It took all her self-control to not give in to the sobs that threatened to rise. It would do no good to howl all through the woods, she told herself. Imagine the racket. The others would think there was something wrong with her.

Erno patted her arm and let go. Part of her wished he hadn't let go, for there was something reassuring about him, while another part was relieved. Normally, she didn't feel miserable things like that. How had Erno dredged that up from a simple touch?

"I can feel your pain," he said, "but please don't think you're alone anymore, because you're not. I take my assignment to you very seriously. You are mine before anyone else. Do you hear me, Deborah?"

"Yes. I do."

"Speak your mind."

She reached out to touch him. Felt his twiggy hair, touched his soft, cool cheek, and found his shoulder to rest her hand while she held Jacob in the crook of her other arm. "I don't belong here. I don't even know where I am, really. These woods are like nothing I've ever known. Are you sure the squatchamn girl has it wrong? How can you know my father isn't near?"

"Just as I know he wasn't east of Smoky Glade when that rumour came to your ears—I don't sense any true word of him. Besides, the rovi have told us where he is. I hope you won't go running off away from me again."

Deborah thought of Nurrel's village and her mad dash away from there. How differently would things have turned out if she had stayed? Where had Father been while she was there—in that region somewhere?

"My sister, custodian of Nurrel's region, had not sensed your father there," Erno said, as if he knew exactly what she was thinking. "So, he really was nowhere near the village like we had hoped. When I got back from speaking with her, you were gone. I'm sorry I didn't look for you immediately, but, by then, my instruction was to go to Hirahi. Besides, you had rejected me as your custodian, so I had to abide by your decision. Still, I was glad when I received word that you were safe with the gehun image-bearers and that I was to go to you. What a tangle!"

"Yes, a tangle," she said. "Sorry I left you. I didn't know."

"O-ho? What—oh! I hear them. They are coming!"

"Who?"

"Guandras. Wait here. Nurrel!" Erno thumped away. "Nurrel, prepare yourself with Oxpeina-life! Five little ones are closing in. Wait here with the others while I go after them."

"Five?" Nurrel said. "Shouldn't I go with you?"

"This light is no good for you. Wait here—I'll scare them off."

Deborah heard the cracks of twigs snapping with each thump of Erno as he bounded away. He couldn't have made more noise if he tried, and, as he grew more distant, he shouted something unintelligible. A series of wails answered him that made the back of Deborah's neck prickle, and she had the sudden feeling that something watched her, that she stood too far from Kasharel and Nurrel, and that if she did not move now then whatever it was would come and seize her. She stumbled in the direction she thought Kasharel was.

"Kash! Kasharel! Where are you?"

"Deborah!"

It was Nurrel's voice and his warm hand that took hers. She held tightly to him as he led her, and, in moments, Kasharel was beside her. She brushed against the folds of his robe as he put his arm around her.

"Let us stand still together," Nurrel said. "I know their voices sound unhinged and bite to the core, but believe me, it's nothing. A few little guandras will run on sight of Erno. Frankly, they shouldn't have had the nerve to try to come near us. Silly of them."

His sensible voice heartened Deborah. "What do they want with us?"

"Oh, what guandras usually want—control. They won't be happy until all of the regions are theirs. I don't think they'll ever be happy anyway, but that's beside the point. They've got it fixed in their twisted minds that they'll have Oxpeina-life if they can get image-bearers under their control. It's a lot of bosh."

"How do you know this?" Kasharel said. "I thought it is death to us that they always seek."

"Right, yes, I suppose that's how it goes. The turning eventually leads to death and we're all in danger of that."

Deborah heard Kasharel murmur in assent. Here again, 'the turning'—something that seemed to be of significance in these woods. Well, it all had nothing to do with her.

"I'm hungry," said Jacob.

Deborah looked down in surprise. She couldn't see him but felt him wriggle in her arms. "You're awake!"

"How are you feeling, Jacob?" Nurrel asked.

"Somewhat tender and bruised, but much better than I was. Yes, I am awake, Deborah. You're as observant as ever."

She pulled a face at him. Jacob could probably see her, even if she couldn't see him. "I'm surprised, that's all. You slept for so long."

"The woods have gone quiet," Kasharel said. "Erno must have sent the guandras running."

"Guandras?" Jacob said.

"Just a few small ones," said Nurrel. There was the sound of rustling. "Now, I have here some dried meat; will that do for you?"

"These woods are indeed quiet," Jacob said. "I don't hear any insects, and I would rather like some right now."

"You'll probably have to wait until we're out of this region to find any," said Nurrel. "Here, have this. Beg your pardon; I can't quite see where you are, so I hope I'm holding it in the right place."

Deborah felt Jacob wriggle again and heard a gulp.

"Thanks," he said. "Where are we?"

"Not far from Silver Lake," Deborah said. She thought of what the squatchamn girl had said—that Father was on the other side of the lake. How could Erno be so sure that was wrong? The thumping sounds of his return were reassuring. She gazed out into the night, looking for any movement of shadows.

"That's that," said Erno, when he had landed next to them. "Feisty wee things, tried to have a go at me, but soon ran instead. The moment one went, the others quickly followed suit. Hello there, Jacob!"

"Erno," Jacob said. "Thank you for the sleep. I am somewhat improved."

"Only somewhat? Well, when we get to Hirahi, I'm sure you'll be more than somewhat. My sister, Fothie, has the Oxpeina touch, so we'll get her to do what she can for you. You sound worried, Deborah."

"What?" she said. "I didn't say anything."

"I hear it in the timbre of your breathing."

"I—*uh*, yes, maybe."

"Do you wish to talk privately with me?"

"Yes, I think so," she said.

"Would you like me to hold Jacob for you?" Kasharel said.

"*Hmph*," muttered Jacob.

Deborah felt around for Kasharel's hand and passed Jacob over to him.

"I may as well be baggage," Jacob said.

"Stop fussing, Beebee," Deborah said.

"*Hoo!*"

"Beebee?" Nurrel said.

"Deborah," said Erno. "Let's talk now before the sun returns."

She felt her way carefully through the woods, following the sounds of Erno thumping slowly away, and left the others to talk about the origins of 'Beebee'. When their voices were indistinct, Erno stopped. He lightly touched her arm.

"It's all right," he said. "That's why I'm here—I'm your custodian. You're not convinced the squatchamn was seeing things in the lake, and you wonder if your father actually is close by."

"Yes, but this is… well, it's… I don't know. You say it's not possible, that she's imagining things in the lake, but what if she isn't? She's not like the others at the lake; she's able to walk away from it."

"She really rattled you, didn't she?" Erno said. "Puzzling in a way as, yes, she seemed ready to leave the lake, but instead she's taken it upon herself to try to get you to change where you're going. I might have to ponder that awhile, as I'd like to know why she would bother with that instead of staying stuck at the lake. The thing is, you shouldn't pay any attention to what she says you should do. In a region such as this, the image-bearers caught in it don't know what they're saying half the time, and they're midway turning. Most of what they say is regurgitated from what they're trapped in. It can look all right and plausible, but they're really not seeing or reasoning clearly."

"I don't understand," she said softly.

He squeezed her arm gently and let go. "I'm sure you will in time. For now, trust me, please. If Sonax has sent word by Val and his pack that your father is on his way to Aric, then that's precisely what he's doing. We will find him together. I will help you. Now, I just heard Nurrel asking me if I could speak to him once I've finished speaking to you—he's suffering, and I'm relieved that instead of suffering silently alone with his thoughts, he wants to talk. Will you stay here and try to get some sleep before the dawn, or shall I lead you back to Kasharel and Jacob? I warn you, Jacob is fully awake and has found his voice." He chuckled.

"I think I'll stay here."

"Rest," he said. "I'm within earshot of your voice if you need me."

"Thanks, Erno."

She sat on the hard ground and tried to get comfortable. There was no way she could get to sleep again despite how tired she felt, but she supposed at least she could rest without having to think or talk or be bothered by anyone.

~ 18 ~

The pale early light crept through the trees, if spindly, broken shards, tall and twisted against the sky, could be called trees. There was a silver touch to the light Deborah hadn't seen the day before, a luminescence that seemed to hint at something beyond, beckoning her to discover hidden depths. She felt as though she stood in deepest shadow and should go towards the light. The allure had the same quality as the lake, and she frowned. Better to be further away from the stupid thing than go off looking for pictures or whatever in it.

Where was the bag of food the rovi had brought? Hopefully, there was something still in it and the others hadn't eaten everything in the night. And, hopefully, Erno had summoned up a spring of fresh water, too.

She got up and stretched, her body feeling stiff and tired. Jacob had her jersey. She wouldn't mind having it back—the morning air had a nip to it. She shivered and rubbed her arms, then spotted the face watching her. Jutting out from behind a tree, the face—was it a face?—had a strange look about it. Something wasn't right. There was a hollowness, a sense of not being there. Perhaps it was only the silver-tinged outline backlit from the light of the lake that made it hard to clearly see what it was.

There was only time for a glimpse, for it darted back as soon as she saw it. Her first thought was that it was the squatchamn girl, but something didn't seem to fit. The head was larger, a different shape, no hair? The eyes—there had been eyes gleaming with some kind of intent and a shapeless mouth. She hadn't seen the squatchamn girl enough times to know what she looked like. Even if it wasn't the squatchamn but was a guandra, then Erno would know. She looked about for him. Where was he?

She spotted a patch of green in the distance, half-obscured by trees. She hurried over and was relieved to find Kasharel sitting crosslegged, his robe tucked neatly about him, Jacob on the ground beside him still wrapped in her jersey, his eyes blinking crossly at her as she approached, and a few steps away were Erno and Nurrel. Nurrel stood with his arms crossed, leaning against a tree, looking downcast.

They all had their backs turned to the silver light, and Deborah supposed that was a sensible thing. She still felt some desire to leave the shadows and head into that light. She told herself firmly that nothing good would come of following that urge—she didn't want to end up fingerless or even limbless like the squatchamn.

"Can't do it," Nurrel said. "Can't leave her. Not here."

"I understand," said Erno.

"No, no, I don't think you do," Nurrel answered.

"Yes, yes, I do," Erno said.

His voice was without its usual cheeriness, and Nurrel looked over at him.

"I'm sorry. I said that without thinking. I should have remembered."

"It was a long time ago," said Erno. "I think I have only spoken once of it to you. But it does bear remembering—it may help us decide."

"I've already decided," Nurrel said.

"Then you decide wrong," said Jacob. "If you go back to the lake, we won't come with you, and you will be alone. How easy will it be to stay and never move on through the regions again? You know there are guandras all around us as we speak. You think they will be content to merely watch you? They will want you to stay. We need to get to Hirahi. We should have left at first light and not wasted time sitting around here talking. This is not a region to spend more time in than necessary—there is hardly any life here, and it feels as though it may close at any moment."

Nurrel covered his face with his hands. "I can't leave. I may as well be leaving Ibelli to her death."

"Then, let's go get her," said Deborah.

Nurrel stared at her. "We can't do that. She has to want to leave."

"Rubbish," Deborah said. "She can come to her senses when we've got her out of this region."

"It doesn't work like that," Jacob said. "Ibelli already wanted to be here before she came into this region. She really does have to want to leave; otherwise, no matter where we take her, she will keep coming back."

"How do you know that?" Deborah said. "You can't know what she wanted."

"Yes, I can extrapolate that from what I know of her and the fact that she's here. I can say with confidence she was never content with Shady Glen—"

"Smoky Glade," said Erno.

"—and silently harboured thoughts of getting away from her own people and finding freedom. Her idea of freedom is here."

"That makes no sense," Deborah said.

"Not to you, maybe, but to Ibelli it does. Therein lies the problem."

Nurrel nodded. Kasharel and Deborah exchanged glances. Expressionless as he often was, she could still tell he was not entirely convinced. She knew her own expression was probably very clear—this stuff didn't make sense. Surely, if they got Ibelli out, then she would be able to think more clearly.

Jacob glared up at Deborah. She knew he couldn't help it; that was just his owlish face. Even so, somehow that look brought everything home to her. She remembered Father saying that once they had left Eblhim, he would be much better. Then he said once they got to the mountain passes, he would be able to think more clearly. Then, once they got to Shilhim, he would really be able to find peace; that living by the woods was what he needed. What had he truly wanted? Had he planned all along to go into the woods? And, where had he got the idea that in the woods there was something he needed?

So, Ibelli had it in her thick head that the Silver Lake was what she needed, and she was happy here. At least Father hadn't been so stupid. At least he hadn't come here, too. She would have dragged him out, kicking and screaming if he had. Deborah looked at Nurrel. Really, if Nurrel loved Ibelli, he should do the same. Ignore all that 'what she wants and going against her will' stuff. That shouldn't apply when someone you loved was in danger.

"Ah," said Erno. "Val and his pack are coming our way." He swivelled on his stumpy leg. "Here! Over here! Soi-nah!"

"*Soi-nah*," was the distant answer.

Rumbling and crackling grew in volume, and through the woods a cloud of dirt was raised. Soon enough, Val and the four others of his pack were seen, a blur of vibrant brown racing along, dodging and weaving through the trees. When they reached Deborah and the others, they came to a halt and stood with scowls and snarls on their wild faces.

Having the five rovi standing so close again caused the air to become more breathable. Deborah realised she had got used to the rancid taint of the atmosphere of the region, and having the rovi rush in seemed to sweep the air clean. She felt a little unsteady on her feet as the sense of Oxpeina-life emanated from the pack.

"It is I, Val," said Val.

"Hello, Val," said Erno. "Of course it's you. Who else could it be? Your heavy-footed stomp is easily recognisable."

Val's lips curled into what appeared to be a growl, but his green eyes lit and sparkled with good humour. Deborah supposed his mouth was not as easily formed for grinning as Erno's was.

"This from a brismun," Val said, "the greatest stompers of all, shakers of the ground."

Deborah noticed that the darker-furred rova with the intense blue-gold eyes was watching her. She looked up at him and felt his question. Again, her instinctive response was to think *no*, she didn't know. What did he want, and what was he asking? He gave an imperceptible shake of his sleek head and looked away. To Kasharel? He seemed almost to flinch and could not return the rova's gaze. The rova's intent eyes then flicked to Nurrel, who smiled and gave a slight nod in response.

"What can I do you for?" Erno asked. "I wasn't expecting to see you back so soon. I suspect this is not a good thing."

"Your suspicions are correct, Erno," said Val. "I also did not expect to see you, but Sonax sent us again. He says guandras are on their way to you. Larger than you have seen here so far."

Erno's grin vanished amongst his mossy face. "Makes sense. There are an awful lot in this region, and they can see we're not wanting to stay."

"How many guandras?" Kasharel asked.

Val shrugged. "It doesn't matter. Sonax thinks we are enough to protect you."

"How close to us are they?" Kasharel said.

"We will hear them when they come." Val turned and motioned to his pack. "Grufful, take Deborah; Hio take Kasharel. Nurrel, I see you."

"What about me?" Jacob said.

Deborah stooped and picked him up.

He wriggled in her arms. "I would rather fight."

"You've already done that, and look where it got you," she said.

He grumbled and stopped wriggling. "It wasn't like that. Sometime, I will tell you what happened to me."

The blue-eyed rova stepped closer to Deborah. "I am Grufful."

The wheaten-coloured rova with silvery eyes went to Kasharel. "I am Hio," she said, and took his hand.

"Watch me," Grufful said to Deborah.

She looked up at him. She could smell his fur, the sweetness of his breath. The others talked amongst themselves; she did not listen. The rich dark brown of his fur was incredible in these dead woods; his gold-flecked deep blue eyes held so much meaning, his beast-like face wild and strong. She could look at him forever. So much life was in him; electricity in the air surrounded him.

"I am going to hold you when the guandras come," Grufful said. "Don't be afraid."

Afraid? How could she be afraid? She would never be afraid of anything ever again if Grufful was with her. Maybe he should be her custodian. She felt bad for that fleeting thought. No, Erno was her custodian, and she was glad for that. But, Grufful? Now that she was so close to him, she felt secure, that nothing could happen. That the guandras, whatever they were, would not touch her.

His expression changed to one of alarm, and he quickly put his arms around her, just as an earth-shattering howl split the air close by. Pain coursed through Deborah's head, and she felt as though her ears would burst with the pressure. She reached up to block one ear while struggling to hold Jacob with her other hand. Jacob was wriggling, and she could see his beak moving. She thought she could hear him shriek and rasp. What did he think he was doing? She couldn't hold him; she couldn't hold anything. Where was Grufful? He was a blur. She felt as though she was falling, that she was losing sensation in her body.

"Grufful," she tried to say, but no noise came from her mouth.

"I am here, Deborah," he said. "Listen to me. Feel me here with you."

His cheek was against hers, his voice in her ear, his arms wrapped around her.

"Where is Jacob?" she cried. "I don't have him! Where is he?"

"I have him," Grufful said. "See? Look at my shoulder."

She drew back a little and saw a mess of brown and white feathers, pink skin patches—what was Jacob doing? He was perched on Grufful's shoulder, his tattered wings outstretched.

"Look again at me, Deborah," said Grufful.

She tried to, but something else caught her eye. An opening of some kind—a huge and towering fissure in the woods, swirling and pulsing with a strange energy. It would suck her in, and then she would be gone, her atoms scattered into nothingness. Grufful could not hold her; this thing would take her. It would be all right to go. This would end everything—no more pain, no more searching, no emptiness, nothing. Father was gone; she would never see him again; she knew that now.

She felt herself lift as her feet began to leave the ground and her hands reached towards the opening. Grufful roared, and the blast of his voice swept through her body. The ground jolted beneath her feet, and she felt his arms wind tightly about her again. She wrapped her arms around him, her hands in his thick fur. The opening in the woods was gone. In its place stood a guandra.

Almost the height of a man, it was slightly hunched and without any vigour of life, instead appearing as a shadow, a dried husk. The loose coverings it wore—were they scales? Metal? She could not tell; it was too hard to see clearly, the woods were too dark, but she saw the featureless head turn her way. The guandra's eyes—where were they? There was only emptiness, light extinguished—and somehow she knew what the guandra was saying to her. *Your father is dead. I killed him myself.*

She seemed to see an image—a ghostly impression, her father, cowering, his arms raised to shield his head, the flash of a knife coming down. The same knife the guandra now drew, tarnished brown with the dried blood of her father. She screamed and thrashed in Grufful's arms to try to get away, try to run. Not stand there as the guandra advanced; no, don't stand there!

"Listen to me, Deborah," said Grufful. "Tuck your arms in against my chest; they're too exposed for my liking. I'll stand you back against this tree, so at least you'll have more protection there. I can cover the rest of you. Pay no attention to the guandras; they're just trying to get you out of my arms. They won't succeed."

His pragmatic voice in her ear and the warmth of his body against hers made her catch her breath and stand still. She quickly tucked her arms in as he said and, for good measure, bowed her head and pressed her face against his fur. She couldn't look at the guandra again; she mustn't. The woods howled around them, shouts and screams intermingled. She held onto Grufful as he held onto her. Father was *not* dead, she told herself. He was *not* dead. Where was the guandra now? It was coming, it was coming. Grufful had no knife. The guandra had a knife. Where was Val? Where was Erno?

"Steady," said Grufful. "Your heartbeat feels like that of a rabbit's."

"How can you be so calm," she mumbled against his chest.

"Easy," he said. "I feel the Oxpeina-life around me as a shield, don't you?"

She was about to say no, but his fingers lightly tapped her back, and a tingle of electricity spread in a fizzing torrent over her back, curving over her shoulders, up her neck, and prickled at her scalp, down her legs, and through into her arms. It was not exactly like the Oxpeina-rich region she and Kasharel had been in and the hum and buzz of life they had felt there—this felt more aggressive, that nothing would stand in its way as it closed in and over her as a protective shield.

"Yes," she whispered, and closed her eyes. Father was alive; she could feel it. She felt she could almost see him if she tried hard enough. He was walking somewhere. The trees in that region were broad with vine-tangled trunks, jagged, four-pointed leaves touched by autumnal colour, a stream nearby turning to a river.

Then she saw something else. A face. Not Father's. Somebody else. He knew her. He saw her. He was saying something to her—what was it? She couldn't make out the words. Then he was gone, and the woods were quiet.

Grufful had let go of her. His lips curled as he looked down into her eyes. "All well," he said. "*Soi-nah.*"

"*Soi-nah*," answered the other rovi of his pack.

19

"What a stench," Nurrel said, as he hoisted a guandra's body and shoved it onto the three he had already heaped together. It landed with a clatter.

The guandras' coverings that Deborah had thought might be metal were in fact more like sheets of dusty stone that were patched together incoherently. As Nurrel piled the bodies, they cracked and split apart. They could have been mistaken for a pile of dead leaves and branches if not for the skeletal hands and misshapen skulls that emerged. Each time one split or broke, a smell issued forth like nothing Deborah had ever encountered. She had to step a few feet away to be able to stop retching and stood close to the pack of rovi where the air was clearer.

"And you should know, with a nose like that," said Erno.

Nurrel laughed. "How you can know that with sight like yours is a mystery."

"I see you well enough close up, especially your nose."

Grufful growled. "Humour in the midst of destruction?"

"Yes," said Kasharel. "This has been a sad encounter, and I cannot laugh. Were these not rovi at one time in their lives? They are of a size to suggest that."

"It is a warning to us all of what can happen," said Val.

"They disgust me," said Grufful.

Deborah heard the silvery-eyed Hio quietly say something in a different language. There were murmurs of assent from the others.

Deborah stared at the heap of guandras and the fifth body that Nurrel was dragging over to it. What did Kasharel mean? These dried corpses that looked like they'd been dead a long time—these had once been rovi? "What happened to them?" she asked.

"They turned," Grufful said. "They chose this senseless way of life rather than the Oxpeina. Despicable."

Nurrel grunted as he heaved another body onto the pile. "I don't laugh at that. I laugh because Erno lifts my spirit, and I'm glad he does."

"I understand that well," said Jacob.

Deborah was once again holding him bundled up in her jersey, for his lack of feathers had caused him to feel the chill of the air. She didn't feel especially warm herself; the woods had an air about them that was unforgiving, harsh, as if the guandras had turned things sour. She moved closer to the rovi pack, glad of the warmth that emanated from them.

She edged nearer to Grufful. There was something about him—yes, she knew that Erno had been assigned as her custodian, and she supposed there was nothing she could do about that, and she did really like Erno too, but she felt a connection to Grufful now. He had held her and kept her safe. She hadn't seen the fight against the guandras, having kept her face buried in Grufful's chest, but the sounds of it had been enough. Now to see them lying there hideously dead and to see the bandage on Nurrel's arm, the sticky area on Erno's side—what was that? Sap? Blood belonging to him or the guandras?—yet she had been completely untouched by what had happened, and it was all due to Grufful.

Nurrel heaved the last guandra onto the pile and wiped his hands on the ground, only succeeding at making his hands more dirty from the earth. "I'll not be able to touch anything now. Not until this stink is off me. Where's the nearest river? I wouldn't mind a swim."

"It was good of you to desire to do this, Nurrel," Val said, "although you did not need to. They had turned and so were dead long ago. I do not know why you wish to heap the dead together. This region does not need such honour, for it is nearly gone. The river, as you know, is at Hirahi, and I would command you to go there if I could."

Deborah saw the sober look cross Nurrel's face. "Val," she said hesitantly, "is there any way that you, us, we could, *uh…* go back to the squatchamn settlement and get a friend of Nurrel's out of there?" She looked up at Val's grizzled face, the life in his green eyes, the force of personality in his bearing. "I'm sure that she would listen to you and leave the Silver Lake if you could just talk to her."

"I don't know where you get your certainty from," Val said.

"The sweetness and innocence of youth," said Hio.

Deborah looked at the silvery-eyed rova, whose intent gaze was upon her. Hio seemed to say something in her gaze, something tender and wistful, and Deborah felt as though Hio looked right into her soul. Deborah's face grew hot with embarrassment. She could not remember the last time anybody had ever called her 'sweet'. What was it with these rovi? Why did they evoke such depth of response?

She thought back to life in Eblhim with neighbours, acquaintances, and even further back to school days that seemed so long ago now. There was no closeness with anyone, no real connection. Family was all she had, and that had fallen to pieces. Here now, standing with the rovi pack, Jacob in her arms, Kasharel flicking dust off his robe with an expression on his solemn face that she knew was relief, Nurrel's heartiness, and Erno's vigour, she felt a connection with them that was puzzling. Perhaps all she needed was a good square meal, and that would bring her back to normality.

"The squatchamn hate and fear me," said Val to Deborah. "Whatever I have to say to them will be fruitless words."

What? How could anybody hate Val? Fear, yes, she could understand, for he was intimidating, but the Oxpeina-life that surrounded him was intoxicating. Surely the squatchamn would be drawn to that and see that the lake in all its shimmering beauty… She sighed. The lake was too mesmerising. Maybe they wouldn't even notice Val. Not many had bothered to look at Erno, and he appeared ridiculously green and brimming with life in such parched surroundings.

"Then what do you suggest we do to help Nurrel's friend?" she asked.

"It can be difficult to accept the choices of those we love," Val said, turning to face Nurrel. "I understand that, truly, I do, but sometimes we must allow them to live their lives and find their own way. That's not something we can bring our own will to control."

Nurrel looked at the ground, his brow furrowed.

What was he thinking? Was he still planning to go back to the lake to keep trying to talk sense into Ibelli or would he stay here with them? Deborah glanced over at the pile of dead guandras. Better to stay with the pack than be alone with creatures like that in the woods. She shuddered when she thought of how rashly she had charged into the woods alone, thinking guandras were just some kind of wild animal she could climb a tree to escape or frighten off with a stick. She clutched Jacob closer. He would tell her she was stupid. He had tried to tell her she was stupid. Well, not anymore.

Nurrel covered his face with his hands and then yelped. "Why did I just do that? *Ugh!*" He furiously rubbed his hands in the dirt again.

"*Hoo*," Jacob uttered quietly and shut his eyes.

Deborah realised he was twitching with laughter but trying to hold it in. "Shut up!" she hissed at him. "Don't you know what it must be like for Nurrel having to deal with seeing Ibelli like this?"

Jacob's eyes popped open, and he stopped twitching.

"And yet," said Erno, squinting towards Val, "if Nurrel can tell Ibelli of his love for her, that may be the only thing that can save her."

"How do I say that to someone who despises me?" Nurrel muttered.

He walked off, still muttering, and Deborah watched him stop and place his grubby hand against a tree. Oddly, she thought of Iff and how he had 'gone to ask Sonax', using his favourite trees. If the trees worked as some kind of message system, Nurrel would be out of luck trying to get any help from those dried up sticks of firewood.

An unfamiliar voice spoke next, and Deborah turned to one of the rovi. She had not heard this rova speak at all before and was interested to hear what he might have to say. He was smaller than the others yet still obviously densely muscular beneath his supple fur, and his eyes were a subtler, darker green than Val's.

"I will go with him to the squatchamn if he wishes to try again," he said. "Erno, I understand you have been assigned custodian to Nurrel, but perhaps here Sonax will give you leave. Val, is this acceptable?"

"It is with me, my son," said Val. "I see your heart. But here, this decision is for Sonax, and he has placed Nurrel in Erno's care. We must not usurp that, for we don't know the reasons behind this. Also, it is entirely the will of Nurrel to accept Erno or turn him away."

"He must not turn," said Grufful in a low growl.

Deborah found all of this strange. Weren't they making this more complicated than it needed to be? If Val's son was willing to accompany Nurrel back to the squatchamn, then that was a good thing. Everyone else could wait here, go back, or go forward; what did it matter? Nurrel would have a rova to protect him, so he would be all right.

"Besides," Val said, "we have not been given instruction to remain with these image-bearers. We were commanded to defend them from the guandras' attack, and we have done that. Now we must move on to our next task."

"Oh, don't go," Deborah said, before she realised the words were out of her mouth.

Grufful immediately embraced her. "It's all right," he said in her ear. "I expect we'll see you again. We've been sent to you three times already, so Sonax has given us a bond."

He stroked her hair, and she swallowed a lump in her throat.

"Can't breathe," said Jacob.

Deborah drew back from Grufful and looked down at Jacob. "Sorry."

Jacob spat a few hairs from his beak. "That's fine; don't mind me. I'm just baggage."

"Shut up, Beebee," she said.

"*Hoo.*"

"As Grufful has said," Val said, "I expect the same. We will meet again. Sonax go with you all until then."

"*Soi-nah*," said the four others of his pack.

"*Soi-nah*," said Jacob and Erno together.

Deborah almost instinctively joined them to utter the rovi phrase, whatever it meant. Farewell? Greetings? Something to do with Sonax? She made a mental note to remember to ask Erno about it when the pack had gone.

To her surprise, Hio hugged her. Deborah stiffly returned the hug. What had she done to prompt that affection in Hio? Val didn't hug. His green eyes were serious, as if he were saying something to her in one steady gaze. She didn't know what, but tried to meet that gaze and instill her own meaning in it that she was all right, she would be fine. His eyes briefly narrowed—did he disapprove? Why? Then, the pack turned and ran through the woods.

Deborah stared after them. The woods were strangely still, and the air felt heavier—each breath needed more effort. Without a word, she, Kasharel, Nurrel, and Erno moved away from the pile of guandras. They went on silently for a while, threading their way through the dead trees, then Nurrel stopped.

"I have to go back to the lake," he said.

"I know," said Erno.

"Well, I can't just leave Ibelli there, can I?" said Nurrel. "She'll die."

"Perhaps," said Erno.

"Perhaps? She can't break free by herself."

"She might."

"We will come with you, Nurrel," said Deborah. She looked down at Erno. "I know, you said we would go first thing this morning to Hirahi, but can't you allow us a little more time? Nurrel, if we come back with you, will you agree to talk to Ibelli just one more time, then leave with us if it doesn't work?"

"Someone's an organiser," Jacob said.

"I don't know if I can agree to that, Deborah," said Nurrel.

"You must, or we won't come with you," said Erno. He leaned towards Jacob. "I'm an organiser, too."

"I thought we were not supposed to coerce by force of will," said Kasharel.

"They're giving me an option, and I appreciate it," said Nurrel. He shook his head and gazed about. "I need to wake up, I suppose. Look at where we are. I can't stay here. Yes, force of will, yes, I get it, but I have to try again with Ibelli. One more time. If that's it, then that's it."

"Let's go before you change your mind again," said Jacob.

Nurrel gave him a small smile. "I won't. I see things clearly now. Thank you, all of you."

20

Deborah stood at the edge of the clearing that held the squatchamn dwellings. Stupid idiots—why would anybody want to stay here? It was foul. Dry, mud huts. Hard metallic light washing the colour out of everything. What in the world did the squatchamn eat for there were no crops anywhere. *Did* they eat? Or did they just sit staring at the lake until they dropped dead?

Nurrel led them over to Ibelli's hovel. Erno's thumps were obnoxiously loud in the quiet again, but none of the squatchamn they passed appeared to notice him. Some winced when Kasharel's tall shadow flowed over them, but that was the only response they gave. Nurrel hesitated a moment at the opening to Ibelli's hovel, took a breath, and went in.

Deborah thought about going in with him but didn't want to face that shrew again. Besides, if Nurrel was going to declare his love, then he probably didn't want an audience. It really was a waste of time talking to Ibelli again, and he would probably not get anywhere with the determinedly senseless lumdil.

There was movement across the other side of the clearing at the edge of the trees by the lake. Somebody was emerging. A rova. Then a man. Familiar somehow. No, it wasn't. It couldn't be.

"Father!" she shouted and ran across the dirt.

It *was* him. He was stooping, tired, shouldering a pack. That same pack he had used when they'd left Eblhim. He looked her way, shielding his eyes with his hand, a look of disbelief on his face.

"Deborah?" he said.

She almost knocked him over, seizing him in a fierce hug. It was true! The squatchamn girl really had seen him by the lake!

"Deborah?" he said again. "How? What are you doing here?"

His eyes were clearer than they had been for a long time. He seemed present. He was there. He saw her.

"Me?" she said. "What about you? What are you doing here? I thought you were going to Aric."

"Yes, I am; I was, but something made me change direction and come this way. I felt the Oxpeina calling me. Now I know why. I can't believe it's you. Is it really you?" He touched her face, stroked her cheek and hair. "My girl, my girl."

She could not remember the last time he had done such a thing. It was like being a child again. He dropped his pack and wrapped his arms around her, holding her tightly as though he could not believe she was real, that he wouldn't let her go this time.

"I've missed you," he said, his voice cracking with emotion. "You don't know how I've missed you. I'm so sorry. For everything. I don't know what I was thinking."

She shut her eyes and leaned into his embrace. Finally. Everything would be all right now. They could go home to Eblhim, try to pick up the pieces of life there, and start again.

"I'm so glad I found you," he whispered. "So glad. I can't believe it; I can't. You're really here." He drew back and stared at her. "Deborah, what are you doing out here? What are you doing all alone in these woods? They're dangerous. I only survived because of Reunta, my custodian. I don't suppose you know what that means, but Reunta has cared for me. Honestly, he has brought me back to sanity."

Deborah looked over her father's shoulder at the rova standing silently next to them. Reunta blinked, a knowing look in his dark green eyes. He was smaller than Val, lighter-furred than Grufful.

"Thank you," she said softly.

Reunta gave a slight nod.

"I'm just—I'm shocked," Father said. "I was never expecting to find you here. All I knew was the Oxpeina had me change direction, come this way, go back. And now, to see you?" He shook his head, still staring at her as though if he took his eyes off her, she would vanish.

"I thought you were miles away," she said. She felt she could hardly say anything. This was so astonishing. And yet, here he was. It was just as well she and the others had headed back to the Silver Lake with Nurrel; otherwise would Father have found them?

"But why are you here?" he asked. "How? What? Who?" He grinned.

She hadn't seen him grin for a long time. Gone was the vacant stare, the melancholy expression that had been prevalent for several years. She wondered what had happened to him in the woods. Certainly, plenty had happened to her.

"I came looking for you," she said. "I couldn't let you go."

The grin fell. "It's all my fault. I'm so sorry I've done this to you. I should have come back for you. I believe I was, really, I was starting to realise that I needed to do this. I haven't been able to think so clearly for ages. It's all coming back now."

It was intense, facing him like this and having him speak the words she had longed to hear, see him a changed man, have him so focused on her. She felt as though she couldn't quite handle it, couldn't quite take it in. He seemed to recognise that in her, and he slipped his arm in hers and turned to the lake.

"Oh," she said, "don't look at the lake. We should really get away from here, or we'll get caught. This lake has a lot of magic. I don't know how, but it'll keep you staring at it forever if it can."

He smiled at her. "That's true if you don't have the knack of it, but strength of will is what counts here. I learned that art as I walked around the shore. Great thanks to the Oxpeina-life for teaching me that as I very nearly got trapped on my first encounter and wondered what in the world this lake is about, but I see it now and have learned from it."

"I don't understand. I felt the lake's power to mesmerise, and, look at the squatchamn! They can't get away from it."

He looked out over the lake. The gaze that used to have such a distant, unseeing look was clear. "They're weak-minded, that's all. Shift your focus. See the lake for what it is—a tool. Don't allow it to take control of you; instead, take control of it."

Deborah glanced back at the silent Reunta. Why did he not say anything? Surely a rova would spit at such things; tell them to keep away from the lake. Like Grufful, who despised this whole region. Or, maybe Grufful despised the lack of will, the lack of control, the small and weak squatchamn.

"It's an interesting place," Father went on. "It took some understanding to grapple with how to be so close to it without it affecting me, but now I think I have finally found a place to rest awhile."

"Well, not here," Deborah said. "The trees are dead, and it's an awful region. It's hard to find drinkable water, and I don't know what food there is here, either."

"The trees are dormant, not dead," he said. "It is not their time to awake. And Reunta always knows where to find water."

What was Father talking about? Rest here awhile? Dormant trees? And how was he not affected by the lake? She still could not look at it without feeling its strange pull.

"We will have ourselves a time of connection," he said. "Get to know one another again and tell each other everything we've seen in these woods. I've missed you, Deborah. I wonder if we could take one of these houses? They seem pleasant."

"Pleasant? Dirt mounds for houses and shacks on the lake? No. It's not safe here."

He laughed and gestured at the clearing. "That's a bit extreme, Deborah. It's a simple life, granted, but I like that."

She looked back at the dirt mounds. They didn't look so bad after all. Simple, yes. Rounded and smoothed by hands that had taken great care in their shaping to provide shelter. And the huts out along the edge of the lake—finely-balanced on stilts above the silver water, connected by rustic wooden walkways—there was something artistically appealing about them.

"Here's what you do," said Father. "You look at the lake, but you don't let it control you. How? By telling the lake what *you* want to see in it and not the other way around. Look with a thought of something already in mind, say, the coast at home in Eblhim, and make sure your will is firm. Success in existing here in these woods seems to be about the strength of will. I never had that until I came here myself and learned."

He might think he had not had strength of will, but she recalled his insistence they leave Eblhim and take up residence in Shilhim. So, despite his apparent lack in other areas, she knew that somewhere deep inside him he had always had that strength. She also knew how vibrant the Oxpeina-life felt in pockets of these woods. How much of that had he encountered, and how had it altered him?

"I'll keep you safe," he said. "If I see you having trouble with the lake, I'll stop you from looking. You'll conquer it. You're strong."

Where was Erno? Where was Kasharel? She couldn't see them anywhere in the clearing. Had they gone into the woods for something?

"Deborah," came Erno's voice. "Stop it."

She glanced down at him, realising he had suddenly appeared at her side. "What? Stop what? Look, Erno. This is my father. I've found him!"

"No, it's not. You're staring at the lake. Stop it."

"I'm not looking at it at all. I'm looking at you. Erno, this really is my father. I've found him. The rova brought him to me. Oxpeina-life brought him to me." She and Father smiled at each other.

"No, Deborah," said Erno.

There was a sharp pain in her arm, and she yelped.

"Deborah!" rasped Jacob. "Look at me!"

He was in her arms. That was weird. Hadn't she dropped him when she had seen Father and run to him? Had she still been holding him the entire time?

"I should never have allowed you to come back here," Erno said.

"Well, I'm not a child, and I'm perfectly able to take care of myself. I was the one who said we should come back, remember? Besides, Father was just telling me there's a knack to handling the lake and its magic."

"Your father isn't here, Deborah. He isn't. You're seeing things in the lake."

She frowned at him. Sickly green moss, twiggy hair—it was kind of annoying the way it all seemed to waver in and out of focus. He didn't look right somehow, and his voice was irritating.

"He is," she said. "He's right here."

"Remember how Val said your father was seen miles from here and that he's heading for Aric? Aric is a long way away."

"He came back. Oxpeina-life told him to. He came back for me."

"No."

"I think your friend is having his mind altered by the lake," Father said. "Pity. Tell him to take control of himself and his thoughts."

She looked at Father. He was there; he was right in front of her. This wasn't the lake. She wasn't even facing the lake. She could see the glimmer of silver out of the corner of her eye, but she wasn't like the squatchamn who sat staring at the thing. What was wrong with Erno? Why couldn't he see Father? Kasharel suddenly stepped in between them, and his tall, tatty brown-robed body obscured Father. She almost pushed him away for being so rude for stepping in between them like that, and the memory flashed into her mind of a squatchamn batting his shadow away.

She gasped. What was happening?

"Deborah," Kasharel said gently. "Can you see me?"

"Yes, but I don't understand. I never looked at the lake. Father is here; can't you see him?"

"You're looking at the lake right now," said Erno. "Will you look at me instead?"

She wanted to, but where was he, exactly? He seemed to have moved from where he had been standing. "Erno, where are you?"

"I'm right here."

And he was. She looked down, and he was at her side again, squinting up at her. She reached out with one hand—she was sure the other held Jacob, for she could feel that lumpy bundle—and touched Erno's twiggy mess of hair. Bristly, scratchy, almost startling in reality. She was going to look over at Father for reassurance but glimpsed the flicker of Erno's dark pupils in his squinting gaze and caught a flash of life, emotion, some vital spark that called to her. He reached up, and his mossy fingers closed around her forearm. His touch shook breath into her, and the squatchamn clearing around them wavered as a mirage, then settled.

Everything came into sharp focus. Father was gone. Reunta, too. She bit her lip, trying to stop the waves of disappointment from breaking over her, and stared at the hard dirt between her feet and Erno's stumpy leg.

"You're here now?" Erno said quietly.

She nodded and blinked away the tears that were forming. How could she have been so stupid? Of course Father wasn't here. Of course he wasn't. He was miles away. He really didn't care anything at all for her and where she was—he was too busy off on his own quest for whatever it was. He had left her without a word and wasn't coming back.

"Was I really staring at the lake?" she asked quietly, not daring to take her eyes from her feet.

"Yes," said Erno. "I sensed that in your breathing a little late, I'm afraid."

"You didn't look for long," Jacob said. "I think you caught us off guard. We weren't expecting you to do that at all. At least, I know I wasn't."

"I wasn't either," said Kasharel. "I still have Iff's words in mind, telling us to not look at the lake, and so I thought you would, too."

She shook her head in the tiniest of movements. It was all too much to take in. Father had seemed so real, *felt* so real. Yet, here she was with the others, telling her it had all been her imagination, or the lake's imagination, or something. This damned place! She shouldn't have come back. She shouldn't have encouraged Nurrel to try again. They all should have got as far away as possible from here.

"Can we go now?" she said, keeping her gaze fixed on the ground. She did not want to move her head an inch, dared not have it all happen again. Who knows what she would see next in the lake? "Let's just go now."

"Can't, yet," said Erno. "Nurrel has only just begun to talk to Ibelli. We'll have to wait for him a while."

"But why wait here? We don't have to wait right here; we can wait under the trees."

"I was able to leave Nurrel here alone before," said Erno, "but I don't think it's wise to now. I want us grouped together."

The sharp tones of a raised voice came from the nearest dirt mound. Definitely Ibelli. Whereas Deborah could barely hear the low murmur of Nurrel's voice as he answered. How did he stay so calm?

"You need to stay close to Nurrel," said Jacob, turning to look at Erno. "Who knows when the verbal attacks cease and the physical begin?"

"Yes," Erno said, "my thoughts, also. Ibelli's arguments are altered from when we first arrived."

"Has Nurrel told her he loves her?" Jacob asked. "I can hear some of his words, but not all."

"Don't be so nosy," Deborah said. Although she also wanted to know the answer to that question.

"I don't see how you can tell someone you love them when they are attacking you," said Kasharel. "I would think it not the best timing for such a conversation."

"This may be the only time Nurrel gets," said Erno.

"So, has he?" Jacob asked.

Nurrel poked his head out of the dirt mound's opening. "You know, we can hear you, or at least I can. Your voices are sort of funnelled into here. All of you move away from the door, would you? Right, thanks." He disappeared back into the mound.

Deborah and Kasharel shuffled away, and Erno made one leap.

"How can the sky be so pure and clear?" Jacob said, staring upward. "You'd think it would be hazy like it is over the lake. Just here, it's stunning. Look across the tops of the trees. Go on, look."

Deborah supposed no harm could come of looking up. At least it wasn't towards the lake. The sky was a clear azure, a blue that was untroubled, uncomplicated, and she felt she could safely watch the clouds, pure white puffy softness, undulating unhurriedly as they moved across the sky. She supposed the sky was just that, the sky, nothing imaginary, and it would not change no matter what region it was over, for it stood over them all. Weather would be regional, sure, and perhaps the pall that hung out over the Silver Lake might obscure it here and there, but the sky stood above them all, unreachable, untouchable. Such a sky with colour and clouds like this could even be standing over Eblhim right now.

She inwardly sighed. Father had seemed so real, looked so real. He had been what she longed for—sane, engaged, truly seeing her. And to find out none of it was real? It was too hard. How could such a thing have been faked? What had she actually been conversing with? The lake? A dream? But, why? What was the point of it all?

She could hear Jacob and the others chatting but didn't listen to them. They could chat all they liked. They didn't understand what had just happened—to see Father then have him cruelly ripped away from her and find out it was only a fantasy. And all the while they stood there waiting for Nurrel; Father was moving further away.

The clouds slowly shifted and morphed, changing shape. She supposed all she could do was keep trying to track him, try to find him. What else was she supposed to do? Go back to Eblhim and try to start her life all over again alone? She had no job, no real qualifications for anything. All that had slipped away when Mother had died. She had finished school—barely managed to scrape through doing that as it was quickly apparent that Father could not do anything to look after the two of them anymore—and then life had become all about managing him. His inheritance had paid for them to be able to do nothing. Years later, he had got it fixed into his head to go to Shilhim, and nothing would budge him from that. It would solve all their problems to be near the woods. He would be better there, he said; he would find himself again. That had hardly lasted two days before he had taken off into the woods, so had that been his plan all along? To leave?

And yet, she missed him. Missed the old him. Seeing him here at the lake, she had briefly tasted that again. Stupid lake. Shouldn't have come back here. The clouds shifted again. She could see a face in profile, a nose, lips moving as the clouds slowly altered. It reminded her of the face she had seen when Grufful had held her. The one that had come right after seeing a vision of Father in the autumnal woods. How could she have forgotten that vision? She had seen Father walking, a rova at his side—it didn't look like Reunta; perhaps that was a stupid made-up name that meant nothing and belonged to no one. The rova with Father in her autumnal vision was larger, the fur almost black. Was that vision nothing but lies, too?

"Deborah," said Jacob. "*Deborah.*"

She looked down at him.

"Finally," he said crossly. "I thought I was going to have to peck you again. Listen to this."

"Nurrel has just told Ibelli that he saw a future for them both," Erno said, his head tilted slightly, his eyes shut. "He asks what she really wants, why she left home… " He paused, listening, "Wasn't it to go with the others to the Oxpeina's region? He has wanted to do that, too. With her."

"Should we really be eavesdropping like this?" Kasharel asked. "Give the man some space."

"*Shh,*" said Jacob.

"I don't think it's right," Kasharel said.

"Wait," said Erno. "She's reacting. 'Stop that', she says, 'I don't want to hear it'. Oddly, she sounds very quiet and controlled. Oh dear, that's not good—I don't think I'll repeat that bit."

"What?" said Jacob.

"She's insulting his parentage."

Deborah grit her teeth. She strode to the front of the dirt mound and positioned herself at the opening, trying to cast as much shadow as she could.

"What are you doing?" Jacob said.

"What does it look like?" She held him lower and to one side so he would add to the shadows. "I'm trying to block Ibelli's view of the lake."

Kasharel immediately joined her, and together they were able to form an effective screen, especially as he held part of his robe out. There was a shriek from inside the mound.

"I don't think this is such a good idea," Jacob said.

"Why not?" Deborah said. "It worked for me when you all took my attention from the lake."

"That was different," said Erno.

"How?"

Ibelli shot out through the opening with speed that took Deborah by surprise, shoved between her and Kasharel, and took off for the lake at a run. Nurrel scrambled out of the mound and ran after her.

"Not good!" shouted Erno and bounded after the pair.

"Stay where you are!" Jacob squawked up at Deborah as she began to follow. "You know what will happen to you if you face the lake again. Don't do it!"

"I've got to help them!"

"No, you don't. Erno will handle it better than any of us."

Deborah turned her back to the lake and stared at the dirt mound, trying her best to stand still and not look over her shoulder. What had she done to Ibelli by blocking sight of the lake? It should have snapped her out of her delusion, not had the opposite effect. She had only been trying to help Nurrel as the others had helped her when the lake had her mesmerised.

"Hold me up so I can see," Jacob said.

Deborah held him against her shoulder. She looked sidelong at him, the orbs of his eyes were hard and staring in his feathery brown and white head. "Don't look at the lake," she said.

"Hush, nonsense," he said. "It won't take me; I know who I am. Now let me listen; it's easier to hear their voices when they're out in the open echoing off the lake."

This was true; Deborah could hear the shouts and screeches of the agitated Ibelli.

"You leave me alone! I'm happy here! Don't you see what I have? How can you be so blind?"

Deborah frowned. That was rich, coming from her.

Nurrel's voice now, but she could not make out the words. Then Erno sounded like he was saying something, too.

"What're they saying?" she said to Jacob.

"*Shh*," he said. "I'm listening."

"Narrow-minded fools!" Ibelli again. Her voice pierced the clearing and echoed faintly across the lake. "I can think for myself! I know what I'm doing! I always wanted to come here to get away from you!"

The murmur of Nurrel's voice, and again, Deborah thought, Erno's.

Ibelli laughed. "I'm not dying! Why would you think I'm dying? Go away!"

"We should just really go and grab her," Deborah said. "Drag her out of here."

"Nurrel is trying to," Jacob said. "It's only making her go closer to the lake. *Ook!* She almost put her hand in, tried to clutch at it… hey… now Nurrel's got her; he's holding her."

"Let go of me!" shrieked Ibelli. "Let go of me!"

"She's struggling," said Jacob. "Kicking for all she's worth. Erno's moving in… no, wait, almost let go of her… "

Ibelli screamed, the sound reflecting off the lake in wild peals.

"Ibelli!" shouted Nurrel.

"*No*," hissed Jacob.

"What?" Deborah said. "Has he got her?"

"No," Jacob said in a subdued voice. "She's gone."

Her heart dropped. "What do you mean? What are you saying?"

"Don't you dare turn to look," said Jacob. "I can't have either of you looking at the lake, not now, not ever again. Don't you do it; do you hear me? Answer me now; tell me you're not going to."

She held him closer. "I won't. It's okay, Jacob, I won't."

"I won't," Kasharel said softly.

He sounded dazed. Deborah did not blame him; she felt in a state of shock, too. She could hear someone sobbing, gut-wrenching sobs that filled the clearing. It could only be Nurrel.

21

They left the squatchamn clearing behind, walking without a word beneath the withered trees, the only sound the impact of Erno's leaps on the hard earth. Deborah cast surreptitious looks at Nurrel whenever she drew level with him, for they walked several feet apart through the woods. His face was wet with tears, and from time to time she saw him pause, lean with one hand against a tree, then continue onward. Kasharel was pale, his face expressionless. Even Jacob did not speak. They merely kept on through the woods, following Erno as he led them through the region.

Deborah could not help but think that Nurrel did not speak to her or look at her because it was all her fault. She was the one who had provoked Ibelli, causing her to leave the dirt mound and run to the lake.

"Let us go on together and leave this region," Erno had said when he and Nurrel had rejoined them outside that same mound.

And they had been silent ever since.

Not that she wanted to talk. She didn't want to hear them all blame her. She knew if she had just kept out of things, it would have turned out differently. Ibelli wouldn't have died, but she and Nurrel would still be there in that mound arguing over the lake. She felt foolish, out of place, out of her depth. Who was she to tell anybody what to do? She had already failed Father; that should have been enough to cause her to be more cautious about trying to help anybody. She had never managed to help him. Now, she had caused someone's death.

It seemed they trekked on in this way for a long time and still had not left the region. Acres of trees, all dead. In some areas they had fallen completely and there was no way through, so Erno led them around or underneath the split and mangled trunks. The sun blazed down for lack of cover, lack of a cooling shelter of leaves.

"I'm too warm," Jacob said quietly. "Let me onto your shoulder."

Deborah unwrapped him, and he climbed up to her left shoulder while she knotted her jersey about her waist. It was a relief to not have to hold him anymore. Her left arm was stiff for having carried him in the crook of it for so long. She flexed it and swung it to ease the ache.

"Are you all right?" he whispered into her ear.

She was startled he was asking her this. It would have been more typical of him if he had started a lecture on what she had done to Ibelli and Nurrel.

"I'm tired and thirsty," she said in a low voice.

"That's not what I meant. Well, I suppose that too, but I mean more so, are you all right after what happened?"

"I don't see how anybody is supposed to be all right after that."

"True. I am still coming to grips with it myself. It was a terrible thing to witness."

She waited for him to go on, to scold her for her part in it.

"Terrible," he said softly. "*Hssh*."

She walked onward, finding her way around the fallen branches, between the scattered broken trees. Jacob said nothing more for some time, then gave a triumphant hoot.

"At last! Trees! Erno, I see trees ahead!"

Deborah stopped, looking this way and that to try and find what he was talking about. "Where?"

"Straight ahead. Look to the horizon above this wasteland."

She saw nothing other than the blue cloud-plumed sky above the skeleton trees. "Must be your super owl vision," she muttered.

"A few more hours, and we will reach them," Erno said.

"Is there any chance of some water nearby?" Kasharel asked. "Perhaps you could call some up for us?"

"Not right here, sorry," Erno said. "I will stop as soon as I detect some."

Nurrel sat on a fallen tree, his head bowed. Erno hopped over to him and placed his hand on his shoulder. Deborah could hear him speaking in a low voice and saw Nurrel nod without raising his head. She turned away and took a deep breath.

She felt Jacob shift his position on her shoulder as he turned back around to face the others. He could eavesdrop all he wanted; she didn't want to. She hoped whatever it was that Erno was saying would bring Nurrel comfort. She thought of her own father and how long it had taken him to speak again after Mother's death. It was as though words would not come for him; he spoke in fragments.

"Deborah. Come, sit here."

The voice was unmistakeably Nurrel's. She was shocked. What did he want? Was he going to vent his anger on her? She slowly went over as Jacob turned around on her shoulder again.

"Sit." Nurrel patted the rough bark next to him.

She did. "I— I'm really sorry, Nurrel. About what happened. About… Ibelli. I'm so sorry."

He glanced up at her, nodded, and looked down again. He looked unspeakably weary, his face drawn and sombre. He exhaled, and for a moment she thought he was about to say something, but he closed his eyes instead. She wanted to reach out to him then, do what Erno was doing, put her hand on his shoulder, let him know he wasn't alone. But she couldn't. She didn't know why Nurrel wanted her to sit next to him, but she was sure he wouldn't want her touching him. Not after what she had done. Saying sorry didn't even seem enough; it sounded hollow.

How long they sat together, Deborah did not know, but finally Nurrel stood. "I can go on," he said. "We've got to leave this region. Erno, do you think we can make it before dark?"

Erno's mossy brow wrinkled. "Don't know. Depends on how quickly you all can move."

"Not very, I'm afraid," Nurrel said. "I seem to have no strength."

"Shall I carry you?" Erno asked.

"I don't think I could stand the jarring of your leaps," Nurrel said.

"Shall I, then?" Kasharel asked. "I could carry you on my back."

Nurrel looked up at him. "I'm heavier than I look."

"I'm stronger than I look."

Nurrel gave a slight nod. "Fine."

Kasharel crouched, and Deborah took the empty cloth bag that hung from his shoulder so it wouldn't be in Nurrel's way. This was the bag the rovi had brought, but what remained of the food packed in it had been finished some time ago. Nurrel climbed onto Kasharel's back.

"Ready?" Kasharel asked.

"Yes. I thank you, Kasharel. It's very good of you."

"It is no problem."

He stood, and Nurrel happened to look down at Deborah as she looked up at him. When their eyes met, she was taken by the look in his dark brown eyes. She felt she could see something raw and deep in him—yes his grief, but also a strength, a tenderheartedness, and something of Oxpeina-life. This was no vacant gaze; she knew he saw her. She looked away. If only that vision of Father had been real. If only he would see her, too.

"Onward," said Erno. "Let's try to pick up the pace if we can. I don't want us to spend another night in this region. If we have to, we have to, but I'd rather not. I'll stop if I sense water and have a go at calling it up."

On they went. Deborah pushed herself to walk faster, but she lagged behind Kasharel's long-legged stride and Erno with his great leaps. It did not matter, for in this stark region it was easy to see where they were. Kasharel and Nurrel frequently looked back to check on her, too.

The trees were thinning, and there were no longer any great broken heaps to bypass. After a while, she saw what Jacob had seen—the dark smudge on the horizon between dead trees and sky. It thickened and grew, forming into the rounded and varied shapes of treetops, green and reassuring. Deborah didn't want to look anywhere else. It was still so far away, enticing, promising better things ahead and the relief of finally being able to leave this cursed region behind. She stumbled once or twice as her foot caught on branches scattered on the ground and Jacob hissed.

"Watch where you're going."

"Sorry."

"Water!" shouted Erno and stood still. He raised his hands to the sky, his face upturned.

From the distance, Deborah thought he looked like a stubby tree. As soon as she caught up with him and Kasharel, she sat heavily on the ground, glad for a chance to stop and rest. She stared at the base of Erno's leg, willing the water to hurry and rise to the surface. Her mouth felt so dry it was hard to swallow.

"Erno, is the air telling you anything?" Jacob asked.

"Just the usual kinds of things," Erno said. "I feel the trees' proximity, the water, the directional pull of the Oxpeina."

"What about guandras?" Kasharel asked.

"There's nothing to worry about," Erno said. "They're too distant, too few, too puny."

"And our squatchamn hanger-on?" Nurrel asked. He shaded his eyes with his hand as he looked back the way they had come.

"She's still following," Erno said. "She's okay. For a while she had her own hanger-on, but I don't hear it anymore."

"That's good news," Nurrel said.

Deborah glanced at him. His tone was sober. He would surely wish that the only one following them was Ibelli. It was kind of him to say it was good news that the squatchamn girl was with them. Deborah gazed into the distance but saw no movement, no sign of the girl. She hadn't realised they were still being followed by her. She thought of the annoying 'Debah, Debah' and wondered why the girl didn't come any closer.

"Yes," Erno said, "but, odd. I don't know why a guandra would give up trying to steer her back to the lake."

"Perhaps a rova stepped in," Jacob said.

"Perhaps," Erno said, "but I have heard none."

He leapt aside, and a spring of water burst upwards from where he had stood. It sprayed all over Deborah, and she yelped with surprise. Jacob jumped clumsily down to the ground and shook himself. Deborah hastily got up as the water pooled towards where she sat. The spring continued to burble up, and there was enough for everyone to crowd around and drink.

The water tasted sweeter, lighter, than it had back at the Silver Lake. Still not quite normal tasting, Deborah thought, still with a bitter tinge and metallic aftertaste, but it was a relief to have any water at all. She splashed some over her face and felt the dust and dirt rinse off. Nurrel washed his hands repeatedly at the edge of the small pool before he drank from the spring.

He sniffed his hands and pulled a face. "I still stink of guandra. I'm sorry, Kasharel, for what you've had to put up with."

"No apology needed," Kasharel said. "I've been glad to help you."

Deborah watched the expression on Nurrel's face change as misery crossed it. He got up and walked away a few paces to stand with his back to them. She supposed he would always be like that now, always in the hands of grief as it shifted him to and fro. She had seen it enough in Father—the way his moods would change, the way that grief would unexpectedly rise from any innocuously spoken word.

"Now all we need is something to eat," Jacob said, busily preening the few feathers he had left.

"I can't help you there," Erno said. "The only thing we can hope for out here is that Sonax becomes aware of our need and sends rovi again with supplies. I think we're still too far from the border of this region to hope to find anything edible."

"What do the squatchamn people survive on?" Kasharel asked. "I've been wondering about that. I saw no crops near their settlement."

"Food drops from guandras," Erno said, his face grim.

"What?" Kasharel said. "How could that be?"

"It's a way of controlling image-bearers," Erno said. "Feed them just enough to keep them from wandering."

"Or, dying," Jacob muttered.

Deborah poked him with her finger. "*Shh*. Don't say that." She glared at him and motioned towards Nurrel. Jacob should be more sensitive in the things he said.

"Or, dying," said Nurrel, as he turned to face them. "Keep them alive; keep them under control; it's what guandras do. Why can't they see it? Why? Why don't they see the hand that feeds them? Nothing good can come from those who have turned, *nothing!* Yet they can't be made to see it. I can't make them. I couldn't do it. I couldn't get through to her. I couldn't! It didn't matter what I said." He clenched his fists. "And now… and now… she… " He grimaced and turned away again.

His short-legged gait was swift as he stumped away across the dirt, and Deborah wondered where he had suddenly found the strength to walk. He uttered an anguished cry and some unintelligible words, accented and nuanced in a way that reminded Deborah of the rovi.

"*Soi-nah!*" he shouted, piercing the air of the region.

In response, Deborah found those words rise to her lips as Jacob muttered them and Erno spoke them. Even Kasharel whispered something, as though he too could not help but respond in kind. Deborah quickly helped Jacob to her shoulder, and they all set off after Nurrel towards the green band of trees on the horizon.

22

In the fading light, the distant trees were a dark border casting long-reaching shadows. Deborah could feel that region's cool air and the change of ambience imbued with what she knew was Oxpeina-life. Her breathing became less laboured, and she inhaled the sweet hint of foliage in the breeze. The weariness that had been with her for what seemed a long time began to dissipate.

As they walked on, she saw a carpet of green ahead, lush grass, empty of trees broken or living, a no man's land that defined the passing of one region to the next. Everyone quickened their pace, eager to reach it.

Jacob's grip on Deborah's shoulder tightened, and he hissed. "What is that?"

"What is what?" Erno asked.

"I think—I don't like to say what I think. It does not appear to be a tree. Deborah, move us closer so I can get a better look."

"Move us closer, where?"

"To our left."

She did not really want to go that way. Why detour now when they were so close to the next region? All she saw was a smattering of twigs, dry rotted branches, the occasional jagged tree stump in the dirt.

Jacob clamped her shoulder again as if urging her. "Please, Deborah."

She wound her way across the dirt, stepping over this and that, trying to see what had caught Jacob's interest. Kasharel and Nurrel stayed waiting where they were, but Erno leapt alongside her.

Then she saw it. A small tangle of twigs beside a sun-dried brown and dark green sunken frame. A body, not a tree. The face upturned to the sky, the moss withered so that she could see the features, gentle, sorrowful in their lines.

Jacob sighed.

"Why have you stopped?" Erno said, squinting towards Deborah. "Tell me, what do you see?"

"A brismun," she said softly.

"Where? Show me!"

She moved carefully closer, not wanting to disturb anything. "Here."

Erno leapt to her side. "I can't sense anything. Place my hand."

She guided his hand to the body of the brismun, and the instant his hand touched, he gasped and bowed his head. "Oh, my brother, my brother." He bent over the body, his hands moving gingerly along the misshapen form. "Senka," he whispered. "Senka. I knew your fate; I knew it, but to have it confirmed is misery. My brother. To die here, so close. Why did you stay?"

His language changed, and Deborah stood silently next to him, listening to the whispering echoes of a bygone dawn, the softness of leaf in the air, the longing of heart and soul in hushed tones. She hardly dared to breathe, not wanting to draw any attention to herself in such an intimate moment. Jacob nuzzled closer to her neck while she looked at the bright green of Erno contrasted against the dull body of Senka. Both appeared to wear crowns of twiggy hair, one shrunken and dry, the other vigorous and abundant.

Erno finally stood up straight. Slowly, he extended his hands to the sky and stood, face upturned, eyes closed amongst the moss. His mouth moved, but Deborah heard no more words.

Then he turned and squinted at her. "Thank you for leading me here. You too, Jacob. I knew Senka was somewhere, but I could not sense exactly where. Life is easier to feel than death. Speaking of which, let's leave this region. I hope I never have to return here."

He leapt away without a second glance at Senka and headed for the wide grassy band. Deborah could see that Kasharel and Nurrel had already reached it, and she made her way across the dirt.

"Seems strange to just leave Senka's body there," she whispered to Jacob, hoping Erno's sharp ears would not hear her. "Why not bury him?"

"I understand it is different for image-bearers, but most custodians don't. Rovi do, perhaps, but I don't think it is the way of a brismun. They lie where they fall. I would think that would be inconvenient. I am surprised how much of Senka's body still remains, as I would have thought his departure from this region was a long time ago. Perhaps the sun has preserved him. I suppose he's a bit like a tree, or something."

"*Jacob*," she said. "That's revolting."

"Is it? Why?"

"Don't talk about him like that."

"It's not him; it's his body."

"*Jacob!* Erno might hear us."

"What do you mean, might? Of course he will."

She frowned sidelong at him. "Then, be quiet."

"*You* be quiet."

She resisted the urge to flick him. Not so far to go now, and she would be ankle-deep in fresh, green grass. Away to her right, Erno had joined Kasharel and Nurrel, who were now sitting. She wondered why they didn't go further on to the trees. Sure, the first line of trees was still some way off, but it would be better to be within their shelter and away from any sight of this region. Strange that the regions were so different yet butted up against each other.

With her first step onto the grass, she felt the change. It was as though she pushed through a screen and was encompassed by a completely different atmosphere. The sense of Oxpeina-life was not as electric as it had been back in the region by the gehun caves, but this felt, well, *busier* somehow, as though life teemed with activity and there was more to touch, and see, and smell. Insects buzzed, speckled bright blues and reds that flew and hopped about the grass that was not just plain green but had a myriad of shades and dimensions of greens to each strand, and each strand moved and swayed with a life of its own, following the breeze, or not, it was hard to tell, and a bird flew down, and it was not just brown and black, but its feathers shone with purple and yellow depending on which way it turned… Deborah took a deep breath to try and steady herself, and even that filled her lungs with a new vitality. It was hard to take it all in. She understood why Kasharel and Nurrel sat, for she did not know what to do with herself. She felt she was not ready to go on any further.

"What are you waiting for?" said Jacob. "Let's get to the others."

His voice sounded nicer, sweeter, less harsh in her ear.

"I don't know," she said. "It's just… difficult. Don't you feel this?"

"Feel what?"

"The Oxpeina-life here."

"Oh yes, it's much better now that we're here. I feel sorry for the squatchamn image-bearers at the Silver Lake and what they have to put up with. They get used to it and don't know what they're missing. Now we're back to some normality, and it's about time—we were too long at the lake."

How he could talk like everything was fine and normal now was beyond her. She sank down onto the warm and springy grass. No more hard earth or crusty, scratchy twigs; just nice cushiony ground beneath her hands.

"What are you doing?" Jacob said.

"Nothing," she said.

"I can see that. What's wrong with you?"

"Nothing."

"*Huh.*"

"You can walk over to the others," she said. "I'm not stopping you."

"I might just do that."

"Go on, then."

He gently nibbled her ear, and she flinched. "That tickles! What are you trying to do to me?"

"*Nothing.*"

She smiled.

The thumps of Erno as he hopped over to them were muffled in the grass, but the ground trembled nonetheless when he landed next to Deborah. "Everything all right?"

"Yes," she said.

He laid a cool hand on her head. "Ah. You're affected the same way as Kasharel. He can't walk on, either. I suspect we'll have to spend the night here and let you both acclimatise before we go on to Hirahi."

She sighed and lay down, and Jacob hopped off her shoulder. It would be good to stay here a while and not have to do anything. Although something to eat would be good. When had she last had something to eat?

"I'm hungry," she muttered, closing her eyes.

"I expect you are," Erno said. "I think, well, I hope, word will get out that we're here and someone will bring us something. Especially if they learn we're not going on to Hirahi tonight."

There was an abrupt shuffling sound. Deborah opened an eye and saw he had swivelled about on his stumpy leg.

"A-ha," he said. "Our squatchamn friend has almost made it to the border."

Deborah didn't bother to sit up and look. "Good."

"I think I will go to the edge to greet her. She may welcome that now, being so close."

He leapt away. Deborah thought it sounded like he went the other way, not back towards Kasharel and Nurrel, but she couldn't be sure. She yawned and snuggled into the warm grass. "Jacob. You still there?"

"Yes."

"Good."

"Get some sleep. I'll stay by you."

That was nice. Comforting, somehow. Although why he wanted to do that… other things he could do… chase bugs… talk to Kash…

She fell asleep.

Some time later, she woke to darkness. There was a crunching, crackling by her right ear, and a gulp. Then more crunching. Another gulp. Something small and sticky fell on her cheek. She grimaced and moaned as she wiped it off.

"Oops," said Jacob. "Sorry about that."

"What are you doing?"

"Erno brought me some grasshoppers. They're really quite tasty."

She sat up and glared at the ground in his general direction. "Do you have to eat them right by my head?"

"I'm not right by your head. Do you want something to eat now that you're awake?"

"I'm not eating grasshoppers!"

"I didn't mean grasshoppers. We had some food brought to us earlier. I didn't want to wake you then."

The vestiges of sleep vanished. Food had been brought? By who? Had she missed seeing Val? More importantly, had she missed seeing Grufful? "Who brought the food?"

"One of the locals, she didn't give her name. She was in a hurry to get back to her home."

"There are homes nearby?"

"Yes, not too far. By Ekiple Lake."

She frowned. Not another lake.

"*Hoo.* I see your face. This is a real lake, unspoiled by the guandras. This region has its custodians firmly in place, and I can't imagine that the image-bearers here would want that to change."

Deborah heard the soft whumps of Erno coming to them across the grass.

"You all right?" he said, when he had reached them.

"Yes," said Jacob. "Have you any more grasshoppers?"

Erno chuckled. "More? I thought I gave you heaps. Deborah, here."

She felt a cloth bundle land on her lap.

"Kasharel was famished," Erno said, "and just about ate the lot. I couldn't get Nurrel to eat much, though."

"How is he doing?" Jacob asked.

"Still in shock. He can't get the images of Ibelli's death out of his head."

Jacob uttered a low hiss. "Neither can I."

"Nobody should have had to see that. These things shouldn't be happening in our world."

"But they do," Jacob said. "With increasing frequency."

"You think that, too?"

"Of course."

"Well," said Erno. "If you're both all right and don't need anything else, I'll get back to Nurrel. He's not sleeping, so we're talking things through. Meantime, Kasharel sleeps like nothing would wake him."

Deborah felt through the cloth bundle, trying to find the opening. "Thanks for this. We're all right—you go back to Nurrel."

She could hear the smile in his voice. "Yes. I know you're always all right, Deborah."

She wasn't sure whether he meant it or whether he teased her. She knew she didn't feel all right. The initial glow from coming to this region seemed to have faded somewhat, and guilt crept over her as she realised she had hardly given Nurrel a thought. Nothing had changed for him—he still had to deal with the pain of his loss. And it was her fault.

Erno leapt away, his muffled thumps becoming fainter. Deborah ate in silence. Whatever it was, chunks of something bready around what tasted like a soft cheese, and a small bottle of syrupy water. Jacob resumed crunching on his grasshoppers—so he really did have more there. Perhaps Erno hadn't sensed them if they were lying dead. Deborah thought of Senka. He lay not so far away from them, left by himself in that horrible region.

"Why did Erno not bring Senka here to this region?" she said softly. "Why leave him back there? I know you said a brismun is left to lie where they die, but still, it's a horrible place to be left."

"I don't know. Perhaps Senka didn't want to leave, and Erno knows that."

"Why wouldn't he want to leave? It's no place for a brismun."

"I don't know that either. You should be asking Erno these questions, not me." He continued crunching.

After Deborah had finished eating, she lay down again. She could hear the distant murmur of voices—Erno and Nurrel, no doubt. She wondered how Kasharel could sleep with them talking right next to him, unless he had moved away. She looked up at the few stars above, tiny sparkles amongst the greyness of cloud that moved slowly across the sky. How long was it since she had been home? Days? It felt like months.

She sighed and closed her eyes, then jumped as Jacob nudged her arm. "What?"

"I'm cold," he said. "Would you mind?"

Where was her jersey? Still tied around her waist. She wriggled around and undid it, then fumbled in the dark to wrap him while he muttered and grumbled.

"Not there. Yes, there. Like that."

Once done, she lay on her side, holding him against her chest as sleep drifted over her.

23

The sounds of munching made Deborah groan. "Jacob, stop it. Don't eat by my head."

"It's not me, you twit," he answered.

He wriggled in her arms as she blearily opened her eyes to an early morning mist. The sounds of munches and snuffles went on uninterrupted.

"It's the rvenan cattle," Jacob said. "Why you would think that's what I sound like when I eat, is beyond me. Not very flattering, I must say."

She sat up. She was covered in a light dew, and her hair was damp and stuck to her face. She shivered and clutched Jacob closer. Moving slowly around grazing the grassy band were several, dozens even, mottled grey beasts. Not quite like a cow, but longer-necked and slimmer with long drooping ears. One of them paused from grazing and looked back at her. It seemed to study her as she studied it, then gave her a wrinkly smirk and mumbled a long, incomprehensible monologue.

Deborah did not know what to think. "Do they bite?"

Jacob craned his neck above the folds of her jersey. "What? No. At least, I don't think so."

The rvenan that had taken an interest in Deborah kept on mumbling while eyeing her.

"What's it saying?" she said.

"Haven't got a clue," Jacob said. "It just sounds like a load of gibberish to me."

Some of the rvenan cattle grunted amicably and stepped aside as Erno made his way through.

"Come warm yourself by the fire," he said.

Deborah got up with Jacob and went with Erno back through the cattle, the aroma of manure and warm beasts around them. Soft plodding footsteps accompanied her, and she turned to see that the rvenan was following her. It had stopped its mumbling, but smirked again at her when she looked at it. Strange thing. What did it want?

Erno led them to where Kasharel sat by a fire ringed with stones. A small, lank-haired, bug-eyed stranger sat cross-legged next to him. The squatchamn girl, Deborah decided. She must have come out of hiding at last. Deborah looked around, wondering where Nurrel could be. Beyond the green border of the region back in the dead lands, she saw him approaching with an armful of sticks. He looked grim—she thought perhaps more so now at the sight of her—and so she turned her back to him and sat opposite Kasharel, the fire between them. Erno stood a few feet away.

"This is Rati," Kasharel said, gesturing slightly to the squatchamn girl. "Rati, meet Deborah, and with her is Jacob."

Deborah half expected her to start chanting 'Debah, Debah', but all she did was nod silently, her wide eyes fixed on Deborah.

"These are your cattle?" Jacob asked.

Rati turned her gaze to him. "My father's."

"They look healthy. You must care well for them."

Rati gave another nod, interest on her face as she looked at him.

Deborah was confused. She looked like a squatchamn; she had the thin build and staring eyes, but was this not the same girl who had been following them? She was about to question this when the mumbling of a rvenan began again at her ear. Hot breath tickled her neck, and she realised it was standing right behind her.

"*Ah!*" shouted Rati.

The rvenan let out a long spiel of baffled-sounding jargon as if it had every right to stand over Deborah and breathe down her neck.

Rati leapt to her feet. "Go!"

"I don't mind it," Deborah said. "What's it saying?"

"Nothing recognisable yet," Rati said, "but it's starting to awaken. Can't understand why, for Sonax hasn't touched it, and I have been careful with them all. The last few days I noticed signs this one could be awakening, but now for sure it seems to attempt to communicate." She fixed her gaze on Deborah again. "Have you been speaking with it?"

"No."

Rati came around to the rvenan and shoved its flank. "*Ah!*"

The rvenan mumbled under its breath and slowly moved away. Rati frowned as she watched it go.

"It'll have to be separated from the herd. We can't eat one that's awakening."

Deborah turned to look at the rvenan. The cattle back home in Eblhim did not look like the rvenan and she ate their meat without thinking about it. No cattle had ever 'awakened' and started trying to talk. She was sure that sort of thing was unheard of outside of the woods. Yet… again, the *Legends Of The Greener Land* storybook came to mind. Despite its obvious flaws about brismuns, such things as dwarves instead of lumdils, not really having a clue what a gehun was, and so on, at least one of the fables had a talking animal.

"What will happen to it?" Kasharel asked.

Rati went and sat next to him again. "Oh, it'll have to be taught to do something useful." She looked again at Jacob. "You've fully awakened. How did that happen?"

"Sonax held me in his hand."

Rati nodded, her gaze fixed on him. "Sure, I've seen that."

There was a clatter as Nurrel dumped his armful of sticks and branches. "Hello, Deborah, Jacob, sleep okay?"

He sounded subdued. Deborah wondered if he had had any sleep at all or if he and Erno had talked through the night.

"Perfectly well," said Jacob. "I tried my best to as I was unable to hunt, of course. But I found myself very comfortable thanks to Deborah."

She glanced down at him. Praise from Jacob? That was a change. "Fine, thanks," she said to Nurrel. She was not sure if she should look at him, not look at him, smile or not smile—how did he feel towards her? He must surely be blaming her for what had happened to Ibelli. As his shadow moved across the ground next to her, she looked away. Her own shadow had been what had caused Ibelli to leave her shelter in a fit of madness and run to the lake.

Nurrel's hand on her shoulder startled her. A light touch, a gentle squeeze, then he went and stoked the fire. "Your clothes are soaked with dew, Deborah. Get closer to the fire and warm yourself."

Deborah said nothing but inched a little closer, just to do what he said. If he was not outwardly angry at her, that was something, and she would try not to antagonise him.

"Not too close," said Jacob.

"Bird," said Rati, "tell me, when did Sonax hold you? How long have you been awake?"

Jacob quickly swivelled his head and scowled at Rati. "*Bird?*"

"I've forgotten your name," said Rati, picking a piece of fluff off her sleeve and flicking it towards the fire. "I'm like that with names. I get introduced to someone, and I don't know what happens—the name doesn't stick."

"*Jacob*," he said.

"Jacob," she repeated. "Let's see if it sticks this time. Probably won't."

Erno chuckled while Kasharel looked down at Rati, an amused glint in his eyes. Deborah half listened as Jacob explained to Rati his meeting with Sonax. She'd heard it before. Besides, what now? It was a new morning; they were in a new region and yet sitting around a fire, not doing anything or going anywhere. Hirahi, supposedly, was not far off. She had been promised that there at last she could get accurate information as to her father's whereabouts. She shrugged to herself. What did it matter anymore. It felt like nothing really was happening. Father was miles away. Perhaps she could at least get a map or something to show how to get to Aric. If Father was heading there, then she supposed she should, too. She set Jacob down—away from the fire—and turned her back to warm that side of herself. The neighbouring region seemed too close. Broken trees cut sharp outlines into the sunrise while the barren ground held confused shapes of nothingness.

What was she even doing anymore? Maybe she should just go home. Back to Eblhim. What work could she get to earn money to live on? She had no qualifications, no training, nothing. She had only been a companion for Father, if you could call it that. More like a servant putting up with his whims and moods. What had she done all day? Looking back, it seemed a blur. A draining, emotional, menial blur, living in a cloud of grief. He obviously didn't care that he had left her.

"Deborah," said Erno.

His tone of voice gave her the impression that this was not the first time he had called her name. She turned. "*Huh?* Yes?"

"How many sausages do you want?"

Rati was cutting through a string of sausages with a short knife, and Nurrel was deftly skewering them onto long sticks.

"Two," Deborah said.

"What about the squatchamn who has been following us?" Kasharel said. "She must be hungry."

"I tried to coax her over into this region last night, but she wouldn't budge," Erno said. "Rati, come with me, and we'll try again. She is still close, and I think watches us. If she spoke with you, it may help her."

Rati glanced back at Erno. "What? Go where? You're not talking about over there in the slaughterland, are you?"

"If that's what you call your neighbour region, then yes."

Rati shook her head. "Not happening. Not going there, no, no. You can see from here what it's like; everything winds up dead there."

Deborah shot a look at Nurrel. His expression was pained as he handed a sausage-laden stick to Kasharel, then he got up to bring her one as well. Their eyes met, and again she was struck by something in his gaze. Tenderness, sadness, but something clear and striking in the depths of those dark brown eyes—a strength that she was drawn to. She wanted to say something to him but couldn't think what. This was weird. Why feel so drawn to Nurrel? She fumbled as she took the skewered sausages from him, almost dropping them into the fire.

"Precisely why you should go and speak to your kin," Jacob said to Rati. "She is so close to crossing into this region, and you could help her greatly."

"My kin?" Rati said. "You must be joking."

"She's squatchamn as you are, or am I mistaken?"

"You're mistaken. They're nothing like us over there. I am a true squatchamn image-bearer, and they've forgotten who they are and who they're supposed to be. It's not my problem."

Kasharel cleared his throat quietly. "You could remind—"

"Nope," said Rati. "Not going over there, and you can't make me." She wiped her knife on the grass, then gathered up a cloth bag that lay beside her. "I've got to tend to my herd."

With that, she headed off to the rvenan cattle.

"I don't understand," said Kasharel.

"She's afraid," Erno said. "That's all. She's right to be—the region is full of death—but I would have gone with her so she'd be safe."

"What happened to your brother?" Jacob asked. "How do you think he died?"

Deborah almost dropped her stick of sausages into the fire again. She wanted to kick Jacob for his abrupt and insensitive change of conversation or at least pull a face at him, but he had his back to her. He had managed to extricate himself out of her jersey and stood looking like a small, half-plucked chicken by the fire.

Erno's cheerful countenance sank into mossy furrows. "I assume it was the usual story—the image-bearers rejected his custodianship of the region as they turned. I could not feel from his body that they murdered him, so his death must have occurred naturally due to that rejection and the ensuing change in the atmosphere. I think that where he stood he was within reach of the feel of the air of this region, but he could not leave his own region."

"Why not?" Jacob asked.

"Senka was very committed, very dedicated to his role, and I believe he would not have wanted to give that up for any means."

Erno sighed and was silent for a moment. There was tranquillity in the crackling of the fire, sizzle of the cooking sausages, and the whispering *shuffs* of the rvenan cattle as they grazed the grass band.

"I should be so dedicated," Erno went on. "It has been several years since Senka and I crossed paths, and I was able to speak to him. He didn't roam as I do. He was the dearest of brothers, the tenderest heart. I saw what was happening to his region in the early days, and he did, too, but he could not change the will of the image-bearers. He was at their mercy and their whim.

"Meredea, his shaseeliany, fell first. Her waters were tainted, and she was lost. Although he searched the whole of his region, he never found what had become of her. I told him then to leave, but he would not. Now to find him so close, so close to this region—he must have stood with such longing for the Oxpeina but could not bring himself to leave the dwellers of this region without his care. It hurts my heart to know that this is how things ended for Senka."

"There don't appear to be any dwellers," Jacob said. "I heard no birdlife, no insectlife while there, and the trees are all dead or mostly dead."

Erno shook his head. Deborah realised the moss around his eyes dripped with tears. She swallowed hard and stared at the stick in her hands, slowly turning it as the fat from the sausages sizzled and sputtered above the licking flames. Why must there be such sorrow and death in the world? Crossing into this region had been a balm, but the grief that was tied to her and the others would still follow.

They ate together silently. The cheerful banter that had sparked between Erno and Nurrel only a few days ago was no more. It had all changed. Just as her life had been irrevocably changed when Mother had died. Now, Father had obviously decided he didn't need or want her anymore—he had left her without a word. Perhaps it was time she came to grips with that. Perhaps she should abandon this fruitless search for him and look at starting a new life for herself. She could not even begin to think of what that might look like. Any dreams she'd had for her life had slipped away years ago. Life revolved around Father and his care. What did she really want? And yet she longed for Father. Longed to see him again, longed to see him return to his old self and to feel safe and secure in their family home together again.

She stared gloomily into the fire, watching the flames burn lower as nobody bothered to toss more sticks on. They would soon be leaving it anyway. On to Hirahi, on to whatever awaited them there. Perhaps there she would know what to do. She would find out how long it would take to travel to the city of Aric and think about if she really wanted to continue onwards. Maybe Father didn't even want to see her anymore. Maybe he wanted to start a new life for himself, and that didn't include her.

Erno leapt towards the region's boundary. "Before we move on, I'd like to give one more try at coaxing the squatchamn girl forward. Deborah, will you come with me?"

She almost choked on her last bite of breakfast. "Me? You've seen what I can do. I don't think I'm the best choice here. Wouldn't Kasharel be better? He's the calm one."

"I'm asking you."

"I can't think why. You know I make a mess of things."

He swivelled on his stumpy leg, and she thought she could see the rumpling of a frown in his face. "Deborah. That's not so."

She wondered how he could say that in front of Nurrel, of all people. "Yes, it is."

"No."

"Yes."

"*Hoo.*" Jacob ruffled and shook his remaining feathers. "Just go, the pair of you. Otherwise, we'll spend the whole morning here doing nothing."

"I will come too, if you wish it," Nurrel said.

"Me, too," said Kasharel.

"Not necessary," Erno said. "The girl is shy of the lot of us. I think she might be better with just Deborah."

Deborah shrugged and got up. "Don't blame me if I make things worse."

Erno squinted up at her. "So, you'll come?"

"Sure, I guess so. If I can get her to cross into this region, that's a good thing, right?"

"Take her this." Nurrel handed her a cooked sausage on a stick. "She must be hungry."

Jacob stared grimly at Deborah. "Be careful, won't you? Don't fall for any tricks to get you to stay there or go back to the lake."

"I'm not going back to the lake; don't be crazy."

"*Hmph.*"

"And watch out for guandras," said Kasharel.

"I know where they are," said Erno. "There are several of them out there, watching, and I find it curious that they haven't moved in and convinced the girl to go back to the lake already. There is something about it I can't quite put my finger on. Is it that she is near enough to me that they dare not move in, or is it something else?"

"I don't like the sounds of that," said Nurrel. "Maybe you shouldn't take Deborah over there. Maybe we should all just get away from here."

"I will do what Deborah decides," Erno said.

Her eyes widened. "Me? You put that decision on me?" She supposed it was something to do with the whole 'I'll-do-what-the-image-bearer-wants' stuff that custodians seemed to be obliged to. She turned away and took a deep breath of the cool air, laden though it was with the aroma of the rvenan as they quietly grazed the grass strip. The line of green was so clearly delineated it was as though a fire had torn through the neighbouring region and stopped at an invisible wall. She did not particularly want to cross that line, but where was the squatchamn girl? Hiding behind one of the dead trees and watching? That region was no place for anyone with any sense. As for the guandras, they hadn't been much of a bother, not really. The fight, if you could call it that, had been over in a moment with Val's pack of rovi doing their part to get rid of them. She supposed the several guandras out there that Erno had mentioned were probably of the smaller variety, and being such would probably just try to look menacing from a distance as they had done when she and Kasharel had first entered the region.

She turned back to Erno. "How far away is she?"

"Not very."

Deborah shrugged. "Let's go, then."

24

Deborah's first step over the line and into the dead lands was like a slap in the face. She almost lost her footing and fell, despite being on flat ground. All the air was pushed out of her lungs, and a heaviness blanketed over her as a shroud. She did well to not let the stick that held the sausage for the squatchamn girl go flying out of her hand.

"What?" She sputtered, gasping for breath. "It—wasn't—" she paused to try to suck enough air into her lungs to speak, "—like this before!"

"You sound weird," said Jacob, and his voice was garbled as though he spoke underwater.

She looked back at him standing with Kasharel and Nurrel on the grass strip in the neighbouring region. They appeared murky, indistinct, and she could hardly make out their faces. Oddly enough, there was more light in the region she stood in now. Sure, all the tree debris and dirt ground were like dry bones whitened under the sun, but it was definitely brighter.

"Erno," she gasped. "What's happened?"

"It's horrible, isn't it," he said.

There was nothing wrong with his voice, and he spoke easily enough. He also, she was relieved to see, looked brilliantly and wonderfully green, retaining all his vibrant mossiness.

"But it wasn't—like this before." Still hard to breathe, but it was getting easier.

"Yes, it was."

"No. I never experienced—anything like this—when Kash—and I—first came to this region."

"Oh? What is Iff's border like?"

"Bit greener. Not as bare. Still some trees with leaves. I think." It was hard to remember. There was a thinning of trees when she had left Iff's region, certainly, but it was not all dead and barren like it was here. "You met us—when we were still among—trees by the lake, didn't you?"

"Yes, but they were dead, too. Perhaps they were the last to let go and hadn't had the time to decay as they have done in this part of the region. If you didn't really feel the shock of crossing into this land, then I would guess that Iff's enchantments on you were stronger than I thought. He's always been a bit heavy-handed." Erno smiled. "It goes with his size; he's a giant in some respects."

She nodded. "Could use him—now. Can't you—shove some enchant—" she gulped for breath, "—ment on me?"

"Give it a moment; you'll adjust as I have."

"Are you all right?" Nurrel's voice, although it too was strangely distorted. "Do you think you should come back?"

Deborah shook her head. "I'm all right."

Erno chuckled.

She straightened up and sucked in breaths. The choking feeling was easing, the pressure on the chest lifting. She could cope with this. It wouldn't be for long. The squatchamn girl was not so far away, or so Erno said. "Okay. Let's keep moving."

Erno hopped slowly onward in small leaps to keep pace with her, deftly navigating across the dirt around and over the broken remains of trees.

"If this is all dead and you don't feel any Oxpeina-life thingy, then why don't you trip on things or bang into stuff?" Deborah asked.

He grinned. "I hear the reflection of sounds and feel the way the air moves around objects, or rather, stuff. For instance, see the larger lump of stuff over there?" He pointed to a heap of branches and tangle of dried brush in the distance.

From where Deborah stood, she thought it looked as though it had been gathered together, ready for a bonfire.

"Our squatchamn is behind it," said Erno. "I can hear her whispering as we approach."

"What's she saying?"

"Oh, bother. She's doing a spell."

"What?"

"She's trying to ward us off." Erno stood still, his brow furrowed. "Well, this isn't going the way I hoped. I don't understand why she would follow us all this way, then when she's so close to leaving this region, she wants us to leave her alone. Odd, odd stuff. Why do image-bearers have to be so complicated? Dwellers are so much easier."

She smiled at him. "I thought you were doing really well at understanding us and caring for us."

He turned a surprised face to her. "Well, thanks. I try." He shrugged. "Let's stand for a moment. I don't want her to run if we try to approach her too quickly."

"Shall I yell out to her?"

"It depends what you yell."

She felt her face grow hot with embarrassment. He was probably thinking of how she had yelled at Ibelli. "I won't tell her to shut up," she said quietly. "I'll just say hello."

He reached out and laid his hand on her arm. She had the impression he was sensing more from her in that touch as he had done another time.

"I wasn't referring to *that*," he said. "I was thinking if you yell 'come here' or 'we're coming to you' that might cause her to dash off. Depends how flighty she is."

Deborah looked towards the bonfire. "Is she still doing a spell?"

"Yes, she's repeating the same thing over and over. As if that'll help."

"Will it? I mean, Iff was able to put a spell on me."

He shook his head, rattling his twiggy hair. "Image-bearers don't have the ability to create enchantments. That is reserved for custodians, simply because we need it to guard our dwellers and image-bearers.

Some image-bearers mistakenly think they can do away with custodians and do the job themselves and somehow obtain their power. However, I warn you, that usually comes from a desire to control, not to care."

"I don't know why you're warning me—I'm not interested in that sort of thing. Why would I want to do away with you?"

"Says the image-bearer who ran away from me at Nurrel's village."

"Hey! What? I didn't know. I didn't mean any harm!"

He grinned. "I know, but the point is, there's the tendency in image-bearers to try to take control of everything around them. And that leads to all sorts of problems." He stiffened. "*Oop*. She's trying to slip away as we talk. Bother! Now the guandras are moving."

Deborah looked quickly about. There were no signs of movement in the parched land, just the sun-faded, splintered tree limbs and stumps littered about the dirt. "What guandras?"

"There're a few keeping distance from her as she keeps distance from us. They're moving closer. Don't worry."

"Shouldn't we get back to the other region?"

"It won't make any difference. Don't think the guandras can't cross into Hirahi's region, because they certainly can. No, there is something going on here that I can't quite fathom. The way they're moving, the fractured words I catch, and the squatchamn's behaviour make less and less sense to me. I had thought she was following us because she was drawn to our Oxpeina-life, but now I'm not so sure."

Deborah stiffened. In the distance, something had just darted out from behind a tree stump and gone behind a pile of branches. Or had it? Was it a trick of the eye? Everything was still again. No—there it was, another streak of movement, this time on the periphery of her vision. She turned her head to the right to see what it was. Then another, this time even further right, as though it danced on the edges of her sight. And, another. She quickly turned. She couldn't seem to see anything definite. Ha! There it was, again to the right.

"Don't do that," Erno said. "Stand still."

"But they're all around us. I can almost see them."

"Yes, I know, but I don't want you getting so focused on them that they catch you in a whirl. Guandras sometimes do that to try and hypnotise their prey. I've seen this happen to dwellers—especially birds—but I see no reason why they wouldn't try this tactic on an image-bearer, too."

Deborah looked at the skewered sausage in her hand. "How about I just throw this sausage to them, and they can fight over that and leave us alone?"

Erno burst into peals of laughter. Something in the atmosphere shrank back under the sound, and the air became clearer to breathe.

"I wasn't joking," Deborah said.

"I know," he said, and wiped his eyes. "*Ha! Phoo.* It made me imagine them as a bunch of scrawny chickens running after whoever has the sausage. *Hee!*"

The squatchamn girl suddenly emerged at the side of the scrub pile. She was very thin, her ragged clothing loose, and her hair clung lankly around her small face, emphasising her wide-eyed, red-rimmed stare. "That for me? Me? My? Food? Me, Debah, me?"

"I wasn't expecting that," Erno said, swivelling on his stump and squinting in her direction.

Deborah smiled at the girl and held the sausage out. "Yes, I've brought you something to eat. Come into the Hirahi region with us, and you can have it."

"No, I stay. No. Give to me."

Erno hopped forward and the girl flinched.

"Wait," he said firmly.

Deborah felt the influence of his command and stayed where she was, even though she was sure he had spoken to the girl. It reminded her of Iff and his commands, yet here she knew she could do what Erno said or not.

Erno hopped forward again. One more hop, and he would be right in front of the girl. "Wait," he said again.

The girl's red-rimmed eyes were wide and uncertain. "I—not… you—"

Erno quickly raised his hands. "Go away!"

The girl squealed and cowered against the scrub.

"Not you," Erno said. "I'm talking to the guandras."

The girl stood up. "No guandras here."

Erno harrumphed. "Yes, there are, and you know it. You brought them, didn't you?"

"No, I didn't, no, no. Why? No."

"Yes, why?" Erno said. "Don't lie to me. I can sense your intent very clearly now. In fact, I don't even need to touch you to sense it. The guandras promised you something if you could bring them another image-bearer, didn't they?"

The girl's gaze flicked to Deborah, then back at Erno. She grinned. "No, not? Nothing, what?"

"Lies," said Erno. "They lie to you. You will never have the power you see in the lake. Believe me. Let that go and come with us out of this cursed region!"

Deborah felt the tug on her heart at his words. Yes, she believed him whole-heartedly and yes, she wanted to immediately leave the region with him.

Yet the girl's grin did not falter. "You don't know. You don't know! I seen!

Erno raised his hands. "Away! I will defend her. I will defend both of them. Leave, now!"

There was a crackling sound. Deborah saw a small swirling mass of something, then two guandras appeared out in the open, a stone's throw away. Where they had come from, she didn't know, for they were not standing next to anything that could have hidden them previously. Wizened, scrawny figures, not quite there if she looked to the side of them, but commanding the space they held if she looked directly at them.

Although they had no faces, no distinguishing features, she had the horrible sensation that they were looking right at her. Not at Erno, not at the squatchamn girl, but her. Why? What did they want from her? It was hard to look away from them; she *should* look away from them, should walk away, should go back to the other region and the Oxpeina-life there.

Erno's hand lightly touched her arm, and she sucked in a deep breath of air, feeling as if she had been underwater, and this was the first breath she had taken upon emerging. She knew then that Erno could snap those guandras like twigs. He *would* snap them like twigs. He had dealt with bigger guandras, and these little ones were nothing in comparison. But then, Val and his pack had been the ones who had killed the guandras. Had Erno actually fought? Deborah had buried her face in Grufful's chest and not seen anything really, so maybe Erno hadn't done anything; maybe Val and his pack had done everything.

Another crackling sound. This time behind her. She quickly turned, so that Erno's hand dropped from her arm, to see two more guandras had appeared, still keeping their distance but also strangely fixated on her.

"There, go. There, she!" The squatchamn girl pointed at her.

Deborah turned and saw something behind the girl. Two more guandras? Yes. That made six. Could Erno handle six? Could she hit them with something? Drat this tiny stick in her hand. She needed something bigger to try and beat off these creatures.

"Deborah," Erno said and touched her arm again.

Her thumping heart calmed immediately.

"I need you to look at me. They will draw you away from me if they can."

It was difficult to look at him. She didn't want to. She wanted to keep watch on the guandras, make sure she knew where they were at all times, make sure she could see if they were moving in. They were all around. Six of them, just waiting to pounce.

"Deborah," Erno said. "Are you looking at me? I can't tell."

"Not yet," she said, her voice strained with the effort it took to speak.

"Come on," he said. "Look at me. Measly old guandras, I'll thrash them if they come any closer. Don't you worry about that. Sonax made me your custodian; I can't think why, but here I am—I'm right here with you, and I'll take care of you. I can put up an Oxpeina shield in an instant if need be."

His words drew her to him in that irresistible pull she was beginning to recognise had hints of Oxpeina-life threaded into it, and she looked at him, feeling the desire to hold his hand, touch his shoulder, keep a connection with him, her custodian. Her breathing slowed, even as she felt uneasy taking her eyes off the guandras. Those things, those guandras were going to close in on her. She needed to watch them, needed to make sure she was ready to fight when they… she exhaled. Erno. He stood, his arms flexed, the vibrant green moss spread across his broad face, covering his broad body and the leg that always made him appear planted where he stood. He was there. He was right there.

"Ah." He smiled. "You're less anxious. You see me? Good. Now, let's go back to the others. Come."

"Debah, come!"

The calm that had come over Deborah at Erno's words vanished, and she spun on her heel and fixed the squatchamn girl with a glare. "Shut up! What do you think you're doing? I come here, offering you this—" Deborah threw the sausage at the ground "—thinking you might be starving out here and find what? You've brought guandras with you? You're trying to put a spell on me?"

"Deborah," said Erno.

"What's the matter with you?" Deborah shouted at the girl. "Get out of this dump of a region!"

The girl shook her head. "No! You wrong. This region is power!"

"It is not!"

"Deborah," said Erno. "I just asked you to come with me, and instead you're yelling shut up and all sorts of other interesting things. Don't you trust me?"

"I wasn't telling *you* to shut up," she said. "I—"

He nodded, rattling his twiggy hair. "Yes, I know. Still, I'd like you to trust that I've got this under control. Let's go." He hopped away.

She felt the impetus of his words and went after him. As soon as she began to walk, she felt a sense of release, as though she stepped through something she hadn't been aware of and had snapped its hold.

"Girl of the squatchamn," Erno called over his shoulder. "You can come, too. Come home. You are from the neighbouring region, yes? Come with us."

Even if the squatchamn girl didn't feel the urge to follow Erno as he spoke, Deborah certainly did. She purposely stepped on each light imprint he left in the dirt as he jumped along. What in the world was going on? What had just happened? All of this didn't seem to make any sense. Erno had brought her back to this region to try and help that girl, try to encourage her to follow them the rest of the way out of the dead lands, and it turned out she had some other hidden agenda. Why all the guandras?

"No!" shrieked the girl. "Debah, back! I tell your father! I seen him!"

Deborah watched Erno leap into the air effortlessly and land, stirring puffs of dust with each impact. If only she could move that easily. Instead, she felt as though she had walked hundreds of miles—and, really, she could have for all she knew—and not got anywhere in particular except plunged deeper and deeper into a bizarre world. The longing for home rose up again. If only life would just go back to what it had been years ago, if she could blink and all of this craziness would disappear.

She trudged after Erno, lost in thought. Any fear that the guandras would come after her had gone, she simply watched Erno as she followed after him. She supposed she should be frightened as she thought about what the guandras looked like, how they had seemed so ready to close in on her, but Erno had turned his back to that nonsense, and so did she. He would hear if they tried to do anything.

Awful how that girl had brought Father into it again, saying that she had seen him. What was with that Silver Lake and its visions? It hurt to think of the vision she herself had seen of Father and to know it was all lies. He was miles away now. She had better get used to the fact he didn't care about her. That he had stopped caring after Mother's death.

Kasharel took her hand and helped her to step over the border of the regions and onto the grass. She didn't know she needed any help to step there, but no matter. Yes, it was all very nice to step back into the region again, to breathe the cool, fresh air; to hear the birdsong; to see the herd of rvenan grazing not far off; and to look at the faces of the others as they gazed earnestly at her. Except Jacob, he never looked earnest, only cross. Although she looked down at his beautiful, feathery owl face and realised there was a softening in his expression. He blinked his golden eyes at her while standing at her feet.

She looked away and stood there waiting. Waiting for the Oxpeina-life-thing to do what it was supposed to do, to fill her with a light-hearted vibrance. It didn't. The weight of sadness wasn't shifting.

"The girl would not come back with you?" Kasharel asked.

Deborah slowly shook her head. It was somewhat of a relief that he could think that was what she was unhappy about. There would be no questions about how she was, what was wrong, and all that pointless stuff. Jacob, she noted, still studied her. She could see out the corner of her eye that his face was upturned to her. Nurrel, meanwhile, went and sat by the dying embers of the fire. Perhaps her failure to bring the squatchamn girl was felt too much by him. Maybe he had even heard her shouting at the girl.

"No," said Erno. "She would not. I was mistaken in thinking she might come with us. I got close enough to her to feel her true intention. She was hoping to be rewarded by the guandras for bringing them an image-bearer."

"Rewarded, how?" Jacob asked.

"What guandras?" said Kasharel.

"I don't pretend to understand the ins and outs of how image-bearers think," Erno said. "Especially as the turning takes them. It's all power and control that are uppermost. So, what reward she was expecting, I can't say."

"The turning does not take them," said Nurrel, thrusting a stick into the embers and pushing them about. "They *choose* to turn. Don't think we image-bearers don't have any choice in the matter, because we do. Will we listen to reason? No. Will we think of our family? No." He snapped the stick over his knee and threw it onto the embers. He got up. "Enough of this. Let us go to Hirahi."

He stumped off across the grass towards the trees. Deborah scooped up Jacob and held him in the crook of her arm as she went after Nurrel.

25

The air was refreshingly cool beneath the wide, spreading branches of the trees. Birds of colours and sizes that Deborah had never seen before darted here and there. Bell-like song occasionally rang out in the forest to be answered by a distant refrain, while the buzz and chatter of insect life went on, flittering transparent wings that flashed gem-like blue.

At first, after the stillness and emptiness of the previous region, Deborah's senses were overwhelmed, but it was not long before she became accustomed to it and no longer felt she had to give attention to every little thing. The atmosphere settled into normality, and she walked onward with ease, holding the bundled-up Jacob in the crook of her arm.

No matter what Erno said, Deborah could not fathom any guandras daring to follow into this region. They did not, could not belong here. Erno looked right at home as he hopped along, the patches of sunlight that filtered through the trees flickering over his body. Kasharel's long brown robe looked slightly out of place, the cloth worn and dull compared with the rich, deep colours of the forest. Nurrel went on ahead without hesitation, the rust-red of his tunic and dark brown of his trousers in hues that seemed more fitting somehow.

Deborah wondered how she appeared and if she looked too much out of place. She was in dire need of a wash; her hair felt like a tangled mess, and her clothes probably looked like they had been dragged through the dirt repeatedly.

The ground sloped downward, and Deborah saw a glimmer of something through the trees. Water. The sparkle of water. As she went on, she could see it extended far and wide, shining like silver in the sun.

Her heart sank. "It's not another Silver Lake, is it?"

"No," said Erno. "This is Ekiple Lake, and it's good water."

She breathed a sigh of relief. As they went further on, yes, it did look different. It must have been a brief play of the light initially making her think of silver. As more of the lake came into view, it had the glassy, mirror-like look of pure water, and she felt no underlying enchantment compelling her to stare at it.

They soon emerged from the trees to a shingly shore. In the arc of the lake that curved to her left, there were scattered huts, some out on the water with wooden walkways, others clustered by the trees. They were the same design as those of the squatchamn, and she could see small figures—were they squatchamn folk?—moving about: someone hanging washing on a line, someone digging in a garden, children running. Little boats were out on the lake. Deborah stood and stared a moment. This was what the Silver Lake community should have been like—a hive of activity, not the numbness of a life spent staring at a cursed lake. It was so strange to think that the two lakes were not so far from each other.

On the distant shore, varying shades of green were smattered with autumn colour, the trees rising, falling, in the contours of low hills. Deborah thought of Father and the vision she had had of him while feeling the electricity of Oxpeina-life in the embrace of Grufful. Had that been a true vision? Was Father travelling through a region among the amber rusts of autumnal trees?

A plashing sound drew her attention. Nurrel had stripped to his undershorts and was wading out into the lake. Deborah was surprised to see the knotty muscles of his back; she had not realised he was of such a build. A large purple bruise was on his upper right arm, and he had removed the strip of cloth that he had been bandaged with after the guandra fight.

He dove under the water, then a moment later burst to the surface. "Woo! It's cold!"

Erno stood at the lake's edge, the water lapping gently around his leg. "Cold but good."

"I don't mind as long as it gets the guandra stink off me," Nurrel said, and ducked under again.

A long call echoed across the water, a high note that trailed off then became low. Erno laughed. He drew a deep breath and shouted a reply—another long note that ended low. The distant call came again. It stirred Deborah's heart. There was something in it—a joy, a familiarity, a fondness.

"That is my sister, Fothie," Erno said. "She has heard me."

"Is every brismun your brother or sister?" Deborah asked.

"Yes, indeed," said Erno.

He hopped along to the right, and Nurrel swam. Deborah noted the hint of distaste in Kasharel's expression as he gathered Nurrel's clothing and walked after Erno. Perhaps it still stunk somewhat. She clutched Jacob and walked along the shore, the water quietly lapping beside them.

She found her thoughts turning to Iff. Iff, the large boisterous brismun, and his anger at the Silver Lake's region and how he would go in there and sort it all out if he could—but only if Sonax told him to. Who was Sonax? Whoever he was, he seemed to organise the custodians and advise them of their duties, not only the brismuns but the rovi, too. Sonax had even sent Erno to be her custodian. How did he know about her? Had he been told about her when she entered the woods back at Shilhim? Had the trees or the birds somehow spread that information? Val had said Father wanted to find Sonax, and that's why he was heading to the city of Aric.

"Jacob," she said. "Who is Sonax?"

Jacob blinked crossly up at her. "I thought I'd told you that already. He is the Oxpeina."

"Oh yes, I remember, but what do you mean?"

"I mean that he's the ancient world-builder who holds all life."

Kasharel paused to walk in step with Deborah. "I like that reference. It conjures up an interesting image. You have... Jacob, you have really met Sonax?"

"Yes. As I told Rati, I came to life in his hand. That's truly how it felt to me. Have you not met him? Hasn't he been to your caves?"

"I think yes, but before I was born. I have only heard the tales. I have been meaning to travel to Hirahi and find my way, but did not have the time or opportunity until now."

Deborah glanced up at him. His grey eyes were thoughtful, and she felt he had more to say; that more was in his silence. Erno stomped ahead of them on the pebbly shore while Nurrel swam further out into the lake. The stomps echoed across the water, repeating thumps that seemed out of rhythm. Jacob turned his head. Deborah realised that the staccato of stomps were not merely Erno's and his echo, but they belonged to another brismun, too. She thought of the brismun who had attacked her when she had left the lumdil village. So, that had also been a brother or sister of Erno's.

Erno faltered and turned back to her. "Troubled breathing? What's wrong, Deborah?"

"*Um*, nothing. Your sister is safe? She won't harm us?"

He came to an abrupt stop, sliding a little in the shingle. "She will not. Why do you say that?"

She felt then that she should go to him, having a strange impulse to touch his hand or shoulder, but instead she stood clutching Jacob uncertainly. "Just thinking of the brismun who attacked me."

Erno's mossy face rumpled into a grimace. "Even we brismuns are not immune to the turning, and Rengo has had a very difficult region to oversee."

"Why do you say that?" Kasharel said.

Deborah heard the slight shift in the tone of his voice. Defensive, perhaps? Sensitive?

"Because there is a deep turmoil in that region," said Erno.

"This is my region you are talking about," Kasharel said. "I don't think you can say 'deep turmoil'. We have our conflict, as any region does, but we do our best to bring unity and balance back under such circumstances."

"And yet you, Kasharel, don't know who you are," Erno said. "How many more of your gehun are the same? I can easily enchant you if I want to, as did Iff. Isn't that right?"

Kasharel was silent, a contemplative look in his expression. He did not seem offended; Deborah thought he might have pressed his lips slightly and his eyes become harder if so. Instead, he appeared to be considering. The thumps of the approach of Erno's sister continued to ring out across the lake.

"It is a sorry, sorry thing when a brismun turns," Jacob said. "It is hard to comprehend."

"Yes," Erno said. "As much as it pains me to hear what has happened to him, and I admit I want to excuse Rengo after hearing what has gone on in his region, but I can't. Not really. It was his choice to make, and in it he found madness." He hopped towards Deborah. "If I did not say it before, I say it now. I'm sorry for what my brother Rengo did to you."

She looked into his mossy face, the squinting eyes almost closed, the faint, softly creased line of his mouth. In that moment, she felt something she had not felt for a long time. It arose in her heart as tears threatened to brim and spill from her eyes. *Love*. Erno was her custodian. Her very own. How curious to feel such a connection with him, a brismun, a creature that, as a child, she had believed was fable.

She swallowed and tried to push away the feeling, looked out to the lake at Nurrel swimming there, purposely widening her eyes to get them to dry up naturally so she would not have to wipe at them in front of anybody. The emotion was uncomfortable. Made her feel vulnerable. She didn't know why. She hoped Erno would not touch her arm gently as he often did. She would be all right. She was tired, that's all. Her body ached from the days of walking and nights of sleeping on the ground, and her shoulder—well, her shoulder still didn't feel quite normal. Erno was nice; yes, he was comforting to have around, but she didn't belong here in his world. Her home was back in Eblhim.

She shrugged and tried to force a smile at Erno. "It's all right. I'm doing well now. Let's keep on and get to your mysterious Hirahi. I need to find out where exactly Aric is and how to get there." As the words came out of her mouth, she wondered if she really had decided to go on to Aric in hopes of finding Father. But then, what else was she supposed to do? She needed time to think about things.

"*Yoi!*" came a shout.

Some distance away, a brismun bounded out from the trees and onto the shore. She sprang in great leaps, her arms raised, a wide grin on her face. Deborah thought if it had not been for Erno standing right next to her, she would have believed that this was him. The impression did not lessen as Fothie approached, even when she had come close and was standing right next to Erno. They reached for one another and clasped hands.

"Erno!" Fothie said. "You're here!"

Her voice was of a higher pitch than his. Deborah looked for differences in the way their twiggy hair grew, in the shades of green moss that covered their bodies, but could find nothing significantly noticeable. Maybe there would be something in their expressions, but as it was, they grinned at each other in mirror image then briefly bowed their heads to mingle their hair.

"I heard you were here a couple days ago," Fothie said, "and I was miffed you left without seeing me, but now here you are again. I've switched with Hemri to watch over these parts—we do that now and then. What are you doing here? I haven't seen you in ages!"

"I've brought those in my care to Hirahi," Erno said.

"Those? You have one owl, no more that I can sense nearby. I sense only my dwellers in the trees."

Erno grinned. "I have two image-bearers."

"Get out! Image-bearers? You? What! That's crazy!"

"Yes, you are," Erno said.

"Shut up, you!" Fothie said.

"Get out of my way. We're going to Hirahi."

"You get out!"

With that, they leapt off together, bounding along the shoreline as if in a race.

Deborah turned to Kasharel. "I guess we just follow?"

"I guess," he said, a twitch at the corner of his lips as he watched Erno and Fothie.

"I'm sure they'll be back," said Jacob. "Besides, I know the way from here. Just keep walking until we get to the river."

26

Nurrel pulled a face and held his tunic away from himself. "I think I'll leave this off; it needs a good wash." He sat on the grassy bank and pulled on his socks and shoes.

Maybe it was simply the cream colour of his long-sleeved shirt that made him appear brighter, but Deborah thought the swim had done him good—he seemed more at ease. She turned to Kasharel as they stood at the edge of the wide river, its waters flowing slowly by as it fed the lake. There were more rvenan cattle across on the far side grazing the grass there and a squatchamn boy sitting on the bank, a fishing pole in his hand. "Now, what? Where have Erno and Fothie got to?"

"I hear them," said Jacob. "They're not so far from us in amongst the trees, standing talking as far as I can make out."

The scent of sweet, woodsy resin was in the air. Deborah looked over her shoulder. The trees there were of a different sort than what she had seen before, straight, in regimented rows, circular marks on their trunks as though the lower branches had been cut, while the upper branches all grew out from the same height. A few long-legged birds were stalking about, digging at the ground with their beaks, but Deborah couldn't see the brismuns amongst the low, scattered undergrowth.

"Shall we keep walking?" Kasharel asked. "If Hirahi is upriver, then they can catch us up."

"I suppose we could," said Nurrel. "Although I would rather wait for Fothie to send for a ride for us." He lay back and closed his eyes.

Deborah sat on the bank a few paces away from him. "I'd be glad of any chance of a ride. I'm tired of walking."

"A ride on what?" Kasharel tucked his robe about him and sat beside her. "A boat?"

Jacob turned his head to gaze up at him. "*Hoo.* If you're lucky, it will be a boat."

Nurrel smiled.

"Whatever do you mean?" Kasharel asked.

"Drat!" said Jacob. "I can't fly. Well, you'll hold me, won't you, Deborah? I don't want that thing holding me."

She stared down at him. "What thing?"

"You'll see."

"No. You tell me now—what thing?"

The muffled stomps of Erno and Fothie came from under the trees, and they leapt into view. Deborah studied them again, trying to tell them apart. Perhaps something in the posture and expression of the one on the left was Erno?

"Don't worry about it, Deborah," he called. "Ubsies are very gentle."

She was correct; it was him on the left. She smiled.

"And, slimy," said Jacob.

"Slimy?" Fothie said. "No. They're really not." She hopped over to Jacob and held out her hand. "Come, little one. You've suffered, and I can help you."

Jacob immediately wriggled free of Deborah's jersey and leapt up to perch on Fothie's hand. He did it so quickly Deborah wondered if he had obeyed the command to do so and hadn't really thought about what he was doing. She certainly felt the instinctive pull and found herself leaning towards Fothie. Deborah watched as Fothie felt along Jacob's wings and around his body.

"Tell me what happened," Fothie said.

"Guandras," said Jacob.

"Yes, but I want to know how it happened to you who are with Oxpeina's life."

"They were going to attack."

"Say again?"

Jacob bowed his head. "I was afraid they were going to attack. I thought they were going to attack Deborah; I really did think they were. I wanted to stop them, distract them."

Deborah was astonished. "Jacob, what are you saying? You mean you put yourself in harm's way for me?"

"Maybe," he mumbled. "Didn't think it would go this far with my feathers; just wanted to lead them away, that's all. Fortunately, they dropped me when they heard the custodian of the region coming, so I was able to escape."

Fothie looked thoughtful. "It was done with love and fear. Hold still. This might hurt a little."

She deftly turned Jacob this way and that, her green fingers moving quickly, firmly, kneading and rubbing his body. Jacob let out a squawk and shut his eyes.

"What are you doing to him?" said Kasharel.

Erno squinted in Kasharel's direction. "You sound like you think Fothie's trying to dismember him."

"Well," said Kasharel. "It doesn't look very nice."

Fothie said nothing to him but whispered over Jacob and continued to manipulate his body.

"*Well*," said Erno, "that may be so, but Fothie is using the Oxpeina touch to bring on Jacob's feather growth. Otherwise he'll be stuck like this for many months."

"*Urk*," said Jacob.

"Almost done," said Fothie.

Deborah was disappointed to not see feathers magically springing up before her eyes. Instead, Jacob looked rather worse for wear, with pink splotchy skin and his remaining feathers in even more disarray, if that was possible. She wrapped him in her jersey again, as he was shivering, and kissed his head.

"*Oik!*" He swivelled his head to look up at her in surprise.

She pretended to not notice.

"Now," said Fothie. "Who's next?"

"Deborah," said Erno. "Take a look at her right shoulder."

Deborah shrank back. "I don't know… "

"Come here," said Fothie, beckoning. "No, wait, hang on, just stay sitting there 'cause you're a big lass and I don't think I could reach up to your shoulder if you stood."

Before Deborah could protest, Fothie's hands were on her, and a warmth spread from the firm brismun fingertips and seeped into her shoulder joint and around her neck. It felt pleasant until Fothie's fingers suddenly dug in.

"Who did this?" Fothie said, a note of alarm in her voice.

"Rengo," Erno said.

"What? No! What's the matter with him? When I see him again, I'm going to give him a piece of my mind. How dare he do this to an image-bearer! How dare he even think about turning away from Sonax?"

"Calm down, Fothie."

"*Ugh!*" she retorted.

Her fingers became less violent in their manipulation of Deborah's shoulder, and she leaned in closer and whispered. Deborah thought she caught a word or two, possibly 'Sonax' and 'Oxpeina', but wasn't sure if it was all in the brismun language or also included the shared common language. The warmth was still there with Fothie's touch, and with it came an easier feel, a loosening, a relaxing of muscles. Deborah realised she had been used to a perpetual dull ache or stiffness.

"Thank you," she said when Fothie had finished, and shrugged her shoulder experimentally. It definitely felt lighter.

"No problem," Fothie said. "Next!"

"That would be me," Nurrel said.

Fothie turned. "Would it? What's wrong with you?"

Nurrel unbuttoned his shirt and exposed his bandaged arm. "Just a wound on my arm from a guandra."

"You surprise me, you who know very well who you are, image-bearer!"

Deborah cast a sidelong glance at Kasharel. This was not the first time that it had been said directly or implied to her that she didn't know who she was. What were they going on about in this strange land? She was Deborah Lakely of Eblhim, daughter of… She stared at the ground. May as well be the daughter of no one.

"Yes, right," said Nurrel. "I know it shouldn't have happened. I had… well, I had things on my mind when we were attacked by guandras."

"Grief," said Fothie, as she investigated his arm, her fingers moving lightly along the bruising. "Shock and grief gave them a crack, an access through the shielding of Oxpeina."

Nurrel's brow furrowed. "Yes, I—yes, that's right. You're spot on."

Fothie shook her head, her twiggy hair rattling. "I'm not saying mourning is wrong. You know that, don't you? Just be careful how you let it affect you. Don't let it be your ruler."

Nurrel took a deep breath, his face serious. "I know," he said quietly.

Jacob wriggled and muttered. "Deborah. You're holding me too tightly."

"No, I'm not," she said.

"Yes, you are. It hurts."

She loosened the jersey about him. "Maybe this is too tight."

"No. It's you. Your fingernails are digging in."

"No, they're not."

"No, they're not," echoed Fothie, grinning back at Jacob. "Your skin will be feeling sensitive with the new growth of feathers. Think of it as your moult season times a hundred and happening in a short burst instead of taking months."

Erno chuckled. "Times a hundred?"

"Something like that!"

Deborah unwrapped Jacob a little to take a look at him. He eyed her crossly. Spread across his belly skin were what appeared to be a multitude of goosebumps. She covered him up again.

"Thank you for that," Nurrel said to Fothie as he buttoned his shirt.

"I know very well you didn't have to give me a gift of health to my arm. I know it was my fault that I let the wound happen in the first place."

Fothie slapped him soundly on his arm, right where the wound had been. Deborah winced, but Nurrel, she was surprised to see, smiled.

"These things happen," Fothie said. "We none of us get things right a hundred percent of the time because we all grapple with the turning."

"I have learned something new," said Erno.

Everyone looked expectantly at him while he stood still with a solemn expression.

"I have learned that Fothie's favourite number is one hundred."

Fothie guffawed, and Erno's face split into a wide grin. They leapt away as one and shoved at each other in mid-air. Each still landed sure-footedly on the slopes of the grassy bank, and they bounded on together.

"*Huh*," said Jacob. "They seem happy."

His tone was gruff, and Deborah thought he looked crosser than ever. She carefully shifted the way she was holding him, trying to ease any pressure she might inadvertently be causing. "Perhaps we can get you some kind of balm for your skin at Hirahi."

"If we ever get there," he muttered. "We're wasting the morning away. First with that silly squatchamn in the dead region, and now we've got to this river, there isn't even a ride waiting for us. You'd think there was no communication going on in these parts."

Nurrel sat on the bank and gazed out over the river. "I think Fothie has been too busy catching up with Erno to call on her shaseeliany to get a ride for us. Erno did have a lot to tell Fothie about, and she may not have known about Senka's death. So, I think we can allow them some time together. I am in no hurry." He sighed, a faraway look in his soft eyes. "It is simply a relief to be here in this region again."

Kasharel sat near him. Deborah wanted to sit beside Nurrel, too, but went and sat on the other side of Kasharel. Most likely, Nurrel still might not want her too near. She looked down at the mouth of the river where it met the lake.

The brilliant blue, cloud-daubed sky, and the curves of the tree-clad hills were reflected in its wide expanse. Speckled white waterfowl milled about the shore, some wading in the water while others paddled, and further out onto the lake, a few boats were dotted about. Deborah thought that on the distant shore she could make out more signs of civilization—huts perhaps, a lower sloping hill with green pasture. Other than that, she was relieved to feel that the lake was just that, a lake, and it held no particular fascination for her other than it being much larger than anything she had seen back home in Eblhim. The three lakes there were surrounded with housing, industrial buildings and were not as pristine looking. And there were not many trees in Eblhim. There was a park near home that Father had often gone to, to sit on a bench there beside his favourite tree—not that there had been very many trees to choose from in that park.

It all seemed such a long time ago. It had been there, on that bench, that he had told her of his wish to move to Shilhim and his desire to find peace, find escape from the city. She had never even heard of Shilhim, but she remembered feeling glad that he was talking to her, that he was sharing something of his thoughts with her. Of course she would move there with him. Why not? If it would help him, then they could spend that time together in a village on the edge of the woods, on the edge of nowhere. She was surprised he had found a house already for them to go to—when had he done that? Dirt cheap, too. She thought of the shack in Shilhim and wrinkled her nose. No wonder.

She sighed and stretched. He hadn't taken long to up and leave her there. What did he think she was going to do there all by herself? Or, did he think she would just return to Eblhim? Maybe she should have.

Jacob shifted uncomfortably, his eyes shut, and made a grinding sound with his beak. Deborah thought if an owl could grimace, that was what he was doing. She lifted the jersey and took a peek. The goosebumps now had dark spots in their centres. She covered him up again and resisted the urge to stroke him. That would probably only irritate him further.

Kasharel gasped.

Deborah turned to see what had startled him. A blue-green man had appeared beside the river, his filmy raiment clung dripping about him, his hair long and flowing, shimmering and refracting the light. He looked intently up at them.

"Must be Fothie's shaseeliany," Jacob muttered. "About time!"

For a moment, Deborah thought her heart was beating loudly, for she was taken aback by the shaseeliany's sudden appearance, then the sound crystallised into the rhythmic thumps of Erno and Fothie's return. The shaseeliany turned his gaze to them and nimbly, lightly, as if hardly touching the earth, walked to the top of the riverbank. As he moved, the light shifted around him so that he had brief moments of appearing almost translucent.

Fothie beamed at him. "Hello, my love."

His returning smile, amongst the glistening contours of his face, was warming to the soul. His eyes were pure and reflective, lakes in miniature. He bent and took her hand. They made an interesting pair, the one rounded and green in bushy earth, the other tall and flowing of water, yet when they touched they were one harmonious whole.

Deborah thought of Iff and Sar. Was it the case that to every brismun there was a shaseeliany? If so, where was Erno's?

"You called me," the shaseeliany said, and his voice was reminiscent of a brook, of a waterfall, of intermingled notes that converged into words.

"Get right to the point, why don't you?" Fothie said. "No, 'hello dearest, how are you?', even though we haven't seen each other for a few days. Where've you been?"

"You're the one who moved and didn't tell me," he answered.

Fothie pressed a finger to her mouth. "Did I? Oops!"

Erno grinned.

"I only found this out from Hemri and Shis when they moved in," the shaseeliany said. "Shis wanted to see my work on the dam and also to show her where I thought the northern ubsies should winter this year and the preparations I'd started making there."

Fothie looked dismayed. "Oh! Did I move us too soon? Hemri and I thought now would be a good time to switch."

"Some consultation wouldn't go amiss at this time of year, although I suspect we both have many seasonal changes throughout the year to manage as it is. I'm interested to see what Shis has done in these parts since we were last here, and already I'm pleased to see she didn't redo my work at the bottom of the lake but instead built further on it and strengthened its productiveness.

"I think she has thinned out some of the plants a touch more than I would do, and I may have to rebalance some of the algae on the western side of the lake. Also, she advised me of one sick ubsy, so I will continue her treatment of it and perhaps bring in something new that I have thought of in encouraging their health."

Deborah wondered if he would ever pause for breath, but the words flowed on. Kasharel, Nurrel, and Jacob were watching him—they were probably as dazzled by his gift of the gab as she was—while Fothie and Erno were all grins. Erno, in particular, had his eyes shut and was looking highly amused.

"Fish are looking good so far from what I can tell, and I have yet to talk to the squatchamn on the east side to find out how things are going for them and whether they are happy with what they are being supplied with, as although I don't think they are overfishing, it wouldn't hurt them to ease up somewhat at this time of year, and Shis also advised me of a problem with snails—"

Deborah began to feel as though she was losing concentration on what he was saying as the sound of his speech had a sleep-inducing quality. She stared up at him, for there was also something soothing about watching his animated face as he spoke and the way his clothing—or whatever it was that he wore because it all seemed to be a part of him—constantly reacted to the slightest move he made or rippled in the breeze.

When Fothie spoke, it brought Deborah back to earth with a grounding bump.

"I'm sure you'll sort it all out, and no doubt you'll enjoy doing it. Shessi, I should introduce Erno's friends. There's Nurrel, thing, and the other one." Her eyes crinkled up in mirth and disappeared amongst the moss.

Erno laughed heartily, louder than Deborah had ever heard him before.

Fothie elbowed him. "You can fill in the blanks; you said their names so quickly before, and I was distracted. Everyone, Shessi is my other half in our unity. We are currently watching over this part of the region which also includes Hirahi, so if you have any concerns, bring them to us."

"Now you sound very official," said Erno, grinning.

Fothie grinned back, for a fleeting moment appearing as his mirror image, then assumed a serious expression. "I would like to inform you all that from time to time we have been experiencing guandra incursions, so if you notice anything untoward or anything that—"

Shessi laid a fluid hand on her hair. "What? Have you really been experiencing guandra incursions? When? What happened? Shis never said anything about that. You'll tell me if you're in danger, because I can protect you. Remember how I told you that Sonax taught me more defensive manoeuvres and also increased my powers? So, I am not foremost vulnerable to the guandras, despite that having been the usual plight of my kind."

Fothie blinked up at him. "Shis really should have told you about the guandras. We need a good catch up, but we'll have to talk all about it later. Right now, these poor things need to get to Hirahi. They're in dire need of a bath."

Deborah thought if Fothie had a nose, she sounded as though she would have wrinkled it in distaste at that moment. She supposed she, Kasharel, and Nurrel probably did have the aroma of those who had spent too much time in the neighbouring region.

"Get an ubsy, would you?" Fothie said. "Are there any close by?"

Shessi pointed at the river behind him. "There are two down there right now. It's interesting—one of them is especially curious about *thing*."

He smiled at Deborah, and his expression was all warmth and kindliness, with an impression of seeing deeply into her. It was very like some of the looks the rovi had given her. She stared at the ground. These custodians were strange. Why did they look at her like that?

"I understand why," he said. "There is something curious about you."

Deborah realised Shessi actually meant her when he said *thing*. She looked at the river. There was nothing out of the ordinary down there, just a few birds, and the squatchamn boy was still fishing on the far bank, the rvenan cattle grazing behind him.

Jacob wriggled in her arms. "Don't want an ubsy," he muttered, his eyes still tightly shut. "No, no, don't let it touch me."

Shessi shifted his limpid gaze to him. "Are you afraid it will squeeze the life out of you? I suppose that's a real possibility, given that you are so small and light and an ubsy has a strong grip. They're more used to tearing plants and shifting rocks, not to mention wrestling with each other, and as I have seen many times they—"

"Not to worry," said Fothie brightly. "Deborah will hold you, Jacob, and the ubsy will hold her. No problem. Shessi?"

He spun and backflipped, leaping in a high arc across the steep bank to land in the river with barely a splash. Moments later, shapes were seen moving to the surface, and a sleek marbled grey-and-white head slowly emerged, round black eyes blinking, a whiskered muzzle twitching and sniffing the air, the widening neck hinting of a large body beneath the water. Bubbles foamed and churned around the ubsy as it looked up at the bank.

Deborah had never seen anything like it and could only stare back in surprise. Then up came another, this time speckled white and brown. The two of them bobbed there together, silently eyeing Deborah and the others standing on the bank, the waters frothing and stirring around them.

Shessi appeared upstream of the ubsies, gliding about like a fish. "Ready!"

"Ready, he says," said Fothie, "as if it's the most natural thing in the world. Well, go ahead." She motioned to Nurrel. "Have you done this before?"

Nurrel nodded. "Yes, Erno and I were carried by ubsy a couple of days ago." His brow furrowed. "It seems such a long time ago. I can hardly believe we were here so recently."

"A lot has happened since then," Erno said.

Sorrow crossed Nurrel's expression. "Yes. Right, well, yes. Here I go." He took a running leap off the edge of the bank.

Deborah gasped. He could not possibly reach the water! Surely, he would fall down the bank instead. "Nurrel!"

Her cry had barely left her lips when two long tentacles whipped out of the water and caught him mid-air. One of the ubsies gave a grunt of satisfaction, while the other looked approving.

Jacob shuddered. "*Ugh*."

The ubsy's tentacles swiftly wrapped around Nurrel's midriff and held him dangling above the river.

"Ready!" called Shessi again.

Erno took a giant bound into the air, and another tentacle shot out of the water and caught him neatly.

"They're very good," said Kasharel. "Very precise aim. How do they manage it?"

"Don't ask me," said Fothie. "Shessi would know, as he's been working with them for years. We didn't used to have them in this lake, but it's nice that we do and to know that they're there."

"Ready!" came the cry from the river.

Fothie turned to Deborah. "Would you like to go next?"

Jacob hissed and burrowed further down under the jersey.

Fothie laid her hand on him. "Don't fuss. You're perfectly safe. Shessi won't let anything happen to you—the ubsies love him and will do anything he says." She squinted up at Deborah. "This might be a little awkward, but I suggest you jump while holding Jacob up over your head. Less chance for the ubsy to catch you around your arms. Think you can do that?"

Deborah went and stood at the edge of the bank and looked down. Sure, take a flying leap at a weird river creature while holding an owl over her head. No problem. She backed up several paces. "I think I'll have to take a run at it. I don't know if I can jump very far. I don't seem to have much strength right now."

"Would you like me to fling you?" Fothie asked.

Deborah saw the amused glint in Kasharel's eyes. "You'd like to see that, wouldn't you," she said to him.

A smile twitched at the corner of his lips. "Yes, I think so."

"Ready!" cried Shessi again.

"*Hup*," said Fothie. "The ubsies must be getting impatient."

Deborah sighed and held Jacob up over her head. He hissed again. "Go ahead," Deborah said to Fothie. "Fling away."

Fothie pressed a finger to her mouth. "I have to think about the logistics of this—you being tall, me being short, my arms, your arms, Jacob." She grinned. "Kasharel, you'd better go next while I consider how to do this."

Kasharel gave a slight nod. Deborah was amused to watch him hike up his robe and take a running leap off the bank. In the blink of an eye, one of the ubsies' tentacles lunged up and grabbed him.

"They move amazingly fast," Deborah remarked.

"*Hmm*, yes?" Fothie said, looking thoughtful.

"Can't they just pick me up if I walk a bit further down the bank, closer to the river?" Deborah said. "That way I don't have to jump, and you don't have to fling me."

"Where's the fun in that?" Fothie said, grinning.

Despite her weariness and all the things that were weighing on her heart, Deborah found herself smiling back. Brismuns seemed to have a way of making her do that, yet it always felt strange to smile, as if she shouldn't somehow after everything that had happened. She sighed.

Fothie lightly touched Deborah's arm. "Oh. I hear that sigh. Everything will be all right. Sonax-Oxpeina will sort things out."

"Ready!" came the cry from the river.

Deborah looked at Nurrel, Erno, and Kasharel swaying to and fro above the water in the ubsies' grip.

"We're not exactly ready!" Fothie called back. "Distract them with something, will you?"

Shessi disappeared underwater, and the ubsies lurched forward after him. They travelled up the river a ways, the three in their tentacled grasp dangling overhead, while Deborah and Fothie stood together on the bank.

"You will know who you are soon enough," Fothie said to Deborah. "Things will become clear to you then."

Deborah looked down at her earnest face, the flicker of pupils like sparks of energy in the near-closed eyes. She was so much like Erno, but the more time she spent with the two brismuns, the more Deborah saw the nuances in their expressions, the way their twiggy hair grew, the subtle shades of moss. Deborah supposed Fothie was talking about image-bearers and how she was one of them. Iff had shown her clearly she was too susceptible to any magic of the custodians and that if she 'knew who she was' that wouldn't be the case. Sonax had something to do with all of that. Was that why Father was searching for him?

"You sigh again," said Fothie softly. "Erno has told me something of the heavy load you carry. Family can be such a pain in the butt sometimes, can't they."

"*Hoo!*"

Deborah wanted to laugh, too. "Yes, mine's not great. I'm still trying to figure out how to deal with it all."

"There's good food and a warm bed at Hirahi," Fothie said. "Recover something of yourself there and then make your plans. I know Erno will stay with you. I've not seen him so dedicated to someone. Well, not for a long while, anyhow."

Deborah looked over at the river. The ubsies were slowly returning. There was something ridiculous about the waving tentacles and the three held in their grasp.

"Come," said Fothie. "Perhaps Shessi can get an ubsy to pick you up. They do love to catch things, but if we do as you suggest and move closer to the water, I'm sure he can explain to them what to do."

27

"They can't, really, and shouldn't," said Shessi as he stood at the top of the bank with Fothie and Deborah. The sunlight shone and refracted off him, causing him to appear many-hued in greens and blues with hints of gold. "They've been taught they're not to pluck dwellers and image-bearers off boats or off the land. Otherwise, they'd go about doing it whenever and wherever to satisfy their curiosity. One of them wanted to pull Nurrel down when he was swimming in the lake to get a better look at him, and—"

"It's just that Deborah is feeling weak and unable to jump," Fothie said. "She's very tired."

"Can't you just pick her up and make the jump yourself?" Shessi said. "I'm sure the ubsies can manage to catch you both at once, and then they'll separate you out to make it easier to hold onto you. They have a lot of dexterity in their limbs; sometimes it's fascinating to watch them peel the—"

"Why didn't I think of that?" Fothie said. "That's a good idea."

"—leaves off the tinka vines and make knots." Shessi turned back to the river. "I don't think it's simply that they play with their food; I think they genuinely believe it makes the vines taste nicer." He started to drift down the bank as if his feet were sliding across the earth, his long flowing garments shimmering around him. "Then again," he said, his voice growing quieter as he moved further away, "there is something to be said for a meal that has been presented attractively and how it enhances the eating experience; sometimes the mind is drawn to certain colours and shapes, and that affects the appetite and I know that I like—"

Fothie grinned. "He does that sometimes," she said to Deborah. "He's thinking and doesn't realise he's still speaking aloud."

"What's that, my love?" Shessi called over his shoulder. "I hope you're ready, for the ubsies are itching to get going."

Deborah looked at the ubsies. They didn't seem in any hurry whatsoever, for they eyed her mildly as they floated, their tentacles underwater stirring eddies, while Erno, Kasharel, and Nurrel were held overhead. Deborah noticed the three were held more closely together and were chatting.

"All right!" Fothie answered.

Deborah checked that Jacob was wrapped securely, and Fothie picked her up. There was a quick, slight crouching movement, then Fothie launched into the air, taking Deborah's breath away and making her feel she had left her stomach behind. Just as quickly, tentacles caught about her in a wet elastic grip, and Fothie and Deborah sank almost immediately as if their combined weight was too much. Deborah saw the river rushing up to meet her, and her feet and legs splashed in, soaking her shoes and trousers. She shrieked, expecting to go underwater, but there was a grunt from an ubsy, and she and Fothie were thrust upward.

Then it was a blur of tentacles, probing, wrapping, turning her, patting her head, the aroma of fish, a firmness grasping around her middle, Jacob squawking and struggling in his bundle while she tried to hold him but found her arms were pinned, and then… stillness. Her arms were free; she looked down at bands of the grey-and-white marbled tentacles that bound her snugly from chest to hip. She felt surprisingly comfortable if a little wet—for the tentacles were somewhat slimy, as Jacob had feared. Her arms rested against the tentacles, and while she did still have hold of Jacob, there was also one small loop around him as well. She hoped he would not notice, for he was burrowed down in the jersey with the top of his head barely showing.

"You all right?" she said to him. "We're okay, we're secure."

"*Huh.*"

They lurched forward, and Deborah looked down to see Shessi swimming ahead while the ubsies followed. There was a popping sound some distance below her feet, and she saw the ubsy that held her had its muzzle half underwater and was blowing bubbles. It looked up at her as if sensing her gaze, and the bubbles ceased. The round black eyes grew inquisitive as the thin nostrils flared and contracted, the whiskers quivering. The ubsy tried to turn its head to look at Deborah the right way up, for they were staring at each other upside down, then instead drew her down and around in front of it so that her feet almost touched the water again. The ubsy blinked at her then gave a great yawn, showing little sharp teeth. There was a translucent flash in the water, and Deborah realised it was Shessi swimming by. The ubsy looked sideways at him, gave a shrug and a snort, then raised Deborah back up alongside Fothie.

"She likes you," Fothie said.

"Deborah has that affect on dwellers," Erno said.

"Oh, that's nice," said Fothie. "You must have the Oxpeina's touch, Deborah. From what I understand, that's not always so common for image-bearers."

Deborah didn't know what to say in return, as both brismuns were smiling at her as if she should know exactly what they meant and that it was somehow something special and a privilege. Jacob grumbled and wriggled again, so she pulled down the jersey to check on him. This time there were banded brown and white spikes protruding from his bare patches of skin. He scowled at her, and she covered him up.

"Your feathers are coming through," she said.

He muttered unintelligibly.

The popping sounds resumed as the ubsy began blowing bubbles once more.

The riverbanks smoothly slid by as the ubsies gathered speed, the water churning and frothing around them. Shessi darted around and ahead, sometimes surfacing to speak to Fothie, sometimes diving and disappearing. Deborah idly listened to Kasharel and the others chatting, not always catching everything they said depending on the swaying of the tentacles and how far away she was held from the others. Not that she minded. It was a relief to not have to do anything. No more walking for now. The ubsy was doing all the work, and she was held snugly.

The river wound through forested land, more grassy clearings where small herds of rvenan grazed, and squatchamn huts lay with areas of crops. Some of the squatchamn turned to look at the passersby.

Before long, the river widened and was divided by a wedge-shaped promontory cutting through the water like the bow of a ship. The grass and scattered trees of the land soon gave way to a steep, high rock face. As she drew nearer, Deborah could see windows dotted here and there in the rock. An immense stone building was perched atop, its sandy grey colours blending so that she found it difficult to tell where the rock ended and the building began. If it had not been for the dark amber pitched roof, she might not have seen it at all but thought it just another protrusion of rock.

"Is that Hirahi?" she asked Erno, who was nearest to her, although she felt she already knew the answer.

"Yes, indeed."

She felt a twinge curling inside her, part apprehension, part relief, along with the feeling of actually getting somewhere in this as yet unsuccessful search. She would decide what to do from here. Whether to go on to the city of Aric or to let go of the pull of finding Father. How could she let go of that? By accepting he didn't want her. Not, really. He was leading his own life, and that didn't include her. She should tell herself that over and over, and maybe it would help her to let go. But was he in his right mind? He hadn't been himself for a long time. Maybe he was still not thinking clearly, and she would be able to help him. Then again, shouldn't he love her enough to want her?

She bowed her head and blinked away the tears that threatened.

28

"Let her go," said Shessi again.

The ubsy blinked as if weighing up his words and deciding whether or not she would obey, then moved Deborah an inch closer to her face. Deborah was held horizontally; more of the ubsy's tentacles had wrapped around her body so as to hold her securely in this position. She felt rather stupid that she was the only one who hadn't been set onto the ground but was instead being studied as though she was some great curiosity.

"Have you never seen someone my size before?" Deborah said to the ubsy. "You can't hold onto me forever."

The ubsy's eyes grew soft and adoring as if thrilled Deborah was speaking to her, and she dipped a little lower into the water and blew bubbles.

"She has certainly seen image-bearers your size," said Fothie, who stood at the water's edge. "Several, in fact. Let her go, you nit!"

"It's not going to eat her, is it?" Jacob said.

He was perched on Kasharel's shoulder, his bare patches bare no longer but covered in mottled brown spikes. Deborah suspected that when the ubsy had offloaded him, he had gone to Kasharel merely because he was the tallest of the group and therefore furthest from the water.

The ubsy gave a startled grunt and looked over at Jacob as if affronted by such an idea.

"Probably not," said Shessi.

Deborah stared at him as he swam breaststroke around the ubsy. "What do you mean, *probably?*"

"I mean probably, as it's been a long time since an ubsy showed an interest for meat, they're more keen on fish and greenery and the odd snail, especially if it's a large, juicy snail, and, oh yes, of course, the lake crawlers if they're small enough and their shells haven't developed fully—"

"My irresistible fishy-man," said Fothie, "get the ubsy to let go of Deborah. This is ridiculous."

Shessi dove in a flash of pale blue and disappeared in the depths. Deborah could see the ubsy's swirling tentacles closer to the surface and something of the plump grey-and-white marbled body. The ubsy glanced from side to side as if wondering where Shessi had gone. She lowered herself slowly until her head was underwater, and Deborah recoiled and tried to wriggle free. The water was so close, any moment her face would be right in.

"Hey!"

"It's okay," said Fothie. "That's a good sign. She's gone under to listen properly to Shessi."

Deborah was about to retort that it didn't feel like a good sign when she was whisked upright and over to the river's edge. The tentacles swiftly unwound from her body as Nurrel took her hand to steady her and help her onto dry land. She looked at him, wondering why he would help her, but he was looking out across the water, a distant expression on his face as if far away in thought. It reminded her too much of Father.

Nurrel briefly squeezed her hand, then let go. That simple gesture was surprising—it showed an awareness that he knew she was there. She swallowed hard. How many times had Father acted as if she were not there?

They walked the grassy slope that led to the base of the rock, passing the occasional tree that stood alone as a showpiece of autumn's splendour of red and amber. Clusters of round, flat-leafed vines grew a short way up the rock and were smattered with pale gold flowers that looked as though they were past their best.

"This is an interesting formation," Kasharel remarked. "Standing alone as it is."

"There are more further into the region," Fothie said as she and Erno hopped slowly together in unison. "I suppose as a gehun you would find them fascinating. We also have some underground caves that used to be inhabited, but this is the largest outcrop."

"Inhabited? By who?"

"More of your kind, but they moved on many years ago. This region has been active in the migration for quite some time, although not as markedly as it is now."

"I did not know that," said Kasharel. "I had not heard of a gehun community being here. I wonder why that information is not in our records?"

Jacob made a hissing, grumbling noise in his throat, and Deborah instinctively reached up to Kasharel's shoulder so he could step onto her hand. His taloned feet closed around her fingers, and she drew him to herself. He bowed his head to his chest and nibbled the spikes of feathers there as if trying to tease them into opening out.

"There seem to be many things in our brother's region that are wrong and souring," Erno said. "Is there noticeable conflict present in the image-bearers there?"

"Conflict?" Kasharel's brow furrowed slightly. "I suppose—no, I shouldn't think so. That is what the council has been working hard on eliminating. We did have conflict at one time, yes, but it is not spoken of so much now, and we do strive for unity."

"Strive and work?" said Fothie. "That sounds difficult and as if there is something brewing underneath that needs addressing."

"Perhaps," said Kasharel.

Deborah thought he sounded uncertain.

"How about you, Deborah?" Fothie asked. "Where is your region and how is it faring?"

Deborah shrugged. "I don't have a region. I'm from outside of the woods. Life is very different there."

Fothie skidded to a halt. "Really? The woods are gone? Is it like how Senka's region is turning?"

Deborah thought of the dead lands and the Silver Lake. "No, I mean I am not from a region at all."

"That's what you think," said Jacob gruffly.

"No, really. We don't have regions outside of the woods."

"Nobody is outside of the woods," said Fothie. "If I understand your meaning, that is. Do you mean the trees and life's growth across Sonax's realm?"

"Yes, well, I suppose so."

"All of the realm has been divided into regions," Nurrel said.

"Okay, then I am from outside of the realm."

Jacob squirmed. "*Huh!*"

"That's not possible," said Fothie, "and now I'm very curious as to what your region is like. Erno, have you been there?"

"Not for a long time," he said.

Deborah stared at him. "You've been to Eblhim? I don't mean Shilhim; that's the village at the edge of the woods. Eblhim is a city beyond the mountains that divide the woods from the plains."

He nodded, and his expression was thoughtful. "Yes, I know it. As I say, it's a long time since I was there." He laid his hand on Fothie's shoulder. "That region was overseen by our sister, Trithan."

She gasped. "Really? Oh, poor sister Trithan!" She gulped and was at a loss for words for a few moments. She bowed her twiggy head, her eyes closed.

"What occurred in this region?" Kasharel asked. "Has it been taken over by guandras? Deborah, you never said anything like this to me."

She gazed into his grey eyes. "Because there was nothing to say. I've never seen any guandras before I came into the woods. Really, I'm not from a region—Eblhim is outside all of this; it's just an ordinary city. There must be some mistake, Erno, you must be thinking of some other place."

"I must, must I?"

"Yes!"

Erno grinned. "Nope. I'm familiar with Eblhim and of the neighbouring city, Albim. Shilhim was formed by those who left both of those cities to escape the turning. They came together and made Shilhim a base not only to begin their migration but for others to come to as they began theirs."

"Hold on," said Deborah, "you're not making sense to me."

"No surprises there," muttered Jacob.

She nudged him. "Shut up. Let me think."

"Don't hurt your brain."

"You know about the turning," Erno said, "and you know there are those who wish to escape it and have no part in it." He briefly gestured with his hands. "As if changing location will make any difference to whether one will turn or not! But anyway, for some of your image-bearers, it was enough to set up a new home in Shilhim, and there they stayed, while for others, they still felt the pull to go further in, to go deeper. This is not the turning but the migration to the Oxpeina's region."

"At least half of my village has emptied out," Nurrel said. "We're feeling that pull, as you call it, to go. It's like a desire to go home—that where we are is no longer home, and we've got to go before our region closes." His voice became subdued. "I would have left months ago if Sonax hadn't told me to wait a little longer."

Deborah's thoughts surged around in a torrent. This was what Father was doing. He was responding to some unseen 'pull'. How had he known about Shilhim? She had never heard of the village until he told her of it. Somehow, he knew to go there. Who had he spoken to about it? Why hadn't he told her more about what he was really doing? He had only said he wanted peace and quiet, to recover by the woods, to get away from the city. He must have planned this all along. Then why had he bothered taking her with him to Shilhim? Why hadn't he just left her in Eblhim? It would have been easier if he had. She would have just tried to pick up the pieces of her life there and make something of it… no, she wouldn't have. She would have tried to track him down, tried to find out where he had gone, and not just simply let him go.

"Deborah," said Erno. "I believe this is what your father has been doing, responding to that pull to go home, to join the migration to the Oxpeina. At first, I thought you were too, but you soon set me straight on that."

There was something painful about the whole thing. Her heart felt wounded, heavy. She was so tired. So, so tired. She looked up at Hirahi. Not far to go to the base of the rock now. Somewhere to rest, at least. Perhaps a real bed, a good meal.

Erno's fingers closed around her arm. He was touching her again in that way that he did. This time she could feel the tingle of Oxpeina-life come through his fingers as he sensitively sought out how she was, how she felt. There was something nice about it. She bit her lip. Don't cry. It would do no good to cry. She wished they would all stop looking at her. She was just tired, that's all, from too much stupid, disorientating, exhausting stuff.

"We will talk later," Erno said softly. "When we are alone."

She took a deep breath and nodded. Jacob nuzzled his head against her hand.

"Onward!" said Fothie cheerfully. "I've got to offload you lot, then get back to my dwellers."

29

In the base of the towering rock was an opening, a wide arching doorway surrounded by a thin strip of engraved symbols. A heavyset rova stood just inside, his salt-and-peppered grey fur unmoving, his shoulders stooped with age. He was so silent and still that at first Deborah mistook him for a statue. Yet, as she looked at him and he at her, she felt there was a vital force within him, that he would roar, he would attack, that there was no hint of frailness in his great age, and the Oxpeina-life power was with him. She thought of Grufful and how he had encircled her in that power as the guandras had attacked.

Again, as with all the rovi she had encountered, this one looked at her with a question in his deep cobalt-blue eyes. Do you? he seemed to say. This was the first time she sensed distinct words in the questioning. There was more; she had the impression of more that he wanted from her in that probing stare. He looked hard for her answer, and she had none to give. It gave her the feeling of being exposed, of being seen. "I don't… I don't know," she found herself whispering, short of breath.

The rova's expression changed to disappointment. Or was it concern?

"It's perfectly safe to go in," said Jacob. "What are you worried about?"

He had mistaken her meaning, and she did not trouble herself to correct him. She adjusted her hold of him. He did not seem to mind that she was carrying him as she would a small toy. He had not asked to be wrapped again in the jersey, and his feather spikes were bristly against her skin.

"Hello Geor," Fothie said. "I'll leave these image-bearers with you."

The rova gave her a nod, his eyes softening as he looked at the brismuns who stood short and squat before him.

"Good to see you again, Geor," Erno said. "I'd come in with them, but you know I'm not keen on the indoors, especially with all the tight spaces you have in there. Yikes!" He swivelled on his leg and squinted up at Deborah. "You'll be taken care of in here. I'm only a shout away if you need me. Just go to a window and call my name. I'd most likely hear you anyway, but throwing your voice out a window will help. I'll remain in earshot of Hirahi while I wait for you. Perhaps tomorrow morning we can meet up and talk over what you want to do next."

She nodded. She had many questions for him. She was still unsettled by the thought that her home city of Eblhim belonged to a region, and Father knew that and had wanted to migrate to another, the Oxpeina's. Wherever that was.

"Thank you, Geor, for allowing us in," said Nurrel. "Now that I see you again, it makes me feel as if I never left, that the past few days are imagined. If only that were so."

Geor lightly traced two of his fur-covered fingers across Nurrel's forehead. Deborah began to wonder if Geor spoke aloud at all.

Nurrel gritted his teeth and shut his eyes as if trying to gather himself. "No," he said quietly. "It's no good, no good. I can't believe it, really. It's like—it's like it can't have happened."

Geor lowered his hand, and Nurrel went on into the tunnel. Kasharel made to follow, but Geor's eyes hardened, and he placed his palm against Kasharel's chest. His gaze was intense, narrowly focused. They stood toe to toe and eye to eye, for Geor had straightened himself to his full height. Kasharel appeared thin and insignificant before him.

"I am sorry," Kasharel whispered.

Geor's hand dropped, and Kasharel went on in.

Deborah took a deep breath. What would Geor do to her before he let her in? Geor stepped forward and caressed the top of her head. His eyes met hers with a fatherly tenderness that caught about her heart and made it ache. How did the rovi do this? They always managed to instill such meaning in their gazes. She blinked away a tear and ducked in behind Kasharel and Nurrel.

The tunnel, pale polished stone that was lit by lanterns, had several twists and turns and steps and off-shoots. Nurrel hesitated here and there as he led them through.

"Where are we going?" Kasharel asked.

"To the mages," said Nurrel. "One of them will sort out rooms for us."

Mages? Deborah suddenly thought of the storybook *Legends Of The Greener Land*. There were mages in that. She remembered having liked them. Wise men and women, wizards of their land, who were always ready to advise, find the solution to the problem, magically produce whatever was needed. There had been one story in particular; she tried to think of the mage's name… Holber? Hol-something. Holber had ridden a gryphon to the dengla to save him from the fires of… whatever it was. She looked at Kasharel's high, straight back as he walked ahead of her through the narrow tunnel, his robe looking in need of a wash. There were no denglas, anyway, just gehun. Were there any part-bird, part-beast gryphons?

A middle-aged lumdil man stepped out of a side tunnel and nodded as he went by. "Hiya, Oxpeina's best."

"Oxpeina's best," Nurrel answered.

Next, a squatchamn girl came through a door and trotted up steps ahead of them. There was the murmur of voices, and Deborah looked down another passage and, to her surprise, saw a man and a woman who could very well have come from Eblhim. She paused, almost called out to them, then hurried to catch up with Nurrel and Kasharel climbing stone steps that had a slight dip in their middle, revealing the aged wear by countless feet.

At the top was a good-sized room, simply furnished with woven wall hangings—mostly depicting trees and animals—and side tables. The buzz of voices came echoing through from the different doorways, and Deborah could see beyond one particular doorway a large hall, tables and chairs in the middle set up for dining, and sofas at the far end. A dozen or so people were milling about there, mostly squatchamn, she thought. Nurrel went through a different door, and there in a narrow room was an inviting plump two-seater against one wall and a low table in front of it. The vague scent of something flowery was in the air. The end door was closed, and Nurrel knocked on it.

"Enter!" came the voice inside.

He opened it, and they all went in. Bookshelves lined the walls; a large desk was in the middle of the room, and a tall woman was bent over beside it, sorting through papers in a box on the floor. She was dressed in long, flowing trousers, blue with a gold shimmer to them, a light gold buttoned-down shirt, and a dark blue and black geometric-patterned open coat over the top of both that went nearly to her knees. Her blonde hair was shining and pulled back into an intricate knot at the back of her head with an amber gem pinned on top.

"Hello, Mage Chila," Nurrel said.

She straightened up and frowned at him as if wondering who he was, then smiled in recognition, her eyes sparkling. "Why, Nurrel! Back again. That's great. We've been missing your delicious cooking here. Please tell me you're staying longer this time?"

"Not sure," he said, "but we need some rooms, please. These are my friends, Deborah, and Kasharel."

Deborah stared at Mage Chila, who was almost as tall as Kasharel but did not appear to be gehun, for her manner and colouring were more expressive and glowing. She was what a mage should look like as she stood with an air of authority about her.

Mage Chila strode over and eyed Kasharel. "Welcome! I do not think I have seen you here in Hirahi before. Are you staying long?" Before he could answer, she smiled down at Deborah. "Are you a wedded couple needing a room together?"

Deborah almost choked as Jacob stifled a *hoo*.

"No," said Kasharel. "That is not the case."

"Oh!" said Mage Chila, as if noticing Jacob for the first time. "Your poor, sweet little bird. Does he need medical care?"

Deborah felt Jacob stiffen at her words. "He's fine," she said quickly. "Fothie has healed him, so his feathers are growing in now."

"Fothie?"

"Fothie has changed places with Hemri," Nurrel said. "She is now in this area."

"Is that so? Well. It would be good if they would let me know their plans instead of going on ahead without consultation, but you never can tell a brismun what to do, can you. They are such difficult creatures." She smiled. "Now. How can we be of help to you here? Will you stay long? If you're just overnight, that's very well, but if you're planning on a longer stay, we'll need to work out some sort of arrangement so you can contribute here. What are your skills? I already know that Nurrel is a fantastic cook."

Nurrel shifted uncomfortably on his feet.

"I have some experience in doctoring," Kasharel said.

Of course he did. Why had Deborah not realised that before? That was why he had been assigned to take care of her in the gehun caves. She really hadn't given any thought to it; she had only been glad he had been there for her and looked after her. It gave her a sinking, disappointing feeling, which puzzled her. She knew the gehun council had instructed him to care for her, so what difference did it make?

"That's brilliant!" Mage Chila said. "We can certainly do with your help here. What with so many coming and going, we don't always have a doctor at hand. You are most welcome here and definitely needed, Kasharel."

"Why would you need a doctor when you have Fothie?" Jacob said.

Mage Chila smiled fondly at him. "You are a dweller, so I can see why you would say that, and I'm certainly impressed to find out you have speech, dear little one! Have you been a long time in Deborah's care, and she has awakened you to speech?"

"No," he said gruffly. "I was held by Sonax himself."

"Wonderful!"

"But you don't answer my question," Jacob said. "Why need a doctor when Fothie has the Oxpeina healing touch? She did not limit it to me, but gave it to Nurrel and to Deborah as well."

Mage Chila went back to the box on the floor and resumed shuffling through her papers. "Aren't you quite the chatterbox. Nurrel, you can take the room you had before, and I believe there are two more rooms off the same passage that are free. We have many spare rooms at present—I suppose it is a sign of the times." She looked over at Deborah. "You were about to tell me your skillset?"

Deborah fidgeted, pretending she had to readjust her hold on Jacob. Skillset? She had none. What should she say?

Mage Chila gave her a sympathetic, knowing look. "That's quite all right, Deborah. There are always hands needed in the kitchen or the laundry, so you can take your pick. I'm sure you will do a wonderful job. Nurrel, make sure you let Taffin know where you all are and what you're doing—she will take care of the rest."

"I will," Nurrel said. "Thank you, Mage Chila."

"Yes, thank you," Kasharel said.

Mage Chila gave him a warm smile. "You're most welcome. It is my pleasure to have you here with us. May the Oxpeina be your guide."

Deborah noted her gaze lingered awhile on Kasharel and did not include her or Nurrel. Kasharel returned the gaze steadily, but as usual, his expression showed nothing. Nurrel turned and left the room; Deborah and Kasharel followed.

"She still didn't answer my question," Jacob muttered.

Nurrel led them back down the steps. He took them along so many tunnelways that Deborah thought she would have no idea how to get out of the place if she wanted to.

"This is very pleasant," Kasharel said. "I like it here."

"You would," Jacob said.

Nurrel threw a door open, and daylight spilled into the tunnel. Inside was a comfortably furnished cream-coloured bed, so low to the ground it was obviously for a lumdil, while a pale green rug covered most of the stone floor, and a wide window opposite was dazzlingly bright with sunshine. "This will be my room. So, you both can take anything else around here that's unoccupied. Go ahead and choose something while I go and find Taffin. I'll be back before long. Bathrooms are in this passageway, too."

He looked so tired as he spoke to them that Deborah almost reached out to touch his shoulder, to reassure him somehow. "Shouldn't you rest first? We don't need Taffin right away, do we?"

He shrugged. "We all need something to eat and clean clothes. I won't take long. You could take a bath or something in the meantime." He didn't wait for her answer but set off back the way they had come.

30

Deborah sat on the bed and gazed out the window. This side of Hirahi had views of the wide, meandering river that led to tree-clad hills in the distance. It was probably a good thing to not have a lake view. She did not feel like looking at any lakes. She could still hear Nurrel's anguished cry and Ibelli's scream; still see Father walking the shore of the Silver Lake towards her, a rova at his side.

"You'll get the bed dirty," Jacob said as he walked down her arm and onto the folded blanket at the foot of the bed. "You're filthy."

They were alone together; the door to the passage shut. Kasharel had gone to find another room that had a bed suitable for a gehun.

"Doesn't matter," she said.

"I'll be able to fly soon," Jacob said, preening the few feathers that had expanded and come in properly while the rest of his body was still in a state of patchy spikiness. "Just as well. I'm starving."

"How can you be starving? Erno gave you tonnes of bugs this morning."

"That was ages ago."

She supposed it was. It felt like the middle of the day, the morning had faded, the sun was high. Time had passed by as it always did, and she was left to fumble along after it.

"Why don't you take a bath?" Jacob said. "You'll feel better for it. You're lucky you got a room with its own bathroom."

She sighed and got up. "I guess so."

"Open the window so I can get out."

She went over and did as he said. Looking out, she could see the ground below, the smooth expanse of grass, a garden, a fringe of trees along the riverbank. She went into the bathroom and shut the door. The stone floor was cold underfoot, but the water that came gushing from the tap was hot. Once the bath was filled, she undressed and eased herself in. She lathered up the spicy fruit-scented soap and washed away the aches and dirt of several days. Too much dirt. She emptied the bath and began filling it again, shivering while she waited for its steaming waters to cover her.

She sat staring at the pale marbled wall. What now? She couldn't stay here in Hirahi. Should she go back home? What was there for her now in Eblhim? Should she go on to Aric and try to find Father? He didn't want her, so why should she?

Finally, after several top-ups of hot water, she reluctantly got out of the bath and tried on one of the pale yellow robes that hung on the back of the door. It was too big, but still wearable. She wrapped herself in its luxurious thickness and went out into the chill air of the bedroom. Jacob had gone. She debated whether she should shut the window but did not like the thought of him coming flying back and walloping into it. She then noticed a stack of folded clothes on the bed and a tray with some food. Had Nurrel silently come and gone?

The clothes were a sensible selection; a stretchy pair of navy woollen leggings; a wraparound plum-coloured overskirt that could be adjusted and tied to fit almost any waist; a selection of different sizes of knit long-sleeved shirts; and a sloppy brown woollen jersey that went comfortably on top. Once dressed, she went back into the bathroom to try and dry her hair some more. She glanced at her own clothes strewn on the floor and was reminded of the rundown shack in Shilhim and the things that had been left lying about by the previous owner. She had tried her best to clean it all up and make a home for Father. Well, no more. Her clothes could stay on the floor—it didn't matter.

She rubbed furiously at her hair with a towel, then wiped the condensation from the mirror and stared at her gloomy reflection for a moment. She had lost weight, and her face was drawn. Ugly. She ran a wooden comb through her hair to bring some sort of order to it, then went back to the bedroom. Socks or footwear would be nice, but none had been provided. Her own shoes were tatty, and she didn't want to put them back on. At least there was a mat by the bed so she didn't have to stand on the cold stone floor.

"You look better," came Jacob's raspy voice at the window.

She almost jumped out of her skin. He folded his wings and stood on the sill, looking pleased with himself. His brown-and-white mottled feathers were shining, and with them all filled in properly, he appeared plump and healthy once more.

"So do you," she said.

Jacob began to preen himself, and Deborah picked through the food on the tray. There was a soft dark-grain bread roll, a wedge of cheese, and a square of something pink-coloured and sticky. It was edible, although the pink thing was very strange, all at once sweet and sour.

She sat on the bed and watched Jacob as he buried his head under his wing, nibbling through his feathers, pausing now and then to look out the window before resuming slowly grooming himself. She supposed it must feel nice to have his feathers all back again. He had said it was because of her that he had lost them in the first place, that he had tried to distract some guandras, fearing that they would find her and Kasharel. He had put himself in harm's way for her. Why? And why was he still with her?

"Now that we're here in Hirahi, what do you plan to do?" she asked him.

He looked up from his feathers. "What do you mean?"

"Well, are you staying here in this region or going back to where you're from?"

"Why would I do that?"

"I don't know. Where is your region?"

He eyed her silently a moment. "I am from the outskirts of Albim."

She was astonished. She had never been to the sister city of Eblhim, but knew it was closer to the mountain range that separated the woods from the plains.

"You see," Jacob said, "I was caught by a young man who found me something of a novelty. His treatment of me was harsh, and he broke my wing. Coop found me not long after that and paid for my release."

She felt as though she should know that name.

"Coop," said Jacob again, as if reading her puzzled expression. "He and Nina own the general store in Shilhim. He brought me back there on one of his supply runs, and Nina did her best to fix me up. Coop knows I can speak, but Nina never did find out. He said she wouldn't understand and it would be best to not let her know. He said she might have thought I was touched by guandras." Jacob's gold eyes were cross. "Completely ridiculous, if you ask me. Anyway, after having experienced the behaviours of the image-bearers in Albim, I was unwilling to trust anyone. I don't know how Coop knew that I could speak. He just knew. He got me talking to him on the way back to Shilhim."

"Why did you never tell me this before?"

"You never asked me before."

"Why didn't the brismun custodian of your region rescue you?"

"Ha! Now you're understanding the way of things. Because there is no brismun custodian of that region. You heard Erno and Fothie mentioning her. Trithan was driven mad and pushed out years ago by the image-bearers, so we dwellers, what there is left of us, had to fend for ourselves. And so, no, I don't want to go back there." He fluffed his feathers out and continued preening.

"It's so strange," Deborah said.

"What is?"

"To think that there was a brismun for my region, and that… well… I was *in* a region. I never knew. Was there also a shaseeliany there?"

He nodded. "There is always a brismun and shaseeliany paired together in a region. It is strange to me that you never knew."

She thought he was about to make some sort of jibe about her lack of knowledge again, but he cocked his head at her.

"I wonder why that is? Why were you never taught these things?"

She shrugged. "I'm beginning to think my father knew something of it, but he never talked about it—not that he spoke much to me. And there was never any mention of custodians or anything back in my school years."

"What were you taught for the history of your region?"

She frowned. "What is history?"

His eyes widened, if that was possible for an owl. "The record of how we came to be. *History*."

"I don't know that word."

"Perhaps you use a different term for the recounting of the past."

"You mean 'memories'?"

He briskly scratched his head. "Well, no, but yes, I suppose. What are the recorded memories of how Eblhim was built and who built it? What were you taught about that in school or by your parents?"

She picked at the edge of the folded blanket beside her on the bed and tried to think if the subject had ever come up. School seemed a long time ago, and most of the lessons had been boring, but as far as she remembered, there had never been anything about who had built Eblhim. She didn't recall Mother or Father talking about it, either. Why would they talk about that?

Jacob hissed and stalked up and down the windowsill. "It's no wonder you don't know who you are. You've never been told, have you. Ridiculous!"

She watched him, thinking he looked like a grumpy old man with his hands in his pockets.

He turned and studied her. "You look gloomy." He hopped off the sill and, with a silent flap of his wings, landed neatly on the bed.

"I'm just tired," she said.

"Understandable." He gently tugged at her sleeve. "What are you going to do now? Go to Aric?"

"Don't know."

"Don't know? Don't you want to continue looking for your father?"

She shrugged again.

"With more good food and a proper sleep tonight, you'll feel better in the morning and be able to think more clearly. You just need to regain some strength, that's all."

She sighed and looked out to the rising and falling contours of the tree-covered land on the horizon. "I guess so."

"Shall we go find Nurrel?" Jacob said. "According to the mage, you're supposed to report to the kitchen and start washing dishes to earn your supper, aren't you?"

Deborah reluctantly went over to the door and opened it. "How am I supposed to find my way there in this maze of tunnels?" She almost bumped into a tall man out in the passage. "Excuse me."

"You're excused," he said.

She looked up at Kasharel in astonishment. He wore dark green trousers and a flecked-grey jersey that made the otherworldly hue of his skin and grey eyes even more distinctive. He looked like a completely different person without his brown robe—somehow, regular clothes made him appear more broad-shouldered and masculine in build.

"You look nice," he said, a hint of a smile in his eyes.

She felt a wave of hot embarrassment—nice? She looked worn out and terrible.

"Yes," Jacob said, as he flew to her shoulder. "Deborah's finally cleaned up and looks a lot less ratty."

"As do you," Kasharel said.

Out the corner of her eye, Deborah saw Jacob ruffle his feathers and puff himself out.

"Well, yes," he said. "Thanks to Fothie, I can put that horrible experience behind me."

Deborah realised she hadn't thought about her shoulder since Fothie had rid it of the lingering stiffness and dull discomfort. Not that it had been bad at all, for the days of being cared for by Kasharel, Shinah, and Bey had helped it heal tremendously. She glanced up at Kasharel as he led the way through Hirahi's passages. He seemed to have a good memory for the twists and turns Nurrel had brought them through, only now and then pausing to decide which way, assisted by Jacob offering his opinion. It was interesting to watch Kasharel's long-legged stride and the way he planted his feet, slightly out-turned and confident, something she had not noticed before beneath the swathes of his robe. He also took the steps two at a time, which she supposed was necessary for him as they were fairly shallow.

Before long, they were outside Mage Chila's library in the small entranceway that led through to the great hall filled with dining tables. Mage Chila herself happened to come through the door.

"Hello!" she said. "I almost don't recognise you both. You look wonderful."

Again, Deborah thought that Mage Chila looked more at Kasharel as she spoke and only glanced down at her once with a sympathetic smile. She began to feel small beside these two very tall people, and it annoyed her. It was not as if she herself was particularly short; she was considered above average in height for someone in Eblhim. But this wasn't Eblhim.

Mage Chila took Kasharel's arm. "I have an office ready for you—come this way, I'll get you settled, and you can tell me what you think. Our last doctor left it in good order, but who knows, you might spot something that we desperately need. I can source whatever you think is necessary."

Deborah stood still, watching them walk away together.

"Aren't you going after them?" Jacob said in her ear.

"Why? I'm supposed to find the kitchen and work there, aren't I? I'm not going to be Kasharel's nurse."

"*Woo.* Ah, look! Here comes Nurrel."

She did look, but no one was nearby or even behind her. She heard distant footsteps and saw Nurrel at the far end of the great hall. She went to meet him, weaving in and around the tables, and felt somewhat dismayed to see his shoulders were sagging as he walked slowly towards her and that he appeared even more tired than he had earlier. She bit her lip, unsure if she should say anything to him.

"You look rotten," Jacob said. "Have you had any rest at all?"

Nurrel looked up at him. "I can't rest. I can't seem to relax. Not yet, anyway. Maybe later."

"Take a bath," Jacob said. "It's what Deborah did, and she was in there for hours."

"It wasn't hours," she hissed at him.

He hissed back.

Nurrel gave him a small smile. "You two are funny. Nice to see all your feathers come in, Jacob."

"Nice to have them in," Jacob said, "and finally to fly. It feels great. So, I'm going out again now that you've found each other and don't need me." He nuzzled Deborah's cheek. "I'll come to you later."

He leapt from her shoulder, spreading his wings wide, and flew along the length of the great hall and out an open window into the bright sunshine.

"No doubt he's off to eat bugs again," Deborah said. She winced inwardly. Her voice sounded overly cheery and unnatural. If only she didn't feel so tense at being left alone with Nurrel.

"I'm surprised he flies so well after his enforced rest," Nurrel said, watching Jacob as he became a dot in the sky. "Then again, I imagine Fothie's Oxpeina touch helped him there as well. She helped me, but… I don't know; I still don't feel right. Sometimes I think I do, but other times, no definitely not."

Deborah thought rapidly. What should she say now that wouldn't be the wrong thing? "You have been through a lot. You can't expect to get over what happened right away."

He sighed, his expression despondent. "Yes." He looked up as if seeing her afresh. "Where's Kasharel?"

She grimaced. "Being shown his new doctor office by Mage Chila."

"Right, okay. I'll show you the kitchens. Things are underway there for dinner; I was actually coming to get you—they could do with an extra pair of hands. People are thinning out here in Hirahi as much as they are at home."

She realised he was talking about his home back at the village of… she wrinkled her brow. Shady Glade. No. *Smoky* Glade. She looked at the row upon row of long tables and chairs set out neatly in the great hall. "There are lots of tables here." Her words sounded stupid and awkward. Of course there were lots of tables there; that was obvious.

"Yes," he said, "but I don't think they're all in use anymore."

She pattered after him in her bare feet across the cold stone. As they approached the tall windows at the end of the great hall, she could see the river curving its way down to the lake, shining in the distance, resplendent greens and blues in the sun. She paused, taking in the view. The great hall must be at the very top or nearly the top level of Hirahi. She wondered if anybody had been standing here when the ubsies had carried her and the others up the river. It must have looked like a strange procession. Where were Erno, Fothie, and Shessi now?

She went after Nurrel as he disappeared through a wide doorway. It took a few moments for her eyes to adjust to the dim light, and she felt her way down a flight of well-worn steps. The mingled aroma of smoke, of vegetable, of bread wafted up to meet them, along with the clatter of pots and pans and the murmur of voices.

She and Nurrel stepped into a well-lit, long kitchen furnished with polished stone countertops, wooden shelves filled with an array of utensils, a fire burning in a hearth. A squatchamn boy was chopping vegetables at a countertop; he glanced up and gave them a quick grin; a woman with a long grey plait had her back turned as she stirred a steaming pot at a stove; two other squatchamn were at the far end of the kitchen chatting at a sink as they worked; and a stocky lumdil woman burst through a doorway to Deborah's right, lugging a crate of fish.

She plonked it down and adjusted her glasses over her enormous nose. Her thick brown hair was swept back from her face in typical lumdil fashion, and her dark eyes sparkled as she saw Nurrel and Deborah.

"Oh, hi there!" She wiped her hands on a rag and hurried over, a beam on her flushed face. "You must be Deborah. I'm Taffin. Nice to meet you. Nurrel has told me about you, I—oh! Bare feet! Nurrel! You haven't got any shoes for her. Your feet must feel like ice." She looked over her shoulder. "Mally! Would you mind going and grabbing some shoes? Size… "—she glanced down at Deborah's feet. "—*um*, try sizes six or seven? Ta!"

The squatchamn boy put down his chopping knife and hurried away.

"Can't have your feet freezing off," Taffin said, smiling at Deborah. "That would not do at all!"

There was something about her, something that warmed Deborah, the look in her eyes akin to a rova's intent knowing imbued with Oxpeina-life, yet something safe and homey.

"You all right?" Taffin asked Deborah. "I take it you've had something of a rough journey here. You don't need to get stuck in right away, but I would really, *really* appreciate it if you could. Wait—" she stuck a pudgy finger to the bridge of her glasses "—that sounds like I'm guilt-tripping you to work right away. What I mean is, no, you don't have to if you're not up for it yet, I completely understand. I mean, I've been telling Nurrel to go away, but he won't."

"I need something to do," Nurrel said. "I can't sit around doing nothing."

Taffin looked sympathetically at him. "I understand that, but is it best right now? You look done in, Nurrel. I don't like it. However, you're determined, so I suppose I have to give you something to do." She smiled up at Deborah. "As for you, make Hirahi your home for as long as you like—you're really welcome. Now, I've got to cut heads off fish. A delightful job." She shuddered and pulled a face.

"Would you like me to?" Nurrel said.

"No! I'm not letting you loose with a knife. One slip in your weariness and you could cut your fingers off. Find something else to do that doesn't involve sharp implements, thank you!"

"What can I do?" Deborah asked.

"*Hmm*. Well, I think Mally could probably do with help chopping the veggies—he'll show you what he wants when he gets back."

It was not long before Mally returned with two sets of soft, woven slip-on shoes, and after trying both, Deborah found that one pair was too big and the other slightly too small. She opted for the small ones, hoping they would stretch somewhat, rather than wear the big ones and trip over herself.

As she and Mally worked together, Deborah discovered that he was from a squatchamn village close by but had decided to live and work at Hirahi; the grey-haired woman at the stove was Sarammi—Sam for short—and was from a city Deborah had never heard of yet she could well have been from Eblhim for she was the build and height of the average woman there; while the two other squatchamn were husband and wife and much older than their youthful appearance made them seem.

Deborah was interested that the squatchamn had the large, slightly staring eyes of those who had lived by the Silver Lake, yet the haunted, red-rimmed look was absent, and their hair, although fine and limp, was soft and clean. Did they know about the squatchamn image-bearers in their neighbouring region? Were any of them relatives? If so, surely they should go there and try to bring them out of that place.

Taffin talked cheerfully as she filleted the fish, the others calling out in response or laughing together. Nurrel was quiet as he made a dessert under Sam's guidance. Deborah cast surreptitious looks at him now and then, but he seemed in his own world. She supposed she was quiet too, other than to answer Mally as he asked where she was from and what she was doing at Hirahi. She was unsure how to answer that last question, and he seemed to accept that.

When the dinner was nearly ready, the tall and imposing Mage Chila swept down the steps and into the kitchen. When she spoke, it was with an authoritative resonance that made Deborah feel that being near a mage was something to not take for granted, that whatever Mage Chila said should be listened to. She found herself straightening up, giving a quick wipe to the mess on her apron.

Mage Chila looked around the kitchen, a benevolent smile on her face. "How is everyone? Is dinner prepared? We have begun assembling upstairs. Thank you all for your wonderful hard work. Oxpeina-life to you all."

She then left the way she had come. The kitchen was silent for a few moments, as if everyone was unsure what to do or say. Taffin spoke first.

"Well, that's it. Grub on plates and let's get going."

The clatter and bustle of the kitchen resumed.

31

By the time Deborah had traipsed up and down the stairs with some of the dishes she had helped prepare in the kitchen, she was ready to collapse into a chair at the dinner table. Two of the long tables had been pushed together around which twenty or maybe thirty people were seated. She couldn't be sure exactly how many, for she didn't like to stare at everyone. As far as she could tell, it was a mix of squatchamn, lumdils, gehun, and she was sure some of her own kind, too.

Mage Chila sat at the head of the table, her back to the windows, her hands clasped together in an attitude of introspection. The sky behind her was bathed in sunset peach, giving the hall a mellow light.

"How did you get on?" Kasharel quietly asked Deborah as he drew out a chair next to her.

"Kasharel, son of Mali," said Mage Chila, her voice echoing through the hall. "You will sit here." She indicated the dinner setting at her right. "As our new doctor, everyone must learn who you are."

Kasharel went over and took his seat. As he did, Nurrel brought the last of the dishes, a tray piled with various roasted vegetables, pushed it onto the table, then headed off through the length of the hall towards the other exit.

"Nurrel," Mage Chila said. "Where are you going?"

"Sorry," Nurrel said over his shoulder, and kept walking.

"Why—" began Mage Chila.

"I'll see to him," said Taffin, getting up and scooping different things onto a plate. "He's finally going to get some rest, and he certainly needs it." She hurried after Nurrel, plate in hand.

Mage Chila looked disapproving. "Very well."

Deborah frowned. Why should Mage Chila be annoyed simply because Nurrel had decided he didn't want to eat with everyone? Didn't Mage Chila know what he had been through, what he was dealing with? He had witnessed the death of Ibelli, whom he had loved, yet here he had helped prepare dinner when he didn't have to at all. Mage Chila shouldn't get her nose out of joint just because Nurrel didn't want any company right now.

Deborah carried on eating, feeling too tired to listen to the hum of conversation around the table. Now and then Mage Chila's voice rose above the others. She said high-sounding things about the Oxpeina-life and Hirahi and this and that. Deborah thought she was worse than Jacob when he got going on those things, but the others at the table seemed to hang on to her every word, and there were many nods of agreement.

She looked over at the evening sky. Where was Jacob? When would he return to her, or would he be out all night? He wouldn't be able to get into the great hall as all the windows were shut. Was the window in her room still open? How cold was it in there now? The room had a radiator, sure, but that wouldn't do much if the window was still open. If only she had thought to shut it.

"Deborah," said Mage Chila. "I am speaking to you."

Deborah paused mid-bite. Kasharel had a tinge of embarrassment on his face. Everyone else had their heads turned Deborah's way.

"We would all like to get to know our new guest," Mage Chila said. "Where are you from, Deborah, and why have you journeyed to Hirahi?"

Deborah did not want to share her life story then and there in front of everyone and was irked by the way Mage Chila was smiling at her as if she were a small child who needed encouragement to talk. "I'm from Eblhim, and because I was told to," she said flatly.

Mally, who was sitting opposite her, gave a snort of laughter.

"And, who told you to?" Mage Chila asked.

"Erno."

"Is Erno a mage in Eblhim?"

"No, he's my brismun custodian." Deborah carried on eating.

There were a few gasps around the table.

"A brismun!" said someone. "How'd that happen?"

"I never heard of such a thing," said somebody else.

"They're so mysterious," said Sam, who was seated at Deborah's right. "How in the world did you get a brismun?"

She shrugged.

"Many years ago," Mage Chila said, "Mage Barmus recounted to me of such a thing, unusual although it was at the time. If I recall aright, he told me it was due to a shortage of rovi available to accompany the travellers."

Sam nudged Deborah and whispered, "Mage Barmus was the mage who began Hirahi—did you know that?"

Deborah shook her head. She couldn't have cared less who had begun Hirahi. However, the potato she was eating now—if that's what it was—was delicious. Buttery and crispy outside, soft inside, with a flavour so creamy and savoury she could eat a pile of them. She looked over at the dishes along the middle of the table to see if there were any more left.

"Such things, although strange," went on Mage Chila, "can occur in the realm when required. I have seen that the movement and unrest of the regions has caused more unusual happenings of late."

"Pass the dish with the yellow flower pattern," Deborah whispered to Sam.

"The Oxpeina-life causes change," said Mage Chila. "It causes growth, and it calls to us to behave in a better way, with more love, more light, and more understanding. Let us consider the truth." She smiled at all seated around the table.

There were nods and murmurs of assent. Sam leaned forward and got the dish Deborah asked for. There was a brief moment where nobody said anything, and it was then that the serving spoon Deborah used to scoop a few of the remaining potatoes made a loud scraping sound. She grimaced at Mally, and he grinned at her.

"Love," said Mage Chila. "It is the goal for us all to live by. How can we escape the turning? With love. When I trained under Mage Barmus, I learned the way of love and how to take hold of the completeness of Oxpeina-life."

There was a collective gasp from several people, and something clutched Deborah's shoulder. She yelped and almost jumped out of her skin.

"Jacob," she said. "I wish you wouldn't sneak up on me like that!"

"It's your fault for having your face in your dinner plate," he said. "If you had been more aware, you would have seen me coming."

"You should have announced yourself or something."

He pressed his soft, feathery head against her neck. "How much longer are you going to be here? We should go out. It's a beautiful evening."

Mage Chila cleared her throat and gazed at Deborah with a persistent smile that did not falter. Deborah felt strangely obligated to smile back, so she did, although she felt her own smile was forced.

Mage Chila gave her a slight nod and smiled around at everyone once more.

"Come on," said Jacob. "Let's go."

"*Shh*," Deborah hissed. "Dinner's almost ended."

"Let us consider," said Mage Chila. "Let us not allow Mage Barmus' teaching to languish and sink into fallow hearts. He heard many a time from Sonax himself; many a time Mage Barmus walked and studied with Sonax."

Deborah saw that all at the table were turned to Mage Chila again, listening to her with rapt attention. Jacob shifted impatiently on Deborah's shoulder, and she absentmindedly reached up to stroke him. She couldn't just walk away from the table with everyone stuck in a kind of lecture or whatever it was. This might be their usual routine at the dinner table—to study under the mage. She felt so tired that most of what Mage Chila said went in one ear and out the other. If only she had followed Nurrel out of the great hall. Taffin hadn't come back, so was she still with him? Hopefully Taffin had been able to get Nurrel to eat something, and he would finally get some sleep after having spent the last couple of nights talking with Erno.

Deborah was roused by chairs scraping across the stone floor, plates being collected, chatter as everyone got up. Had she nodded off? She wasn't sure. It felt good to have had a decent meal at long last. She got up and looked around. Mage Chila was surrounded by a huddle of half a dozen people, Kasharel included. It was hard to get used to how different he looked wearing ordinary clothing; he did not seem to be the same Kasharel anymore. If it had not been for the hue of his skin and hair, she could have mistaken him for someone from Eblhim who was very tall.

"Come on," said Jacob.

She frowned, watching as Sam and Mally stacked plates. "I don't think I can. I'd better help clear up. You know I'm supposed to be working in the kitchen while we're here."

"*Hmph.*"

"*Hmph* yourself," she said. "It's got to be done. What do you want me for, anyway? You can enjoy the night air by yourself."

"I wanted to show you something."

"Show me tomorrow."

She felt him shift as though preparing to spread his wings and launch himself into flight. "Wait," she said. "I'll close my bedroom window later, so make sure you don't bash into it. Yell at the window if you really want me to open it."

He nuzzled her neck again. Funny that he was being so affectionate with her. Well, it was nice. He leapt from her and flew the length of the great hall and on out through the far door.

She set to stacking plates and utensils. She was about to head off for the kitchen when she realised Mage Chila was standing right next to her.

"Deborah," she said, a kindly smile on her face. "Thank you for your wonderful cooking. I hear that you were in charge of the fish. I thought it was fried to perfection and so very gorgeously seasoned. I have never had such a perfect piece. You must be super experienced with cooking fish; not everyone can fry it so well."

Deborah recalled hurriedly throwing salt over the fillets as she had flopped them onto the serving dish. She had done nothing special. Yes, it was true; she had cooked fish many times back home in Eblhim, so knew what she was doing even though she didn't usually cook so many fillets at one time. But, *perfect?* Hadn't Mage Chila eaten a decently cooked piece of fish before? "Oh, okay. You're welcome. Glad you liked it."

Mage Chila smiled again, then strode away, her long coat sweeping about her. Deborah looked around the great hall and sighed. Kasharel was no longer there. He hadn't bothered to wait to see her.

Down in the kitchen, she was soon elbow deep in soapy water, washing everything up at one of the sinks. Sam had said she would go up and down the stairs and bring everything else down from the great hall—which Deborah was grateful for—and Mally was busily wiping down countertops and clearing things away. The squatchamn couple were nowhere in sight, and neither was Taffin.

It wasn't until all the cleaning was nearly at an end and Deborah was beginning to wonder how she would find her way back to her bedroom, when Taffin came into the kitchen.

"Sorry about that," she said. "I hadn't meant to leave it all to you three."

"We understand," said Sam. "How's Olly?"

"He's a lot better. He's still in the barn and determined to carry on, though. I said I would feed the inmates for him, but he wouldn't hear of it, so I just helped as best I could."

"Inmates," said Mally with a snort.

"Animals," said Taffin to Deborah. "My husband Olly takes care of the livestock here. He's been unwell, and I can't get him to slow down. He does feel so responsible for the barn, and I suppose that's understandable as we have less people staying here to help out." She sighed and swept a hand through her thick hair. "Anything I can do here, or have I missed it all?"

"We're pretty much done," said Mally. "All that's left is to take the scraps down to the barn, and I can manage that."

"You sure?"

"Yep."

"Goodnight all," said Sam. "Oxpeina's best."

Deborah watched her leave through the same doorway Taffin had come in by. "Taffin," she said. "I don't know how to get back to my room. Would you show me?"

"Sure thing."

Taffin got a lamp from under a countertop, and when it flared into life, it shone up into her ruddy face, reflecting a glow of amiability and kindliness in her dark brown eyes, softening her crinkly smile lines. In a flash, Deborah thought of Ibelli illuminated in the harsh light of the Silver Lake, the angry glitter of her red-rimmed eyes, the fixed, unseeing stare, the fading vibrancy of life in her whole being.

Deborah silently followed Taffin out of the kitchen. How could Nurrel have loved someone like Ibelli? What had he seen in her? She must have been different when she lived in his village, but what had made her change so much? Or, had she always been that way and no one had really known what she was truly like? Nurrel had said she was quiet. What thoughts had she harboured?

"Nurrel was pretty muddled up about how to get back to your rooms," Taffin said over her shoulder, the lamplight swinging shadows around the narrow passage. "So it's no wonder you don't know how to get back there yourself. He said when he led you, he'd been doubling around and back on himself while he tried to remember where to go. I don't blame him—he's exhausted. But Hirahi's really not that big and muddly of a warren. The rock has only a few excavated areas linking the natural caves, and the rest is what was built on top. So, once you figure out what connects where, you're golden." She lightly touched the wall of the sloping passage. "Right now we're going around under the back of the great hall. Once we come to this next branching of ways, we take the left and then go on down the next flight of steps. Then it's just along to the end of the passage there, and, bingo! at the next branching we take the righthand way. That's where your rooms are."

Deborah wondered if Kasharel knew that or if he was still wandering up and down steps and in and out of different passages as he found his own way back. "Thanks very much," she said. "That makes things simpler." She half-expected Taffin to stop and go back by herself now that she had explained the route, but the lumdil woman walked briskly onward.

"Sorry, we don't have electricity up here," Taffin said. "I have no idea how difficult it would be to run all the wiring through the place and make that happen. We've got the pump at the mill, and thankfully, that helps power the kitchen. Some of Hirahi's building is caught in the past, but I think it adds to its charm."

"How long have you been here?"

"Oh, about twelve years now. Olly and I came here and finished raising our kids. We've got three—two boys and a girl. They've gone on ahead of us to the Oxpeina's region, but we'll stay a while longer. Until we get the word from Sonax to move on, of course."

Here again was someone talking about Sonax as if Deborah should know exactly what was meant. "Okay," she said.

"Nurrel said your father has gone on ahead of you?"

Deborah bit her lip, and for a moment, their pattering footsteps were the only sound. 'Gone on ahead' was one way of putting it. 'Left her and forgotten about her' was more like it. "I've been told he's on his way to Aric."

"*Hmm*. I'd have to look at the map of the regions to figure out exactly where that is. I think, if I recall, Aric's about four regions over, but we'd have to look at the size of them and see what would be the best way to get through. I can definitely do that with you tomorrow. I have some time after breakfast. Remind me then."

"Okay." It gave Deborah a sinking feeling to think of figuring out how to get to Aric. Why go there? Father didn't want her; that was clear.

It was not long before Taffin opened a door and stepped aside. "Here you are. All good? Anything else you need?"

"I don't think so," Deborah said.

It was cold, a breeze whistled through the open window, the deep blue sky was dotted with stars. Deborah shut the window then stood close to the small radiator set against one wall.

Taffin opened a cupboard. "I'd better get out your lamp. Wouldn't do much good to leave you fumbling around in the dark!"

The lamp was lit and set on the tiny table next to the bed; then Taffin chuckled as she picked up the tray that had been left earlier. "I'd better not drop this while I'm trying to hang on to my lamp. Imagine the racket I'd make if I did that! If you need anything, Olly and I are back up the steps and along the right branch, third door along." She shook her head and pulled a face. "Or, at least, he should be. Knowing him, he's probably still down in the barn." She smiled up at Deborah. "Goodnight. I'll see you in the morning. Breakfast duty starts as soon as you're up and able to come join us. Also, the laundry folk come by the rooms every morning, so put out any washing you've got and they'll take care of it. There's a basket in your bathroom; just toss things in there and put it out in the hallway."

Deborah nodded. "Thanks."

She shut the door after Taffin, then went and stood by the radiator again, warming her hands. The lamp cast a cosy yellow glow over the bed. The last time she had slept in a bed had been back in the gehun caves. At least here she did not feel completely shut in but had a window to see out of. Were Kasharel and Nurrel in their rooms? She quietly opened the door to the passage and looked out. All was silent and dark. Well, if they wanted to know where she was and if she was all right, they could come to her. She waited a while, half-expecting Kasharel would come and check on her. But he didn't. Nurrel wouldn't, and she didn't expect him to. He had enough to think about.

She shivered as she got under the bed covers. The bed was a little lumpy, but it was comfortable.

She must have slept like the dead, for the next thing she knew, daylight was streaming in her window. She got up, washed and dressed, found the basket in the bathroom, and stuffed her travelling clothes in it. Should she try putting her shoes in there? They were caked in dirt. She set her shoes next to the basket outside her door to see if the 'laundry folk' would take care of them, then headed off to the kitchen.

She smiled as she passed the first set of stairs that led downward—she knew now to not take those!—and found her way back to the kitchen without any trouble. Lights were on, and the warm, steamy smell of yeast filled the space. The squatchamn couple were there already, shaping rows and rows of bread rolls and knots onto trays.

"Oh, hello," Deborah said. What were their names? Taffin had introduced them while preparing dinner last night, but everyone had been so busy and Deborah hadn't interacted much with them.

"You're nice an' early," said the woman.

She had the typically wide, round eyes of a squatchamn. Her fine hair was pulled back into a neat ponytail, and her hands and apron were covered with flour.

"Heya," said the man as he set an empty tray down onto one of the countertops. He was like Mally, although older, good-humoured in his expression, his hair tucked back behind his ears, his wide eyes keen, patches of flour on his face.

"We're up before dawn, o' course," said the woman. "That's the bakers' life. First to come an' first to leave."

Deborah tried again to think of what her name was. Nothing sprang to mind. "Is there anything I can do to help?"

"I'm nearly ready for the eggs; would you fetch them?"

Deborah looked about the kitchen. There were bins of flour, stacks of veggies, all sorts of other condiments and ingredients, but she didn't see any eggs.

"They be down in the barn," said the man. He stooped and brought out a basket. "Here y'ar, Debrah, fetch'em in this."

He remembered her name even if she didn't remember his, and at least he wasn't calling her 'Debah'.

She took the basket. "Where's the barn?"

"Straight down," said the woman. "I'd say follow your nose if you were a lumdil, but you ain't." She grinned, a chummy gap-toothed grin. "Get all the eggs you can, 'cause we'll need them not just for glazing the bread but cooking up for brekky."

She tied a knot in one of the rolls, and Deborah was shocked to see that most of the fingers of one hand were missing.

"Are you—were you… from the Silver Lake?"

"Yes! How'd you know that?"

"Your hand."

"Hey, I just about forget it sometimes; look at that!"

"Years gone by," said the man with a nod.

"I didn't think anyone could leave the Silver Lake," Deborah said.

"Right?" said the woman, shaping and patting a roll. "Me neither, but it happened. I was there for years an' couldn't get out."

"How did you?"

The woman pulled off another lump of dough from a bowl. "It's like this—Sonax knew I was trying to get out, an' he came an' got me. Knew my heart wasn't in it, not really. Not like the others. Those others, I try to talk to them, an' they reckon they're all right, they're happy, an' don't want for nothing, says they know what they're doing. Not me; I knew I wanted more, an' the lake wasn't giving it to me." She deftly shaped more rolls. "Tried to get out, couldn't. Muttonheaded me all caught up by the magic. My cousin's still there, an' I can't get him out."

"Aye," said the man, his face sombre. "We try many a time to get him come here, but he won't."

"Strong magic, strong turning," said the woman. "I hate going back there an' seeing it all. But it don't get me no more. It's nothing to me now."

Deborah looked at her as she worked busily with the dough. "You mean the magic doesn't affect you?"

"Sure, it don't. Sonax stopped that on me. Still got to be careful; can't be cocksure, but I know where I am now an' who I am." She wiped her nose on her sleeve and grinned at Deborah. "You been there, have ya?"

Deborah nodded.

"Rotten, ain't it."

"Morning, all," said Sam as she came into the kitchen and got herself an apron. Her grey hair was tied back in a bun, and she had the heavy-lidded look of someone not fully awake.

The squatchamn man glanced over at her. "Heya."

"Hi, Sam," said Deborah. "Well, I'd better go get the eggs."

"Ta very much," said the squatchamn woman as she placed more rolls on the tray.

32

Deborah had a multitude of thoughts as she went down the winding stairs. To think, someone had actually got out of the Silver Lake's grip after years of being stuck there. Maybe she should have left well enough alone and not tried to jolt Ibelli back to reality. If she had left Ibelli alone, things could have been different. Maybe in time Ibelli would have wanted more, realised that the lake was empty of any meaning or real life, and let go of that whole region, or Sonax, whoever he was, would have recognised she wanted to leave and done the same as what he had done for the squatchamn woman.

She sighed. She had made such a mess of things. Someone had died because of her. Now here she was, safe in this region, as though nothing had happened, as though she hadn't done anything wrong. It was hard to fully grasp what had happened—that it really wasn't some horrible dream. What must Nurrel think of her? He had been prepared to wait, had wanted to keep talking to Ibelli, but she, Erno, and the others had pressured him to move on. Why had it been so important to Erno that they all stay together? Nurrel hadn't seemed bothered by the magic of the lake, so he could have stayed there longer by himself. However, she had ruined all of that. She was the one who had forced Ibelli out of her mound. Forced her to go to the lake and die. Why was Nurrel even still speaking to her after what she had done?

The aroma of the barn drifted up the stairs, and before long Deborah stepped down into a comfortable warmth to see fowls contentedly clucking as they scratched about in pens, the mottled grey backs of rvenan cattle in a row of stalls, and small pale blue woolly animals in pens further along. There was a repeated rhythmic swooshing of water from one of the stalls nearby, and she looked in to see what it was.

"Oh," she said, as she saw a man sitting on a stool at the side of a rvenan, milk foaming into a pail as he worked. "Hello."

He paused and looked up. He was an older man and could very well have been from Eblhim; he had such a familiar build and colouring, even down to the shape of his face. His clothing was different from what she was used to at home—he wore a leather jerkin over a cream long-sleeved shirt and baggy, rust-coloured trousers that were tucked into his boots.

"I'm Deborah," she said.

He gave her a nod. "Olly."

So, this was Taffin's husband. That was a surprise—he was not a lumdil.

"I've just come to get the eggs," she said. "Where are they?"

"In with the hens," he said. "They're the ones laying them, you know."

No, she did not know. Her experience with animals was limited and mostly came from books. She went over to the fowls and started hunting around the hay for their eggs. As she did so, a mumbling sound from one of the stalls drew her attention. She looked up to see the grey muzzle of a rvenan over the half door, his long, floppy ears framing his inquisitive face. Was it the same one from yesterday morning? He kept up a steady stream of incoherent mumbling.

"What is it?" she said as she went to him. "What are you trying to say, fella?" She tentatively reached out to stroke one of his ears. It was as velvety soft as it looked, and the rvenan closed his eyes and tilted his head, a blissful expression on his face. His rubbery lips twitched, but he fell silent.

"Brought in last night," said Olly, as he came out of the stall. "He's a talker."

"I think I met him yesterday," said Deborah.

Olly gave her a nod and went into the neighbouring stall. The hissing sound of milk striking a pail soon resumed.

"You're a talker, huh?" Deborah said softly to the rvenan.

He opened his eyes and smirked at her. She wanted to stay there, patting him in the warmth of the barn, but remembered the others in the kitchen waiting on the eggs. She went back to the fowls' enclosure to check she had found them all. Before she left the barn, she leaned over the stall door where Olly was.

"Do you mind me asking if you're from Eblhim?" she said.

"Sure am," he said as he steadily milked the rvenan cow.

"Me, too," she said. "How in the world did you get here? Why did you leave Eblhim?"

"Drawn by Sonax."

"Drawn, how?"

"The enchantment. Felt him pull me in. Knew he was there, felt the Oxpeina-life. Could see it ebbing away in Eblhim; no pun intended. You saw that, too?"

How should she respond to that? She had seen nothing of the sort.

"As to how I got here," Olly went on, "I walked, same as you, I guess. Stopped in Shilhim, wasn't enough. Had to keep on going."

It was hard to listen to, and she felt a painful throb in her heart. Olly could well have been the same as Father—mysteriously drawn away from Eblhim, feeling the compulsion to go into the woods. Why did they have to be like this? Why couldn't Father have just stayed in Eblhim?

"When were you last in Eblhim?" Olly asked. "Haven't been there for many years. Expect it's pretty far gone now."

"Not at all," Deborah said. "I was there not long ago. There's nothing wrong with the city."

"Is that so?"

His tone of voice made Deborah feel as if he didn't believe her. "Yes, that is so," she said. "I would be back there now if it wasn't for—if it wasn't for… circumstances."

"The edges of the realm go first," Olly said, his head down as he watched the milk streaming into the pail. "Folds in on itself. Oxpeina-life is at its centre, and you've got to follow it in. You've got to follow him in."

Deborah remembered Taffin saying Olly hadn't been well. Perhaps that was why he was talking gibberish. She picked up her basket of eggs. "I'd better get back; the others will be wondering where I am."

As soon as she returned, she saw the busyness in the kitchen had stepped up a notch.

"Whoops," said Taffin as she scooted past Deborah with a pan of water. "Morning! Hope you slept well last night?"

"Yes, I did," said Deborah.

"Good-o." Taffin plonked the pan onto a stovetop. "Mally! I'm just going to fetch the milk; you keep an eye on that!" She bustled off out the door.

Deborah was just about to ask the others what she could do when Mage Chila came down the stairs that led from the great hall. She wore a white high-necked jersey and tan trousers; both were close-fitting and accentuated not only how tall she was but her feminine shapeliness. Her golden hair was pulled back into a sleek ponytail, and the large amber gem that had been in her hair yesterday was now on a chain about her neck, stunning against the white of her jersey.

Deborah felt suddenly conscious of the sloppy brown jersey she was wearing and that her own hair was loose and untidy. She surreptitiously stepped behind one of the kitchen counters.

"Greetings, all beloved ones," Mage Chila said. "Oxpeina-life and health to you."

"Oxpeina's best for you, Mage Chila," said Sam, Mally, and the squatchamn couple.

Deborah hoped Mage Chila wouldn't notice she hadn't joined in with the others in what seemed to be their usual response.

Mage Chila looked over at her, smiling. "What a beautiful basketful of eggs. Were you the one who collected them this morning, Deborah?"

Deborah glanced at the dirt-smudged eggs she had set on the countertop, then back at Mage Chila. "*Um*, yes."

"Thank you very much," said Mage Chila. "Your help here is very much appreciated." She turned her smiling gaze to include each of the others in the kitchen. "We will be assembling for breakfast soon. I will send Aurath down when we are ready."

And with that, she left the kitchen. Deborah let out the breath she had been holding.

"Mage Chila is so lovely," said Sam. "Such a kind mage, always so thoughtful."

"Right," said the squatchamn woman. "Now, give me those eggs; we've got to get cracking." She laughed, and Mally snorted.

Breakfast went on much the same as dinner the night before. Now and then everyone's conversation was broken into by Mage Chila—not intentionally, Deborah thought; it was just how it happened, for when she spoke louder, others paused to listen. She was like that; she had such a commanding presence that she could not help but draw the attention of others. She talked of Mage Barmus' goal for Hirahi, his desire for unity and life amongst the regions, and the instructions he had given her for her role now.

Nurrel was not at the table, Deborah had not seen him all morning, and Taffin was not there either, for she had taken breakfast down to Olly. Kasharel was at the far end of the table, again seated next to Mage Chila. Occasionally, Deborah saw him and Mage Chila conversing together. He seemed even more serious in his expression and preoccupied in thought when he was not speaking with Mage Chila, and only once had he looked Deborah's way and caught her eye as if to silently greet her.

As for Jacob, he was nowhere to be seen. Deborah did not join in the conversation around her but ate silently. It was hard to think of what to do. What was she even doing here? She didn't belong. Why had she made the journey in the first place? It was a complete waste of time. She thought back to that night in Shilhim when she had woken to discover Father had gone. She should have let him go instead of running madly into the woods after him. Should have let him go. She set her spoon down, her appetite dwindling as gnawing despondency took its place.

"—and brismuns meddle in life that they do not understand," said Mage Chila.

Deborah stared at her. Brismuns did not meddle, and what did she mean: 'in life that they do not understand'? Brismuns were incredibly understanding and insightful.

"They are here primarily to tend the trees and the dwellers within, not to influence and dictate to the image-bearers. A brismun should understand that it is here only on request of the image-bearers and therefore should do as it is told."

Deborah frowned. Mage Chila made it sound like Erno and Fothie were some kind of trained animals.

"They are flighty, disrespectful, and throw their weight around."

"No," said Deborah. "Brismuns are not like that!"

Everyone at the table turned to look at her.

"They are not," she said. "The brismuns I know have been nothing but caring, understanding, and loving."

"It may be that you do not know many brismuns," said Mage Chila. She smiled, sitting very tall and upright in her chair, her eyes on Deborah. "I have had many, many experiences with brismuns—different from your own experiences, it seems. I am sorry if I have offended you, Deborah. As mage, it is my duty to share what I know with you all to better equip you for your journey onward."

It was uncomfortable to have that smile fixed on her. Deborah could not smile back, even though she had the impression that was what Mage Chila wanted. It was wrong; what Mage Chila had said was wrong. Wasn't it? She had the fleeting thought of the brismun who had attacked her. She looked at Kasharel. He said nothing but merely had the slightly sympathetic curl to one corner of his mouth while the look in his grey eyes hinted at discomfort. All of a sudden, Deborah longed to see Erno's grin and his vibrantly green, mossy face. To have him gently touch her arm and know exactly how she was feeling. What were he and Fothie doing right now?

"Let us all carry on with our morning tasks," said Mage Chila. "We have much to do, don't we."

There was a collective murmur of agreement around the table, the shuffling of feet, the scraping of last morsels on plates, and chatter resumed. Deborah sat staring at her plate. People got up around her, and still she sat. Everything had gone wrong. It had been wrong for a long time, ever since Mother had died, but now things were about as wrong as they could get. Here she was, out in the middle of nowhere, and she would never see Father again.

A hand touched her shoulder. She flinched and looked up, half-expecting to see Kasharel.

"Oh, my dear," said Taffin. "You look like you've swallowed a lake eel, and it's wriggled down the wrong way. Are you all right?"

"Yes," Deborah said.

Taffin's brow wrinkled, and she pursed her lips. "You could have fooled me. What can I do to help?"

Deborah shook her head. What could be done? She did not know.

Taffin got a thick cushion from one of the other chairs and put it on the chair next to Deborah. She climbed onto it and sat, her feet resting on the first rung of the chair. Like Deborah, she wore a loose knitted brown jersey, along with a skirt and leggings, although with her shorter legs, her skirt appeared longer than Deborah's. "Awkward," she said. "One size does not fit all with these chairs and tables, but we do our best. I think sometimes it makes me miss my village, but that has gone now, and here we are. Olly and I make do. He told me that you're from Eblhim just like he is."

Deborah nodded.

"It's okay," Taffin said softly. "Do you want me to call for your custodian? A brismun, isn't he? That's wonderful."

Deborah looked at her. Taffin had not been there when Mage Chila had spoken about brismuns. "Do you think so?"

"Yes, I really do. There's something special about them. It must be incredible to be able to spend so much time with one. To travel with their knowledge of the woods, well… I imagine it would give an interesting perspective."

Interesting was one way of putting it. Even though not all of Deborah's travels in the woods had been with Erno at her side, she had come to depend more on him and found it hard to think of going on without him. "Yes. It has."

They sat silently together for a moment. Through the great windows, the sun was rising over the lake, and Deborah could see puffs of white clouds slowly moving across the azure sky.

"Where are all the rovi custodians?" she asked. "I mean, with everyone who stays here, I thought I'd see more rovi around."

"Custodians are assigned when we travel," said Taffin. "It can be difficult crossing through the regions, so Sonax sends out a custodian to watch over the image-bearers then. It's different with brismuns; their custodian role in the regions is more a caretaker type of thing."

So, Father really would have had a custodian assigned. Yes, Deborah had been told a rova was with him, but there was some consolation in hearing that again. He would have all his needs taken care of so wouldn't have any need for her. That much was clear—he was not making any effort to come back to her.

"Fothie has just changed over with Hemri around here," Taffin went on. "That's probably for the best, as we're soon to start felling some trees we've been growing for use. Hemri's a bit sensitive to that sort of thing, so I suspect he wanted to get away before we start on that. Fothie's more practical, and she'll be a great help to us in how we go about things." There was a contented look in Taffin's eyes as she gazed towards the great windows.

"Mage Chila said the brismuns meddle, and they're disrespectful," Deborah said.

Taffin's expression grew thoughtful. "Did she? *Hum.*"

The sound of footsteps echoing through the great hall drew their attention. A young squatchamn man was approaching, his face serious, his eyes staring.

"Deborah?" he said.

"Yes," said Deborah.

"Mage Chila has requested you to come and speak with her. She has two times available—either at the morning's break or right after the lunch has finished. Which of those do you prefer?"

Deborah wasn't sure she preferred either. She didn't particularly feel like speaking to anyone, much less the mage. "What's this about?"

The young man shrugged. "I don't know."

She sighed, supposing she may as well get it over with sooner. "I guess the morning's break will be okay."

The young man nodded and turned on his heel.

"You don't have to do that, you know," Taffin said to Deborah. "If you're not feeling so well, you can leave talking to her for another day. You could always go down to the barn and help Olly out with the new rvenan instead. He's going to start training it to be ridden, and he says it has a liking for you."

Deborah thought that should be an appealing idea, but she felt nothing. There didn't seem to be enthusiasm for anything. Maybe the only thing she had any desire to do was go back to her room, to sit alone, to try to think of what she should do, where she should go. To wait and see if Jacob would come, then ask him what he thought she should do, whether she should go on to the city of Aric or just go back home. Perhaps that was what Mage Chila wanted to talk about—her journeying plans.

"Maybe later," Deborah said.

Taffin looked as if she was about to say something else, but bit her lip and leaned back in the chair. Sam came up the stairs from the kitchen and started collecting plates from the table.

Deborah got up. "Oh! I should be helping."

"So should I," Taffin said with a grin and got down from her chair.

33

Deborah supposed 'morning break' was once everyone had finished clearing things away in the kitchen, scraps had gone down to the barn, dishes washed, bread rolls covered with light cloth and set aside for the lunch and dinner meals. She was the last to take off her apron and leave the kitchen.

She reluctantly climbed the stairs back to the great hall. Hopefully, Mage Chila wouldn't talk for long. Hopefully, she would just offer whatever advice mages did for travellers, and that would be that. Then Deborah would go back to her room and see if Jacob was about.

She padded quietly through the great hall in her soft shoes, wending her way past the rows of dining tables. It was easy enough to find Mage Chila's library; she remembered the foyer right outside the great hall and the little side room off that containing the sofa. Deborah went through there and opened the door to see Mage Chila sitting at the desk in the middle of the library.

"Hello," Deborah said. "You wanted to talk to me?"

Mage Chila glanced up. "Yes, that's right. Wait outside."

That was oddly abrupt. Deborah backed out and shut the door. She went over to the sofa and sat, pondering what she should say to Mage Chila. She had no real idea what she wanted to do, whether to go on to Aric or to go back home to Eblhim. It would probably help to take a look at a map and see how close Aric was, but somehow, as she thought about it, her stomach turned. Why bother going? What would she find if she did? Would Father want her there? She had been told he was on his way to Aric, but that was days ago. Maybe he had already been there and moved on. Was there really any point to chasing him all over the regions? If he really loved her, he would be chasing her; he would come back to her. He was supposed to be her father. He was supposed to take care of her.

She took a deep breath and fidgeted with her skirt, smoothing the wrinkles from it. Mage Chila was taking her time; when was she going to want to talk? Deborah thought of Taffin and Olly down at the barn, wondering if they had started training the mumbling rvenan.

The door to the library finally opened. Mage Chila looked down at Deborah. "Come in, please." She held the door open, giving a swift gesture for Deborah to go through. "Take a seat."

As they sat at opposite sides of the desk, Deborah looked at Mage Chila expectantly.

Mage Chila smiled back at her. "Good morning, Deborah. I wish to speak to you of your tendency to talk out of turn, your lack of sensitivity to others, your brash hardness."

Deborah felt as though she had been slapped across the face and was breathless from surprise.

"I have been mage for many, many years. I trained under Mage Barmus himself. You may not be aware that he was the well-respected mage who founded Hirahi. Nobody was like him, and nobody will ever be like him again, but I am most thankful that I can carry his knowledge and offer my services here as mage. In all my years, I have never come across someone as ungrateful as you. We offer you a place to call home, somewhere to live and breathe and work in the love and power of Oxpeina-life, and yet you have acted very disdainful of this."

Deborah was so confused she was unsure how to respond. Mage Chila did not give her the chance to, however, as she barely paused for breath.

"You sit at our dining table with a very frowny face. A *very* frowny face. It is most unbecoming. I would think that because of the opportunity you have freely been given, you would show us more appreciation. You have been here barely a day and already have spoken against me. I find this very shocking and uncouth."

Deborah could only stare at Mage Chila, who kept smiling as she spoke.

"I understand you may have some little experience with brismuns—not all pleasant as you were physically attacked by one, I hear—but I won't have you spreading untruths about brismuns in Hirahi. I have many, *many* more years of experience with brismuns, and I have been entrusted with sharing my knowledge." She tilted her head, smiling sympathetically. "Such a frowny face, Deborah. When you have experienced the love, and life, and light of Oxpeina as I have, it is easy to smile. I smile to show you the life of Oxpeina flowing through me."

Well, Mage Chila was batty; that much was clear. Deborah began to think of how to leave the library. Should she just get up and walk out?

"You have no such life," said Mage Chila. "I only need to take one look at you to know that. I can see that you are a child who has been left and that you have driven away your family by your own actions. And, now that you are here, you drive away others. I see it happening all around you—this is the low quality, the flimsy substance, the *air* of life you send out. No one wants to be close to you, for they have all felt that air from you, Deborah. You do not want love; you do not want life."

It was like needles stabbing into the heart, finding their mark exactly, knowing where all the weak points were to sting and harass. Mage Chila's smiling face was in sharp focus amongst the cloud of shock that bore down onto Deborah.

"I tell you this because I love you," said Mage Chila. "I have such great love for all of the image-bearers and desire them to live, to truly feel the Oxpeina-life."

A memory stirred, remembrance of the region just outside of the gehun tunnels where the electricity of life was felt in the ground, in the rocks, and where she and Jacob and Kasharel saw each other more brightly. Then came the memory of being held in Grufful's arms as the guandras attacked—the warmth of his rova fur, his voice in her ear, the surge of Oxpeina-life across and around her back at the touch of his fingertips. *That* was Oxpeina-life, not this strange fixed smile from Mage Chila and her hard, glittering eyes.

"Your mother died," said Mage Chila, "and your father left you. These things are connected. They are a part of who you are and reveal your involvement in these events. They would not have happened if not for you. And I hear there was another death at the Silver Lake—"

Again, the words were so stunning they were like a slap in the face. Deborah felt her breath coming more quickly, felt it choke in her throat, her sight beginning to blur with tears. "No," she said, struggling to get the word out. "*No.*"

"Yes," said Mage Chila. "I see it all. I see it in you. Let me help you."

Deborah sprang from her chair and fled the library. She ran through the great hall, stumbling and slipping in her cloth shoes. Must go back to her room, get away from everything, get away from everyone. Would have to go down to the kitchen to find her way back to her room from there. She clutched wildly at the tunnel wall as she almost slid down the steps to the kitchen. No one was in the kitchen, no one was around. She could get to her room without anyone seeing her.

How did Mage Chila know her mother had died and that Father had left? Had Kasharel told her? It must have been Kasharel. She also knew about the brismun attack; had Kasharel told her that as well? And about Ibelli at the Silver Lake? Why would he talk about her to Mage Chila? Why? These were personal things, private things. He shouldn't have spoken of them, least of all to Mage Chila, someone they hardly knew. And to imply that it was her fault that Mother had died, her fault that Father had left... how dare she? Why would she say such things? All with that smile on her face as if she were doing Deborah a favour. Saying that her smile was 'showing the life of Oxpeina flowing through her'. Some kind of life!

She shut the door to her room and sat on the edge of the bed. Mage Chila had better not follow her, had better not come to her room. Maybe she should have gone somewhere else, gone outside. That would mean going back to the kitchen, down to the barn, finding the way out there. What if Mage Chila was in the kitchen right now, looking for her? Terrible woman. She didn't want to see her again.

A scrabbling sound came from the window. Jacob was perched on the outside sill, glaring in at her. Deborah got up and let him in.

"What are you doing in here?" he said. "I thought we'd be talking to Erno by now, making plans to leave. Half of the morning is gone already. I think Nurrel is pretty keen to get going—he's been up most the night talking with Erno and Fothie. Hemri came over for a while, too. He's interesting—very different to his siblings."

Deborah looked at Jacob as he folded his wings and walked along the inside sill. She could not think of what to say; shock still had its disorienting tendrils around her.

"What's up with you?" Jacob said. "Your face looks all strange."

Frowny face, Mage Chila had said. Frowny face, most unbecoming. She might as well have said outright that Deborah was ugly.

"You don't want to stay here, do you?" Jacob asked.

"No," she said quietly.

"Have you looked at a map and got a mage's advice?"

Deborah bit her lip. No, she was not going to cry. Why bother crying? She shouldn't care what Mage Chila thought of her. If only it hadn't been so incredibly personal, as if she saw right into Deborah and knew her life. Yes, she had got the mage's advice, all right.

Jacob hopped from the sill with a silent flap of his wings and landed on her shoulder. "What's wrong? Are you tired? Didn't you get much sleep last night?"

"No," she said. "It's not that."

"Then, what?"

"Nothing."

"Don't give me that load of rubbish. I can see that it's not nothing." He pressed his head against her cheek, his feathers cool and soft against her skin.

She drew a deep breath. "It's just… well, I don't know. I've just been talking to the mage. She—well, she was… I don't know, it was all so bizarre."

"Which mage?" said Jacob.

"Mage Chila, of course; who else?"

"Mage Taffin, of course."

She looked sidelong at him in surprise. "Taffin is a mage?"

"Sure she is. I thought you knew that."

"No. Nobody told me."

"*Huh.* So, now you know. I seem to be in the habit of telling you things you don't know. What would you do without me?"

She shrugged, and he stepped about on her shoulder to counteract her sudden movement.

"Talk," he said firmly. "Tell me what happened, *now*."

34

"Do you want me to go and peck her eyes out?" Jacob said, after Deborah had recounted her experience with Mage Chila.

He stalked up and down her bedspread while she sat on the bed, and she gave him a small smile.

"The nerve of her!" Jacob said. "And this from a mage. She's got a screw loose in her brain. I knew there was something funny about her; I knew it! The way she talked down to me about brismuns like I was a moron. *Gah!* What's she doing here in Hirahi? It's supposed to be a safe outpost under Sonax's good name. What about Mage Taffin? Is she crazy, too?"

"Not so far," said Deborah. "She seems nice, but then what do I know? She could be fake, too."

"We've got to tell Fothie and Hemri. This could be very dangerous for them."

"Dangerous, how?"

"It could push them out; it could turn the image-bearers against them. It'll unsettle the region. Let's go!" He hopped to her shoulder and gave her a pinch as if to urge her to get up.

She winced. Clouds were gathering in the sky, grey and unappealingly wintry. The little radiator in the room was doing a reasonable job of keeping the small space warm. She would much rather crawl into bed and not do anything. "You go," she said. "You know everything. You can tell it all."

"Where's your spirit?" he said. "It's not like you. You should be hopping mad and ready for action."

"Just tired, I guess."

He leapt back down onto the bed and glowered up at her. She could not help but smile. If anyone had a 'frowny face', it was him, but then he couldn't help it. Maybe she could, but did she really want to go around smiling inanely like Mage Chila? No. Showing love and life. Sure, showing love and life then attacking with all sorts of vile comments—she had pretty much outright accused Deborah of having something to do with Mother's death.

"Well," said Jacob. "I'm going. This kind of information can't wait. I need to tell Fothie right away because it affects her."

Jacob seemed focused on what Mage Chila had said about the brismuns and not what had been directed at Deborah. Maybe that didn't matter to him as much. Maybe he already had those kinds of thoughts about her—he no doubt found her argumentative and probably thought she was stupid travelling through the regions trying to find Father.

She nodded dolefully.

He flew to the windowsill. "I'll be back soon."

She opened the window for him, and he launched himself with a magnificent spread of his wings. He soared around in a wide arc and was soon gone from view. She leaned against the sill for a while, looking out over the river, the trees, to the ranges in the distance. Maybe she really should go home now. Find a job, find a new life. The house in Eblhim hadn't been sold; it was only rented out. She could take it back. Could she take it back without Father's authorisation? Or she could live in the house at Shilhim. She grimaced. Live in a shack at the edge of the woods doing what? That would have to be the last-ditch option if she couldn't get the house in Eblhim.

A light tap came at her door. She stared at it. That had better not be Mage Chila. Although, would she do a light tap? She would more likely bash the door in with great dominant thuds of her fist. The taps came again. Deborah held her breath.

"Deborah, are you in there?"

She exhaled. It was Kasharel's voice.

She let him in and sat on the bed while he leaned against the windowsill, his tall, slim frame traced by the light. They eyed each other for a few moments.

"I haven't seen you to talk to you since we got here," Kasharel finally said.

"I've been busy. I'm sure you have, too."

He folded his arms. "I suppose. I've been finding my way around the treatment room and getting set up. I haven't treated anything other than a cut hand so far."

"We've been here barely a day," she said. "I'll sure you'll get more customers."

The corners of his lips twitched.

"*Patients*," she said. "You know what I mean."

He gave a slight nod. "So, do you think you will stay here long?"

She shook her head. "I don't think so. This place is nuts."

"Nuts?"

"I've just had Mage Chila tear into me and basically tell me it's my own fault my mother died and my father left."

His eyebrows raised infinitesimally. "Surely not. You must have mistaken what she meant."

"Oh no, I didn't. She also told me I've been really ungrateful and rude—that I have a brash hardness and lack of sensitivity to others, oh, and I also have an air about me that pushes everyone away."

"I can't believe she would say anything like that. Are you sure you didn't misunderstand what she was saying? Perhaps all she was trying to say was that you have kind of a barrier to getting close to anyone—that you like to keep your distance."

She frowned at him and immediately became conscious of the feel of her face. *Frowny face*. She tried to assume a more neutral expression. It was not fair of him to say that to her—she had shared plenty of her life story with him, maybe too much when she had been unwell in the gehun caves. He knew how hard things had been for her with Father since Mother had died.

"I understand," Kasharel went on. "It's hard for you to trust others. Maybe that's what Mage Chila was trying to say."

Why was he defending Mage Chila, not her? "She is a nauseating excuse for a person, putting on all smiles then sliding a dagger in when no one's looking."

"Deborah!"

"She thinks her sickening smiles are showing love and Oxpeina-life. She's a phoney! There's nothing loving about how she talked to me. Or, how she talked about brismuns! She hates them."

"I think you're being a little extreme. Mage Chila has been nothing but kind and helpful since we got here. She is very well-educated—she told me something of her years of training, and I have looked at some of the books in her library—and she also has a lot of knowledge about the Oxpeina-life that we could benefit from. Why are you picking on the way she smiles? She is simply trying to show others that she cares about them. I think that's nice."

"Did you not hear me? I said she accused me of having something to do with my own mother's death and that I'm the reason my father left."

He drew a slow breath. "What did she say exactly?"

"And how did she know that my mother died?" Deborah said, glaring at him. "Have you been talking to Mage Chila about me? You told her about Ibelli at the lake, too?"

"She only wanted to know something of your background so she could help you. That's her job here as mage."

"It was none of her business, and you shouldn't have told her anything about me."

"I only wanted to help you. I thought that was why we are here—to gain help and direction for the way ahead. I think that is all Mage Chila is wanting to do, to help us."

"She attacked me, and she attacked Erno, Fothie, and Hemri. How is that helping?"

"What do you mean, attacked? She hit you?"

"No, I mean she verbally bashed me."

"What about the brismuns?"

"She said things about them. She said they meddle in life that they can't understand; they're disrespectful and throw their weight around. You heard her; she said it at breakfast in front of everyone."

He shrugged. "Well, she does have a point."

She stared at him.

"They do interfere, and not always for the best. I mean, you were attacked by the brismun custodian of my region, and amongst my people, he is known for being unpredictable and unsafe. Then, what about the brismun we met who threatened to 'put us in the ground' just because we were walking through her region? And, Iff. Don't get me wrong, I liked Iff, but he certainly threw his weight around."

She felt as though she was talking to someone she didn't know anymore. Kasharel really thought that about brismuns, too? "But we wouldn't be here if it wasn't for Erno," she said. "He's kept us safe. We would be completely lost without him."

"Erno's different. Still, how long have you known him? I have only known him for a few days, and I don't know if I agree with everything he has done. Why did he take you back into the Silver Lake region to talk to the squatchamn girl? What sense was in that? I don't think that was a good idea. Also, he didn't prevent what happened to Ibelli at the lake, and I'm sure he could have."

Her heart hurt as she listened to Kasharel criticising Erno. Erno, who had protected her; Erno, who was so cheerful yet full of tender-heartedness, insight, and care. If anyone was full of Oxpeina-life, it was him. She wished she had gone with Jacob to find him. Wished she was anywhere but in this stupid place. "Well, I have only known you for a few days, too," she said, "and I'm beginning to regret it."

He was silent, but she could see from his expression that she had dealt him a blow. It made her feel angry. He shouldn't be the one who acted hurt; *he* was hurting *her* by failing to see anything wrong with

Mage Chila's accusations. "You don't need to stay," she said, gesturing towards the door. "I'm sure you want to get back to Mage Chila and hear all her amazing wisdom on the meaning of life!"

"I don't see why you're so angry," he said. "We've been offered help here, and we should take it."

"Have you not been listening to me? She accused me of having something to do with my own mother's death and my father's leaving me!"

"You haven't told me exactly what she said. I think you must have misunderstood her."

"No, I didn't! I also didn't misunderstand her when she said I have a low quality air of life about me that drives away others, and no one wants to be close to me! Who says stuff like that? She doesn't know me; she's only just met me!"

"She's a mage. She must have seen something—"

"*Kasharel!*"

"We can't know the things that mages perceive. We should listen to them when they offer their insight."

She glared at him. Did he believe she had 'low quality air of life'? Did he think no one wanted to be close to her, too? On some level, he must agree with Mage Chila if he was talking like this. He was not indignant at all about what had been said to her; he failed to see anything wrong with it. At least Jacob had said he would go and peck Mage Chila's eyes out, so *he* knew it was wrong.

"Go on, then," she said. "Don't sit here talking to me anymore. Go back to Mage Chila and kiss her feet and see what kind of insight she gives you!"

He got up, his brow furrowing ever-so-slightly. She resisted the urge to call him 'frowny face'.

"We will talk again on this later when you have calmed yourself," he said.

"No. We won't."

He left the room with no further word.

35

Deborah did not know how long she sat in her room, fuming, thoughts tumbling through her mind. Kasharel had obviously had his head turned by Mage Chila, her face all loony with fake smiles and her so-called 'wisdom'. What about their friendship? Did it mean nothing? He had cared for her after the attack by the brismun custodian of his region; she thought they had become close, and now he was turning his back on her. For what? A mage? If this was what mages were like, he could stick it.

Yet, Taffin was also a mage. Why hadn't she said she was a mage? She wasn't like Mage Chila, unless she was putting on an act, too. It was hard to think she was—the little lumdil had oozed friendliness and practicality as she got on with her jobs about the kitchen. She had been kind. She had not said anything about an 'air' and she hadn't acted as though Deborah was some kind of horrible freak to keep away from.

Deborah went into the bathroom and splashed water on her face. She looked at herself in the mirror, all splotchy-faced and frowny. So, it was her face; it was just how it was—she didn't mean to frown. She smiled at her reflection and immediately felt stupid. It was not a proper smile; it looked like a grimace. She did not glow with Oxpeina-life, and why should she want to? If Mage Chila was full of Oxpeina-life, then she could have it, but she wasn't. She *wasn't*. Being around her was nothing like the feeling of being with the rovi. The very air around Val, Grufful, and the rest of the pack was infused with life. The *air*.

She rubbed her face with a towel and turned away from the mirror. So what if Mage Chila didn't think Deborah had that air? Kasharel obviously didn't think she did, either. Father didn't. Who knows what Mother had thought; they hadn't got along because they were too different.

She went back to the bedroom and stood at the window. The clouds had broken and rain was streaming in great sheets, driving against the windowpane and blurring sight of the distant woods. She was not going to go out in that stuff and search for Erno. She would have to stay put.

She sat on the edge of the bed and grimaced, supposing she ought to really go back to the kitchen. The others who worked there might already be back preparing for lunch. What if Mage Chila came waltzing down the stairs? What about the lunch table? Would Deborah have to sit there while Mage Chila went on and on about Oxpeina-life? What if she said something about Deborah in front of everybody? The thought made her stomach queasy. This would not do. She wasn't a child anymore, and she shouldn't care at all what Mage Chila did. No. It didn't matter.

The nerve of her, saying Deborah had something to do with Mother's death and implying she was the reason why Father had left. Absolutely vile and ridiculous. As for Kasharel, thinking that Mage Chila was just trying to be helpful—what was wrong with him? Well, he could stay here and play at being a doctor. She didn't need him anymore. As soon as this weather cleared, she would talk to Erno, tell him she was going back to Eblhim. Gain his help in getting what supplies she could for the journey home. He was her custodian; he would travel with her. Forget about Father. He had forgotten about her. He could live his own life, free of her.

She swallowed a lump in her throat and frowned at the tears that threatened. Yes, she would frown. She would frown as much as she wanted to! She stood and straightened her shapeless jersey. Time to go to the kitchen, do what jobs needed to be done as payment for the use of this room and hopefully as payment for the supplies that she would need to leave Hirahi for good. Her legs felt a little wobbly. Shut up, legs! No need to be nervous. She could face Mage Chila if she had to.

Deborah left the room and marched along the passageway. Her breathing felt shallow, and she forced herself to take deeper breaths, to calm down, to try to relax. So what if Kasharel was not on her side and did not believe her—she had only known him a matter of days. It was not like they had been friends for a long time. He could do whatever he wanted; Erno had not been assigned as his custodian and didn't have to stay with him or travel with him. Kasharel had no custodian. That was weird, but it had nothing to do with her. Erno was her custodian. And, Jacob's. And, she suddenly thought, Nurrel's. She remembered Erno saying he was Nurrel's custodian, too. What did that mean? She did not know where Nurrel was or what he was doing. Jacob had said Nurrel had spent most of the night talking with Erno. Were they making plans to travel on together? They would not do that, would they? Surely Erno wouldn't leave her. The thought gave her stomach an anxious turn.

The kitchen was empty. She looked around for a moment. What should she do? The sight of the stairs leading up to the great hall was off-putting. She didn't want Mage Chila to come down and find her alone. Better to go down to the barn. She pattered down the flight of steps in her soft shoes.

In the barn, the warm aroma of hay and beast intermingled. The fowls clucked quietly to themselves as they scratched about in the hay, the whatever-those-animals-were-in-the-pens grunted and snuffled, and the rvenan cattle munched contentedly in their stalls. The stall that had held the mumbling rvenan was empty. Had they taken him outside in this weather? Deborah walked through the barn, past buckets, stacks of hay, and other metal and wooden implements. The natural cave ceiling, uneven ripples of smooth veins of stone, was not so high overhead. She thought if Kasharel was here, he would probably be able to just reach it if he stood on tiptoes. She frowned again at the thought of him, then took a deep breath. Drat being acutely aware of her own face and the frowns it made!

The murmur of voices came from the far end of the barn. Deborah rounded a stack of hay, atop which a small furry orange-and-grey-striped animal lay sleeping. It opened one eye and cocked a pointed ear at Deborah as she passed and let out a tiny *chirrup*. At the end of the barn, wide doors were open, the rain pelting down like a curtain. Olly and Taffin were there before it, sitting on a hay bale together. Seated, their differences in height did not seem so apparent. The mumbling rvenan looked over their shoulders out at the rain. Olly patted the rvenan's flank, and it leaned over and nibbled the top of his head.

Deborah paused, unsure if she should approach or go back to the kitchen. Taffin was a mage—what did she 'see' in Deborah? It did not matter—she would be leaving here soon, so they could think what they liked. She went on, steeling herself for any kind of encounter that may come.

"Hi," she said, attempting to put cheeriness in her voice. "Not great weather for taking the rvenan outdoors!"

Olly and Taffin turned and smiled at her approach. Warm smiles, real smiles, not forced or fixed, as far as Deborah could tell. The rvenan smirked at her, wrinkling and twitching his upper lip. She couldn't help but smile back at him.

"Not at all," said Olly.

"I think it's more us, not him, who want to stay in," said Taffin, reaching up to stroke the rvenan. "He's used to being out in all weathers. You'd go out in it now, wouldn't you, huh?"

The rvenan bobbed his head and mumbled. He turned neatly, swinging himself around on the spot, and went over to Deborah, his large hooves clopping on the stone. She stood still, unsure what to do as he approached. He let out a mumbling stream of nonsense as if he were trying to tell her something.

"What is it?" she said softly.

"What a funny old character!" Taffin said. "What's he trying to say?"

"He's professing his love to Deborah, I think. Sounds like how I did when we were young."

"Olly!" Taffin said, laughing.

He grinned at her. Something in the profile and shape of his nose and chin made Deborah catch her breath. Yes, Olly was similar to Father. But when had she last seen Father smile—a real, true, light-hearted smile? Years ago.

The rvenan gently lipped her hand. She stroked his long velvety grey ears, and he shut his eyes and sighed.

"Soppy sook," Taffin said as she watched.

"He is, that," said Olly. "Would you like to name him, Deborah? He seems to have a soft spot for you."

Deborah scratched the rvenan's head between his ears. "*Um*, sure. I'll have to think about that."

"Good-o." Olly got up. "I'd better get back to it—the barn doesn't clean itself."

"More's the pity," Taffin said. She smiled up at Deborah. "I guess you've come looking for me because I promised we'd go over the maps of the regions and sort out the best route to Aric?" She got up and picked pieces of hay off her skirt and leggings.

Deborah bit her lip. "Well, I… no, not really. I have decided to go back home after all, so I won't be going to Aric. Thanks, anyway."

Taffin's eyes widened in surprise. "Oh! Okay. Really? I haven't heard anything good about how Eblhim is doing. Are you sure you should be going back there?"

"It was rotting when I left," Olly said over his shoulder as he got a rake and bucket, "and that was years ago. Image-bearers getting more and more self-absorbed, not caring for anyone but themselves. Would think it'd only be worse by now. That region must be near to closing."

"Well, it's not," Deborah said. "It's fine. My home is there. I was in Eblhim only a few weeks ago, and there was nothing out of the ordinary going on." Although, his remark about people being self-absorbed was unsettling. Mother had been just like that, caring only about herself and what she wanted, thinking only of her own happiness, not Father's and certainly not Deborah's. And what about Father? He had retreated into his own world when Mother had died, and now he was gone.

"Still," said Taffin, "do be careful. If Erno's travelling back with you, look after him. I don't know it would be safe for him to go near the city with you."

"Most likely he'd be attacked," Olly said. "Eblhim image-bearers had no tolerance for custodians back then, and I would think it's no better now."

Deborah stared at him. "I don't know what you mean. Before I came to the woods, I'd never heard of a custodian, and we in Eblhim certainly don't label ourselves by the term 'image-bearers', so I think that sort of thing is probably not even relevant."

Olly nodded. "*Humph*. Yeah, that's about right."

"Hey," Taffin said.

He gave her a significant look and headed off to the rvenan stalls.

Taffin turned to Deborah. "He doesn't mean to be hard on you—it was very difficult for him to watch his region begin to turn."

"Perhaps he should go back and see it's not so bad there now," Deborah said. "If he hasn't been there for many years, he might be surprised at how well Eblhim is doing."

Taffin looked thoughtful. "Still, take absolute care with your return to that region—rely on the advice of Sonax as to how to go about it."

Deborah gave what she hoped was an amiable smile. All of this sort of Sonax-Opxeina thing wouldn't matter once she was back home again. She had other things to think about—how to get the family home back, how to find work and build a life for herself. The rvenan nudged her arm, as she had stopped stroking his ears, and mumbled at her.

Taffin chuckled. "Perhaps we should call you Mister Needy!"

The rvenan flicked her a sidelong smirk and snorted.

36

Deborah carried the last of the lunch dishes to the table as all the inhabitants of Hirahi gathered and began taking their seats. She could see Mage Chila standing a little apart, Kasharel beside her as they talked. It made her feel sick. Why was he befriending someone who had treated her so badly? She had told him how Mage Chila had accused and attacked her—did that not matter to him? Yet here he was, being all chummy with her.

As soon as Deborah had entered the great hall, she had the impression that Mage Chila was watching her. She tried not to look, for each time she inadvertently glanced over, the mage's eyes were on her in a hard, penetrating gaze.

She had hardly set the dish onto the table when she had a voice in her ear and a hand on her shoulder.

"Marvellous!" said Mage Chila, smiling brilliantly. "We are so glad to have you here with us, Deborah!"

Deborah began to edge out from under the light pressure of her hand, but Mage Chila moved position to rub Deborah's upper arm.

She smiled indulgently down at Deborah, her eyes gleaming. "We will have to keep you on in our kitchen. You're doing such a great job!"

The smile didn't falter but remained fixed as if Mage Chila was trying to coax a smile from Deborah and would not move until she got what she wanted. It was a strange sensation, and Deborah felt trapped somehow, as if moving away without responding would be more proof of her rudeness, of her unfriendly air. A smile inadvertently twitched across her face, and she kicked herself for it—she should not have to smile! She should not have to do anything! Why was Mage Chila acting so friendly, anyway?

Mage Chila's smile took on a gratified quality, then she strode away to take her place at the head of the table, her long pale blue cloak sweeping along behind her. Deborah sat quickly, her legs feeling suddenly wobbly.

Taffin drew the chair out at her right, settled a thick cushion, and climbed onto it. The chair at Deborah's left scraped along the floor as someone drew it out, and she looked to see Nurrel setting another cushion onto it.

"Nurrel!" she said.

It was a relief to see him—to see that familiar face, his soft brown eyes with the sadness behind them.

"Deborah," he said, giving her a nod.

At least he didn't smile. Deborah didn't think she could take another one just yet, for she felt confused by Mage Chila's behaviour. One moment glaring from across the hall, the next moment that beaming smile and a great show of friendliness.

"Welcome!" called Mage Chila. "I am so very glad to have you all here again today! We have exciting things ahead of us here in Hirahi. Oxpeina's best to you all!"

"Oxpeina's best," murmured several at the table.

Oxpeina's best? How? By telling someone that they were basically responsible for the death of their mother and why their father left?

"Love and light to you all," said Mage Chila.

"Love and light," murmured some.

Taffin and Nurrel weren't among those who responded. Across from Deborah, Mally and Sam intently watched Mage Chila with smiles on their faces. Well, they could smile all they wanted. Mage Chila wouldn't tell them they had frowny faces, that's for sure. She looked down at her plate. Was Kasharel right? Had Mage Chila actually been trying to help her with her insight? She supposed she wasn't the friendliest of people, she did feel a certain amount of caution around others.

But then, how would she have caused Mother's death? Mother had been knocked down, hit her head on pavement—it was all an accident. Then again, would it still have happened if she had been with Mother? She was a child in school, but would it have been different if they were out together that day? Maybe she would have seen what was about to happen—Father hadn't been very clear on how the accident had come about, and he hadn't witnessed it, either—and maybe she could have somehow prevented it. Is that what Mage Chila meant? And now Father had left because she didn't care enough for him? She hadn't understood well enough what he really wanted; hadn't known anything about how he might have been trying to answer the pull, the enchantment of the Oxpeina-life drawing him into the woods.

Watching Mage Chila now, she was full of smiles—the Oxpeina-life, she said—and talking to others about love. Deborah felt as though her own thoughts were muddly and conflicted. Was she being too sensitive about what Mage Chila had said to her? Too quick to take offence? Should she have listened to the mage—someone who knew a lot more about Oxpeina-life than she did?

The distant sound of thuds broke into her thinking. Steady, *thu-da thu-da*, repeating, sometimes offbeat, out of sync. Mage Chila stopped talking, and a hush fell over everyone at the table. Louder and louder came the thuds. Deborah's heart echoed the thuds—could it be? Was it Erno? And Fothie as well, for the thuds were not singular, sometimes coinciding, sometimes apart.

Everyone turned to watch the far end of the great hall. Deborah found herself almost holding her breath, and then—there they were. Leaping through the open doorway, vibrantly-green bushy figures against the stone of Hirahi, their thick legs impacting the floor as they landed, then gathered themselves to leap again. Deborah felt as though she wanted to leap too, leap from her chair, and run to them. Erno was following Fothie, dodging around the empty tables. She knew it was him by the way he carried himself. Deborah wanted to cry his name, have him know where she was, but Mage Chila stood.

"Why are you here?" she said in a loud, calm voice.

"Why not?" said Erno.

Deborah realised there was a third thumping—ponderous amongst the sounds of Fothie and Erno's entrance. And then, a third brismun stood in the entrance to the great hall. Deborah supposed this was Hemri. He was less rotund than his siblings, a little taller, his twiggy hair longer and spikier, and there was something about him that made her heart ache for him, something that made her want to go to him. He stood still in the entranceway, his chest heaving, the green of his body intermixed with patches of grey and brown.

The facial features of all three were lost in their mossy countenances, giving them a starkly creature-like appearance in comparison to all the people around the dining table.

"This is no place for brismuns," Mage Chila said.

"Beg pardon," said Taffin, and she got down off her chair and stood, although it made little difference to her height to do so. "You are all most welcome here, Fothie, Hemri, and brother. Hirahi is as much your home as it is ours. How may we help or assist you?"

By now, Erno had come around the table to Deborah while Fothie had gone straight to Mage Chila. Deborah turned to Erno as he placed his hand on her shoulder—a very damp hand, as indeed all of his mossy body was glistening with moisture.

"Deborah," he said. "Jacob told me what happened. Please, come with me."

"Don't touch me," Mage Chila said, drawing back from Fothie. "You have no right to touch me, for I do not give you permission."

"Well," said Fothie, "I don't exactly need it, and in all truth it is my right. But I didn't reach to touch you, so you needn't be afraid."

Deborah got up. As Erno had spoken, she had felt a certain measure of relief. He had come for her. He knew what had happened and he had come.

"I am not afraid," said Mage Chila. "However, I know your place, and it is not here."

Fothie leapt away at that and went over to Taffin. "Hello, sweetie. How's Olly?"

"Do not move away from me when I am addressing you," Mage Chila said.

"I have no business with you, Chila," Fothie said over her shoulder. "I'm here with my brothers for Deborah. Carry on; don't let us disturb your meal. It looks quite tasty."

Erno beckoned and Deborah followed. Nurrel got up quietly and went with them. As Erno leapt ahead, a fine mist of water shook out around him each time he landed. The voices of Fothie, Taffin, and Mage Chila became indistinct as Deborah half-walked-half-ran to keep up with Erno. They soon joined Hemri, who led them to the door of the library. Deborah grimaced and hung back at the sight of it.

"What's the matter?" Erno said.

"I don't want to go into her library," Deborah said. "Can't we go somewhere else?"

"It's not her library," Hemri said, and his voice was low and hoarse. "Here will do for now for us to speak. It's raining heavily, and as much as I hate the indoors, it's better for you to not go out in this weather."

There was a thud behind them.

"You image-bearers would get sopping," Fothie said. "Then you'd probably get the sniffles, and it'd be all our fault."

Erno grinned.

Hemri opened the door to the library, and they went in.

37

"It's worse than I thought," said Fothie, after Deborah had told of her encounters with Mage Chila, and the three brismuns had questioned and clarified certain points until they felt they had the information they needed.

Nurrel had said nothing but sat with his head bowed as he listened. Erno's hand was on Deborah's arm the entire time she had spoken. She was sitting in the same chair she had been in by the desk when Mage Chila had spoken with her, and, while she did occasionally feel unsettled and hoped that the mage wouldn't come in at any moment to find them all there, Erno's touch was reassuring. He was with her now. Everything would be all right.

"It's really all right," Deborah said. "I'm going to leave here as soon as the weather clears."

"No," said Erno. "This is about more than how badly Chila has treated you; it's about what she is doing here in Hirahi to all the image-bearers around her. She is turning, and she is opening the way for others to turn."

"Hemri," Fothie said. "Why didn't you tell me it had got this rotten? I didn't know it was one of the mages who has done this to you."

Hemri stood with his hands clasped in front of his stomach. "It is one of the many things we had yet to discuss."

Able to look at him more closely, Deborah could see that the patchiness in the colour of his moss was due to areas that seemed dry.

"Is Taffin still all right, or does she show signs of turning, too?" Fothie asked.

Hemri cleared his throat. "She is well. She will readily come to us. She will touch any of us before we touch her and allow us to sense her life. She needs that, for she struggles to exist here."

"She knows what is happening to Chila?"

"Most definitely. That is the source of her struggle. She would leave here but instead stays on to try to provide balance for the travellers coming through. I am surprised you have not met with Taffin yet—she has often sought me out for reassurance and to share her heart."

"Well," Fothie said, "you and I have only just switched over our areas of the region, and what with Erno here now and all the catching up we've been doing, I hadn't found Taffin yet. Or rather, she hadn't found me. I probably need to make myself more available. Yes, I do recall that the last time I took charge here, she was always the one to seek me out. She had some misgivings back then about Chila. While Chila herself was often too busy to come and speak with me when I was here."

Hemri nodded, his twiggy hair rattling. "Yes, busy. Very busy. Too busy to take time to meet me and yield herself to any of my assessment, or any discussion of the Oxpeina-health for the image-bearers and dwellers of this region."

"She begins things with flattery," Nurrel said, looking at Hemri.

"What?" said Erno.

"Flattery," Nurrel said. "I experienced this a few days ago here and then again yesterday when we returned. Chila says things that flatter. Somehow, I don't think she's sincere, and it made me uncomfortable."

Deborah thought of how Mage Chila had praised her cooking of the fish at dinner last night and how 'perfect' it was.

Hemri clasped and unclasped his hands, his fingers moving slowly as if stiff and uncomfortable. "An image-bearer seeking control over other image-bearers can often do that. They start with praise that can be excessive, and thankfulness, expressing approval—this manipulates the flattered image-bearer into feeling good about the flatterer and therefore more likely to be compliant towards them."

"When you lay it out like that," said Nurrel, "how am I supposed to say anything good to anyone about anything without it having the wrong effect?"

"Motives," said Hemri. "It's all in your motives. If desiring control over another image-bearer has anything to do with your motive for praising them, then this is evidence of your own turning. What we see now with how Chila has behaved with Deborah shows another strategy: the slap down, the attempt to knock another into submission. Deborah spoke out against Chila's opinion—in front of others, no less!—and Chila then moved against Deborah to try to regain control and dominance."

As he spoke, Deborah felt as though things were beginning to make sense.

"An image-bearer who has high self-importance must be bowed to by others, you see?" said Hemri.

"Not really," said Nurrel.

Hemri was silent and stood as a shrub-like statue in the library. Deborah could not tell if he was gathering his thoughts or taking a moment to rest. She could see more now that in him there was something very different to Fothie and Erno. Not just in the careful way in which he moved or spoke, or even his discolouration, but something else in his manner. She realised it reminded her of Geor, the rova who stood at the entrance to Hirahi. Perhaps they were both very old.

"Who is as Sonax?" Hemri muttered. "Who has become as one who holds the Oxpeina-life? An image-bearer? No. Yet, this is the image-bearer's weakness—the desire for the life and power of Sonax for themselves. It becomes the desire for control over others, the rising self-importance, the higher position, the need to be recognised as greater. And now I hear another strategy for increasing the self-importance—reflected glory! Deborah has said that Chila referred often to being a student of the great Mage Barmus." He raised his hands slowly and turned his subtle-contoured face upward. "Oh, the great Barmus! As one image-bearer claims closeness and connection to another of higher stature, so then to others she shines in that reflected glory."

He lowered his hands, and, for the first time, Deborah thought she could see expression appear in his mossy face as his eyes briefly opened a little wider. Was it anger? Disgust?

"Never mind that Barmus became rotten through and through," Hemri said, "and turning to a guandra was his fate—nobody here knows that, for none of those present in Hirahi now were present then. Barmus' position of power went to his head so that he no longer served Sonax. He served himself, as an image-bearer consumed with self-importance does. Barmus ceased stewarding the image-bearers who pass through Hirahi. He should have been stripped of the title of mage, which is a shame, because he was not like that when he was young; he was eager to learn, eager to serve. It appears Chila is walking in his ways."

"Can we warn her?" Fothie asked. "Tell her she's in danger of turning?"

"You can try, but in my experience it only makes the self-importance burn hotter and angrier to suggest such a thing."

Erno grimaced. "Hemri, I think you should have been made custodian to image-bearers, not me. You have a better understanding of them than I do."

Hemri bowed his head. "If Sonax made you Deborah and Nurrel's custodian, accept his choice."

"Rather you than me," Fothie said, grinning.

"Turning is turning," Hemri said, "and neither of you need me to tell you how to recognise that in ourselves or in others."

Erno hopped to one side of the library and laid his hand on a row of books. "I never had to bother about that when caring for dwellers. Unless they had been awakened as Jacob is. Dwellers are uncomplicated and never in danger of turning."

"Where is Jacob?" Deborah asked.

"Sheltering in a tree hollow," Erno said. "He shouldn't fly in the rain because his feathers aren't waterproof. I am sorry I didn't come to you sooner, Deborah. Once Jacob told me what had happened to you, I had to find Fothie and Hemri. As it was, I met Nurrel first, and when he learned of it all, he said he would go to you. So I knew you would have his support, at least, until I could come."

Deborah looked over at Nurrel, who was gazing at the floor with a brooding expression. Yes, Nurrel had come and sat quietly next to her at the lunch table. He who had been making himself scarce from the great hall mealtime gatherings. So, he had come because of her?

"It is wrong," Nurrel said. "It is all very wrong. A mage shouldn't have said such terrible things to you, Deborah."

"But where is Kasharel?" Erno asked. "I sensed him there at the table. Why has he not come with us?"

Deborah felt the frown beginning to steal over her face. "He doesn't think Mage Chila did anything wrong. He thinks she was trying to help me."

Hemri shifted on his stumpy leg. "*Humph!* Rot!"

Nurrel looked at Deborah, his brow furrowed. "What's wrong with Kasharel? Has he let her flattery get to him?"

She was unsure what to say. It hurt to think about Kasharel. He should be there with them all, not staying with Mage Chila and taking her side. Deborah had told him plainly about Mage Chila's accusations, so why didn't he care? Why was he throwing away their friendship?

She thought of how Mage Chila had come over to her at the lunch table and rubbed her arm in a great show of friendliness. Yet, was it really a show? Or, was it genuine? Kasharel seemed to think so. The brismuns and Nurrel didn't.

Erno leapt over and laid his hand on her left shoulder. "Oh, Deborah. You're still holding some confusion about this matter."

Fothie also leapt closer and laid her hand on Deborah's right shoulder. The brismuns' touch, although still a little damp, was steadying. She felt they knew her and accepted her and were trying in their own way to watch over her.

She took a deep breath. "I suppose I don't completely understand your talk of 'turning' and what it is and why it's so damaging to the image-bearers. I do feel better to have shared with you all what Mage Chila said to me, but I also can't help feeling maybe I have blown everything out of proportion? Kasharel seemed to think she was only being kind and trying to help, and Mage Chila also told me she was speaking to me with love. So, I don't know."

"Deborah," said Hemri, "don't think that you are the first to have been treated this way by Chila. Many others have. Those who have left, those who have gone on. Just because she has not permitted me to touch her does not mean I have not been able to sense her and feel the deterioration of Oxpeina-life in the very air around her."

Deborah stared at him. It was surreal to hear almost the same words Mage Chila had used coming from Hemri. Was that just because Deborah had told him what had been said?

"I have felt it, too," said Fothie.

"Me, also," said Erno. "And no, Hemri does not use the words you gave him, Deborah. He knew them first."

She was sure she had not said that out loud. How had he known what she was thinking?

"I have felt that about Chila, too," said Nurrel.

Erno smiled. "I would expect as much from you. Nurrel, you know who you are and can see in others who they are, too."

Nurrel glanced at him then looked at the floor again. "I don't know why you would say that when you know how blind I have been."

Erno hopped over and placed his hand on Nurrel's shoulder. Nurrel covered his face in his hands. Deborah felt her heart ache, for she supposed Nurrel was referring to Ibelli. Fothie's hand smoothed and caressed her shoulder lightly.

"Fothie," Hemri said. "I am beginning to have second thoughts about changing places with you. Do you understand what living closer to Hirahi will do to you now?"

"Hemri," she said. "I need you to get away from here. I've done all I can to bring healing to your body, but I can't seem to do any more.

The will of the image-bearers has the power to keep causing damage. I need you to recover. Shessi and I can live here for a time. You and Shis need to get out. Do as you're told, little brother."

Hemri permitted himself a smile. Deborah looked at him. Was he younger than Fothie? Was this aged appearance, the weathering, the dryness of moss, due to some influence of whatever was going on here with the image-bearers?

"Yes," said Fothie softly, leaning over her. "Chila is against us and is leading and influencing this part of the region."

"I think we would be gone from here if not for Taffin," Hemri said.

Deborah looked up at Fothie. Somehow, she too had read her thoughts as Erno had just done.

Fothie grinned down at her, seeming very like Erno. "You are especially open and trusting towards us right now, so it's easier to get a sense of you and your thoughts. Which is awfully nice, considering what life has been like here for us with many of the image-bearers."

The door of the library opened quietly, and Deborah turned to look, a sick feeling in her stomach. Was it Mage Chila? But, no, the small figure of Taffin stepped in and closed the door behind her. She stood a moment, looking uncertainly from Erno to Fothie, then hurried over to Hemri, her hands outstretched.

"Hemri," she said, as they clasped hands. "I've calmed things down out there, but I don't think you all should stay here. I didn't think Chila would be so outspoken against you, but I guess she's been chipping away at things with her words for some time now. She's got them pretty easily convinced you're up to no good. I'm so sorry."

Fothie hopped over to Taffin's side. Taffin looked at her, then at Erno. "Fothie?"

Fothie nodded. Taffin immediately extended her hands. Fothie took hold of them and carefully felt them and along her forearms.

"It's not your fault," Fothie said softly. "It's not."

Taffin's eyes filled with tears as she held onto Fothie. "I've tried. Honestly, I have tried, but it seems like every time I try to correct things, nobody listens." She glanced over at Deborah and Nurrel. "I shouldn't be talking like this. Fothie, I need to speak to you and Hemri privately."

Fothie shook her head. "You are with us. There are no image-bearers in this room who belong to this region other than you. Deborah and Nurrel's will is for Erno, my brother, to be their custodian."

Taffin wiped her eyes and took hold of Fothie's hands again. "That's—well, that's something special, and I hope they treasure him as I do the pair of you. You know that I do, don't you?" She touched Hemri's arm. "Hemri?"

"Of course I do," said Hemri.

"Then, why haven't I been able to stop this from happening to you and Geor? I should have been able to stop it."

Hemri smiled at her. "Taffin. Think of all the image-bearers you've aided—all those you encouraged and sent on from Hirahi with the supplies and direction they needed. These ones who saw, these ones who knew. They were not satisfied here but wanted to go further in to Oxpeina-life. They felt Sonax's sublime enchantment drawing them in. Your role has never been to stop the image-bearers from travelling. If the image-bearers who stop here think that Chila is going to give them all the Oxpeina-life they need, then you and I both know that they have forgotten who they are and who Sonax is."

"It hardly seems possible," Taffin said. "I don't know how things could have gone so wrongly. I mean, yes, I know I have seen it coming, but just now out there amongst the others, you would not believe the things that were said—"

"We heard them," said Erno.

"Just outright lies about you, really," said Taffin, "and, all the while, Chila smiling and acting like she knows everything. I don't know how I managed to calm everyone; really, I don't. Someone saw you come in here, and they were all ready to do something about it—although I think they're probably too afraid to come near you—so I told them I'll ask you to leave Hirahi and go back to the woods. I don't like to, Hemri; really, I don't, but I must."

"I understand," Hemri said. "We will go. We only came for Deborah. It seems we have inadvertently caused Chila to show herself more plainly."

"Too plainly for my liking," Taffin said, frowning. "I don't know what I'm going to do about this. If only we had a third mage here—a true mage, I mean—then we would probably be able to shift the balance of Oxpeina-life." She went over to the far door of the library and opened it. "Probably best to go out this way so nobody sees you. They'll hear you leave, no doubt, but I'd rather they didn't see you in case someone tries something foolish."

The three brismuns thumped across the floor. Deborah and Nurrel got up and followed them out. A short flight of steps led down, then the tunnel went a few steps around a corner and joined with a larger passageway that Deborah was sure was the same one she had been using to get to and from her room. She shuddered to think that when she had fled from Mage Chila and gone the long way around through the kitchen, the mage could have easily stepped out from the library and met her here.

"Why does Sonax not come in and change things?" Nurrel said, raising his voice to be heard over the ricocheting thumps of the brismuns. "Hirahi's his outpost, after all. You'd think he would see what Chila is doing and throw her out."

"That's the question I struggle with, too," said Taffin. "However, I'm fully aware he has his own ways of doing things, and in due time he might very well do just that."

"He may do," said Erno, "but he's also attentive to the will of the image-bearers and what they want for their region."

"Well," said Taffin, turning to look at him, "this is not what I want for my region, but I see that I'm in the minority."

Deborah felt gratified to see the deep frown on Taffin's face and that she didn't go around smiling at anything and everything. Most likely, she wouldn't call Deborah 'frowny face'.

"Olly says it's the natural way of things," Taffin said. "He says the outer regions of the world die off as life moves further inward. Which reminds me—Hemri, Olly wanted to know how Shis is doing. Is she all right?"

"She's very weak and needs rest," he said.

"Wait, what?" Fothie said. "You didn't tell me that."

Hemri paused and rested his hand against the stone wall, his breathing laboured. "We still… have plenty to discuss."

"So it seems," Fothie said. "Should I be worried for Shessi?"

"I think," said Hemri, his chest heaving, "we should all be able to cope if we change places regularly. We are—we are well-positioned in this region in that respect. With two each of us. Not all regions have that. We will be stronger for longer."

As they came to the top of the long flight of steps that led down into the barn, Fothie took hold of Hemri's hand.

"Hold me, my brother," she said. "I don't want you falling headlong."

He squeezed her hand. "That idea does not fill me with joy."

There was just room for the two of them to be side by side, and they leapt together down the steps, Fothie steadying Hemri when the need arose. Down in the barn, the fowls and other animals pressed eagerly against the walls of their pens, jostling for position with excited grunts and clucks, and all the rvenan cattle looked over their stall doors, their noses snuffling and twitching as the brismuns passed by.

"Wait," said Hemri, stopping at the last stall.

The rvenan there smirked at him.

"Oh yes," said Fothie, reaching up to touch the rvenan's mouth. "He's very interesting."

"He's in because he's beginning to awaken and attempting to talk," said Taffin. She looked here and there about the barn. "Olly!"

"I hear ya!" came Olly's voice from somewhere over the other side of the barn behind stacks of hay and barrels. "Give me a moment, I'll be right over!"

"If I'm not mistaken," said Hemri, "he's trying to get medicine down a dengla's throat."

Deborah stared at him. A dengla? That was the storybook name for the gehun—the one who stood plain and expressionless. "What's a dengla?"

"A small furry animal," said Fothie. "You think they're so sweet and cuddly until you try to give them a pat, then you find out what they're really like." She grinned.

Deborah wondered why the author of the storybook had used the name dengla instead of gehun. "Does the word dengla mean anything in particular?"

"Yes," said Fothie. "Two face. Why do you ask?"

Deborah sat slowly on a hay bale. Kasharel had been a good friend, or so she had thought. Yes, she had only known him for days, perhaps weeks—it was hard to know exactly how long she had spent recuperating in the gehun caves—but he had been caring and thoughtful. Yet, now, he did not believe her in what she told him about Mage Chila; he had not taken her side at all and did not stand with her. That was hard to take, and it hurt.

"I think it's more like double-mind than two face," said Hemri.

Erno hopped over to Deborah. "What's wrong?"

She bit her lip, trying to think of how to explain. "It's just… I had a storybook when I was a child, and in it was a picture of a gehun, but he was called a dengla."

Nurrel sat beside her. "I can understand that. It's not a very nice generalisation, but I get it—gehun have the reputation for not knowing their own minds. I think that's why many of their clans wear those robes; they say—let me think how it goes—in conformity there is unity, or maybe it's: there is unity in conformity. One of those."

Footsteps came from behind them, and Deborah turned to see Olly walking over. Her breath caught. He was so like Father in demeanour. Was there anything that her own people were known for, as the gehun were?

"This storybook of yours," Taffin said. "Is it *Legends Of The Greener Land?*"

Deborah looked at her. "Yes."

Taffin's expression was difficult to read—there appeared to be hints of amusement and puzzlement.

"Hello, Olly," said Hemri. "Keeping them all in because of the weather?"

Olly nodded. "I'm not up for it myself, even if they are. 'Though, the hens won't venture out in this stuff, the rvenans love it." As if an afterthought, Olly leaned over and grasped Hemri's hand briefly. He looked at Erno and Fothie, his brow furrowed. "Fothie," he said, and took Erno's hand.

Fothie snorted with laughter while Erno grinned.

"Picked wrong, did I?" Olly said, smiling at them both. "You can't blame me; you look like twins."

"This is our brother, Erno," said Fothie.

Thunder boomed into the barn, and the sheet of rain outside the open doors burst into hail. Conversation was impossible for several moments. Deborah sat quietly watching Erno as the cool air swirled into the barn. How was he going to react when she would tell him she wanted to go home? Would he still accompany her and be her custodian? Or, would he want her to go 'further in' and keep trying to find Father? That desire seemed to have died. He did not want her in his life, so she did not want him in her life. That was all.

38

Shessi stood outside the barn doors, smiling in the pouring rain. Water streamed over his body, his filmy blue-green clothing swaying and moving as if with a mind of its own, his hair sleek and ethereal. "It's a beautiful day."

Fothie stood next to him, her mossy body glistening. "For us, yes. Not so much for the image-bearers."

Shessi's pale, almost colourless, eyes flickered to Nurrel and Deborah. "Too cold out? It is not that cold yet, winter is still some way off, the waters cool only slightly, the fish turn to other activities, and I think—"

"The wet, not the cold," Fothie said. "That's why we're waiting for Taffin to bring coats. I'm glad you're here, though. Why didn't you tell me that Shis is sick?"

"It's one of many things that we have yet to discuss."

"Not you, too," said Fothie and grimaced at Hemri. "I begin to feel that I am very remiss and have handled this changeover badly."

"It's all my fault for distracting you," Erno said.

Fothie punched his arm. "Yes, that must be it."

"Here we are," said Taffin as she hurried over, holding a bundle of shiny dark green material over one arm and a satchel on the other. "This one was my daughter's," she said, separating out one oilskin coat from another, "so it should fit you, Deborah, seeings as you fit her other clothes pretty well. This is one of mine that will do for you, Nurrel." She handed the smaller coat to him.

Taffin helped Deborah with the coat and fussed about straightening the collar. "Our girl Trinni left a lot of her things when she went to the Oxpeina's region. She won't mind you having this."

Deborah happened to glance up and see Olly looking at her, a wistful look in his eyes. A father's longing for his child, she supposed. It gave her an uncomfortable feeling and brought a lump to her throat. If only her own father would feel that way.

She looked down at the coat and busied herself buttoning it. "Thanks, Taffin."

Taffin looked her up and down, then stared at Deborah's woven shoe-encased feet. "Shoes! You can't go out wearing those things; they'll get sopping. Have you got a pair of shoes back in your room? I'll fetch them."

"No. I put my shoes out with my laundry this morning."

"Right, okay. I might have an old pair of Trinni's somewhere."

Deborah smiled at Taffin. "It's fine. I'll dry off at the house when we get there."

It didn't matter if her feet got wet—at least she would be away from Hirahi and wouldn't have to go back. Hemri's suggestion of using one of the vacant houses across the river until the rain had eased had been a welcome idea.

"Well, okay," said Taffin. "I'll bring your things over tomorrow morning. Even in this weather, the laundry crew have got hearths set up for drying the washing, so it should be done by then." Taffin handed the satchel to Nurrel. "Eggs in here, bread, and other bits and pieces to tide you and Deborah over 'til tomorrow in case the house has nothing in it." She looked at Hemri. "Which house will it be, Hemri?"

Hemri stirred, as if he had been sleeping, and raised his head. "Most likely Justyia's. Unless it has been taken already, in which case I'll try the neighbouring houses."

Taffin nodded. "See you tomorrow, then."

"I think you will not see me," he answered. "I must go and patrol my area of our region."

Taffin kissed his mossy cheek. "Until we meet again. I will do my best for you and Fothie."

Hemri gently clasped her hand. "I know you will, my Taffin, and I want you to remember that none of this is your fault. It is not within you to hold back the will of the image-bearers."

She took a deep breath and nodded, her expression suddenly sad. "Sometimes I wish I could so that none of this would happen."

"Never wish that," Hemri said.

Deborah put up the hood of her coat and followed the brismuns out into the rain, the air fresh and clean once away from the barn. Her woven shoes were immediately useless as she squelched across the sodden grass and the icy water seeped through to her feet. Each time the brismuns landed, sprays of water shot up around them. After being splashed once in the face, Deborah kept her distance. Shessi led everyone down a grassy slope by some trees and to the riverbank. Three ubsies were there waiting, their sleek marbled heads just above the waterline, their black eyes placidly watching.

Fothie turned to Deborah. "Do you need me to carry you this time?"

"No," said Deborah. "I can jump."

And, when it was her turn, she did, from the small height of the bank, feeling sure she was going to land in the river, but the ubsie's tentacle whipped out and caught her. Even so, her feet dipped into the river, and the ubsy grunted. Its tentacle wound about her several times and held her snugly—so snugly she felt short of breath.

She did not look back at Hirahi as she was slowly ferried across the river. Stupid place; Erno should never have taken her there. So much for Hirahi helping her and giving her the supplies and direction or whatever she needed. Mage Chila was crazy and caught up in some weird kind of power play. And, Kasharel—she bowed her head and watched the ubsy as it swam beneath her, her heart filling with hurt—she had better forget about him. He was no friend.

It was not long before the ubsy set her down on the far bank with the brismuns and Nurrel. Shessi vanished into the depths of the river with the ubsies. The rain kept on as the brismuns leapt across the field, with Nurrel and Deborah striding after. Rvenan cattle grazed here and there, and Hemri headed for a line of trees in the distance. And, Deborah soon realised, a line of houses. Little, steeply pitched wooden houses painted green were set under the sweeping branches of the trees.

The houses were at neat intervals, and Hemri passed the first one, the second, and stopped at the fifth. "This is it."

"I must go," said Fothie.

"Yes," said Hemri. "That doesn't sound good. I will continue onward, for I have left my area long enough. We will meet again here tonight?"

"Yes," said Fothie and Erno.

Fothie dashed off into the woods behind the houses while Hemri continued on down the field at a slower pace.

"Get yourselves indoors and dry," said Erno to Deborah and Nurrel. "I won't come in. I've had enough of being indoors for one day." He grinned, his twiggy hair and mossy body dripping wet. "We've got more to talk about, but that can wait. So, I might as well go off to Jacob now and let him know where you are."

"Why did Fothie rush off like that?" Deborah said.

"Oh, you didn't hear it? There's a bird in distress."

"I can't hear much beyond the rain on my hood," said Nurrel. He went up the steps of the house and opened the door. "I think this place is more me-sized than you-sized, Deborah."

She ducked her head to avoid the doorframe as she went in after him. "It's fine. At least I'm not tall enough to hit my head on the ceiling like Ka—" she bit her lip and turned to look back through the doorway. "We'll see you again soon, Erno?"

He nodded. "Yes. Rest well, Deborah. You too, Nurrel." He leapt away across the field.

"Rest," muttered Nurrel as he took off his coat. "I think I've done enough of that."

"I haven't," said Deborah. "I mean, yes, it was good to sleep in a real bed last night, but I feel like I haven't got over the last few days."

"You and me both," said Nurrel. He went over to the fireplace.

She took off her coat and hung it next to his. Trust her to open her mouth and say something thoughtless. Her last few days were nothing compared to his.

He set to making a fire while she peeled off her sodden shoes, got the satchel, and set it onto the countertop. A squatchamn-height countertop, she supposed, as she stood over it. The room was small, but everything was tidy. A two-seater couch in front of the fireplace, a little table and two chairs, and a kitchenette in the form of the countertop against one wall with fitted cabinets above and below.

At least she wouldn't have to do any cleaning, not like the shack in Shilhim. This house had the stillness and faint musty smell of something unlived in, but it was clean. It had only one bedroom—she supposed she could curl up on the couch if Nurrel wanted the bed—and a tiny bathroom that made her feel like a giant as she squeezed into it. She opened a cupboard to see it housed an array of switches and a low white cabinet with geometric markings.

"What's this thing?"

Nurrel came over. "Looks like a generator to power the house. *Hmm.*" He leaned over the cabinet, undid a cap, and sniffed. "Yes, it takes water to get it running. Seems to be enough there to get it going for now." He threw a number of switches, and the cabinet let out a slight cough then began to hum. He went over and tried a wall switch in the living room, and a light immediately flicked on.

"Do you want anything to eat?" he asked as he emptied the contents of the satchel onto the countertop. "We didn't get to have much lunch after all that."

"Yes," she said. "Come to think of it, I don't think I had any."

He pulled a book out of the satchel. "What's this?"

It was green, had a wide, worn cardboard cover, and Deborah recognised it even before she saw the flowing script title. *Legends Of The Greener Land* by M. Boggerns.

"My goodness!" she said, grabbing it. "This book is from my childhood!"

"Nice," he said, and began exploring the kitchenette's cupboards.

She went and sat on the couch by the fireplace, the book in hand. It felt different, and she realised it was because it had a back cover whereas her old copy hadn't had one. Father's copy, really, as it was something he had occasionally read to her—usually at bedtime when she had trouble getting to sleep. She smoothed the book with her hand, thinking of him. It was always Father who would tuck her in at night; Mother never did anything like that.

She thumbed through the book and was surprised to find that it was full of old, uncommonly-used language and had many more words in it than she remembered. The drawings she knew, and she smiled to see the one of the brismun, a bird perched upon its head. It was a pretty good rendering of a brismun, too. She looked at the block of text beneath. Puzzling. That wasn't the tale she remembered. Here and there were familiar parts: 'he flies as fleeting as the night holds true' and 'all amiability is his heart untarnished'.

How old had she been when Father had read these tales to her? She remembered the soothing sound of his voice; remembered leaning against him and studying the picture on the page as he read to her, but did not remember reading many words for herself at all. Had she read *any* words, or had she been too young to read? She turned the page. This one had a drawing of trees with intertwined branches and a path beneath. 'Journeying together, beware the seeing path divulging your failings to guandra-kind' read the first sentence. The picture was less familiar; she didn't recall Father telling that particular tale as often, and she certainly didn't remember him saying anything about guandras there. She flicked through the pages—more familiar drawings, pieces of story she didn't remember—then additional pages at the end of the book, each with drawings she didn't recognise at all. Had Father's old copy been missing pages along with the back cover?

"It's ready," said Nurrel, as he set plates onto the table behind her.

She looked up and realised he had been busily cooking eggs and slices of meat and had cut up some of the bread while she had been absorbed in the book. She went and sat opposite him in the squatchamn-sized chair. At least her knees fit under the table.

They ate silently together. Deborah did not feel like talking; the book filled her thoughts. And, Father. How bittersweet to think of those times with him as he read bedtime stories to her, the closeness she had felt, the warmth and security of him being there for her. Had she been too hard on him when he had changed after Mother's death? Was it unrealistic to expect he would be the same again, be the same father he had always been? Their roles had changed uncomfortably; she felt she had become the parent and he the child in need of care. She didn't want that; she wanted Father to be Father again.

She glanced at Nurrel, and he looked up as if aware of her eyes on him.

"I think I'll go for a walk once I've cleared the dishes," he said.

"Out in this stuff?" she said, looking over at the rain striking the windowpane.

He shrugged. "Makes no difference. I can't sit here doing nothing all day. I need to get out."

It was like Father all over again—his need to get out, to walk, to go and sit in the park under a tree. His need to be alone.

"Come with me?" Nurrel said.

She almost choked on her piece of bread. "What?"

"You're welcome to come with me if you want some company."

"*Uh*, thanks. I think I might wait here for Erno."

He nodded.

39

'Turning from the one who bestows the image, the image-bearer loses sight of one; nay, I cannot illustrate his likeness even-though he who holds all images elects the one as himself.'

Deborah looked up from *Legends Of The Greener Land* and gazed at the flames wreathing about the logs of wood in the fireplace. This part was odd. It was at the end of the book, where it had things about the Oxpeina. Or, rather, Sonax. As the author put it, 'All the realm life outflowing from Sonax-Oxpeina enraptures the traveller into the deep and narrow way to see Sonax-Oxpeina and not oneself.'

She could not help but think of Father yet again and wished he had explained more of his own thinking and what he was intending when they had left Eblhim together. It was more than just sitting at the edge of the woods in Shilhim and being satisfied with the life there; it was *more*. He must have been intending to be a traveller, to journey 'further in' and find something of Sonax-Oxpeina-life. Had he been incapable of telling her his real intention? He had been incapable of a lot. He had always been a good and loving father until Mother's death had broken him. *Broken* him. She should have been more understanding instead of expecting so much of him.

She set down the book and wiped her eyes. This book—it had brought back to her those precious memories and the rawness of how she felt.

The fire had burned low, so she put another log on and settled back onto the couch. The rain had not let up and steadily pattered on the roof. Life would never be the same again. Father was gone and had been gone for a long time. Over the past few years, she had really only seen glimpses of who he used to be. It was strange, for she had not thought Father's relationship with Mother was good—they argued so often—so why had her death changed him so much? This was a question for him, and he was not here. He would not talk about such a thing anyway. She should get on with her own life; she was grown; she had no need for a father anymore, so why did she feel such a need for her father? Why feel so very alone without him?

She got up and looked through the kitchenette cupboards for a mug and something to make a hot drink out of amongst the smattering of supplies there. All this brooding over the past wasn't doing her any favours; it merely made her feel as though a cloud of misery was hanging about her.

She made a malty sort of drink and sat at the table. Away from that book, away from that cosy blanket of sweet sadness on the couch. Sit upright, try to breathe, try to get some perspective, try to look forward to starting a new life back… home. What was home? She sipped the drink, staring at the wall.

And, then, Sonax-Oxpeina-life sat opposite her. In a flash of shifting faces, she saw Nurrel, she saw Father, she saw Taffin, she saw herself; then his face became still and was someone she had never seen before, and yet she knew. Wavy brown, almost unkempt hair framed a strong masculine face, his amber eyes—such an unusual colour!—fixed on hers as if he too knew her. And, his eyes, they silently communicated more than the rovi's ever had, more than anyone had in one glance, and there was no question in them for her to answer, for he already knew. How did he know her, and she know him? His broad hands rested on the table, and she instinctively reached for them, almost as one would reach for a brismun.

"I've just been reading about you," she said softly, as his warm hands closed around hers.

He tilted his head back and grinned and, in that moment, was gone and her hands were empty.

She sat in stunned silence. She had not imagined that, had she? He had been there, right there, and she had felt his hands and looked into his face and seen something of his thoughts in that brief instant. He knew her. She, strangely enough, was part of him, for she had his face. That is, the image of her face, of Nurrel's, of Father's, of Taffin's, had all shown on his face for a fraction of time before he became himself. She put her hands to her face, felt it experimentally—felt strange for doing that—but it felt as if her face was something different, was something given to her. And was something beautiful, something cherished. She, plain Deborah Lakely from Eblhim, was something special. *Someone* special. She? Special?

She laid her head down onto the table as waves of emotion, grief, tears, swept over her. She cried like she had never cried before, as if something had unlocked inside her. The pain of Mother's death and the pain of never feeling close to Mother, the pain of Father's leaving, his rejection of her… it all seemed to burst out in a flood.

She did not know how long she lay there sobbing, but, after a while, distant thumps were noticeable over the pattering rain. She sat up and wiped her eyes. Erno was coming back. She took a deep breath, got up, and went over to the window.

There he was, across the field, leaping towards her. In no great hurry, simply bouncing along, some of the rvenan cattle lifting their heads to look at him as he passed.

She put on the oilskin coat and stepped out from the warmth of the little house into the cold air.

"Erno!" she called, wondering if she had to let him know she was there or if he knew it anyway and that his sensitive ears had heard her open the door and step out.

A wide smile split his face as he leapt nearer, and it was only a few more bounds until he was there before her. "Hello," he said. "How's things?"

She found herself hurrying down the steps to take hold of his wet hands.

"Hey!" he said, drawing back in surprise. "What? This is—*oh!*" His fingers gently probed her hands. "You've had recent contact with the Oxpeina, with Sonax!"

"Trust you to feel that," she said, looking at her hands. How did they feel to him that he knew that?

"Because they feel tingly with life, and I can just about feel where his hands met yours," he said.

"Stop reading my thoughts!" she said.

He grinned at her. "Yes, it would be disagreeably wet to hug me right now, but I think it nice that you'd still like to."

"Stop!"

"I will when you want me to. For now, I'm relieved to sense that some of the depression that had been deepening and darkening your spirit has lifted. It had me worried, Deborah. And, no, don't tell me not to worry about you because you're *all right.*"

He had spoken the words she had instinctively been going to say, and, as they held hands, she felt something from him, something of his thoughts for the first time.

She nodded. "You're here to watch over me. You're doing what you've been assigned to do by Sonax, but I'm not just a job to you." She swallowed hard as emotion began to rise. "Thank you, Erno. For caring about me." Not many do, she wanted to add, and quickly let go his hands, knowing he would have heard that.

"Sweet heart," he said. "Okay, we'll talk about other things. Jacob's still sheltering, and I've told him where to find us when this rain finally stops. He's somewhat bored, I think, so I stayed awhile to talk with him. Where's Nurrel?"

"He went out for a walk. I don't know where."

"I never got to ask what your plans are now. I suppose I thought we would talk sooner about this. I had no idea you'd get caught up in what's going on in Hirahi. Are we going to the city of Aric, or what?"

She gazed out across the field, unsure of what to say. "Honestly, I really don't know. I did think I was going back home to Eblhim, but now… something has changed, and I need some time to think. I feel… I feel some kind of reluctance to go back there. I don't know why."

"Discuss it with Nurrel when you can. Because I've been made custodian to both of you, you'll need to agree on where you travel. Jacob, he'll likely go wherever you go—he seems to be like that—so it's really down to you and Nurrel to decide. He's an easygoing fellow, so it shouldn't be difficult."

Puzzling that they were connected in this way. Deborah did not know if she wanted to be connected to anyone. She had known Nurrel for less time than she had known Kasharel, and that had turned out badly. It might be better to be alone.

❧ 40 ❧

Deborah moved her feet as close as she dared to the fire and tried to rub some feeling back into them. Erno had gone in search of Fothie rather than stand outside waiting for Deborah to come up with a decision on what she wanted. What did she want? She was still trying to come to terms with seeing Sonax-Oxpeina—she hadn't dreamt that, it had *happened*—and the ensuing gush of emotion when he had gone.

Everything felt different. Erno was right. That gloom, that depression, had lifted. She didn't feel happy; there were too many unpleasant thoughts swirling around for that, but the dark cloud that had been pressing closer had gone. What to do with Father's rejection of her? Had he truly rejected her, or was he lost in his own cloud of depression?

She thought of how it felt to have Sonax's hand close around hers when she had reached for him. She had felt anchored; she had felt as if she belonged. Still did, when she thought about it. Is that what Father was looking for? Then she recalled that Val and his pack had said Father was going to Aric to find Sonax. One of the other rovi, Grufful, maybe, found that strange. Aric was thought to be a birthplace, someone else had said.

All along, Father wanted peace. All along, he wanted to be himself again. If, Deborah thought, *if* she could somehow meet Sonax again, she could tell him that Father was looking for him, needing him, needing that Oxpeina-life to flow through his veins so that he could be himself again. She got up and faced the empty room.

"I know you were here, Sonax-Oxpeina. I don't know if you can hear me or if you've gone too far away by now, but I need you to go to my father. He's looking for you."

She waited, hoping to hear something, see something, but the room remained still.

She sat on the couch and tucked her legs beneath her. Perhaps that wasn't the way things were done. Perhaps there was some other way to make contact. She would have to ask Erno.

A knock at the door made her jump out of her skin. She went over to open it and was aghast to find Mage Chila standing on the step, the rain running off her pale green hooded cloak.

"Why, hello!" Mage Chila said, smiling.

Deborah noted the amber gem she had previously worn either in her hair or around her neck was now hung on a silver-string headpiece so that the amber stone lay on her forehead. Amber, the colour of the Sonax-Oxpeina's eyes.

"I've brought you some buns," Mage Chila said, producing a small paper packet from under her cloak. "I thought you might like them to munch on while you're enjoying your new surroundings. You are most welcome to come back to us at Hirahi—we miss you, Deborah—but it is a fine outlook here." Despite that irritating smile that never seemed to leave her face, her eyes were hard and slightly widened.

Deborah felt caught off guard. How did Mage Chila know where to find her? Had Taffin told her? What was she doing—bringing food and acting like nothing had happened? You don't accuse someone of having a hand in the death of one parent and driving off the other, then bring them buns.

"I don't want them." Deborah pushed at the packet Mage Chila held out to her. "Go away and give them to someone else. I don't know what you think you're playing at, but I want nothing to do with you. How dare you tell me I don't have Oxpeina-life? How dare you talk the way you did about my parents? You don't know me. You're a hateful person and shouldn't wear the eye of Sonax on your head—how ridiculous of you!"

Mage Chila's smile grew more disdainful. "You are exactly as I said you were. You need help and love, poor thing. I will be right here at Hirahi, right where Sonax himself assigned me to be, and I will continue to spread Oxpeina-life and love. You appear unable to do that." She set the packet of buns down on the doorstep and strode away.

Deborah kicked the buns so that they burst out of their packet and went flying in all directions, then slammed the door. She yelled with frustration and restrained herself from kicking and throwing more things about inside the house. What did Mage Chila think she was doing? Spreading love? That was so screwed up it was ridiculous. How could she go from saying despicable, judgemental things to then acting like she had done nothing wrong and pretending to be nice? Didn't she remember the things she had said? The accusations? And, now again, saying 'you need help and love' and 'you are just as I said you were' with the attitude as if she was talking to the lowest form of pond scum. Hateful woman. And, so bizarre. Who does that? Who acts all nice and kind in front of others, then behind closed doors does a 'slap down', as Hemri had called it, to try and knock her into submission, and then brings buns and says she's spreading love? What?

Deborah sat on the couch and glared at the fireplace. Well, she had given Mage Chila a slap down in return. She had shown Mage Chila who was in control. Mage Chila would not get the better of her. Shouldn't even call her a mage. What was a mage, anyway? Deborah looked over at the *Legends Of The Greener Land* on the couch beside her. She hadn't come across the part with mages yet. If Chila was claiming to represent and speak for Sonax-Oxpeina somehow, then she was all wrong. Sonax-Oxpeina was nothing like her.

The anger seeped out of her at the thought of him. He was nothing like Chila. In that brief moment of seeing him, she had known him, she had sensed him, and she had found her self in him. She took a few deep breaths and shut her eyes.

All of this was so strange. All of it. In that moment, she knew what she would do; she knew what she wanted. She *would* find Father. He was in trouble. He needed help. He needed to find himself again. He had not meant to reject her; he had *not* meant to. He was lost and trying to find his way out of it all. She would find him, and she would take him to the source of Oxpeina-life, wherever that was, the city of Aric or somewhere else—maybe Taffin or Erno knew—and that would be that.

41

Deborah looked up from the book as Nurrel came through the front door.

"Hi." He set a bulky cloth bag down onto the kitchen countertop and took off his oilskin coat. "I've got some fish and vegetables for dinner. Hey, it's warm in here!"

She closed the book. "I've had the fire going all day."

"Feels like it." He smiled at her. "I had to push past some rvenan to get in the house; they're busy eating the bread you put out for them."

Puzzled, she looked at him, then it dawned on her, and she laughed. "Buns!"

His expression became unreadable as he stood there looking at her. "What?" she said.

"I don't think I've seen you laugh before. That's good. You're feeling better?" He turned and began unpacking the bag.

She went over to him and watched as he placed item after item out onto the countertop, mostly odd-shaped and leafy vegetables. He seemed absorbed in what he was doing, his face inexpressibly sad. Had she offended him somehow or had his grief come up again? He was not quite like Father in his grief-stricken behaviours, but there were similarities. Was Nurrel thinking she had no right to laugh, not after what she had done to Ibelli?

"I am sorry for everything," she said in a low voice.

He glanced up at her. "What? Everything? What do you mean?"

"For what I did."

He turned to face her, leaning side-on to the countertop. "What are you talking about, Deborah?"

She supposed she may as well out with it and confront things head-on. "It's my fault Ibelli died; I know it is. If I hadn't blocked the view of the lake, she wouldn't have left her mound. I'm so sorry, Nurrel. I was stupid. I shouldn't have done it."

He stared at her, and the silence between them went on for too long. She didn't feel any relief in saying all of that to him, just tight anxiety in her chest. He was saying nothing, only staring at her. She went over to the coat hooks.

"I think I'll go for a walk," she said, putting on her coat.

He still said nothing.

Out she went into the chilly air, shutting the door behind her and buttoning her coat as she went down the steps. At least the rain had eased off, and it was now merely drizzling. The sky was still clouded over and turning a darker grey—perhaps it was later in the afternoon than she had supposed. A few rvenan cattle were milling about near the house, but there was no trace left of the buns.

Where would she go now? What was she supposed to do—wander around the field and try to guess when it would be all right to go back to the house? Maybe she shouldn't have said anything; maybe she should have left Nurrel alone. Well, too late now, she had done it. Opened her big mouth and put her foot in it again. Maybe she really did have a bad air around her, something in her that drove others away.

The sound of thuds impacting the ground caused her to stop and turn. Erno was coming out from among the trees behind the row of houses.

"What are you doing?" he said as he landed next to her. "You shouldn't have said all that to Nurrel, then run out the door."

"You heard me?"

He grinned. "Of course, I did."

"Then, you know I made a mess of things again."

His cheerful expression did not waver. "Rubbish. I thought what you said was from a loving heart, a caring heart. Completely wrong, but loving all the same."

"How can you say that?"

"Quite easily. I can see how you'd imagine that it was you who caused Ibelli to bolt from her mound, but really that wasn't how things went. I think you would have to talk to Nurrel about it and have him tell you what happened."

She snorted. "He's not talking to me!"

"Give him a chance. You waited all of five seconds for him to respond to what you dropped on him—he needs a little more time than that to frame his thoughts. You probably shocked him into silence, plus he's been dealing with a lot the last few days and has spent his nights talking to me instead of getting the sleep he needs."

She looked back at the house and saw Nurrel's dark head at the window. He was still at the kitchen counter and was probably getting on with preparing dinner. "Are you saying it wasn't my fault that Ibelli left her hut?"

"Yes, I am saying that."

She didn't know whether to feel relieved or confused. "I always thought it was because of me, because of what I'd done."

"You should know by now that not everything is as it appears."

She watched the rvenan cattle wandering further from the houses, cropping grass as they went, and thought of the buns they had eaten. "Did you see Mage Chila come to the house earlier?"

His mossy face wrinkled into furrows of concern. "No. What happened?"

"She gave me buns."

"Buns?"

"Yes. She said I was welcome to go back to Hirahi and that I'm missed. All the while smiling and acting like nothing had happened. But I refused her stupid buns and told her to go away, and then she told me I needed help and love and that I was just as she thought I was—meaning, no doubt, that I am the lowest of the low. She said she was at Hirahi, where

Sonax told her to be, and she was going to keep spreading Oxpeina-life and love, and that I was unable to do that."

"Isn't she charming," a sarcastic, husky voice said at Deborah's left ear.

She shrieked and jumped as Jacob landed on her.

"Don't hit me!" he cried, his wings flapping as he tried to maintain his balance on her shoulder.

"Jacob! You're supposed to warn me, not sneak out of nowhere!"

"I wasn't sneaking."

"Yes, you were!"

"*Humph*. It's nice to see you, too."

She took a deep breath, her hand on her chest. "It would be nicer if it didn't give me a heart attack."

He nuzzled her cheek, and she petted him.

"You feel a little damp," she said.

"Yes, and I'd like to get indoors before it starts raining properly again."

"You two do that," said Erno. "Deborah, I wouldn't worry about what Chila is doing—I think it's all a manipulation game, and she's trying to regain some control over you."

"*Bleh*," said Jacob.

Deborah shrugged. "If you say so." It didn't make a lot of sense—why did Chila care about having control over her when she wasn't going to stay at Hirahi or in this region?

"Is Fothie coming tonight?" Jacob asked.

"I expect so," said Erno. "Hemri, too. We have a lot to catch up on together."

"I'll join you if it's not raining," Jacob said.

"Great," said Erno, and leapt towards the row of houses.

Deborah slowly followed. What was she going to say to Nurrel when she went back in? Apologise all over again, or just say nothing?

"Call out if you need me," Erno said, giving her a grin before he bounded away into the woods.

"This looks like a nice place," Jacob said as Deborah went up the steps of the house.

"*Um*, yes."

She went in and was enveloped by stuffy warmth. "Nurrel, look who I found." Hopefully, he wouldn't notice that her voice sounded forced in its cheeriness. "Get off," she muttered to Jacob. "I want to take off my coat."

He hissed. "I should think you'd want to take off more than your coat; it's like an oven in here." He flew to Nurrel's shoulder. "Hello."

Nurrel was busily filleting fish at the countertop and glanced sidelong at him. "Hi there. Do you eat fish guts?"

Jacob's gold-ringed eyes blinked as he turned his head. "You image-bearers have an interesting way of saying, 'How do you do?' One yells, and the other one offers me fish guts."

Nurrel smiled, and Deborah stifled a laugh.

In the evening, when the dishes were cleared away and Jacob had gone out, Nurrel and Deborah sat on the couch in front of the fire.

"Dinner was nice, thanks," she said carefully.

"*Hmm?* Oh yes. Thanks for cooking the fish."

"I hope you enjoyed it." Stupid stilted conversation, why couldn't she relax? She felt so tense sitting there beside him. If only Jacob had stayed.

"Yes, I did. It was a little dry, but still nice."

She felt tired, half-hysterical, giggles rising up, and bit her lip. "So, it wasn't perfect, then."

"What?"

"The fish. It wasn't perfect."

He looked at her, puzzled.

"Mage Chila said the way I cooked fish was perfect. I fried it to perfection!"

Understanding dawned on his face, and his soft eyes glinted with humour. "Dried it to perfection, more like."

She laughed then sighed, feeling able to relax into the couch cushions and sit less rigidly. She and Nurrel sat together silently a moment gazing into the flames of the fire, then he cleared his throat.

"*Hum.* So, about what you said earlier. I want you to know that you didn't have anything to do with Ibelli going… running to the lake. I don't—well, I don't want to talk about it right now, but I just want you to know that. I—*hum*—can't, *don't* want to say exactly what happened. Another time, maybe."

"That's all right," she said quietly. "I mean, you and I have only known each other a few days, and it's none of my business."

"Yes, right, we haven't known each other long, but that's not why I don't want to talk about it now. I've, well, I've been going over and over it in my head—and to Erno—and still trying to sort it all out, and you have enough of your own sorrow to cope with, let alone mine." He stared at the fireplace. "I'm relieved that you're looking more rested and been able to get away from Hirahi for a while."

His tone had changed, and Deborah had the sense he was closing the door on any further talk about Ibelli.

"You've always looked so very tired whenever I've seen you," he went on. "So, it's good."

"Have I?" She thought back to when they had first met at the lumdil village. She supposed she had been weary of the travel then, and again when she had met up with him at the Silver Lake. Was that what gave the impression of her having a bad air and lack of Oxpeina-life? She could see again the smile on Chila's face as she said all that and when she had been at the door with buns. Smiling, always smiling. Deborah wished she could forget about her and not think of her at all. Kasharel had said she was only trying to help, and that was what mages do.

"You can take the bed, and I'll have the couch," Nurrel said.

"Funny. I was going to say the same thing."

"I think the bed is longer than this is and may fit you better. I don't know that I'll get much sleep tonight, anyway."

She turned to him as he sat fixated on the fire, a brooding look in his dark eyes. "I hope you do get some sleep."

He shrugged. "I might wind up going to talk with Erno again. Then again, might not. I'm starting to feel drowsy with the warmth here."

She put another log on the fire. "Me, too."

They chatted of inconsequential things, sometimes with long silences; sometimes another thought would come. Deborah found herself thinking of Kasharel. She supposed she was very aware that Nurrel was also someone she had only known a few days. Better to not become too close as she had done with Kasharel. Yet she was reluctant to leave the fireside and go to a bed that was bound to be too short to stretch out on, and there was something comforting about sitting with Nurrel. He did not demand anything of her.

At one point in the evening, she saw something in his expression that made her remember what it was like to see his face appear on Sonax-Oxpeina's. Her hand instinctively went to her own face, and she touched her cheek. Image-bearer. What she had read about that sort of thing in *Legends Of The Greener Land* needed going over again to make better sense of it all. It didn't help that the language used was almost poetic, somewhat complicated. How endearing that Father had used the book mainly for its pictures and turned it into a storybook for her. He must have loved her. Once. Must have loved her once. He would again when he had found himself and had Oxpeina-life to fix things. Oxpeina-life felt different, did something. She yawned, her eyelids closing of their own accord. Probably should move. Probably should get up and go try the bed.

42

In the morning light, she woke and looked around, trying to get her bearings, then realised it was the living room of the house she and Nurrel were making use of. She was curled up on the couch, a blanket over her. Nurrel wasn't there. The fire had burned down to embers.

She moved slowly about the little house, her body stiff from sleeping in an uncomfortable position. At the small window at the rear of the house, she looked out and saw Erno, Fothie, Nurrel, and Jacob among the trees. Jacob's head swiftly turned towards her, and she waved, then went to find something to eat.

It was not long before the front door opened, and they all came in.

"Morning!" said Fothie. She and Erno hopped carefully into the living room. "Don't jump high and hit your head, brother."

"Don't you punch a hole through the floor, sister," he said, grinning.

"We can all go outside again if you'd prefer," said Nurrel.

"Nah," said Fothie, "it's no problem."

"At least the rain has stopped," said Jacob, and flew to Deborah's shoulder. "We can make a start on our journey as soon as you're ready."

"Yes," said Erno. "About that… Deborah, we've been talking, and I know you said you hadn't decided what you want to do yet, and I said talk to Nurrel—well, Nurrel would very much like to go back to Smoky Glade and tell Ibelli's parents what has happened to her."

Deborah nodded. "Oh, yes, I understand. *Um*, how many days do you think that would take?" She tried to not let any disappointment show, hoping that if Father had made it to Aric, he would stay there and not journey even further ahead of her.

"I am unsure, as that relies on how quickly Nurrel can walk. I would say at least three days, perhaps?"

"Okay."

"Will you come with us or would you prefer to wait here?" Nurrel asked.

Deborah thought for a moment. What if Chila came again with more buns, or what if Kasharel tried to talk to her? She wouldn't let either of them try to push her around or say more hurtful things. Then again, why should she care if they did? It shouldn't matter; she should be able to shrug off and ignore anything they might have to say. Still, the idea of seeing either of them was disagreeable.

"I would stay with you," said Jacob.

She smiled at him. "Well, I think—"

There was a knock at the door, and she felt suddenly sick. That had better not be Chila again.

"*Ah*," said Fothie, smiling. "Here's Taffin."

Nurrel opened the door, and Deborah was relieved to see the little lumdil woman on the step, a large bag slung over her back and another bag in hand.

"Hello there!" she said. "I've got all your belongings, Deborah, fresh from the laundry, and some more bits and pieces. Hello, Fothie, Erno, how're you getting on, Nurrel?"

"Fairly well," he said. "Come in."

Taffin dumped her bags on the floor. "That's a load off! Now, I can't stay long; too much to do, but I do have something interesting for you, Deborah. Mister Needy is asking for you; can you imagine that!"

"Mister Needy?" Deborah said.

"Our awakening rvenan. You were going to name him, remember? I'm afraid I've been calling him Mister Needy, and it's sort of stuck. He was saying 'where she?' over and over. Olly's been trying his best to coax a bit more out of him as to who he meant—and it certainly wasn't me;

Mister Needy said a firm 'no' to that—and now he's saying 'Debah'." Taffin laughed. "Isn't that funny? What it means, of course, is that he wants to go with you. Olly is pretty sure you'll be able to ride him. I really do think that was Sonax's intention all along."

"That would be great," said Erno. "It would make our journey much easier. I don't suppose you have another rvenan you could spare for Nurrel to ride?"

"Well," said Taffin. "I don't know, but I'll certainly pass that on to Olly and see what he thinks. Do you all want to come now and get Mister Needy?" She frowned. "I must stop calling him that. What did you want to call him, Deborah?"

"I haven't thought of anything, sorry. I forgot."

"No problem. I'll leave it to you to come up with a proper name if you think you'll take him."

It would be good to have something to make travel easier—she would be able to catch up with Father a lot faster. Deborah nodded. "Yes, I will, thanks."

Taffin beamed. "Come along over when you're ready, and Olly will give you a few tips on how to look after him."

Deborah looked at Erno and Nurrel. "When are you planning to set off for Smoky Glen?"

"Glade," said Erno, chuckling. "As soon as Nurrel and you, if you're coming, are ready."

"I'm ready now," said Nurrel.

Deborah bit her lip. Would it mean going back through the region that held the Silver Lake, or was there another way of skirting around that? She didn't want to go back through there, and Smoky Glade seemed very far away. Yes, she wanted to be with Erno, but Fothie would stay, and so would Jacob. Perhaps it was better to let Nurrel do this alone, and in the meantime she could prepare for journeying on ahead when he and Erno returned. "I think I'll stay here for now."

Erno lightly touched her arm. "Don't leave without me."

She knew he was thinking of when she had left him at Smoky Glade and set out on her own. She did not want to repeat that mistake. "I won't. I'll wait for you."

"You'd better," muttered Jacob.

"So, I take it that you've decided you want to go to Aric rather than head back to Eblhim?" Erno said.

"Yes," Deborah said.

"Very well."

"Would you all like to come back with me now to Hirahi?" said Taffin. "Nurrel, I'll fix you up with whatever supplies you need and see what Olly says about a rvenan you could have, and, Deborah, we'll get Mister N—*oops*—sorted out for you. I'll need to send for a barge to get them across the river, but hopefully that won't take too long to organise."

Deborah looked at Fothie. "The ubsies can take them across, can't they?"

Fothie shook her head. "Shessi probably wouldn't agree to that—ubsies and rvenans aren't a good combination."

Deborah did not see the necessity of going back to Hirahi with the others, as surely Mister Needy could be brought to her by barge. On the other hand, if Chila saw everyone arriving, then Deborah didn't want her to think she wasn't with them because she was afraid of her in any way. She would go, and she would show Chila she didn't care about her stupid opinions.

They all set off together across the field to the river. The morning was chilly as the sun rose bright and glorious in the pale blue sky. Taffin and Nurrel climbed into a small rowboat at the river's edge and set off, ripples of shining water in their wake. Fothie let out a shout for Shessi that echoed across the water. Taffin and Nurrel were almost a third of the way across by the time Shessi leapt onto the riverbank and stood dripping next to Fothie. He embraced her, briefly obscuring her like a waterfall. They spoke quietly, then ubsies were summoned for Deborah and for Erno, who might damage a rowboat by jumping into it.

"*Yuck.*" Jacob shook himself. "No way am I letting an ubsy's creepy tentacles near me again." He flew from Deborah's shoulder out across the deep blue water.

Erno and Fothie clasped hands as they bowed their heads, their twiggy hair mingled. Whispery language flowed from their lips, so Deborah left them to their goodbyes and jumped towards the waiting ubsy.

In its secure grip, she felt a twinge of sickness in her gut as she looked at the towering visage of Hirahi across the river. Maybe she really should have waited at the house instead of going back there. But, no, she would show Chila that she was not intimidated by her.

The ubsies overtook Taffin and Nurrel, grunting and blowing bubbles as they passed, so that Deborah, Erno, and Jacob were waiting on the other side of the river by the time the rowboat slid into the bank. Nurrel got out and dragged it into a low, shingly area.

"Nice to have someone else do that for me," Taffin said, taking his hand as she stepped out. "Although I must say I'm jealous that the others got a ride from an ubsy. I don't see that every day and it was very funny to watch!"

Deborah looked at Erno's grinning face. So, not only was it unusual for her to have a brismun custodian, but being carried by an ubsy was also not the norm.

"If you want, I'll ask Fothie for one of them to take you for a ride out to the lake," said Erno.

Taffin beamed. "Oh, I would *love* that."

"*Yerk*," said Jacob. "Revolting."

Hirahi seemed higher than ever as Deborah gazed up at the cliff face to the dark windows. Was anyone at any of them looking down at her? She turned away and walked with the others to the barn entrance, trying not to feel self-conscious.

"Taffin," she said. "Did you tell Chila where I was?"

Taffin's brow furrowed as she thought. "Chila? No. I did tell your gehun friend, Kasharel, when he came looking for you. I hope my directions were clear enough and he found you all right."

Kasharel must have told Chila where she was. How infuriating! Why would he do that? Why hadn't he come himself to see her? She did not answer Taffin, and the others began to chat together, so that was a relief. She didn't want to talk about Kasharel, some friend he was!

43

The rvenan trotted over, his grey coat shining in the lights of the barn. "Debah!"

Deborah didn't mind that he called her that, even though it reminded her of the squatchamn girl by the Silver Lake. "Hello, Mister." She stroked his floppy grey ears.

His eyes widened as he looked at Jacob on her shoulder, and in the light she could see fine veins of green in their dark brown. "Whassat, whassat?"

"What do you mean, what's that?" Jacob said. "Have you never seen an owl before?"

"Ow."

"*Owl*," said Jacob.

"Be nice to him," Deborah said. "Weren't you like this when you awakened?"

Jacob shook his feathers. "Not at all. I was fully awakened in one breath."

"Give him a chance," said Olly. "He's had just a small touch, and it'll take time for him to become himself. Nurrel, let's see if Maqua suits."

He and Nurrel walked along the row of stalls.

"I'd better pack some food for the journey," Taffin said. She smiled at Deborah. "I'll be in the kitchen if you need me."

She went briskly after Olly and Nurrel, giving Olly a playful slap as she passed him.

"I really wonder if you ought to come with us after all, Deborah," said Erno. "I don't know that I like to leave you here."

"I'll be fine. It's only for a few days."

"Don't engage with Chila if you can help it."

"Why not? If she comes my way again, I'm not going to let her walk all over me. I'm beginning to think I shouldn't have left Hirahi and gone to that house. I should have stayed here and shown her that she has no power over me."

"That's what I mean," said Erno. "If you get caught up in a battle of wills, then I'm afraid it'll shift your focus off what really matters. You talk like you care what Chila thinks. Do you?"

Deborah pushed Mister Needy's soft muzzle away as he nosed her. "No, of course not. I don't care at all what she thinks of me, and it's not a battle of wills!"

"Really," said Jacob. "Then why bother showing her she has no power over you?"

"Because she shouldn't think that she does!"

"Why does that matter?" Erno asked. "Sec, what I want you to grasp is that this place has the potential to be the same as the Silver Lake, and in fact is headed that way if it's not corrected."

"I don't see how," Deborah said.

"You would say that," said Jacob.

She scowled sidelong at him.

"It's all a question of who or what has control over image-bearers," said Erno, "and that includes yourself."

"Well, Chila does not have control over me."

"Exactly. Don't let her."

"But she shouldn't think that she does. Yes, I know, you say I shouldn't care what she thinks, and I don't, but she still shouldn't think that, because she's wrong. I don't want her to have any power over me or think that she does."

Jacob trembled with laughter on her shoulder. "*Hoohoo!* The more you try to explain, the worse it gets."

Deborah vigorously scratched the rvenan's cheekbone. He shut his eyes and tilted his head, leaning into her hand.

"I guess it sounds like I do care what she thinks," she said. "I wish I didn't. It's all so annoying. I just want her to know that she's wrong in everything she's said about me. That's all."

"Of course she's wrong," said Jacob. "You know that, I know that, Erno knows it, and of course Sonax knows it, too."

Deborah remembered that fleeting glimpse of Sonax-Oxpeina, the touch of his hands, and the impression of being seen and known for who she was and cared about. If only he could come back and sort out this mess. If he knew what was happening at Hirahi, which was supposed to be one of his outposts for travellers, then why didn't he fix what was going on here and stop Chila from presenting herself as a mage?

"Yes," said Erno. "I do know that."

The sound of clopping on the flagstones drew their attention. Another rvenan emerged from one of the stalls, Nurrel on her back. She was not as tall as Deborah's rvenan and was a pretty grey with black speckles over her nose and rump.

"Good, Maqua," said Olly as he walked alongside, his hand on her neck. "Good. Give her a push with your left leg, Nurrel. Get her to turn right."

Nurrel must have done just that, as Maqua turned slowly.

"You remembered," said Olly. "Good girl. Take her out on the green, and we'll work her, Nurrel."

As they went slowly by, Deborah's rvenan turned and followed them out.

"Don't mind Mister Needy," said Olly. "It'll be good for him to watch and pick up a few tips."

"Actually," said Deborah, "I was thinking of calling him Ned, or just Mister."

Olly gave a nod. "I s'pose 'Needy's' not the most flattering moniker."

Deborah pulled a face. "Ned's not very imaginative, either."

"You're telling me," said Jacob.

"I can't think of anything else right now."

"Get to know him and see what fits," said Erno.

Deborah tickled Jacob's feathers. "How did you get your name? Did you think of it yourself?"

"No. Sonax said, 'Hello Jacob,' and that was that."

She smiled. "It's better than Beebee."

"Well," said Erno, "I think I'll head outside again. There's only so much indoors I can take." He leapt away across the cobblestones.

"What about you?" Jacob said to Deborah. "Coming outside to learn to ride Ned?"

"Later," she said. "I think I'll go and help Taffin."

She did not know why she said that, for part of her didn't want to venture any further into Hirahi, while another part of her wanted to see Chila again and show she would not be cowed by her.

"Suit yourself," Jacob said. "I'm off." He flew from her shoulder and into the halo of light from the open barn doors.

Deborah felt weak in the legs as she ascended the flight of steps to the kitchen. It made her feel cross. She shouldn't be intimidated, and she wouldn't be intimidated. And she shouldn't care what Chila thought. So, why was she going up into Hirahi?

When she reached the kitchen, she found no one there. A bag lay on one of the countertops with an array of vegetables and breads next to it—appearing far too many than what would fit in the bag—but Taffin was nowhere to be seen.

She would go up; she would go further in and find Kasharel. Say goodbye; see if their friendship really was dead and if he was set on staying with Chila.

The rattle of utensils came from the other end of the kitchen over by the sinks.

"Taffin?" Deborah called.

She expected to see Taffin's head pop up from behind a counter, but instead something else emerged. What was it—a rumpled piece of grey cloth? An old tarnished pot, dented and strangely shaped?

"Who's there?" Deborah called. "Taffin, is that you?"

In one quick move, a long-limbed, shrunken creature leapt over the counter and galloped straight for her. Deborah tried to scream but could not take a breath. She turned and tried to run, but the creature had her before she could take a step. It tore at her, raking nail-sharp fingers down her cheek, down her body, plunging stabs into her stomach. Deborah tried to scream again, but not one breath could she draw. She kicked and struggled, trying with all her strength to fight the creature off, trying to fend off its blows, desperate to gasp for air, to breathe.

A flash of amber swung in front of her—this creature was wearing the eye of Sonax! She clutched wildly for it and felt the cold, hard gem as her hand somehow managed to close around it, let out a shriek—air, finally, air! able to breathe!—then she fell onto the stone floor, the creature on top of her.

They wrestled, she kicked and thrashed, the pungent aroma heavy in the air of something rotting, sickening, nauseating, she tried to fight, tried to block the creature's blows, could not get it off her; it was too strong, could not get free…

Then came distant screams, shouts, and an electrifying sensation surged around her, the feeling of Oxpeina-life rushing in and surrounding her as a shield, just as it had while in Grufful's arms. Fizzing with passion and fire, it swept away the raking, stabbing fingers of the creature, which let out a blood-curdling howl as it leapt away, crashing into pots and pans as it hurtled over the counters and up the stairs.

Taffin rushed to Deborah's side. "Deborah! Are you all right? Are you hurt? Where did it get you?"

Deborah looked up at Taffin's horrified face.

"Dear, Deborah!" Taffin cried. "You're bleeding! You're hurt!" She turned her head and screamed at the top of her lungs. "Olly! *Olly!*"

"Erno," said Deborah faintly. "Erno."

She heard the answering thumps in the depths of the building. Steady, quickly, thump after thump. He was coming. She was safe. She lay back and sucked in breath after breath.

They were all around in her in a blur, Erno—so green! so bright! his face close to hers—Nurrel, Taffin, Olly, Jacob. Saying something—she couldn't decipher what. Urgent voices, Nurrel going, Jacob, where was Jacob…

Everyone faded into darkness.

44

"You've got to stop the bleeding!"
"I'm trying!"
"Oh, where is Fothie? We need Fothie!"
"What happened? Who did this?"
"It was a guandra! A guandra!"
"Are you sure?"
"Of course I'm sure! I saw it with my own eyes. If only I'd been there a moment sooner, I could have prevented it. I could have put the shield around Deborah sooner; I could have been there with her and stopped this from ever happening!"

"Help put this on those wounds. Press that other one. There."

The voices were those of a man and woman. Familiar. Echoing as though in a tunnel. Shadowy shapes hovered about.

"Deborah, stay awake."
"Where is Fothie!"
"Deborah, can you hear me?"
"Keep the pressure there. Put the salve here and here to seal those ones."
She drifted into nothingness.

"This would never have happened to her if I had been her custodian," came a low growl.

"Grufful, you don't know that," said a calm, authoritative voice. "You can't watch an image-bearer every moment of every day. What is disturbing is that apparently she does not know how to defend herself. Why has she not been taught?"

"I did not think it necessary here." Erno's voice, sounding very subdued.

"You did not think," snarled Grufful.

"Don't blame him. It's not that simple, and you should know that." A woman's voice. Taffin. "You can't just teach someone how to bring Sonax's life-shield around themselves. It requires trust, and that trust only comes through getting to know him."

"They had only just met," said Erno.

"Have you caught the guandra?"

"Yes, and killed it myself. It had all the hallmarks of having been a mage."

"Chila."

"No, that can't be. You must be mistaken."

"Oh, Chila! She was turning. I knew she was, but I never imagined she had turned so far."

"I'm sorry, I cannot understand why you would think this. Mage Chila is very wise and caring, and this could never happen to her. Why, only yesterday I spoke with her about a food drop she was planning for the Silver Lake. How can someone do such good for others, then turn and become a guandra? You are mistaken; it was not her. Perhaps Mage Chila is at the lake now as we speak, and that's why you can't find her."

"You are the one who is mistaken. Self-importance can use many guises, but the intent is the same; it puts oneself above all else."

"Deborah can hear us again now. I sense her thoughts."

"How is she?"

"Confused. Wondering where she is and why she can't move or see anything. Deborah, Grufful is going to put sleep onto you now as Fothie works on healing your body. You understand? I'm here. It's me, Erno. We're all here. You're safe."

The voices were silenced, the shapes gone. Deborah drifted, as though lying on her back in water, held up in the buoyancy of otherness. Soft, muscles relaxed, snugly at home, all worries ebbing away. Awareness that she could not move even if she wanted to, but that did not matter. She did not want to, did not need to.

"I'm scared."

The voice belonged to Fothie. Very near. Overhead? Why did she sound clearer and lighter? Oh, because there was no ambient background noise, nothing for her voice to cut through.

"You, scared? Why?"

A new voice. Something comforting about the warmth and timbre in his few words.

"Because she's so close to death," Fothie said. "I don't know if I can save her."

"She's close to life now," he said, "and I'm holding you, too."

Now, things made sense! The familiar Oxpeina-life held her up, had her secure. She could breathe freely again.

"I can't see you," said Fothie.

"Yes," he said. "I know, but you hear me, don't you?"

"Yes."

"Then, stop being scared," he said. "Don't let fear turn you from me, Fothie."

Strange to think of Fothie being scared. She who was so boisterous and confident.

"Sorry, Sonax. It helps hearing you. I just—well, you see how she is."

Sonax? So, that was who the other voice belonged to. Yes, that made sense. If only she could see his face again. He and Fothie sounded very close by, but she could see nothing of them.

"Fothie," said Sonax, "don't look at that. I'm here, you're here, we can help her together. I gave you this ability so you can use it. Let's use it now."

"I'm trying."

"Just relax. There, that's better. You can see me now?"

"Yes, yes, I can."

45

Daylight streamed into Deborah's eyes as she woke. She squinted at a pale ceiling overhead—stone?—and realised she was lying in a bed. The mattress beneath her was comfortable enough, but it was firm and tangible. There was no longer the sense that she was floating.

Erno hopped over to her, a wide grin on his face. "There she is, finally awake!"

"About time," said Jacob, and flew to the bed, landing neatly at its foot.

"You hate being inside," Deborah murmured, looking at Erno.

He chuckled. "'Tis true; I'm not a big fan of it."

"Where am I?"

"You're still in Hirahi."

She slowly sat up. Yes, it was that same small room in which she had spent a night. The view from the windows looked out to a cold blue sky, the river below snaked by the dark forest carpeting the distant low hills. "How did I get here? What happened?"

"What do you remember?" Erno asked.

Her brow furrowed as she stared at Jacob.

"Don't look like that at me," he said, his eyes widening. "I didn't do it—it was a guandra."

She hugged the bedclothes to herself as the image of the long-limbed creature rushed to mind. "A guandra tried to kill me."

"Yes," said Erno.

"Is it gone?"

"Yes. Val killed it."

"Val?" She thought for a moment. "Grufful was here, too. Where is he? Is he still here?"

Erno shrugged. "Yes, I think they're still somewhere in this region."

She lifted the bedclothes and looked at herself. "I was stabbed. The guandra stabbed me." She could only see faint round marks and light scratch lines on her skin. Yet she had felt the guandra stab her; she was sure of that.

"Yes," said Erno. "You're all right now. Fothie has healed you."

"So did Kasharel," said Jacob. "He, Taffin, and Olly saved your life while we went looking for Fothie."

"Kasharel?"

"Yes."

An amber glint caught her eye. There on the tiny side table by the bed lay a sparkling gem. The eye of Sonax.

"Where's Sonax?"

"What?" said Erno.

"Is he still here, too?" she asked. "I heard him and Fothie talking."

Erno tilted his twiggy head. "Really? That's interesting."

"He wasn't here," said Jacob. "You must have been dreaming."

"No," said Erno. "I think it more likely that when Fothie was using Sonax's healing power and tapping into his Oxpeina-life, Deborah heard some of what went on between them."

"*Huh*," said Jacob.

Deborah considered getting up out of bed, but her legs felt heavy and unwieldy when she tried to move. Fothie had obviously healed her, so she should be fine. Why feel this way? Then she remembered that Grufful had put her into a sleep. Perhaps it hadn't worn off properly. "How long have I been asleep?"

"Two days," said Erno.

"You've been here all this time?"

"Yes."

"I haven't," said Jacob. "I can't go without food like Erno can. Otherwise, I wouldn't have left you. Really, I wouldn't have."

She stroked his feathers. "I know, Beebee."

He lightly bit her finger.

"I don't understand what's happened," Deborah said. "Why did the guandra do this to me? I didn't do anything. I was in the kitchen, looking for Taffin. Then it came out of nowhere and attacked me. Why?"

"It's what they do," said Jacob.

"Are you sure you want to talk about this now?" Erno asked. "How about having something to eat first?"

"In other words," said Jacob, "you sound groggy and look dopey. Wake up first, then we'll talk."

She frowned at him. "I *am* awake." She managed to wriggle her legs over the side of the bed, and her feet touched the cool stone floor. She wrapped a bedsheet about herself then took the eye of Sonax into her palm, studying the amber glow that flickered like fire as she held it.

"They could barely prise that thing out of your hand—you were holding onto it so tightly," said Jacob. "Where'd you get it?"

"Off the guandra. Why did a guandra have it?"

"Because it belonged to Chila," said Erno. "And Chila became the guandra."

Deborah turned the gem over in her hand. Yes, it looked like the same one she had seen Chila wearing, but Chila, a guandra? "I don't understand."

"You really should do by now," said Jacob, hunching down into his feathers and glaring at her. "If you turn from Oxpeina-life, what do you think you're turning *to?* And, once you've taken that final step into the narrowness and bleakness of your own life, then you can't go back—your transformation is complete. Why do you think so many are trying to journey deeper into the regions of Oxpeina-life? We're all trying to get away from the inevitable creep of death as the outer regions die off in the cold."

"Very poetic," said Erno. "In other words, Chila's desire for her own self to be held up above other image-bearers turned into a consuming desire for control. This is always what guandras want—control. There is no embracing the otherness, no Oxpeina-life for them; there is only embracing the desire for self, and that leads to a collapse in on oneself."

"Now, who's trying to be poetic?" said Jacob.

The door to the room opened. Deborah tucked the sheet closer in around her body. It was a relief to see Nurrel, and, as he looked at her, his expression showed his relief, too. Close behind him towered Val and Grufful. They brought into the room with them that sense of electricity, that invigorating sense of Oxpeina-life, so that the air seemed brighter and clearer. Both rovi looked at Deborah, that question in their eyes, the question that always seemed to be there whenever she met a rova. This time, Deborah felt she knew what they were silently asking.

Do you know the Oxpeina-life?

"Yes," she whispered.

Grufful's blue-gold eyes glinted with satisfaction, but Val showed no emotion. Another question came from their gazes. *Are you going deeper into the realm after Sonax-Oxpeina or are you turning?*

Deborah faltered, uncertain what to think or say. Grufful frowned, and Val still did not let on his thoughts by any change of expression.

"Deborah," said Grufful. "This is the second time I have laid sleep on you to assist someone to heal you. Erno does not do his duty as your custodian—he has allowed two attacks on your life."

The second time? It dawned on Deborah that when she had been attacked by a brismun back near the caves of the gehun, she had been told that rovi had fought off that very brismun, then sent her into sleep. So, that had been Grufful? She had him to thank for the heaviness of sleep that lingered and clung to her now?

"Erno does his duty just as well as Deborah lets him," said Jacob. "You know very well that the image-bearer's will must be respected, and if she chooses to go her own way, then that's not the custodian's fault. Besides, who are you to question Sonax's choice for Deborah's custodian?"

"Who indeed," said Val. "However, that is not why we are here. It is good to see you awake and well, Deborah. I have news for you."

Her heart gave a painful thump. She knew what he was going to say next.

"It is about your father."

Her breath caught in her throat. "Yes?"

"He has left the city of Aric and has been led another way. He is being taken into the Wrion region."

Nobody said anything for a moment. Deborah had no idea what it could mean, and yet Val had delivered the news with the kind of solemnity as if the Wrion region was a bad thing.

"We will find him, and we will rescue him together," said Erno.

So, it *was* bad.

"Love seeks after, and love finds," said Val.

Nurrel nodded.

"As soon as you're ready to go, Deborah," said Erno.

"I'm ready now," she said, and stood, the bedsheet swaddled about her. Her legs gave way almost immediately, and she sagged back down onto the bed.

"*Hoo*," said Jacob. "Not quite ready."

46

Deborah stood at the window of her room, looking out at the morning mists rising off the distant trees curling into wisps evaporating into the grey sky. "I wish you would take this feeling of sleep off me. We're wasting time."

"Not at all," said Grufful. "It has given time to Erno and Nurrel to travel to Smoky Glade—"

"Shady Glade," said Jacob.

"—and time for you to heal. Besides, by the time they come back, I'm sure you'll be ready to travel. So, time," Grufful said, his upper lip curling into a snarl in the way that Deborah had come to learn in the last few days was a sardonic smile from him, "has many uses and fits the purpose that it has been given."

Deborah leaned closer to the window and peered down. There. Another one. This must be the fourth person she had seen going by, a rova at their side. "What is going on? Why are so many of your kind here, Grufful?"

Grufful joined her at the window. "Many of the image-bearers are leaving, and so they need a custodian for their journey."

"Why are they leaving?"

Jacob coughed uncomfortably and stalked away from her along the windowsill. He turned his head this way and that as though pretending to look out and that he did not notice his little act had drawn her attention.

"Is there something you're not telling me?" she said.

"The death of Chila has had an impact here." Grufful's wild face became even more ferocious as he spat the words. "Some of the image-bearers can't accept she has died and that she did in fact turn and become a guandra. Some know this has happened, oh yes, and that knowledge has hurt and confused them badly. Others have decided that Chila did not die but must have gone on to travel through the regions to the Oxpeina."

"*Hmph*," said Jacob. "Didn't they see what she was really like? Deborah can't have been the only one Chila tried to control and manipulate."

"But I'm not travelling, and yet you're here with me," Deborah said, looking at Grufful.

The wildness of his face softened as he looked at her, his blue eyes bright against his dark brown fur. "Sonax has assigned me to protect you while Erno is away."

"Protect me?" She drew her cardigan closer about herself as she thought of the guandra's attack. She could still feel the claws raking down her cheek, the plunging stabs into her stomach. "Are there more guandras nearby?"

Grufful laid his hand on her shoulder, and, in his light touch, she felt the tingle of Oxpeina-life. The memory of the attack faded. She drew a deep breath and smiled at him.

"Not protection from the guandras," he said, "but from the image-bearers who are angry and looking for someone to blame."

"They should be angry at Chila, nobody else," said Jacob.

Deborah stared at Grufful, aghast. "Is everyone blaming me for what happened?"

There was a light tap at the door, and it opened. Taffin came in carrying a tray with breakfast, and Val followed. The tall rova blinked at Deborah in the way she had learned was his greeting—no more silent questioning from his green eyes whenever she saw him, which was every time Taffin came.

"You're up," Taffin said, smiling. "You're looking much better today, Deborah."

Deborah said nothing. It was too shocking to think that the image-bearers of Hirahi might be blaming her for Chila's death.

Taffin set the tray down with a clatter on the table next to the bed. "Oops. Almost lost half your drink in my haste. Didn't mean to slop it everywhere." She dabbed the tray with a napkin.

"Is this why I'm confined to my room?" Deborah said. "You're afraid of what the others might do to me?"

Taffin pulled a face at Grufful. "What have you been telling Deborah?"

"Only what is true of the image-bearers here in Hirahi," he said.

"There's time enough for talk of that another day."

Jacob fluffed his feathers. "*Hoo*. Time!"

"Don't worry about it, Deborah," Taffin said. "We're doing our best to calm things down—Val, I'm so thankful you're here to help me!—it's just all in disarray at the moment, that's all. I think I'm still in shock, and others are too, and yet others are—well, let's just say they're struggling to process what has happened and they're not coping with it very well."

"They have been blind to it and Chila for too long," said Grufful. "Why did she hold herself up so high and maintain such a position of self-importance? Because she was able to here."

"Now, yes, well, that may be so, but you can't expect everyone to see the inner workings of the way someone thinks."

"The outer workings can be indication enough," said Val. "You saw them."

Taffin burst into tears. Grufful darted over, and both he and Val embraced her so that the little lumdil woman was almost engulfed by the two of them.

"*Oh!* Sorry," Taffin gasped from under Val's arm. "It just gets too much, sometimes. I just never—well, it shouldn't—you know. To have watched Chila turn and be powerless to help—I never thought it would go so far—and then attacking Deborah, who of all people did not deserve anything like that! Not that anyone does—*oh!*" She buried her face against Val and sobbed into his fur.

Jacob hopped to Deborah's shoulder. She instinctively reached up to touch his feathery breast. Strange to see this outburst of emotion from Taffin, she who had been so loving and calm, bringing the daily meals with a smile and kind words and never letting on what was going on in Hirahi.

Taffin wiped her eyes and smiled up at Val and Grufful. "You're both lovely. Val, I've missed travelling with you, you know? Missed it so much. Olly and I will stay here as long as Sonax wants us to—really, who knows what is going to happen to Hirahi now, I don't—but one day I hope we'll be able to journey on deeper in with you again and go to the Oxpeina's region together."

"One day," said Val. "We will."

Taffin turned to Deborah. "I guess I'm now free to tell you that Fothie has been wanting to visit you, but I've told her not to. It's not safe for her to come into Hirahi right now with everyone's fractious tempers. The feeling towards our brismun custodians is very dark."

So, Fothie hadn't forgotten about her. Deborah felt a rush of relief to know that she would have come if she had been able to. "If you see her, tell her I am so thankful to her for saving my life, and I hope to see her again soon, but of course I don't want her to come here if it's dangerous." She frowned, thinking for a moment. "Is this why Kasharel has not come to see me?"

"I'm sorry," said Taffin. "I didn't know he hadn't. If you like, I'll find him and tell him you'd like to see him."

It was painful to see the look of surprise on Taffin's face. So, Kasharel really had no reason for not coming. Deborah shook her head. "No, it's okay."

Grufful uttered a low growl.

"Oh yes," said Taffin. "Before I forget—Fothie had good news. She believes Erno and Nurrel will be arriving tomorrow. Don't ask me how she knows that, but that's what she said, and she was very sure."

"Good," said Jacob. "We can finally leave."

"If I can," Deborah said, looking pointedly at Grufful before sitting heavily on the edge of the bed.

"I am not preventing you from going," he said.

She feigned a frown at him. "Yes, you are, by not taking this sleepiness off me."

He attempted to frown back at her. She almost giggled at the sight but caught herself. When had she last giggled? It felt unnatural.

"The sleepiness, as you call it," he said, "will stay on you for as long as it is necessary."

"Give it *time*," said Jacob.

He dodged away from Deborah as she reached up to flick him.

"Anyway," Jacob said, "all you need be able to do is hold onto Ned. You won't have to walk."

"Reminds me of someone else I know," she said to him. She looked over at Taffin. "How is Ned? Is he all right?"

"Needy Ned is still grumbling and whining every day for you," said Taffin. "I'm afraid his speech hasn't developed any further, but he has come leaps and bounds in knowing how to handle a rider."

"Reminds me of someone else I know," said Jacob. "*Hoohoo!*"

Deborah did giggle then, but the bubbling up and release of mirth suddenly mingled with wanting to cry, as if laughing was wrong, that she should not laugh, that there was too much pain over Father being gone. She caught her breath and smoothed her clothing just for something to do, acutely aware that Grufful and Val were watching her closely. Perhaps they did not read her thoughts and emotions as well as Erno could, but she still felt self-conscious.

"Well," said Taffin, "I must be off. Too much to do. Glad you're looking better this morning, Deborah. See you at lunch."

She and Val left the room.

"You can't call him Ned," said Jacob. "It's a dumb name."

"I know," said Deborah. "It's sort of stuck."

"Unstick it and come up with something nicer."

"Ned is not a dumb name," said Grufful. "It has come from mine Edgren, as in mine Ed or my Ned. So, it is born of affection."

"How do you know that?" Jacob said.

"I know a great many things, dweller."

"You would, rova custodian." Jacob hopped down onto the bed and looked up at Deborah.

She smiled at him. "I suppose you're going out again?"

"I suppose I am. I suppose you're going to nap for most of the day again?"

She sighed. "Yes, but I want to try to walk some more today and get stronger."

"Only in this room and the corridor," said Grufful.

She sighed again. "Yes."

After breakfast, she got into bed as Grufful stood by the window looking out, his bright eyes far-seeing. Jacob had gone; the room was silent. It was easy to fall to sleep.

Hardly a moment later, or so it seemed, Deborah was woken by a tapping at the door. Grufful padded noiselessly across the stone floor as Deborah slowly sat up and blinked, trying to find her bearings again. Jacob was there on the windowsill, preening. Surely, it was too early for Taffin to be back with lunch; besides, she usually knocked then came right in.

A male voice murmured in response to Grufful as he opened the door. Kasharel? Had he come to see her?

"Hello, Olly," said Grufful.

Deborah's heart sank. She forced a smile as Olly came in, bringing the aroma of the barn with him.

He held a pretty bunch of flowers out to her. "Val said you're ready for a visitor. How are you getting on, Deborah?"

She took the flowers, looked unseeingly at them, and gave them an absent sniff—why did Olly's mannerisms seem so much like Father's? To see him again brought up a hollow ache and longing for Father. "Thanks. These are very nice. I'm improving. I feel fine actually, just sleepy."

"Good," said Olly. "Glad to see you doing so well. I won't stay long; thought I'd pop in and give you these and tell you that Mister N asks for you every day. I've been working him whenever I can, teaching him riding aids. He's picking it all up quickly, is our Mister. He's a clever fella."

"Uh-huh."

"Have you ever ridden before?"

"No."

Olly nodded. "Yeah, guess there's not much opportunity for that back in Eblhim. Don't have so many animals there, do we." His expression grew thoughtful. "You know, when I lived there, I didn't see a lot of clues that Eblhim was fading out. I've been thinking a lot about what you said about how there was nothing wrong there. I can kind of see why you'd say that. I mean, I used to think that, too. I don't mean to say I know better than you; I really don't; it's just you reminded me of how it was when I was there. Been thinking about it. Brought back memories." He smiled at Deborah. "I s'pose I'd better not keep on talking when you need your rest. Better let you get your strength back. As soon as you're able, come down to the barn and see Mister."

He went over to the door.

"Olly," Deborah said. "Why did you leave Eblhim? I know I asked you before, and you said something about being drawn away, but what was it that really made you leave?"

He turned and was silent a moment, considering. "My life there… well… everything was humdrum, went on like clockwork, and in the back of my mind I kept having the nagging thought there was something more, something I was missing out on. Then one day, you know what? I saw him walking down Main Street. Sonax-Oxpeina, I mean. You know Main Street? Sonax walked right by one of the clothing stores there—forgotten its name. Lots of people about, didn't seem to notice him. I saw him; he saw me. Was the weirdest thing. Then he vanished, and I thought I have to find him. He had *something*. That Oxpeina-life. And, that was that; the enchantment got me, and here I am." He shrugged and gave her a grin.

It was startling to think Sonax had been in Eblhim. Why had he been there? Was this what had happened to Father, too? Had he seen Sonax? Father had only said he needed to be by the trees, by the woods, to find peace in Shilhim. She did not think she believed that anymore. He must have been planning something else; must have felt the enchantment as so many seemed to. She didn't know if she felt any enchantment.

"See you later," said Olly.

"'Bye," she said.

Grufful shut the door after Olly. Deborah watched as he took her empty mug into the bathroom, heard the tap going there, then came back and set the flowers into the mugful of water. He fussed a little with them to get them to balance right. It was curious to see a rova doing such a menial task.

"What is it?" he said to her. "You look at me so strangely."

"Nothing," she said.

There was another tap at the door. Deborah felt hope spring up.

"Hello, Mally," said Grufful as he opened the door.

Deborah sighed. Where was Kasharel?

"Val said Deborah's ready for visitors," came the squatchamn boy's voice.

What was it that Val had seen in her that he thought her ready for visitors? Still, it was nice of him. She wondered if he had spoken to Kasharel and told him, too.

"Yes, she is," said Grufful. "Come in."

Mally did so, a beam on his thin face, his eyes wide. "Shocks, Deborah, I was so worried about you when I heard what had happened. Are you okay?" He handed her a jammy cake in a pastry case that was small enough to sit in her palm.

"I'm all right," she said.

"*Bah*," muttered Jacob.

She cast him a sidelong look. "I am fine now, and I'm healing well. I'll soon be up and about and able to help you in the kitchen, Mally."

"I thought someone had butchered a rvenan, there was so much blood on the floor! Then when they told me it was your blood, *wowser!*"

He grimaced and gave her a searching look. "Yet, here you are, and you look pretty good, Deborah. Taffin told me you're all right, but there was so much blood I don't know how you survived! Took me ages to mop it all up."

She set the little cake onto the table, trying to stop her hand from shaking as she did so. If only Grufful would take away this weakness! "Fothie, the brismun custodian, gave me Oxpeina healing."

Mally's eyes widened. "Really? For a while there, some of us thought the brismuns had done it, but the rovi that came here said no, it was Chila, that she had turned all the way. Taffin says that, too. Was it? Was it really Chila?"

"You have been told the truth, Mally," said Grufful in a low voice.

Mally's face reddened. "Yes, I have, yes, sorry."

Deborah frowned. "It was *not* a brismun who attacked me. It was a guandra. You should trust the brismuns here in your region—they're lovely and special, and I don't know why anyone wouldn't like them."

"I will, I mean, I do. It's just… odd times, odd times. Never thought I'd see all this going on here. I mean, it's Hirahi; we're one of Sonax's outposts; we're not supposed to have this happen here. I think I've been really dunderheaded, honestly." He sat on the end of the bed and looked up at Grufful, awe on his face.

"Why do you say that?" Grufful asked.

Deborah had the impression from the tone of his voice that he already knew the answer.

"Looking back, I don't know," said Mally. "There were things I should have noticed. I *did* notice them, but I didn't. Am I making sense?"

"No," said Jacob.

Mally picked at the bedcover, pulling and teasing a stray thread. "It's all… well, I should have done something. I know very well what we're supposed to be here." He glanced sheepishly up at Grufful, then down again. "Hirahi is to equip and assist the travellers. We're supposed to work together, to make it all easier for everyone. We're not supposed to sit around and treat Chila like she's the all-knowing high mage of all the regions and knows how to get the most Oxpeina-life better than anyone, as if she's bigger than Sonax." He grimaced. "I look back at my time here, and I feel so chunder-dunderheaded, like, so dumb! I knew it wasn't right. Why did I go along with it? I shouldn't have, that's how. It's only now that I see all the things I should have paid more attention to. So, why didn't I back then?"

Deborah suppressed a yawn. It would be nice to lie down again. Mally's stream of words was beginning to run in together, and it was taking an effort to listen, especially as he spoke with more intense feeling. She looked at him as the words kept pouring out, his thin face fretful. She reached over and gave his shoulder a light pat.

"You'll be all right, Mally," she said. "Taffin is here, and she'll help you." She looked up at Grufful. Would he see in her expression she had had enough and it was time for the visitor to go? Erno would have known what she needed. She would only have to touch Erno's hand, and he would know.

"Yes," said Mally. "Taffin's the best, but I won't treat her like she's any different from the rest of us even though she's a mage. I won't! I'll keep working here and do what I can to have Hirahi be the way Sonax wants it and be useful to travellers. We're supposed to be useful!"

Deborah nodded and pulled a face at Grufful. His bright eyes blinked affectionately back at her. She glanced meaningfully in Mally's direction. Grufful blinked again. That was annoying—he wasn't getting the message. She didn't want to be the one to tell Mally to go, especially when he was in mid-conversation about something he clearly felt very strongly about. Maybe she just had to summon the energy to break into his chatter again and ask him to come back another time to talk.

"There's less to do now that people are clearing out," said Mally. "Even the new doctorer has gone. What are we going to do without someone here to do the doctoring? I might have to go around the lake houses and see if they can spare anybody."

She could hardly breathe. Kasharel had left?

Jacob hissed and looked crosser than ever. "The new doctor has gone? Are you sure?"

"Yes," said Mally. "Went last night. He didn't have a custodian, which was weird, but when he heard Sam was going and she had one, he went with her. I think they were from the same region, or close regions, anyway. She said she's going back. Why would anyone go back? She should go on, not back. Who knows when their regions will close? Why aren't they going to the Oxpeina's region? I don't get it."

Deborah shut her eyes, holding back tears. Why would Kasharel leave without even saying goodbye? Did their friendship mean nothing to him? Obviously not. Yet he had helped her; she was sure he had helped save her life. At least, that's what she had been told, that he had helped stop the bleeding while everyone waited for Fothie to come. Maybe he had only been doing his duty as a doctor and really didn't care anything for her at all.

"—although some are still deciding," said Mally. "What about you, Deborah?"

Deborah came to herself with a jolt. What else had he said that she had missed? "Sorry, what?"

"Are you going to stay or go on? Don't tell me you'll be one of those going back. I would go on myself; actually, I'm still tossing that option around and figuring out what I should do, but I still think someone needs to be here for the image-bearers coming through. I guess there will be more coming through? I don't know, maybe after this there won't be?"

"I'm getting a headache," said Jacob.

He stretched out then folded his wings in what Deborah thought was an overdramatic and exaggerated way, and turned deliberately around, placing his taloned feet carefully, and glared at Mally.

"Can I get you anything for it?" Mally asked. "'Though I don't know what birds have for headaches. Should I go find the brismun?"

"*Birds?*" Jacob hissed. "I am an owl."

"I thought that was a bird. Aren't you a bird?"

Jacob made a grinding sound with his beak. "*Humph.*"

"Poor little thing," said Mally, getting up. "You don't sound well. I'll see if I can get the brismun for you."

47

Deborah stirred as the door opened quietly.

"It's only us," said Taffin, as she came in with Val.

Deborah slowly sat up and eased her legs over the side of the bed. This was lunchtime, or was it dinner? Too many naps, the day was a blurry collection of people talking too much—the squatchamn couple who worked as bakers in the kitchen had come after Mally; 'we ain't goin' nowhere!' was what she remembered of their chatter—eating, drinking, getting up to the bathroom, Grufful standing staring out the window, Jacob coming and going, more naps.

Deborah blinked up at Val as he blinked down at her. Her blinks meant nothing; she was only trying to wake up in the midst of grogginess, while his were a greeting.

Taffin set down a tray. "Good morning, Deborah."

"*Morning?*"

"Yes, indeedy!"

Deborah groaned and gave Grufful a look.

He frowned at her, his upper lip curling into a snarl. "For the last time, no. I won't take the sleepiness, as you call it, off you. When I place a protective sleep on you, I do not specify how long it stays. That timing is not in my power but only responds to your need."

"Fine then," she muttered, "how do I get it to recognise I don't need it anymore?"

"How do you know that you don't?"

She frowned back at him. "You're as bad as Jacob."

"Please," said Taffin, "let's not be having an argy-bargy. I've had enough of that kind of thing around here."

"Very true," Val said in a low voice.

Grufful bowed slightly. "Apologies, Taffin."

She gave him a small smile. "You've been stuck in here together for days; that's enough to make anybody crotchety. Well, I have good news on that. Deborah, you don't have to stay shut up in here anymore. Anyone who would cause trouble has gone. The last decisions were made yesterday, and I wouldn't be surprised if you heard some of the shouting carry all the way here to your room."

"I didn't," said Deborah.

Taffin sighed. "Just as well. Anyway, feel free to come out whenever you want to. We're a very small number now, but we're banding together and figuring out how we're going to keep Hirahi open."

Later that morning, Deborah went to the door and tentatively touched the handle. She had meant to go ahead, turn it, leave the room at long last, but when it came to the act of doing it, found she couldn't. The thought of going to the kitchen or the great hall made her weak in the legs, and her breathing become shallow. Yet it was safe now, she had been told it was safe. No Chila, no guandra—she still didn't fully understand how they could be one and the same—no other image-bearers who might behave disagreeably.

"I am here at your side," Grufful said.

She glanced at him. "I just… well, I… this is stupid. I should be able to do this. I feel stronger; I thought I was ready. Now, I don't know."

"Are you afraid?"

"I suppose I am."

"Think of the pleasanter things. What would you most like to do, or who would you like to see?"

She bit her lip. "I suppose Erno's not back yet; otherwise, I would have heard. I would like to see Fothie and Hemri. Oh, and also Ned.

And I want to go outside and feel the fresh air and see the river." She turned the handle and took a deep breath as she looked out at the empty passage, the stone walls smooth and grey. It was so quiet and empty, she could not help but think of Kasharel. Had he really gone?

She took hold of Grufful's arm, her fingers sinking into his thick, warm fur, and they walked together. Not so long ago, she had walked with Kasharel in the gehun caves, him giving her the support and help she needed as she recovered. Had that only been out of his sense of duty? She had thought his care of her was genuine, as was their growing friendship. Now, it appeared it had all meant nothing to him.

"See?" Grufful said. "You are doing well. I sense the sleep is fading from you."

Deborah shrugged. "At least my legs aren't collapsing under me anymore."

They came to the first bend of the passage, and she hesitated.

"Let's see if we can take Ned outdoors," Grufful said. "Perhaps you could have your first ride."

She squeezed his arm. "You're just saying that to distract me so I don't turn back."

"Yes, I am. Is it working?"

She smiled up at him. "Maybe."

With his closeness and the vitality of Oxpeina-life she felt from him, she found herself wondering why he had not been assigned as her custodian. He was assigned to care for her now, so why had he not been right from the beginning?

"Why do you think I was given a brismun for a custodian?" she said, as he helped her down a flight of steps. "Why didn't Sonax give me a rova? I mean, I'm not sorry Erno is my custodian, but I know it's strange. I should have had a rova, maybe even you. Why am I different to everyone else?"

"Why do you think it is solely to do with you? This custodianship is for Erno's benefit as well as your own."

She felt slightly chided by him. Was he implying she was self-centred?

Yet, it had never occurred to her that the custodianship might be for Erno as well as herself. She had only thought of it from her own point of view. "You sound very sure of yourself. How do you know that?"

"Because I asked Sonax, and that is what he told me."

She stared at him. "When did you see Sonax to talk to him about that? Where is he? I need to tell him to go to my father."

"He is aware."

"What do you mean? He knows I want to tell him, or he knows my father is looking for him?"

They passed a lamp affixed to the wall, and Grufful's dark brown fur took on a burnished sheen.

"Both," he said.

"So, is he doing anything about it? Does he know Father is going to…" She paused, trying to think, "Whatever that place was you warned me about?"

"The Wrion region. Yes, Sonax is aware of all of this. He has been trying to reach your father and turn him back but has had no success as of yet."

"What? Why?"

"If I knew all the ways and thoughts of image-bearers, then I could tell you. However, I do not, and because your father is not my responsibility, Sonax has not told me why. He only told me some of his thought and dealings on the matter. I suspect only what would be of benefit to you."

She supposed it was reassuring that Sonax now knew that Father was looking for him, but it was puzzling to think that somehow they had not connected, that Sonax had apparently tried to 'reach' Father and not been able to. For someone, or something, that could suddenly materialise out of thin air and could also connect with a brismun's thoughts, as Sonax had done with Fothie while she was healing, why had he not reached Father?

She held tightly to Grufful as walking grew more tiring and she needed to lean on him more. No, she would not go back to the room; she wanted to get *out*. Out into the fresh air.

"Have you not thought it curious that Kasharel did not have a custodian?" Grufful said. "I have been waiting for you to ask that question."

"Oh, yes, I meant to. Do you know why?" She tried to sound bright, as if she were not feeling waves of hurt roll in at the mention of his name.

"His particular gehun clan has had many woes and great unrest over the years. Their method of conquering this was what I thought unusual, that in their strivings for unity they would curtail their individualities in an attempt to overcome differences. They aim to think the same, to believe the same, on all manner of issues to rid themselves of conflict, and they allow no room for independent thought to be expressed."

Grufful steadied Deborah as she stepped heavily off the end of another flight of stairs. "What this has done is that Kasharel's clan has become insular, fearful, reluctant to trust outsiders. Included in that distrust are the custodians of their region. The gehun no longer wished to work with custodians in the natural symbiotic way for the care of their region or even for their own image-bearing selves. Their council set themselves up as custodians over all. When image-bearers do that, it leads to an imbalance in a region, so that in time it is more and more difficult to maintain Oxpeina-life. The more that Oxpeina-life is sought without using the practices that Sonax has set up for a region, the more out of reach that life becomes. So, they will wear their robes, they will try to stifle differences, and all the while the image-bearer will silently groan and strain under the pressure of constraint, and discontent will grow."

Deborah sighed. "I don't think I quite understand all that. Maybe I'm too tired right now."

"Think of it as trying to have Oxpeina-life for oneself while doing away with the Oxpeina."

"That's even more confusing," she said, smiling at him.

"Yes, it is," he said, his lips curling into the sneer that she knew was his smile.

"But I thought the gehun seemed to have great respect for rovi," she said. "Who was it that came to the caves when I was there and spoke to their council? Was it you? Also, Kasharel really seemed to want a rova custodian when we were travelling together. He said his had been killed. How could that happen?"

Grufful gave a low growl. "Yes, it was I who was sent to the caves, and it is a mystery to me why Sonax still chooses to send messages to such unyielding image-bearers. As for Kasharel's custodian, this is what I know of the matter: many years ago, Kasharel and two others attempted to journey from their home, part in rebellion against their clan, part in response to the desire for Oxpeina-life. They were, of course, immediately assigned a custodian in their travels. Her name was Tira."

He paused. Deborah looked at him; his forehead was furrowed in thought and his blue eyes misty. She was about to ask if he had known Tira, but he spoke before she could.

"Fear beset the gehun image-bearers as they ventured into the woods. They were unable to travel far, as their fear brought confusion and muddled their ability to feel the pull, the enchantment of Sonax, and find their directional bearings. Fear is like hounds to the blood for guandras desirous of control over others, so it brought in several. Kasharel and his companions did not listen to Tira, did not relax and allow her to place a shield about them. In fact, in their panic, they fought against her. I do not know all of the details, but I know the outcome. Kasharel made it back to his caves—I cannot say for certain how, but I suspect the guandras let him go as he no longer wished to leave his region. Tira was overcome and unable to stand up to attack on all sides. She was killed. She should not have been. Should *not* have been. The will of the image-bearers had too great an influence on her, and she lost her hold on Sonax."

He went on in silence for a moment, his feet padding quietly on the stone while Deborah walked slowly with him, clinging to his arm. He looked down at her, and she sensed affection in him in that enigmatic way of a rova's gaze.

"It is a reminder to us all to hold steady when under attack and have confidence in the shielding of Sonax-Oxpeina."

She knew he was referring to how he had held her when the guandras in the woods near the Silver Lake had attacked. He had calmed her, and the electricity of the Oxpeina shielding had spread in a fiery surge across her back as she buried herself in his fur. What would have happened to her if she had not listened to him telling her to hold onto him?

"And," Grufful went on, "as Kasharel has not faced Sonax and admitted his hand in Tira's death, that mark remains on him for all of my kind to see."

Deborah thought back over what she knew about Kasharel: his fear of guandras, his mistrust of brismuns, even the way the rova, Geor, at the entrance of Hirahi had treated him, and yet his seeming respect for Sonax and the rovi.

"So, you mean that Kasharel will never be able to have a custodian again?"

"He will if he has an honest conversation with Sonax and admits his culpability in the death of Tira. Then, Kasharel's mark will be erased, and Sonax will be able to trust him to another custodian if he wishes to travel again."

"I didn't see any mark on him?"

"We see it when we look into the eyes of an image-bearer. A brismun would sense it by touch, and a shaseeliany would hear it by the sound of the voice."

"But Kasharel really seemed to respect Sonax, or as he called him, Sonashi."

"Respecting is not the same as truly talking with someone and forming a connection or an understanding."

Deborah's heart began to pound, and she stood still. She was nearly at the open door to the kitchen. She could see the counters, pots, and pans, and smell the yeasty bread aroma wafting through the doorway. Her grip on Grufful's arm tightened.

"I don't think I can go in there," she said, her voice tight.

"Why not? Merely because it is the place you encountered a guandra and were almost killed? *Fah!*"

She looked at him, and he at her, his clear blue eyes contemplative, a light in their depths, the liveliness of Oxpeina-life in him even as he was motionless. As she felt that quality of life in the air around him, Chila's words came back to her again. You have a low quality air of life; no one wants to be close to you; you drive people away. Chila was right; even now Kasharel had left her without saying goodbye as if she was worth nothing, meant nothing to her. Father had left, and now so had Kasharel. Was Erno going to come back, or had he and Nurrel decided to go a different way and leave her here, too?

"I see progression of thought," said Grufful. "The variation of emotion as it passes through memory, the manipulation of a guandra, and the piercing thorn words of one who turned. Why do you hold onto those words?"

She sucked in a breath, trying to calm herself. "Because they are true. I have driven everyone away."

"Because you *believe* those words are true. They are not true."

She looked away from him. "How do you know that? You can't say that. You must know I don't have Oxpeina-life like you do."

He gently touched her cheek where the guandra's claws had raked, his soft fingers causing her skin to tingle. "It is strange how an image-bearer thinks something must be true simply because they believe it so, as if all the effort of their will must *make* it so. As if all the elements of the world were shaped and in place only because of their belief. Yes, strange."

His fingers moved to her forehead. Immediately, her breathing steadied, and the kitchen, the stone walls around them, faded into the periphery. When he spoke next, she was unsure if his words went directly to her mind or if he spoke aloud.

"You do not yet know yourself, image-bearer, so I could easily order you to step through this doorway now, but I will not. Shall we return to your room or shall we continue onward?"

He let his hand fall. Their surroundings sharpened into focus once more. She looked again at the kitchen. It would be all right. All right.

Grufful was there at her side. She only needed to take a few steps through, get to the steps that led down to the barn, get out into the open air. She clutched Grufful's hand and went on.

48

"Debah, Debah!" cried Ned, his rubbery lips twitching into a smirk as he trotted to her.

She stroked his long, floppy grey ears and smiled at him. "Hello, my Ned."

"I learning riding," he said. "You riding."

She sat on a hay bale. "Yes, but not yet."

He nudged her hand. "Go! Go!"

"No, Ned. I'm not ready. When I'm feeling stronger, then I will."

He pursed his lips and his brow wrinkled, his ears flicking to and fro as he seemed to puzzle out what she had said. He looked sidelong at Grufful, his large, docile eyes narrowing. "You make Debah do. Do make. Go."

Grufful caressed the length of Ned's face down to his muzzle. Ned shivered and closed his eyes, his lips trembling.

"Ned," Grufful said, "you are a very good boy. I am glad you want to go riding with Deborah. She wants to go riding, too, but she is not yet well enough to. You must wait nicely, like a good boy."

Ned shook his head, flapping his ears, and looked down at Deborah. "Go riding. Do!" He stepped closer, almost onto her toes, and would have nudged at Deborah again but Grufful pushed him back so that he staggered, his hooves slipping on the cobblestones.

And then there was movement on the other side of Ned, a rush of air as the atmosphere contracted and expanded. Sonax appeared faintly there, wavering as if behind a wall of water, tall and broad-shouldered, his wavy brown hair windblown about his rugged face.

"Good boy, Ned." Sonax placed his hand on Ned's side, looking intently at Deborah.

In his gaze, she felt him say he knew her, and also had the impression that if she stepped through that wall of water between them, she would find what it was she was looking for, what she needed.

Then he was gone, and the barn became dark and dull as if all the life had drained from it. There was an excited murmuring from the rvenan cattle in the stalls, clucking and whiffling from the fowls and the other barnyard animals.

"Oh!" said Ned. "That felt unexpectedly peculiar, sort of like a rushing, burning sensation in my side that travelled all the way through to my brain and cleared out all the muddliness. I'm sure I can see things more clearly now, too."

Deborah looked at him. His eyes were sharper, more comprehending, as though the dimness of sleep had been washed from them. She said nothing, for she felt unable to utter a word. What had just happened?

Ned raised his head, looking this way and that about the barn. "Very nice. I like the gradation of colour, even in that wooden beam there."

Grufful burst into a roar of laughter.

"My!" Ned turned to Grufful, his eyes wide. "How is that funny? I wasn't trying to be funny."

"I know you weren't." Grufful laid his hand on Ned's back. "It was simply quite an abrupt change to watch you given speech by Sonax. I'm glad for you."

Ned flicked his ears. "Why did Sonax have to leave? I liked him—I liked what he said to me, and yes, you're right, it did all happen very quickly." He gazed down at Deborah. "Are you feeling all right? I missed you very much, and I'm looking forward to showing you what I've learned. Olly taught me riding aids and what they mean. At first, it felt very strange having someone up on my back; sort of threw me off balance, but now I like it because it makes me feel like I'm not alone and that there's someone to go adventuring with. As soon as you're feeling well, I'll take you out and show you what fun it is."

"He will settle," Grufful said to Deborah. "Once speech bursts forth, it truly does burst forth!"

"Are you talking about me?" Ned asked.

"Yes. Try not to overwhelm Deborah, for she has had a very difficult time in the last few days. And, sometimes, when there is a lot of talk and chatter, it can be too much, too tiring, for an image-bearer who is unwell."

"Is that right? Thanks for telling me. I can see I'll learn a lot from you." Ned gently nudged Deborah's hand. "I'll try to stop talking; I really will. I will try my best, now that I know it might be too much for you, I will try to hold things in instead of talking."

She stroked his muzzle. "I don't want you to stop. You've only just begun to talk, and I don't want to ruin it for you."

He smirked. "Ruin it? Never, Deborah! But I can see what the rova says is right—you look tired and you have a droopy face. I'll go outside and find Olly. I think I'll creep up behind him and say something and see if I can give him a fright." He gave a snort and trotted the length of the barn.

Grufful sat next to Deborah on the hay. "I have seen this happen countless times, but it never fails to amaze me as speech and comprehension leap into being at the touch of Oxpeina-life. Ned will settle as he finds himself in this new born element, and will no longer need to speak incessantly. Unless that is his personality."

She nodded. She needed time to breathe, to rest, to try and process what had just happened in the briefest span of a moment in time. Why had Sonax suddenly appeared in that way? He had been less clear than the first time she had seen him, as though he was reaching out from behind a barrier of some kind. Why had he given speech to Ned?

A rhythmic thumping in the distance caught her attention, and her heart lifted. "Erno?"

The thumps grew louder and then took on a flatter, harder quality as the brismun landed on the cobblestones.

Deborah got up and headed for where she thought the barn's outer doors were, while the thumping sounds bounced off the walls and seemingly came from different directions. "Erno, is that you?"

"Sorry!" came Fothie's cheerful voice. "It's only me!"

"Very good." Grufful put his arm around Deborah to steady her. "We will ask you to touch Deborah again with Oxpeina-life and bring her more healing."

"Ask away, then!" called Fothie.

She leapt out from behind a stack of hay bales and grinned at them both. Deborah hurried forward, her hands outstretched to grasp and touch Fothie's, then she faltered and gasped. Fothie was thinner, her twiggy hair appeared brittle and was missing pieces, and a large pale blotch was spread over her chest and stomach.

"Fothie!" Deborah cried.

"Yes," said Fothie, "I'm sure I look a bit of a mess to you. I feel it myself. This region has had a rough few days, and it all seems to have come out in my health. Rather me than Hemri, though. I've made sure he stays up the other end of our region, so I think he's well out of it."

"But, will you be able to get better now?" Deborah said. "Taffin says that the image-bearers who would cause trouble have left."

"*Hum.* There's a bunch of turmoil and confusion going on with the villagers as they try to make sense of what happened with Chila. That still has its affect hereabouts, so I'll need to wait and see what is decided."

"Decided?"

"For some reason, one of the main rumours they're believing is that Erno, Hemri, and I killed Chila. They think Shessi was in on it, too. So, the villagers are thinking about getting rid of us."

"What? They can't do that!"

Fothie shrugged. "Yes, they can. The will of the image-bearer holds sway over a region, and that's all there is to it."

Grufful growled. "They would not be so foolish! They must not do away with the natural order. Do they not see what happened to their neighbouring region?"

"I'm sure they have," said Fothie, "but maybe they have their own ideas for what happened there. Image-bearers tend to be like that, seeing only what suits them."

Deborah leaned heavily against Grufful and looked around for somewhere to sit.

"Take my hand, Deborah," said Fothie. "I hear a lot in your breathing that I don't like. I'll do what I can for you."

Deborah grasped her hand, finding it drier and firmer than a brismun's normally would be. "What about you? You need healing more than I do. Can't you get the Oxpeina-life for yourself?" She gingerly touched Fothie's chest, where the moss was discoloured.

"Hey!" Fothie smiled as she squinted up at Deborah. "You're trying to heal me! That's a lovely thought. Hold still now; let me get a good hold of you." Her fingers closed firmly around Deborah's hands, and she pressed her thumbs into Deborah's palms, then felt carefully along to her wrists.

Warmth suddenly went up Deborah's forearms as though she stood too close to an open fire and was touched by its heat. Fothie whispered, and in the closeness of the barn, sounded as if leaves were rustling or straw was being scattered. Deborah watched Fothie's face; her pupils flickered in the green of her face, and she felt as they touched that Fothie saw past her and was talking to someone else, to Sonax, and that if she could concentrate well enough on Fothie's thoughts, then she might hear his answer. Then, it occurred to her that Fothie could be a conduit through which she could say something to Sonax, too. Tell him to give healing for Fothie. Also, find Father. *Find Father. Bring him back.* The warmth in her arms faded.

"Hang on a moment," said Fothie. "You're distracting me a bit, Deborah. Those are some forceful thoughts you've got going on there! I'll pass your request on to Sonax, sure, but right now just let me do my thing."

"Oh, sorry."

Grufful laid his hand on Deborah's shoulder. "There is no need to use a custodian as a go-between. You are free to speak with Sonax yourself."

Deborah felt a little silly, acutely aware she had done something that they thought was pointless. She supposed she still did not quite understand how things worked in the regions, or even what or who Sonax-Oxpeina-life was. She thought back to when she had first come to the woods with Father, leaving the gloom of the city behind, and their first sight of the never-ending sea of trees as they stood together on the mountaintop. She had not known they had been at the brink of a new land, of places and creatures of magic. Had he known? If only he had spoken more of his thoughts to her.

She drew a deep breath, finally able to breathe properly again after days of weakness, days of heaviness. The barn smelled. Seriously, Olly needed to give it a good clean, as manure was the odour of the day.

Fothie grinned up at her. "There! You're much better now."

Deborah felt she was standing taller, that she did not need to clutch at Grufful for support, that she could climb a mountain if she had to. This new strength had happened almost without her noticing, and she realised she also felt something else—the zing and zip of life she had experienced back in the woods after leaving the gehun tunnels, when she and Kasharel had emerged to the region that was rich with Oxpeina-life. Why weren't all the regions like that? She recalled the brismun custodian's wariness, defensiveness, that she had no image-bearers in her region and seemed to prefer it that way.

Deborah began to sense something else as she stood with Fothie and Grufful—an underlying current of disagreeability, a discord that permeated the air of this region. She felt that if she reached out her hand, she would touch it, or if she stepped outside the barn and into the open air, she would feel its full force. What was it?

"A pushing away of Oxpeina-life," said Fothie as she held Deborah's wrists.

Deborah looked down at her, suddenly conscious that her thoughts were known.

"The image-bearer's desire for having one's own way," said Fothie. For taking Oxpeina-life for oneself.

Deborah was not sure if Fothie had spoken that aloud or if they had shared that thought together. Yet, it was all so puzzling and contradictory. How could one push something away yet also try to take it?

"Enough now," said Fothie, and let go of her.

The sense of the region vanished immediately, along with much of the electrifying touch of Oxpeina-life. Deborah felt her shoulders sag as a heaviness spread over her, as though something vital had been taken from her, and she swayed a little on her feet. Thoughts rushed back of Father and his abandonment, memories of Mother and never really feeling close to her, of Kasharel up and leaving her without a word. She did not want any of that. She wanted to feel lighter, freer, again.

"I showed you that so you'd understand some of what goes on here," said Fothie. "I know you want healing for me; I know you do, but I'm immersed in this region and deeply connected with it. What you ask for isn't possible at this time and place. I'm subject to the will of the image-bearers of my region."

"Can't you leave?" Deborah asked.

Fothie shook her head, her twiggy hair rattling. "I don't want to. Sonax placed me here to take care of the dwellers, and that's what I want to do. I love my dwellers, even the grumpy ones! But if the image-bearers push me out, then that will be that. I'll have to go. Either that, or death."

Deborah remembered the desiccated and shrunken body of Senka lying in the region of the Silver Lake amongst the broken and dead remains of trees, the parched ground. She lightly touched Fothie's soft green cheek. "Not death. Don't stay in this region if it turns. Get out while you can."

Fothie bowed her head. "Yes, Deborah."

Deborah was taken aback by her reaction, as if she were responding to an order. But, as an image-bearer who didn't belong to this region, she shouldn't have any power or command over Fothie… or, something like that, however these mysterious things worked.

49

Outside the barn, Olly stood in the middle of the grassy area, looking at Deborah as she sat astride Ned. "Heels," he said.

Deborah brought her heels in against Ned's sides for the umpteenth time and tried harder to sit up straight. It was too easy to leave her feet dangling and flapping while focusing on holding Ned's shoulders with her hands. His fur was too short to get a proper grip with her fingers, and the small bumpy knot at the peak of where his neck and shoulders met was only big enough for one hand to cup. And there was no way she was going to try holding onto him with just one hand; it was hard enough to keep her balance as he walked onward—she rocked in every direction with each step he took.

Olly walked alongside them. "Feel your legs. Try to be more aware of how they're holding Ned. Riding is all in the legs."

"It's all in the legs, Deborah!"

Ned sounded too cheerful, and he tossed his head, a quiver running through his body as if he were eager to leap and race away as soon as possible.

She gripped him more tightly. "Ned! Don't you run or I'll fall off!"

He gave a slight gurgle. She did not know if it was laughter or surprise.

"Don't look down," said Olly. "Keep your eyes straight ahead. Same for you, Ned. Stop turning your head to try and see what Deborah is doing. Your job is to be aware of where you're going and what hazards might be about."

"There're no hazards," said Ned. "We're on flat grass. I could walk around with my eyes shut and it wouldn't matter."

"Actually," said Olly, "that's a good idea."

"What, that I shut my eyes?"

"No, that Deborah does."

Deborah stared in dismay at Olly. "You can't be serious!"

He gave her a quick smile. "Yep, I am. Close your eyes and focus on how Ned moves. You'll find your balance that way. And you, Ned, focus on where you're going and what it feels like having Deborah on your back."

"I'm going in circles," Ned said. "Deborah feels like a big lump."

Olly patted his shoulder. "Okay, I mean more, do you feel how tense she is? What else can you feel that she's telling without words?"

Ned shook his head, and his ears flapped. "Oh, I get it. I'll try to figure that out." He turned sharply.

Deborah grabbed at the small knot between his neck and shoulders as she lurched sideways. "Hey!"

Olly pushed her upright. "Close your eyes. Work on your balance. I'm right here to catch you."

"Olly!" came a shout from the distance. Taffin appeared over by the barn doors. "I need you for a moment!"

Olly pressed his hand against Ned's chest, and Ned stopped walking. "Be right back."

Deborah watched Olly stride across the grass, feeling suddenly vulnerable. Sure, Ned wasn't that tall, the ground wasn't so far away.

Ned snorted. "I'm right here to catch you, he says. Then, off he goes. Don't worry. I think we can do this ourselves. We don't really need Olly."

She dug her finger into his fur. "Don't you dare move!"

"Come on," he said, turning his head to look back at her. "I think what you should really do is sort of scoot back and lie down and put your arms around my neck and hold on to me that way. Then I'll walk, and you can find your balance like Olly says, except you won't be sitting up high, so you can hold better. Ready?"

"No! I'm not going to lie down; I'll most likely slide off!"

"Really, Deborah, you are a baby. I didn't know you were such a baby. We can do this! You just need to sit still and relax. Otherwise, we're going to be here all week stuck doing circles and nothing else. So boring! Come on!"

She supposed he had a point. She didn't want to be walking circles all week, either. She took a deep breath and shut her eyes. "Okay, okay. Just go slowly. *Please*, Ned."

"Sure thing!"

Again, he sounded too happy, too excited, like he would leap away as soon as he had the chance to. He chattered away while she willed herself to hold on with her legs and be conscious of how he moved. Block out his chatter; it was too distracting. Focus on how he moved, how to maintain her balance. Grasp that small knot, which really did fit well in the palm of her hand; feel a rising awareness of the sense of life throughout his warm body; the gentle rocking as he took each step; his hooves softly *thud-thudding* on the grass. It was better, it was easier; she could do this. Feel the balance, *breathe.*

Something clamped her right shoulder; she jumped with fright and yelled as she slid around Ned's tummy until her legs hit the ground, and she ended up in a heap there.

"*Jacob!* Why didn't you warn me!"

He glared down at her from where he perched on Ned's back. "I did! I said your name!"

"You never did!"

"Yes, I did."

Ned smirked. "Yes, he did. I heard the bird—I mean, *owl*—clear as anything say your name, but I was talking at the same time, so maybe you were distracted by what I was saying. Owl wasn't all that loud, though, I must say, and those wings don't make any noise, either."

Deborah got up, dusting herself off.

Jacob swivelled his head and eyed Ned. "I see you've found your voice. How did that happen?"

Ned's brow wrinkled. "First, I was looking at Debah, I mean *Deborah*, then the rova shoved me, and then Sonax braced me so that I didn't fall over, and, when he did, something happened. I hadn't seen he was there until then, but I felt all that Oxpeina-life go into my head and lungs and everything. I feel like I woke up from a long, strange dream."

"I know exactly what you mean," said Jacob.

Deborah spent much of the day trying to find her balance on Ned. By the time dinner came around and Olly called her in, she realised she had forgotten about helping Taffin in the kitchen. The flight of steps from barn to kitchen was cool, each lamp a halo casting a yellow sheen on the smooth stone, and, as she ascended, Jacob on her shoulder, the reluctance to go any further choked into her chest. Where was Grufful? He should have come back by now from wherever he had gone. Maybe he thought she didn't need him any longer, but she did. The thought of the kitchen—what had happened there—she paused and stood silent on the steps. The guandra—Chila? Had it really been Chila?—had been caught and killed. There was no longer anything in Hirahi that would harm her, or so she had been told. But then, nobody had known *that* would happen.

"What's the matter?" Jacob said.

"Just thinking," she said.

His talons shifted on her shoulder. "The guandra's gone. Don't worry."

She looked sidelong at him. "It doesn't make any sense to me. This turning, Chila, and guandras, and all that, I mean."

"I don't know why it doesn't. It makes perfect sense to me. You turn from one thing to the other; you can't have both. Either you have Oxpeina-life and all it brings, or you don't. Simple."

She sighed and shook her head. "It's easy for you; you're used to all these regions and the way they work."

"You'll get used to it, too. Now, let's go on up so you can get your dinner, then I'll go off and get mine."

She lightly touched his feathers, took a moment to gather herself, then, with trembling legs, resumed climbing the steps. Voices drifted down towards them, along with the clatter of pots, the aroma of fish frying and vegetables sizzling, and it heartened her. Everything was fine; all was normal. Taffin and the others were there.

She stood in the kitchen doorway and looked in at Taffin, Mally, and the squatchamn couple. "It's all right now," she said to Jacob. "You can go."

"See you later," he said.

She felt his small weight lift and the brush of wings as he left. She went over to Taffin. "Sorry, I should have been helping you with dinner."

Taffin smiled up at her. "Not at all! We are so few now that apart from us four and Olly and you, there are only two others left in Hirahi. I could have done dinner all by myself, but the others wanted to help and act like everything here is carrying on as normal. Well, it's not!"

Mally glanced up from where he stood cooking fish. "But it will again!"

"Says you! The whole place is in a terrible mess and might never be the same again. Do you think Sonax is pleased with how things went? He has every right to shut us down! Why keep this place as his outpost? Some outpost! What use are we to anyone now?"

Taffin sucked in shaky breaths, her chest heaving. The squatchamn couple and Mally set their utensils down and hurried over to surround her in a small huddle.

"Calm youself down," said the squatchamn man. "'Tis all right. We're here, ain't we? An' we'll go on as long for as Sonax wants it. We all got in a muddle with Mage Chila, but doesn't mean all's lost. You'll see, rovi'll keep on bringin' their travellers, an' we'll be right here to help 'em go on. An', if no rovi come, we'll know we ought go on further in ourselves, an' that's that. All good."

Taffin wiped her eyes and looked miserably at him. "I know what you're saying is true. I just… I feel like I failed Sonax. I should never have let this happen here."

Mally shrugged. "You're the one who always goes on about letting image-bearers have the freedom to turn or not turn and that we can tell them what route to take from here, but the decision on what they do is on them. That included Mage Chila—she was an image-bearer just like the rest of us, and more fool me if I ever treat anyone as though they're better than me ever again. Yet, I've somehow got to balance that by not thinking *I'm* better than *anyone*. *Phew!* We're all image-bearers."

Taffin smiled at him.

Mally turned his head and sniffed. "*Yow!* My fish is burning!" He ran over to the stove.

The squatchamn woman—Deborah could not think what her name was and vaguely remembered being introduced, but it was too awkward now to say, 'Sorry, what's your name?' when they had spoken and interacted several times—rubbed Taffin's back with the palm of her fingerless hand. "Magey-mage, let's get on. Chin up. We'd a humongous explosion clear the air, is all. Maybe it's what we all needed, right? Clear out an' begin again."

"Yes," Taffin said soberly. "I guess so."

Dinner was a quiet affair. Just eight at the table in the waning sunset light that cast its long shadows into the great hall. Deborah could not help but think of Mage Chila sitting at the head of the long table, nodding knowingly, speaking with great authority, Kasharel at her side. It pained her to think of him. He really had gone without saying goodbye. She thought over their last conversation. It was bad; she knew it was bad. She had lashed out at him. But then, he had defended Mage Chila. Not defended her, as a friend should do, but Mage Chila. And left Hirahi, even as she had been recovering from a brutal attack. He had not even stayed to see if she was all right, had not come to visit her. She pushed her vegetables and singed fish uselessly around the plate, feeling too churned up to eat anymore. Was Mage Chila right? Did she have a 'bad air' that nobody wanted to be around?

Faint thumps sounded in the depths of Hirahi. Faint and steady. She smiled. Was that Erno? He was due back today, and the day was almost over. It must be him. She turned this way and that, trying to determine which door he was approaching. The far one at the end of the hall? Or, from the kitchen?

From the kitchen, she decided, as the thumps grew louder, resounding through the passage as he leapt up the steps. She got up and rushed to meet him, and he grinned at her as he landed with a pronounced thud at the top of the steps and into the great hall. It *was* him. She bent and threw her arms around his mossy, round body, breathing in the scent of earthy sage.

His cool cheek pressed against hers. "There you are. I missed you more than I thought I would. Which, I suppose, is only half a compliment."

She smiled. "I missed you, too."

His firm hands probed her arm. "You feel much better. In great health. Good!"

Footsteps drew her attention, and she looked up to see Nurrel. His brown eyes lit with glad recognition, and she almost let go of Erno to go and hug him, but thought better of it. He might not want that. They hardly knew each other after all. Besides, she did not normally go around hugging others. Grufful was the only other she had hugged, and, besides that, hugs were not something she normally did. Mother had certainly never hugged her, and Father had stopped hugging years ago.

"I see," said Erno softly.

She let go of him immediately, realising he had discerned all of those thoughts tumbling through her mind. Nurrel came over, arms outstretched—intending to hug her!—and, instead of backing away, she bent down to return his embrace. It was all right—a bit strange, but nice. He let go just as she was getting used to it.

"So good to see you well, Deborah," he said. "I didn't like to go off and leave you while you were so ill, but I knew you were in good hands here."

"How was your visit to Ibelli's parents?"

"Difficult. Very hard. They're devastated and want to know why Ibelli's companions left her at the lake and what happened to their rova. Too many questions that I don't think we'll find the answers to."

Of course—Ibelli had been travelling with others; Deborah remembered Nurrel saying that, and of course they would have had a rova custodian with them. At least, to begin with. She thought of what Grufful had told her about Kasharel. Had Ibelli and her companions turned their rova away? Or, had the rova gone on with the others while Ibelli stayed behind?

"We don't know what happened," said Erno, "but as I said, we shouldn't rule out the possibility that Ibelli's friends also perished at the lake."

Nurrel looked dubious. "I don't see why she would stay if she had seen that happening to them."

"She may not have seen it. She did not appear to truly see anything other than the lake."

Deborah thought of her own hallucination, or whatever it had been, of Father at the lake. That had been so real she had been unable to see beyond it until Jacob had pecked her and snapped her out of it.

Taffin called out from the table. "You must be hungry after your journey, Nurrel! Come join us; we've got plenty to share."

50

Deborah slid from Ned's back and stood on the grass beside him in the misty morning light. "It's no good; I can't do it! Balance? What balance? I have none."

Jacob fluffed his feathers. "You're telling me—it was like riding a twig in a storm."

"You'll get better, Deborah," said Erno. "Just be patient."

She grimaced at him. "No. I can't muck around doing this. We've got to leave today, and I'm sorry, Ned, but I can't ride you. You may as well stay at Hirahi."

Ned turned his head and gave her a doleful look. "We've barely practised together, and you're giving up already? I don't want to stay here—I'm supposed to be with you. I'm supposed to carry you to help you travel much faster than you did before. That's my job. Sonax wakened me just for that job; I know he did. Just let me come with you. We can practise riding on the way."

She stroked his side. It would be good if she could master riding him, but her attempts so far had been worse than useless. It should be a lot easier. All she had to do was sit on his back and let him carry her, but it seemed like every step he took threw her off balance. She could not find any pattern to his motion, no predictability, no sense of how to hold herself. She turned to Erno. "I don't suppose you can magic me up some balance? I think Iff would have been able to do that, so can you?"

A flurry of movement in the distance caught everyone's attention. A blur of brown took shape as it emerged from the mist, materialising into three rovi running lightly across the grass. It was Val, Grufful, and one other, slightly smaller, who Deborah thought might be Val's son. Her heart lifted at the sight of Grufful, his blue eyes gazing fondly at her as he approached.

"We have come to say farewell," Val said. "We are leaving this region."

"We will soon, too," said Erno, "but I expect you know that. You and your pack seem to be shadowing us through the regions."

Val cocked his head, a thoughtful look in his green eyes. "It does appear so, yes. I think Sonax intends for us to maintain something of a connection."

Grufful wrapped his arms around Deborah and lightly pressed his chin to the top of her head. "For that, I am glad."

She snuggled into his warm fur. "Me, too."

"Is there anything you require before we go?" Val asked.

Erno grinned. "Balance for Deborah. Do any of you have that to give her? She strives to ride Ned, and balance does not come easily for her."

"It does not come at all," said Jacob.

Val turned to the other rova. "My son, this ability could be obtained from Sonax's gift to you. See what you can impart to Deborah."

Grufful let go of her as Val's son stepped forward. Deborah had thought him smaller and somehow of less import than Val or Grufful, but as he stood close to her and the air of Oxpeina-life emanated from him, she felt cowed, and that she should bow, and that she was small. A question arose in his dark, woodsy-green eyes. Again, with the questioning rovi, why did they do that? She kept trying to look steadily back at him and resist the urge to back away or lower her gaze.

Do you know the Oxpeina-life? Are you going deeper into the realm after Sonax-Oxpeina or are you turning?

Why did the rovi always ask this?

"Yes," she whispered, although she felt less sure as she said that. Did she know the Oxpeina-life? What did he mean exactly? As for going deeper into the realm, or if she was turning, she uttered a low: "I—I don't know."

He blinked at her as if he understood. "Shall I give you balance?"

"Yes. Please."

He covered her eyes with his soft, warm hand, and she felt her breathing calm. Clarity and sharpness came to her mind. She saw something. Saw Sonax sitting again with her at the table and the way he had laughed as she told him she had just been reading about him. She remembered the way she felt when seeing her face appear briefly on his face. That she was *somebody*, that she was wanted, that she belonged.

It was no mistake that she had left her home region and travelled into the woods. Sonax wanted her here. Wanted her to come deeper into the realm and leave the dying regions behind.

Val's son lowered his hand.

She looked at him in the morning light, the mist beading in his brown fur as tiny, glistening drops. "What is your name?" she asked him softly.

"Linnfel."

"Let's see if that worked," said Jacob. "Try riding Ned again."

Ned, who was standing very still and had not moved a muscle since the rovi had joined them, cleared his throat self-consciously. "*Er*, yes."

Deborah smiled at him and stroked one of his floppy ears. "What are you so worried about? These rovi are our friends."

"Yes, yes, *um*, yes."

Erno gave Deborah a leg-up, and she tried to mount Ned less clumsily in front of the rovi. "Let's go, Ned."

He took one step, and the movement of his body caused her to lurch backward. She grabbed for his neck while Jacob flapped his wings to maintain his balance on her shoulder. Ned stopped and looked back at them, his eyes wide.

Jacob shook himself. "*Hoohoo!*"

"Stop laughing," she muttered to him. "I don't know what happened." She looked over at Linnfel. "It didn't work. I still have no balance!"

"What were you thinking about?" he asked.

"Nothing."

"That could be the problem. Try thinking about the vision you saw."

She shrugged. "Okay." She took a deep breath. "Go, Ned." She shut her eyes, almost wincing as she waited for Ned to move. She thought of the vision of Sonax at the table; the feeling of being somebody, the thought of going 'deeper into the realm', that somehow in all of that there was a warning to leave the dying regions, a warning she hadn't heard before. Sonax wanted her to escape the city of Eblhim, leave it far behind, and be free of the death there.

Ned took a slow step forward. She felt herself move with him in a fluid action, sensing he was one who had been woken by Sonax, a beast who had been gifted with Oxpeina-life, who knew himself now and had speech. He stepped forward again and again, and she went with him, conscious also of the life on her shoulder, the light weight of Jacob who came with them, too, that together the three of them were intertwined in life.

She opened her eyes. "I did it!"

"Yes, amazing," said Jacob. "Ned took three steps forward, moving as slowly as he possibly could. At this rate, we'll reach the Wrion region in ten years."

"Joke's on you," said Ned. "I'm still walking and Deborah's still sitting comfortably, so what do you think about that, hey?"

He was right. Deborah had almost been about to flick Jacob with mock annoyance and realised it was true; Ned was still moving. And she wasn't rolling about on his back like a drunkard. It felt good. The ground wasn't so very far away, not really; she no longer felt like she was up too high and would fall at the next step. She could do this; she really could.

"Faster," said Jacob.

Deborah resisted the urge to tense with fear at his words. It was all right; everything was all right. "Yes, Ned, go faster."

His hooves were muffled thuds in the grass as his steps quickened, and Deborah adjusted her balance, *felt* balance within herself, causing her to relax her seat. Her shoulders lowered, and she gripped Ned's sides firmly with her legs. As she did so, it seemed to cue Ned to break into a lope, and the world became a smooth, rocking motion that flowed and swept her along as life coursed through her body. *Oxpeina*-life. She needed to go more into it; there wasn't enough; this region was cold, the edges frayed, a warning again that it was dying, that it was indeed curling up from the outside in, and that she needed to get further in before everything changed. Puzzling. Is this what Father had sensed? Is this why he had left her and gone 'further in'? Why hadn't he told her? Warned her of this himself? She thought of his brooding silences, his turning away from her, and pain choked up into her chest. She felt herself slipping, felt herself falling… Ned shouted, Jacob flew…

"*Soi-nah!*"

Hands caught her, and she found herself looking up at Grufful, then at Linnfel's intent woodsy-green eyes.

"You turned," he said gently. "You turned from life and fell."

They set her on her feet. Val and Erno were right there, too. Deborah looked to each of them, feeling small and surrounded by an energy she did not have—wanted to have, wanted to feel again—while they gazed back at her as if they could see right into her. She reached out to touch Erno.

I didn't mean to.

I know you didn't.

It was reassuring to have him hear her thoughts and know his response. Yet, there was sadness there that made her feel she had failed him. She looked at the ground. Someone kissed her forehead. Val. She tried to stop the tears from welling up, as this was what she desired from Father. To be loved, to be accepted. To be wanted, not left alone as though she was worth nothing to him. Tears slipped down her cheeks. Why was she even doing any of this? Just to find him again?

Sensing Grufful was about to enfold her in his arms, she turned and walked away from all of them. Down to the water's edge to watch the slow-flowing deep blue river slip by the grassy banks. The air was chilly, the mist still clung in drifts to the land, smudging the shapes of the distant rvenan cattle across the river. What world had she come to? A world of natural laws and rules that were hard to make sense of, custodians and image-bearers, and all of the regions held in their sway, somehow centred around Oxpeina and Sonax. Nothing like the simplicity of life in the city of Eblhim, the endless drudgery of day in day out. Yet, that was predictable, safe. Guandras were not real there; guandras were a thing to make fun of, or make fun with. Not real, long-limbed death that leapt through such a mundane thing as a kitchen and attacked without a word. It had wanted to kill her. Had tried to kill her. Why? And this had been Chila, somehow transformed?

Softly *thu-thunking* hooves approached. Ned nudged her elbow. "Deborah, what's wrong? Did I go too fast?"

"No." She stroked his forehead. "You were good, Ned. Just… I need… some time to think, that's all." She wrapped her cardigan more closely about herself. What was there to think about, really? She was only stuck in the same situation—wondering if she should rescue Father, wondering why she should bother if he cared nothing for her despite the thought that he had loved her once, had made up stories for her as a child. What did it matter anymore?

Jacob landed on her shoulder. Oddly, she did not flinch or jump, for it felt natural for him to alight there. She waited for him to make a sarcastic remark about her having fallen off Ned, but he pressed his feathery head against her cheek briefly and said nothing. Perhaps he had heard her comment to Ned about needing to think. He grasped her shoulder, the points of his talons not uncomfortably pricking through her clothing, but just enough to make his presence known.

"I like to think, too," said Ned. "I find it an interesting experience being able to have thoughts run clearly through my mind instead of being in a state of oblivion. It's as though I did not truly exist until now. There is so very much to think about and ponder." He nudged her arm again. "Grufful would tell me to leave you alone, as I expect you need some quiet to have your thoughts unclutter and rearrange themselves. So, I'll just go over there and graze awhile, Deborah."

She nodded. "I don't know," she said quietly to Jacob. "It all seems pointless."

"What does?" he said in his low, raspy voice.

"This. All of this. Being here, trying to find Father. I don't know why I'm doing it anymore. And now, it's like I feel I'm being warned somehow that the regions are dying and I should get away from them. Get away where? I don't even really know where I am." She glanced over her shoulder. Four rovi were some distance away where she had left them—who was the fourth?—and Erno. She could hear the murmuring rise and fall of their voices. Erno would most likely still be well able to hear what she was saying to Jacob. She turned back to the river.

"They are dying," said Jacob. "The outer regions, at least. I too have had that warning ever since I was woken by Sonax's hand. I did not know exactly what to make of that. I'm still trying to understand it myself and figure out what to do."

She looked sidelong at him. He was admitting he didn't know something? The all-knowing Jacob?

"All the image-bearers who speak of this tend to set off and travel 'further in' to find Oxpeina-life," he said. He fluffed his feathers and hunched down into them. "I don't know where that is, but I feel something. A pull towards the centre of *something*. But I am not an image-bearer. I'm a dweller. Perhaps I should have stayed in my own region."

"And, die?"

"We all must die eventually."

The unmistakeable thumping sounds of Erno coming towards them caused Deborah to look back again. The grin spread on his face as she did. She supposed that even if he did not see her clearly, he had felt or heard the shifting of currents of air around her.

"We all must die, must we, Jacob?" he said. "Whoever told you that? If that's true, then why bother trying to find Oxpeina-life? No, you listen to that warning of death's approach, and you move. You move where you're told to, and don't just sit there and let death come and swallow you up."

He held out his hand. Deborah felt a strange tug towards him and involuntarily swayed on her feet. Jacob flew to Erno's hand.

"See?" said Erno. "You felt that?"

"Of course, Custodian," Jacob muttered.

Ned also went to Erno and stood silently, his grey coat damp with mist, and lowered his head so that his chin almost touched Erno's twiggy hair.

"It is the same," Erno said. "I can draw you to myself with what little taste of life I have from the Oxpeina, and you will feel a sense of invigoration. Feel it?"

"Of course," said Jacob.

"Yes," whispered Ned. "Of course."

Erno looked up at Deborah. "I know you do, too."

She sighed. "Yes, but that's what's so confusing. I don't understand any of it."

51

Jacob shook himself, tickling Deborah's neck with his soft feathers. "Here's Nurrel, at long last."

Nurrel led Maqua out from the barn, the sheer rock face of Hirahi towering above them, the windows dark amongst the marked and pitted variation of stone, the vine that clung to its base dotted with the last of the pale gold flowers.

Maqua, shorter and finer-limbed than Ned, had bundles tied about her, small ones on either side of her neck, and a stretch of cloth for a saddle seat with larger bags attached behind. Taffin and Olly came after, carrying more bundles.

Olly let out a rallying shout. "Ned! Come!"

Ned set off towards him at a trot. When he got to Olly, the bundles were fitted on his back with ties that secured across his chest and under his belly. He nosed at them with interest but stood still as they were settled and tightened.

Now that they were about to leave, Deborah felt uncertain. She supposed she had sort of figured out how to ride Ned, but she would have to make a decision now as to where they were all travelling to. What had seemed so sure a day ago now seemed muddly and confusing again.

The four rovi were still in deep discussion, and, as Deborah and Erno approached, she recognised the fourth was Geor. Tall and stooped, grizzled grey, but he who had been silent on her entry to Hirahi many days ago was speaking now.

"I will never see another like this," he said grimly. "I failed, and that is all. I am no longer worthy to remain but must go."

"Then, you have not heard us at all," said Val.

Grufful frowned at Geor. "You have not listened at all."

"Brother," said Geor, "you will likely never understand how it is to have an image-bearer in your care that turned, and I pray you never do. Speak no more to me, for this is my fate."

"Fate!" spat Grufful. "*Pah!*"

Linnfel let out a low growl, his face twisted into a snarl as he eyed Geor.

"Brother," Grufful said to Geor, "this is wrong. You must not leave. Not now! Let go of she who turned and give yourself to Oxpeina. Be restored!"

Geor slowly shook his head and walked away. The three rovi stood watching. Deborah saw different expressions cross their faces—disbelief, anger, sadness—mingled with the wildness of a rova. The life glow around them seemed even more distinct as Geor faded into the mist.

"He makes his choice," said Val.

"And it is wrong," growled Grufful. "He thinks only of himself; thinks only of his own shame, his own heart. What of the need of those who pass through Hirahi? What of the need of another image-bearer journeying further in? Does he choose to go against Sonax's way and order of life? Geor chooses to not give himself in love to others but instead decides to turn?"

His words struck Deborah's heart. Was she choosing her own way? Was she giving up on Father? It hit her that she always seemed to focus on how much or how little he loved her. But what of her love for him? How loving was she, his daughter, when he needed help? He was searching for peace, for Oxpeina-life, and now, by all accounts, he was travelling the wrong way into the Wrion region. She took a deep breath and smiled at Nurrel as he and Maqua approached.

"You ready to go?" he said.

She nodded. "I think so."

He took folded oilskin from one of Maqua's bags and handed it to her. It was the coat Taffin had given her that had been left back at the little house across the river, along with the storybook Deborah had read by the fire.

"Thanks." She put on the coat. "Do you have the book Taffin gave me?"

Nurrel nodded. "Yes. Everything you own is packed up, and more."

Everything she owned. What was that? A change of clothes, the storybook, that was all. Ned trotted over to her, the bags on his back jiggling but holding firm. He smirked at her but said nothing, which was unusual. Perhaps he was still intimidated by the rovi.

It was all kind of a blur as the rovi, Taffin, and Olly enveloped her, all wanting to hug and kiss her, wish her well, offer words of advice. There was no turning back now. No matter how unsure she felt about it all, she had better forget Eblhim and just do this: find Father and get him out of whatever fix he had got himself into. She would love him, even if he would not love her.

Further along the river, a barge was waiting to ferry them across the lake. A squatchamn man sat at the wheelhouse reading a book and barely looked up at their approach.

"I hope we will meet again, Deborah," Grufful said, his warm breath against her hair.

He gave her a leg-up onto Ned, where she sat snug between the bags. She sat tall, telling herself she could do this; she could ride Ned if she focused on the right things, on *Oxpeina*-things. She pulled the collar of her coat a little higher against the chill morning air, and Jacob adjusted his grip on her shoulder. She looked about, hoping to see Fothie somewhere or Shessi swimming in the river.

"*Ugh*." Ned nosed the edge of the barge. "I never liked this thing."

Maqua got on and positioned herself plumb in the middle without Nurrel telling her anything.

"Show-off," Ned muttered.

Erno landed with a *thwack* onboard, causing the barge to shudder. Ned stepped slowly after, his head lowered.

"Turn around," Deborah said to him. "I want to see the others as we go."

He did so, and she was relieved to feel a connection with him as he moved, to feel herself well-centred on his back. It would not have made for an elegant goodbye if she had fallen off the moment he turned about.

She smiled as she looked at the three rovi on the bank: Val, serious and commanding; Linnfel, quiet and thoughtful; Grufful, fierce and full of suppressed emotion; Olly, who had similar mannerisms to Father; and small Taffin, wiping her eyes as if she were seeing off a beloved daughter. Deborah's breath choked in her chest as her gaze went back to Grufful, his blue eyes fixed on hers. He who would be her custodian. Is that why it felt hard to leave him?

The rumble of a puttering engine broke the silence, and Ned flinched. The barge eased away out onto the river and headed towards the lake.

"Goodbye!" Taffin called.

52

Jacob stared out across the dark blue waters of the lake, his gold-rimmed eyes intent. "Why are we going this way?"

The barge sliced through the water, leaving feathered ripples in its wake, the engine louder and more conspicuous now that it was out on the lake. The mist was clearing, but the day was grey, and the far-off slopes of tree-clad hills looked dark and impenetrable.

"I don't know," said Erno.

Deborah looked with puzzlement down at him as Ned sidestepped slightly to keep his balance. "What? You mean we're not going the right way?"

Erno squinted up at her. "Didn't you look at a map?"

"No!"

"I did," said Nurrel. "Taffin pointed out some different routes to Wrion. I thought this way would be better for us to manage—the terrain isn't as difficult. Sorry, I should have consulted everybody first instead of making the decision myself."

"*Huh*," said Jacob.

Deborah nudged him. "It makes no difference to you. You can fly!"

"Feels wrong," he muttered.

"Of course it does," said Erno. "Nobody ever said the Wrion region is close to where anybody should be; it's further out. But, yes, Nurrel, I probably would have made that decision, too. You're thinking we should go around the Hictin region instead of through it?"

"Yes," said Nurrel. "The map showed a lot of ravines there, so I thought it best to avoid them."

"How long will it take to get to Wrion?" Deborah asked.

"A day, perhaps two."

His answer took her breath away; a pang of nervousness gripped her, and it took a moment to form words. "So soon? So close?"

Nurrel leaned over and patted Maqua's neck. "All thanks to Maqua and Ned. We could never get there as quickly without them."

At the sound of her name, Maqua turned her head to glance sidelong at him, her soft grey ears framing her docile face. Her eyes were uncomprehending, a dull naivety in them that made Deborah think of how Ned had appeared before he had been 'awakened'. And indeed, Maqua was quiet for the rest of the barge journey while the others chatted lightly. Deborah did not join in, for her thoughts were occupied. Would she really see Father again so soon? How would it be? What would she do once she found him? What if he did not want to see her? It seemed like she had not seen him for the longest time, and now the thought gave her an uncomfortable twisting feeling in her stomach.

Ned stepped onto the shingly shore, and Deborah roused herself. She had to focus now, not lose her balance. A little practise on level ground was not going to be the same as what the rest of the day would involve. She had to pay attention to Ned and where he stepped, pay attention to the feel of Oxpeina-life, remember that Sonax knew who she was and was warning her to leave the regions behind.

She frowned. It was all so strange. Even now she could feel it— something about the air, as though life waned and was seeping away as they moved through the region. Jacob was right; it did feel like they were going the wrong way. Yet, to see the forest as they rode under the covering branches, to hear the scurrying birds, the chirruping insects, as all the while nothing looked out of the ordinary, nothing looked wrong, she could not help but wonder if she imagined things.

Erno thumped on ahead, winding in and around the trees, some of whom imperceptibly shifted and bent closer towards him as if he were someone they were drawn to. As Deborah watched him, she felt her heart lift with the knowledge that they were travelling together again, leaving Hirahi and all its nastiness behind. And, Kasharel. She sighed.

Following close to a stream that rushed and tumbled down towards the lake that they had left behind, Maqua and Ned trampled across the leaf-litter, dodged fallen branches, and broke into a lope when the ground was easier. Uphill sometimes, then down the slopes, always under the trees, always with few glimpses of sky, the forest floor shadowed but lit well enough to see their way. Deborah's confidence grew as she rode Ned, and she found she could observe more of their surroundings instead of focusing so hard on centring herself and how he moved.

Late afternoon, a rush of bitingly cold air stung her face. "Stop, Ned!" She looked about, wondering what had caused it.

Ned shook his head, his ears flapping. "That felt horrible."

"We've just crossed into a different region," Erno said.

"I don't like it," said Jacob.

Erno shrugged. "It's empty, that's all, and that's a good thing."

"Then, why the cold air?" Nurrel said. "That was more than an autumn wind."

"Is this the Wrion region?" Deborah asked.

"No," said Erno. "That will come next. As for the cold air, well, I suppose it's just the emptiness. There are no dwellers here anymore. No image-bearers, either."

Nurrel dismounted. "We should stop awhile for Maqua and Ned's sakes."

"I feel kind of sick," said Ned. "I think it's the air."

"Now that you mention it," said Jacob, shifting uncomfortably on Deborah's shoulder, "I feel that way myself."

Erno hopped over to Ned and touched his muzzle. "Breathe. I'm here." He went to Maqua and laid his hand on her cheek. She whiffled and gently lipped his twiggy hair. Erno turned back to Deborah. "Jacob?"

Jacob leapt in a spread of wings and flew to his hand.

445

Nurrel patted Maqua's rump, then began to undo the straps that secured her bags. "It's all right, girl. Erno, isn't there a brismun custodian here?"

Erno grinned at him. "There is, now! I must confess… this was my region."

"What?" said Deborah. "Erno! Your region?"

He laughed.

"How can you be so cheerful about it?" Deborah said. "This is horrible. It's empty! What happened here?"

"Everyone moved out," Erno said. "Good, huh?"

"How can you say that?"

"*Hrm*," said Ned. "I suppose if the regions are dying, and you say this is good, then does that mean those who were here have gone to find the Oxpeina region?"

"Yes," said Erno, "I should hope so. At least, all the image-bearers I spoke with before they left intended to go on deeper into the Oxpeina-life. All I could do was encourage them and watch them go. As for the dwellers, it's only natural that the will of the image-bearers affects them one way or another. So, they went, too."

"I hope they went in the right direction," Jacob said.

"Erno, why didn't you go with your dwellers?" Deborah asked.

"They don't need company like image-bearers do when they travel—they have the care of my brothers and sisters throughout the regions." He leapt to the nearest tree and laid his hand against its rough bark. "When I knew everyone had gone, I waited and waited in case others came through here. Such a very long time of waiting. Finally, Sonax released me from my region." He tilted his head as though listening. "I suppose I shouldn't call it my region anymore. It no longer belongs to anybody."

"Where's your shaseeliany?" Jacob asked.

Deborah shot a look at him, wondering if that was prudent to ask. She wanted to ask the same thing but felt reluctant to. Erno did not have a shaseeliany with him, and according to what she had learned about brismuns, he should have a counterpart, an opposite: water to his earth, female to his maleness to make a complete circle. Something must have happened to her.

Erno was silent a moment and bowed his head, his eyes closed. "My Sasaris, my sweet, dear one. I never expected she would turn; never thought the dissatisfaction and departure of the image-bearers would affect her so. But none of us is immune to the turning." He looked in Deborah's direction. "You want to know why she turned, don't you."

"Yes," she said quietly.

"She was happy here, happy to rule the region with me over many, many years, and I think that feeling went deeper than I ever realised. When the image-bearers began to leave and the dwellers to follow, that was an insult to her. We were no longer looked to as the stabilising life force keeping our—*this*—region healthy, and we were no longer looked to as rulers. We never should have thought of ourselves as rulers, and while for me it was easy to let go of that notion and realise my mistake, for Sasaris, she could not. Her self-importance had grown too much; she had forgotten that we were merely custodians given our role by Sonax."

Again with the talk of 'self-importance'. That, according to the brismuns, had been Chila's problem. Her self-importance had caused her to turn, and in that 'turning' she became a guandra. Deborah got off Ned's back, trying not to get caught up in the bags as she did, and patted his neck. It was a strange world—these woods, these regions—and she still did not know what to make of it all. "I'm sorry that happened to Sasaris. It must have been hard for you."

"Yes, it was. It all happened a very long time ago, but now that I'm here, the memories are fresh."

"Sorry to interrupt," said Ned, "but is there anything to eat around here?"

"You'll have to make do with leaves," said Erno. "Unless you want to run until nightfall, which is about how long it'll take for us to reach a grassy clearing. If it's still there."

Ned pulled a face. "Now that we've stopped I feel very tired and want to rest."

Jacob flew back to Deborah's shoulder. "I think we all do."

She tickled his breast. "Why do you need any rest? You should be the one sorting out everybody's dinner, as all you've done the whole day is sit there."

"*Hoo.*"

Nurrel undid the chest and belly straps that held Ned's baggage and hefted it all onto the ground. Maqua was already lying down, her legs tucked alongside her body, eyes shut, her head drooping so that her chin brushed the ground.

Erno held out his hand to the nearest tree. It shivered and released leaves that swirled down to him in a rain of gold and green. He took handfuls over to Maqua, who blearily opened her eyes and began munching, while Ned browsed amongst the lowest hanging branches he could find.

"No bugs here for you, Jacob," said Erno. "Not even the smallest dweller remains in this region."

Nurrel rummaged through one of the bags. "We've got plenty here you can eat. Dried fish, dried meat, berries, bread, all sorts of things."

Jacob fluffed his feathers. "Bread? *Bleh.*"

53

White hot fire claws raked her face; knives plunged again and again into her stomach. Deborah woke with a gasp and sat bolt upright, her heart furiously pounding. She felt her face, felt her stomach. No, it was all right, it was all right. Fothie had healed her. Fothie and Sonax had healed her; it was all right. Chila wasn't here. No guandra was here.

In the blackness of night, she heard a rustling movement.

"Deborah?" Erno whispered.

"I'm all right," she whispered back.

He thumped to her side—surely that would wake the others—and his mossy hand was soon on her shoulder. Her heart rate began to slow. She sucked in the cool air, deep breaths, *steady*.

"Bad dream," she said. Or, did she only think those words?

About Chila.

His words were definitely in her mind and were not a question, but stated as though he knew now that he touched her. The woods were eerily quiet, with only a slight sighing in the trees, accentuating all the more that they were empty of insects or wildlife. *Dwellers*. The only life there was centred around herself, Erno, and the others. Yet the trees were alive; what of them? Aren't they dwellers? Don't they speak?

Erno squeezed her shoulder lightly. *Yes, they do. These ones still have voices. It's nice to hear my old friends again and to know they're at peace. But they are not dwellers in the same sense as animals. Sonax planted them for shelter, food, and tools when he set up all the regions.*

Set up all the regions?

Yes. This is his third building of a world. I was there at the beginning of the first, my siblings, too. Sonax always placed us in the regions. They were much the same each time he rebuilt them, except death and guandras were cleared and everything renewed.

She could see in her mind's eye the memory of being placed in a region, set down as if by an invisible hand, delighting in the trees, the birds, the sky, and the invigorating freshness of a world newly formed. She felt that Erno smiled as she remembered, and she was acutely conscious of his hand on her right shoulder. She reached up with her left hand and grasped his, not wanting him to withdraw, wanting to keep this connection with him. She saw through his eyes, bounding through the woods, leaping, twisting, moving at incredible speed—he had been travelling so slowly with them now as he kept pace with Ned and Maqua loping along—all with an exhilarating awareness of Oxpeina-life in his veins. She wanted that. Wanted that feeling for herself. She could feel all the old things—all the pain, the wounds from her past, the indifference from Mother, the abandonment from Father—all that had gone, and she could see herself now, placed in the region by Sonax. Thought of, planned for, *wanted*. She took a deep breath and mentally shook herself. No, none of that was for her; she was simply feeling what Erno felt, knowing his memories.

Wrong. You were placed in your region, too, Image-bearer.

I don't see how—my life has been pointless.

The thought startled her as she released it to Erno, even as she realised that deep down it was truly what she believed. She felt his dismay and, in the dark night as they were close together, began to see more of his thoughts, his memories. At first, something like a map was laid out before her, the regions charted in thin, green lines. A vast map, so large she could not see all of it. Trees, mountains, rivers, lakes, dotted and unfurling wherever she looked in ribbons and swathes of emerald, lapis lazuli, richest brown. A man's hand hovered over the map, pointing here, there, a voice explaining, while she, *Erno*, nodded in agreement, understanding. She turned her head to look at the speaker, and there he was, *Sonax*. Amber eyes deep with life, sparkling with vitality as he spoke, his fingers smudging something on the map, flicking, *drawing*. Something dancing from his fingers, an energy, a magic, a power, the map twisting and changing under his touch, but it was no longer a map, it was a world, and she looked out over it as a bird.

Standing on a mountaintop, looking at the land spreading out in all directions, Sonax's hand outstretched with a power she could not comprehend, *making the world*. Fothie was there, Hemri was there, and other brismuns, *my siblings*. Then, the shining shaseeliany clustered together in a pool of light, water, separating out as each went to their brismuns. Then, the rovi, their wildness tamed and in deference as they stood tall in a long line before Sonax.

"Take care of the regions as the image-bearers come forth," he said.

These were the first words she had comprehended in this vision, and they puzzled her. "Why?" she said.

Sonax turned, and his hand, the hand of power, touched her cheek. He looked into her eyes. With a gasp, she knew that he saw her, wasn't looking at Erno, but was there with her as she sat in the woods with Erno.

"Because I want the image-bearers to come to life," he said.

As he said that, surrounding him was a different region, enormous and bright, dazzling to the eye in the array of colours. Already there were image-bearers come from the previous worlds or who had travelled from this one and found their way there, living in harmony, building, growing—the true region of the Oxpeina. The regions Deborah had travelled through were dull, muddied by discord, small, and inward-looking, yet they held glimpses reminiscent of the Oxpeina's region, hints that pointed towards that life, and she felt if she looked again, looked more closely, she would see them all.

"Why don't you just put all the image-bearers in your region if that's where you want them?" she asked.

"Then they'd have no thought or will and have never learned to make any decision on their own. These outer regions are lands of discovery for the image-bearers to grow in. Only then will they understand Oxpeina-life."

The bright vision vanished, and Deborah was back in the slumbering woods again, Erno beside her, his scent of sage in the air, Ned mumbling in his sleep as he lay nearby.

"Erno," she whispered, still holding tightly to his mossy hand on her shoulder.

Now do you understand? came his thought.

Her first impulse was to say no, but she found that was not entirely true. The vision, Sonax's hand on her cheek, had somehow imparted something even more to her. He had touched the same part of her face that the guandra, Chila, had torn with her claws, and now she was left with a lingering feeling of warmth as though his hand was still there. And, as she sat there in the dark, she sensed the existence of the region of the Oxpeina, felt she knew in which direction it was—she sat now with her back to it—and felt the need to go there and leave all these other regions, these trying grounds that were made for discovery of one's true self, far behind. She was an image-bearer, born of image-bearers—*mother and father*—who, right or wrong, in their passion had brought her forth. They had made their own decisions. Now, she must make hers.

Sonax had stood before her as custodian over all, origin of image-bearers, maker of worlds. She could find her way to him and his region or turn from him. As that thought came, in one quick moment there was a dizzying awareness of life that overwhelmed and erased even the smallest hint of sorrow, while alternately she felt within herself a baulking sense of refusal to have anyone or anything over her as custodian and the wish to push it all away.

It dawned on her that this was the turning; this was what everyone kept referring to, and she could feel it now distinctly and clearly, that either she could choose to go fully into the life of the Oxpeina by entering Sonax's region, or she could turn her back and go her own way and refuse any idea that there should be someone over her as custodian.

Erno's fingers twitched on her shoulder. *This is the danger of self-importance—it's the belief that no one is over you but instead you are over all.*

She turned her head to try to see him in the dark. *But why should that matter?*

Because it's not what you were made for. Your connection to this world and the reason you have any life at all is to belong to the Oxpeina.

Again, as he passed his thoughts to her, she could almost see the glimmering border of the Oxpeina's region. She sensed Erno's longing to go there, his weariness from living through three worlds that Sonax had formed one after another, and that he wondered if Sonax would again assign him as custodian to another region in a new world. This current world, Erno felt as surely as he breathed, was on the cusp of closing.

He shook himself, an awareness of Deborah seeing his thoughts. She heard him in formless words telling her that even if he was assigned to a region again, it was all right. She sensed him grin at that, as if he teased her for the way she always said she was 'all right' even when she wasn't. But, he reassured her, with every assignment to a region came an initial boost of Oxpeina-life and the knowledge that his role as custodian mattered. That brought him joy.

Yet, if Sonax was going to build another world after the closing of this one, then he would miss Deborah, miss Nurrel, Jacob, and now Maqua and Ned. He thought dolefully of them going on into the Oxpeina's region without him, as had the others he had come to love over aeons of time.

Deborah got up and wrapped her arms around Erno's cool, mossy body. "I love you, Erno," she whispered, her face pressed against his soft cheek, an intense love filling and brimming over in her heart. It felt different, as if she had never truly felt love before or been able to express it properly. Was this sensation something that Erno gave to her in this moment of connection, or was it something that had been unlocked from deep inside herself? Either way, it felt good. "Jacob, where are you?" She would hold him close to herself and tell him she loved him, too. And Nurrel, she loved him, and Ned, and Maqua.

54

Deborah got up shivering in the dim morning light, her hair stuck to her forehead from the dew. So stupid and achey from the cold and from sleeping on the hard ground. What a horrible morning. Where was all that overflowing love and warmth she'd had in the middle of the night? Now she felt grouchy and cold. Perhaps all that love and Oxpeina-life stuff had been a dream.

She rummaged around in the bags and found her old jersey, whipped off her coat and cardigan, then put on the jersey, the cardigan, then the coat back on over the top. She swung her arms to try and generate some warmth.

Something made her turn and gaze through the woods. Oxpeina's region. Back that way. She could still sense it. So, it hadn't been a dream, and, yes, like Jacob had said, it did feel like they were going the wrong way. What was Father doing? He was the one who had been drawn to the woods, its power, the Oxpeina-life, and seen trees that looked like a doorway, so why was he so far out in the wrong direction? Of course he must have taken a completely different route to her, so maybe now he was heading in the right direction from wherever he had come from.

She turned back to the others. Nurrel, somehow, had got a small fire going under the dripping damp of the trees and was cooking breakfast. Ned and Maqua were grazing on whatever greenery Erno brought them while Jacob perched on a low branch of the tree closest to the fire, gazing inscrutably at her, his gold-rimmed black eyes hard and intent.

She smiled at him affectionately. There! She did still feel love flowing and bubbling up more easily in her heart. Strange to feel that way.

Jacob flew from the branch to her shoulder. "You look different, Deborah."

She rumpled her wet hair, flicking him with drops of water. "Yes, very different."

"No, I don't mean that. I mean your whole appearance. You look healthier and have a less faded look about you."

She stared sidelong at him. "Less faded? What do you mean?"

"Just what I said. You've brightened up. Remember how you, me, and Kasharel looked when we were in the region outside of his caves? You look like that."

Yes, she did remember. It all seemed so long ago that she had left the gehun caves and entered that Oxpeina-rich region. Kasharel and Jacob had looked brighter with life there, too. Again, it hurt to think of Kasharel. Is that all image-bearers did? Hurt each other? She watched Nurrel stir the fire, his face grim under his hood. There he was, doing what was needed, making sure they had a good breakfast, when all the while he held onto his own pain. Pain that must still be fresh.

"Nurrel," she said. "Anything I can do to help?"

He glanced up and gave her a brief smile. "It's almost ready, I think."

She nodded and walked a short distance away from everyone to the small stream Erno had shown them yesterday. It trickled sluggishly across the ground as if prompted to move only through the force of gravity and not through any life of its own. She dipped her hands into the ice-cold water. It tasted pale, lacking in any kind of flavour. She sat back on her heels, looking at the trees hanging apathetically over her. Erno's former region really was nothing. Deserted and cold, lacking any kind of appeal, *empty*.

When breakfast had been eaten and everything was packed up and loaded onto Ned and Maqua once more, Erno stood before them all.

"Late this morning we will reach the Wrion region. I've been listening to the trees and the whispers they've heard from across the border, and, from what I can tell, some guandras are definitely there."

A sick feeling clutched the pit of Deborah's stomach.

"Some?" said Jacob. "How many is *some?*"

"Not sure," Erno said soberly. "But, where there are image-bearers, guandras are usually found. So, this news should come as no surprise."

"I don't want to see a guandra," said Ned. "I've never seen one before, and I don't want to now! What if it attacks me?"

Maqua mumbled a little as Nurrel led her over to a rock. He stepped up onto it and mounted her. "Nothing to worry about," he said. "All our other encounters with guandras have been easy. If we need help to deal with them, Sonax will give it. Most likely, he'll send Val and his pack. If not, we can manage."

"Says the one who got slashed on the arm," said Jacob.

"It was only a small cut. Besides, that was my own fault—I let my guard down for a moment."

Deborah gripped Erno's hand tightly. "I don't know how to protect myself. You know I don't. Why is it the first time you knew guandras were near; you made me run until I almost dropped? Now, you think I can go where they are?"

"You were different then," he said. "You didn't know anything about anything."

"*Hoo.*" Jacob butted Deborah's neck. "That was our first day in the woods together. Seems ages ago!"

"And," said Erno, "we've seen other guandras since then. Remember the Silver Lake? You managed fine there when they tried circling you. Also, when Val and his pack came to protect us, that went well, too."

She let go his hand and frowned at him. "You're forgetting something. *Chila.*"

"No," he said softly, bowing his head. "I haven't forgotten."

His expression was so pained, she took his hand again to get his thoughts.

… not being there when I should have and failure to teach Deborah how to protect herself. He glanced up at her. *So, it's like this now, is it? Getting hold of my thoughts whenever you feel like it? I'll have to watch what I think when I'm in grabbing distance of you.*

She smiled at him. *Well, it's an easy way to communicate, and I like it—there's something open and true about it.* She gently squeezed his hand. *Don't blame yourself for what happened with Chila.*

But I'm your custodian. I shouldn't have let this happen to you. Grufful was right—I didn't do a very good job.

Oh, so you're telling me you were supposed to know somehow that Chila was going to turn into a guandra and attack me?

He shrugged. *I should have recognised more what was going on. Hemri understands image-bearers better than me.*

"Are we just going to stand here all morning?" Jacob said. "You've both gone peculiarly quiet, and it's weird how you're staring at each other."

Erno chuckled. "Yes, we'll get moving soon. First, let me teach Deborah how to raise a shield about herself, then I'll show Ned."

Ned lipped and tugged Erno's hair. "Teach me how to fight. I know I have to. I can't just stand still and do nothing if they're attacking me." His words came quickly, his sides heaving and his breathing loud.

Deborah stroked his neck. "Calm down, Ned."

"You can talk," said Jacob in her ear. "Your shoulder feels as tense as a rock."

"The first thing to do," said Erno, "is not be afraid."

"*Ha!*" said Deborah. "Don't be funny. How am I supposed to do that?"

"Well," said Jacob, "you'll have to. Fear gives them power and control—everybody knows that."

She frowned at him. "I can't just turn it off like a tap."

Nurrel rode over to her, Maqua's hooves quietly thudding on the earth. "Yes, you can."

Maqua whiffled and sniffed Ned's muzzle. He bared his teeth at her and nudged her nose away. "This is no time for flirting, woman. I've got to listen to our custodian!"

Maqua stepped back, her eyes fixed adoringly on him.

Erno patted Deborah's hand. "Linnfel already taught you one of the basics when he showed you how to ride Ned. What you focus on is very important. You can't let the guandras draw you into their world. You've got to stay in this one; got to stay holding onto Oxpeina. You know who you are; you're an image-bearer, and you will not turn."

She grimaced. She supposed she had sort of learned all of that while in the regions, but how that kind of knowledge would raise a protective shield around her she did not know.

Ned's ears drooped and he looked dolefully at Erno. "I'm not an image-bearer. How's all that going to help me?"

"You are an awakened dweller," said Erno. "The principle is the same. Sonax awakened you to life, and you've got to remember that and not be lulled back to sleep. Follow me, keep close to me, and remember who you are."

"And I can kick and bite too, can't I?"

"If you need to, yes, of course. Deborah will be on your back, so you'll fight for the both of you."

Deborah thought of the guandra she had grappled with on the kitchen floor and how she had thrashed and fought with all her might to try to get it off. Its grip had been too tight, its strength too much. What had she now to fight with? There was no knife other than what Nurrel had used at breakfast, and that was an ordinary-looking thing. A dagger or sword would be much more useful.

Ned lowered his head and bucked, swiftly kicking the air with his hind legs. "I can do that. I'll look after Deborah!"

Maqua snorted, and her eyes widened.

"As long as she doesn't fall off when you do that," said Jacob.

"No, she won't," said Erno. "She will be focused!" He squeezed Deborah's hand.

If you say so, she thought at him.

Change your focus. You're thinking too much about that fight and not enough about how you were rescued. Taffin threw a shield around you, didn't she? You can summon your own shield now.

She bit her lip. *Can I?*

Of course you can.

But, how exactly? You say to focus and think of Oxpeina and who I am, but I still don't see how that can summon a shield.

Try it now while I help you.

She took a deep breath.

"You're staring at each other again," said Jacob. "It's weird."

"Hush," said Erno. "I'm teaching Deborah how to raise a shield."

As he spoke the word *hush*, Deborah glimpsed the nearest trees bow slightly towards him, stilling their autumn-tinged leaves in the cool air as if not daring to let them fall. Jacob's grip on her shoulder loosened, while Ned's side slowed as his breathing relaxed. Maqua let out a soft sigh. Deborah looked up at Nurrel, and their eyes met briefly—she could not look long at him, for the pain in his eyes seemed more present than ever. She stared at the ground and at the vivid green mossy stump of Erno's leg planted before her in the decaying leaf litter.

Ah! he thought at her. *You felt Nurrel's heart just then; I saw it.*

She spread her fingers across his cool hand. *Isn't there anything we can do to help him?*

I am helping him. I'm taking him to the Oxpeina's region, and his heart will heal there.

She looked at him, his pupils briefly visible amongst the green of his round face as he squinted up at her. *But*, she thought, *you're all coming with me to find my father instead of going straight to that region.*

Yes. No other custodian has been provided, so you and Nurrel must journey on together.

She felt him mentally shrug.

Don't ask me why, he thought, *because I don't know why that is. It just is. Now, focus. What are you going to do if you face a guandra's attack? How will you respond?*

She mentally shrugged back at him. And then he showed her. In one quick moment, she was acutely aware of his face as the periphery of the woods faded. Then, the light weight of Jacob was gone from her shoulder, and Erno vanished, too. In the stillness and haze of being unable to truly see anything, she was gripped by a pang of confusion, panic at being alone, then Erno squeezed her hand.

I'm still here. Who else is still here?

She thought over his question, and the pull—the enchantment of the Oxpeina region far, far behind her somewhere beyond the mists of all the other regions—felt more distinct. It was there. Oxpeina-life, there in that region, a shining fire of promise.

Again, she was aware of her face and how she had seen Sonax briefly bear her image on his own face and that she bore the image now. Image-bearer, whatever that meant.

She felt Erno grin. *Yes, whatever. Now, imagine you're under attack.*

She could not, did not want to, for the first image that came to mind was Chila, the guandra, long limbs reaching, claws scraping, and she swiftly pushed back against that memory.

Let it come, Erno thought.

She shook her head. *Don't want to.*

It's only a memory—a good thing to practise with.

Nope.

Deborah.

She sighed. Perhaps if she could just allow a corner of that image, a small fragment of memory, rather than picture it all so clearly and fully, then it would be more comfortable to practise with.

Maybe, thought Erno. *Allow a small piece, then. Just the claws.*

Her hand swept to her cheek as she felt the sting and pain of the claws raking down her face. The face that Chila had called 'frowny' and had drawn such hateful attention to as if Deborah had no Oxpeina-life in her at all, and that was shown all over her expression, all over the 'air' around her.

Not true, is it. Erno's thoughts again, trying to encourage her, his tone conveying the expression he saw something more in her.

I—I don't know, she thought, wishing she could see him standing in front of her instead of this haze of nothingness. His cheerful countenance always lifted her spirits. A cheerful countenance that she didn't have, for she was frowny. She was tired; she was lost; she was abandoned. Mother had gone, and Father did not care anymore but had left her to go off on his own quest for Oxpeina-life. He had left her to somehow piece together what he had done, had not spoken of it to her or shared anything other than his desire to move to the village of Shilhim and find peace there by the woods. Liar. He had wanted more than that. Why drag her along, too? Why hadn't he just left her at their home in Eblhim?

He wanted you to go with him.

Was that Erno, or her own thought?

Neither.

In a flash, she saw Sonax before her in the void, faint as if far off, his hand outstretched. She instinctively reached for him. Electricity shot all around her; she knew the shield had come—it felt exactly as it had when Grufful had held her tightly in the midst of the guandras' attack. Then, Sonax was gone, and the woods came back. Erno was there, Jacob upon her shoulder, and Ned stood staring wide-eyed at her.

"You did it!" he said.

"I guess I did," she said, puzzled as to how exactly the shield had come. Hopefully, she could do that again, whatever that was, when faced with real guandras.

55

Ned trotted onward, following Erno as he wound his way through the trees. As the morning progressed, Deborah found that her balance on Ned's back came almost without thinking. She rarely had to focus herself in the Oxpeina-life but simply reminded herself of it whenever Ned took a more difficult turn or clambered over a patch of uneven earth. The terrain sloped downward through the cool, moist shadows, ragged drifts of leaves releasing a faint musty scent as the trees sleepily clung to an old region that was slowly fading.

Deborah shielded her eyes with her hand as Ned emerged from the forest into pale sunshine. A great expanse of feeble, yellow grass lay at their feet, and, in the distance, geometric shapes of wood and stone filled the horizon.

"There it is," said Erno. "The first town in the Wrion region."

Deborah felt her heart thump painfully in her chest. "Is Father there?"

Nurrel rode Maqua out from the trees and drew alongside her.

Erno hopped slowly onward. "I can't tell. Too many voices mingle together, and I don't know your father."

"He is here," said Nurrel. "Val told me so when I was looking at the map of the regions. He said Deborah's father would be found in the first town we come to, and to beware of this region and how it will try to keep us here." He grimaced. "I suppose that's much like the Silver Lake. Val said only a few image-bearers have been able to leave and answer the call of Oxpeina that this world is drawing to a close."

"When will it close?" Ned asked.

"I wish I knew," said Nurrel.

Erno shrugged. "When Sonax decides it is time."

Deborah felt Ned suddenly tense.

"We won't get stuck out here in the middle of it closing?" he said.

His question arose in her own mind. Stuck in the outer regions when Sonax closed the world and began a new one? What would happen to her if she did not get to the Oxpeina region before then?

"That's why we go on," said Erno. "I can't say with certainty what happens, as in the other two times of closing the world I always got to Oxpeina's region in time. The call to go home comes on suddenly, and those of my siblings who listened were swift to answer."

Deborah thought of the memory Erno had shared with her, his experience of flying through the woods and the incredible speed with which he could travel. It was all right for him and the other brismuns—it probably did not matter where in the regions they were, the rate they could move. But, for her, Ned, Jacob, Nurrel, and Maqua, it was different. She *had* to get to Father as soon as possible, and then they all had to get to Oxpeina's region. There was no point ever going back to Eblhim now, not when she had tasted a glimpse of the Oxpeina region. There did not seem to be anywhere else to go, not if the other regions were dying. Besides, she felt it again—the distinct impression that she was going the wrong way, that the Oxpeina region lay behind them, and she, an image-bearer, belonged there.

They continued onward across the grass plain, and she stared at the town as it grew on the horizon. Father was there. He was there. Why did she feel sick at the thought? A huge lump of anxiety gripped her stomach, making it harder to breathe. She should be happy. Should be relieved that her journey to find him was almost over. So, why feel this way instead?

She thought of him, his sullen quietness, how they had hiked together all that way from Eblhim to the village of Shilhim, just because he had said he would get better there, he would find peace there. Yet, the gnawing feeling she had always had that she could never get close to him, that ever since Mother had died, he had closed himself off to her. She had tried her best to look after him, tried her best to keep their home warm, food on the table, clothes washed. He never acknowledged anything she had done; only wanted to leave, wanted to go to the woods. How much of that had been 'answering the call of the Oxpeina'? Had he thought the regions were coming to an end? Why did he not love her enough to tell her?

As Ned and Maqua trotted through the grass, their muffled footfalls *thud-thudding* behind Erno's ground-shaking thumps, something further on caught Deborah's eye. A dirt path. Something felt all wrong about it as she looked, and a dizziness came over her. Somehow, the path seemed to look back at her as if telling her to come. 'Beware the seeing path' the *Legends Of The Greener Land* storybook had read, and also something about how a path would show—exposing?—failings to the guandras. She couldn't quite remember how the book phrased that.

Ned went towards it. "Here's an easier way through."

She grabbed the small knot of his neck as Jacob's talons clenched her own shoulder. "No, Ned, stop! Keep away from it!"

"What?" he said. "Why?"

"It belongs to the guandras," said Jacob.

Ned quickly looked this way and that, as if he expected to see a guandra spring up in the grass. "How do you mean?"

Erno slowed, shortening his leaps so that he was not as far ahead of Ned and Maqua. "Some guandras have the ability to spread tendrils—feelers, I suppose you could say—to warn of anyone coming and also to give them an advantage in battle."

Ned tossed his head and snorted. "Battle?"

"If guandras can catch you on a path and keep you there, then it's less work for them to win control. Plus, they can use a path to see into you and find your weaknesses. How dare they stretch a path into my region?" He shrugged and bounded across the yellow grass. "Not my region anymore."

Deborah thought of her encounters with paths and how her face, her image, had been captured and whisked away, and how when she had walked on a path it had become progressively difficult to think clearly until she was almost somnambulant. Then had come the attack by a brismun. After which, Kasharel cared for her in the caves. She sighed. Why had he bothered, if all he was going to do was turn against her and leave her without saying anything, as if their friendship meant nothing?

Nurrel rode closer to her. "Stop looking at the path, Deborah," he said quietly.

She came to herself with a start and glanced over at him. "Thanks. I—I didn't realise I was."

"I didn't realise you was, either," said Erno.

"Do you hear any yet?" Nurrel asked.

"Any what?" said Ned.

"Guandras," said Erno. "Yes, I do indeed. They're just beyond the border."

Ned stopped dead. Deborah fell forward onto his neck, clutching wildly at him and his baggage to keep from falling to the ground. Jacob flew from her shoulder and in a wide circle around them.

"Ned!" Deborah cried. "Don't do that. You almost had me off!"

Nurrel turned Maqua and rode back, Erno leaping alongside them.

Ned stood there, and Deborah could feel all the quivers and trembles that ran throughout his body. She stroked his neck. "Hey. Calm down, Ned. It's all right."

"No, it isn't. It isn't!"

Erno went to him and cupped his muzzle in his hands. Deborah felt Ned's breathing slow, and the trembles became less violent. Erno's eyes were almost closed, lost again in the moss of his face, but his mouth moved as though he spoke. Ned muttered words that Deborah could not catch, and then was quiet.

Jacob landed on her shoulder and folded his wings. "Well, that was fun. Nothing like a good jolt to feel alive."

"Don't be a grump," she said.

"If Ned had been going any faster, you would have flown over his head, too."

She smiled at him. "Perhaps you're right."

Ned shuddered and yanked his muzzle out of Erno's hands. "Why do we have to go in there? Why?"

"Steady," said Erno. "Now, Ned, you know we're going there because we're looking for Deborah's father."

Ned lowered his muzzle again into Erno's waiting hands and sighed heavily.

It was easier now to make out the rooflines, partial facades, and shadows of the town buildings as they lay exposed in the bleak sunshine. Deborah could not see any signs of movement. Perhaps she was still too far away to see that. Erno could hear guandras. Exactly how many, she did not know. Could any of them see her? Were they at the windows now, looking out across the withered grass plain?

If only Val and his pack were here. If only Grufful was beside her, ready to protect her with an Oxpeina-life shield. She looked down at Erno, seeming small as he stood in front of Ned, whispering quietly to him. One brismun to watch over all five of them. Nurrel could throw his own shield; presumably he could protect Maqua, too. So, that left herself, Ned, and Jacob for Erno to shield if he had to. How could he fight guandras and maintain a shield at the same time? He wanted her to throw her own shield. She was not even sure she fully understood how to do that.

As for Father, what was he doing in a town full of guandras? Was he trapped?

"You look troubled, Deborah," said Nurrel. "We'll manage this all right. You'll see."

She looked over at him. He calmly faced the horizon, unseen thoughts deep in his soft, brown eyes. He did not need to be here with her. Surely, Sonax could have given him another custodian so he could get more quickly to the Oxpeina region. She drew a sharp breath. Why did the awareness of the Oxpeina region behind them suddenly become more acute when she thought that? She could almost see it in her mind's eye, feel it sharpen and shift in a flash of light as if to draw her attention.

The world will close soon.

Jacob shook his feathers. "Did you hear that? I thought I heard Sonax say the world will close soon. Where is he? I don't see him anywhere."

"I heard him." Deborah could not see Sonax, either, but the voice had seemed to be more in her mind rather than words spoken out into the open air.

"Me, too," said Nurrel.

Erno grinned. "Me, three."

Maqua mumbled and nudged Erno.

Ned stamped a hoof. "How soon?"

They were all silent together, listening, but no answer came.

"Strange," Jacob said finally. "I would have thought I had imagined that if it hadn't been for all of you hearing it, too."

"Yes," said Nurrel. "He spoke barely louder than a thought. I suppose it means we must hurry on. Really, how soon *is* the world closing?"

It was an uncomfortable question. What world had Deborah stepped into when Father had brought her to the woods? None of this, no closing of the world, no dying regions; *none* of that had ever been a consideration. Now, here she was, astride a talking beast, a talking owl on her shoulder, a brismun custodian—it had all become so normal in a short span of time. How much had Father known? What had he believed about this world and not told her?

"I don't know," said Erno to Nurrel, "but let's get on. Ned, are you okay now?"

"I guess so," he muttered.

56

A wispy, sheer curtain slowly undulated at the open window, and the distant sound of voices carried on the breeze. Beyond the square of neat lawn, the low shrubs, and flowering garden bed that lay alongside the white house was a low wooden fence. On the other side of that began a long, straight street between rows of houses. Many were painted white with flat grey roofs, while others were painted light grey with angled copper-coloured roofs. Square, boxy buildings, each window symmetrically placed. Deborah stared in astonishment at it all. This could be a neighbourhood of Eblhim. The size of the buildings, the style of them—it was all so familiar. And the image-bearers walking in the distance—surely they were as she was? They appeared to be the right height and build. Was one of them Father? She could not tell.

"Ready?" said Erno.

"Yes," she said quietly, unsure if she really was.

They were poised at the border of the region, just steps away from the house. Oddly, there was no garden fence this side of it, just a faint line snaking across the yellowed grass of Erno's old region. The others murmured their assent, and even Maqua mumbled a little as if reluctantly agreeing.

Deborah gritted her teeth as Ned stepped onto the lawn, waiting for the unpleasant sensation that must surely come from crossing into a region known to have guandras. To her surprise, the air felt clearer, better, sweeping into her lungs with a certain clarity, and she felt there was a liveliness, a lightness, in the atmosphere.

"*Huh*," said Jacob, adjusting his grip on her shoulder. "I don't like this."

"Why?" she said. "It feels all right."

"Exactly," he said. "But it's not. Don't go by feelings."

Ned snorted. "Look at the size of that path. How can we get around it?"

Deborah looked about, wondering what he referred to.

"No," said Nurrel. "That's a street, not a guandra path. You can see the difference if you look more closely. Wait... I think... yes, look... I think the guandra path is over there, on the right side of the street. See the way it lies? It doesn't sit quite right. Watch where you walk, and you'll be fine."

Deborah looked where he pointed. At first glance, it merely seemed as a shadow on the street, but then she saw it shift slightly as if breathing, and it blurred a little in her vision. Unnerved, she held tighter to Ned.

There was the sound of a door opening, then a shriek. "Who you? What you want? My property get off!"

A woman stood there, faded somehow as if not all there, grey in her clothing, skin, and hair. Yet she did not appear old, and neither did she stand in shadow. Deborah stared at her, trying to make sense of her appearance.

"We're very sorry," said Nurrel. "We didn't mean to trespass. We've just come from the neighbouring region. We'll leave your property at once."

"See you do!" She turned.

"Wait!" said Erno. "Do you know Ben Lakely? We were told he's here in this town."

"Don't know." The door slammed. Moments later, her face appeared at the window, and she stared out at them, the sheer curtain a ghostly veil drifting around her.

Nurrel dismounted Maqua, opened the garden gate, and led her through. Ned followed, his head down as if carefully watching each step he took. Erno leapt over the fence itself, and his impact on the outside paving was so heavy, or the stone so brittle, it cracked beneath his stumpy leg.

"Whoops! That does not feel sturdy."

"Yet, it looks sturdy," said Jacob. "The stone must be thinner than it appears."

Erno stumped along the street, and, each time he landed, crazed cracks sprang into being with each impact. "This is no good," he said, spreading his fingers as if feeling the air. "But it can't be helped."

Nurrel led Maqua after him, as Deborah rode Ned. She looked at each house they passed, crisp, clean facades that might well be freshly painted. The guandra path shifted and writhed as though sensing their presence, and edged closer to the line of houses. Ned felt very tense, and she stroked his neck. She realised she did not feel much better than him—her stomach gave an anxious lurch each time she saw any hint of movement in the town, whether it be a curtain fluttering at a window or a flower bending in the breeze in one of the gardens between the houses. Was it a guandra? Was it Father? Where was he? How close was she to him now?

At her left, a front door opened and out stepped a grey man, his features and outline pencil-sharp, while the rest of him was fuzzily smudged. "Morning," he said, and gave them a nod. "Sonax's best." He strode off down the street ahead of them, the daylight passing through his body so that he left no shadow.

Nurrel looked at Deborah, his eyebrows raised. "You'd think seeing a brismun and all of us was perfectly normal to him. Look at us, look at our colour compared to his! Didn't he notice and think that was strange?"

"Compared to his?" said Erno. "Why, what's his colour?"

It was easy to forget Erno's sight was different from her own. "Grey," said Deborah, gazing after the man, disconcerted by the way he faded from sight the further he went.

"Not like Ned's grey coat, either," said Nurrel. "Ned's grey is warm and alive. This grey is empty somehow. Deborah and I look like clowns in comparison, and our clothing is not even very bright."

Erno nodded. "The Oxpeina-life is dim in some of the image-bearers here—I'm finding them hard to detect. I hear them all right, but the two we just encountered… the air currents move oddly around them."

Further in the distance, Deborah could clearly see other people who, from what she could tell, had a more normal appearance. Perhaps one of them was Father. She should urge Ned on, but the anxiety churned in her stomach again, and she felt she could not move. Why was she like this? She should be glad. She was about to find Father. Everything would be all right. They would be together again.

"The man looked creepy," muttered Ned. "Now, I can't even see him. It's like he's gone into nothing."

"You're telling me," said Jacob. "He reminds me of the image-bearers back in my home region. I was glad to get out of there. Everyone was turning."

So, that was why these people were faded. They were midway between being a person and becoming a guandra. Deborah thought of Mage Chila. She had not been faded, and her transformation had been sudden. Why were these people different?

Ned shook his head. "He even said, 'Sonax's best'. I don't understand why he's not bright with Oxpeina-life if he knows Sonax."

"It doesn't mean anything," said Nurrel. "People can say Sonax this and Sonax that, and it doesn't mean a thing."

His tone of voice was so gloomy Deborah thought he was referring to something, or someone, in particular. She remembered in his village the lumdils' greetings were 'Oxpeina's best', and 'Sonax sees you this bright day'. Yet no one there had been faded, had they?

Nurrel led Maqua on, and Ned clopped slowly next to them down the street, while Erno continued to fracture stone each time he leapt. A flock of birds flew swiftly in arrow formation overhead, and Erno raised his hands. One of the birds left the flock and returned to Erno, green wings flashing in the sunlight as it circled him, the red feathers of its head as bright as its eyes. Erno said a few words Deborah did not understand; the bird sang a brief melody and darted off to rejoin its flock.

"*Ha!*" Erno said. "My sister *is* still here. Now I know where to find her."

Jacob ruffled his feathers. "'By the river'. Yes, very informative. Where exactly by the river? And, which river? There surely can't be just one in this region."

"No," said Erno, "there isn't, but you had to listen to the inflection of how that bird spoke, not just his words, for the answer is there. He meant the narrow part of the river in the east of the region. My sister, Sofi, is in a copse there."

"You got all that from 'by the river'?"

Erno grinned. "Indeedy."

"Shame he didn't know anything about Deborah's father. What are we going to do now? Wander the streets of this town and hope we bump into him?"

Erno laughed. "That's a stunning plan, but, no. I'd like you to go and question any birds you can find—yet, there are very few in this region—while we go on to meet Sofi. She will certainly know where he is, but I'd rather we didn't have to leave the town and take more time to find Deborah's father if we can help it. Stay high in the sky to be out of reach of any guandras, and also make sure you keep an eye on our whereabouts."

Ned shivered. "Guandras."

Jacob nuzzled Deborah's cheek, then flew from her shoulder. She watched him ascend over the rooftops and glide high above before decisively heading off in a straight line.

The town broadened and became busier, streets intersected, houses gave way to shops, and there were more people going about their business—washing windows, sitting at cafés, sweeping the streets, walking alone or in pairs, standing chatting. Some of them were faded, not quite there, yet still moved with purpose, while others were more substantial in their appearance but covered with what appeared to be a layer of dust. Father was not amongst them. No one seemed at all bothered by Erno thumping through their midst or Ned and Maqua plodding by, and any questions as to whether anybody knew Ben Lakely were met with blank stares. Occasionally, Jacob soared overhead, then flew on again as he searched for birds.

"I'm surprised we haven't seen any guandras," said Nurrel.

"They've seen us," said Erno. "I heard several, and two are following us."

Ned faltered. "What?"

Deborah patted his neck. "Don't worry. Erno will take care of us." She hoped she was right. She wriggled around on Ned's warm back to look behind them, but could not see any guandras. It was all so surreal—she could have been back home in Eblhim apart from the way the people were. Didn't they notice they were faded and dusty? Surely, those who were faded would be able to see right through their own bodies and realise that wasn't normal? Why didn't anybody look at Erno? He, who was so vibrant and green and growing, did not draw their attention at all.

They left the busier areas of the town and went along a lane where the houses were smaller, further apart, with dingy, unmown patches of grass between them. Down the end of the lane, Deborah could see a narrow river, the one she supposed Erno was leading them to. The murky green water did not show signs of flowing in any particular direction, and Deborah was about to ask Erno how much further he thought Sofi was when the door of one of the houses abruptly opened. Out came a thin man. He glanced over at their approach and his face was clearly visible in the sunlight.

Deborah gasped. "Father!" She hurriedly slid from Ned, disentangling herself from the bags that hung about him, and stumbled across the lane, her heart thumping wildly. Was it him? Was it really him? A strange sheen in front of her feet caught her eye, and she froze with the realisation it was a guandra path. One more step, and she would be on it. When had it appeared? She had not noticed this one before, yet there it was hugging the left side of the lane, hardly discernible. She jumped over it and onto grass. "Father!"

He looked at her, his expression vacant as it had been for so many years, then recognition dawned. "Deborah?"

She was horrified to see that he was dusty; parts of him were translucent, some of his right arm and leg, part of his face. And he had always been thin, but he had lost weight. She threw her arms around him, part of her wondering if that was all right, would he mind her showing such emotion, the other part damning it all, needing to hold him, and feel for herself that he was really there and she wasn't imagining him. He was rigid in her embrace, she could feel an awkwardness in him that did not yield or soften.

"Deborah," he said against her hair. "You? You?"

She drew back and looked at him. Why did he speak so?

He smiled. "Deborah, you."

Then she saw his eyes had a cloudy blue film as though they too were dusty.

She looked back at the others. "Erno! What's wrong with him? Why's he like this?"

"He is turning," said Nurrel.

57

"My house," said Father. "My." He beckoned to Deborah and motioned to the open door of the house. "I show. My."

This could not be real; it must be a dream. Even now she could see the light passing through Father's forearm, and, more alarmingly, a patch of skin beside his mouth was seemingly not all there, as if his face was in the process of disappearing as a mist began to seep into his body. Deborah could not utter a word as she stared at him, feeling as though the world spun out of control around her and nothing was as it should be.

A warm hand touched her arm. She looked down to see Nurrel at her side. "Just keep talking to him," he said. "If you keep talking gently—don't get frustrated or angry—he'll regain some speech simply from hearing you."

What could she talk about to Father when he was in a state like this? This was all wrong; he should not be like this. He was supposed to be finding Oxpeina-life; that was why he had come to the woods and come to the regions. Not *turning* as the others said. He wouldn't turn. Turning meant becoming a guandra, and Father would never do that. Something had been done to him, something had happened.

"It's a very nice house, Ben. I'm Nurrel, by the way, and your daughter, Deborah, is my travelling companion."

Father turned his cloudy gaze to Nurrel, and Deborah could tell from his expression he was listening intently.

"See the rvenan cattle standing out on the lane?" Nurrel said. "They're Ned and Maqua. Erno is our brismun custodian, and Jacob, an owl, will join us presently. He's flying around at the moment trying to find other birds to talk to."

Father looked out to Erno, Ned, and Maqua. "Brismun."

"Yes," said Nurrel. "He's kept us safe and led us through the regions. We've been looking for you, Ben, and now we've found you. Deborah has missed you a lot, and I'm sure you've missed her, too."

Father jabbed a finger at his own chest. "I, Ben."

It was painful to watch him. Deborah reached out, tried to brush the dust from his thin arm, found it wasn't dust at all but was rough like sandpaper. She clutched his rough hand. "Father… what happened to you?"

"Home." He smiled. "Found home."

She frowned. "No, Father, this is not home. We're not in Eblhim; we're miles away from there."

Bewilderment came into his cloudy eyes. "Yes, this my home."

"No, it's not! We're not home. This isn't Eblhim!"

Nurrel nudged her. She drew a deep breath.

"You know it's not Eblhim, don't you, Ben," Nurrel said softly. "You've found a new home. It looks solidly built and has a good roof. The outside is very clean and looks recently painted. Did you do that yourself or did someone else?"

Relief swept over Father's face. "Yes. Paint. New home." He glared at Deborah, and his eyes became hard, accusing, even beneath that film of grey-blue. "I found new home and this Oxpeina-life."

It hurt to see the way he looked at her—what had she said that was so wrong? And what on earth did he mean? "Oxpeina-life?" she said hesitantly. "No. It isn't. You're in the wrong region for that."

The film of his eyes thickened, and he frowned back at her. For one split second, she felt he was going to strike her. She let go his hand and stepped back. He would not hit her, he had never hit her. Why would she think that? Then, she noticed the colour of his hand, the one she had been holding, had changed. Warm, living flesh was there in a small circle on the back of his hand. Had the dust, the grey, rubbed off? She looked at her fingers, but no residue was there.

"Look at his hand," she said to Nurrel. "Some of his colour has come back."

"That happened fast," said Nurrel. "That's great."

She wanted to step forward, take Father's hand again, and see if she could bring more warmth and life into it, but the hard look in his eyes stayed her. She bit her lip, wondering what to say, wondering how to stop him from looking at her like that. She would not cry, why should she cry? She usually never did around him anyway, so those tears she could feel threatening, that lump in her throat, should all just go away right now.

"Ben," said Nurrel, "do you want to show us about your house?"

Father's eyes lost some of their hardness, the anger in them subsiding. Why did he do that for Nurrel and not her?

"Yes." Father nodded. "My house. I show."

Deborah looked back at Erno. He had said nothing in all this time but simply stood planted in the middle of the lane with Ned and Maqua solemnly beside him, their soulful eyes watching her. She felt the urge to go to Erno, to touch him and hear his thoughts, stand close to him and his Oxpeina-life, to get away from Father and his house. Instead, she followed Father and Nurrel into the house.

"My." Father pointed at a hall table in the entryway. "My." He touched a small framed sketch of a boat that hung on the wall.

Everything they passed, every stick of furniture, every knick-knack, he said "My" to.

"That's very nice," Nurrel said more than once and sometimes asked a question about its construction—which Father was unable to answer.

Deborah could not say a word; the lump in her throat was burning, and she rubbed furiously at the tears pricking her eyes as she walked behind them, pausing at each thing in the house. Father did not seem at all happy to see her. He asked her nothing about where she had been, he said nothing about having left her. There was no remorse, no feeling, *nothing*. All he talked about—if it could be called talking—was the stupid stuff in his house. Pointing at himself, pointing at the things. How Nurrel could act like everything was fine and normal and keep speaking gently was beyond her. She wanted to shake Father, get him to wake up and see that nothing about this was normal.

"Why did you come here, Ben?" Nurrel asked as they sat in comfortable chairs in the living room.

Father thought a moment. "I don't know."

It was the first sentence that he had spoken in his real voice with nothing halting or strange in his tone.

"Something led you here," Nurrel said. He gazed out the window to the small, grassy yard, as if uninterested in the answer. "What was it?"

"The path. I found the path and walked here."

Deborah was alarmed at his words. Surely, he couldn't mean the guandra path that lay outside his house. "What path?"

His eyes looked vacantly at her, and he was silent as if wondering who she was.

"What path did you find, Ben?" Nurrel asked.

Father shrugged. "I'm tired of your questions. Don't talk to me anymore."

"Father!" Deborah cried. "How can you say that! I've only just got here, and you act like you don't care at all and like you don't even see me! What is wrong with you? You just talk about *my my my!* Can't you think about anybody else except yourself? I—"

"Deborah," said Nurrel. "Don't."

She frowned at him and stood. "I can't sit here and pretend everything is fine. Everything is *not* fine. Father, there's something really wrong with you. What's that strange coating of stuff all over you? Why are you fading? Don't you see that you're fading? Look at your arm! Look at your leg!"

"Go away!" Father shouted and stormed from the room.

Deborah stood trembling with rage, listening to his footsteps thumping up the stairs.

Nurrel went to her. "Deborah. Look at me."

She did, and something about his steadiness helped her—the calm way he looked at her, even though she knew he was in pain, knew his thoughts were still with Ibelli and what had happened to her, yet here he was trying to help her connect with Father, even though he didn't have to.

"Yelling at him isn't going to help, you know," he said.

"I know."

His eyes crinkled into a smile. "I know you know. But, it's hard, right? Hard to see them like this and try to get some sense out of them. You've just got to love him."

Love him? What had she done for Father for all these years since Mother's death? It had all been love, trying to care for him, trying to watch over him. She exhaled heavily. "He doesn't love me."

"Give him time to remember." Nurrel went to the hallway. "Come on. Let's get out of here for a while. We'll come back later and try again."

She waited a moment, listening, but there was no sound from upstairs. She went after Nurrel, her heart heavy. It had all been a waste of time. She never should have bothered trying to find Father.

They went out to the lane, and Deborah felt immediately sheepish as she saw Erno standing there waiting with Ned and Maqua, Jacob perched in his twiggy hair.

"No doubt you heard me make a mess of things," she said.

Erno's expression was solemn. "No doubt. It was an impressive explosion, but I'm sure it could have been worse. You didn't say a lot of the things you're holding inside."

"Deborah, what happened?" Ned said, looking puzzled. "I heard some yelling."

Jacob flew to Deborah's shoulder and pressed his head against her cheek.

She sighed. "Nothing. That's what happened, *nothing*."

"Oh," said Ned.

Nurrel went over to Maqua and patted her neck. "We'll come back later and try again."

"Okay," said Erno. "Well, I would like to get to Sofi before she moves away from the river, as there don't seem to be many birds around to let me know where she is, and I don't want to leave you all to go and search."

Deborah looked back at Father's house. There was no sign of movement at the window, and the front door remained shut. "Let's go."

~ 58 ~

Deborah walked silently between Ned and Maqua as Erno led the way down the lane. The occasional chatter from the others drifted over her, and she mumbled one word answers if Jacob said anything to her. This was what she had been waiting for, for countless days? This kind of meeting with Father? She shouldn't have bothered looking for him at all. All this time, all this trouble… for what?

The river was still, the dark green depths hemmed by scruffy grass banks and drooping trees devoid of any birdsong. There was not the freshness of air that had been in the town, but a staleness clung about. They walked on, leaving the houses behind, and the stillness only deepened, broken intermittently by the sound of Erno's thumps that seemed quieter than usual in the soft earth. Even Ned and Maqua's footfalls were muffled and near silent.

They passed paddocks, their fences in disrepair and grass left long, and soon saw a distant copse of great, tall, gnarled trees that looked as though they had stood there for centuries.

"Sofi," said Erno. "Are you here?" After a moment, he smiled. "Yes, it's me, Erno; who else? I thought you would have heard me ages ago and come! Are you going deaf?" After another pause, his smile fell, and he quickened his pace.

"What's wrong?" Nurrel asked.

"She says she can't move," said Jacob.

Deborah broke into a run, and Ned gave a startled snort as she ran ahead. Anger rose in her as she raced after Erno. Yet something else wrong in this region, and another brismun had to suffer for it. What had the image-bearers done to Sofi? And, no doubt, her shaseeliany was in trouble too, if the river was any indication. And Father thought he was 'home' and was proud of all his stuff as if having idiotic pictures on the walls and boring pieces of furniture was some great achievement. It wasn't any better than what they had shared back home in Eblhim; in fact, it was less. They had plenty of stupid, pointless stuff back home. She would never go back there. It wasn't home anymore; it was nothing. He obviously had no thought of going back, obviously had no thought of her.

Jacob's wing brushed against her neck as he flew from her shoulder. She hadn't thought of him when she started running. Just like Father. He didn't think of anyone but himself. He didn't care. She had come all this way for nothing.

"Sofi!" cried Erno as he leapt into the copse and dodged around the first tree.

Beneath the great, tall trees, their twisted and gnarled limbs held high in all directions, the light fell through their knotted fingers, casting shifting shadows. Deborah saw Sofi then, yellowed and stained, leaning against the trunk of a tree. She turned her head slowly, as if the effort was too much, yet smiled the cheery smile typical of a brismun, framed by her crown of broken, twiggy hair.

"Erno," Sofi whispered.

He clutched her dry hands that were stiff at her sides. "Sofi, I'm here. It's all right, I'm here now."

Deborah gently held her arm, dismayed as she felt its roughness. It was exactly how Father had felt. "Sofi."

Sofi blinked in surprise. "Who is this? Image-bearer, you're not mine."

"This is Deborah," said Erno.

Jacob landed lightly on Sofi's hair, and Deborah winced, hoping he would not break it any further.

"Oh, beautiful," Sofi whispered. "A mottle-backed Picaymy owl. I haven't known one for years."

"Hello," he said.

"Sonax-awakened," she whispered. "That's fab. I thought you had a different air around you."

Deborah immediately let go of Sofi. She did not want Sofi to feel her air; the air that Chila had said was so bad.

"Deborah," said Sofi, "don't do that. Hold me again; I need you. Your thought turned rotten and untrue—drop it."

Deborah hesitantly touched her arm again.

"She does that a lot," said Erno.

"Because she's been hurt a lot," said Sofi.

Deborah took a deep breath and resisted the urge to let go again. Yes, another brismun was seeing into her in their uncanny thought-reading way. It was fine; it was all right.

The *thud-thudding* of hooves burst into the copse as Ned and Maqua joined them.

Sofi gasped. "What! Rvenan cattle, one awakened, and the other almost? That's so cool!"

Ned pushed in and sniffed her face, noisily blowing air. "Brismun custodian, why do you stand here and look like that?"

Sofi smiled faintly. "Too tired to explain with words. If you truly want to know, touch me."

"I do truly," said Ned.

He bowed his head to Sofi's breast, his ears softly drooping against her as Erno shuffled over to make room while still keeping hold of his sister's hand. Deborah stood at Sofi's shoulder, one hand lightly on Sofi's rough arm and the other on Ned's warm, life-filled side. Everything faded as Sofi made her thoughts known to them. Deborah began to see green fields dotted with rvenan cattle, flocks of fowl, belts of flourishing trees, the shining blue threads of rivers and streams. Then came the feeling of bounding freely through the region—a *vast* region, farms and mills surrounding the towns. One town became grey, dried, *died*, then two more, three. The farms emptied, vanished, as the image-bearers became inexplicably angry. Some left the region, going on to search for the Oxpeina-life, while others pushed their own people out. She felt a pang in her heart—no, *Sofi's* heart—there is no need for a brismun; there is no need for a custodian, get that water creature out of our town, out of our water supply, we will manage everything, we don't need you.

But, why? Ned's thought came piercing through in childlike innocence.

Self-important control, thought Erno. *It's always about control, the opinion that they're not image-bearers. They think they are the true image, not a copy or bearer of one, and that they're not honour-bound to anyone.*

The aggressive face of an image-bearer thrust itself forward; Deborah could see it close to hers, to *Sofi's,* away with the old things, the custodians, the regions; we don't need you. She felt herself shrink, felt herself wither as the natural order of the region altered.

I am dying.

Hold on a little longer. Erno's thought, insistent, clear. *Sonax said he is closing this world soon. Hold on a little longer.*

I can't move, Sofi thought. *I can't get to the Oxpeina region when he closes the world.*

You don't have to try. I was like this in my region in the first world. My region turned, and I couldn't move, just like you now. But, as Sonax closed the world, he gave a last call, and that was what loosed me.

As Erno remembered, Deborah felt the strange pull of that call, tugging at her feet, her heart, that she must run *now*, much like the influence of Iff or Erno when they commanded something and the trees irresistibly bent in while she felt drawn and compelled to obey.

All you have to do is wait and not turn, Erno thought. *Don't let despair turn you from life. Hold on. Then, when he calls, you'll be able to move.*

I'm not turning, Sofi thought. *Never turning. I'm just so tired, and I can't wake Sessa.* The beautiful shaseeliany—he lay at the bottom of the river, just near where they were, so close, lying there. Still alive, his heartbeat was faint, but her calls didn't wake him. Dead water dwellers floated to the surface around him—fish, eels, tangled knotty vines that no longer grew.

As Deborah drew back in horror, another presence came into the thought as someone touched Erno. Nurrel. In one brief moment, he infused a sadness, a searing pain, the harrowing memory of Ibelli, fresher now after seeing Ben, talking to Ben and trying to bring him back, just as he had with Ibelli, but he would do that for Deborah; he didn't want her to suffer what he had; he must try and help Ben come back to life, but it was so painful.

Deborah let go of Sofi and stumbled away, away to the edge of the river, where she stared down at the murky depths, knowing Sessa was there lying still, his body pale and dull. Her breaths were jerky, shallow. This was all too much. Life held too much pain; it was all wrong. Nothing was right. Father… what was he doing? His mind had gone, and his body was following. He didn't care anything at all for her, and she never should have come. Never should have come into these woods, hurt Nurrel by forcing Ibelli out of her dirt mound—Nurrel said it wasn't her fault, but, really? Wouldn't Ibelli have stayed there if she hadn't blocked the light of the Silver Lake? And all of this custodian, image-bearer, region whatever-it-all-was… just an incomprehensible muddle. She sank down onto the bank of the river. Never should have come. Never should have tried to find Father. What was the point of that, anyway? Why had she? He didn't love her. He was just like Mother, had never loved her, not really.

Something lightly touched her shoulder, and she instinctively reached up to caress Jacob's feathers. He wasn't there. She realised it was not the familiar feel of his talons on her shoulder; instead, it was a hand. Not Erno's, for his would be cool and mossy while this was warm and broad. Nurrel? She wiped her tear-blurred eyes and turned to look. And, there he was, Sonax Oxpeina-life, his large form and outline springing into the space as if her very look had summoned him. His clothing and wavy brown hair blew and rippled about him as he appeared, then became still. He sat giant-like next to her, close enough that she could lean against his side if she chose to. She almost did, for intoxicating power surrounded her as it did whenever she was around Gruffal or the other rovi. Each breath she took eased the sting and ache of Father's rejection and heaviness lifted from her lungs.

Sonax gazed at the river, and Deborah knew he was aware of what lay in their depths. "I'm going to close this world soon," he said. "Don't stay out in the darkness of these regions. Come home, Deborah."

It took her a moment to be able to speak. "Why do you want me?"

He looked at her, and his face changed, first becoming Nurrel, then Taffin, Olly, and on through other image-bearers she had never met, until finally her own face appeared on his. Soft, lovely—something in her eyes and appearance she had never seen before in any mirror. No hardness, no tiredness, no hint of any bad air.

"Because you're my Deborah," he said, as the image of his face returned to Sonax.

She opened her mouth to speak, unsure of what she should say, but he was gone, and the air was chill, the banks of the river grey, the water stagnant. The hand on her shoulder was still there.

"Are you all right?" said Erno.

She hadn't heard him come, but he stood just behind her, brightly green in the sickly surrounds.

He squinted earnestly down at her, his cool hand resting on her shoulder. "You were breathing very painfully not long ago."

"I'm all right," she said.

He grinned. "Of course you are. Yet, somehow, I believe you this time. It feels as if Sonax was just here. Was he?"

She nodded.

"Good. I must go back to Sofi."

Deborah sat quietly, staring at the river. *You're my Deborah*. Nobody had ever said that to her, not even Father. How could those simple words give her such a keen sense of belonging, that she truly belonged to someone when she never had before? Words from someone she didn't even really know. A world-builder. It was all so strange to see her face on Sonax's, to realise again that she was somehow connected to him and that the Oxpeina-life was something real, something tangible. She had felt it many times now amongst the mysterious mouldering of the regions, the onset of death and decay that pervaded, and—as much as she didn't like to recall Chila's hurtful words—the air.

She thought over her travels, the longing for Father mingled with half-suppressed feelings of unbearable loss, grief, of never really belonging anywhere or to anyone, and the discovery of what was occurring now in the regions. The world was closing soon, and she must not get caught up in it; she must get to the Oxpeina-life region.

Tiny bubbles rose as strings of pearls in the river before her, and the water churned as a shape moved in the depths. A hand outstretched, an arm, a flowing mane around the upturned face of a shaseeliany. He surfaced, his head and shoulders almost white above the dark waters, any colour he had merely hints of green and blue, and he squinted as if finding the daylight harsh. He slowly swam to the bank and rose from the water, each movement stiff and laborious, until he stood on the grass beside Deborah, his off-white clothing dripping in a continuous waterfall. Puzzlement was on his face as he looked down at her, his eyes so pale and cloudy as to give the appearance of blindness.

"You did not wake me," he said in a low voice. "Sonax woke me." He looked around. "Where is he?"

"He has gone, Sessa," Deborah said softly.

He eased himself down carefully and sat next to her. "You have not come to kill me," he said, looking at her.

"No." She touched his hand lightly. "I would never do that to you."

"No," he said. "I see that. You have Oxpeina-life; I see the true air around you. It is beautiful. Who are you? Have you come to take me home?"

She swallowed hard and turned away from his intent gaze. How could he see any good or true air around her? It must only be because Sonax had just sat there; it could not be anything in herself.

A heart-wrenching cry came from the copse. "*Sessa!*"

Sessa turned. "Sofi. Why does she not come to me?"

"She's not able to move," Deborah said.

Sessa slowly got up. He looked down at her. "Don't stay in this region, precious image-bearer. Escape while you can." He walked to the copse.

Yes, she must leave this region, but how could she leave Father? It did not seem to matter that he no longer wanted her; she still wanted him. Still wished he could be her father. How could she leave him here? Whatever was happening to his body, to his mind, she could not just go and leave him to that fate.

But what about Erno and the others? She could not ask any of them to stay, especially Nurrel. Now that she had felt his pain and heard something of his thoughts, she knew he must go on to the Oxpeina region and find relief there, find the life he needed. She could not ask him to stay or travel with her any longer. It did not matter if he was better at talking to Father than she was; he must go. As for Erno, assigned as custodian to them both, he must go, too. He must take Nurrel to the Oxpeina region, get him safely home. She did not know how far that was. Perhaps Erno could return for her. Until then, she could keep trying to convince Father to leave this region, that he must come with her.

How she was supposed to do that, she did not know. It was plain he did not care for her, did not want to be her father anymore. How could she make him see that he must not stay in this region and that death would come for him if he did?

Jacob's raspy voice called out behind her. "Deborah, I'm coming. Don't wallop me!"

He landed on her shoulder and folded his wings in a flurry of cool breeze against her cheek. She stroked his breast, and he butted his head against her.

"You've been sitting here deciding what you're going to do, haven't you," he said gruffly.

She gave a small smile.

"Well?" he said.

"I have to try to get Father to come with me. Don't know how, but I have to try." She stared gloomily at the murky river. "I can't ask anybody else to stay here. I don't know how long it will take to convince Father to leave. You all should go while you can."

"*Huh.* Don't talk rubbish. You think I'd go off and leave you here in this region? Not a chance."

"Nurrel has to go. You must have felt, I mean, heard his thoughts. And, if he goes, Erno has to take him, and then that leaves us no custodian. I don't think you should stay anywhere without a brismun who can—"

"Will you shut up? I just told you I'm not going to leave you. Think of the trouble you'd get yourself into without me. Erno can take Nurrel and the hairy beasts off to Oxpeina-land and then come back for us."

There was relief in hearing him say that—to know that he would stay even if no one else did. She said nothing but lightly touched his taloned feet.

59

Nurrel looked up at Deborah, his expression set with determination. "I'm not going. You need my help."

"You *are* going," said Deborah. "You've travelled with me long enough. I don't know why. I'm grateful I've had you as a companion for as long as I have, I—" her breath caught in her throat. Even though she felt that the heaviness in her heart caused her to speak without much feeling, it suddenly struck her. Nurrel had been her quiet companion, never demanding anything, just there, a friend. Somehow, she depended on him more than she had realised. "I—you—I think you really must go on without me now. I don't want to be the cause of any more pain to you. Please, go." She turned to Erno, who stood watching her. "Take Nurrel home to Oxpeina-life. You know it's the right thing to do."

It was hard to look at him, his usually cheerful face now so full of dismay. She wanted to touch his arm, have him know her thoughts, yet she did not really want to know his. The expression on his face was enough. She might as well have told him outright that she didn't want him to be her custodian anymore. She swallowed hard, willing herself to not let out those tears that threatened to come. "You can come back for me. I'll wait for you, Erno. Please come back if you can."

"What about me?" said Ned. He stood a few paces away and had been silently listening to their discussion. "You don't say anything about me."

Deborah went over to him and laid her hand on his long face. "You must go, too, Ned."

"No, I don't want to. You can't make me. Sonax woke me so you could ride me and travel faster. I know he did. You can't make me go. I won't."

"You will," said Erno.

Deborah felt the authority of his words shift the air around them, and Ned bowed his head. "I—I don't want to."

"You are my dweller," said Erno. "You are not an image-bearer who has the right to your own will and your own decision. I know this is hard for you to hear, Ned, but in this case I want you to obey me. Deborah has told you to go, and you must listen to her and to me. She is trying to protect you."

Ned gave a gulp. "Don't want to," he muttered.

"I know you don't," said Erno. "Neither do I, but this is Deborah's decision, and we must heed it."

"Yes, right," said Nurrel, "but I don't have to, and if I stay, then you must also."

Ned's face brightened and he nibbled Deborah's sleeve.

She turned to Nurrel, and they gazed at each other a moment. He so steady, so serious, his brown eyes with an intrinsic quality that now tangibly reminded her of Sonax and the life running through his veins.

"Nurrel," she said, "you know you can't. It will do you more harm than good to stay here, and I can't have that on my conscience. Ben's my father; he's my responsibility, not yours. You need to go to the Oxpeina region, you *know* you do. The world is closing, and I am not going to be the one who makes you miss your chance to get out while you can."

From the look on his face, she could see he was thinking, trying to frame his thoughts, trying to suppress the pain he felt. The trees of the copse towered behind him, branches outspread to block the sky, their life seemingly inert as they stood in silent grandeur with faded scent of bark and leaf.

"It doesn't seem right to leave you," Nurrel said in a low voice.

"It seems right to me," Deborah said, and walked away along the grassy bank of the river.

Jacob's talons tightened on her shoulder. "What are you doing? Don't just walk off like that. Go back!"

She shrugged, trying to ease the discomfort of his grip. "No."

The *thud-thudding* of hooves followed her.

She turned and gestured at Ned. "No! Stay with Erno." She quickly moved away from him so she did not have to see the confusion on his face. "Come back for me once you've got them safely home, Erno," she whispered.

Even though they were not touching or even facing one another, she could almost sense him hearing her words and saying, *thinking*, that yes, he would.

The sound of running feet padded across the grass, and Nurrel grabbed her arm. "Deborah! Stop and think for a moment. You can't think you're going to get back into that town without any trouble whatsoever—there are guandras about, or have you forgotten?"

She had never seen such a look of frustration on his face.

"Food!" he shouted. "Take some food with you! I didn't load up all of Ned and Maqua's bags just to feed myself and nobody else! What do you think you're going to eat if you stay here? They've hardly any supplies in this wretched town. Most of the farms in this region have been shut down—what a brilliant decision that was by the image-bearers!"

She stared at him. It was so unlike him to yell—he who always seemed so unflappable.

"Hold on," said Jacob. "You've been around Deborah too much. I didn't think you were one to blow your top, Nurrel."

"I waited!" Nurrel's ruddy face flushed with anger. "You don't know how long I waited. I could have left my home much earlier, wanted to, was ready to go! I wanted to get to the Oxpeina and leave all this behind, but no, Sonax had me wait. So, I did. Did he tell me why? *No*. Not until you came." He gestured back at Erno. "Not until all of you came. *Then* Sonax told me. I was to travel with you; I was to take care of *you*." He jabbed a sturdy finger at Deborah. "I saw it all so clearly then. But you ran off! Ran off and left us. I thought I'd made a mistake, hadn't really understood what Sonax meant. Then, Ibelli..." He sucked in a deep breath. "You can't think I'm going to leave you now, right when your father is on the cusp of turning. You think he won't attack you when he turns? He could kill you!"

Deborah shook her head. "No—"

"Yes," said Nurrel. "Just like Chila tried to. Your father could kill you when he turns. You think I'm going to listen to you telling me to go now? What do you think I am? Some kind of coward? Deborah!" He exhaled loudly and grimaced. "Look, Deborah, I know you want to spare me pain; I get that, yes. You heard my soul's thought when I touched Sofi, but let me tell you, I heard yours just as clearly. You can't tell me you're only doing this to save me. You're also doing this because you think nobody really cares about you, nobody really loves you, and that you're all alone and you have to do this on your own. Look around you!" He swept his arms wide. "Sonax brought us all together to look after each other. We're supposed to be trying to look after each other and get through this together. We will get to the Oxpeina *together!*"

Ned raised his head and smirked, and a smile spread across Erno's face.

Jacob nudged Deborah's cheek. "I couldn't have said it any better myself."

Deborah's breath came in shallow gasps as she tried to hold her emotions steady, tried to will away those tears that began to blur her vision. How did Nurrel know that? He had felt that? She hardly knew that herself, but as he said it, each word struck painfully into her heart. Yes, she was alone. Yes, nobody truly loved her. Father, Mother, neither of them loved her.

Nurrel's warm hands closed around hers, and he looked earnestly up at her. "Deborah. Come now; you're not alone. Stop pushing us away. We're not leaving you to do this by yourself. I'm not going anywhere without you, and neither is Erno."

"Nor me," said Jacob.

"Nor me," echoed Ned.

Maqua let out a mumbling sound.

Deborah threw her arms around Nurrel.

He hugged her tightly. "It's all right," he said against her hair. "It's all right. We'll do this together. You're not alone."

She gulped back the sobs, shutting her eyes furiously against the rivers of emotion. It was all so hard to understand—why anybody would care about her or want her, yet they did. Nurrel did, Erno did, Jacob, Grufful, and even Ned. And, Sonax, why did he care? Why have her face appear on his like she meant something to him? She did not even know who he was—world-builder, Oxpeina-life, overseer of the custodians in this strange world. Her home city of Eblhim seemed inconceivably distant now, as if it were merely a faint echo of past times, a life that had never really seemed complete. The stress and strain of dealing with parents who did not truly care, did not truly love her.

"Well," said Erno, "I didn't expect rovi to join us so soon."

Nurrel drew back, and Deborah wiped her eyes. By the copse or by the river, across the yellowed fields, she could not yet see any rovi, but her heart lifted at the thought. Was it Grufful? She glimpsed a dust cloud far along the riverbank, and it soon grew and materialised into the distinct rich brown of rovi travelling together at speed. The tattoo of feet beat across the dry grass like a heavy rain. She recognised the darker brown fur of Grufful, the smaller muscular build of Linnfel, and the strong bearing of Val. She smiled to see their wild and snarling faces and hear their familiar cry of greeting: "*Soi-nah!*"

In hardly a moment more, Val stood tall before her, and the air was charged with Oxpeina-life. She saw the question again in his green eyes, the question that always came when meeting a rova: *Do you know the Oxpeina-life? Are you going deeper into the realm after Sonax-Oxpeina or are you turning?*

Why did he insist on asking her that again? Didn't he know her? But, as she met his stern gaze, her annoyance soon faded as she saw something more in his eyes. An awareness, the knowledge that anyone could turn, even Val himself if he was not careful.

"I am not turning," she whispered. "I am going to find the Oxpeina's region. I will get there before the world closes."

For the first time since she had known him, she saw an expression of relief cross his face.

Grufful stepped forward, his blue-gold eyes glinting, and wrapped his arms around Deborah. She sank into his warm fur and buried her head against his chest. Everything would be all right now; he would help her get Father out of this region, too.

"Hello, Val," said Erno. "I wasn't expecting to see you so soon."

"I, too, was not expecting that," said Val. "Yet, here we are, summoned from one task to another. What have you got yourselves into, Erno?"

"Guandras, I expect," he said cheerfully. "We've been observed by several, and while they let us get through the town without any bother, I suspect we might have a bit of trouble getting back in."

"Then, why return?"

"We're hoping to get Deborah's father out of there."

"I see. You have located him?"

"Yes," said Erno.

"Very good."

Erno's face fell. "Not really—he's altered… well, somewhat."

Deborah knew he was trying to spare her feelings by not explicitly saying what was wrong with Father. "He is turning," she said against Grufful's fur.

Grufful's grip tightened on her, and he growled.

"He's not too far gone," said Nurrel. "We already had one talk with him, and he regained some language ability."

"Now, *that* is very good," said Linnfel. "It means he hears you. There is hope."

Val glanced back towards the town. "Are you all on your way now to him? We should go quickly, as I am unsure for how long we are able to assist you before Sonax moves us on again. In only the last day, events in the regions have changed. Erno, I expect you saw what was happening to your former region."

"Nothing was happening when we were there just hours ago. All was quiet and cold, just as it was when I left it a long time ago."

"Oh?" Val tilted his head. "I can tell you that the region is starting to clear. We observed many trees vanish even as we passed through. The gloaming has begun."

"The world builder gathers his belongings," said Linnfel quietly.

Grufful released Deborah and scowled at her. She smiled, knowing that was an attempt at a loving expression from him. Jacob fluffed his feathers and resettled himself on her shoulder.

"We should not return that way," Grufful said. "We will travel through the other neighbouring regions that still contain more life and are not ready to be cleared."

Val gave a nod.

Ned cleared his throat quietly. "*Uh*, excuse me," he said in a small voice. "Shouldn't we really just leave here now? Go to Oxpeina right now if the regions are clearing out?"

Val moved to Ned and laid his brown-furred hand on his cheek. "Hold steady."

That was all he said, and Ned gazed up into Val's grim face with a mixture of awe and shyness in his eyes. His lips trembled as if he was about to say something and his left front hoof turned inward.

"Erno," Val said, as he let go of Ned, "we will come now with you to the town, if that is your desire. I'm sorry that not all members of my pack are with us—our women Hio and Sil have been assigned elsewhere by Sonax. There is so much movement now occurring in the regions we must let go of the joy of always being together. Until the end comes."

"Until the end comes," muttered Grufful under his breath.

"*Soi-nah*," said Linnfel.

"Must you always be so serious?" said Jacob.

Val turned to him, his green eyes sparkling as he threw his head back and snarled.

Deborah wondered if she had just seen him laugh.

60

Nurrel's eyes narrowed. "I see them. They look as though they're waiting for us."

"I expect they are," said Erno. "They won't want Deborah to come for her father."

The first of the clean-painted houses that lined each side of the street cut geometric shapes into the sky, and Deborah saw nothing out of the ordinary. She did notice the nearly transparent guandra path as it lay on the street twitching in the shadows and frowned, thinking of Father's admission that he had used such a path to come into this region. She was about to ask where the guandras were when a row of shadowy figures materialised, standing like statues shoulder-to-shoulder as if they had always been there barring the street.

Daylight passed through some of them while others were like blocks of rough-hewn stone, and the path took on an unnatural hue beside them. Deborah realised with horror that the guandras had no faces, that they were image-bearers who bore no images any longer. Yet, somehow, she knew they watched her, waited there for her. Told her that she was one of them, that this town was the beginning. This town, this region, was Oxpeina-life. She felt as if she sank sideways, that it was difficult to stand as weakness came into one side of her body and her thoughts became difficult to focus.

Sonax is no world builder, but a controller, and we are no longer under his control. We are free. Free of bearing any image. This is the new Oxpeina-life;

feel it now surge through your veins; feel it now give power; throw off the shackles of image. There is no image. All is one.

Deborah could not hear the voices of the brown beasts who stood near her, of the small image man, the four-legged beasts, the thing on her shoulder—where, *who* were they? Nothing. No one would have any control over her anymore. So dizzy, so hard to stand, something pressing down, a buzzing in her ears.

Let go of it all and enter in. No one will have any power over you anymore. You will stand tall; you will have our power. We have the true Oxpeina-life.

She stood face to face with a mirror of herself. Her face was smoothed away; nothing was there—no features, no skin, only grey. No one could see her to hurt her anymore; she would be shielded and hidden once she lost her image; no one would see her to hurt her. She would take back control over her life, she would shed her image and all the pain that it brought.

"But I like my image," she heard herself whisper.

The guandra standing before her staggered back as if she had struck it a blow.

Like her image? A surprising thought. Had she ever really liked herself before? She, who had always been so focused on others, on *Father*, and his lack of love for her. Yet, the last time she had seen her face on Sonax's, she had felt at peace with her image and connected with her own self in a new way.

The line of guandras twitched and shifted akin to the movement of the path. Deborah sensed they wanted to take her for their own, wanted whatever life she had as if they believed it would give them more power if only they could control her. She quickly stepped back, reached to the side where she would find—what was it? *Think*. Yes, that was it—she was trying to touch Erno, her custodian. Her hand connected with the texture of moss, and she clasped hold of his shoulder. Clarity surged up her arm and into her mind.

Are you all right? Erno thought.

His connection swept away the fog, the confusion. The street, the town—it all came back into focus along with the sight of him, Nurrel, and the rovi alongside her.

I am now, she thought back at him.

Good. They're very focused on getting you and Nurrel to join them. I suppose it's to our advantage that they're not immediately fighting us physically, but only mentally. "Stay back, Ned and Maqua," he said aloud, his voice clear and commanding.

She was glad he did, for in her connection with him she felt what he sensed—the guandras' rage against dwellers that would have anything to do with image-bearers.

Why? she thought.

Because you love them, and they're dwellers who are dependent on you.

What about Jacob? Is he all right?

'Course I am, came Jacob's gruff thought. *I've got my shield up, and you haven't. You're only using Erno's shield. Lazy!*

She frowned sidelong at him. *I am not lazy!* She realised his mottled brown-and-white feathers shone and rippled with traces of orange light, and then saw that the same colour flickered around Val, Grufful, Linnfel, Nurrel, and Erno. She glanced back at Ned and Maqua. They stood uncertainly, their eyes wide and trusting as they looked at her, but no shield was around them. She had the fleeting thought that Linnfel must go and shield them. She was about to call his name when Erno thought at her: *No. The dwellers are your responsibility and mine. The rovi are the ones who will fight for us—this is Sonax's way of things.*

All the sharing of thoughts with Erno and Jacob had occurred faster than speech—it seemed only the briefest moments of glancing here, there, and realising what must be done, even as the three rovi shouted "*Soi-nah!*" and advanced as one to the line of guandras.

A boom split the air, and she was thrown by a force she had never felt before and inhaled a suffocating bitterness. She scrambled to get back onto her feet and, as she did, saw the furthermost guandra stoop and gather the path as though it were fabric. The guandra whipped the path, and it flew out, spreading in a sheer loop. As it drew in around Deborah, she swung her arms wildly at it—this path, this thing, was going to wrap around her, just like Mother had been wrapped in a shroud for burial, and it would bind her tightly, lower her into the grave, take her breath, take her life.

What life? It would be better to lose herself. No one would ever be able to hurt her again if she lost herself. If she became something else, not her self, then she would not, *could not* be hurt, she would be free.

She stared down at the path beneath her feet, those shoes she wore so old and worn from many steps, many days of walking, walking in the woods, and never finding what she searched for.

What was she searching for? The guandra knew. The guandra—why call it such a name now that they were connected? It had no name; it was free of such things. She felt its nearness as they both touched the path; both drew breath at the same time, felt it watching her.

Why was she standing on the path? It had been trying to wrap around her, but instead it was beneath her feet. She had power over it. She stood on it. Her face appeared in the path before her feet as it had done so long ago, and her features—what were features?—began to fade. Erase it all and start again. Be without. No image.

"Deborah!"

A familiar voice, a familiar hand. Jolting her awake, wakening sense into her.

"Deborah!" cried Erno again.

"Put up your shield, drat it!" squawked Jacob, pecking her ear.

Erno's shield surged around her, tingling electricity all over her body, an orange light fizzing and sparking before her eyes; the connection with the guandra instantly severed. Val, Grufful, and Linnfel moved in a blur while their swords of fire and shining steel were clearly visible. Swords? Where did they get those? The guandras fought back with strange implements—not straight and true as swords, but twisted and knotted things of rust.

A squeal rang out behind her. She turned to see a guandra launching itself at Ned. Claws swiped his grey neck, and lines of red appeared. She dashed to the guandra, grabbed at its sandpapery body, couldn't get hold of it as it twisted and turned beneath her grasp, scraping her fingers raw.

"Get back, Deborah!" shouted Erno.

The strength of his command caused her hands to drop, her legs to step back, and she knew he would save Ned. Erno leapt, wielding high a sword—where did he get that?—and down, down it went, smashing into the guandra. The guandra fell apart, sliced in two so that a hollow shell clattered before her feet.

"Sonax!" Ned screamed, and orange light flickered into life around his body.

He had summoned his own shield, all while she had not, could not, did not know how to.

"I'm sorry I did not—" Ned gasped, his eyes wide beneath the flickering orange, as blood dripped from his neck, "—did not get a shield quick enough. I'm sorry. Sorry."

Who was he talking to? He did not look at her but stared ahead, stared at nothing, then bowed his head, his sides heaving as he gasped for breath. Why could she not move? Why did everything feel so strange, so heavy? Even sound became muffled.

"Shield!" rasped Jacob, from a great distance.

How to summon a shield? Something to do with centring, with Sonax and Oxpeina-life.

The path was beneath her feet. She could see herself walking. She did not need Father anymore. Did not need anyone. She would leave them all behind and be free.

Something stung her forehead, snapped her awake, and she saw Erno's face close to hers. He was shorter than her; how could his face be close to hers? He was bending over her. The cold, hard stone of the street pressed against her side. Lying down?

"Deborah," he said, his mossy hand touching her forehead.

The coolness of it was blessed relief, and she felt a calm wash over her.

Erno? she thought at him. *What's happening? Why am I lying down? I thought I was standing. Is Ned all right?*

He's wounded; I don't know how badly. I can't go to him now; I need you to stay awake. Hold steady and look at me, Deborah. The rovi have almost finished dispatching the guandras. Stay awake.

Awake? She blinked at him. Such vivid green, his round, mossy face, the beautiful and familiar countenance of her custodian, her companion. She suddenly thought of Nurrel. *Where is he?*

Nurrel's with Maqua. He's holding her steady with his shield around them both.

She exhaled slowly. *That's good. He's done what I've failed to do—I failed to protect Ned. I don't know how to. I'm useless.*

Strong hands took hold of her, raised her up, lifted her like she weighed no more than a feather.

"What happened?" Grufful snarled, cradling her in his arms.

She leaned against his chest, stared at the sleek, dark brown fur of his arm, and weakly reached to stroke it.

"The path got her," Erno said. "It has done something—I'm not sure what; it wrapped around her body for only an instant."

"She was all right," said Jacob.

Where was he? Not on her shoulder.

"She was able to run to Ned," he said, "but then she collapsed. Help her!"

"None of us has the healing power," said Val.

"All I can do is put her into a healthful Oxpeina sleep," said Grufful.

Not again. Not the sleep that lasts for days. She tried to shake her head, tried to open her mouth to speak a protest.

We won't go against your will, Erno thought at her, his hand on her side, *but don't you see it is the only thing we can do for you right now? Even I don't have the healing power as strong as is needed here.*

Stay with me, she thought back at him.

Of course I will.

Then I agree. Sleep if I must.

61

She woke to darkness. Her heartbeat swooshed in her ears, but other than that, there was no sound. She was in a bed, but where? She rolled over slowly, her body stiff and clumsy. Was she in Hirahi? Shilhim? Eblhim? She felt for a wall, not knowing which side of the bed she should attempt to get out from. Her hand connected with nothing but air. She struggled to get herself up into a sitting position, the swooshing quickening in her ears. There was a smudge of pale green light. Square-ish. A curtained window? No wall that side of the bed, at least, so she pushed away the blanket and got up, clutching at the bed to try and steady herself. The swooshing in her ears grew ever louder, and she stood still a moment, trying to gather herself, find her balance.

"Erno?" she said. "Are you here? Jacob?"

She managed to stagger over to the pale green. It was indeed a curtain, and, as she pulled it aside, it made a terrible screeching noise that drowned out her swooshing. The sky had an eerie green glow away to the left—too wide and expansive to be a single light—while clouds slowly shifted and gathered in daubs of moonlit hues in the rest of the night sky. That green glow—why did it look so familiar? She had stared out a window just as she did now, out at that green. Where? Beneath trees. In Shilhim. That's where she had seen it—the first night she and Father had spent in that old house. Was she in Shilhim now? Couldn't be. But, where? It was hard to make out anything in the dark. Beneath the sky, there was nothing but murk. Wait—her eyes began to adjust now that she wasn't looking at the green—she could see a shape. The lines of a roof?

Then she remembered. She was in that stupid region Father had decided was his home. Guandras, the path, the rovi… Was she in Father's house?

A faint creak made her catch her breath, and the sound was followed by a soft tapping. Someone knocking at a door? Father?

There was the quiet noise of a door opening, then a man's voice. "Deborah. Are you all right?"

Nurrel's voice. Of course, it wouldn't be Father.

"Yes, I think so," she said. The swooshing in her ears hadn't stopped, and she didn't exactly feel like trying to walk again just yet, but other than that, nothing else seemed off.

"How are you feeling?" he asked.

"Disoriented."

"That's understandable. Are you hungry?"

"I don't know. Where are we?"

"In an abandoned house. There's plenty of them. We're actually right next door to your father's house."

Her heart sank. Why wasn't she in Father's house? Did he know she was here?

"I haven't got a lamp," said Nurrel, "and the electricity isn't working, so I'm afraid we'll have to wait for daylight. Do you want to come downstairs now to eat, or would you rather I bring you something?"

"How long have I been sleeping? Where are the others?"

"You've slept almost two days. At least, this is your second night, so I suppose it's more like one and a half days. Erno, Ned, and Maqua are down in the yard. Erno can't come in the house; he's broken two of the floorboards already, so we decided he'd better stay outside. Things are oddly flimsy in this region. He heard you say his name, so sent me to check on you."

"Is Ned all right?"

"He is, mostly, although the wounds on his neck aren't good. I haven't found anything except honey to put on them. I thought that might act as an antiseptic. Ned says it has soothed the pain somewhat."

"Where's Jacob?"

"Gone to see if he can get Fothie to come heal you and Ned. He should really have been back by now."

"Where's Grufful? Val?"

"They had to leave right after they brought you here. Sonax gave them another task, so that was that. Grufful was pretty angry at what happened to you—almost attacked Erno until he came to his senses. I don't think I've ever seen anyone so repentant so quickly. Grufful, I mean. He blamed himself for not keeping a better eye on you. I'm sure he would have stayed with you if he could have, but you know how he is—he's not going to turn; he'll always be the custodian he's asked to be."

Too many words, too much *swooshy swooshy* in the ears. Deborah leaned on the windowsill, willing her legs to behave and hold her body up. "Does—does Father know I'm here? Does he know what happened to me?"

"Yes. I've been talking often to him, and he's more coherent."

"Did he—has he—come to see me?"

There was silence for a moment; the air felt heavy between them, and she knew what his reply would be.

"No. Sorry, no. I did ask him to, but he hasn't been able to yet. Don't pay too much attention to that—he's not himself."

How did Nurrel know Father was not himself? This was exactly like Father—only thinking of himself and what he wanted, nobody else.

"Come and have something to eat. You must be hungry."

Eat? She couldn't eat. The thought of Father and his inability to check on her, inability to care… caused a dullness to sweep over her, a suffocating feeling in her chest. Of course, Father would not come to see her. This was just like Kasharel not bothering to see her when she had been attacked. Father did not love her.

The floorboards creaked, and Nurrel came and stood by her at the window. She looked down at him; even in the pale green light, she could see the tiredness, the weary lines in his face. He gave her a brief smile, and in that strange light she saw the warmth, the Oxpeina-life, in his dark eyes.

Somehow, it hurt her heart, and she looked out the window. "What is this green light?"

"Erno calls it the gloaming. I described it to him as he can't see it very well, but he definitely feels the change in the atmosphere. He says it's coming from what used to be his region, and it's probably all that's left there now."

"I'm sure I've seen it before."

"Where?"

"Back in the region I came from. It was one of my first experiences coming to the woods."

"Sounds like you were near the border of another empty region."

She shrugged.

"I don't think I'll ask you for the umpteenth time if you're hungry," he said, "but at least let me get you a drink of water. The plumbing here works, even if the electricity doesn't. Not very nice tasting water, but it's drinkable."

She nodded.

He moved away from her, and she heard a thud.

"*Ow!*" he said. "Can't see a darn thing. Stubbed my toe on whatever that was. I'll be right back."

She felt her way back to the bed and sat heavily. Still with the noise in the ears, the unsteadiness on her feet, yet she couldn't pinpoint what was wrong—nothing in her body felt tender or sore. The guandra hadn't physically attacked the way that Chila had; it had only thrown a path around her. She shut her eyes. Perhaps she should just go back to sleep, wait for Jacob to bring Fothie. What could Fothie do? She wouldn't be able to fix anything, not really. How could she fix what had gone wrong? Everything had gone wrong. All of this—all of the search for

Father—was a waste of time. She had poured her whole life into trying to take care of him since Mother had died, and it was never good enough. Her whole life. Come to nothing. It was all pointless. He didn't want her now, didn't want to be her father. Didn't love her.

What was it all for? She could look back at her life and see nothing. Nothing real or important. No meaning. It had all been so hard, so much work to try and help Father, try to make him better again, try to regain the old him, the way he used to be. Yet, what had he been like all those years ago? It was hard to remember. But he should be different; he shouldn't be like this. He should care. Why didn't he want to be her father anymore?

She sighed and wiped the tear that slid down her cheek. It was all for nothing. Probably better if she had never been born. Better to never have existed if this was the life she had to live. She could see her face looking back at her and the way the features slowly dissolved, wiping the image away just as she wiped her tears away, leaving blankness, nothingness. No one would hurt her, no one would know her, for she would not be.

A creak on the floorboards startled her.

"Here you go," said Nurrel. "Deborah? Where are you?"

She took a deep breath and sat up straighter. "On the bed."

"Wherever that is," he muttered.

"Over here," she said.

After a little more guidance, he put a cold glass in her hand. She sipped the water. It was lacking in flavour, thin, but he was right, it was drinkable.

The bed dipped as he sat near her. "I'm sorry."

"It doesn't taste that bad," she said.

"No, I mean, I'm sorry for what happened. I should have watched out for you. I—really, I thought you knew how to put up your own shield. Erno had taught you, after all. I was caught up trying to calm Maqua, but I should have been watching you, too. I'm afraid I was not a very good friend to you, and I'm sorry for that. Maybe all this could have been avoided."

Well, it didn't matter. Nothing mattered any more. "It's fine," she said. "I'm all right."

A shout rang out below in the dark night. "You are not!"

Deborah glanced over at the green window. "I should have known you could hear everything, Erno." She imagined him grinning at her response. The thought of him, fresh and vibrant, while she sat under the heaviness of her wasted life—the contrast between them was clear. He was so lively and energetic and always knew the best way to go about things. She was nothing like him.

"I think I begin to see why Sonax assigned him as our custodian," Nurrel said.

There was silence, as though he waited for her to say 'why'? but she sipped the water instead. Custodians didn't really matter anymore, either. If this region was ending soon, she may as well be swallowed up into it and nothingness, and all the hurt, the pain of life would then be over.

"Rovi don't thought-share," Nurrel said. "Brismuns are the only custodians who do. I did not know that, but now that I do, it makes sense. I expect brismuns need that to understand the dwellers—the unawakened ones who can't talk, I mean. And, really, for me, it has been, well, a boon to be able to have that kind of communication."

Why was Nurrel so chatty? He wasn't normally so chatty. She thought of the evening they had spent together in the little house near Hirahi, sitting by the fireplace, occasionally chatting, other times just quietly gazing into the fire.

"I have spent so many nights with Erno," he said. "I haven't been able to sleep well since—" he drew a deep breath, "since Ibelli died. Can't seem to get the sight of that out of my head. But, he helps. Erno helps. Just to be able to have him know my thoughts when I can't speak, can't articulate everything. I think you've also found that. So, that's what I mean. I think I understand why Sonax assigned him to us. He knew we would need Erno and that he can do what a rova isn't able to."

World-builder, she thought to herself, and immediately the memory of Sonax saying, 'You're my Deborah' sprang to mind. She shut her eyes. Why would he have said that to her? He didn't know her. He didn't know what a mess of everything she had made and how her life was worth nothing. All that longing for Father—what was the point of it? He didn't love her, didn't want to be her father anymore. If he ever had.

"It's cold in here," said Nurrel. "Maybe you should come downstairs and I'll get a fire going. Probably good if you could go out and see Ned, too. He's been worrying about you."

She supposed she ought to. Ned was innocent and didn't deserve what had happened to him. It was all her fault for failing him. She should at least go and tell him she was sorry. Then, why didn't she want to? "I'll come down the morning," she said.

"It's almost that now," said Nurrel.

"I'm tired."

"Grufful said he put the sleep only lightly on you this time, but I'm sure everything you've been through in the last weeks has been exhausting."

It didn't matter. It was all for nothing. She sat there, clutching the cold glass in her hands, her head bowed.

"Get some more sleep if you can," Nurrel said. "I'll check on you later."

The bed shifted, and she listened to his footsteps, then the door, then the creak of floorboards or stairs or whatever was outside the door.

You're my Deborah, she thought again.

No, she was nobody's Deborah. She shivered and pulled the blanket up around herself. She did not know how long she sat there numbly—why bother thinking? There was no point going over everything that had ever gone wrong; her whole life was a waste of time—but the green light from the window was eventually overcome by dawn. The room became visible. Not that there was much to see. It reminded her of the shack in Shilhim—someone's clothing hanging out of the open drawers; an open closet half-empty; items heaped on the floor as if they had fallen off the hangers; a circular rug in the centre of the room with just one sock lying there. Either someone didn't care about cleaning up or they had left in a hurry.

How hard she had scrubbed at the floors in the house she and Father had taken in Shilhim, done her best to clean and make it liveable for the two of them. All because Father had promised he would feel better if they could live there close to the woods. Why had she believed him? He had only made use of her to get there, while obviously secretly planning to go into the woods. He hadn't thought of her at all.

The creak on the floorboard outside the door told her that Nurrel was back. She sighed.

His eyes widened in horror as he looked at her. "Deborah!" He rushed over and took her right arm. His hand felt strange, almost as though it wasn't quite all there.

"Deborah!" he said again.

"What?" she said.

"What's happened to you?" He rubbed her arm vigorously, as if trying to get some warmth into it.

She looked down at his hands. Why didn't she feel much sensation? Something didn't look quite right. Was that dust on her sleeve, dirt from lying on the ground? He took her right hand and began rubbing it as though he was again trying to bring warmth to her. As she stared down, she realised part of her hand was not quite flesh-coloured. Seeing it gave her a horrible chill.

Nurrel pulled her to her feet. "Come with me to Erno. Come on, Deborah. Come with me."

Erno. Yes, she wanted Erno. Erno would make all things right. Erno cared about her even if no one else did. Although, he hadn't come to her, so maybe he didn't really care about her after all.

She stumbled more than once down the stairs as Nurrel pulled her along. The rooms he took her through seemed to sway, the walls bending and refracting.

"Deborah," he said. "You hear me, don't you? You understand what I'm saying? We've got to get to Erno. Everything will be all right."

"Of course I understand you," she said, the words feeling thick and difficult to speak.

Yet, he was right, she knew he was right—she had to get out, get to Erno, stop the world from spinning.

Nurrel dragged her outside into the cold air. She had gone far enough, she had better stop now or go back inside. Didn't matter that things were moving before her eyes. Shut her eyes, then it would stop. She sank down onto the ground.

"Let me in!" cried Erno.

Where was he? Over there somewhere. Didn't matter.

"Oh!" said Nurrel. "Yes, right."

Deborah heard footsteps, voices. Where was Erno? She needed Erno.

Thumps shook the ground, her body trembled with each beat. She managed to open her eyes, squinted at the blue sky overhead, then a face, bushy hair blocked everything.

She smiled at him. "Erno."

"What have you gone and done?" he said brightly. "You know I can't have you turning. It's not allowed, Deborah."

Not allowed. That was funny. Wait, what—turning? No! She reached out and caught hold of his hand.

That's better, he thought at her. *But, goodness, is this what the path has done to you? Given you a huge dose of guandra thoughts? What a load of rubbish. You're not worthless or unloved, Deborah, you hear me?*

But it's all true, she thought back at him. *Father doesn't want me. I don't even know why I call him Father. He's no father to me.*

That's only because he can't be. It's nothing to do with you; it's all him. He let me touch his hand briefly—only briefly, mind!—before he backed away. I'm going to share with you the memory of that touch, then you'll understand. Are you ready?

She nodded. Well, why not. It didn't matter anym—

A memory flashed into her mind, and she saw Father standing before her, looking down at her, no, looking at *Erno*, a puzzled expression on his face. "Brismun," he said.

"Yes," came Erno's voice. "I'm your daughter's custodian."

"Daughter? I have none."

"Yes, you do. Her name is Deborah, and she's worried about you. We're here to bring you out and take you to the Oxpeina's region."

The opaqueness of Father's eyes thickened. "I'm already in the Oxpeina's region. Here. Better than the Oxpeina's region. Brismun… I always liked the brismun." He frowned as if he were trying to remember something. "Brismun in the book."

He remembers the storybook, Deborah thought. *Does he remember reading it to me?*

Don't know, thought Erno, *but this is why he touched my hand. Here, listen to the consciousness that came when he did.*

Deborah took a deep breath. She felt a dry hand touch hers—no, it touched Erno's—and in that connection a myriad of emotion, of thought, swirled around her.

… doesn't want me, afraid, can't let anyone close, can't let them see me, Charlotte hated me yet she was the only one who loved me, and she knew me, so must have had reason to be disappointed. Can't let anyone close to me, they won't like what they see, I'll be a disappointment to them, too, was never good enough, don't let anyone in, Charlotte always told me I was no good, worthless, let her down, don't want that to happen again, must go…

The hand let go, and Father looked blankly upward, then walked away.

What does all of that mean? Deborah thought, clutching tightly to Erno's hand. *What does he mean? Charlotte was my mother's name. Why is he thinking of her even now? It's been years since she died.*

Erno squeezed her hand. *Calm yourself. I know it's disturbing to sense his innermost self, but steady your breathing and your heart. You have answers now as to why he is the way he is and why he left you. Do you see it's not your fault?*

I don't know what I see. It's confusing. He's never spoken like that before.

Don't expect him to. Those were his innermost thoughts, and they were all about not letting anyone get close to him. You see why he left you?

I suppose you're saying it's because he didn't want me to get close to him. But, I'm his daughter!

So what?

512

"Erno!" she said and sat up.

He grinned at her. "Maybe speech is slightly better than thought in this instance—you heard my instinctive reaction too well. What I mean is, I don't think it matters who you are, whether you're his daughter or not. If he doesn't want anyone to get close to him, then, well, that applies to everyone."

She hugged her knees and stared at the ground. "But, I'm his daughter," she said in a low voice. "He's supposed to love me."

"How do you know he doesn't? He's afraid, that's all, and it looks like his fear has made him push you and others away." Erno sighed. "I wish Hemri was here. He's better than me at explaining image-bearers."

"I think you're doing all right."

He touched her cheek, his mossy hand fuzzy and cool against her skin. *Don't turn. Don't let this region and all its troubles work the wrong kind of power on you. I wouldn't have left you alone if I'd known the guandra's path would have this affect on you.* He grinned. *Mind you, I did wreck a couple of the floorboards trying to get into the house to see you. The stairs might have collapsed if I'd gone up them.*

She gazed up at him. *I'm not turning, but I don't know what that means anymore. I'm lost.*

You're an image-bearer.

She saw the suggestion of another face superimpose over his, other eyes look out from his, and realised it was the essence of the Oxpeina, something of Sonax, in Erno's bearing. The feeling of warmth, of belonging, came over her, and she felt the ground centring beneath her, the sky above, the world around, and she knew where she was. She was in the wrong region. She shouldn't be here. She should find the Oxpeina's region now that the world was closing. She was an image-bearer, her image decided upon by Sonax.

Why, thank you, Erno thought at her. *Nice to know I can reflect Sonax back to you in an odd sort of way, even though I'm not an image-bearer. Hold onto this now; shake off the path's attempt to erase who you are.*

Why did it do that? How?

He mentally shrugged. *Beats me how that all works. Guandras always have an obsession with control and the belief they'll get more life-power if they can make others turn. Or, something like that—where's Hemri to explain things when I need him? Anyway, the guandra that owned the path had been a rova—or, forbid me from even thinking it, one of my brothers or sisters.*

How do you know that?

Because that guandra controlled the path, I know it was a custodian before it turned. Custodians have all got a distinctive kind of power in one way or another, generally useful to image-bearers and dwellers. Whatever the path was originally intended for, I don't know, but now it's twisted up like its owner.

She looked around at the yard. At least no path was there. The yellowed grass was short and stubbly, while high wooden fences surrounded on three sides—or, almost surrounded. The right side fence was broken, with a large gap.

I did that, Erno thought at her. *Ned and Maqua ate all the grass here, so I had to break through into the neighbour's yard. Nobody lives there, so it doesn't matter.*

Deborah looked over at the lefthand side of the yard and the glimpse of the narrow two-storey house over the fence. Nurrel had said Father was next door. That must be his house.

Yes, it is, Erno thought.

Where is he now?

He's inside.

Was he upstairs? Could he see her out of his window now? She could see no sign of movement, no shadow, at any of the upper windows.

"He's downstairs," said Erno. "I heard him come down not so long ago, and now he is quiet."

"He was always quiet," she said softly. She did not know how to feel. She had found Father at last and did not know what to do. She got up and suddenly realised that the swooshing in her ears had gone and she could stand and move about normally again. She held out her right hand and turned it this way and that. Her skin was normal, and she felt as though she had dreamt seeing it a strange colour, that maybe it had been a trick of the light. But, no, she felt better, clearer in her thinking. Erno had helped her.

"Custodian," she said, and briefly touched his face. "What do I do now?"

A pleased smile spread across the vibrant greenness of his face. "You are not turning."

"No, I don't want to."

"Good. Let go of all that self-importance, as Hemri would say. Thinking of yourself as worthless and your life as meaningless places far too much terrible importance on your own opinion of who you are." He swivelled on his stumpy leg. "Nurrel! Ned can come and see Deborah now."

Nurrel appeared at the broken fence and stepped through, then he turned and beckoned. "Come in," he said.

Ned pushed past him and trotted to Deborah, as Maqua followed at a more sedate pace.

"Deborah!" Ned cried. "You were hurt and then sleeping, and I couldn't see you, and they made me wait, and are you all right?"

She gasped at the sight of his neck, smeared and glistening with bloody streaks. "Ned! Oh, Ned. I'm so sorry I didn't protect you. Are you all right?"

He nosed at her hands. "I'm all right, are you all right?"

"I'm all right." She cupped his face in her hands and kissed his nose. "Does it hurt?"

"What, my nose? No, you mean my neck. Yes, a bit. Nurrel puts honey on it, and Erno speaks to me, and that helps, but it does sting and feel funny."

She could hardly bear to look at his neck. She cradled his head and laid her cheek against his. "I'm so sorry," she whispered.

The sound of rhythmic thumps rapidly drumming the earth grew louder and louder. It soon became so loud and so heavy, the ground trembled beneath her feet.

"Erno," she said, "is that Fothie?"

He tilted his head and shut his eyes. "No. Over here, my brother!"

There was a crash from around the side of the house.

"*Youch!* Mighty!" shouted a familiar voice. "What magic is this? I bounced off like a dratted ball. You all right, little fella? I almost threw you."

"Who is that?" Nurrel said.

"Iff," said Erno, grinning. "Let him in."

Nurrel hurried around the side of the house while Deborah stayed with Ned. "It's Iff?" she said to Erno. "What's he doing here?"

The last time she had seen Iff was before she, Kasharel, and Jacob had gone to the Silver Lake. Iff, the large brismun, who had placed magic on her so that she would keep walking until she got to Erno.

The thumping began again, and Iff sprang forth from between the houses. As she had been when she had met him, Deborah was struck by how big he was. He stood at least twice the size of Erno, and the energetic way he moved and appeared made the tall houses behind him seem dim and frail.

"Erno!" he shouted. "I found out the hard way you've got rovi magic keeping everyone out. Did you hear me bash into the barrier? I almost brained myself!" He made a quick gesture with his hands. Jacob flew out from them and swooped straight to Deborah's shoulder.

He nuzzled her, and she stroked his feathers.

"Are you all right?" he said.

"Yes, I'm all—

"Everyone's all right," boomed Iff. "It's all you lot say around here."

Erno leapt to Iff, and they clasped hands. He seemed like a brismun child next to Iff as they grinned at each other.

"Haven't seen you for ages," said Iff. "You little dunderhead."

"Big Oof, I mean, Iff."

Iff squinted at the sky. "What is it with this region? I tore up half the ground just getting here. It's all flimsy and dry-rotted. Your region has gone; I bet you're chuffed about that. Mine's on the way out, too. Sar has gone already to the Oxpeina. I've been hanging about making sure things are clear, waiting for word to be able to go after her. Then, I get this little fella," he pointed at Jacob, "coming at me and asking for help."

"Jacob," Nurrel said, "I thought you were going to get Fothie? What happened?"

"She wasn't able to come," Jacob said. "She wanted to, but she's too busy. Lots of image-bearers are clearing out. I could hardly believe it was the same region; it looked so different and was so much colder. Fothie couldn't leave the dwellers; she was getting as many as she could to leave, so she told me to try Iff."

"It pains me to know I'm not first choice," said Iff, grinning.

"Can you help Ned?" Deborah asked. "He's wounded."

Iff hopped over and squinted down at her. She felt small and insignificant under his intense gaze. Was his sight better than Erno's? How well did he see her?

"You sort of know who you are now, don't you, image-bearer Deborah? Stand on one leg."

She felt one of her legs buckle under his command. She gritted her teeth with the effort of trying to hold steady and not do what he said.

"Ha!" Iff cried. "Much better. Still, not as good as it could be, but better all the same. Release."

She felt her body slacken and ease at his word, and no longer had to desperately try to stop herself from standing on one leg.

There was something potent about having both Erno and Iff so close to her. It felt similar to the intensity of Oxpeina-life the rovi had in the air around them, but this had something else, something growing, something responding in the ground beneath her feet as if the whole region would shift and break apart if they commanded it to. She did not remember this sensation with the other brismuns she had encountered, but then again, Iff was not quite like them.

Jacob huddled closer to her neck as if he too was cowed. Iff continued to stare thoughtfully at her, his steely blue eyes just visible amongst the moss. She wondered why and felt the desire to reach and touch his arm, to hear his thoughts, but could not bring herself to. It seemed too audacious to do such a thing with him.

She gestured feebly towards Ned. "Are you able to help him?"

Iff shook himself as if she had woken him from a reverie, rattling his twiggy hair, and swivelled about. "Come here, my lad," he said, holding his hand out to Ned.

Both he and Maqua stepped forward, and Deborah noticed that even Nurrel started forward instinctively then stopped himself.

Erno laughed. "We always said Sonax gave Iff everything in double measure."

"That may be so in some things," said Iff, "but I wasn't given the healing power in the same measure as Fothie. I have felt a tad envious of that—perish the turning thought! So, I need your help here, Erno."

"Will do."

"Now, my Ned," said Iff. He stroked Ned's nose, who quivered and gave a little jump as if the touch gave him a shock. "Let us have a look at what's bothering you."

Ned slowly turned so that his neck was on full display in front of Iff and Erno.

"Nasty!" said Iff.

Deborah grimaced at the sight of the bloody gashes, shining and matted with the sticky honey. She quickly looked away and at Ned's doleful eye as he gazed sidelong at her. This was her fault. She should have been looking after him and putting a shield around them both, as Nurrel had with Maqua. She went and stood at his head and gently took his face in her hands.

"Hold still, Ned," said Iff. He leaned towards Erno. "You do down there, and I'll do up here."

"That goes without saying," Erno said.

"Haha!"

Erno spread his thick green fingers along the underside of Ned's neck while Iff laid his hands along the top. The whispery language of the brismuns came from them both, and they turned their heads to each other, Iff bowing so that his twiggy hair almost touched Erno's. Their hands did not move, yet Ned winced and shut his eyes. Deborah glanced around at his neck, willing for the gashes to disappear, but saw no change. She also waited to hear the thoughts of Erno and Iff, assuming she would as she was touching Ned at the same time as them, but her mind was quiet with her own thoughts. She wondered what they said to each other as the whispering continued.

Finally, Iff lowered his hands. "You'll be right, my Ned. We'll have to do this several times a day. Tell me why you didn't raise your shield the moment you saw a guandra, because you can, can't you."

"Yes, Iff," said Ned. "I was—I was afraid."

"Good lad. An honest admission staves off the turning." He looked at Deborah, his steely eyes thoughtful once more. "I was brought here to help you, too, image-bearer," he said, his voice quietening. "Come here if you are willing, and we will tend your wound."

If you are willing? She was not sure if she was; she felt strangely reluctant. "I don't have a wound."

"Yes, you do. I see it plainly."

Was he referring to the scars that Chila had left on her cheek? Or was there something else the guandra's path had done to her that nobody had noticed? She looked down at herself. There was no blood on her clothes, and she didn't feel any pain anywhere.

"Erno and I will tend it together," he said. "Don't be frightened."

"I'm not." She busied herself, stroking Ned's face. There was nothing wrong with her now; Erno had brought her out of the turning. Why Iff thought she had a wound somewhere, she did not know. Nobody else was agreeing with him that they could see such a thing; Nurrel and Erno were both silent, and Jacob was, too.

Iff turned to Erno. "She doesn't want me to help. Well! If that's all I'm wanted for here, I may as well get going. Are you all coming, too?"

"I thought you said you would need to help heal Ned several times a day," Deborah said.

Iff glanced over his shoulder at her. "I did say that, yes. But, really, the main work has been set off and running and truly only needs Erno to keep it going. I sense you don't want me here, image-bearer, so I don't see any reason to stick around. I'd much rather leave for the Oxpeina's region. You all should, too."

"Don't be hasty, brother," said Erno. "You can understand Deborah's reluctance—you bound in here like a world basher, yet she needs time to think about what you've said."

"Time? There is no time. You know that. I know that." Iff swept his hands upward. "You feel this, don't you? The very air is changing. This region will be closed soon. Why the image-bearers here don't pay attention to the signs, I don't know. Daft, the lot of them. We shouldn't stay here a moment longer."

"I do feel it," Erno said. "But we can't leave just yet. Deborah needs to ask her father to come with us. He's trapped here."

"Where is he? I'll have at him, if you like."

"If only it were that simple," Erno said, "but we can't go against an image-bearer's will. If you used any of your mind's influence on him, then you'd violate Sonax's natural laws and no longer be the custodian you're supposed to be."

Iff sighed and muttered. "You're right, brother. I'm impatient to leave. I feel the urgency to clear out. That might be slightly affecting my judgement."

"Only slightly," said Erno.

"*Hoo*," said Jacob.

Deborah looked over at the house next door. Erno had said Father was there now. She could imagine him sitting by the window, looking out to his yard, lost in a daydream. "I'll go now and try talking to Father again." She was about to, when she thought of Nurrel. He was much better than she was at talking to Father and keeping his cool. "Nurrel, will you come?"

He nodded soberly, and they set off together.

62

Deborah stood with Nurrel on the front doorstep of Father's house, Jacob on her shoulder. Her hand was poised to knock, but she could not do it. The thought of Father's angry stare, how she had felt he was almost going to strike her, the sight of his strangely disfigured body—what was she doing? Why was she even trying to speak with him again? He had made it clear he didn't want to be a father to her.

She lowered her hand and stepped back.

"It's okay," said Nurrel. "Let me."

He rapped sharply at the door. They waited a while, then he knocked again more loudly. After repeated knocking and what seemed an age, the door opened.

Deborah was aghast to see Father again. Even though she knew what he looked like, it was still a shock to see the translucent patches on his face and body, his glassy, opaque eyes, the dusty coating on his clothing. He smiled slightly at Nurrel, recognition dawning on his face.

"Oh, it's you," he said. "Good morning."

"Hello, Ben," said Nurrel. "Can we come in?"

Father stepped aside and motioned them in. "Yes, my house. Come in. See my house."

Deborah took a deep breath. He had better not be intending to show them through the house again while saying 'my' at everything.

"Well," said Nurrel, as he went inside, "we've come to see you, not your house, Ben. You remember Deborah?"

Father's gaze flickered to her, and she looked steadily back at him. It hurt to see his eyes, vacant and cold.

"Yes," Father said softly.

That was a surprise.

"My daughter." He turned as soon as he had uttered the words and went ahead of them through the narrow hallway.

"That's right," said Nurrel. "Deborah is your daughter."

Deborah followed them, feeling as though her heart was going to pound right out of her chest. She took a few shaky breaths to try to gain some composure. Didn't Father know what he looked like? Surely, he must. She had seen the way the skin of her hand appeared and the dusty coating on her sleeve. Surely, he must see himself, too. Yet, what was causing him to turn, and how could she stop it?

Jacob nudged her cheek gently, as if he felt the tension in her shoulder and the struggle she was having to remain calm.

"Have you had some breakfast, Ben?" Nurrel asked.

Father paused and looked down at him. "Breakfast?"

"I've got plenty of food next door if you want to come join us for a meal," said Nurrel. "I don't think you've got many supplies here in this town, have you, Ben? Have most of the farms closed down, and now the regions nearby aren't delivering anything?"

Father's brow furrowed as if he were trying to think. Nurrel took his hand and held it in both of his, smoothing it gently as if willing life to come back. Deborah supposed she should probably try to touch Father, too, but she stood watching, feeling unable to move any closer to him. He looked up from Nurrel and pulled his hand away. As he did, it reminded Deborah of the memory Erno had shown her. Father's thoughts of being afraid, his thoughts of her mother, his not wanting anybody to get close to him.

"Father," she said. "Come and have breakfast with us. Please, come."

He glared at her, and she shrank beneath his gaze. Jacob flapped his wings as if trying to keep his balance.

"Stop telling me what to do," Father said.

"I'm not," said Deborah. "I just want—I want to help you. We need to leave from here. You can't stay in this region. Please, Father, come with me."

"No," he said sternly. "This is my home. Stop trying to take it from me."

"I'm not trying to take it from you; I'm trying to tell you that this region is… you can't live here… the region is going to close. The world is closing. We've got to get to the Oxpeina's region as quickly as possible. Please don't stay here."

"I *am* in the Oxpeina's region. Why can't you see that? You're a blind, stubborn, useless child."

He swiftly turned and went into the living room, where he eased himself down in a chair and stared out the window. Nurrel went after him, while Deborah remained where she was, reeling under Father's insults. After everything she had done for him, the way she had cared for him for all those years since Mother's death, this is what he thought of her?

"He's horrible," she whispered to Jacob. She stood in the hallway looking at Father sitting in his chair as if he had done nothing wrong. "This is all horrible and pointless. What do I do? How do I make him see what's happening? How am I supposed to get him to come with us?"

She could hear Nurrel begin to chat in his sensible and unflappable way to Father. She did not know how he did that. She wanted to slap Father. Shake sense into him. Get him to see what was going on around him.

"I don't know," Jacob answered. "Perhaps ask Erno what he thinks you should do."

"We're wasting time," she said. "I'm not just going to sit around and talk about farms and the weather. Father needs to snap out of it and turn back to being himself again."

She strode over to him. "I want you to come with us. You can't stay here. You're obviously not eating properly, and no one is looking after you." She took hold of his crusty sleeve and tugged at it. "See what your arm looks like? You see it, don't you. This isn't right. You must see this strange coating all over it. Look at your leg! It's not all there. Father, do you see it?"

"Let go of me!" he roared as he got up out of his chair. "Get out of my house!" He shoved her so that she stumbled backward, and stormed from the room.

"Don't you run away from me!" she yelled. "Get back here!"

She was about to run after him, but Nurrel caught hold of her arm. "Don't," he said.

She stood, her breathing shallow and rapid, listening to Father's footsteps as he ran up the stairs until a door slammed. "He never used to yell at me like that. This isn't him. Why can't I make him see?"

"Get out of my house!" Father shouted from upstairs. "Get out! Get out!"

"Come on," said Nurrel. "We'd better go. We'll try again later."

"Try again?" Deborah said, frowning at him. "How? This is useless!"

The shouts began again. "Get out! Get out!"

"I'm going!" she yelled back.

She stomped through the house in exaggerated fashion, making sure he would hear her leave.

"Calm yourself," Jacob said. "I don't want you turning, too."

"What?" She glared sidelong at him. "What in the world do you mean? I'm not turning; he's turning." She flung open the front door.

Nurrel hurriedly stepped outside with her, then she slammed the door. "Are you happy now?" she shouted, looking at the upstairs windows.

"Please, Deborah," Jacob said. "Hear me. Don't turn."

"I'm not! What are you talking about?"

"Look at your right hand," he said.

She held it out and felt a stab of shock as she saw the dusty coating over three of her fingers. She rubbed at them furiously. Surely, it was only there because she had touched Father's sleeve? But, the coating did not come off. "What's happening?"

"I think it's this region," said Nurrel. "Every hint of turning seems magnified somehow. We've got to be more careful."

"But, I'm not turning," she said. "I'm really not."

"Give me your hand," he said.

She hesitated. Why did he want her hand? He was going to hold it in his warm hands, going to try to coax life back into her. She didn't need him doing that. She was all right. She would be all right. Jacob pecked at her ear.

She flinched. "*Ow.*"

"Give Nurrel your hand. Let him help you. Don't be like your father."

That hurt. She was not like Father; how could Jacob even think she was? She would show him she was nothing like Father. She thrust her hand at Nurrel. He took it in both of his and looked up at her. It was hard to look back at him, his earnest brown eyes filled with so much deep thought as if he saw right into her. Her breathing suddenly felt trembly; she could feel the hint of tears pricking at her eyes—stop it!—and she clenched her jaw to try to remain calm. Why was he doing this for her? He looked at her as if he loved her. He did not love her. Nobody loved her. Nobody but Erno. And, Grufful. Grufful did love her; she knew that, felt that whenever she was near him. But, he had left. Jacob loved her. Ned did, too. They all loved her.

She looked at the ground, blurry through the tears, and became aware of a feeling in her right hand. She had been so cold and hadn't realised it. This feeling in her hand was not just the warmth of Nurrel's hands, but a tingling sensation travelled up her arm to her elbow. It was like Erno's shield. It was the Oxpeina-life. Yes, that's what it was.

She wriggled her hand out of Nurrel's grasp. "I'm all right now. Thank you."

"Yes," said Jacob. "You're all right, we're *all* all right. Just fine and dandy."

"Don't grump," she said to him.

"Let's get off the street," he said.

She looked around. There were no guandras about. She could not even see where the path had got to. What she did see was a line of large potholes, widely spaced, leading around to the side of the house next door. Iff's work, no doubt, as he had bounded along. She gazed up at the windows upstairs. Whatever Father was doing, he wasn't looking out at her. He was probably sitting in a chair brooding over nothing again.

"Yes," said Nurrel. "Not good to stay out here. We don't know if any guandras will try again. They haven't so far, so that's good."

"Because they're weak," said Jacob.

"Right, yes, true. They haven't got much life left in them."

"If any."

Deborah went over to the house next to Father's and, as she tried to step up onto the front doorstep, her leg inexplicably swung around so that she wound up facing the street.

"Oh, sorry!" said Nurrel. He trotted up the step and opened the door. "It's Val's barrier around the property. I keep forgetting no one can get in without my say-so. Come in, both of you."

Deborah cautiously took the step up to the door, and this time there was no resistance. A barrier? It reminded her of when she, Erno, and Jacob had gone to Nurrel's village in the woods and how she had tried to climb over the low stone wall but had been turned about by magic.

"It was good of him to do that for us," Jacob said, "but you should have seen Iff trying to cross it! *Hoo!*"

"How is it that you can get in?" Deborah asked Nurrel.

"Val made me the gatekeeper. Made sense for me to be that, I suppose, as Erno can't come into the house without damaging it. So, if your father comes to the front door, I can let him in."

"He's not going to come," she muttered, and went through the house to the small kitchen that looked out to the backyard. The others weren't there. She supposed they were through the hole in the fence.

In the kitchen, the bags that had been tied onto Ned and Maqua were lying against the wall, and all sorts of supplies—jars of preserves, paper packets, bread, eggs, folded clothing—were set out on the small table and the countertop. A lone book caught her eye and she picked it up.

"My storybook," she said, looking at the cover of *Legends Of The Greener Land*. "I'd forgotten we brought it along."

"I'd packed all your things," Nurrel said. "Not that you had many."

"This wasn't really mine; it was Taffin's."

"Oh well, never mind." He set to getting plates and utensils out.

Deborah sat at the kitchen table and thumbed through the book. She paused at the page describing brismuns. There again was the sketch of a brismun with the bird perched in its twiggy hair. Father had always told her such interesting stories about the brismuns. She felt angry at the thought and clapped the book shut. Jacob jumped.

"Sorry," she said. She stared a moment at her hands. Grubby fingernails, but other than that, her hands were normal, their usual colour and texture. "If I can see signs of turning on myself, why can't Father?"

"You don't have his eyes," said Jacob. "Yours are clear. His aren't."

"So, all I need to do is clear his eyes, then he'll see?"

"Easier said than done," said Nurrel as he spooned something out of a jar onto a plate.

Deborah fidgeted with the cover of the book. Maybe she should take it to Father, see if he recognised it, show him the picture of the brismun. He had been interested in Erno and wanted to reach out and touch him. That was something. Maybe Father would remember the times they had together many years ago, reading the book. Or, at least, the stories he had made up from looking at the pictures. The language in it was so old. She opened the book again to a page that had the scowling face of a rova, its teeth bared. She studied it for a moment, smiling to herself at seeing something of Grufful's expression in the sketch.

"Looks like Grufful," said Jacob as he leaned over her shoulder.

"Doesn't it?" she said. If only Grufful hadn't left so soon.

She thought over how she had reacted to Father and stomped through the house like a child, yelling back at him out on the street. Perhaps it was better Grufful hadn't seen her do that. But, it was all so infuriating. Surely, Father knew on some level that this wasn't what he had been searching for. He hadn't travelled into the woods, these regions, just to sit in a house by himself and waste away. Why did he think it was okay? Why wasn't he travelling onward to the Oxpeina's region? It made no sense to stop here.

"What does it say?" Jacob asked.

"What does what say?"

"The writing beside the picture."

"Oh." She smoothed the page of the book. "'Herein the untamed heart of a beast drew fathomless passion unlike which I have never seen fore, nay, solely in Sonax, the hand of time. Oxpeina's provision for the humble image-bearer, shepherd alongside each tremulous step—'"

"Blah blah blah," said Jacob.

She smiled at him, then suddenly thought of something. "What happened to Father's rova? He had one, didn't he?"

"I remember someone saying that." Nurrel set a sandwich-laden plate onto the table. "Erno, wasn't it? Didn't he think a rova was seen with your father near my village?"

Deborah pushed the book out of the way. "I don't remember. Father must have had a custodian at some point, though. Although… we never had one when we left my home in Eblhim. We travelled all the way to the edge of the woods and saw no one else."

"Same region," said Jacob. "Sonax usually only assigns a custodian if you're leaving your region and heading towards his."

"*Hmm.*" She took a bite of a sandwich. "But, still, Father must have had one when he left Shilhim—that was entering a new region, right? Erno came to me not long after I left there. So, what happened?"

"He probably pushed his away," said Nurrel. "You see how he is. I don't think any rova would tolerate that. Besides, the will of the image-bearer has to be respected, no matter how offensive it is."

She looked across the table at him and the brooding expression he wore. He was probably thinking of Ibelli. She must have lost her custodian, too, there at the Silver Lake. The thought triggered a memory. "Wait, I do remember. Val told me that one of his brothers was my father's custodian. He told me so at the Silver Lake. That's when he said Father was journeying to Aric, wherever that is." She sighed. "I suppose none of that matters anymore. He's here. We're all here in this stupid place."

Jacob shook himself, his feathers ruffling. "Not for much longer, I hope."

63

Deborah sat at the kitchen table, gazing out the window to the closely cropped backyard boxed in by the high wooden fences. Through the gap on the right side she glimpsed Ned ambling past in the neighbour's yard. She looked pensively at the unbroken fence on the left side bordering Father's yard. "I'm going to try again. This time I'll show him the book. Maybe he'll remember something of it and how he used to read it to me."

Nurrel glanced over his shoulder at her as he stood at the counter washing the breakfast plates. "Give me a moment to finish clearing up."

She thumbed through *Legends Of The Greener Land*, pausing now and then at the familiar pictures. Surely, this would help; Father would remember happier times. If she could just try and keep calm this time and get him to listen.

"Do you want me to come, too?" Jacob asked.

She tickled his soft feathers. "Sure."

He nibbled her ear.

When Nurrel was ready, they went out into the backyard and over to the gap in the fence.

"Do you all need to come through here?" Nurrel asked.

Erno thumped over to the gap. "We need more pasture—Ned and Maqua have cleaned this lot up. We can't break into the next yard as that house is occupied. The back houses are, too. I don't really like to go to Sofi and Sessa's patch, as I don't want to be too far away from you three."

"Break into Father's yard," said Deborah. "He might like seeing you and Iff there."

Erno nodded, his twiggy hair rattling. "I did wonder if that might be an option."

"Come in," said Nurrel. "All of you."

Erno hopped through, Ned squeezed after him, then Maqua, and finally Iff leapt through.

He grinned down at Deborah. "You're somewhat better than when I last heard you, but you still need that wound looked at."

She looked up into his mossy face, so similar to Erno's but broader, and his grin was more intimidating somehow. "I don't have a wound."

"Yes, so you said. I didn't mean a flesh wound, I meant a mind wound."

"I don't have one of those, either. What makes you think I do?"

"I don't think it, I hear it. I can touch it in the air around you."

She tensed at his words. If he was about to tell her she had a 'bad air' then he could go jump over the fence and not come back. She was about to open her mouth and tell him so when he caught her hand in his strong, cool one. For one moment, she considered pulling away, but that changed the instant she heard his thoughts.

Gentle hearted one, he said to her. *I don't mean to be such a terrible bully forcing my way in like a great lump, but it hurts me to see your hurt. Won't you let me tend it for you? Erno can too, of course, but I think in some of these healthful things Sonax gave me an extra helping. Don't think I don't know how huge and overbearing I am compared to my brothers and sisters!*

As they held hands, she knew that he did not believe at all that she had a 'bad air' and he was furious she had been told that by Chila. He knew it was the wound that caused her to pull away from others, the wound that caused her to not feel loved, the wound that made her work so hard to try and gain Father back into her life and fill the void in her heart.

She did not know what to say or even to think back at Iff as he stood over her. The way his thoughts and perception burst in seemed almost too much, filling her mind so that she could hardly hear or see anything else.

Whoops! he thought, and she felt a sense of the deep affection he had towards her. *I can cut myself off if you'd like, and we can go back to speaking aloud.*

She let go his hand. "Perhaps that would be better." Yet, once her hand left his, she felt suddenly abandoned and aware of the emptiness of the region, the cold breeze whistling around them, and that it was better to have Iff in her mind.

Jacob nudged her cheek. "What's going on?"

She had almost forgotten he was there.

"I have been chatting in thought to Deborah," said Iff. "I cut you out from hearing anything, my little friend, as it's fairly private stuff."

"Oh."

Deborah tentatively took Iff's hand again and was immediately enveloped by his strength of presence. The air was warm, the sky brighter, and Oxpeina's region not so very far off now. Iff would make sure she got there, he would care for her. Why did he feel this way towards her? He hardly knew her.

Maybe he thought at her, *but maybe I just like you anyway, so what's the big deal? I can like who I want to.*

But why me?

That's your wound flaring up, making you think you're unlovable.

She looked searchingly at the flitting glimpses of his steely blue eyes amongst the moss as he blinked and squinted back at her, a smile on his face. Her next thoughts came out of the depths of her soul, bubbling to the surface in bursts. *I don't seem to feel connected to love. I can't seem to feel what love is. All these—Erno, Nurrel, Jacob, Ned, others—seem to love me, but I'm left disconnected, cold, something, like I don't truly feel emotion.* She grimaced at him. *You're going to tell me that's the wound talking. What wound is this? I can't seem to feel anything. What is love? Why can't I feel? I thought I could. Now I don't know.*

Peace, he thought, squeezing her hand gently, just like Erno would do.

Where was Erno? She needed him; needed her custodian. Needed him now.

Iff whispered something in the brismun language. Erno hopped to Deborah's side and laid his hand on her arm.

I'm here, he thought at her. *Oh! That wound's much clearer now. What a nasty thing it is, cutting through your mind as if that's all you are, or all you ought to be, separating you from what you should be.*

Her breathing quickened. *What do you see? What do you mean? I can't—I don't—why can't I feel?*

You can feel, thought Iff, *it's coming out in a gusher. Hold steady; it'll be painful.*

She didn't want to feel it, didn't want to face it, but there was something sharp, something that gnawed and burned at the edges of her consciousness. She tried to push it back as it threatened to overwhelm her.

I'm here, Iff thought. *I'll hold you.*

Me, too. Erno's thoughts were quieter, gentler than Iff's, but still present.

Mother never loved her, had always been distant. Father, she thought he had loved her, but that had vanished, and he had become even more distant than Mother. Why didn't they want her? Why did nobody want her? Why even exist in this life? Now, Father kept pushing her away, kept telling her to leave him alone. Why did she keep trying? Why couldn't she let him go as easily as he could let her go? Why didn't he love her? Her own parents. She loved them, tried to love them, but they didn't love her, didn't want her love.

She was alone. Tears slipped down her face, and she shut her eyes. She could see Father's cold, angry gaze at her as if she was a nuisance, as if she was hated. It had come to that? She had spent all this time searching for him, wanting to help him, wanting to rescue him, and this was the way he treated her? As if she was nothing and nobody. Not wanted at all.

She bowed her head. *I can't bear it*, she thought at Iff and Erno. *Why don't they want me? My own parents?*

Because they're stupid buggers, Iff thought back.

She wanted to laugh, wanted to cry, at his blunt response.

No, really, he thought. *They had their own problems and spilled them out onto you. Yes, Erno saw inside your father and saw that gunked-up fear oozing all around and affecting his actions, but it's no excuse, not really. So what if he's crippled by fear? He chose to stay that way. He set off to get rid of it all and be freed by Oxpeina-life, but then he stopped midway in his search. He didn't keep trying, and now he's turning. He might as well have taken a sword and whacked you with it, just in his attempt to not let anyone get close to himself. His own-self, his selfish self. That is self-importance at its miserable height. You know all this, Deborah. Erno's talked to you about it, and you know it. This lack of love from your father is not your fault. It's nothing to do with you being good enough or worthy enough.*

She clung to Iff's hand. *But I just thought that if Father wanted to love me, then he would. His fear wouldn't stop him. But he doesn't even want to love me.*

How do you know that? Wanting and doing are two different things. My point is, your father should have kept going after the Oxpeina-life instead of turning away from it. If he had, then he would have been freed to love, and his self-importance would have fallen off. He's made the wrong choice here. That has nothing to do with you, it's all to do with himself, his own-self.

Deborah, thought Erno, *your father is pushing you away to protect himself. His own-self has become more important than anything else. He can't love anyone when he's like that, and, once the turning is complete, there will be nothing left—his life or any part of Oxpeina-life will be hollowed out and gone.*

She thought of the guandra Erno had killed and how it had been a hollow shell.

Oof! You've seen that? Iff thought. *I've seen it over and over. Pretty disturbing stuff to see an image-bearer turned into nothing. Bizarrely, the desire for control remains but not much else. Reason, thought—it's all distorted and, as Erno says, hollowed out. Once Oxpeina-life has completely gone, it's gone, and that's that.*

She did not know what to think. Surely, life could not go completely; there must be a way to turn back from being a guandra. It would not happen to Father. Her own hand had cleared and become normal again, so there must be a way back from the turning.

In the middle of turning, there's always a way back, thought Iff, *but once you've fully become a guandra, there is no more. I wish I had better news for you, but it's just the natural order of things, and nothing anyone can do can change that.*

She felt he was simplifying it all for her in his thoughts, and that beneath an almost superficial summing-up he knew profoundly what it meant to turn and had observed it many times. She sensed his memory of watching, *listening*, as Sonax had drawn the map of the regions and spread out the world, the creative sparks flying from his fingers as he set in place the axis of order. His memory of Sonax was not the same as the visual encounters she had had; instead, there was the brismun sense of pulses of sound, awareness of thought, and the feeling of an almost overwhelming intensity of life from standing so close to Sonax, so much so that she, *Iff*, could hardly move. Not that she, *Iff*, wanted to; *Iff* wanted to stay there immersed in the Oxpeina-life that fostered colour, sense, and time.

Then, in an instant, she felt the sensation of flight, of being whisked off one's feet as Sonax's attention shifted from his map to the brismuns as he assigned each to their regions with a word: go. Iff, together with the beautiful water-bride Sar, stood amongst the trees of their region, feeling the boughs sway and whisper overhead, and the birds burst into song at the emergence of image-bearers.

The image-bearers stood glowing with Oxpeina-life freshly-made, over time that glow ebbing and flowing at the force of each individual will, to take life, to give it, deciding who they were and wanted to be, and for some the final severing of the link and a cold, empty statue left in its place. Iff's sense of loss as he felt the image-bearers turning was unbearable, and Deborah stumbled backward, letting go of his hand.

The region was cold again. She shivered and pulled her coat more closely about herself. She looked up at Iff's face, feeling a closeness, an intimacy with him for having seen his memory and felt his experience. Everything made sense now—the regions, the way life was interconnected, the Oxpeina underneath it all. This world was a growing ground, a proving ground for the image-bearers to find themselves and understand who they were as they developed personality and found existence. She was an image-bearer, bearing the image Sonax had assigned her, and her true life would begin once she entered the Oxpeina-life region. Her childhood, her growing ground, would be put to rest, for its purpose had been to show her how to recognise life—for how could she know what life was if she did not know the turning?

Had it all been accidental that, with Father, she had stumbled upon the existence of the regions once they had left their home in Eblhim? Had Father known somehow they needed to move, and she had gone with him just because she was so focused on him, on needing him and his life? Her focus needed to shift. She could not have everything bound up in him; her life did not depend on him. He was an image-bearer just as she was. They were equal.

Somehow, Iff had imparted all of this to her.

He smiled at her and gently touched her cheek, the same cheek Chila had raked with her claws. "Your wound has faded," he said. "That's a relief."

"Thank you, Iff," she said softly.

She turned to Erno and Nurrel, who stood behind him with Ned and Maqua. They were clear images in a fading region, the light and atmosphere not quite right as though ailing, and she could almost see the glow of Oxpeina-life in her friends. Yet, here they all were, staying in this region because of her. She was holding everything up. They should be going; should be getting to the Oxpeina's region before the world closed. She glanced over at Father's house. One last try. She would take the storybook, try to find common ground with him, see if he remembered the love they had shared over the stories, and hope his eyes would clear somehow with her love. Yes, she loved him. Father.

64

"I've had enough of this," Nurrel said, after he had knocked at the door for the umpteenth time. "Let's just go in."

Jacob shifted his weight on Deborah's shoulder. "That's crossing the will of the image-bearer."

"So what?" said Deborah. "We're running out of time."

She opened the door and quietly went inside, resisting the temptation to march in and yell for Father to come. No, this time it would be different; she would be different. She could be as calm as Nurrel.

It was easy to find Father; he was sitting in the living room gazing out the window, a blanket about his thin shoulders. Erno and Iff stood as shrub and tree in the backyard, while Ned and Maqua grazed. Father seemed fascinated by them and did not stir as she approached.

"Father," she said softly. "I'm here."

His gaze did not leave the window.

She went to his side and set *Legends Of The Greener Land* on his lap, open to the page about brismuns. "Look, Father. Remember this storybook? You used to read it to me when I was a child. We always liked the brismuns."

Still, he did not move. Did not even lower his gaze to look.

"Hello, Ben," Nurrel said as he sat in the opposite chair.

Father looked over at Nurrel. Deborah stiffened. Why look at Nurrel and not at her? She took a deep breath. Now was not the time to get angry. Father was ignoring her for some reason, acting as though she wasn't even there. Was it because of his fear?

She tentatively reached out and laid her hand on his shoulder. He flinched and shrugged her hand off without looking at her.

Jacob let out a disapproving hiss.

Deborah stared down at Father. Why did he want to hurt her so much? Why shrug her hand off? Yes, yes, the others said he had fear of getting close to anyone, but still, she was his daughter, his only child, and this is how he treated her? She stood silently, unsure what to do; hurt feelings mingled with a pitying understanding as she looked at him. He was so thin, looked so terrible with the patches on his face, his arm, and leg. This was almost too horrible to be real, yet it was.

She swallowed hard, her throat feeling dry. "The book, Father. Remember those happy times we used to have? You used to read me bedtime stories."

Again, no response. He was back to staring out the window.

"Nurrel," she whispered. "What do I do?"

Nurrel leaned forward in his seat. "We care about you, Ben. We're here because we want to take you home with us."

"I am home," Father said under his breath. "This… my home."

"But, you have nothing to eat," said Deborah. "How can you live like this? You're wasting away."

He glared up at her. "Quiet!"

At least he acknowledged her, as much as it pained Deborah to see those cloudy eyes turned in anger to her.

There was a thump outside the window, and Deborah saw Iff had hopped closer. He peered in, his round face framed by his twiggy hair. Father stared back at him.

"Image-bearer!" Iff shook his finger at Father, his voice carrying clearly through the glass. "Be who you are supposed to be, image-bearer!"

Ned paused from grazing and raised his head. He smirked as he noticed Deborah, his large trusting eyes fixed on her. He and Maqua would soon finish the straggly grass in Father's backyard. Then, what?

None of them should stay in this region. They were only doing it for her. How much more would they endure, waiting for her to go with them to the Oxpeina-life region? What if they didn't make it in time? What if the world closed before they could get there? She could not, would not be responsible for that.

"Father," she said. "I have to go. I want you to come with us. This is not right. You shouldn't stay here. You're going to die if you do. We're going to the Oxpeina's region. Please, please, come with us. Remember how you wanted peace by living in Shilhim by the woods? Remember what you said you wanted? You didn't get that, did you. You went into the woods to try to find it. This region—"

"*Quiet!*" he roared. "You know nothing! You are a child! An unwanted, worthless child! You—"

He was cut off as another voice, familiar and compelling, spoke over everything.

The world will close soon. Come to me now.

"There!" gasped Deborah. "You heard that, didn't you, Father?"

His chin sank to his chest, and he scowled.

Her breathing was shaky; she felt the sting of Father's cruel, unjust words and fear at Sonax's warning. "Father!" She put her hand on his shoulder again, and Jacob moved uncertainly on her own shoulder. "We have to go! I know you heard Sonax's call; I know you did. Don't try to pretend you didn't."

"Leave me," he muttered.

She grabbed his arm, tried to pull him up out of his chair, but he struggled against her and pushed her off. The storybook fell from his lap to the floor.

Nurrel hurried over. "Ben. Come now. We're here for you. We love you and can't leave you on your own."

Father glared up at him. "You don't love me. You hardly know me."

"That may well be," said Nurrel, "but Deborah, your daughter, loves you. She's come all this way to find you."

Father turned his cloudy stare to Deborah, his expression morose.

She should say now that she loved him, but how could she? Such hate was in him he would surely sneer and insult her again if she said such a thing. Why make herself vulnerable only to be hurt again by him? It was bad enough looking back at those eyes of his, so foreign from what they used to be. She could not keep meeting that terrible gaze, so looked at the floor. The storybook lay there at his feet, open to the page of the rova. Something of Grufful's fierceness snarled up at her and she was immediately heartened. Over at the window, Iff stood there still, listening, watching, Erno behind him with Ned and Maqua. Erno smiled, as if he sensed she was looking his way.

She took a deep breath and spoke as calmly as she could, despite the feeling she would burst into shouting at any moment. "Father, I do love you. I left Shilhim to look for you as soon as I discovered you were gone. It hurt me that you left, but I have travelled a long way to find you and bring you home. Come with me now and let me take you home."

The cloudy blue dissolved from his eyes and revealed the familiar hazel-tinged brown, tender and wistful, but, as Deborah's hope rose at the sight, the cloudiness swirled and covered his eyes again.

When Father spoke, his voice was a dry whisper. "Leave me."

"No, I won't," she said. "How can I? You're my father. I think—I believe you love me as I love you. I—you—can't you feel what has happened? Things aren't right. You don't have the peace you were looking for. This isn't home."

"Be silent," he muttered, his chin sinking to his chest again.

"I know you heard Sonax's warning that it's time to go," she said.

"You know nothing," he said. "Nothing. This is the Oxpeina region. I'm here."

"How can you even think that? Why then would Sonax tell us to leave?"

"Didn't," Father muttered. "Not. This my region. My."

Jacob hissed again. Deborah stared at Father. Why was he such an unmoving, stubborn lump? Then, she noticed his feet and the lower part of his trouser legs. They had turned even greyer with that strange, crusty coating that now appeared to be embedded with shards of stone.

This had happened in an instant—she was sure they were not like that a moment ago. Her heart beat faster. Was he now turning completely, and nothing she could do would stop it?

"Ben," said Nurrel, "I know you want to stay. I know you want the safety of home, but we're telling you the truth—the outer regions are closing and all image-bearers have been asked to come to the safety of the Oxpeina's region. It is what it is—what you think about it all doesn't matter, it's going to happen regardless. Stop closing yourself off to your daughter's love. Stop pushing her away."

"No," Father said, hunched over, his head bowed.

Deborah tugged at his arm, chafing her hand on the crusty coating of his sleeve. He did not resist or try to shake her off, but still she could not budge him out of his chair, for he was as heavy as stone. "Father!"

The thicker stone coating spread to his knees.

"Please, don't," she said. "Please, Father!" She dropped to the floor in front of him, looking up into his face, hoping he would raise his head even a little and look back at her. "Father! It's me. Deborah. Your only child! Please don't turn away from me." She looked at Nurrel. "Why is he turning so quickly? What's happening. Look, it's spreading!"

Iff tapped on the window. "It's because you're trying to impose your will on him! You're only making him get all feisty and resistant with his own self-importance. Step back and leave him be. You've said all you need to say right now, Deborah. Come out here to us."

Deborah got up and stepped back from Father. How could she leave him? The moment she did, he might turn completely and be gone forever. But then she saw the spread of stone slowing as she moved away. How infuriating! She gritted her teeth to stop herself from shouting at Father and trying to shake sense into him. "Goodbye, Father," she said grimly. "I'm going now. I will be right outside if you need me. I don't know how long for. I am leaving this region."

She waited for him to look at her, to respond in any way, but he stared fixedly at his lap and acted as though he had not heard her. She clenched her fists and left the room.

Jacob nuzzled her cheek. "I'm sorry."

"I am, too," said Nurrel.

Deborah marched through Father's musty-smelling kitchen to the back door. She flung it open. "Well, that was a waste of time!" she shouted to Erno and the others.

Erno hopped briskly over and caught her hands in his. *I'm sorry.*

Everybody's sorry, she fumed. *I am so angry, and I've wasted everybody's time! You all came with me to find Father; you all stayed with me; I don't know why, and here we are—it was all for nothing! He's turning, and refusing to listen to me!*

Erno's love and affection flowed over her without utterance of thought or word, soothing and untangling the burning anger she felt. Then came piercing sorrow, for he had known it all before; he had seen it with his own shaseeliany, his water-wife, who had decided to leave him and all others behind, and he did not want Deborah to experience that agony.

Deborah bent and hugged him, laying her head against his mossy cheek, and, as she felt his arms wrap about her, she burst into tears. "I've failed," she said between sobs. "He doesn't love me. I've lost him forever!"

"You haven't failed," he whispered in his leafy voice. "You told him you loved him, you told him where we're going, and you asked him to come. That's good."

"How is that good? It achieved nothing."

"You don't know that. Let him sit and think now."

"Sit and think?" She drew back. "There's no time for that." She was about to wipe her eyes but thought better of it and turned her hands this way and that to check if the rough dusty coating on her fingers was there. "My hands are clean," she said, surprised.

"Why wouldn't they be?" said Erno.

She wiped her eyes. "Because of how I feel. I thought all the negative stuff would bring on the turning again."

He smiled. "There's nothing wrong with grieving for someone—the danger is only when your self-importance pushes itself forward."

She sighed heavily and looked back at the windows of Father's living room. Iff stood there, immense and green, facing away from Father who was still hunched over in his chair. "I don't know how to leave him," she said softly. "How can I leave him?"

Father abruptly got up, bent briefly to the floor, straightened up, and walked away from the window. As he did, Deborah spotted the storybook clasped in his hand.

"Did you see that?" she gasped.

"No," said Erno, grinning, "but I hear him walking through the house."

"He took the book," she said. "Our book! He's got it."

"Interesting," said Jacob. "Perhaps that will help him remember who he is."

"I hope so," said Nurrel. He went over to Maqua, who stopped grazing and mumbled contentedly to him.

Deborah watched them together, observing the slump in Nurrel's shoulders. This experience with her father had no doubt freshened his memory of watching Ibelli turn. "You all must go, Erno," she said in a low voice. "I can't make you wait here with me any longer."

Iff thumped to her side. "I will take the children. This is no place for them now."

He touched her shoulder briefly, so that she knew he was referring to Ned, Maqua, and Jacob. She nodded.

"I am your custodian, Deborah," said Erno. "I stay with you."

"But you can't! I don't want you getting caught up in the closing of the world."

"I won't," he said simply. "But if it truly is your will to send me away, then I must oblige. Oh, that reminds me. Grufful left a message for you before he left."

He took her hand and, in her mind's eye, she saw Grufful standing tall, his dark brown fur sleek and smooth, his wild face in a scowl as he looked down at her, *at Erno*. "Tell Deborah I did not want to leave her and that I do so only at Sonax's bidding. I am needed elsewhere as the world is closing. I will see her again soon in the Oxpeina's region. Make sure she gets there, Erno. Tell her I love her and would gladly have been her custodian. You are her custodian. Hold that responsibility with all seriousness and gravity. I am depending on you to stay with her."

"Will do," Erno had said.

He let go Deborah's hand and squinted up at her. "So, you see? Even Grufful says I must not leave you. Not that I would. And, before you object, no, I won't get caught in the closing of this world. That's just not possible."

It was reassuring to hear him say so. She knew he could move far more quickly than she ever could. If it came to that, and the world closed before they could get to Oxpeina's region with Father, Erno could leave her then.

"All right," she said.

He grinned.

❧ 65 ❧

Deborah stroked Ned's face and kissed his soft grey nose. "Behave yourself," she said to him. "Do what Iff tells you, and keep moving as fast as you can."

His dark eyes were the most miserable she had ever seen. "I want you to come," he said.

"I will, my Ned, but I can't leave Father just yet. Not while there's hope he might come with me. Don't go too far into the Oxpeina's region—I'll be hoping to find you as soon as I get there. Wait by the border for me."

He sniffed and curled his lip. "I'll stay two steps in, watching for you."

"Good boy," she said, and kissed him again.

Nurrel smoothed Maqua's grey coat and talked quietly in her ear.

Iff bent over Deborah, his green face close to hers. "Don't stay here so long you turn to stone, image-bearer. I don't know that what you're doing is the best idea. I understand it, sure, but there comes a time when you've got to think of your own future." He swivelled to Erno. "And you, my big little brother, same thing. Hear me?"

Erno clasped Iff's hand.

Deborah took Jacob from her shoulder and held him. He glared crossly at her.

"See you soon, Beebee," she said.

He blinked. "*Hoo!* Think you're funny, do you, Debbie?"

She smiled at him. It was hard to think of what to say next—she did not realise how much she loved him until now when they had to part, and how light and empty her shoulder felt without him there. Anyway, this was not a final goodbye. It *wasn't*. Somehow, Erno would help her reach the Oxpeina's region in time, even if he had to carry her. She looked up at the sky. Clouds drifted across the pale blue expanse. She had thought the 'gloaming' would appear in this region, or maybe houses would crack and start falling down, but all was quiet. Nothing showed that the world was closing. Yet, Sonax had said to come now.

"Don't be an idiot and wait too long," Jacob said curtly.

"Don't fall off Iff," she said. She had meant to be funny or make some snappy retort, but it fell flat as she started feeling choked up at the thought of Jacob leaving. It was *not* a final goodbye. Things shouldn't feel so serious.

"I'll try not to," he said.

She handed him over to Iff. Before she had a chance to say anything more, he shouted, "Run!" and leapt away. Ned and Maqua galloped after, no doubt compelled by his order, for Deborah staggered on her feet and almost went with them. They disappeared around the side of the house, leaving by the narrow way there. She stood listening to the thumping of Iff and the *thud-thudding* of Ned and Maqua's hooves, and imagined them tearing up the street.

"Will they be safe from guandras?" she asked Erno.

"Any guandras out there will be bowled over by Iff, no doubt."

"No doubt," said Nurrel.

Deborah looked down at him. "Nurrel, I still think you're crazy for staying. Call out to Iff now; I'm sure he'll hear you. Go with them. Please."

He shrugged. "Somebody has to stay and make sure you don't turn."

She frowned at him. "But not at the expense of your own life. You should be thinking of yourself, not me."

"Should I? That's not what Sonax told me to do when you came to my village. He said to take care of you, and that's what I'll do until he says different."

"He *has* said different. He said to come now. You should do what he said and make sure you get out of here in time."

"So should you."

They eyed each other, he quiet and solemn, she unsettled and anxious. She didn't want to stay in this region, but what would she be going to, anyway? What was the Oxpeina-life region really? She had only a glimpse, an idea of it, yet still did not truly know. There was the promise of life and warmth; she knew only that. She slipped her cold hands into her coat pockets and shivered. This region, she knew for a fact she did not want to be here, yet she could not leave Father. He was her father, how could she just walk away from him? It did not seem to matter anymore that he didn't want her or love her; she still felt as though she could not let him go.

She looked over at his window. He was back in his chair, staring out at them. Or rather, she decided, staring at Erno. Even then, Father seemed as pale as a ghost—she did not know if it was the reflection in the glass making him appear that way or if the dusty coating had spread further over him. She waved and beckoned to him. "Come, Father!" she called, her voice piercing the cold air. She pointed at Erno. "Come meet the brismun!"

Father looked away.

She jammed her hands into her pockets again. "I can't understand this. Why is he like this?"

"What did he do?" Erno asked.

She scowled. "Oh, just ignored me again."

"I hear and sense very little life in him now," said Erno. "Deborah, are you sure you want to stay and watch him turn completely? Because this is what seems to be happening now. I'd prefer you didn't witness that. I think we should go."

"I can't."

"Why can't you?"

"I don't know. I just can't."

He touched her arm, and she took her hand out of her pocket and clasped his fingers tightly.

I can't let him go, she thought.

Why do you think that is?

I don't know.

Yes, you do.

I thought there was hope. He picked up our book; I thought he was going to look at it and remember. Remember me, remember the times we shared together when I was a child and how we loved each other. Yet, now he's back in the chair, just staring into nothing again. And you say he has hardly any life left.

Erno pressed her hand. *If he has gone from you, if he has almost completed turning, then why can't you leave him? What is it that holds you to him?*

He's my father.

Not good enough. That's no reason for you to die here.

He… I… need him. I want him to be my father again. I don't seem able to let go of that. He's a part of me.

Deborah felt understanding sweep over Erno. *The familial connection of the image-bearer*, he thought. *I have sensed something of that in Sonax, too, in how he thinks towards the image-bearers and, to a lesser extent, the dwellers. The painful longing you feel now reminds me of that—not only the need for love but also the need to share love.*

She frowned at his hand in hers. *I still feel as though I am unsure of love, what it is, how to feel it.*

He grinned. *Like love is supposed to be a feeling and that's all it is? You know love is more than that. Why do you think you came all this way to find your father? It wasn't just for your own need of him; it was also because you wanted to help him, to care for him, to look after him. I can sense that very easily in you. You wanted him to be okay, or, as you say, 'all right'. Now you want to get him out of here and bring him to the Oxpeina's region and find peace of mind. That is love.*

I don't know. I have needed, have wanted, his love, though. I haven't been as selfless as you make me out to be.

Of course! We all need to be loved; that's only natural.

There was a sudden shift in the air; an icy wind whipped her hair and chilled her to the bone. The atmosphere took on a paler hue as if the sun had dimmed, and the fence, the houses, the ground, all faded to a silvery-grey.

"What was that?" she said, looking about.

"That," Erno said, smiling, "was my sister, Sofi, leaving. She's been released from this region, and Sonax has gathered her and Sessa in. They're safe now. That's good."

"Does that mean we haven't much time left?" Nurrel asked, buttoning his coat.

"Hard to say," said Erno. "I can feel more of Sonax's pull on me, but it hasn't reached the urgency I felt at the closing of a previous world. The first world, I was almost in a panic, for I was left at very nearly the last moment. While, in the closing of the second world, I made it to the Oxpeina region ahead of time."

Deborah almost reached out to take his hand again, desiring to discover his memories of those events, but thought better of it. There was no time for that anymore. "I'm going to try one last time to reach Father," she said in a low voice. She did not feel hopeful.

66

Deborah sat silently opposite Father. She could not think of what to say. If she tried again to push him, then all she was doing was crossing his will and asserting her own self-importance. What could she say to change his mind, anyway? She had said it all before. She had warned him that the world was closing and was sure he had heard Sonax saying that to all of them, too. What more could be done?

Father gazed straight ahead through Deborah as though he didn't see her. His eyes were so filmy that perhaps he couldn't, anyway. He was very grey now; the stony texture had covered most of his body. She was not quite sure he still lived, although, before she and Nurrel entered the house, Erno had assured her there was life present in him. She thought she could see a slight rise and fall of Father's chest as he breathed, but perhaps that was imagined.

"Father," she whispered. "I'm here."

How long they sat in silence as time slipped by, she did not know. After a while, Nurrel got up and went to the window to look out at Erno, who stood as a statue in the failing light. Why did they both stay for her? She did not want them to stay. They should leave and get to safety.

"Deborah."

Father had uttered her name so quietly she wondered if she had dreamt it.

"I'm right here with you," she said softly.

He made no sign he had heard.

Outside, there was a tremendous cracking sound. Deborah looked out to see the peaked roof of the house beyond the backyard was sliding. Had broken, was falling, drifting, collapsed, and crashed in a cloud of dust against the neighbouring house.

She got to her feet. "Nurrel! You should go."

He turned and looked at her.

"You're taking this task of caring for me too far," she said. "It's all right. You can go now. You've been a good friend to me, much better than I deserved."

"It's been easy to love you, Deborah," he said.

"Well," she said, "I love you, too, Nurrel, and that's why I want you to go. Now."

"Sonax hasn't told me to stop looking after you," he said.

"Don't be so stubborn," she said. "It's time to let go. You've got to think of yourself now."

He shrugged. "What about you?"

"What about me? I can't just walk off and leave my father. Not while he's still alive. Even if he can't see or hear me anymore, I—I just can't. I don't want him to die alone." She stared at Father. So still, so unmoving. She went to him and touched his shoulder. So hard, so cold. She smoothed his hair gently. Some of it broke and crumbled beneath her touch. Was he still alive? She bent and put her arms around him and kissed his cheek. There was a little warmth in that cheek, and she thought she felt his breath. He had not gone yet.

There was another cracking, groaning sound from outside, followed by a thump. The fence had crumbled and fallen in a hazy sheen of dust. Two of the neighbouring houses began sliding into one another. Upstairs in Father's house, there was a bang.

Deborah leapt up. "Nurrel! Go, get out of here!"

Something clasped her wrist. It was Father's hand, and it was not all grey but had tones of flesh. She gasped and looked at him. He had turned his head and was looking up at her, his filmy eyes unseeing.

"You love me?" he said, his voice dry and hushed.

"Of course I do," she said. "I always have."

"Don't leave me," he said.

"Don't be silly." She put her arms around his cold, thin shoulders. "Why would I do a thing like that? You know I came all this way to find you, and I'm not leaving now. Nurrel must, though." She pulled a face at Nurrel. "Go on," she hissed. "Get out of here. Everything is falling down. You and Erno, go!"

Erno swivelled at her words and leapt aside as roof tiles slid and clattered beside him.

"Sonax didn't tell me to go yet," said Nurrel.

"Yes, he did," Deborah said. "He said ages ago to come now. You heard him; do as he says! What is wrong with you?"

"No, I really think if he wants me to look after you, then there'll be an easier way to get to the Oxpeina region as the world closes."

"Don't be daft!"

"I'm not. I'm serious."

She never thought she would be arguing with Nurrel as the world came to an end. Yet, he stood, a determined look on his face as he watched her. He, who had always been so mild, so kind, always there. He had shown her love when she hadn't even truly known what love was. He had not left her and was unwilling to now. Surely, he could not be willing to lose his own life just to keep stubbornly 'caring for her' as Sonax had told him.

Sonax, world-builder, had given him the task of looking after her. Why? And, given Erno—the custodian she had needed. *You're my Deborah*, Sonax had said, and her image had appeared briefly on his face as though she was important to him. Strange, yet he was the world builder and now was dismantling his world. In preparation for a new one? Would he start the process all over again? Settle the brismuns and shaseelianys back into the regions, then plant the trees, position the image-bearers, and send the dwellers?

"Deborah," said Father, his voice stronger.

"Yes, Father," she said. "I'm here."

More crashes came from outside. The sky brightened somewhat as the neighbouring houses fell in. Then, in Father's house, she realised the walls were collapsing. She shrieked and tried to shield Father with her body. All around her arose the deafening sounds of wood and metal grinding and crashing as the house twisted and broke apart.

She shut her eyes and held tightly to Father. This was the end. They would be buried and die together. Things pattered on her head, her shoulders, and she winced, waiting for the ceiling and upper storey to come next and crush them, but the *pat-pattering* continued as a light rain. It continued so long she opened one eye to see what was happening. As she did, Father's chair disappeared, and they both fell to the ground. Into dirt, for there was no floor. There was no house. Flimsy pieces of nothing, of dust, showered down around them.

Erno hopped to her, his stumpy leg leaving sandy impressions. "Well, that was fun. Are you all right?"

Deborah coughed and sat up. The dust in the air spiralled and melted away in wisps of grey. The sky was pale, faintest green. She looked all around but could see no houses, no town, no people, nothing. All that remained were Erno, Nurrel, herself... and Father. He lay unmoving on his side, and she rolled him over.

"Father," she said. "Can you hear me?"

He blinked and feebly raised his hand to try to catch hold of her, his fingers struggling to close on the fabric of her coat. "Deborah?"

"It's all right, Father, I'm here. Can you get up?"

Nurrel crouched beside them. "Come on, Ben. Let's get you on your feet."

He took one arm while Deborah took the other, and they managed to get Father into a sitting position.

"I can't move my legs," he whispered. "I can't get up."

"It's all right." Deborah knelt and rubbed his feet, trying to get some warmth into them, grazing her hands in the process on the rough, grey coating that covered most of his body, hoping that somehow she could massage some life into his feet, his ankles, or get his knee joints to bend.

He reached out and caught her hand. "Stop. It's useless."

"No, it's not," she said. "Your arms can move, and look at your hands—colour is coming back into them."

Father peered at his hands, and Deborah wondered if he could see anything through the thick film covering his eyes. An icy breeze whipped around them, and it began to get more difficult to breathe, as if something substantial was lacking in the air. Each time she inhaled, she felt life and energy seeping from her as if she too would fade and disappear like the buildings if she did not get out of the region.

She looked up at Erno. "Can you carry Father?"

"I can if that's what he wills," Erno said, "but if he resists me, then I'm afraid he will turn and we'll lose him completely." He bent over Father. "How about it, Ben? Want to come with us out of here? Allow me to carry you?"

"Brismun," Father said.

"Yes, that's me," said Erno.

Father's next words were spoken so quietly, Deborah leaned in to try and catch what he said. She missed the first few words but heard:

"I told my custodian go away."

"I figured as much, Ben," Erno said. "That's all in the past now. I'm Deborah's custodian, and she wants me here and wants me to help you. I'm willing, if you are."

Father's nod was almost imperceptible.

Deborah began to feel lightheaded and a heaviness pressed down on her chest. How could she keep breathing in this air? It was stifling—as though her lungs struggled to push air in and out. She looked about. The dirt ground seemed an immeasurable expanse. How far was it to the border of this region?

Nurrel caught hold of her hand. "Come on."

He was breathing more heavily, too, and his face had taken on a strange colour, but he pulled her to her feet with a strong hand.

"Now you, Ben," he said. "Let's get you up so Erno can lift you more easily."

Father grabbed for Nurrel's shoulder, but his hands moved clumsily, and he was unable to grasp hold. Deborah heaved at his other arm, and somehow she and Nurrel raised him to his feet. Deborah let go and bent over, coughing and gasping for air.

"Take her," Father whispered. "Brismun, take Deborah, not me."

"No," Deborah said.

"Deborah."

She turned her head to look at Father and was amazed to see the hazel-tinged brown of his eyes as the grey-blue film melted away. It was him; it was really him, and he saw her. She smiled but felt unable to form another word as she struggled to draw breath. She let out another hacking cough, willing herself to draw in air—where was the air? Why couldn't she breathe? She tried to reach out to Erno to touch him—she could not speak but she would tell him in thought to take Father and to leave her, to come back for her once he had got Father safely out of the region—but the coughing took over again.

She heard the voices of Father, Erno, and Nurrel, but her own coughing fit drowned out what they were saying. If she could just draw a breath… just draw breath… too dizzy… darkness.

You've fainted, she heard in her mind. It was Erno. *You can still hear me, yes?*

Yes, she can. Another voice. A man. Familiar. She'd heard him before. When Fothie had been healing her. Sonax.

What are you doing here? she thought at him.

She felt a sense of amusement at her question, as if she should know. *I'm gathering up my image-bearers caught in the dying regions.*

I meant to get out sooner, she thought.

I know, and I understand why you stayed.

Father. Where was he? *Take my father out of here*, she thought at Sonax. *Please.*

I already have. It's now your turn.

Nurrel?

I've got him at the same time as you. Take my hand.

She tried to move, tried to wake up. *I don't—where? I don't see anything.* A hand took hers and an electric shock coursed through her body, and the darkness turned to orange, brightest orange that even though she knew her eyes were shut, it shone through her lids, lit her body, burned away the struggle to breathe, cleared her lungs, and she took in a deep breath, the deepest breath, and Oxpeina-life coursed into her.

The potency of it scared her at first, for it was far greater than she had ever felt before. Being with the rovi pack was nothing, being with Iff and Erno was nothing, nothing but dregs compared to this. She could not stand, could not get up; this Oxpeina-life would tear her apart if it kept flowing in an unceasing current. Her grip on Sonax's hand loosened.

In response, he gave her hand a brief reassuring squeeze. *It's all right. Hold on.*

Can't. How could she possibly hold on? She could not move at all, and Sonax must know her hands were useless and wooden. *What's happening? Am I dead? I can't move, can't open my eyes.*

Not dead, Sonax thought at her. *That's the whole point of this—I'm getting rid of the dead. Another moment more... there!*

The orange light softened and faded, the Oxpeina-life settled and calmed, and her body was her own again.

Something brushed her face, tickling across her cheek and nose. She pushed it away and opened her eyes. Grey was all she could see, brilliant in hue as if grey was more than a colour but something alive. The grey moved, and lips curled into a smirk. Ned. It was Ned! She sat up and looked into his big eyes sparkling with veins of gold, his wonderfully grey face framed by floppy ears.

"You're here!" he said, and his voice was clear and stripped of all uncertainty. "It was the weirdest thing, Deborah. We heard a crackling sound and then all of a sudden you all appeared on the grass next to us. I think I should have been startled, but I wasn't. Somehow, it was so normal."

She could not speak for a moment. Beyond Ned, trees were not so far off, and she had never seen anything like them—trunks embossed in rippled patterns, muscular branches reaching to the sky or spread in welcome, power and strength in their poses, their greens, browns, and greys in sharp and detailed colour. She felt the pulse of life in the earth and in the warm grass beneath her hands. What sky above them! The blue, the white, the azure. It reminded her of the times she had seen Oxpeina-life in some of the old regions, but this was clearer, purer, had no undercurrent of rot, no impurity.

Ned nudged her. "We've been waiting at the border just like you told me to."

Something alighted on Deborah's shoulder, and she felt Jacob nuzzle her cheek. "Took you long enough," he said.

His voice was its usual rasp, but any hint of grouchiness had gone, leaving only good humour. She took him from her shoulder to look at him. His eyes were still black with rings of gold, but the crossness of an owl was no longer there. Instead, she saw guileless innocence and beauty in his expression amidst the soft details of his brown and white feathers. The pupils of his eyes, rich and vibrant black, expressed deepness of thought as if he knew and had seen much. It was still Jacob, her same dear Jacob, but he seemed stronger as if who he was before had been flawed and fragile.

She smiled at him, smoothing the feathers of his head, then lightly scratched his neck. "Why do you say that? You surely can't have been here for very long. It doesn't seem long at all since you left me."

"Time is different here," he said, "and I missed you. There, I admit it. I missed you." He blinked as if the thought was funny. "*Hoo!* At least you're all here now."

"All?" She set him back onto her shoulder and got up.

Ned nosed her sleeve, and she stroked his warm neck, his perfect, clean, wound-free neck, and looked over his broad back to the trees. Beneath them were three bushes, one large, two small, no, not bushes, *brismuns* with their hands linked. Iff and Erno, and, judging by the mirror image of Erno, Fothie, too.

"Where are Father and Nurrel?"

"Behind you," Ned said. "Look, right there by the border."

She turned around. Not so far away, a wall of pale misty green—through which nothing could be seen—rose high into the sky. Close to it, two men lay several paces apart in the long grass. The nearest, Nurrel, had Maqua lying beside him, her legs folded beneath her, and she was nibbling at the grass next to his head. Deborah ran to him. His eyes were shut and his breathing slow.

"Nurrel," she said, shaking his shoulder. "Nurrel! Are you all right?"

He slowly opened his eyes. "Catching up on some sleep," he murmured. "Haven't slept for days."

He smiled at her, and she saw not only the Nurrel she knew and loved, but more of his heart and who he truly was as the weariness was no longer a part of him, the unfathomable burden of grief had lifted, and she saw peace.

"You're finally here in the Oxpeina-life region, and the first thing you want to do is sleep?" Jacob said. "*Hoohoo!*"

Nurrel shut his eyes, grinning, and shrugged. "Feels good. Relaxing. Nice."

Deborah hurried over to Father. All his dusty, stone coating was gone. He was clothed simply in dark grey trousers and a white long-sleeved shirt that appeared clean and freshly ironed. He lay on his side, his back to her, and she stepped around in front of him and saw his eyes were closed in sleep, too.

"Father," she said softly. "Wake up."

"I'm not asleep," he said, and sat up. "I'm thinking."

Sparkles of mirth were in his hazel-brown eyes instead of the dullness of depression, and vitality of youth was in his whole demeanour. She felt as though she could look at him forever, astonished by his transformation.

His eyes widened as he looked at her. "Deborah, is that you?"

She grinned. "Of course it is."

Why did he look at her like that? How different was her own appearance now? She thought of the last time she had seen her face on Sonax's, and the soft loveliness he had shown her as if in a mirror, with no hardness, no tiredness. And, it was true, she no longer had the life-clenching, ever-present feeling of pressing on, of trying to overcome, of striving to keep going in difficult circumstances. She could breathe now.

Tears slipped down Father's face, and he wiped at them.

She put her hand on his shoulder. "Don't cry. We've made it. We're here in the Oxpeina's region. You're safe now."

"Oh, I know, I know," he said, and buried his face in his hands.

"What's wrong?"

"Nothing. Nothing at all. I'm—it's just—it's all overwhelming. I shouldn't be here. I know I shouldn't. I was turning away from all of this. You stopped me. If it wasn't for you, I wouldn't be here."

She sat in the grass next to him. "I thought I was losing you completely. It seemed like nothing I said mattered."

"It did. It did. Don't think it didn't. For some reason, I just couldn't let you close to me." He shook his head. "Not for *some* reason. I know why. I was afraid. I was consumed by fear." He took a deep breath and gazed upward at the sky. "So different now. I've been thinking about it all, finally understanding. The choices I made, the things I did, the way—the way I treated you." He took hold of her hands and looked earnestly at her. "I'm so dreadfully sorry. Saying sorry doesn't seem enough. I never should have done what I did. I've wronged you in many, many ways."

She thought she should feel hurt by the acknowledgement, should feel the pang of regret, or even anger, as was her habit. Instead, as she looked at Father, she saw what had been taken away from him—the aloofness, the despair, the anguish he had sheltered inside himself—and felt only affection and relief that he was like that no more. How could she feel bitter? The very ground thrilled with life; the air they breathed together soothed and calmed the spirit. She didn't want anything to spoil that.

"We are going to rebuild our lives," he said. "I'm going to look for some work, and you can be free to do whatever you want to, Deborah. When Sonax was bringing me into this region, he said we're welcome to settle in any of the cities or towns here, that there will be a house set aside for us. Plenty of room here, he said. And if you don't want to live in a city or a town, then we can live out in the countryside. And," he said, smiling at her, "if you don't want to live with me, then you don't have to. You should be free to spread your wings and rediscover who you are."

"*Hoo.*"

Father's gaze moved to Jacob, and his eyes lit with interest. "You speak and understand, don't you."

"Certainly. I didn't mean to interrupt you but you have me imagining Deborah with a giant pair of wings. *Hoohoo.*"

Deborah laughed and tickled Jacob's feathers. A deep *thump-thumping* in the earth caused her heart to leap. She got up and turned to see Erno, Iff, and Fothie approaching, the wide grins of the brismun on their faces.

She threw her arms around Erno. "Thank you so much for getting me here. For getting *us* here."

"Well," he said, his voice irrepressibly cheery, "I only helped hold you steady while Sonax pulled you in."

"Where is he?" she said, looking over his shoulder. "I want to thank him, too."

"He'll be in the centre of the region," Fothie said.

"No doubt still gathering in all of his belongings," said Iff. "Not just trees and rocks and rivers, but image-bearers like you who want to be here."

Deborah saw a blur of brown moving in and around the trees as shadows shifting, and heard the sound of a gentle rain. She smiled as she saw Grufful, Val, and Linnfel take shape as they ran towards her.

Grufful gave her an endearing snarl. "We were told you had arrived. I came the moment I heard. I am most relieved you did not turn. How are you now, my Deborah?"

"I'm all right," she said, and felt at long last it was not something said out of habit or to push anyone away but that it was deeply true.

Erno burst into peals of laughter.

Printed in Dunstable, United Kingdom